W9-BFC-614

GODSCHILD COVENANT

DOUGLAS
EVERY DAY IS GIFT!
Marshall
03-AUG-03

GODSCHILD COVENANT

RETURN OF NIBIRU

MARSHALL MASTERS

YOUR OWN WORLD BOOKS

GODSCHILDCOVENANT.COM
MARSHALLMASTERS.COM
RETURNOFNIBIRU.COM
YOWBOOKS.COM

Godschild Covenant
Return of Nibiru

No part of this book may be reproduced or transmitted in any form or by any means, graphic, electronic, or mechanical, including photocopying, recording, taping, or by any information storage retrieval system, without the written permission of the publisher.

All Rights Reserved © 2002 by Marshall Masters
ISBN: 0-972-58950-3
2nd Edition

Your Own World Books
an imprint of Your Own World, Inc.
Carson City, NV USA

For information address:

Marshall Masters
P. O. Box 67061
Scotts Valley, CA 95067

GODSCHILDCOVENANT.COM
MARSHALLMASTERS.COM
RETURNOFNIBIRU.COM
YOWBOOKS.COM

Printed in the United States of America

This book is a work of fiction. Names, characters, places, and incidents either are products of the author's imagination or are used fictitiously. Any resemblance to actual events or locales or persons, living or dead, is entirely coincidental.

To Morris for My Gift

and to

Aron for My Inspiration

TABLE OF CONTENTS

ACKNOWLEDGEMENTS

THIS BOOK IS a labor of love that could not have happened without the support of my wife, Yelena, and my dear friends who contribute articles to my web site, YOWUSA.COM.

To Janice Manning, my greatest thanks for sticking with me through thick and thin during the many months it took to complete this novel. Through it all, Janice was with me each step of the way, offering kind and nourishing words of support, especially when I needed them most.

To Steve Russell and Jacco van der Worp my deepest thanks for superb technical editing and insightful analysis. Their keen eye for technical details and plot lines was of immense help in ensuring the flow and scope of the story.

I also wish to thank Lisa Mastramico, Tina Mastramico, Mike Crawford, Michelle Turley, Kari Tsujimoto, Toby Gerst, DeWitt Weaver and Margarita Gantman for their contributions and kind support.

Cover design by Steve and Nadia Russell.

FOREWORD

ANCIENT VOICES FROM our distant past warn us that we of today may soon face the fearful challenge of a majestic but violent universe. With life as we know it hanging in the balance, we may find ourselves perched upon a fulcrum of evolution, de-evolution or worse yet, extinction. If a planet five times the size of Earth passing through our solar system does not threaten catastrophe, then certainly something else will. For this reason, this book is not about catastrophe. Rather, it is about the awesome strength of our own humanity and how it gives us the strength to carry on when all we have left is hope itself. In essence, this book is focused on the most important question of catastrophe — how will the human spirit survive?

Godschild Covenant: Return of Nibiru, is about the enduring strength of the human spirit and is based on a fictitious flyby scenario of the planet Nibiru in 2012, as described in the various works of the noted historian and scholar, Zecharia Sitchin. As this book goes to press, there are many who feel certain that Nibiru will again pass through our solar system sometime within the next decade. They further believe this next flyby will be as catastrophic as a previous passing that caused the "Great Deluge," as the ancient Babylonians called it. For Western civilization, the "Great Deluge" is more commonly known as the Old Testament (Hebrew Torah) story of "Noah's Flood."

Assuming you know little or nothing about Nibiru, you're probably wondering: Does it really exist? If so, when will it appear next and what would that mean for mankind?

Without question, Nibiru is a historical fact, according to ancient texts, dating back to the earliest civilization of Sumer, in the region now known as Iraq, Syria and Iran. In terms of scientific fact, nothing conclusive in terms of credible astronomical observations of Nibiru has yet emerged. This is not to say that Nibiru does not exist. Any astronomer will tell you that failing to observe an object in space is not proof that it does not exist. So are astronomers still looking? They are — and until scientists can offer conclusive proof, all that we have are historical facts handed down to us from the ancients.

What ancient texts tell us, according to Sitchin, is that with the exception of the Great Deluge flyby, the coming of Nibiru had always been greeted with great enthusiasm. Visible to the naked eye after dusk, the appearance of Nibiru in the night sky would prompt great parades and feasts in celebration of life. This was because our ancient forefathers held the firm belief that the coming of Nibiru brought with it dramatic technological and sociological advances.

A previous flyby of Nibiru, as recorded by the ancients, has been inseparably linked with the Great Deluge as a time when the "gods" of Nibiru warned mankind of the impending disaster, in much the same manner as the Old Testament tells us that God warned Noah and ordered him to build an ark.

From what scholars on the subject can gather, Nibiru passes through our solar system well beyond the orbit of Jupiter every 3,600 years. Some have expressed the opinion that Nibiru is actually a small captive planet of a collapsed star that orbits our system. This is not such a far-fetched idea as systems with two suns are more prevalent in the universe than our own single sun system.

So could Noah's Flood have been caused by Nibiru, or perhaps by a collapsed star holding it captive? That depends on the positioning of the planetary bodies in our system, or simply being at the wrong place and at the wrong time. Other Nibiru scholars have expressed the opinion that during the Deluge flyby, the positioning of Earth relative to Nibiru was uniquely catastrophic. So, could another flyby of Nibiru through our solar system cause a repeat of Noah's Flood — during your lifetime?

Be forewarned: contemplating this thorny question will net you many long and sleepless nights. While gazing upward from your bed at the little cracks in your bedroom ceiling, your mind will dwell upon horrific flyby catastrophe scenarios until exhaustion and sleep finally overtake you.

However, there is an eventual bright side. At some point in the process, you will decide to put all these doomsday "what-if" catastrophe scenarios behind you and to focus on what really matters — the survival of the human spirit, no matter what comes. (And while you're at it, it probably wouldn't hurt to paint your bedroom ceiling, just for good measure.)

The fact is that while the ancient Sumerian texts link the passage of Nibiru through our solar system to the time of Noah's Flood, they do not suggest or imply any causal connection, such as tidal gravitational forces being exerted upon the Earth by Nibiru. Simply put, Nibiru's flyby and Noah's Flood could have been a matter of coincidence and nothing more. Then again, the ancients did not possess modern technology as we know it, and so it is unlikely that they would have been able to establish such a causal connection.

In the final analysis, the next coming of Nibiru is more likely to herald another celebratory event as the ancient texts suggest, as opposed to creating a modern day catastrophe for our lovely blue-green planet. Sadly, though the chances are remote, the risk of catastrophe remains.

If the worst were to happen — another Great Deluge — that would certainly mean the end of civilization as we know it. A global catastrophe of that scope could certainly endanger the very survival of mankind if we blind ourselves to the threat. For this reason, the flyby scenario in Godschild Covenant, The Return of Nibiru, presents a level of catastrophe that falls somewhere between the Great Deluge and a harmless celebratory flyby as reported in the ancient texts.

It is also important to keep in mind that mankind faces even greater threats than a catastrophic Nibiru flyby, such as a major impact similar to those portrayed in blockbuster movies Armageddon and Deep Impact.

Is that the worst the universe can throw at us? As terrible as those cinematic impact scenarios may seem, there are even more terrible things to consider. For example, if a star within twenty-five light years of Earth were to suddenly go supernova, the result would certainly become an extinction level event for mankind.

In this context of all this, Nibiru, which is often called "Planet X," is something we can survive! This is one of the reasons why I chose a Nibiru-based catastrophe scenario for this book, because it allows me to focus on the issue that is nearest and dearest to my heart — how will the human spirit survive?

After years of study and deliberation, it has become my firm belief that a catastrophe, such as the one portrayed in this book, would become a catalyst for change. It would jar us out of our present self-serving, materialistic rut and force us to evolve into the more intelligent and compassionate beings to which we aspire. God willing, later generations would reflect upon our deep suffering as mankind's unavoidable price of admission into a millennium of peace, as foreseen in prophecy long ago.

— *Marshall Masters*

THE GODSCHILD COVENANT

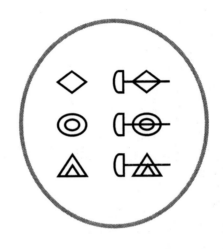

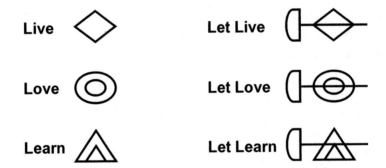

Live	◇	**Let Live**	
Love	◎	**Let Love**	
Learn	△	**Let Learn**	

Destiny finds those who listen,
and fate finds the rest.

So learn what you can learn,
do what you can do,
and never give up hope!

CHAPTER 1

2011: THE YEAR OF LIES

THE WARM, MOIST night wind and driving rain, unusual for December in Berkeley, buffeted the windows as Dr. Justin Taylor tucked his 9-year old son Russell into bed. "Hey, Tiger, I wish I could read more of Moby Dick to you tonight but my eyes are killing me. I've been grading papers all day. Such is the life of an English professor, my son. I do dread the end of the semester."

"That's OK, Daddy," Russell answered. "I understand. There will be another time." Born and raised for the early part of his life in Oklahoma, Justin Taylor had that rugged, tall Texan look and gentle accent similar to that of boy's biological father, Anthony Jarman.

Standing up to his full height of six foot three, Justin looked down upon young Russell with adoring love in his deep blue eyes. "You're my hero."

"And you're my hero too, daddy," said Russell. Self-confident, slender and just over four feet tall, the boy had broad shoulders which made him look similar to Justin in many respects except one. While he decidedly shared his mother's facial features and black, curly hair, the difference was in the eyes. In this regard, fate had made Russell a perfect clone of Anthony Jarman, though the boy had never known the full truth of his lineage.

While the secret of Russell's true biological father had been kept from him, his mother and stepfather often talked in hushed tones about Russell's intense, steel blue eyes. Like those of his biological father, they could pierce through you in a single glance, like a hot knife through butter.

"Well, that makes us the dynamic duo, I suppose." Justin replied with a proud glowing smile as he finished tucking the boy into bed.

"You sleep tight, and don't let the wind bother you. It is just this crazy weather right now because of the sun activity, and it will pass in a few months. Or at least that's what the government says, and we must trust them for now."

As he reached over to turn off the light, the young boy rose up from his bed and hugged him closely. "I'm afraid, daddy. My friend, Ernie from school went with his father to some astronomy club observation event, and he said he saw Nibiru for the first time now that it is far enough away from the Sun to be seen through a telescope. I don't like this planet, daddy. I'm afraid of it."

Justin held on to him, gently patting his back. "Everyone is, son, but NASA tells us that nothing major will happen except for these crazy weather patterns, like this rain and floods, which, thank God, we do not have to worry about. In a few months, all of this will pass and things will be better, so buck up. There are brighter days ahead."

They sat like that for several minutes until Justin could feel his son sag into a deep sleep. With tender care, he laid the boy's head back upon his pillow, tucked him in again and kissed him gently on the cheek. Switching off the light, he carefully closed the door to Russell's room, adjusted his house robe and softly walked down the stairs to his living room and waiting wife, Roxanne.

Curled up on the end of their massive couch in a matching robe, Roxanne had uncovered her shapely legs to a suggestive length, then unpinned her long, deep auburn hair and provocatively drew it over the front of her ample and shapely bosom. Even after nearly 10 years of marriage, the exotically beautiful five foot eight beauty could still arouse her husband with her enduring physical grace and delicate facial features. On the coffee table, she had set various tidbits of cheese, fruit and a decanted bottle of

Justin's favorite Petite Sirah, a young but incredibly promising wine.

As he drew close to her on the couch, she held up a box of natural tear droppers she'd acquired from Justin's optometrist earlier that day to treat the lack of tearing in his eyes he usually experienced under the crush of having to grade final exams. "I've got the drops for your eyes, so put your head on my lap, darling, and let mamma Taylor fix you up with some drops and a scalp massage."

"You are my angel," he sighed as he slipped his head onto her lap. "My eyes feel like someone took sandpaper to them. The damn shame of it is that I couldn't read to Russell tonight."

"Hold still," she commanded as she applied the drops to both eyes. "Now remember to keep your eyelids shut and to gently roll your eyes around a few times."

"I'll just pretend I'm sneaking a peak at you in the shower and getting a good look at everything," he teased.

She play slapped him on the cheek. "You're a naughty boy."

"Just the way you like them," he flirted back.

She sighed. "I've been found out. We'll need to discuss this in greater depth later on this evening."

He felt pulsing in his groin. "Oh yes, in much greater depth, indeed."

Roxanne giggled and play slapped him again. There had been a time in her life when she thought she could never be this happy but there she was, with a loving son and a devoted husband, the envy of any woman. The rain outside was driving in sheets across the large picture window facing the street in loud staccato pelts. As she began to massage his scalp, she casually asked, "So tell me, my adorable husband, is Russell sound asleep?"

Continuing to keep his eyes closed, he turned his head slightly with the motion of her massage. "Yes dear, but he's terribly frightened by this Planet Nibiru flyby. The weather is pretty weird now."

"I'll say. Last week, the FAA announced that they are going to extend their virtual cancellation of all daytime domestic flights because of the freakish wind shears that have caused those three horrible crashes last week. The airlines are scrambling to reschedule flights, but people are opting to take the trains."

"Between this and the drop in air travel because of the Chinese-made Stinger missiles the Islamists used to down all those flights a few years back, it looks like the major carriers are not going to make it out of Chapter 11 this time."

"Yes, I think they're their done for. The only planes in the air today are chartered jumbo jets with advanced avionics and military. Damn pity. I can remember when flying was easier than taking the bus. I guess the government will finally have to step in and nationalize the airlines after all."

Justin snuggled his head deep into Roxanne's lap and slapped his thigh. "Oh darn me and these accursed papers. I forgot to tell you earlier, but you got a ninety-percent keyword hit on a Fox News report with Rose O'Hara. I was busy grading a paper when the notice popped up on the screen and I didn't bother to look at the TIVO listing. I just saved it under your favorites box and went back to grading."

"Oh thanks; now you tell me. You know O'Hara is my favorite news reporter."

"Yeah, I know; she's an all-American red-head with an attitude and brains. And, if I may add, a bodacious body."

She play slapped him again. "You are really being a naughty boy, tonight."

He ran his tongue across his lips. "Best of all, I get to stay behind after class is dismissed."

She grasped his chin and shook it. "Open your eyes, and sit beside me. I'm just itching to see O'Hara's report." As he sat upright, Roxanne switched on the wall size mural

HDTV and thumbed her way to the report saved in the TIVO favorites folder for immediate playback."

It began with the usual Fox news bumper and cut to a close-up of O'Hara standing in front of the Homeland Defense induction center in Reston, Virginia with a line of men and women behind her. As usual, O'Hara had pinned up her coppery light auburn hair, which she always let down while at home and shopping. A fiercely proud Irish-American from head to toe, she could roll with the punches like the best of them despite her smallish figure. Some in the media liked to think of her as much younger Christiane Amampour, but with a credible feminine side to counterbalance her biased and blistering intelligence. However, for the management at Fox News, she was simply nothing more than pure gold because she could connect with their audience like a stuck slot machine.

"Good afternoon, I'm Rose O'Hara for the Fox News Channel and behind me is the latest batch of draftees called up by the Homeland Defense for duty." The facility was ordinary by military standards with the usual scrub pines set about the facility, which would be used to train inductees for immediate field commissions.

"Chosen for their skills and education, these draftees are usually commissioned as officers and immediately begin within just weeks. When we come back, we'll learn the story of one these draftees standing behind me. His name is Anthony Jarman, a political consultant and campaign manager for the Progressive Libertarian Party and he's been designated to serve as an End of Life Management Officer or ELMO for short."

Roxanne shot upright and cupped her mouth to muffle her scream as Justin rolled over to catch the reporter's final words before cutting to a commercial break. "Some people call them trench killers, while others call them unfortunate saints. When we return, we'll talk with Anthony to see if he sees himself as a trench killer or an unfortunate saint."

"This is fucking political payback," Justin spat in a disgusted tone as he quickly twisted around to seated position next to Roxanne. "They couldn't beat him fair, so now they're going to kill him."

Roxanne rocked back and forth and wept, "Oh, God! Justin, you're right. They're doing this to kill him. Remember those ELMOs in Redmond last year after the Microsoft Corporation was bracketed with Islamist dirty nukes and all those poor people in Redmond and the surrounding areas began dying horrible deaths?"

"Oh yeah, I remember," Justin replied. "There were four ELMOs and they worked day and night performing assisted suicides for the terminally ill. Then on the last day, after that last of the assisted suicides, they in turn all declared their right for assisted suicide except for one, and he went insane."

Roxanne wept, "Oh Anthony, my dear Anthony, what have these filthy bastards done to you?" In their shock, they had let the commercial break roll on without fast-forwarding the media file, and the return announcement caught Roxanne's eye. She put her hand on Justin's knee. "They're coming back from the break."

"Rose O'Hara here at the Homeland Defense induction center in Reston, Virginia outside of Washington D.C." She stepped aside and pointed behind her. "Behind me is a line of men and women who have just been drafted into the Homeland Defense as pre-trained specialists and will be serving in the field as commissioned officers in just a few weeks." She took a step closer towards the camera, which pulled out to show her standing next to Anthony Jarman. He was wearing blue jeans and the classic maroon-colored Texas A&M sweatshirt with the letters spelled across his chest in large, bold white type.

He had been a cocky, skinny college kid during their 6-year affair at A&M, but now Roxanne could see that the intervening years had pushed back his hairline a little farther than she might have expected and that they had also put a little extra weight on him, but in a flattering way. He looked both powerful and exhausted at the same time, and there was a new gentle softness in his face now, as though the years have finally managed to temper him in a more kindly way.

O'HARA CONTINUED with the interview. "While many of the people you see behind me are the doctors, nurses, bridge builders and so forth desperately needed to fill the upper ranks of our Homeland Defense forces, the man standing next to me, Anthony Jarman, a political consultant and campaign manager for the Progressive Libertarian party, has been drafted and assigned to duty as an End of Life Management Officer. His job will be to help those who have declared their right of assisted suicide under the terms of the UNE treaty to end their lives. Anthony could have moved to another country or filed for a deferment, but he hasn't, which has left many people wondering if his call-up is politically motivated in some way. So what does Anthony think about this call up? Let's ask him." She turned the microphone towards Anthony.

"I would have never asked for something like this under any circumstances," he cleared his throat. "Accepting this call up has been an agonizing decision, but in the final analysis, my family didn't raise me to be a shirker. I can't say for sure whether or not this is some kind of political retaliation, as I've been in volunteer hospice work for the last few years. You know, just trying to be there when I can for the folks dying from the bugs and the bombs and all the horrible stuff going on these days."

O'Hara pointed the microphone back at herself. "But of course you do know that the odds of you completing your tour of duty without committing suicide yourself or going insane are one in ten. Given that your efforts directly resulted in a one-third increase in the size of your party, which is calling for America to abrogate the UNE treaty of 2011, do you not feel that this call-up is in some way politically motivated after all?" She directed the microphone back to him.

He looked down at the ground as he shuffled his feet his feet for a moment. Rather than draw the microphone back for a follow-up question to keep the air filled, O'Hara waited patiently, just as she knew her viewers would be doing, hanging on to this pregnant pause for as long as it would take to look into Jarman's eyes when and if he finally chose to answer.

Anthony looked back up and directly into the camera. He blinked a few times, as the internal conflict in his face became clearly apparent. Clearing his throat a second time, he spoke in deep, firm, measured tones that carried his words with a lasting impression. "It doesn't matter whether this call-up is politically motivated or not. After all, in the final analysis, what isn't political? So, how I got here is not important. What is important is what I will do next. Yes, I've been given a difficult job; I understand the personal risks; and my greatest concern is whether I will be able to put my life back together after this. While I really do not understand how and why fate has led me to this point, I do believe that things happen for a reason and I am confident that my enduring belief in God will help me pull through. In the meantime, this is an important job regardless of how unenviable it may be. It will require my most careful, compassionate and professional attention at all times. This is all that matters now."

She drew the microphone back for the next question. "Anthony, have they told you where they're going to send you after your training?"

He nodded slowly, "They're going to send me to New York. A lot of people are still dying from the low-yield nuke used on the UN headquarters, and a lot of them are tired of the fight."

O'Hara held up a hand briefly; "Excuse me, Anthony." She put a hand over her ear to better hear the instructions of her producer in New York and pointed the microphone back to herself again. "Anthony, my producer tells me that callers from all across the country are simply melting our phone system. Many are asking the same question. "Will you go back into politics if you survive your tour of duty?" She pointed the microphone back towards him.

Lacking a 'smoking gun', he had been forced to sidestep the issue of political revenge as being the reason for his call-up. However, he instinctively knew that it was precisely the cause and that now was his time to send a message back to whomever it was that was trying to destroy his future. He leaned forward into the camera lens with a fixed jaw as his steel blue eyes shot through the camera lens and into homes all across the world. Surprised by his sudden movement, O'Hara quickly reacted by learning forward as well, to keep the microphone near his face.

From the back of a darkened control room in New York, the show's producer watched his wall-sized bank of monitors with keen fascination. He rocked back in his chair and muttered to himself, "He knows he's been screwed and he probably has a good idea of who did this to him. If someone from the IRS showed up on my doorstep with that kind of a look, I'd just start writing checks until the bastard went away."

Indeed, Anthony's steel blue eyes had focused his message with a laser-like intensity that would forever be associated with him and his future accomplishments: "I'm coming back," he said firmly. Then, as quickly as he had leaned forward, he leaned backward and stood upright. Slinging his carry bag over his shoulder, he silently strode away from the glare of the halogen lamps to find his place back in line.

Rose directed her videographer to keep the camera trained on Jarman, with her quietly standing off to one side in the foreground, as he disappeared into the background.

She watched him with her usual keen attention and knew that this man was connecting with her audience in a big way. His story would have legs, damn long legs, and she instinctively knew it as the camera zoomed in on her for a closing medium shot. "Was this call-up politically motivated? While Anthony Jarman cannot say, he was not raised to be a shirker, as he just said, but that doesn't mean the issue is resolved by any means. In the coming weeks, we will attempt to report more about this, and if we can get permission from the Homeland Defense information department, we will interview Anthony once he is stationed in New York for his first tour of duty as an ELMO."

She put a hand to her ear to hear her earpiece. "Our producer just advised me that we've just posted a special chat room for Anthony Jarman, and that the link will appear on our home page at foxnews.com momentarily." At the Homeland Defense induction center in Reston, Virginia outside of Washington D.C., this is Rose O'Hara for Fox News."

ROXANNE SWITCHED OFF the HDTV and the room became silent except for the sound of her voice as she slowly repeated the words, "oh my God."

Justin rose to his feet and paced the floor back and forth in front of the coffee table until he finally turned and faced Roxanne with a stiffened jaw. "All these years, I had hoped you would tell him that Russell is his son. You had no moral right to bear a child by him without telling him. All these years, I'd let you talk me into remaining silent, so who am I to criticize, but things have just changed. This man is very well walking to his death now. Roxanne my love, he has got to know. Not only for his sake, as I hope it will give him something to hang onto, but for Russell's sake as well."

She turned her face away from him. "I've told you a hundred times Justin. It is not about morality. You know about my past and that sometimes, even the most precious things in life must remain precious." Tears began to stream down her face. "Honey this is hard for me too, but we cannot tell him — especially now that powerful forces are aligned against him and determined to destroy him." She looked up into his eyes. "Please honey. You've got to trust me on this. When the time is right, Anthony will be told, and so will Russell, but not now! Not this way!"

"Damn your reasons Roxanne! If you can trust your brother to know who Russell's true father is, then Anthony Jarman has the right to know."

Roxanne could see a terrible fight brewing, one that would tax all of her persuasive powers to their farthest extremes. It would be a terrible evening and she would have to manipulate a man she loved and respected even more for his integrity.

The ring of the front buzzer suddenly interrupted the tension of the living room, gratefully so for Roxanne. "I'll see who it is," Justin said in a highly agitated tone.

On the digital touch screen next to the front door, Justin could see the lone visitor standing under his porch. It was one of his new teaching assistants, Eddy Abubakar from Lagos, Nigeria. He could see that the tall thin 24-year old TA was wearing a surplus Army poncho, now popular with the students on campus. While his dark face was difficult to make out, his pearly white smile and booming friendly voice was unmistakable. "Please, Dr. Taylor. I know this is late, but I have an urgent matter to discuss with you, professor, about the papers you've given me to grade."

"If it isn't one thing, it's another," Justin sighed as he unlatched the door. "Come in, Eddy," he said as he opened the door. While the young man removed his poncho, Justin fished out a pair of house slippers from the hutch in the foyer and handed them to Eddy. "Take off your shoes and put these on so you will not ruin my carpets."

The teaching assistant smiled wide as he unslung his bulging backpack. "Of course, Dr. Taylor."

"When you're ready, I'll be waiting for you in the living room. And, Eddy, let's keep this short, OK?"

"Of course, Dr. Taylor." Eddy could see that Justin was deeply troubled by something and straining to be polite.

"I'll be right along," he said as began to untie the laces on his soaking wet high-top sneakers.

Holding his backpack in his left hand, Eddy paddled into the living room wearing the undersized house slippers. It was immediately apparent that Dr. Taylor's wife Roxanne had been crying. There was a distinct air of tension in the room, and it troubled him. He had expected them to be relaxed mood. Things would be more difficult now.

"Eddy, you must be chilled from the rain," Roxanne observed. "Why don't I make you a nice hot cup of spiced Chai?"

"Thank you very much for your kind offer, Mrs. Taylor, but I'll only be here for just a moment. I just came by to drop off the papers before leaving town for a while. You see my parents back in Lagos want me to stay with my aunt in Atlanta until this Planet Nibiru crisis has passed. She's very worried, you know."

Seated next to his wife on the couch, Justin answered, "I understand, Eddy. Now what do you have for me."

"Oh yes, Doctor," Eddy replied with a toothy grin. He unzipped the backpack and reached his hand in but it wasn't a stack of graded papers he withdrew. Justin and Roxanne suddenly found themselves looking down the barrel of a silenced Beretta 9mm semi-automatic pistol.

"Cooperate, Doctor, and nothing will happen to you or your family," Eddy commanded in a very determined voice.

"You arrogant, little shit," Justin hissed. "How dare you hold a gun on me in my own home?"

Eddy hefted the pistol, "I'll use this if I have to, so again, Doctor, I am asking you cooperate for the sake of your family."

Justin's hands trembled with rage as his eyes beamed in on the dark Nigerian holding a gun on him. "What do you want?"

Eddy knelt down slightly and laid the backpack on the floor. Rising back up, he wrapped both hands around the pistol grip. "We want your son, doctor, and no harm will come to him. In time, we will return him to you."

"I have no reason to believe you, so you can go to Hell as far as I'm concerned."

The calm Nigerian raised his chin. "If a demonstration is necessary my good doctor, then so be it."

Roxanne studied Eddy carefully and determined that he had been trained as an intelligence operative and not a professional hit man. Otherwise, they would both be lying dead in their own blood right now. No, whoever had sent him wasn't interested in drawing blood just yet, but in time, they would be. They most always do. "Eddy, let me help you," she said in a soft comforting voice as she slowly placed her hand upon Justin's leg.

She turned to Justin and nodded once. "Do as he says, Justin, and call Russell down from his room."

"But, but..." he stammered.

"Please, darling. Do as he says. Above all, please don't do anything rash or sudden. I beg you."

Justin bit hard and giving Eddy a hateful glare turned his head toward the head of the stairs. "Russell!" He shouted in an excited loud voice that shook the glass in the china cabinet. "Russell, come down here!"

As Justin repeated his calls to Russell, Roxanne's eyes remained fixed on Eddy, who now focused entirely on Justin. Whoever sent him should have trained him better, Roxanne concluded. With a bit of luck and timing, she would have a chance to drop him with a kill shot before he could react.

The moment Roxanne hoped for finally came as the young boy appeared at the top of the stairs rubbing his eyes.

As Eddy looked up at Russell, Roxanne smoothly shoved her extended hand between the side of the couch and the seat cushion and wrapped her fingers around the small grip of her small yet highly lethal Kimber Ultra Carry EC10 .45. The welcome buzz in the handle told her that the electronic safety system of the lightweight semi-automatic recognized her fingerprint and had just released the safety.

She continued to study Eddy's face in an unassuming way, waiting for her moment to strike. Undoubtedly, Eddy would turn to face Russell as he approached and would, she hoped, turn his back on her for a split second. It would be all the time she needed. The only thought that haunted her was that her son would have to watch the Nigerian's face explode after the hollow-point bullet tore through his skull. Fate had been doubly cruel this evening.

Russell walked slowly down the stairs. The child recognized the menacing pistol in the Nigerian's hands but continued his hesitant descent as Eddy began to sidestep away from his spot in front of the coffee table towards the landing. "This guy is no pro," she silently thought to herself.

The frightened young boy stopped at the bottom of the stairs, his eyes darting back and forth between the gunman and his parents. "Come to me, son," Justin said cautiously. Russell obediently shuffled slowly across the carpet towards his parents on the couch.

At that moment, Eddy chose to speak his first words to the boy, who now eyed him great alarm. "We're going to take a little trip, Russell and I'm going to give you all the ice cream you can enjoy on the trip. Wouldn't you like some ice cream, Russell?"

Russell took a step back; appearing to ready himself for flight, and Eddy turned the pistol on him. It was the exact moment Roxanne had been waiting for, so she drew her Kimber .45 out from between the arm of the couch and the seat cushion. To her dismay, Justin had also been studying Eddy closely and sprung up from the couch, lunging clumsily at him. In that moment, he not only threw his own life away, but also had unknowingly blocked Roxanne's line of sight on Eddy.

The moment the Nigerian caught sight of Justin leaping at him from out of the corner of his eye, he instinctively whipped around and shot. Justin grabbed his chest and stood there for a moment in the realization that he was mortally wounded. His jaw moved and he tried to speak but couldn't form any words. Then, his knees buckled and he fell forward over the coffee table causing it to tip forward.

As Justin's body fell, Eddy could see Roxanne rising from the couch and taking a bead on his head. Turning his pistol towards her, he squeezed the trigger a tenth of a second before his own head erupted in a blinding flash of light, as Roxanne's well-aimed .45 shredded his brain matter like a subsonic meat grinder.

While her shot had brought instant death, the Nigerian's shot had also found a mark, striking Roxanne in the right side of her abdomen. Stunned by the impact of the bullet, she fell backwards into the couch as her breathing became shallow and forced.

She saw Russell standing speechless in the middle of the living room, frozen with fear as he wet himself. She looked down at her wound. The darkness of the blood that had just begun to ooze from her wound was a bad sign. "Damn. Why did the son-of-a-bitch did have to get me in the liver?"

Pressing a hand over her wound to help control the bleeding, she motioned to Russell to join her. "Come to mama, darling. Come to mama."

Russell moved towards her with leaden feet as he approached his father's body then leapt towards her excitedly. "Oh mama, daddy's dead and you're hurt too! Oh mama I'm so scared!"

She wrapped her other arm around him and kissed him sweetly. "I know you are, honey, and I'm so sorry, but your mama is hurt very bad — too bad I'm afraid. Darling, you've got to save yourself." The burning sensation from her wound began to spread and she drew a deeply pained breath that made the young boy start to cry. Girding herself, she gripped his shoulder. "Honey, you've got to be strong. Very bad men want to hurt you, and more will come."

"I want to be with you, mama," Russell pleaded. "Please don't send me away, mama."

Just then, Roxanne could hear the squeal of tires out on the street. Given the lack of a siren, that could only mean that Eddy was not alone. Whoever wanted her son was obviously willing to go to great lengths to get him, and to no good end, no doubt.

She gripped his chin tightly. "Russell darling, you've got to listen to me," she commanded. The boy obeyed. "Do you remember the secret door in the walk-in pantry that leads to Nancy's house next door?"

The trembling young boy nodded. "Yes, mama," he replied dutifully.

The previous owner had built an underground pathway between the two homes. He had used it to secretly visit his mistress who also happened to live in the house where Nancy, a retired nurse and a close friend of the family, now resided alone.

"Good." She pointed towards her cell phone sitting on the edge of the coffee table. "Honey, take the phone. I want you go right away to Nancy's house and when you get there, I want you to call an old friend of mine. His name is Vigo Jones. He is number 27 on the auto dial list. Tell him that you are my son and that I never told him about you and my client. Do as he tells you."

"I don't know this Vigo man, mama and I don't want to leave you," Russell protested.

She could hear heavy footsteps in the rain and the silhouette of man crossed past the picture windows. "Oh damn; shotguns," she sighed as she raised her Kimber at the silhouette and fired. The shot struck the dark assailant in the side of his chest just below his armpit, spinning him down to the ground. There wouldn't be much time now.

She kissed her son one last time and said forcefully, "Run, Russell. Your mama loves you more than anything in the world, but bad men are coming to hurt you, and I can't stop them! All I can hope to do is to slow them down. Please, honey, don't make me cry. Now run!"

There were more footsteps in the rain, racing towards the loud cries of the man she had just shot. The boy took a step back and looked at his mother one last time as dark blood oozed between her fingers, bleeding into her house robe at a frightening pace. "I love you, mama," Russell said as tears streamed down his face. He then turned and ran into the kitchen.

"Thank God," she sighed, as she watched her son disappear into the kitchen. A moment later, she could hear him opening the pantry door as the men outside her house prepared to break in. She reached forward, tapped the remote control and shut down all the lights in the house. She was outnumbered and dying but at least the dark would give her one last chance to buy some time for her son.

She slipped off the couch, sending agonizing waves of pain through her body. Gripping the edge of the coffee table, she was able to use the weight of her husband's lifeless body as added leverage to push it the rest of the way over, away from her. She hoped that the table's thick Marbleite top would at least offer some limited protection from the shotgun blasts. She then dragged herself across the floor behind Justin. Using his body as a parapet, she raised her pistol and waited for whatever would come next.

A shaped plastique charge blew the front door in and the first shooter came in spraying bullets in every direction with a 9mm HK MP5K submachine gun. Roxanne immediately returned the fire, striking the man three times. The first two shots failed to penetrate his bulletproof vest but her third ripped out his throat. In the dim light from the street lamp, she could see him with his back pinned against the wall of the foyer. As sprays of blood shot out of his neck, he slid limply to the floor.

Certainly, that caused a commotion outside the house, and she could hear muffled voices from outside. The next time, they'd come at her from several directions. This would probably be her last stand, she realized as she struggled to breathe, but if not, she would bleed to death anyway.

The pain in her side was burning like fire now, and between that and her loss of blood, keeping her mind focused was a real struggle. She laid her head on Justin's limp body. "You're right, my dear husband," she said with a weak and raspy voice. "I should have told Anthony about his son a long time ago. I was wrong." She grimaced as dark blood continued to ooze from her wound.

She drew pained, shallow breaths as she waited for the next attack. Feeling the fog of death beginning to envelop her, she wondered who it was that had sent assassins to kill her and her husband and to kidnap her son. It just didn't make sense. Who would go to such great lengths to do such a thing and why? Neither she nor her husband knew anything of value, and her child was completely innocent. There was no good reason for it; at least not one that she could see and the pain of that uncertainty now troubled her more than the fatal wound in her side.

Finally, she heard them moving into position outside the house and gripped her pistol tightly as she fought to maintain consciousness. She gave one last great effort and screamed as loudly as she could, "Whoever the hell you are, the police are on the way!"

She knew the police were not coming, but she hoped to push the assassins to make their final move before she lost consciousness. That way, she hoped to buy Russell a little more time with whatever time remained of her own life. "Come on you miserable shits," she hissed under her breath, "let's dance!"

THE TUNNEL BETWEEN his home and Nancy's was only three feet in diameter and used to have a wheeled dolly on a track but that had been taken out many years ago. Clipping his mother's cell phone to the neck of his pajamas, Russell crawled on his hands and knees in the darkness as rodents scurried around his disturbing presence in their underground domain.

Two thirds of the way through the tunnel, he could see the light from Nancy's basement filtering through the old wooden boards that covered the entrance to the tunnel on her side and the safety of Nancy's home.

Suddenly from behind him, came the sound of another barrage. Loud, echoing booms from shotguns and then the dull bursts of his mother's Kimber automatic. There was a long pause before several more shotguns returned fire. After that, a final silence prevailed. The boy's life was twisting around like a bad dream, yet he kept the presence of mind to find safety even knowing that his mother had given the last few minutes of her life to buy him time. Tears continued streaming down his face as he moved towards the light.

What Russell didn't know was that while he had been careful to close the secret trap door in the pantry behind him before starting through the tunnel, the force of the plastique charge that blew off the front door of the house had also jarred open the secret doorway in the pantry, revealing the child's desperate escape.

CHAPTER 2

WHATEVER IT TAKES

THE UNITED NATIONS of Earth conference in Sydney Australia had been an unqualified success for US Senator Merl Johnston, a Democrat from the great state of Louisiana. His late vote on the floor had broken the deadlock in the United States Senate for America's ratification of the UNE Treaty in 2011 and allowed the new world governing body to pursue the final defeat of Al Qaeda after years of deadly terror attacks and destabilizing conflicts.

Upon receiving a private invitation to fly to Washington with Secretary General Antonio De Bono, head of the United Nations of Earth (UNE) governing council, he publicly expressed his gratitude and privately wondered why he had been offered such a singular honor.

The Secretary General had recently been honored with the first Gulfstream G-900 Hypersonic executive scramjet to roll off the assembly line. With its Boeing, high-efficiency Podkletnov Anti-Gravity assist device and liquid hydrogen fueled General Electric engines; the G-900 was simply the fastest way to travel, short of exotic military aircraft.

The trip from Sydney to Washington would take just under two hours. Even better yet, he would be the Secretary General's only guest on the trip. No doubt, Johnston's fortunes were on the rise. As he followed De Bono up the staircase, Johnston turned back for one last wave at the media. With the 2012 elections coming up, this kind of publicity was pure gold.

Standing just less than six feet with a fair complexion and receding dark blond hair, he sported a small paunch from the stresses of political life, which had crept up upon him in his early forties. Yet, his regular visits to the gym had helped him to retain his muscular build. Strong-willed and competitive, he had never lost his virtually indomitable aura of confidence. Many still called him by his college-days nickname, Gator Chaser.

Entering just aft of the rakish delta wing jet cockpit, he was astounded by the lavish interior of the Gulfstream. Cramped, yet functional, the smell of new leather added to its intoxicating sense of privilege. The seating was lavishly spacious for six passengers and was organized around a large center table between the middle rows just forward of the wing. While the small interior could easily accommodate twelve passengers in more frugal corporate configuration, it was relatively spacious for six. Luxury with no expense spared.

Johnston followed De Bono and his 27-year old personal secretary, Yvette Cochereau. An exotically beautiful woman of French-Vietnamese descent, Yvette's trim and curvaceous figure transcended her unassuming business attire.

He quickly noticed her eyes. They were not almond-shaped, as he has expected. Rather, her French lineage had given her soft, widely spaced doe-eyes that seemed to say, "come hither, but only if you've got the price of admission,' and that had obviously been paid by De Bono. It was also apparent that she enjoyed the arrangement as well, given that she exuded the sensual patina of happily kept woman with shoulder-length black wavy hair, which was so well cared-for that it bounced joyfully with each movement.

For most men, her beauty alone would have been enough, but De Bono was more demanding, and Johnston could sense a keen mind lurked behind those shiny doe-eyes. Their controlled darting movements told him that she could scan a person for telling body language in a single fluid pass.

An accomplished linguist, she was completely fluent in six languages and had graduated Magna Cum Laude from the Sorbonne School of Language. Obviously, she was the kind of woman a man such as De Bono would demand, a fusion of great beauty and intellect. This time the grapevine had gotten it right. She was De Bono's secret mistress and that meant she was out of bounds.

Perhaps this was the measure of success, he mused to himself. Senators get to bed eager but clumsy interns seeking their own ambitions with the grace of a cattle stampede, while men like De Bono could lavish themselves in the arms of remarkable women like Yvette Cochereau.

She gestured to Johnston to take a seat opposite De Bono who was now buckling himself in. He quietly slid into his spacious seat facing De Bono, across an elegantly engraved, Merbau hardwood table.

As he sidestepped towards the window seat, he looked down at Yvette with a gracious smile. While her dark business jacket complimented the scarf and her short skirt, he could see she was not wearing a blouse or a bra.

He drew a small quick breath as his eyes instinctively craved to search into the gentle bulge in her jacket to follow the curve of her shapely breasts. In another situation, he would have done so, but his cautious feelings towards De Bono stopped him cold in his tracks. There was something about this man he had never understood, other than it was something to be feared and respected – at all times!

Taking his seat, he glanced out the window as he buckled in. Glancing out the window, he immediately noticed that their seats were forward of the main wing and that he would enjoy an unobstructed view of the Earth during their flight.

One of the technicians on the ground caught his attention. She reminded him of his wife Ginny, approaching middle age and a little pudgy.

Over the years, Ginny had become a practical woman, as he liked to think. She had given him healthy and successful children and now had the good sense, as he saw it, to look the other way when he bedded an intern. Yet, he wondered how his devoted wife would react, if she learned that he had taken a mistress like Cochereau. Would it send her over the edge? Or, does there come a point where a man could obtain enough political power to cower his own wife without having to raise his hand?

This made him wonder if De Bono's wife knew of his mistress, or more to the point, was she honest enough with herself to accept the truth of it. The thought tickled his mind as he settled deeply into the seat and flashed De Bono a gracious southern smile.

De Bono nodded with a smile and checked to see that Yvette had finished buckling herself in. Satisfied, he casually pressed the intercom button on his armrest. "Captain, how soon can we take off?"

The response was almost immediate. "Sir, I've already cleared our departure with Sydney control and all flights have been already been suspended. We can lift in 15 seconds, once you've prepared yourselves for launch."

De Bono glanced at Yvette who smiled back pleasantly to signal that she was ready. "We're ready. Or as you pilot types like to say, it is time to kick the tires and light the fire."

"Very good, sir," the pilot replied.

De Bono and Yvette began discussing the trip ahead, while Johnston stared out the window as the service vehicles pulled away from the Gulfstream to a safe distance. He continued to glance occasionally at De Bono, admiring his presence.

In his late fifties, the UNE Secretary General swam underwater laps in his private pool each morning to maintain his trim and dignified figure, and, unlike other men his age who had already gone gray or bald, he still had a full hairline with chestnut brown wavy hair. Gracefully trimmed by a touch of gray at just the right places, his youthfully thick hair accentuated his strong facial features.

But what Johnston noticed most, was how De Bono's deep brown eyes could flash at you with enough intensity to make you freeze like a startled deer caught in the headlights on a pitch black Louisiana night.

"Prepare for takeoff," the pilot announced. "Starting launch countdown on my mark..." The cabin began to fill with a loud hum and Johnston felt a strange and unnerving sensation pass through his body as the craft began to levitate inches above the launch pad

"Relax," De Bono assured him in a comforting voice, loud enough to be heard over the din. "It's the anti-gravity system. It has to stabilize an EM field. The odd sensations you're feeling will pass quickly. So will the noise. Relax Senator, you're about to have a rather stimulating experience."

Just as De Bono had said, the whirring noise of the anti-gravity device quickly diminished to a slightly audible hum as the nose of the Gulfstream rose steeply towards the sky. The craft hung in that attitude for what seemed an eternity to Johnston before the small low altitude rockets kicked in with a muffled roar, pushing him back into his seat at one and half times his normal weight. He looked at De Bono with surprise, which only made the Secretary General chuckle. Somewhat embarrassed, he turned his head to look out through the large oval window that stretched down past the right armrest of his seat, to watch the Sydney skyline fall below the craft at an incredible rate.

Ten minutes later, the hurtling craft's nose pitched downward to normal flight just below the stratosphere. Johnston marveled at the curvaceous sight of the earth below them as the craft's scram engines propelled them to a speed of Mach 7.6. The noise cancellation system in the Gulfstream's elegantly appointed cabin lowered the sound level such that one could even talk in loud whispers.

The ride was breathtaking and one he would relish telling his friends and family about. No doubt about it, this was air travel such as the common man could never hope to dream about except through the vicarious accounts of media stories.

"Quite remarkable, isn't it," De Bono commented. "You know the first time I ever flew as a very young boy was in a Boeing 727. Oh my," he laughed, "I thought I was an astronaut!"

With his gaze still fixed at the earth below, Johnston could only say, "Secretary General, I definitely catch your meaning. This is real Buck Rogers stuff."

Yvette was amused by Johnston's remark and studied him with a pleasant smile, as watching him reminded her of her own first experience in the Gulfstream. The first time would always be the best, at least for her. She looked over at De Bono and laid her hand gently upon his. "Dom Perignon and Beluga Caviar?

"A delicious idea," De Bono purred back. Yvette winked as she unbuckled herself and walked forward to the small kitchen area just aft of the cockpit. He watched her lithe undulating hips through the space between the seatbacks and whispered to himself, "delicious indeed."

He then turned his attention back to Senator Johnston who was still mesmerized by the view below. It was time to attend to the business at hand, as the purpose of this private excursion was not simply to entertain a recklessly greedy politician with the ride of a lifetime. Rather, he viewed Johnston as an over ripe lemon, about to fall of its own weight from the political tree and with a thud that could interfere with his goals. That was, unless he could manage to turn this particular lemon into lemonade, which was precisely the reason for this trip.

Others would have judged Johnston for what he was, an unabashed and self-serving politician who had held the Senate ratification of the UNE treaty in suspense until the price was sufficient to buy his vote. For De Bono, it was simply a matter of politics as usual.

What De Bono liked about the cagey Louisiana Senator, was that he had earned his reputation for wheeling-and-dealing and knowing when to appease his electorate with highly visible pork-barrel projects. A self-fashioned radical populist, Johnston had developed a dignified Huey Long style approach to politics with his keen sense for politics could not be denied. Yet, his greed had finally gotten the better of him even though he lacked the cleverness to realize it. However, he would, and very soon.

With Johnston's attention diverted, De Bono flipped back the spacious arm to reveal the two large envelopes Yvette had placed there moments before they had boarded. He laid them on the seat next to him, crossed his legs and relaxed. One of De Bono's greatest assets had always been his impeccable sense of drama, timing and the patience to let events flow at a natural pace.

Several minutes had passed as the two men sat quietly together, and Yvette's reappearance went unnoticed by Johnston as she set the table with champagne and caviar, served on chilled bone china.

Yvette quietly poured the champagne while glancing occasionally at De Bono with a knowing smile. She yearned to personally witness what she knew would happen next, but had already resigned herself to spending the remainder of the flight chatting with the pilots. They were handsome, especially the co-pilot, so she reasoned it would not be such a terrible sacrifice after all.

As she finished setting the table, De Bono announced in an exaggerated voice intended to capture Johnston's attention, "Thank you so, Yvette. Perhaps you might like to see if the pilots might enjoy your delicious cappuccino drinks?"

The voice got Johnston's attention and his head snapped away from the window. "Oh my gosh; I've been so rude." Had he blushed it would have at least seemed a bit more sincere, Yvette thought to herself. "Please forgive me, but the view is most breathtaking. Don't you agree?"

"Of course it is," De Bono responded graciously. "I too was equally taken on my first trip, so no apologies are needed. Now perhaps you might like to join me in some champagne and caviar." He pointed at the small black roe on the chilled plates. "This is Beluga caviar from the Caspian Sea. It was harvested at the beginning of the spawning period when the Roe is at its best. At least I think it is. That is why I had a special refrigerator installed on this craft. It keeps the caviar between zero to four degrees Celsius at all times, so I trust you'll find this of excellent quality."

"Well thank you, Secretary General. This is simply marvelous!"

"You're welcome, and if there is anything else you require please Yvette know it now, as she intends to visit those handsome young men in the cockpit while we ramble on here." He winked at her.

Johnston looked up at her and had to force his eyes from searching the parts of her firm, shapely breasts exposed by the somewhat deeply cut, yet conservative business attire. "I'm just fine, Yvette. Please just go on, and do what you need to do."

"Well then, gentlemen, I'll bid you adieu until it is time for us begin our decent." With that, she turned and walked back up the aisle with a gentle, yet alluring slither.

"I've got to admit something, Secretary General. It has been a long time since I've enjoyed a delicacy like this. You know, all we mostly eat on the campaign trail is rubber chicken, BBQ, road kill chili and such."

"We all have our little sacrifices, Senator, as well as our rewards. May I suggest the optimal way to enjoy this caviar?"

"By all means. Please."

De Bono picked up one of the small golden spoons set next to the bone china and carefully spooned the caviar and held the spoon up. "The best way to enjoy such a delicacy, Senator, is to burst the eggs between your tongue and palate, rather than swallowing them whole." He took a mouthful and visibly enjoyed the explosion of flavor in his mouth as the small black roe burst under the pressure of his tongue.

The Senator followed his lead, enjoying the same delightful sensations. He had eaten caviar several times before but had never been taught not to chew it. The difference was noticeably pleasing.

De Bono filled their glasses with champagne and the two men proceeded to eat caviar and drink as they idly chatted about the various rewards and punishments of public life.

After several glasses of champagne, De Bono could see that Johnston was relaxed, at ease and glowing with light inebriation. The moment in time he sought now floated before him like a leaf in a slowly trickling stream. "So tell me, Senator, how are things going on your upcoming 2012 reelection campaign. I understand you're getting some nasty competition despite your surge in popularity as the man whose vote changed American history forever?"

"Oh come now, Secretary General, that wouldn't be of much interest to man of your importance." De Bono noticed that the man's natural accent had grown stronger. As was the custom of his dialect, the words softened at the edges and blurred into one another making them more difficult to deduce. Consequently, his pronunciation was no longer considered and slow for the benefit of a man who spoke European English.

"Oh, quite the contrary, Senator. Perhaps you take me too seriously. Might I quote a line from the cinematic classic, Amadeus, when Mozart says, 'All those old bores! People so lofty they sound as if they shit marble!' Now senator, do you think I'm the kind of man who shits marble?"

Both the question and the statement flabbergasted the Senator. "Uh, no Secretary General." He nervously cleared his throat. "Uh – not at all."

"Well then, a good fight is a good fight regardless of the stakes. Wouldn't you agree?"

"Yes. Absolutely."

"Well then, tell me about your reelection campaign. After all, I'm rather taken by the bravado of American political races if you didn't already know that."

"In fairness I didn't know that Secretary General, but well... OK. I'm not worried about the primaries. I beat the field with one hand tied behind my back on that account. No, sir; I'm a bit worried about the election itself. It seems that I'm getting a lot of heat from an upstart young gentleman by the name of Buck Weaver, who's running on the Progressive Libertarian ticket."

"Oh I've heard of them. That new upstart political party formed from a coalition of disaffected Greens, Libertarians, Progressives and so forth. Do you really take them that seriously?"

"Well yes, Secretary General. They've got twelve percent of the registered votes now, and they're gaining more each day. Worse yet, they've got this hotshot young political strategist by the name of Anthony Jarman running my opponent's campaign. This Jarman fellow is a real pain in the ass. I can tell you that!"

"But what about this Buck fellow, who you'll be running against?"

"Oh him. He's a do-gooder. He runs a tax business during the week and preaches in a few small churches on the weekends. You wouldn't believe it, but he does magic tricks while giving his sermons. Gets the whole bunch of them eating out of his hands, he does, but charisma alone ain't enough to win an election. No, sir."

"So what is his edge?"

"Like I told you, this Anthony Jarman fellow. He used to run campaigns for the Republicans before he switched sides, and he's damn good at it too. In one of the biggest upsets I've ever seen, he helped Senator Connie Chavez win an election in Northern California and she's a Mexican and a Republican to boot! He was a consultant on her election committee and mapped out her entire strategy. She followed it to the tee and won, even though it was a recount squeaker. Go figure I say."

"And so now this Jarman fellow wants to unseat you?"

"Yes, I don't like it one bit. He likes to play things cool till the general elections and then he comes at you from out of the blue. My insiders tell me he'll probably push the affinity insurance and fair trade issues at me."

"Affinity insurance?"

"Yeah, he wants to break the insurance monopoly and let people collectively bargain for health insurance through their clubs, churches and neighborhood associations."

De Bono raised an eyebrow. "But wouldn't that possibly save people a lot of money, especially in difficult times like these with all the residual problems from the Al Qaeda weapons of mass destruction used on America?"

"Sure it would, but there is a bigger picture, Secretary General. It would crater the financial markets. They depend on the large reserves the insurance companies invest from their health insurance premiums. Cut that down and you'll upset the markets for sure."

"I'm sure that is a convincing argument for the insurance companies to fund your campaign."

That insight caught Johnston off guard. "Uh — well, yes."

De Bono waved his hand in the hand in the air to show that it was a not a matter of importance for him. "Now what is this fair trade issue? Is this position similar to free trade?"

"The two things are completely unrelated if you ask me. Free trade is what we presently have; it works great for America and the industrialized nations of the world. However, this Progressive Libertarian fair trade thing is a totally unrealistic plank. In essence, they're saying that goods imported from abroad must be subject to local labor laws of the importers. In other words, sweatshop workers in third world nations should get a minimum wage and safe working conditions just like the consumers who buy their goods in America. It is just plain dumb if you ask me."

"Well I could see how that would fly in the face of exploitation," De Bono noted with a wry smirk. "However, I do believe you're right. It is just one of those things that sounds good but usually ends up creating a terrible mess."

"Exactly Secretary General. In the end, I think the voters will do what they always do — vote with their wallets; and paying twice as much for a hair dryer or go-to-meeting Sunday shirts just won't cut it at the polls."

De Bono studied Johnston carefully. The man was now slightly agitated and focused on the precise issue he needed to use as leverage. "This Jarman fellow certainly is a troublemaker," he said as he refilled the Senator champagne glass. "Not only for you, but oddly enough, for me as well."

The words took a moment to sink in, but Johnston finally caught them as he took hold of his glass. "Excuse me Secretary General. Did you say that Jarman is a trouble maker for you too?"

"Yes I did, Senator and that is precisely why you are going resign from the Senate next week for health reasons."

Johnston lurched forward against the table. "What!"

"You heard me." De Bono said calmly. He then reached into the armrest compartment, drew out the thicker of the two large clasp envelopes, and pushed it across the rich red-colored wood of the Merbau table. "Open it," he commanded in a firm voice.

Johnston immediately recognized the stamped seal of the Senate Ethics Committee on the envelope. "What is this?"

De Bono retrieved the envelope, opened it and dumped the contents on the table before Johnston. "Digital prints of you in the Bahamas, Senator, bank records and so forth."

"How did you get this?" Johnston hissed.

"That doesn't concern you. All that concerns you is that Senator Chavez, who won an election thanks to political genius of Anthony Jarman, has always opposed ratification of the UNE treaty. Further, she is using her seat on the committee to secretly investigate you and as you Americans like to say, she's 'got the goods on you.'"

Visibly shaken, Johnston began thumbing the digital prints and certified document copies with trembling hands.

"Senator, we paid you an exorbitant amount of money for your vote and one of the conditions was that you would not do anything to jeopardize the ratification of the treaty."

In fact, Johnston could have asked for three times as much in bribe money at the time and would have gotten it without hesitation.

"Thanks to your blunder, Senator Chavez is going to take you apart piece by piece in the hopes of forcing the Senate to abrogate the treaty on the basis of fraud." He pounded his fist on the table; "she has enough here to implicate the UNE as well, you greedy fool."

"But, but..."

"But nothing. The minute you stepped off the plane in the Bahamas to stash your ill-gotten gains into your own offshore corporation, your beloved Internal Revenue Service was there, clicking pictures of you every step of the way."

Johnston pushed the documents and pictures apart to reveal images of him with his Bahamian bankers and lawyers along with several damning documents signed in his own hand. He had survived many scandals but there would be no weaseling out of this one. At best, his political career was finished. At worst – the possibilities were too dark to consider. He dropped his head into his hands and moaned, "I'm done for it. Oh Lordy, I'm done for it."

De Bono leaned back in his chair and crossed his legs. "Senator, I have no qualms with avoiding tax collectors and wives. As I recall, the State of Louisiana still adheres to Napoleonic community property laws, so no doubt you didn't want to ever have the risk of sharing this particularly sizable nest egg with your wife in the event of a divorce." He leaned forward and picked up his glass. "After all, one cannot be a successful capitalist unless he knows how to stick his hands in the pockets of others."

"I've done a terribly foolish thing and now I'm going to pay for it."

"Foolish; no. I'd like to think of it as an incredibly naïve blunder. Had you been wise, you would have had your attorney hire a lawyer in Liechtenstein, who would have then hired a lawyer in the Bahamas to set up your corporation and in turn issue bearer stocks to a blind trust you controlled. Now that would have been the smart way to do it. But no, you had to trump up a political junket with the clever notion it would mask your efforts to personally see that things were done properly."

Johnston leaned back in his seat and pushed his head against the headrest. "So what's next?"

"There is where you are most fortunate Senator. Politics is indeed an odious profession, no doubt because it rewards unforgivable blunders with advancement."

Johnston had been in politics long enough to know when he was drowning and more importantly, when someone was throwing him a lifeline. "I take it you're about to make me an offer I cannot refuse," he said with a resigned voice.

"Make no mistake, Senator. I'm not a Godfather. I am the leader of the free world, but let me be very specific. As the Romans used to say, 'either you're for me or against me,' and this is your one and only chance to decide. If you let this opportunity slip by, you will no doubt meet an untimely and unfortunate end and not necessarily by my hands, if you understand my meaning."

Johnston studied De Bono carefully. It was obvious. He still had something of value to offer. If not, someone would have already found him dead in his own bed from some mysterious and sudden affliction. "And if I am for you? What does that mean?"

De Bono kept a straight face even though he was relishing this moment like an angler bringing in a large fish on a lightweight line. "From this day forward, Senator, you will serve me with unquestioning loyalty for the remainder of your natural life. If you do this, you will be rewarded with power and wealth beyond your limited imagination." He leaned forward to accentuate his point, "but be advised, this commitment comes in the form of a bloodline oath. Betray it and you and your entire bloodline will cease to exist."

"I take it I'll not have a few days to consider this decision."

"You're already trying my patience," De Bono replied with an icy stare.

The now weary senator looked at the documents spread out before him again, then turned his head to gaze out the window at the blue Pacific Ocean below. Perhaps somewhere down there would be a cruise ship filled with carefree vacationers. Common people who had worked hard, saved their money and bargained as hard as they could for cabin upgrades, while those with true money and power relaxed in the spacious suites on the decks above them. Given his current predicament, a part of him deeply wished that he was swabbing the decks of his imaginary ocean liner, yet another part knew that this was a fate of his own making and that there were no other options. The realization was sobering and the last vestige of the champagne blur faded away.

He turned to face De Bono. "As we say in America, 'in for a dime, in for a dollar. I accept your offer."

De Bono rewarded him with a satisfied smile. "You've made a wise choice Senator. We'll prepare a resignation statement for you to deliver next week. You will claim that you've been become afflicted with a rare disease and that you will be leaving for Geneva to undergo a radical new treatment not as yet approved by your Food and Drug Administration." He waved his hand across the documents spread across the table. "Then, it will be a simple matter for us makes all of this unpleasant business go away once and for all. After all, you'll be a dead horse politically speaking after your resignation, albeit an immensely popular one. Even if Senator Chavez wishes to pursue this Senate Ethics committee, we can stop her most handily."

"A dead horse pretty much sums it up. But more to the point, what will I really be doing in Geneva?"

"We will be preparing you for a new and more appropriate role; one with considerably more power and prestige – not to mention money. That is all you need to know about that for now."

Johnston nodded and took a deep breath. "Then may I ask you a personal question?"

The question piqued De Bono's interest, "I do not see why not."

"Are you a religious man?"

"How odd you should ask that question. As I recall, the only time you go to church is when the media is there to cover you. But yes, I am in a manner of speaking."

"Of what faith my I ask?"

"This is indeed personal, but I see no harm in answering as you will come to understand this in much greater detail later on. I am a Rosicrucian."

"You mean the Illuminati?" Johnston ventured.

"In answer to your query – yes," De Bono answered without showing a hint of emotion.

"Then can I take it that you're a Jew?"

De Bono frowned. "No doubt you're referring to the 'The Protocols of the Learned Elders of Zion?'"

"Well, yes."

"No I am not a Jew and as to that document, let me inform you of something you'll come to understand in greater detail later on. The Protocols of the Learned Elders of Zion' was a hoax, a decoy, written, crafted, by us to deflect investigators by playing upon their anti-Semitic prejudices to divert their attention towards the Jews instead. At the time, that document was published, the world already knew about us and the investigations at that time had become a serious threat. Simply put, we were in danger and we desperately needed a convenient scapegoat. In addition, as history has well taught us, the Jews have always made superb scapegoats. We just simply played to history to save ourselves."

Johnston sighed. "Then what have I gotten myself into?"

De Bono finally smiled. "You're asking the wrong question Senator. Rather, you should be grateful for such a fortunate turn of events. Trust me. It will all make sense in time and you will look back on this day as a personal turning point of great import in your life."

"I truly hope so, although I've got to be honest with you. Right now I feel like I've been kicked in the gut by the meanest mule in the corral if you get my meaning."

De Bono nodded. "In time, you will find comfort in your decision."

"I'm counting on that, Secretary General. Now, if I might ask another question."

"Another personal question."

"No. Actually, I'm interested in knowing what is in that other envelope."

De Bono laughed and slapped the table. "Good! You're beginning to think clearly, Senator." He drew out the second envelope and passed it across the table. Johnston opened it and found a dossier for Anthony Jarman of the Progressive Libertarian Party.

"Him again."

"Yes. In a manner of speaking, I believe we've already agreed that this young man is a stone in both of our shoes. Wouldn't you agree?"

"Yup. He's that, alright."

"I've read the dossier on him and watched him on televised panels, but I've never met him personally as you have. I'm curious to know what you can tell me."

Johnston thumbed through the dossier. "Well, you've pretty well covered his current history but what I can see is that you don't know about what makes him tick."

De Bono rubbed his chin. "This is beginning to sound interesting. Tell me more."

"Well as you already know, he jumped ship from the Republican Party back in 2008 when he first got wind of the fact that the Republicans and the Democrats were beginning to leaning towards ratification of the UNE treaty."

"That much I know. I also know that he strongly opposes the UNE."

"I believe you're wrong on that assumption Secretary General. He is savvy enough to understand that some form of a single world government is inevitable. Therefore, I wouldn't say that he is opposed to the UNE in theory. Rather, he's opposed to those who control it in fact."

"Then that makes him our enemy."

"Yes it does." Johnston closed his eyes for moment as the realization that he was suddenly talking in plural pronouns with a man who had just threatened to exterminate him and his entire family. What a sudden turn! One minute he was on top of the world and then next – he couldn't even hope to know where fate would eventually carry him. "Let me be frank Secretary General. Your Peacekeeper and Homeland Defense policies are grating on the American psyche and driving more voters to his party each day. In time, the Libertarian Party will be large enough to combine their votes with disaffected Republicans and Democrats and they'll break the treaty or force a major restructuring of the UNE. Rest assured of that."

"And how influential will this Jarman fellow be in that effort?"

"Let me put it to you this way. Since he switched sides, his strategies and efforts have caused the Progressive Libertarian party ranks to swell by half again as much."

"Yet he holds no official position within the party."

"Not him," Johnston sighed. "He's definitely the voice behind the throne type and always will be."

"Then you think he can be easily bought or bribed?"

"That's where you're missing the boat. You don't know what makes him tick. If you knew his early history before he got into politics, you'd know he's the principled sort."

"So what is it that I do not know?" Actually, De Bono knew a great deal about Jarman, far more than he had revealed. Yet, he knew his own intelligence had a few blank spots as well. With luck, he could pry the answers to some of those nagging blank spots from Johnston without tipping his hand prematurely.

"Well, that begins back in his childhood. He was raised in a quaint, little town called Kerrville, Texas south of Austin. Kerrville is a white flight community for affluent yuppies, who've blended in with the local ranchers and farmers and built what many consider to be the best public schools in Texas. Jarman's father was successful mortgage broker, but his mother was a former mayor of Kerrville and heavily involved heavily in state and local politics. That is where Jarman learned his craft. On his mother's knees if you will. At twelve, the boy was out canvassing neighborhoods and planning events. A somewhat precocious child, he did show a marked brilliance early on and demonstrated remarkable public speaking skills. As I recall, he was the oldest of three siblings, which probably contributed to his heightened sense of responsibility I suppose."

"But then there was that terrible accident. My details on that are rather sketchy," De Bono admitted. The fact was that an undisclosed, high-ranking official had permanently sealed all information regarding Jarman prior to his eighteenth birthday in the American government. Despite Yvette's many efforts, she had never been able to get a copy of those records.

"Well, there, I had a little luck," Johnston volunteered. One of my campaign workers had the luck to bed Jarman several times. From what she pieced together from him and those who know, a cruel turn of events happened to him while he was a 15-year old sophomore in High School. Apparently, he was an ungainly kid when it came to girls and couldn't find a date for prom night so his family decided to take a 4-day trip to Galveston as a diversion. Three days before the family was scheduled to leave, a young gal he had a crush on was dumped by her boyfriend and Jarman became her Plan B if you will."

"Oh, now this is getting interesting, please go on."

Johnston nodded solemnly, "As the story has it, he talked his parents into leaving a day later so he could take this gal to the prom. That evening, as he was being used as a decoy for a young girl bent on making her former boyfriend jealous, his family went out for dinner at a restaurant in Austin. Keep in mind, the road from Austin to Kerrville is windy and a bit dangerous, or so I've been told. Anyway, a drunk in a large SUV swerved across the center line and hit them head-on and killed Jarman's entire famiiy." Johnston snapped his fingers and said, "Just like that!"

"Most unfortunate. What happened to the drunk?"

"He survived and is still doing time in prison. Seems he had long history of drunk driving arrests, not that such things ever seem to slow these people down anyway. Later that evening when the girl's parents drove Jarman home from the prom, a sheriff's deputy was waiting for him to give him the bad news. Since they had no other family, Jarman had to identify the bodies and then wound up in an orphanage called Hillview in Austin till he turned 18. As for the girl, she died of a drug overdose two years later.

Guilt most likely drove her to it. Damn shame how one stupid drunk can ruin two perfectly fine families."

"Yes, a pity. Please continue."

"Well, his parent's had left him a sizable estate along with the proceeds of the life insurance, litigation and so forth and he enrolled as a political science major at Texas A&M in College Station where he eventually got his Masters degree. A damn fine school if you ask me."

De Bono pensively tapped his fingers on the table. "But what did this experience do to him? That is what really interests me."

"Well, that's pretty easy to sum up. If you meet the guy, he's an affable character with a dry Texas wit, but what the ladies say about him is even more revealing. Even my gal said the same thing. Get past all the gracious behavior and he's nothing more than an unaffectionate, cold fish — but not just with ladies either. He never lets anyone get close to him, even his fraternity chums at A&M although he could swill beer with the best of them. As I hear tell it, the Sigma's nicknamed him Spock because he reminded them of the Star Trek character."

"So did he get average grades and hop from one sorority girl's bed to another?"

Johnston chuckled, sensing that he finally had come upon something of real interest. "Now, there is the quirky part. Yes, he bedded a few sorority babes, but he quickly settled into a long-time affair with a rather attractive divorcee by the name of Roxanne LeBlanc, a local bank manager as I'm told. A real looker as we like to say. He mainly slept with her all the way from his first year till he finally got his Masters degree. After that, she mysteriously disappeared, but rumor has it she was buying EPT kits in the local drug store for a few months before they parted and most folks guess she got pregnant by him. If she did, he sure doesn't know it."

De Bono's smiled. Knowing the answer, he asked, "So do you think she got an abortion or did she have the child?"

"We checked the local abortion mills, and nothing turned up. My guess is that she left town, went to ground and had the kid without ever telling him."

"And what was her name again?"

"Roxanne LeBlanc and I really can't tell you more than that."

De Bono brushed his finger along the bottom of his jaw. "You've given me two very useful bits of information about this Jarman fellow.   First, I had no idea that he had consulted with Senator Chavez while he was consulting for the Republican Party and that his strategy won the election for her. We cannot afford to underestimate this man."   Both admissions were outright lies, but the real goal was to give Johnston a sense of value.

"I'm here to shout about one Secretary General.   He's a hand full and damn dangerous if he's got you in his political sights."

"And obviously he does, if what you say about his feelings towards those of us who run the UNE is true, of which I have no doubt. This then leaves us to dealing with him before he becomes an even greater threat. Perhaps, this Roxanne LeBlanc pregnancy angle can offer us some leverage."

"You mean find the kid?"

"Yes, but as far as you're concerned, this part of our conversation goes no further. I'll give this to someone else to handle."   It would be a month before Johnston would actually learn how De Bono's operatives had kidnapped the boy and his whereabouts.

"And what about Senator Chavez? I just got dropped on my head thanks to her and I'm itching for some payback."

Johnston's desire for vengeance was welcome news to De Bono. Vengeance was something he could work with; something he could control — a reward for loyal service to be coveted like gold. "Trust me, you'll get your chance,

Senator, and it will come from your hand if you like but you must be patient. Do you understand me?"

"Yes Secretary General."

De Bono grinned from ear to ear with great relish. He had turned this lemon into barrels of the most wonderful lemonade imaginable. "When the time is right you get your revenge on Chavez. In the meantime, the bigger threat is this Jarman fellow. He's not only dangerous to us, but to all mankind as well."

"I don't get your meaning, Secretary General. How could some hack political consultant be a threat to mankind?"

De Bono relaxed back into his chair and rubbed his chin. He hadn't planned to broach this subject just yet but given the confidence of Johnston's eagerness for vengeance, he didn't see the harm in doing so. After all, he had this man right where he wanted him and it was obvious that he fully understood it. Johnston would be the perfect minion. "If you want to understand why well meaning fools like Chavez and Jarman are a threat to mankind, I suggest you begin by looking out your window." He nodded towards the window.

Johnston immediately picked up on his queue and looked out the window to see the familiar coastline of California spread out below the Secretary General's private Gulfstream. "My gosh; time has passed quickly," he noted. "I can even see the San Francisco Bay. Beautiful as ever."

De Bono pretended to look on, while keeping his attention focused on Johnston. "Next year, it will not look so beautiful. Nor will much of the planet, for that matter. You see, Senator, next year our dear planet will experience a series of regional if not global disasters that will defy imagination in their scope and severity."

Johnston's jaw dropped as he turned to face him, "But I thought the wars were over. My God, is there more to come?"

"While the UNE has ended the threat of war, the threat that now faces us is not from mankind my good Senator. Rather, these next disasters will soon occur as the result of Nibiru's flyby through our solar system."

"But NASA said that…" Johnston protested.

"NASA is a toothless giant and has been controlled by America's intelligence agencies, since the Challenger disaster. Think back, man. Remember when the shuttles began flying again after the Challenger disaster. They would say 'another successful shuttle launch with an undisclosed military payload.' Like all good scientists, they'll do whatever it takes to keep their funding. As to Nibiru, they know what's coming, and they know we're powerless to do anything about it. So they tell everyone what they're being told to say, which is basically nothing more than misleading propaganda."

"So, the Planet Nibiru flyby disasters the conspiracy nuts have been warning us about since the turn of the century are true." His face sagged. "Heck, I remember my wife driving me nuts with it for years. She read every book by that whacko, Zecharia Sitchin and pumped my ears full of words like Enki, Nefilim, Anunnaki and Sumerians till I thought I'd go nuts."

"Sitchin is no whacko as you put it, Senator. He is a brilliant scholar and his works will be required reading for you during your indoctrination in Geneva. Trust me; the end of the Mayan calendar is a warning about Nibiru, and it could very well cause another "ending" of human civilization in 2012."

Johnston slumped in his chair. Hearing this from his wife had been one thing, but hearing it from De Bono was entirely another. As the reality of it sunk in, he felt a dark, cold cloud of fear envelop him as his breathing quickened. "I just didn't believe," he finally mumbled.

"Believe it!"

"You know, it was all so incredible. Have you ever seen this Sitchin fellow personally?"

"Not personally. I do not believe he would be the kind of man who would enjoy my company."

"Probably so. You know, my wife made me watch an interview of him on some television program called In Search Of some years ago. He's this little Jewish guy with a serious face and a no-nonsense approach. The funny thing is that he reminded me of this delicatessen owner back in D.C. by the name of Saul. I used to have late night cravings for lox and bagels back then and after doing business on the Hill and I'd drop by Saul's place for a late night fix on my way home. Saul always used to make a big deal out of cutting the lox for me just the way I liked it and would never let any of his kitchen staff serve me. When I saw Sitchin on the TV for the first time, he looked and sounded just Saul so I blew him off as just another friendly lox and bagels Jew. I never gave much thought of it more than that."

"But we're not talking about lox and bagels, Senator; we're talking about a planet that is nearly five times the size of Earth."

"So will it hit us? Is NASA lying about that too?"

"No; even at opposition, which will be the moment when Nibiru comes closest to the Earth, it will not get any closer to Earth than just beyond the planet Mars. Nevertheless, it doesn't need to get any closer to wreak havoc on the earth because of the powerful tidal gravitational forces it will bring upon our planet. Forces so powerful that even though it is still at the outer reaches of our solar system on the opposite the sun from us, it is affecting our planet even now. Nibiru is mostly responsible for the growing increases in global temperatures, droughts, floods and other natural disasters over the last decade."

De Bono leaned forward against the table, his eyes drilling into Johnston's head. "But it gets worse. Seven weeks after it becomes visible to the naked eye, Nibiru will be in perfect opposition, and at that moment, our scientists tell us it will begin triggering massive, catastrophic events on Earth, to include incredibly violent earthquakes, volcanic eruptions and tsunamis. It is truly, as you Americans like to say, 'end of the world stuff.'"

"If this is so… No, check that. If you're telling me, then it has to be so. But then what we are going to do about it?"

De Bono clasped his hands and slowly rubbed his thumbs together. "You'll be shocked to hear this, but there is no way to save everyone and after Nibiru's flyby the planet will no longer be capable of sustaining eight billion souls. Consequently, the only thing we can do is to prevent widespread panic before opposition, which would surely wreck everything. This is why NASA is being made to spew its dismissive propaganda. After opposition, we can just say that we miscalculated and those left alive will be in shock and malleable. They will be glad to accept the explanation, provided we move quickly to help them."

"My God, we're going mislead billions of people without telling them that they are unknowingly doomed, so they will go about their everyday lives to the very end!"

De Bono cleared his throat. "You're missing the point here, which is that we must prevent widespread panic. Imagine entire populaces stampeding in search of safety. They'll flatten precious farmlands and ruin water resources with their mindless stampedes. Then, there will be nothing left for anyone to eat or drink. Trust me; those who will perish in the early days will be considered the lucky ones. "

"Yeah, but it still sounds pretty damn heartless!"

De Bono had expected this reaction and now it was time for Johnston to learn the truth. "Senator, I'm going to divulge a long held secret that you will become increasingly mindful of during your indoctrination in Geneva. The simple fact is that the Illuminati has always known about the coming of Nibiru and feared it. With each passing of this planet, every 3,600 years or so, advanced human civilizations have been thrown back into primitive dark ages leaving their technology behind as they once again fashion flint and bone to make their primitive weapons.

Such is as it has always been. Each time mankind has built an advanced civilization; Nibiru has come along only to knock it apart like a flimsy set of bowling pins. However, this time will be different. No matter how Machiavellian or sordid our methods may seem, it has always been our singular goal to see to it that this time, human civilization will persevere and we will not be cheated of this by unwitting fools like Chavez and Jarman."

Johnston studied the serious lines in De Bono's face as his breathing slowed to a hesitant series of deep chest falls. The two men sat quietly, studying each other for what seemed like an eternity to Johnston. Finally, he spoke in a weak voice. "Pull America out of the UNE and it could fall like a house of cards, Secretary General. My God, if these fools manage to cause that to happen, then where will that leave us?"

"Looking for flint to make our cutting tools and arrow heads, once again."

"I see your point precisely. They truly are a threat to mankind."

Johnston closed his eyes, leaned back into his seat again and held his head with his hands. "Nothing could have prepared me for this," he sighed. "My purpose in life has changed in just an instant and there is no going back now." He dropped his hands limply on the table and stared at De Bono with stunned disbelief.

De Bono's face softened and he reached across the table and gently laid his upon Johnston's forearm. "You've had enough surprises for one day, Senator. May I suggest that we just relax for the remainder of our trip?"

The warmth of De Bono's touch was reassuring to Johnston. He no longer saw the Secretary General as a twisted politician who had hoisted him on his own petard to serve his own sordid interests. He now saw a man who, while flawed in a certain ways, was driven by the desire to save mankind from repeating the failures of the past. In spite of all the dark maneuverings, it was an urgent agenda to which he now felt privileged to serve. However, the fact that this turn of events also happened to save his ass was the deciding factor.

He laid his other hand upon De Bono's and said with a deep newfound determination, "Whatever it takes, Secretary General. Whatever it takes."

CHAPTER 3

POLITICAL LEVERAGE

THE WORLD HAD been finally been shocked into reality when, in the spring of 2010, a Saudi Wahabi terror cell financed and armed by Al Qaeda delivered a deathblow to the United Nations building in New York. In what was a brilliantly executed attack, they managed to transport a suitcase size, low-yield nuclear device to the very steps of the UN building itself and became holy martyrs, shahids, when they turned the UN into a smoldering radioactive pit of death and destruction. The whole world soon knew who had perpetrated the attack and this final torment by Islamist terrorism pushed the American leadership past all sense of self-restraint. In one defining moment that shocked the world, America retaliated by obliterating every city in Saudi Arabia with new strategic scalar weapons based on Tesla technology. Without the residual radiation common to nuclear devices, America's new scalar weapons literally melted everything from ground level up across the entire surface of Saudi Arabia. Not even the scorpions survived.

The Islamists had finally pushed the world to the reality of wholesale nuclear extermination. This realization stunned mankind more than the devastation of Saudi Arabia, and in the aftermath, the world's nations chose to rebuild again. This time a more enduring form of global rule would emerge as the United Nations of Earth. Headquartered in Geneva, Switzerland, the main headquarters of the UNE was built on the left bank, known as the 'rive gauche,' whereas the massive home in which the Secretary General lived had been built on the older and more prestigious 'rive droite,' Right Bank. Designed by Italian and Japanese teams of architects, the massive buildings tastefully blended in with the surrounding architecture, while being constructed in such a manner as to survive a magnitude 9.5 earthquake. A secret underground tunnel connected the two with a high-speed tram.

White with blue trim, the Secretary General's private residence was appropriately named the Blue House and was nearly twice as large as the American White House in Washington D.C. Adjoining the main office wing of the Blue House was the Secretary General's private indoor swimming pool. Housed within a spacious timber lined pool hall, the water in the pool was constantly heated to a minimum temperature of 80 degrees. A private changing room and bath adjoined the pool area, as did a private hallway that led from the pool to the Secretary General's private library and office.

As was his custom each morning, De Bono relished his underwater laps. Rather than splashing about and swallowing pool water, he preferred the eerie peace and silence he enjoyed as he propelled himself from one side of the pool to the other. One aspect of swimming underwater that he liked was the reward of discipline. Rather than paddling madly through the water he would sweep his cupped hands back against his thighs in sure, powerful strokes, then streamline his body so that his momentum would carry him as far as possible. Then, with a minimum waste of motion and effort, he would repeat the process until reaching the other side of the pool, a disciplined study of time and motion that could be measured and fine-tuned with each successive stroke.

Swimming let him focus him mind on each issue of importance that day without the clutter and demands of other thoughts and people. On the final leg of his last lap, his thoughts centered on Senator Johnston and how he delivered his resignation speech exactly as instructed. Further, the most recent status from his instructions showed that his indoctrination was proceeding more smoothly than planned, which would serve to further validate his acumen with the inner council. However, now the time was coming at hand for the Senator to be given his first assignment, and De Bono had the perfect one in mind.

Finishing his swim, he stood up and stepped across to the elegantly contoured stairs leading up to the pool deck. Standing at the top of the stairs was Yvette with a large towel and a terry cloth bathrobe draped over her arm. Dressed in a scant, low-slung string bikini that covered the barest of essentials, the appearance of hair on Yvette's shapely body was limited to her sculpted eyebrows and coiffured hair.

She silently held out the towel first as he removed his cap and earplugs. He dried himself briefly, dropping the wet towel to his feet. She then drew herself close to him and embraced him with a wide mouth kiss. As he kissed her back, she gently tongued the crème-filled chocolate she'd been holding in her mouth into his. He accepted it with his usual delight and crushed the chocolate against his palette allowing the sweet viscous filling to wash away the aftertaste of the pool chlorine.

They kissed lightly again and then she walked with him to the shower where she washed him as he scanned the waterproof webpad in his shower for the latest updates. He had just flipped a page with his eyes, when an alert from Phillip Boretti, his head of staff popped up. He pointed his eyes to the dialogue and blinked twice. "Sorry to bother you in the shower Secretary General," his head of staff said politely, "but Chinese President Chop is online and wishing to have an immediate and urgent dialogue with you."

Yvette was rubbing the small of his back just to be mischievous, hoping he'd lose his usual poker face for just a split second with his head of staff, thereby sending a veiled message as to who was really standing behind the throne.

"Phillip," De Bono ordered, "Prepare the security dome in my library. I'm on my way."

"I have already done so and I will be awaiting you in the library, sir," Boretti replied smartly to send a reply in kind to Yvette's attempted subliminal message.

De Bono turned off the shower, switched the webpad off and turned around to face Yvette. "You little prankster," he scolded her playfully. "I'm going to have to teach you a lesson this afternoon."

She ran her tongue across her lips. "I love being the teacher's pet," she cooed as he took a fresh towel in hand.

"And I love being the teacher, but for now, darling, we need to take care of the business at hand. Did you finish your research on the Three Gorges Flu epidemic? I'm hoping to bring it up during my conversation this morning with President Chop."

"It is all finished. You'll see it in the secure side stream folder as 3G. I believe President Chop will find the contents of that file to be most convincing."

"No doubt he will. Tell me, you really despise them— the Chinese, that is."

Yvette turned away from him. "They killed my maternal grandparents at Lang Son when they invaded Vietnam in 1979. They're filthy pigs, and now these idiots have unleashed a new horror upon mankind that could be like no other. You'll see everything in my report."

"Which as usual will be detailed and brilliantly organized." He put his arms around her. "I didn't know how your grandparents had been killed. Perhaps I read it in passing and forgot it long ago, but this is the first time I've seen your personal pain. I'm sorry for that."

She turned to face him. "So go deal with them and be firm or they will destroy you and it is not my prejudice that is speaking."

"And if they did, what would come of you."

"With my luck, your replacement would be old, fat, toothless and suffering from chronic flatulence, a fate worse than death, so don't let me down."

De Bono laughed hard as he finished drying himself. "Yvette, the only man who could ever hope to break your heart would have to be a diamond cutter."

She pointed her finger at him. "That was not fair. Now I'm really going to teach you something this afternoon." She stepped close as her face softened. "Antonio, please remember; give Chop a millimeter and he'll take the whole planet."

DE BONO STROLLED briskly into his private library dressed in a cream-colored turtleneck sweater with black sports jacket and slacks. Phillip Boretti had already elevated his security dome, which was normally recessed under the floor, and stood next to the open door holding a pair of thin, wireless VR gloves. "President Chop is waiting on standby, Secretary General," he said matter-of-factly. "Your heads-up display is already organized and link-ready."

De Bono groaned as he slipped on his gloves. "Just between us, Phillip, I think Chop is an inept ass."

His chief of staff chuckled. "My sentiments exactly, sir," he agreed with delight as he closed the door to the secure dome behind him. "Happy hunting, sir."

De Bono quickly checked the heads-up desktop for the familiar setting and Yvette's file. He'd seen most of it the day before but opened it once again to scan it briefly, as his security dome transmitted password keys and encryption ciphers with President Chop's security dome in Beijing.

"Yvette, my darling," he hummed admiringly to himself, "You can be as nasty in politics as you are good in bed — a woman of unique talents and passions." President Chop's face appeared in front of him floating patiently in space as the encryption routines completed the exchange of the single use complex encryption cipher they'd use during this dialogue.

The leader's face looked just like the posters papered all across his country. Rigidly stoic with broad jowls and narrow eyes, Chop had the face that could only win the seat of so much power through internal machinations. Finally, the secure transmission icon appeared telling both men the conversation could begin. "President Chop," De Bono greeted. "To what do I have the honor of this call today?"

Chop nodded his head respectfully; "I thank you for accepting my call, Secretary General. The matter I need to discuss with you today is most urgent. As you are aware, only three nations still refuse to sign the UNE treaty, Great Britain, Israel and Taiwan which the UNE has regrettably recognized as a country against our voiced protests."

"Excuse me, President Chop, but so far we're covering old news. Can we dispense with the histrionics and move forward?"

Chop's jaw quivered. Obliviously, De Bono was not going to give him a free hand in setting the agenda and pace of the dialogue. "To be specific, we now have absolute proof that Taiwan has nuclear and biological weapons of mass destruction aimed at us.   We presented this information to your offices last week and you have not responded."

"President Chop, we've been evaluating your request for withdrawal from the UNE with very close attention and are close to a formal response."

The Chinese leader seemed satisfied knowing that his demands were being taken very seriously. "I trust that you now understand our need to withdraw from the UNE in light of Taiwan's possession of weapons of mass destruction. As a member nation of the UNE, we have surrendered control over our weapons of mass destruction to the UNE."

"President Chop, this is a requirement of member states in exchange for a global mutual defense mechanism. If America and Russia, who have considerably more weapons of mass destruction than China, are satisfied with this arrangement, then I'm frankly hard pressed to understand your latest demand."

Chop was feeling an edge over De Bono. He sensed that De Bono was now trying to buy time. "As you can see, circumstances have changed and we cannot afford this terrible risk from Taiwan without regaining control of our own weapons of mass destruction."

"And so China, after careful deliberation of its international agreements, has decided to abrogate the treaty."

"I find the manner in which you express it to be most regretful. Rather, there is a simple matter. Circumstances have changed, and, unlike you, we have an adversarial, non-aligned nation armed with weapons of mass destruction close to our own shores."

De Bono held up his hand. "President Chop, rather than belabor the point, which you have made so very clear in your previous communiqué, perhaps let's revisit some of the benefits of UNE membership. For example, what about the massive medical aid we are providing to your country to combat the spread of the Three Gorges Virus, known as the 3G flu, which first appeared in the settlements near your Three Gorges Dam on the Yangtze River? We are quite concerned about this new airborne virus, as it seems to be over ninety percent fatal, and some people can be carriers for a year or more before evidencing any symptoms."

The sudden broach of the 3G flu was discomforting for Chop, who quickly steeled himself. "Yes Secretary General, it is a most distressing situation. As you know, our country has spent over thirty billion Euros on the construction of this dam, which we hope will finally go into service in two years. The problem has come from displaced populations living near the future reservoir. These settlements are very crowded, and health services, water supplies and sanitation are inadequate. As you know, the residents of these settlements already suffer a high incidence of rheumatic fever, hepatitis B, pneumonia, measles and diarrhea."

"We know about that," De Bono replied sharply, "As well as the other health risks which have included outbreaks of malaria, paragonimus, epidemic hanta virus and hemorrhagic fever."

"Yes, yes, this is sadly true, and the people of China are deeply grateful to the UNE for its kind assistance. However, the point of this conversation is that of Taiwan, an adversarial and unaligned state with weapons of mass destruction near our shores."

"Now President Chop, we both know that Taiwan is not the problem and that they have already indicated a willingness to ratify the UNE treaty once they are convinced that mainland China has no further interest in attacking them." De Bono leaned forward for emphasis as his eyes drilled into Chop's stoic face. "The problem Mr. President is that you are losing control of the PLA."

"That is an insult, sir," Chop shot back. "The leadership of the People's Liberation Army is completely devoted."

"From what we hear, they are annoyed with the leadership over this 3G flu situation."

Chop's jaw stiffened. "Your sources are wrong. There is no such conflict."

De Bono leaned back with a warm smile. "Please, sir, I did not mean to anger you. Rather, I'm simply trying to understand you better." He could see Yvette's file slowly blinking off to one side. With a sweep of his glove, he pushed it into the secure data side stream transfer bucket. "President Chop, I've just sent you an important file, and I need you to review it with me before I can offer my own recommendations on China's intentions to remove itself as a member state from the UNE."

The file arrived in Beijing even as De Bono was speaking, flashing an acknowledgement on his side. "Please open the file now, Mr. President." He then watched quietly as the square jawed leader opened the file. It took only moments before his eyes opened wide with alarm as he manipulated the information objects in the file.

"How did you get this information?" he spat.

"You know, people always ask me that very same question," De Bono replied with relish, "and I always give them the same exact answer: It is none of your business."

The tide had suddenly turned against Chop. The file offered irrefutable proof that the Chinese had originally bought the virus from the Russian Mafia. Developed originally by the Soviets, the intended use of the virus was to cause severe bouts of diarrhea and nausea. The goal was to incapacitate ground forces and civilians without killing them. However, the Chinese had taken the virus one step further with their own bio weapons lab research and turned it into the killer know known as the 3G flu.

De Bono watched with invisible amusement as Chop closed the file with a sweep of his hands. The Chinese leader took a deep breath. He had been out-maneuvered and now it was he who needed to buy time. "Secretary General, this, of course is highly speculative and requires an internal investigation before we can formally respond."

His moment had finally come, the perfect combination of timing and momentum. "President Chop, you've lied to me twice already and if you do it a third time, then I'm quite prepared to let you face your own military alone. However, if you are going walk the path of truth with me, then perhaps I can help. Either way, be advised that my patience is greatly strained with you and that I'm excessively tired from your manipulative tactics."

Chop breathed deeply and considered De Bono's words. After a lengthy pause he tersely answered, "I will walk the path of truth with you Secretary General."

"Now we're finally getting somewhere," De Bono observed wryly. "The problem you're having, President Chop, is that you personally ordered the execution of the bio weapons researchers after they tried to go public about the 3G flu, because they realized that they had created a virus that could literally wipe mankind from the face of the earth."

"I was not aware that their research had achieved such results," Chop protested.

De Bono jabbed his finger at him. "You were aware, and I have proof. That's three. Game over."

"Please, Secretary General," Chop pleaded. "Yes I knew. After creating such a monster, I thought I had killed it and all those connected with its development. That is why we did not declare the virus when we ratified the UNE treaty. We thought it no longer existed."

"But it didn't work out that way, President Chop. Did it?"

By now, the man was humbled and trembling. "Please understand, Secretary General, I had no idea that a janitor at the bio weapons center which is located near the Three Gorges Dam had become infected and would carry the virus to the outside world. Unfortunately, the virus couldn't have had a better breeding ground than the crowded settlements near the dam reservoir."

De Bono allowed his face to soften with a more compassionate demeanor. "Now that we're talking like honest men, President Chop, we can likewise help each other as honest men. Now as I see it, a major problem for the PLA is the food shortages. After all, a starving army is a difficult army to control, and when you boil all the issues away, this is the crux of the problem."

"You understand the situation very well," Chop replied gratefully. "In anticipation of the coming problems to be caused by Nibiru, the Americans have stopped exporting grain, which has put a great hardship on our country due to the devastating floods and droughts that have decimated our crops this year. If there is anything you could do to help us in this regard, we would be most grateful."

"As a matter of fact, there is something we can do to help you. We've already conferred with the leadership of the PLA and the American government. The Americans would rather give your PLA four ships full of grain than have to face the prospect of coming to Taiwan's defense.

While the PLA wants more grain than that, the American offer was final and they accepted it without reservation. I was most pleased to see a practical accommodation from both sides."

Chop was stunned by the arrogance of De Bono's revelation that the UNE had already gone around him to negotiate a deal. Like a mouse unaware that he had been cornered by a crafty feline, Chop realized that he had only been deluding himself. The Secretary General could take him any time he pleased, and Chop knew it.

"Then I presume that everything has been arranged. Therefore, this brings us towards the end of our conversation."

"Not so quickly, President Chop," De Bono shot back. "We also happen to know that you destroyed the original virus, which was an incredibly stupid thing to do given that it has now mutated. Further, you are still in possession of fifty thousand doses of the vaccine, which, according to the PLA, is only about seventy percent effective now that the virus has mutated. In exchange for allowing you to remain in office, you will deliver to me half of all the vaccines you now possess."

Chop's jaw simply dropped. "Excuse me, Secretary General, but if we dilute the vaccine as we plan that would mean a shortage for our own government workers as the PLA is already in possession of their share of the vaccine."

"That is your problem President Chop. You work it out with your people. After all, you're the blundering fool who let this genie out of the bottle. I'll be sending former United States Senator Johnston in my private scramjet to Beijing tomorrow to pickup the vaccines. You, in turn, will give sailing orders for four of your Panamax-size grain ships to make way immediately for the Penney Newman Grain Elevator at the Port of Stockton, California. The crews are not to leave the ships, and after the Americans load them to capacity, they must sail with the next high tide. Keep in mind; the American people have not forgotten that a

Chinese owned company was responsible for wrecking the Panama Canal."

"In all fairness, Secretary General, the vaccines are my only guarantee now that you have taken it upon yourself to exclude me from the negotiations. Therefore, it would be more appropriate to us to deliver your share of the vaccines after the PLA has received its grain shipments. After all, the PLA is not going to be as easy to do business with in the absence of a more peace-minded political leadership, should events take a turn for the worse."

"So you're offering to keep the PLA from become a problem in exchange for this one condition and ending this treaty abrogation nonsense once and for all?"

Sensing that he finally had regained some semblance of power, albeit a minor one at that in the relationship, Chop tried to display his most sincere smile. "You are absolutely correct, Secretary General. I admit your advantage over me, but likewise is it not wise to ensure the success of future relations with a simple gesture of trust?"

De Bono studied the worried man's face pensively. On one hand, the request was not entirely unreasonable. On the other, Yvette's words were still burning in his ears, "give Chop a millimeter and he'll take the whole planet."

He smiled and calmly said, "I'm sorry, President Chop, but I cannot afford to trust you this far. Not now. The deal stands as offered. You give me half the vaccines tomorrow, and we will insure that your grain ships are filled to capacity when they arrive in Stockton. That is the bargain on the table."

"But perhaps it is an unwise bargain, Secretary General," Chop replied seeking an opportunity to bargain.

De Bono's face stiffened with resolve. "I'm going to count down from ten. After that, you and I have nothing to bargain for, or to say to one another." He began the count down, "Ten, nine, eight..."

"Secretary General, this is rude and most unwise," Chop interrupted.

"Seven, six, five…"

"You owe it to me to discuss this further; after all it was I who brought China into the UNE. You at least owe me that much."

"Four, three, two…"

Chop finally collapsed. "I accept Secretary General. We will have your vaccines ready for pickup anytime tomorrow at the Beijing airport. Please let us know when to expect Senator Johnston."

"You can expect a call later this afternoon from Phillip Boretti, my Chief of Staff with the details. As always, Mr. President, it is has been a pleasure meeting with you."

Chop could only nod in agreement. "Good day, Secretary General," he said limply as he broke the connection.

De Bono opened the door allowing a cavalcade of room light to flood through and laughed to himself as he peeled off his VR gloves. "Yvette was right!"

Boretti overheard his gleeful remark, and it drove through him like a nail. The "little slut" as he referred to her in private had trumped him again. Well, there was always another day, so he straightened his back. "Sir, former Senator Johnston is waiting for you in your office."

De Bono tossed him the gloves. "Thanks Phillip. You'll need to make travel arrangements for the Senator. I'll fill you both in on the details in my office.

Boretti followed De Bono dutifully to his office where they found Johnston waiting patiently for them. "I have good news, Merl," he announced. "You're going to China tomorrow." The sudden announcement was welcome news to Johnston, who had become book weary by now.

De Bono discussed the details of his meeting with President Chop with them along with his preferences for the actual execution of the agreement. Following that, he dismissed Boretti for a final word with Johnston.

After Boretti left the room, he said with a beaming smile. "I have some interesting information for you about Roxanne

LeBlanc and her son. It seems that LeBlanc had been a highly successful intelligence operative for the American National Reconnaissance Office and resigned without advising her superiors that she was pregnant by Jarman. Had she informed them, they would have no doubt forced her to have an abortion."

Johnston slapped the arm of his chair. "Damn, who could have seen that one coming? NRO you say?"

"Yes, and there is one even more interesting fact. We have the boy Russell in custody and after running an exhaustive DNA profile on a blood sample taken from him, we learned something more remarkable."

"And you found?"

"He has the mystery gene. Have you read learned all about that yet?"

Johnston shrugged, "Not entirely."

"Well I know you've already been instructed on the Kabala so let's begin there. Aside from all the metaphysical mumbo jumbo, the Kabala is based on the universal knowledge, which was taught by the ancient Egyptian Mystery Schools and used to construct the great pyramids. This knowledge is so mind-expanding that the realization of a significant portion it will drive you mad, or leave your sanity intact by changing your very own genetic code. It is one of the lesser-known reasons why the Pharaohs practiced incest. They wanted to prevent the proliferation of the gene. Then, along comes this fellow by the name of Moses and everything changed. Moses was taught in the Mystery Schools and managed to keep his sanity by changing himself genetically. The important thing to remember, Merl, is that Moses passed the mystery gene along to the Jews through his own children. He also imbued others with the mystery gene near the end of his journey when he taught what he'd learned in the mystery schools to the children born out of slavery during their wandering years in the desert. Moses selected his students very carefully, and under his careful tutelage, most of them survived the awareness and lived to pass their own mystery genes onto their heirs as well."

"So this is why the Jewish people have always had more than their fair share of radical thinkers like Einstein, Marx and Freud," Johnston noted.

"And let's not forget Jesus either, while we're at it" De Bono added. "You see, the mystery gene has a habit of skipping several generations at a time, so when it does manifest itself, someone either writes something brilliant or wastes away in an obscure asylum somewhere, which is what happens in nine out of ten cases. For this reason, Jarman's son is doubly valuable to us now."

"But I thought you wanted to use the boy as political leverage to keep Jarman from causing us any further problems with his efforts to withdraw America from the treaty?"

"Yes, there is that, but perhaps the boy can be of even greater value to us, as only a handful of people alive today possess the mystery gene. As for Anthony Jarman, I've arranged for him to step down from politics in such a way that he'll never be able to return. I doubt that his sanity will survive the harsh duties awaiting him in New York. I understand the suffering from the 2010 Al Qaeda-Hamas attack on the United Nations headquarters in New York is far worse than we had anticipated. The assisted suicide requests are flooding in now."

"I have no sympathy for Jarman, but what do you plan to do with his boy?" Johnston asked.

De Bono waved his finger in the air. "With things like this, it is always best to keep your distance for as long as you can. When and if I feel you need to know something more, I'll tell you. In the meantime, I'm very certain that you will enjoy your trip to China tomorrow."

"It is just a milk run. What's to enjoy?"

CHAPTER 4

ALWAYS AN OFFICER

THOSE WHO DIED immediately in the 2010 Al Qaeda-Hamas attack on the United Nations headquarters in New York were the fortunate victims. For the rest, the extremely crude and hence "dirty" nuclear weapon left tens of thousands of victims in its wake, destined to die from radiation and burns in the short term, or a host of cancers and other terminal health problems in the long term. One such victim was Henry Wheelwright, a military studies professor from the Monterey Institute of International Studies in Monterey, California. He happened to be in the basement auditorium of a New York government office building attending a seminar at the time of the blast, which occurred some three miles away.

Aside from falling ceiling tiles in the auditorium, those in the basement of the building had fared much better than those in the offices above and those on the street did. Those unfortunate enough to be on the street suffered massive wounds from flying debris and glass along with the other serious injuries such as severe burns, burst eardrums from blast overpressure, as well permanent retinal burns and temporary flashblindness.

While some fled the area as quickly as possible in mortal fear, Henry chose to remain with the brave and dedicated New York City emergency personnel, who disregarded their own personal safety to help evacuate the wounded to hospitals in safe areas.

During his six-year enlistment in the Navy as a Nuclear Propulsion Officer on an Ohio Class Submarine, Henry had come to learn the lasting dangers of radiation exposure, and it was his own unequivocal decision to remain that drew a firm line across his future. Because of his heroic efforts, he, along with the other rescuers, was exposed to sub-lethal doses of radiation.

Henry had not received enough rads to kill him outright. Rather, it would kill him slowly through testicular cancer, which first evidenced itself late the following year.

Before being exposed to radiation in the 2010 attack, Henry was a robust man who enjoyed exploring the coastline of Northern California on his lightweight, custom-made mountain bike. At five feet, ten inches, Henry had a barrel chest and thick, muscular thighs and calves in the Greco-Roman wrestler style. Unusually bushy eyebrows and a prematurely receding hairline (which he liked to conceal with colorful variety of seasonal hats), trimmed his dark eyes.

With his cancer well advanced, Henry's muscular build had withered away in a devastating weight loss along with what remained of his hair and eyebrows. A shadow of his former physical self, he still retained the natural stature of a proud naval officer even as he sat propped up in his usual bed at the outpatient chemotherapy clinic at the Dominican Santa Cruz Hospital, where his wife Tanya Wheelwright worked as a senior hospital administrator.

Ramona Baker, a Physician Assistant in the Cancer Resource Center stopped by to check on his progress and to make sure he was receiving his IV medication for nausea as well. A large-breasted and pleasingly plump bleach blond, Ramona had a warm and infectious smile of a down home girl who knew her way around, "How you doing today Henry," she said as she glanced at the webpad on his lap. "Still working on your weird planet theories?"

"Yeah, weird, my ass, Ramona. I've been tracking planetary weather patterns going back twenty years and I think this Nibiru flyby is going to be a lot worse than NASA is willing to let on."

"Well, you know what they keep saying. Things won't get much worse since Nibiru will pass through our system no closer than a hundred thousand miles past the orbit of Mars. Sounds like a miss to me."

"You know, I hear the same thing from my wife. She's buying the NASA spin hook line and sinker, but check this out." Henry's fingers flew across the webpad. A flash file showed all of the planets of the system in a line, with the date, January 2000 displayed below the planets in bold white letters. "Now watch this," he said as he pressed the play icon.

Ramona and the chemotherapy patient in the next bed watched the surface features of some of the planets change as the years progressed towards 2012. Some planets were strongly affected, such as Mars and Jupiter, but all seemed to show increasing levels of changes in their weather patterns. However, what was most striking was the Sun, itself. The coronal mass ejections that scientists now faulted for the mysterious daytime wind shear problem that was bankrupting the airlines seemed to burst with striking rapidity. The violence really stood out because of the animation.

After the animation stopped playing, Henry looked up at Ramona. "I think NASA and the government are feeding us a crock of shit. Last week, Nibiru became visible to the naked eye. I know, I got up at four in the morning and found it in Taurus sure as shooting. At nearly five times the size of Earth, this thing is a real monster. Heck, the largest of its three moons is almost the size of Mars, and I could see it too! With that much mass floating through the solar system, I'm worried that something could happen when Nibiru is finally in opposition."

"Opposition is when it gets real close to us, right?" Ramona asked, concerned by what she'd seen in the animation. It had gotten her to thinking about whether it might not be a good idea to find a nice medical contract someplace a bit more removed from sea level.

"Well, opposition is when Nibiru will be nearest the Earth to be more exact. But you've got the general idea." His animation had drawn the interest of waiting patients and family members in the room and they crowded his bed, asking him to replay his animation and to explain his theories in more detail.

Delighted by the attention, Henry did not notice Ramona as she glided away towards the nursing station, where she would call his wife to tell her that he would be ready to go home in a few more minutes.

BY THE AGE of thirty-three, Tanya Wheelwright's career as a hospital administrator had quickly skyrocketed due to her instinctive abilities to manage people and numbers with interchangeable ease. She had met Henry in 2001 while finishing her Masters degree in social systems at the Moscow State University. Henry had just finished six years as a submariner, which he often said felt more like eighteen years, and become a junior professor at the Monterey Institute of International Studies in Monterey, California. He was visiting Moscow as part of a cultural exchange program group and Tanya was one of the tour guides assigned to his group because of her superb English language skills.

They first become involved after he became separated from the group during a city excursion. Tanya had combed the Moscow subway system searching for him and, once she found him, the rest, as he liked to say, "was history."

She came to America the following year on the fiancée visa, and Henry lost no time in whisking her away to Las Vegas for a quick wedding followed by a long and luxurious honeymoon that included a romantic cruise along Alaska's inside passage. Henry was simply the kind of man who knew what he liked when he saw it and had the class to show his appreciation in memorable ways. For Henry, it was simpler than that. He had the good fortune to fall madly in love with and to marry an incredibly beautiful and brilliant woman nine years younger than he was. She was indeed a catch.

Exactly the same height as Henry and in her prime, Tanya avoided wearing high-heeled pumps at formal events to keep from appearing taller than her husband, which made no difference, as her long legs seemed made to order for a full-length gown. Her light brown hair and green eyes suggested an exotic mix of her Ukrainian Jewish heritage with that of strong-featured Siberian beauties with a pleasing touch of Mongol blood to round out their features. A long, graceful neck supported her distinctive jaw and slim but shapely high-slung breasts.

From head to toe, Tanya was a stunning woman in an evening gown, such that Henry, who usually frowned on what he called "strutting peacock parades," would accept invitations at once. He especially loved to watch her drink champagne, to watch her long, graceful fingers as they supported the glass. Tanya on the other hand was not as infatuated with herself; she considered herself a normally attractive woman and thought nothing more of it. However, she admired Henry, the man who had become the love of her life and the father of her child, with equal intensity and affection.

As Tanya walked through the halls toward the outpatient clinic, she finalized a few remaining details with her assistant and handed over the last of the folders she carried in the crook of her arm. "I'm taking the afternoon off to take my family to the beach," she said, "I'll be on my PCS if you need me." Her assistant accepted the files extending his best wishes to her and returned to the main suite of offices in the center of the hospital complex.

As was her usual habit, Tanya went directly to the break room in the outpatient clinic before meeting Henry. She found Ramona Baker seated on the couch, nursing a hot cup of chocolate. "Been waiting for you," she said in a subdued but friendly voice. "Would you like a cup of hot chocolate?"

"No thanks," Tanya replied as she sat down in the threadbare armchair opposite the couch. "So, how's tricks?"

Ramona twisted the foam cup around in her hands, searching for the right words. "Do you remember the first words you ever said to me?"

"I believe I made a comment about your figure," Tanya replied coyly.

"That's putting it mildly, my dear," Ramona shot back. "As I recall, it was a New Year's Eve party, and you were three sheets into the wind when you looked me straight in the eyes and said, 'with tits that big, you and I are going to be the worst of friends or the best of enemies.'"

Tanya blushed and cupped her hands over her mouth. "Oh my God, that was so rude of me. I…"

"Rude, hell," Ramona interrupted. "It was the first time a woman in a suit ever had the guts to tell me the straight truth, and I've admired and loved you and Henry for it ever since. Hey darling, ol' Ramona has been with you through the thick and thin and not because I'm punching a clock. You folks are like my family and that is why what I've got to tell you next really hurts."

Tanya girded herself. Ramona had routinely shared Henry's chart with her, and she half-expected what would come next. "Honey," Ramona said softly, "It's not going back into remission this time. The doctors do not want to say anything now, but most likely they'll start talking with you about long term hospice care in a month or so."

Tanya began to tremble as she stood up. Each day, she worked with grieving families; yet when the shoe was on the opposite foot, she could not disconnect herself from her own feelings. Ramona tossed her cup in a wastebasket, rose and embraced her in a smothering hug. "Let it go, honey; you can't hold it in. Let it go." Tanya buried her face in the wide cradle formed by Ramona's thick neck and broad shoulder, then sobbed.

One of the floor nurses walked in on them and Ramona shot her one of those 'you and everyone else need to be somewhere else' looks. The woman quickly backed out of the room and made sure they would have their privacy for as long as it took. Ramona consoled Tanya for nearly fifteen minutes until she was able to regain her composure and freshen her makeup to meet Henry at the clinic's reception desk. He was wearing one of his more colorful caps and his favorite old blue windbreaker with the huge pockets that always seemed to be half-stuffed.

"So where are you two lovers off to," Ramona asked in a cheerful voice as Tanya took hold of Henry's wheelchair.

"To Seacliff beach," Henry chirped with his hands wrapped tightly around his webpad. "Svetlana and her grandfather are building a massive sand castle on the beach, ten feet wide by three feet tall! We're going to watch the fun."

"Sounds like a pretty big undertaking for an eight-year old girl," Ramona laughed.

"You'd be surprised," Tanya answered. "Her grandfather made his fortune building high-rise apartments in the suburbs of Moscow. I think helping our daughter to engineer a sand castle will not present much of a problem."

"Well, I should say not," Ramona replied brightly as she walked with them to the door. "By the way, Tanya, if it wouldn't be much of a bother, all the girls on the floor just adore your mother's piroshki. Hint, hint."

Tanya patted Ramona on the shoulder. "Let the girls know that the cavalry is on the way," she said. Then, she pushed Henry's wheelchair through the automatic pneumatic door to their GM electric minivan that an orderly had already parked in the wide driveway next to the clinic entrance.

"You know I don't need this damn wheelchair," Henry protested as Tanya set the wheel locks while the orderly looked on.

"I know, dear, but it is hospital policy, and I should know." She pressed the remote and the side door slid back to reveal a spacious interior with plush captain's chairs. She helped him into the minivan and sat opposite him as the orderly unlocked the wheel chair and began pushing it back towards the clinic entrance.

They buckled their seatbelts and Tanya touched a large blue button on the overhead display. "Computer, drive us to Seacliff beach, parking area two."

"Driving to Seacliff beach, parking area two," the minivan's state-of-the-art auto navigation computer replied in a pleasant mechanical voice as the side door closed. The minivan made a gentle start and drove towards the main Soquel road drive leading to and from the hospital complex as Tanya opened her purse. She took out a large brown prescription bottle, "I renewed your medical marijuana prescription," she said as she opened the bottle and removed one of the machine rolled cannabis cigarettes. Henry accepted it gratefully.

"The IV nausea therapy barely keeps me from tossing my cookies," he said as he fished a lighter from out of one of the large pockets that dotted his favorite old blue windbreaker. "It's a damn shame I couldn't keep the pills down. Heck, I don't even get a buzz off of this stuff anymore, but thank the Lord; it's the only thing that really works to kill my nausea." Tanya smiled and switched on the van's ionic high-volume air purifier.

Henry inhaled deeply as the air purifier drew the smoke out of the minivan's cabin nearly as quickly as he could exhale it. He smoked half the cigarette, snubbed the rest in the ashtray and pressed his head against his headrests while the air purifier finished scrubbing the last of the smoke from the minivan's interior.

"Feeling better, dear?" Tanya asked sympathetically. She'd been with him through enough of his vomiting spells in the past to be grateful for the drug's efficacy; even if it did have what she felt was a somewhat unpleasant odor.

With his eyes still closed, he replied. "Much. Thank you, dear. I really appreciate the way you help me to do this without Svetlana having to watch."

"She'd understand, Henry."

"I know, but I just hate the thought of her having to see me this way. It's bad enough that I haven't been able to get an erection in over eight months."

"Henry, it is not because you're unwilling, honey. It is a medical condition and I am your wife, not some hot-blooded young school girl who needs to feel like a woman five times a day."

He raised an eyebrow. "Five times a day, huh?"

"Let's not even go there," she flipped back.

He chuckled. "OK. Actually, I had something else I wanted to talk with you about while we're alone." He looked out the window as the minivan moved off the freeway onto the exit ramp for the beach exit. There would be enough time he reasoned. He opened a buttoned pocket and drew out a folded envelope. As he handed it to Tanya, she could see that he had already opened it.

She held the envelope in her lap without opening it. He nodded towards the folded envelope. "I'm really disappointed in you, Tanya. Instead of accepting your call-up, you requested a deferment. Well, you got what you wanted." He turned to look out the window. "Congratulations."

"Don't do this to me Henry," she begged. "I've got you and Svetlana to think of. They practically begged me to take the deferment when I explained your medical condition."

He turned back to look at her with hard eyes that burned with humiliation. "I've never been a shirker, Tanya, but if you're going to take the easy way out when your nation calls for you then why shouldn't I do the same. You think I don't know that I'm dying from cancer. How many more battles do we have to lose before we can all be honest about it?"

"Henry, we're still waiting for the prognosis, so how can you say such a thing?"

"I was an athlete, Tanya, I know my own body."

"And what?" She shouted in a worried voice.

"And I'm dying. That's what. To boot, I'm sick of it, and if you're going to be shirker and take the easy way out, then I might as well demand my right of assisted suicide as granted under the UNE treaty."

"No," she screamed.

"Don't worry dear. You and Svetlana will be taken care of. Our portfolio is strong and my life insurance has to pay. It's the law."

"I don't want your damn insurance. I want you!"

"Yeah, well I'm going the way of the dinosaurs, so let's buck up and face facts here."

Tanya turned away and bit her forefinger. Why did he have to find that damn deferment certificate in the mail? Damn the luck! Her life was falling apart, and all she could do was watch it happen. It was all like a terrible dream to her.

Henry reached out his hand to her. "Honey, a lot of people like us are facing the same situation, and they're doing the right thing. Sure, there will always be shirkers, but they'll be the ones bullshitting themselves for the rest of their miserable lives every time they look in a mirror. Dear, I'm certain this Nibiru flyby is going to be much worse than the government is telling us."

She pulled away from him and waved her hands wildly in the air. "Always with this doom-and-gloom, end-of-the-world craziness. If the government is telling us that this is as bad as it's going to get, then that's good enough for me." She pointed out the window. "Look outside, it's a beautiful day. Why do you have to go on and on about this gloom and doom crap?"

"It's not prophecy," he answered calmly. "It's science. Honey, we're just in a very unique place. The jet stream has been behaving fairly well, and northern California just happens to straddle a benign latitude. Look at what is happening at the equatorial latitudes and those nearest to the North Pole. The weather is crazy and getting worse every day."

She clasped her hands over her ears. "I don't want to hear any more. The government says it is not going to get that much worse, and I see no reason for them to lie. Maybe it's all this pot smoking that's making you imagine all this!" That remark cut through Henry like a hot laser and his hand fell away as he withdrew into himself. She turned away with tears flowing from her eyes and meekly said, "I'm sorry. That was a terrible thing to say."

Henry did not reply. He only watched through the window as the minivan slowly navigated the final hairpin turn leading down to the beach. In a few moments, their daughter and Tanya's parents would be greeting them in lot number two.

"So what do we do," she finally said.

"You accept the call-up, but request ready reserve status. They'll approve that, especially since you've already got a deferment. Then go to Washington as ordered for you're your eight-week indoctrination and training. We'll all be waiting for you when you get home."

The minivan slowed to enter the parking lot. Tanya could see Svetlana and her parents waiting next to the ramp leading down to the beach with their hands full of towels, chairs and other beach paraphernalia.

"All right," she sighed. "I'll do it."

"You're doing the right thing, darling," he whispered softly as the minivan slowed to a stop.

"I hope so," she replied.

The minivan's side door slid open and her jubilant daughter shouted, "Hurry, mother; the tide is coming in!"

Tanya smiled warmly. "Go ahead and get started. Daddy and I will meet you on the beach. Now go ahead."

THE HOMELAND DEFENSE draft board had granted Tanya's request for ready reserve status so she could remain at home with her family until she would be urgently needed, just as Henry said they would, but with one little twist. Her job assignment was changed from general hospital administrator to that of triage center administrator with the rank of Lieutenant Colonel instead of Captain. The promotion in rank meant that instead of sharing a small room, she'd get her own private room at a reasonably good hotel once a suitable room could be found.

After her initial two-week officer indoctrination course in Reston, Virginia, she was transferred to George Washington University Hospital in Washington D.C. for her six-week course on triage center management and was assigned a private room within walking distance at the nearby Hotel Lombardy on Pennsylvania Avenue.

The training had been intense with one twelve-hour day after another without letup and she was grateful for her tastefully appointed room with its massive old cast iron bathtub. She tried to call home each day, but some days were simply too exhausting. Thankfully, the first day at George Washington had been mercifully short. That evening after dinner, she promised herself a long, hot bath, followed by a long chat with the family. Even if long distance rates had gone through the roof, she missed her family terribly and didn't care about the cost.

Refreshed and feeling up to a lengthy call, Tanya stuffed a few pillows behind her back and made herself comfortable on the bed. She placed her webpad on her crossed legs and adjusted the webcam. Once everything was perfect, she dialed the access code.

Svetlana answered and squealed "Daddy. Its mommy!" Tanya could see Henry sitting down at the desk next to her daughter.

"Hi dear, we've been waiting for your call. You look a bit more rested than before. Are they starting to treat you with a little respect now?"

"Thank God, yes" she replied with a warm smile.

"Mommy," Svetlana blurted. "Guess what. Charlene had four kittens after you left and Daddy videoed the whole thing. Isn't that great?"

"Don't worry dear," Henry assured her. "I've already made arrangements to have the kittens adopted out by a wonderful animal rescue group once they're old enough. Trust me, you're not going to have to go into the cat raising business," he said with a wink. Tanya laughed wistfully.

She wanted to talk with Svetlana about the little things that mean so much to a child, but there were larger concerns that she needed to address with her husband. "Svetlana dear, do you mind if your daddy and I speak privately for a while? We have some important things to discuss."

"OK, momma, but we get to talk too. OK?"

"Of course, darling."

Henry kissed his daughter tenderly on the cheek. "Honey, please go downstairs and help grandma and grandpa pack. I'll call you back up when mama is ready to talk with you."

"OK, daddy. I love you, mommy," she waved into the camera and skittered off downstairs to help her grandparents. After she left, Henry closed the door to his private office adjacent to their bedroom and sat back down at his desk.

"I take it," Tanya said, "You're getting the family out of town."

"We're pretty damn lucky dear; I swung a special favor from the institute. We're leaving for Las Vegas tomorrow on the first evening charter flight out of town. The institute

has been designated as a contractor for the new Las
Vegas research center."

"Yes, I've seen some mention of that in the news. What
is it really all about?"

"It seems the government has decided to start this huge
technology center in Las Vegas. It is a perfect situation,
given all those empty hotels on the strip with their massive
halls and casinos and virtually unlimited power from the
dam. Mitch at the institute has slotted me for a research
position, and we'll be staying at the Luxor. He's even
arranged for me to bring your parents, thank God!"

"Mitch is a real saint," she said with relief. "Please
thank him for me when you see him. I really mean it." She
gently bit her lower lip. "Honey, you were right about this
Nibiru flyby. Opposition is in four days, and things are
really getting strange. Most of America is having small
quakes and it seems like every major river in Europe is
overflowing its banks. Then, they had that seven point two
quake on the Ramapo fault line in New York yesterday. My
God, the destruction!"

"It's crazy here too honey, so let me fill you in on the
details. For starters, all of the roads leading out of the bay
area are closed to everything except military, emergency
services and trucks. Also, there are no flights out and no
trains. They're using the railroads and trucks to haul out as
much equipment and supplies as possible from the Silicon
Valley to Las Vegas. For all intents and purposes, we're
landlocked and the only things moving out of here that
aren't controlled by the government are FedEx and UPS
flights. It's kinda scary."

"Thank God for the institute."

"Amen to that. They'll pick us up tomorrow afternoon
in a special bus with a military escort and we should be in
the air by eight o'clock that evening. They chartered an
entire 747 for the staff and families. They also tried to
schedule an early morning flight out, but Oracle and IBM
have them solidly booked. Worse yet, people are starting to

panic a bit, since the deep tremors started yesterday and I'm concerned about our bus making it to the airport."

"Deep tremors?"

"Yeah, we've been having a lot of deep micro-quakes and they've been building over that last five days and now they're happening almost every hour now. We can't feel the small ones, but the seismic station at Mount Umunhum, which is the closest monitoring station to our house, is going ballistic. I'm trying my best to keep everything on a positive note here, and so are your parents, but I've got to tell you, we're starting to crap our pants. I'm not going to sleep a wink tonight."

"Henry," she pleaded. "You've got to try dear or you will not have energy for tomorrow. Even if you have to smoke a dozen cigarettes."

He suddenly slapped his head. "For the love of God! How could I forget to tell you? Honey, I think I may have some really good news. The doctors decided to pull out the stops and increase my chemo dosage and it seems to be working. It is too early to tell, but my cancer may be going into remission. Like I say, it is way too early to tell but the initial signs look good."

"Oh Henry," she sighed. "I'm so glad to hear that," she said as happy tears began to stream down her cheeks. "We're going to make it honey. All of us." She pounded her fists on the bed. "I just know it!"

"And by the grace of God and the skin of our teeth," he added thoughtfully as Svetlana reentered the room.

"It's my turn to talk to mommy," she blurted out. Tanya and Henry laughed together.

"Talk about timing," Henry quipped. "OK princess, up on my knee. It's your turn with mommy."

The child gleefully scampered up upon her father's knee and started right in. "Guess what mommy, daddy and I sent you a secret surprise this morning, but I'm not supposed to tell you what it is because it's a secret, you know."

Tanya smiled warmly. "Well, we wouldn't want to spoil a secret now, would we?"

CHAPTER 5

NIBIRU IN OPPOSITION

HENRY HAD SMOKED two more cannabis cigarettes after his conversation with Tanya the night before, to relax as she suggested and to control his persistent nausea. However, what brought him the most relief were the live seismic activity feeds on the USGS web site. Much to his relief, the San Andreas Fault line had mysteriously settled down to the usual scribble of colored lines. As he studied the readouts, he wondered if he hadn't been too pessimistic, after all, about Nibiru's flyby. Things were obviously settling down, and it would still be another three days before Nibiru would be in perfect opposition with the Earth. "Maybe I was a bit harsh on those NASA experts," he thought aloud to himself.

Tanya's parents had returned home to their spacious ocean view cottage at the base of Seacliff beach to pack for the move to Las Vegas. Tanya's father was unimpressed with the prognostications of doomsayers; he had purchased the property for an excellent price and had just finished redecorating the home. He often remarked that living so close to the ocean had been the best thing he'd ever done to enjoy his sleep.

Henry's in-laws had packed through the night, arguing over this and that piece of memorabilia or artwork. The Monterey Institute had set very clear weight and size limitations for luggage, and Tanya's parents wanted to use every ounce of it to pack their most precious things.

Clothes, they reasoned, they could buy in Las Vegas; the immediate concern was to take as much as they could with the fear that looters would ransack their home.

One of Charlene's kittens had passed away the night before, so Henry and Svetlana had taken the visibly tense Persian and her remaining three kittens to the rescue that morning. Svetlana had cried bitterly, but taking Charlene and her kittens with them to Las Vegas was simply not possible.

It would still be several hours before the bus would arrive at their predetermined pickup point in Soquel, so rather than fret around the house, checking and rechecking his packed bags, he decided to take Svetlana for a short drive to his in-laws' house on the beach.

Henry helped his daughter into their minivan as the captain of the oil tanker *Exxon Ayala* walked out of the ship's control center, onto the port wing of his flying bridge.

A mile off his bow was the 4,200-foot long suspension span of the Golden Gate Bridge that spanned the mile wide entrance into the San Francisco Bay. Inhaling the fresh morning breeze, he watched the San Francisco Bay harbor boat come alongside his ship.

He noticed a shark swimming near the surface a hundred yards beyond the harbor boat. It was a 20-foot Great White shark swimming towards the Golden Gate in search of calorie-rich seals around Seal Rock, near San Francisco's Western shoreline.

The *Exxon Ayala* tanker had been named in honor of San Juan Manuel de Ayala, who first sailed through the Golden Gate and into the San Francisco Bay in 1775. The fine ship was the pride of the oil company's fleet. A thousand feet long, she could carry 1.4 million barrels of crude from the marine terminal in Valdez, Alaska to the marine terminal in Richmond, California, at the Northeast corner of the San Francisco Bay, in less time than any other vessel her size. Featuring an advanced double-hull design, the naval architects who designed her bragged that while it could carry as much crude oil as the ill-fated Exxon Valdez could, the Ayala was four times stronger.

As the harbor pilot walked up the gangway, the captain noticed the rapid pace of wide body jets taking off from the San Francisco International airport. The heavily loaded 747 jumbo jets were taking off to the West as other waiting in queue to land from the East.

These jets were not loaded with the usual tourists and businessmen jockeying for a window seat. They were loaded with the best and brightest of Silicon Valley software and hardware engineers and their families. The push was on now to move the much-needed Silicon Valley talent to the new technology center in Las Vegas, Nevada.

The top managers and the brightest engineers and designers had been flown in first and given the best rooms available. The next wave would be the middle managers, staff engineers and engineering support staffers, such as technical writers and quality assurance testers. These were the people in the jumbo jets the Captain of the *Exxon Ayala* watched taking off from the San Francisco Airport that morning, slowly climbing into a gentle banking turn that would put them on course for Las Vegas.

The last wave of those bound for Las Vegas would be the junior engineers and administrative personnel who were responsible for packing manufacturing gear and computers into shipping containers bound for the rail yards in Oakland.

The captain of the *Exxon Ayala* thought about his niece, a security officer at the Oracle Corporation Redwood Shores campus. South of San Francisco, the campus hugged the Western shoreline of the San Francisco Bay. Each time his ship made port he'd call her and offer to take her to diner at a fine restaurant, and seldom did she refuse. He looked at his watch; she'd be at work by now. He was in the mood for prime rib that morning; that was her favorite. He smiled to himself and decided to give her a little more time to settle into her day before ringing her up on the satellite phone.

As the captain's niece clocked in at the Oracle security office, the first hints of danger flashed their way from the USGS seismographic station at Mount Umunhum, South of San Francisco, and from the Stanford Telescope, San Bruno Mountain and Hamilton Field stations to the South. As the needles of the drum recorders began swaying back and forth with large, abrupt races across the paper, the seismologist on duty knew it meant only one thing – a superquake was about to happen!

THE MINIVAN FINALLY coasted to a stop behind the home of his in-laws, having been forced to weave through rocks and tree branches that had fallen down on the private drive leading to their home from the cliff face above.

Henry looked up at the homes above, perched on the edge of the cliff. Several had already been damaged by the small quakes of the previous few days, and he could see where the foundations of some now jutted out into thin air.

Tanya's mother met them at the door and told them they'd be ready in a less than an hour. They'd argued a great deal through the night and she was visibly exhausted. Henry decided to fetch up a beach blanket and to sit out on the sand and wait for them with Svetlana who took a small red plastic bucket with her.

As he laid out the blanket on the beach, Svetlana began playing in the sand. Moments later, Tanya's mother walked out from the beach with two large mugs filled with steaming hot tea and a plate piled high with freshly baked piroshki, filled with various tasty homemade fruit compotes. He asked her to join them, but she said she had to return to the house to help her husband finish the packing.

In unusually good appetite, Henry had already started on his second piroshki as emergency alert sirens began wailing all up and down the northern California coastline. He grabbed Svetlana close, and they heard a massive rumbling sound, like that of a hundred freight trains racing at them. He tried to scream to his in-laws to get out of their house, but the roar drowned him out. Before he could get to his feet, the impact of the quake struck so hard that he could barely continue to hold on to Svetlana, who now clung to him, screaming hysterically with fear.

The whole length of the beach began to ripple like the waves on the ocean. He watched with horror as the land under the cliff homes above gave way and a huge, blue colored four-plex slid down the collapsing cliff face, landing directly atop his in-laws' cottage and crushing everything in its path. "Oh God," he screamed, "No! No! No!"

THE SAN FRANCISCO Bay Area harbor pilot had just walked onto the bridge of the *Exxon Ayala* when all hands on board the ship first heard the wail of sirens in the distance. Then, an odd sight caught the captain's attention. The old WWII gun emplacements of Fort Funston, high up on Marin Mountain overlooking the North end of the Golden Gate, began crumbling to large pieces of reinforced concrete debris and began falling into the sea below.

The impact had come shortly after the captain's niece had reported for work at the Oracle headquarters at Redwood Shores, next to the San Francisco Bay. She too noticed a sound of huge freight trains, just as Henry did even though they were separated by the Santa Cruz mountain range.

Trained to handle quakes, she grabbed a large flashlight and a radio from the charging cradles and rolled down beside an old, massive metal desk, just a split second before the shock wave hit.

It was her great fortune that the founder of Oracle had spared no expense in designing his buildings. Each floor sat on its own quake rollers, and any of the main buildings on the Redwood Shores campus could withstand a 9.0 quake. Workers in the other buildings surrounding the Oracle campus were not as fortunate as floors collapsed one upon another, crushing the hapless office workers into human pancakes.

Worse yet, the quake was not only intense – it was lengthy and it was flattening every bridge and highway overpass within a hundred-mile area, crushing thousands of helpless people in their cars under tons of reinforced concrete. In less than two minutes, the ability of people to freely drive about the San Francisco Bay had become a distant memory as highways, roads and bridges were torn asunder.

The violent shaking stopped, and Henry slowly rose to look at the in-laws' cottage. It was almost completely buried in dirt and debris from the cliff behind it, which eliminated any hope that Tanya's parents could have survived. Their home wasn't the only one destroyed in this manner, and the devastation ran the length of the beach. He'd have to wait for the aftershocks to pass before risking the effort to hike out, given that all the roads and trails leading to the beach had been destroyed.

He comforted Svetlana who was still crying and terribly distraught at the death of her grandparents, and his thoughts turned towards Tanya.

He unclipped his cell phone and pressed the auto dial for the Hotel Lombardy in Washington. At least he could leave a message if nothing else. The phone bleeped and displayed a "no service" message. He switched it to mesh mode hoping it could connect via the slower but reasonably good peer-to-peer mesh network. That too, returned a no service message.

Holding the handheld videophone in front of his face, he thought aloud, "Sitchin was right. Every time mankind gets to thinking that he is the king of the universe, this miserable planet comes back and slams us back into another Stone Age." Disgusted, he threw the now-useless phone into the sand. He knew it would be months and perhaps even years before a minimal level of service could be restored and it would take days before he could get a message to her through the Red Cross. "At least," he tried to comfort himself; "Tanya will get the FedEx package we sent her with the video."

Then the unimaginable happened. The shelf just off the coast of Central California, from Monterey in the South to Bodega Bay in the North, collapsed by more than fifty feet in some places, while rising twice that much in others, as the Pacific Plate suddenly and violently subducted under the North American Plate.

This immense Earth change dropped the waters of the San Francisco Bay by 25 feet in just under a minute as Henry watched the waters of Monterey Bay rush out to sea, revealing a sandy bottom strewn with sunken fishing boats and other man-made litter. It was nature's way of announcing that it was about to unleash a 150 foot tall Tsunami on the West Coast of California.

He realized what was now happening, and that they would not survive it. He kissed his daughter tenderly and said, "Honey, I want you to hold on to me real tight and close your eyes. You and I are going to Heaven with Grandma and Grandpa today."

"I'm so afraid, Daddy," she cried.

"Hush, my darling, it will all be over soon and then everything will be OK."

As the boiling waters of the Pacific rushed out to sea, they pulled the *Exxon Ayala* along with it as though it was a child's toy in a bathtub. The captain ordered the tanker's engines to full speed, but before the ship's huge screws could begin to turn, a massive vortex of spiraling, angry water formed ahead of the tanker's bow.

Caught in a vortex several times the size of the *Exxon Ayala* itself, the bow of the hapless vessel was sucked forward, down into the funnel of boiling water as the stern of the ship whipped around in a circle, as though it were a spinning top.

Holding on for their lives, the captain and pilot glanced at each other and could see their fate in each other's eyes seconds before the bow of the ship slammed itself into the seabed floor.

With the ship half sunk and the other half surrounded by a funnel of angry water, the bow struck bottom with a crashing thud as hull plates and bulkheads crumpled and collapsed. The impact was so great that the ship's bridge was torn away and the last thing both men would see was the watery ocean floor rushing up to meet them.

With a fury that could only be called hell, the ocean heaved once again and formed a one 150 foot tall Tsunami wave that stretched across the Central California coastline. The center of that horrific wave faced the Golden Gate that spanned the entrance to the San Francisco Bay.

Crude oil was already pouring out of the mortally wounded ship as the frenzied Tsunami wave picked it back up off the seabed like a child snatching a toy and hurled it eastward, toward the Golden Gate Bridge.

Carried along like a log in a slough, the *Exxon Ayala* rolled side-over-side as it was pushed along by the wave. In the boiling waters around it, several lifeless bodies of the ship's crew swirled around the ship along with the wrecked and lifeless remains of the harbor boat and several other small craft.

AS THE TSUNAMI wave slammed into the Golden Gate Bridge, it slammed the mortally wounded *Exxon Ayala* sideways into the majestic north tower of the bridge. Other ships would have certainly split apart long ago, but even the massive pilings that supported the bridge's north tower could not break the *Exxon Ayala* in two. Caught amidships, the doomed oil tanker wrapped itself around the north tower until the massive steel structure finally buckled and failed.

Up on the bridge itself, those who had not already been swept off the bridge had been thrown down onto the pavement and snapped in half by the suddenly freed suspension cables. With the combined fury of the sea plus the stranded mass of the oil tanker, the bridge's suspension span between the towers began to sway drunkenly as the large steel cables that supported the upper structure began snapping and whipping about.

Finally, the north tower of the bridge collapsed in towards the bay, freeing the trapped *Exxon Ayala*, which was once again carried eastward by the raging waters straight towards the old prison on Alcatraz Island in the center of the bay. There, what remained of its battered and twisted hull ran aground, never to move again.

As the Tsunami wave pulled out, what was left of the 1.4 million barrels of crude oil in the holds of the *Exxon Ayala*, along with the Great White Shark that the Captain of the ship had spotted that morning near the harbor boat, were now being carried towards the Horizon's Restaurant in Sausalito, with its unobstructed view of San Francisco from across the San Francisco Bay.

A pricey, but favorite restaurant catering to tourists, the Horizon's restaurant featured a large outdoor patio overlooking the bay, plus immense picture windows for the diners inside.

The morning crew had just arrived to open the restaurant when the superquake first hit, and they had huddled together on the outdoor patio hoping to avoid being cut by glass. Thinking they had survived the worst of it, they were stunned to see the bay rise up in front of their picture windows.

As the boiling water smashed through the windows, the Great White Shark now coated in oil, sailed through as well. The last thing the bartender would see would be a wall of black, oily water and the shark's gaping mouth heading straight for him. Even in its final moments of life, the shark remained faithful to its instincts and tore the bartender in half with a single massive bite as his co-workers screamed out their last breaths of air before drowning.

WHILE DEATH WASHED through the northern side of the San Francisco Bay, the worst of it was turning around the San Francisco peninsula, towards San Jose to the south, shattering famous San Francisco tourist spots like Pier 39 into kindling and dragging them under the Bay Bridge. The black, oily water then whipped around the western side of the city where famous San Francisco sites like China Town and the financial district were likewise smashed apart and ruined.

Running parallel with the Bay Bridge that connects San Francisco with Oakland, the now half exposed BART tunnel that had been laid along the floor of the bay was ripped in half by the raging Tsunami wave, drowning thousands of helpless subway riders in the cars. The foamy black edge of the still powerful wave was festooned with oil-covered debris and bodies, as it rushed onward towards the San Francisco International Airport.

The sea level San Francisco airport was filled to capacity with airliners and Las Vegas-bound passengers hoping to leave before the airport closed in accordance with the newest FAA daytime wind shear departure rules.

When the first quake hit, tens of thousands had been working in the airport, waiting in departure lounges or had already been seated in their jumbo jets, anxiously waiting for their captain to announce that they would soon be taking off.

The initial jolt had been so violent that the main runways of the airport immediately fractured as buckling tarmacs sank and wrecked the undercarriages of several parked airliners. Several of the jets were already on the taxiways, loaded with fuel and passengers.

As the tarmacs and taxiways failed, several of the heavily laden jumbo jets crumpled to the ground like mortally wounded fowl. Upon impact, the hot exhaust from their engines sparked a horrendous series of explosions all across the breadth of the airport as desperate passengers spilled out of the fractured airframes like maddened ants on fire.

Those who survived the first jolts in the airport departure lounges watched the carnage with horrified faces, each grateful he or she had not met a similar fiery fate. However, they soon realized that their destinies had also been sealed as people began pointing at a large Tsunami wave now pressing down upon them with merciless fury.

Some ran, but most froze with fear as they watched the wave reach the airport, now dotted with burning airliners and collapsed air terminal buildings. As it swept across the helpless facility, it brought a quick, merciful death to the many burned, crushed and dying passengers and carried away several of the grounded airliners towards the communities lining the southern end of the San Francisco Bay. They, too, would soon be swamped by a wall of oil soaked water, fire, and a God-awful mixture of debris, death and smashed airplanes.

SHEATHED IN DARK tinted glass and shaped like old-style computer hard drives, the Oracle buildings at Redwood Shores had miraculously survived the superquake by wobbling back and forth on the rollers built in between the floors.

While the captain of the *Exxon Ayala*, along with the other members of his bridge crew, had already met their fate, his niece, a security officer for Oracle, had been in the basement of her building when the superquake had first hit. Suffering only some minor bruises and cuts, she had raced up the stairs through the dim glow of the emergency lights to search for survivors once the shaking had stopped.

She had run to the top floor of the building and had already worked her way down to the fifth floor by the time the Tsunami wave hit the building. Fortunately for her, the wave had reduced in height by some fifty feet and taken out the northernmost buildings in the campus, which had absorbed the brunt of the impact.

As the building shook from the flooding and damage happening on the floors below her, she looked out a window in time to see the fuselage of a Boeing 747 slam through a similar Oracle building next door. To her amazement, the building withstood the impact, swaying back and forth.

The next danger would come as the wave washed back out to sea. She knew they'd handily survive that, so she returned to the task at hand; giving aid and comfort to the few office workers that had stayed behind to crate the remaining equipment and computers for shipping.

Unlike her uncle, the captain of the ill-fated *Exxon Ayala*, she would survive the day, but only to face a future that now resembled an open Pandora's Box, out of which would spew dark consequences of misery and death for years to come.

AS THE WAVE moved further south, the rushing force of the wave destroyed all of the small cities running along both sides of the San Francisco Bay. However, in terms of lasting misery and death, the worst was yet to come.

As the wave bore down on San Jose and the heart of the Silicon Valley, it washed through the myriad number of computer manufacturing firms, sweeping up the millions of gallons of toxic chemicals and heavy metals used to manufacture printed circuits and computer chips.

With its forward momentum finally spent, the wave receded. On its way back to the sea, it dragged along with it thousands of dead bodies and a deadly witch's brew of petrochemicals, crude oil, solvents and heavy metals. Some of it eventually washed out to sea, but most of it washed up on the banks and low lying areas of the Silicon Valley.

Some of those who survived would come to envy the dead, whose deaths had been quick and violent. This was because their deaths would be slow and agonizing because of the witch's brew of toxic chemicals and rotting bodies. The foul stench of it all burned their eyes and choked their lungs while the man-made chemicals destroyed their immune systems and ate away at their skin and internal organs till they were susceptible to every imaginable disease and infection.

It is said that in everything bad, there can always be found little bit of good. Such came to be after the catastrophic event that Californians would simply call "The Wave," for centuries to come.

After the carnage, a few survivors turned up who would later come to epitomize the hope of the world for an eventual light at the end of the tunnel. They were the engine room crew of the *Exxon Ayala*. Because of the security systems and strength built into the ship, most of the men in the engineering compartment of the doomed oil tanker survived the ordeal behind double-thick watertight doors and bulkheads.

The day after the ship was run aground upon the barren rocks of Alcatraz Island, the Chief Engineer, along with handful of his able-bodied men, had finally managed to cut their way out of the uplifted stern of the twisted ship and literally walk away from the disaster unscathed.

Their emergence proved to be a much-needed beacon of hope. Four months later, enough of the Golden Gate Bridge wreckage had been removed to clear the ship channel, and ships of trade once again began to make San Francisco and Oakland a regular port of call.

The communities of the San Francisco Bay area also struggled to return to a shadow of their former greatness, and communication was restored in only a month, as opposed to the initial estimates of three months. However, it would still be decades before San Francisco could again call itself "the beautiful city by the bay."

It was during this hectic period of reconstruction following "The Wave" that one of the first foreign ships to dock in San Francisco would bring with it a young sailor from the Orient who chose to jump ship for a better life in America. Little did he know that he had also brought the dreaded Three Gorges flu to America. Dormant until its carrier began to exhibit to flu like symptoms, the Three Gorges Flu spread quickly. A single cough could infect an entire audience as they watched a film, or a train full of commuters on their way to work.

So deadly it was, 3G had already decimated the populations of Taiwan, Vietnam, Cambodia and Laos and now would become western civilization's deadliest plague ever as well. A threat that would be suffered, challenged and finally overcome but at a terrible price.

THE EFFECTS OF the Nibiru flyby had been the most catastrophic event in the recorded history of mankind, and Northern California was not alone it its misfortune.

Similar disasters had dotted the globe during the three days leading up to the perfect opposition of Nibiru, such as the massive Hollywood quake that single-handedly destroyed California's lucrative film industry. During those days, the worst imaginable happened as a whole host of volcanic eruptions, earthquakes, floods and fires beset the planet and continued at a diminishing rate for another five days following opposition.

By the fifth day following opposition, the many volcanic eruptions and fires that dotted the Earth obscured the sky to the point that the entire planet spent three full days in perpetual darkness — a fearful period that would haunt the memory of mankind for generations to come.

Oddly though, while some had expected global disasters that would affect every habitat of man, the carnage was randomized. Like a tornado that can raze one home clean to the foundation and then pass by a neighboring home without so much as moving any of the roof shingles by so much as a millimeter, the devastation wrought by Nibiru struck randomly across the globe. While great cities like San Francisco, Paris and Rome were torn asunder, others like Geneva and Denver escaped the carnage intact.

Overall, the countries in the middle latitudes, such as America, fared the best, while countries in the most northern and southern latitudes were more dramatically affected. However, it was equatorial and third world nations in general where human life virtually seemed to disappear.

After the Nibiru flyby, the "haves" of the world, became those nations with a ready supply of fresh water and water exporters like Turkey. In a strange twist of fate, Turkey would eventually become the wealthiest Islamic nation in the world and well regarded by all other nations in the region as being generous and fair.

The technology center in Las Vegas, Nevada had also escaped the destruction. Consequently, it put itself to the task of building more efficient hydrogen fuel cells for small uses and large magnetic electronic generators sufficient to power small cities and the desperately needed desalination plants required around the globe to save lives and the rich farmlands needed to feed the world's hungry. Lucky for mankind, its technology had survived this particular flyby of Nibiru for the first time, and it would progress beyond a point where all other preceding civilizations had failed.

Nibiru had destroyed a fourth of mankind during its flyby, and six months later, it finally reached the outermost fringes of the solar system, where it would not return for another 3,600 years. However, the news was not as widely celebrated as one would think, as half of those who survived the flyby would die lingering deaths because of thirst and hunger along with plagues and diseases never seen before. Mankind would still have a lot more dying to do, before it could hope to the find time to properly celebrate Nibiru's departure.

CHAPTER 6

LEGACY OF NIBIRU

FLANKED BY A UNE security team dressed in conservative business suits, Secretary General Antonio De Bono stood at the front doors of the ornate covered entry way into the Blue House, dressed in a tasteful maroon evening jacket, with Yvette Cochereau on his arm. She was dressed in a full-length sheer white evening gown topped by a stunning diamond necklace. As former Louisiana Senator Merl Johnston stepped out of his limousine, he waved at De Bono and Cochereau and they walked forward to meet him. As he stepped closer, Yvette took Senator Johnston's breath away just as she had that first day on the Secretary General's private Gulfstream scramjet.

A month after opposition, his wife Ginny was heartbroken by the suffering of her family and returned to Baton Rouge, Louisiana with their children to help her family. For the remaining five months, he slept as often as he needed with expensive call girls to satisfy his primal needs in the most erotic ways imaginable, but none could satisfy the emptiness he continued to feel in his heart.

After the disasters caused when Nibiru went into opposition, the former US Senator had managed to contact his few remaining relatives to let them know he was still alive and to ask how they had fared. After that, he never contacted them again as his own family seldom cared for his company and the feeling was mutual.

However, his wife, Ginny, had come from a traditional, large Louisiana family, and her sense of family was strong. Had he paid more attention to her and their children, perhaps she would have stayed, he reasoned. She had also been deeply annoyed by his mysterious comings and goings and his persistent evasiveness about what he was doing. Wives despise secrets, which he figured was her right, and that probably had been the last straw. He missed her and the children, but with them gone, he was free to pursue his studies and other activates without the distraction and he grew to like that new sense of freedom and power very much, despite his loneliness. Tonight would be different however, as he now had good cause to celebrate.

De Bono greeted him with outstretched arms and wrapped his arms around him. "Congratulations, my friend," he said as he hugged Johnston. "Tonight, we shall enjoy a feast in honor of your good fortune."

The former Senator hugged him back feeling warmed and especially welcomed. Over the last six months, the two men had cultivated a warm and mutually valued friendship.

They stood back from the embrace with warm smiles. Yvette leaned towards him and kissed him gently on the cheek. "Congratulations, Senator," she cooed.

"Well, let's proceed to our modest celebration then," De Bono said as he led them through the massive bulletproof double doors of the expansive UNE estate. As they strolled through the elegantly appointed hallways and chatted, the security team followed from a discrete distance. "I'm sure you'll enjoy this evening, as I gave Yvette a free hand in organizing this little celebration dinner." He looked at Cochereau who had until now been walking silently between the two men. "Yvette, you might want give him a little description of what he is going to experience this evening."

She smiled coyly and turned to the Senator. "It will be the four of us alone this evening in a small dining room that I happen to adore because of the chandeliers."

"The four of us," Johnston asked.

She smiled. "I've taken the liberty of inviting a friend this evening. Her name is Danielle Peters. She works in the UNE public relations office. She was born and raised in England and received her Ph.D. in Public Relations from Stanford University in California."

"Get to the best part, my dear," De Bono teased.

She twitched her nose at him. "Well it also seems," she continued, "that Danielle is a culinary genius and will be preparing our meal tableside this evening."

"And what a meal it's going to be," De Bono added with relish. "She will be preparing Angus beef filet mignons this evening, pan-seared with a delightful Cabernet Sauvignon and fresh Bing cherries. Along with that, we shall enjoy fresh spargel from one of my own family's private farms near Heidelberg. The season is young, but I believe you will find it a real treat."

"This sounds wonderful," Johnston exclaimed. "Pardon my ignorance but what is spargel?"

De Bono laughed boisterously. "My dear friend, it is heaven on the tongue and well loved in Germany as a seasonal delicacy. I believe you Americans call it asparagus, but what you get are green stalks that frankly leave me quite unimpressed. This is because German spargel is cultivated with a covering of earth to keep it pale white. Tonight, Danielle will serve it in the traditional manner. She will sauté it in pure creamery butter, and it will literally melt in your mouth."

"Sounds heavenly," Johnston replied with growing enthusiasm.

"And speaking of heavenly, wait till you see Danielle Peters," De Bono added. As they approached the entry to the small, private dining room, Phillip Boretti, De Bono's

Chief of Staff, greeted them politely as he opened the double doors with a refined flourish.

Johnston walked through the door, stopped in amazement, and quickly realized why Yvette so adored the chandeliers. Their dazzling cut crystal designs accentuated the flickering lights given off by concentric rings of pleasantly scented candles that filled the room with a warm, golden glow.

In the center of the room was a square, hardwood dining table with four, velvet padded high-backed chairs close enough that they could enjoy a casual conversation during their meal. The carefully laid place settings featured De Bono's favorite bone china, silver and crystal glassware.

However, the most dazzling thing in the room was standing to one side, in front of the large cooking cart positioned next to the table. It was Danielle Peters and she was nothing like Johnston had expected just a few moments earlier.

Dressed in a black low-cut, mid-length evening dress, her long shapely legs dominated her five foot eight height. He was immediately drawn to her large, dark blue wide-set eyes and her soft full lips accentuated by her small delicate jaw line, high forehead, perfectly framed by a tempest of full-bodied, ash blonde hair that fell gracefully along her shoulders and down to her mid-back.

She was wearing a white apron that seemed to accentuate her melon shaped breasts that hung firmly above a short, curvaceous torso with a narrow waist. His eyes followed the outer edges of the apron along her perfectly shaped hips, which seemed to him to be naturally made for holding close in the passion of the night.

On cue, Boretti closed the doors, leaving the four of them alone in the room. Gently flowing like water, Danielle walked up to Johnston and extended her hand. "Congratulations, Senator, and I hope you've brought a good appetite with you this evening."

Johnston took her hand and quickly realized that his stomach was not the only thing beginning to growl. "Thank you Ms. Peters," he replied in a polite, gentlemanly tone with a distinctive flourish of southern accent. "And may I add that I do so look forward to enjoying your artful cooking this evening."

She nodded with an approving smile and gestured towards the table; "Shall we begin?"

They talked about little things as they took their seats, and Danielle immediately served chilled iceberg lettuce salads with her own special raspberry vinaigrette dressing. "Secretary General, I took the liberty of decanting the wine about thirty minutes ago, if you like."

"Excellent, Danielle; I'll pour," he said picking up the bottle. "Tonight it is just the four of us, with no servers standing about trying to be inconspicuous, which was my request, so Yvette and I will help Danielle serve the meal this evening."

"Can't I help as well, Secretary General?" Johnston asked.

De Bono laughed. "Tonight, you are my guest of honor, and you will be served by us all and let's not be formal. Everyone, please just call me Antonio this evening," he pointed in Johnston's direction, "especially you, Merl. And," he quickly added, "Tonight, you can feel free to talk about anything, because we are all Illuminati and whatever we say in this room tonight will remain here, so relax and enjoy!"

"Pinch me, somebody," Johnston replied, "I think I'm in heaven." The remark filled the room with laughter that sounded like pure honey to his ears.

After five months of feeling a sense of loneliness creeping up on him, with his wife and family now living in Louisiana, he now felt a new sense of companionship and belonging. Finally, something had managed to soothe that persistent ache in his soul for close companionship.

De Bono rose and began filling the wineglasses, then set down the bottle. He picked up his glass, "Everyone, I propose a toast." They all picked up their glasses. "Not only has Merl successfully completed his studies and rightfully earned the title of Temple Priest, he has also managed to earn the attention of the Grand Secret Master himself, who made a special mention of his appreciation for Merl's excellent work on the 3G project to myself and the other Secret Masters of the Inner Council. I might add that he completed his work on the 3G project while completing his indoctrination studies in record time. Here is to Merl for a job well done!"

They all shouted cheers, causing Johnston to blush gratefully with the feeling that he had finally become a member of a new and very powerful family of world leaders. "Antonio, this wine is something else," he said with admiration.

De Bono smiled broadly. "I'm glad to hear you like it. It is wonderful American wine! I bought several cases of it while vacationing in the Northern California back in 2000. It has always been one of my favorites."

"Could you tell me about it, Antonio," Johnston asked as they all sat to enjoy the first course.

"It is a 1999 Beaulieu Vineyard Signet Syrah," De Bono replied after savoring another sip. "As I recall, 1999 was the coolest year of that decade which caused slow ripening conditions. However, in the last week in September there was a strong heat wave, which caused rapid sugar accumulation in the grapes. This accounts for the strong flavors and rich fruit of the wine. Yes, it is an excellent vintage."

After the first course, Danielle began preparing the steaks as the conversation began to flow like the wine. They enjoyed the rest of the meal with great gusto, talked and teased each other about movies, plays and other forms of entertainment. It was a magical time that pushed away all thought of a world where millions were now dying of starvation each day, the necessary fodder of mankind's survival.

Yvette cleared the plates as De Bono, insisting that Johnston remain seated, served dessert of Tiramisu and steaming cups of freshly roasted Sumatra Lington coffee.

De Bono took his first bite of Tiramisu as the others followed suit. "Isn't this heaven in your mouth," he sighed as he savored the fragile dessert. He pointed his fork at Johnston; "It is said that Tiramisu was the favorite of Venice's courtesans, who often needed a "pick me up" between their amorous encounters. It may not be true, but it sure makes a good story."

Sitting across from Johnston, Danielle kicked off her shoe and extended her leg to rub his manhood with her toes. "Tell us, Merl, do you think the story is true?"

His eyes widened slightly with pleasure, "I'm not an expert in such matters, but I will gladly defer to your professional judgment, Danielle." He cleared his throat and winked at her to signal that she had his full attention now.

De Bono and Cochereau quietly watched the chemistry and lust forming between their two guests with vicarious pleasure, pretending not to notice.

"While I'm not well versed in the history of Venetian courtesans, I must say that it does sound colorful. What I can tell you is that Tiramisu first became popular in San Francisco and not New York, as some may think."

"Bravo," De Bono said while clapping his hands. "You know, Merl, we may have an assignment for you soon if you're interested. Speaking of San Francisco, it seems that we may be looking for a new Southwestern America UNE Governor to replace Melissa Chadwick. She's been doing a great job and the Inner Council has decided to give her a promotion. The UNE district is rather large and covers the entire Southwest, west from Texas all the way to California. I took the liberty of confirming this with the Inner Council and they are for it, so just say the word and the position is all yours."

Johnston's eyes lit up with glee, "Of course I want it," he replied eagerly.

"Then it is done. Next week you will announce your full recovery to the world and the week after we will announce your new post in America."

Johnston sat back in his chair with a deep feeling of satisfaction. "Wow!' was all he could say.

"Of course," De Bono added, "this position also offers a nice perk. You get a personal assistant like my lovely and talented Yvette."

Johnston could see where this was going and glanced over at Danielle who was now looking back at him with bedroom eyes. Was Santa going to leave him an unforgettable gift under his tree this year? "I'll need someone with a strong background in media and public relations," he hinted out loud.

Danielle stretched her leg out once again to caress his manhood with her bare toes. "If you're offering, I'd love to jump on your – offer — as soon as possible after we've had a chance to discuss the position at — further length."

"By all means," he replied in a deep, soothing voice. "And the sooner the better."

"Well ladies, would you care to join us in a cigar and some brandy to celebrate Merl's new governorship?" It was Yvette's pre-arranged cue for the two men to be left alone for a private conversation.

"No, honey, I think I'll pass. Besides, it will give Danielle and me some time for girl talk, but after you're finished with your cigars how about a skinny dip in the pool before we retire for the evening.

"I'm up for that," Danielle chimed in.

"Works for me, Antonio."

De Bono laughed and stood up. "Well then, we have our plan. So ladies, we will briefly bid adieu while enjoy our cigars and brandy out on the veranda." He pointed a playful finger at Yvette. "Are you going to be mischievous tonight and start a water fight in the pool?"

"I'm not making any promises," she answered coyly. "Now, go smoke your cigars."

"Come on, Merl," De Bono said with a gesture of his hand, and the two men walked out on the wide, covered veranda overlooking Lake Geneva. They sat down at a table in the center of the veranda surrounded by electric heaters that took the chill out of the night air with a gentle, warm breeze.

Before the flyby of Nibiru, the night above them would have sparkled with stars in a cloudless sky. Now, the perpetual overcast of volcanic ash streams had turned the sky into a dark, gritty canopy where only a few of the brightest stars could be seen. Most sadly, the familiar, white glow of the moon had become tinged with a red wash that was clearly more pronounced during the day. Pictures taken from distant space probes made the Earth look as though it had become another red planet, as though it had become the larger brother of Mars. How long would it last? The experts debated the point endlessly, citing one conflicting study and theory after another. Consequently, their answers were as murky as the sky above, leaving a consensus that it would take at least another two years before Earth would once again shine like a cool, blue-green sphere in space.

As Johnston stared idly at the red-tinted half-moon, De Bono opened the lid of the large cigar humidor that sat upon center of the table. It had a large glass top with a handcrafted inlaid Spanish cedar interior and a featured a built-in humidification device. He removed two large, hand-rolled cigars, a super-precise double-blade butterfly cutter and a special cigar lighter. After clipping the cigars, he handed one to Johnston as he ran the second under his nose. "What a wonderful smell," he exclaimed. "These are Montecristo Gran Corona cigars from Cuba." He flicked the lighter and held it to the end of Johnston's cigar. "You know, before the flyby of Nibiru, they sold for thirty Euros apiece. Now you cannot buy them for love or money.

Thankfully, I had the presence of mind and the convenience of time to acquire a substantial supply of them before the flyby, so please enjoy."

"I will," Johnston replied as he gently puffed the cigar to life. "This is a cigar!" he said after taking a few mellow puffs.

"We can talk openly out here, Merl. These heaters also serve as a sound and microwave disrupters to prevent us from being overhead."

"Have you got something specific on your mind?"

"Yes and no. Tell me, Merl, how did you manage to do so well with that 3G project?"

Johnston took a puff while he considered his answer. "Well, when I went to China I spoke with their few remaining scientists and spotted one I felt might be helpful so, as you know, a young college intern, I took him back with me."

"And President Chop had kittens about that stunt, but we worked it out, although getting his family out of the country cost us a bundle."

"Well, it paid off. This kid had read through all the lab notes and lucky for us, he has a photographic memory and a good command of the English language. He stayed with me in Geneva and reconstructed the notes in about two weeks. He explained everything to me the best he could, and when we pulled together a research team to work on the problem, it didn't take long for me to see where I fit in."

He took another puff, while De Bono poured the brandy. "This is the best cigar I've ever had," he commented. "Anyway, I only understand this virus stuff enough to be dangerous so most of what these hot shots were talking about went over my head like vapor trails and they were going nowhere fast. That was when I could see the problem clearly. They're all egotistical, just like us politicians. The only difference is that they really don't know when to shut up long enough to hear a good idea. So all I did was to make them stop arguing with each other long enough to hear what the others were saying."

"Well, it worked. Thankfully, there was enough of the original Chinese vaccine for us, our families and key government and military affiliates. Plus, enough for your research program which yielded a promising range of inhibitor drugs for use by our medical and emergency personnel."

"Promising, yes, but the fact is that they are only 70% effective, provided everyone follows the protocols. I only wish we could find a more cost-effective way to mass-produce these incredibly expensive drugs. Otherwise, all we can do is to hopefully slow the spread of 3G, which will soon become the number one killer in the world, closely followed by 3rd world famine."

"Let's just hope that breakthrough happens so that we may end these horrible quarantines and triage centers that are disrupting our already weakened economies. Dying workers are not terribly productive, nor do they generate tax receipts, which are needed now more than ever before. The question is, when can we hope to have this vaccine?"

"You may not care for the answer," Johnston sighed heavily.

De Bono replied "Then, tell me straight," as he began to light his cigar.

Johnston took a large sip of brandy. "As you know, the 3G flu is nearly always fatal. The one in one hundred who survives is usually left with permanent disabilities and a lifetime of suffering. Frankly, if you catch it, you're better off dead. However, if someone somewhere out there in the world will have the right kind of strong natural defense to 3G we have a chance. If that someone not only survives, but also has a full recovery, then his or her blood will hold the key to creating an inexpensive and effective vaccine. After that, everything else is a straightforward, downhill process."

De Bono took a few puffs and then noted dryly as his voice fell off; "then, let's keep our eyes peeled for that certain someone and hope for the best before this miserable plague reduces mankind's chances of survival to non-sustainable numbers." His paralinguistic show of mild interest did not go unnoticed by Johnston and it sent the Temple Priest's mind in motion.

"Antonio, if I'm off base just let me know," he ventured cautiously. "I sense that your thoughts are troubled or preoccupied by something more important than defeating the 3G flu?"

"You're right. There is something I find deeply troubling, and for a little while this evening I was able to completely forget it." He held out his cigar and admired it; "Nobody rolls a better cigar than the Cubans. I hope they can put their island back together. I'd sure hate to run out of these."

"They are great cigars," Johnston noted softly with the assumption that he had transgressed into a sensitive area.

De Bono took a large puff and blew a series of perfect smoke rings. "You were right. I wasn't trying to avoid you. It's just that talking about this is difficult for me, but talk we must."

He opened the humidor again and this time took out what looked like a large brown and rust colored rock the size of a small apple. "What does this look like to you?" he asked Johnston.

"A rock. As to what type I have no idea. I'm not a geologist."

De Bono extended his hand. "Take it," he ordered softly.

Johnston did as he was asked. Hefting the rock in his hand, he struggled to keep from dropping it and noted with surprise, "This is a lot heavier than it looks. What is it?"

"It is an iron meteorite with a weathered exterior," De Bono replied. "While most meteorites are made of stone and weight about three times as much as a terrestrial rock, iron meteorites like the one you are presently holding in your hand is four times as heavy as the others. Now, I want you to hold that meteorite with both hands and close your eyes."

Johnston laid his cigar down in the large cut crystal ashtray on the table and did as he was instructed.

"As everyone knows, Nibiru had three small moons, or to be more precise, satellites. The smallest of the three was a small almond shaped moon approximately 40 miles in diameter and entirely comprised of highly dense iron. The moon was discovered in 2010 and aptly named Shiva by the Indian Astronomer who discovered it. Our scientists believe that Nibiru once had a planet-sized moon, slightly larger than Mars and that Shiva is what remains of the of the larger moon's molten core. Think of the iron meteorite you're holding in your hand as an excellent scale model example of Shiva."

"I'm getting a very bad feeling about this," Johnston said, his voice filling with trepidation and dread.

"As well you should. Seven days after opposition, an unusual celestial event happened involving Nibiru and Mars during the three days of darkness here on Earth. From what I saw in the NASA deep space probe imagery, it seems as though a huge bolt of lighting leapt from Mars towards Nibiru, only to strike Shiva first. The resulting impact fractured Shiva into two pieces. The first piece was approximately 5 kilometers in diameter and plummeted harmlessly into Nibiru. The other, is approximately 40 kilometers in diameter and was thrown into an elliptical Earth-crossing orbit around our sun."

"My God! Is it going to hit us?"

"If you mean us in terms of our planet – no. However, there is a strong possibility that it could impact our moon in 2019 and a virtual certainty that it will do so in 2035. Due to its mass and density, it could alter the Earth's moon's orbit with catastrophic consequences for the Earth. The mantle of our planet could shift suddenly and tear the surface of the planet apart, flipping the poles. The end result is that after Shiva hits the moon, the Earth could become a hellish to live for hundreds of years." He extended his hand across the table to receive the meteorite. "You can open your eyes now."

As Johnston handed it to him, he noted sadly, "It is a queer twist of fate that Nibiru's infant moon could be the one to destroy mankind and not Nibiru itself, as we had feared."

"Yes, Merl. It is a queer fate, at that. For over 150 years, the Illuminati have been working toward ensuring that our species and our technology would survive the Nibiru flyby. In this, we were successful. Now, Shiva and 3G to a certain extent, threaten our very existence in ways that Nibiru never could. Now, we are faced by an even darker threat and we do not have a century or so of time to deal with it."

Johnston felt his chest tighten. This was dark news indeed. "Since I haven't learned about it till now, no doubt there is a pretty tight clampdown on the news about Shiva. Is it because we're afraid of starting a panic?"

"Preventing a panic is obviously business of the first hand. However, we are rising to the challenge. A month ago, we finished negotiating a plan with the Americans and the Russians. The Inner Council has chosen Melissa Chadwick to take the lead on this and she'll run things from Las Vegas, which, by the way, is why you'll be replacing her as the Southwestern UNE Governor in America. Once she tells us that we're ready to launch the plan into action, which we estimate will be in another six to twelve months, we will tell the world. We'll have to; the resources needed for this plan will simply be too great to go unnoticed."

"Finally an upbeat note," Johnston sighed. "So what's the plan?"

"In terms of an upbeat note, keep in mind that due to the metallic density of Shiva, all of the nuclear weapons of Earth can neither stop nor destroy it, so don't get giddy. Nonetheless, the Russians have accepted the task of trying to divert or destroy Shiva before it causes us any harm. However, we cannot afford to hold out much hope for their effort, despite their eagerness. Rather, our primary emphasis is on the American effort. America is tasked with building four nuclear powered space arks to carry handpicked populations of able-bodied astronauts, scientists and engineers into space. Two of the arks will go to Mars, after which, we will begin the process of Terraforming the planet. The other two arks will be used to build permanent L5 Colonies in space. Of course, all members of the Illuminati and their immediate families have been selected."

Johnston held his head with both hands and grunted as he scratched his scalp. "My God! We just don't seem to catch a break, do we?"

"No, Merl. All we can do is play the cards we're dealt to the best of our skills and abilities and hope for the best. Between us, what concerns me most is that we're moving too quickly now, and that is when mistakes happen. The Illuminati is now challenged with a greater threat to mankind than Nibiru, and we've already lost the advantage of time."

"Then, I just can't sit by the sidelines on this and be happy biting my fingers. Antonio, I've got to be involved in some way. What can I do?" Feeling nervous, he picked up his cigar and began puffing it back to life.

The evening had finally worked its way to this moment, the crux of De Bono's main goal for the evening. He picked up the lighter and relit Johnston's cigar for him. "The Secret Grand Master is personally interested in Anthony Jarman's son."

"Because he carries the Mystery Gene?"

"Precisely. The Mystery Gene is the key to celestial navigation. If we are to go out there, it will give us an edge, provided we can raise the boy to become a willing member of the Illuminati."

"Well, I read about the kidnapping and the brutal murder of his parents, so I doubt that you'll be able to get him to participate willingly."

"If it comes to that, we'll clone him and start over. It may take several attempts to regenerate the gene, but it can be done, even if we only use him as breeding stock. However, we have a plan and we need your help."

"The contractors we used to abduct the boy, who also killed his parents and the neighbor, were Nigerian Muslims."

"Neighbor?"

"During the assault, the boy escaped the home through a hidden passageway to the adjacent home of a neighbor, where he placed a call to an unlisted number at the American National Reconnaissance Office. We later learned that the number was assigned to Major Arthur Jones, one of their top men. He is also known as Master Sergeant Vigo Jones; he has been conducting an intensive search for the boy ever since the kidnapping and pulling in every personal marker he has with other national and international intelligence agencies to do so. He has yet to learn of the boy's whereabouts, nor is he aware of our involvement, but, given that he has gotten close to discovering us on a few occasions, he undoubtedly has his suspicions."

"Then, he has to be dealt with. Likewise, we can assume that there is a connection between the boy, his mother, Jarman and this Jones fellow. Dealing with Jarman and Jones is one thing, but what about the boy?"

"The Nigerians actually work for a Syrian operative by the name of Colonel Yasin. Normally, we would be directly involved at this point, but we cannot with Jones snooping about looking for the boy. Therefore, the Inner Council Illuminati has decided to keep the child in the custody of Colonel Yasin, who will now command an elite Syrian Peacekeeper unit to be stationed in an abandoned missile silo at Fort Hood, Texas. The missile field itself is deserted, and the silo is impenetrable and well defended."

"And the last place Jones will look for the boy is on an American military base," Johnston added, "which just happens to fall within the supreme authority of the Southwestern UNE Governor."

"Now, you're catching on."

"Back to the boy. How do you intend to recruit him?"

"We view this as a critical task, and you will be interested to know that your mentor, Secret Master Hans Gebhard, will also raise and mentor the boy. A few weeks after we've transferred the boy to Ft. Hood, Hans will be introduced to the boy as his new male nurse. In the course of spending time with the boy, Hans will form a relationship of trust with him. Once we've dealt with Jarman and Jones, we will stage an escape for the boy and Hans, who will secret him away to a remote place. There, he will raise him as his own son and in such a way as to let us trigger the boy's dormant mystery gene without driving him to madness."

"That's tough assignment, but if anyone can do it, Hans certainly can," Johnston noted solemnly. "So, what about Jarman and Jones? I don't know about you, but the words 'dead men tell no tales' come to mind when I think about how to deal with them."

"Well put, Merl! Rather than wracking our brains on that one, I took the liberty of asking Danielle to formulate a plan. She's has the right background for this and been following the news coverage on Jarman very closely. Let's see what she has to suggest before we make any further plans."

Johnston whistled appreciatively. "And she can cook too!" He winked at De Bono; "tonight was a blind date, wasn't it?"

De Bono scratched his ear. "So far, your training has been largely about history and theory. In this regard, you have come a long way, Merl. However, there is still a lot you do not know, especially when it comes to our operational capabilities." He poured a brandy into the glasses with a devilish smile.

"This brings me to Yvette and Danielle. They are more than you think. Our own School of Assassins has trained both of them as personal bodyguards. This evening, you'll find Danielle to be an incredible lover, which was also part of her training. But you should also know that she has been trained to kill a man twice her size using her hands alone, and she knows at least a dozen different ways to do it. Further, you would not have met her this evening had she not already proven herself in mortal combat."

Johnston gulped. "Antonio, I'm not so sure about this."

"Relax, Merl. It gets better." He puffed his cigar and then took a sip of brandy. "If you choose her and she accepts, Danielle will be totally devoted to you and everything you do for the Illuminati. She will help you in anything you do without question and you will surely come to appreciate her abilities as I have come to appreciate Yvette. Yet, Danielle's most important role will be that of your last line of defense. We may be powerful, but we do have our enemies, and sometimes they can get too close for comfort. If that happens to you, know it in your heart without any reservation that Danielle will eat a bullet for you, if that is what it will take to save your life. Again, as I said, you must offer and she must accept. Only then is the bond made."

"A dozen different ways with her hands?"

"At a minimum, and trust me, the day could come when you'll be damn glad of it." With that, De Bono drained the last of his brandy and snubbed out his cigar to signal that their conversation on the veranda had ended. "Let's find the girls and go skinny dipping."

"Works for me," Johnston said happily as rose up out of his chair and followed De Bono back into the dining room where the found the women waiting patiently for them.

De Bono put his arm around Yvette and said, "We'll see you two at the pool. Yvette and I are going to stop by the kitchen first. It seems that she has prepared some tasty tidbits for us to enjoy later on."

Yvette smiled and waved as they walked out of the room. Turning back at the door, she said, "Don't be long."

"OK; we'll be there shortly," Johnston answered as the double doors closed behind the Secretary General and his mistress. He then turned to Danielle. "Let's sit down and talk for a moment."

"Certainly," she said with a soft smile.

They both sat in their same seats at the table and he emptied the last of the Syrah into their wineglasses. "I know all the basic details about Jones and Jarman," he said frankly. "The Secretary General told me that you might have a suggestion or two as to how we can deal with them."

"Politically speaking, Jarman is definitely the more dangerous of the two and must be neutralized before we can deal with Jones. The problem is that Jarman has become a tragic global figure, thanks to the continuous news reporting on him by Fox News reporter Rose O'Hara. Other End of Life Management Officers would have already gone insane or demanded assisted suicide by now. However, Jarman has broken the mold. He refuses to show any signs of instability or any self-destructive tendencies. The man is becoming a tough egg to crack, and killing him now is impossible, given his global popularity. Even though Jarman has avoided making any political statements, it will only be a matter of time before he does, and that is when he will become extremely dangerous to us. In my opinion, this man knows who did this to him, and he's waiting for payback."

Johnston picked up his glass and gently rolled the Syrah around. "So, how do we neutralize Jarman?"

"Right now, he's in New York and things are starting to ease. However, a rash of breakouts of 3G has been reported in Northern California, especially in the Bay Area. I've studied all of the triage centers being constructed right now and the one that I like the best is the Los Gatos Triage

Center south of the Silicon Valley. It is nestled in the Santa Cruz, hills and access is easily controlled. My suggestion is that the outgoing governor should order Jarman to this new triage center, so that you're not connected with that decision. After you become the new Southwestern UNE Governor, you declare the triage centers as quarantine sites, which means only military personnel can leave the centers until the quarantine is lifted."

"OK, but why?"

"I examined all of the media coverage on Jarman since his call-up. The first thing you notice is that it is not continuous. As a matter of fact, O'Hara only runs a story on him about once every ten days on average, mostly to help boost her ratings. If she enters the triage center as a reporter, she'll also be entering as a civilian. In other words, she'll be trapped there, and I doubt that Fox News or any other network is about to devote any news crew to cover Jarman on a permanent basis. These people work on budgets. Once we bust their budget, they'll move on. After that, it will be a simple matter for Jarman's health to fail, if you get my meaning. Once he's gone, the task of neutralizing Jones can be left to the School of Assassins."

"Damn, but you're good!"

"I try my best," she answered demurely.

"Yeah, well I know good when I see it. But I still have one question, though."

"And that is?"

"If you had evidence that I was doing something to betray the Illuminati, what would you do?"

She slowly waved her finger at him. "Tsk, tsk, that's a tough question, but then you have the right to ask. In terms of what I would do, I believe you really want to know if I would kill you. The answer to that is no as it would be against the code. I cannot harm you because of our bond, and even if I did suspect you I would still forfeit to defend you, but if I have solid proof that you've betrayed our cause, I would have to report it to the Inner Council. If they come to believe that you are a traitor, the first sign of that change will be my sudden departure from your life. Then, the assassins will come for you in the night."

Johnston cleared his throat. "You can be pretty damn direct, too, but that's OK, since I have nothing to fear." He took a sip of wine. "As a matter of fact, I liked your answer. Better yet, I like most everything about you. So why not? Let's bond."

Danielle dipped her finger in his glass and rubbed the wine-moistened finger gently across his lower lip. "Let's not rush this. You know I like to get 'it' too, and a hard man is good to find. I'll give you my answer in the morning."

CHAPTER 7

ASH STREAMS IN THE SKY

THE TRAIN RIDE from New York to Louisville, Kentucky had been long and tedious, with several grinding and jolting stops, but for Homeland Defense Captain Anthony Jarman it would be remembered as the more luxurious segment of his cross-country trip from New York to his new duty station in Los Gatos, California. The next leg of his journey would be a gut-wrenching affair in the minimally pressurized cargo hold of a C-130J Hercules II air transport.

A grizzled, potbellied old weekend warrior who had retired from the Air National Guard six years earlier met him at the train station. His name was Sergeant Mike Tompkins, and Anthony was bored to tears by his 'happy to be back in the saddle' attitude. Unlike Anthony, who had been drafted into the Homeland Defense, Tompkins had been recalled as the result of a severe manpower shortage after the Nibiru flyby. This, despite the consolidation of all branches of the National Guard, Reserve and Coast Guard into one huge, barely manageable force called Homeland Defense after America ratified the UNE treaty in 2011.

Another aspect of the UNE treaty was that America could keep its active service branches, the Army, Navy, Air Force and Marines, but they now served under UNE command as UNE Peacekeepers when deployed outside the country. The UNE Peacekeeper plan was simple. America was responsible for maintaining its own military services, which would train in America for deployment in foreign lands under UNE field commanders. Likewise, foreign armies from around the globe now served as UNE Peacekeepers in America with authority over the Homeland Defense forces, which could only be deployed within their own national boundaries.

Sergeant Tompkins met Anthony trackside and threw his gear in the back of the dilapidated, old HUMVEE. The Army National Guard markings had been crudely spray painted out and replaced with stenciled letters bearing the new Homeland Defense designations.

Exhausted and hungry from the train ride, Anthony crawled into the HUMVEE as Tompkins kicked the old diesel engine to life. "So, you're that ELMO guy from New York I've been seeing on Fox News ain't ya?"

"I guess today is your lucky day, Sarge," Anthony answered laconically.

"You bet your sweet ass, it is. Me and the old lady think you're a damn hero, we do. We see all those poor folks dying of cancers and bugs and what all and how you do such a kind job of sending 'em across to the Lord and all. Yes sir, you're a damn hero."

Anthony patted the old sergeant on the shoulder and said, "I'm not sure I caught your first name. Mike isn't it?"

"At your service," Tompkins chirped back as he whipped the HUMVEE around a corner.

"Well, Mike. I appreciate it and I want you and your missus to do me a favor."

"Sure enough, Captain. What is it?"

"Stay alive."

The sergeant pounded a fist on the steering wheel and burst out laughing. "By God, we will. I'll tell the old lady you said that first thing I get home. Damned if she won't split a gut and gossip across the fence till the cows come home! Yes sir."

In good spirits, the sergeant talked about his wife and hunting dogs as they drove towards the Louisville International Airport, home of the 123rd Airlift Wing, former home of the Kentucky Air National Guard. As they approached the airport, he pointed a thumb towards the back of the HUMVEE. "By the way, I got two cases of fresh .22 ammo for you in the back that are supposed to go with you to California."

"Thanks," Anthony replied. "Make sure they get on the plane for me."

"Will do, Captain," Tompkins replied in a more somber tone. "I guess them rounds are for folks wantin' to die, now."

"Yeah. With the current shortages of drugs, the decision came down from the folks who seem to know better and live better than the rest of us, that anyone requesting their right of assisted suicide who can still walk gets that instead of an injection."

"That's a damn shame, Captain. Getting a bullet in the back of the head isn't my idea of how to go, if you know what I mean."

"I know what you mean, but that is the way it is. Only children and the bedridden will get lethal injections now but a bullet in the back of the head is quick. Before I left for New York, they trained me on it with cadavers. It's amazing, but a well-aimed .22 in the base of the skull goes right through the medulla oblongata, and death is instantaneous."

The sergeant shivered. "Orders is orders, but this stuff really gives me the willies. What do you think about it?"

Anthony looked at the sergeant with a calm face. "It's the way it is, Mike. Plain and simple." He then decided to switch the conversation to another track. "Say look, tell me about this night flight to California. I've heard a lot of horror stories about these wind shear crashes. What are my chances of making it there alive?"

"Ah, hell, Captain, fer starters, you're flying with 123rd AW. We're the best damn Herky Bird drivers there is, and you're in luck! We mostly fly the C-130H Hercules for humanitarian operations, but you'll be going to California on the newer J model we use for special night drops and high priority cargo runs. She's a real beauty, too, called The Flying Circus. I hear tell she used to fly as a weather reconnaissance bird for the Brits before we got her, so I guess her first crew named her the Flying Circus in honor of their favorite English TV show."

"That's interesting, but will I get there in one piece?"

"You bet you will. Let me tell you why. For starters, she's got extended range fuel tanks, and she's an all-weather airdrop-capable bird, which means she can get around these damn volcanic ash streams. Something our H model Herks can't do so well, so they fly mostly during the day. Now, that is damned dangerous flying. Yes, sir. Last month, we lost two Herks to wind shear. One crew walked away. The others didn't, the poor bastards."

"So what does a J model do differently?"

"Well sir, the Flying Circus ain't your run of the mill Herk. She got better engines, propellers and avionics and an upgraded cockpit. She's got four humping Allison turboprop engines that can develop a whopping 4,591 shaft horsepower each, which really comes in handy when the pilots are trying to climb above an ash stream. But if they do hit an ash stream, the J Herk has got six-bladed composite propellers that are a mite tougher than the ones on the H models, which comes in handy considerin' the sandblasting effects of an ash stream."

"Well, that's reassuring," Anthony replied with a little bit more enthusiasm.

"It ain't that simple, sir. Even something as sophisticated as a six-bladed composite propeller ain't enough to prevent a heavy intake of volcanic ash from grinding one of them Allison turboprop engines apart. Ask any stick jockey and he'll tell you that losing only one engine at a time to volcanic ash is a rare and exceptional blessing, as in most cases you lose more than one engine. If you're in a overloaded Herk, that can really tear you a new asshole, if you know what I mean, or as the stick jockeys liked to say, 'The only difference between wind shear and volcanic ash is the amount of time it takes to crash. Either way, you buy the farm.'"

"Thanks," Anthony sighed. "You're really giving me a lot of hope, here."

"Ah hell, don't get down in the dumps, 'cause here's the good part. The original H model cockpits were configured for a crew of three: Pilot, co-pilot and loadmaster, but the Herk you're flying on tonight has an extra station for an engineer-navigator equipped. I've seen it too, and man, is it slick! The station has its own set of fully integrated digital color multifunctional LCD displays for radar, navigation and engineering plus engine controls. But what takes the cake is this new weather radar installed in the nose of the craft. They can see up to 300 miles ahead of them, so they can usually fly around the big ash streams without much of a problem. The little ones are hard to spot, and they're the only real danger, but the crew of the Flying Circus has this uncanny ability to avoid the little ash streams too. Yup, you'll get there with no problems at all, providing the engines hold up."

"Did you say 'engines'?"

"Yeah, seems they're all overdue for a major overhaul but they'll keep 'em turnin', anyway, so don't sweat the small stuff, sir."

OVERLOADED AS USUAL, the tired airframe of the Flying Circus creaked and groaned as it clawed and bucked its way to California through the dark and turbulent skies. Mindful of his precious cargo of supplies and souls, Captain Jerome Richard, peered through his ash-pitted windshield into the gritty darkness. The forty-year-old knew that piloting his C-130J Hercules through the reddish black sky would depend upon combination of skill and luck, with a special emphasis on luck. However, he often wondered if his luck was receding and graying as fast as his medium brown hairline.

He had piloted this route more times than he cared to remember and was well aware of Mount Shasta's tendency to spew ash storms now. Scanning the reddish black night before them through his heads-up display, his dark brown eyes moved in quick jumps from right to left and back again. Even though his eyes were red with strain and buttressed by recently formed deep bags and worry lines, he still relied on his own peripheral vision to aid him in spotting trouble before it found them. However, this time, things were worse. During his preflight briefing, he and his crew had been warned about the unusual pattern of the current stream of volcanic ash working its way across the lifeless, black and red colored night sky.

This new violence seemed a bit pointless to him, yet inevitable. Mount Shasta had already snuffed the life out of everything within its immediate reach. "Maybe it wasn't satisfied with that much death," he wondered to himself, "and now it wants to add us to the toll as well." Which is exactly what would happen if they flew through a small volcanic ash stream. The big streams were easy to spot with their advanced radar system. It was the little ones that worried them all.

Nearly invisible at night, the only sign of a small ash stream would be in the form of sound jokingly referred to as flying through sandpaper and the blackening of his windshield. If they didn't react in time, the next sound they'd hear would be the engines grinding themselves to pieces. Then would come the screams of tearing aluminum and the helpless cries of the crew and passengers as men and machine plummeted downward, forging a fiery trail to the life-bleached landscape below.

Craving sleep, he peered ahead into the starless night and remembered how Northern California had once been famous for its good weather and sunny, blue skies. He mumbled in a prayerful tone, "I don't know where you are, Dad, but at least I know you can see your beloved stars again. I sure wish you were here."

He glanced back at his young navigator-engineer, Second Lieutenant Jeff Stanton. With his medium height and small shoulders, the glow of the radar display seemed to envelop him. Time-and-again, the young Stanton had displayed an almost psychic ability to find ash streams in the night sky even when they failed to appear on the color LCD radar display on the pilot's own instrument panel.

There were still forty-five minutes out from the Livermore airfield and that landing would be tough. During the preflight briefing, they'd been advised that a recent quake had left a huge fracture in the main runway at Livermore, which meant he'd have to make a tough short-field landing in a fully loaded aircraft. Crabbing a beat up old Herky Bird at night to bring it down on the runway numbers would be challenging, to say the least. He doubted if his mental sharpness was up to it and decided to take a quick power nap to refresh himself.

Over the last few months, Jerome had trained himself to power nap, and was able to quickly find that fuzzy but refreshing state between REM sleep and full consciousness in as little as ten minutes. Minutes later, he could awake rested enough to remain sharp and focused for at least another hour. In the meantime, he would be comfortable in the capable hands of co-pilot First Lieutenant Al Chan. Al had been born and raised in the bustling China Town district of San Francisco and had tried his hand at standup comedy clubs while finishing his engineering degree at Berkeley. At five foot nine, his thick frame and slight paunch made him look more like a Chinese warlord than a comedian — a fact that he managed to work in his favor with the audiences.

Instead of pursing a questionable career as a stand up comedian, the thought of which had driven his entire extended family to frenetic distraction, he opted for a more respectable commission in the Air Force as a pilot. To everyone's delight, he graduated his training at the top of his class and was regarded as a natural born stick-and-rudder man by his instructors and classmates. Yet, the glare of the stage lights had never fully left him.

"Take over," Jerome said to his co-pilot; "I need to give it a rest for a bit." Lieutenant Al Chan nodded, and Jerome felt his steady hand take the controls with the familiar 'I'm in control' tap. After flying together for over a year, the two men knew each other so well that a grunt or a tug on the control wheel was all they needed to communicate.

With his co-pilot in control, Jerome slumped back into his seat and closed his eyes, but rest would not come immediately.

"Say, Captain," Al interrupted over the cockpit intercom so that all four men in the cockpit could hear him, "Why don't we have one of the stews back in first class cut up some cool fresh cucumber slices for your eyes? After all, Captain, don't you want to be looking your best for the folks at Livermore?"

Jerome squeezed his eyes shut. "Crap," he muttered to himself. He had been the one who first started this whole vegetable joke thing, and now it was coming back to haunt him like a Mafia leg-buster. He stretched his neck and decided that he could do one of two things. He could be a hard-ass, or he could play it out until everybody got tired of the gag. The latter suited his instincts and he keyed his microphone, "Well Al, you're certainly an officer and a gentleman tonight. While we're at it, why not have that stew toss what's left of the cucumber in a blender and make you up a nice cucumber-cleansing enema?"

Stanton looked up from his radar display and slowly shook his head. They were at it again. 'An officer and a gentleman — oh puhllleeeezzzeee...' he thought to himself. The only time Jerome and Al acted like officers and gentlemen was when someone with greater rank was watching them, or when they happened to watch an attractive young woman with an hourglass figure pass by. When the young engineer-navigator had first been assigned to the Flying Circus, he had expected a cool-headed military style cockpit. What he got was a virtual locker room where grab-ass wit ruled supreme and where thankfully, he could rightly hold his own, or so he thought.

"Say, Captain," Jeff chimed in, "I hear we've got a half case of some new non-carbonated French mineral water with a refreshing twist of lemon added. Ah yes, an invigorating filler for Al's cucumber enema. Whaddya think, Captain?"

Before Jerome could answer, Al keyed his microphone, "OK, you two done shut my mouth 'cause you got my butt squirming! All right, all right! You won this round. Now let me fly the damn plane!"

Grinning ear-to-ear, the pilot and engineer-navigator keyed their microphones in silent acknowledgment. Still the same, Al felt he could hear them laughing over the drone of the engines, which was almost as bad as knowing that he would have to buy next round to shut them up. That was, if they could actually find an Officer's Club with refreshments to sell.

Grateful for a bit of cockpit humor to break the tension, Captain Richard finished rolling his head to stretch the muscles in his neck in preparation for his power nap.

Starting the power nap would be easy now, as always. As before, he'd think back to his childhood memory of when he and his father, Dusty Richard, a lineman for the local power company, first began looking at the stars together.

He remembered how his father emptied the last of the cash from an old coffee can he used for his fishing trip fund, to buy him a 4.5" Meade telescope after it became apparent that he would never become a fishing enthusiast. He was interested in the stars, as was his father, and the telescope became a way for them to spend memorable evenings together marveling at objects in the night sky.

Now, the night sky was dominated by a blood-washed moon set against a reddish-black background that only permitted viewing of the brightest of the stars through the seemingly endless muck.

As he slipped into his power nap, he thought of how deeply he missed his deceased father. "I hope the viewing is better where you're at now," Jerome said to himself as his consciousness descended into a still darkness.

DUSTY RICHARD HAD passed over peacefully two years earlier from pancreatic cancer. It had come on suddenly just after Jerome's wing had been deployed to Germany for special airlift missions, and his son had been asleep at the moment of his passing over. Jerome had intended to call his father before turning in, but was so exhausted he decided to put off a promised phone call until after he'd awakened; a decision that would haunt him with guilt. His lingering guilt over missing that last chance to tell his father how much he loved him now seemed like an impenetrable wall between them. Even though Dusty had clearly heard his son's question, he knew his son would not be able to hear his answer because of his own sense of guilt, so he kept focused on the issue at hand: the outboard starboard engine of the Flying Circus.

As he examined the inner workings of the tired turboprop engine, he could see the failure that was soon to come. It was one that could spell disaster for his son as well all the other souls aboard the Flying Circus. He also sensed the presence of another spirit sitting calmly on top of the starboard wing between the fuselage and the inboard engine — a soul that had not fully crossed over. Perhaps one of the passengers was already near death and had begun crossing back and forth.

In personal accounts, the dying often recall leaving their bodies for brief periods to visit loved ones. As an End of Life Management Officer, Captain Anthony Jarman had been exposed to this phenomenon so often that he had developed abilities far beyond those of common men and women — even beyond those of the most religiously devout. He had found a pathway from one side to the other — one he could travel time-and-again as easily as walking from a backdoor stoop to a well-cared-for garden in the yard.

The deafening roar of wind and turboprops, jarring turbulence and the reeking stench of fuel, hydraulic fluid and vomit had made this flight a long roller coaster ride from hell. Anthony finally decided to step outside his body to escape the sheer physical agony of the trip if for only a brief moment in time.

Invisible to the crew and other passengers in this state and unaffected by the elements, he floated close to the outer surfaces of the lumbering transport and perched himself on the leading edge of the wing between the fuselage and the inboard starboard engine. He could see the spirit of Dusty Richard examining the outboard engine and gave it no other thought, as he was preoccupied with the experience, itself. Being outside of his body, turned everything eerily peaceful as he imagined himself sitting on the wing with his feet dangling over the leading edge. Before him, the red and black night sky presented him with a macabre, red and black beauty.

In time, Anthony's attention was drawn to Dusty as he moved around the outboard engine. He sensed that something beyond the usual was happening as the troubled engine's mighty propellers continued to slice through the night sky; then he realized that this other spirit was somehow connected to the pilot and oblivious to Anthony. Anthony, however, was used to being ignored by spirits on the other side; besides, he had not come to visit him, anyway. Yet, that clear connection between this other spirit and the pilot still intrigued him, and he listened for the thoughts of the pilot, who was now entering a controlled slumber. Bingo, a father and son match, just as he has first thought.

Anthony now turned his attention to Dusty and said, "So what is so interesting about that engine."

Moving closer to him on the wing, Dusty answered, "That pig of an engine is on its last legs. It should have been swapped out a long time ago. By the way, I'm Dusty Richard, or at least I was. Well — you know."

"Yes, I know," Anthony replied warmly.

Looking at him more closely, the other spirit added, "You know, I thought there was something different about you. By golly, you're one of those Indigo kids. Only Indigo kids can step out like you are doing, but I'd say you're much better at it than most. Say, just how long can you stay out, anyway?"

"It varies with time and distance," Anthony replied, sensing that his own body was beginning to teeter. "I've got to be going back shortly," he noted with reluctance.

"Well don't worry about buying the farm tonight in this old heap," Dusty answered, "That engine will make it far enough, and you couldn't have a better pilot than my son, Jerome. He's the one flying this thing."

"I sensed the connection between you two," Anthony replied. "While you were inspecting that engine, I listened to his thoughts. He was thinking about that telescope you bought him and all the good times you two shared while viewing the night sky together."

Dusty smiled. "Some fathers and sons have sports or travel to share. We had astronomy. Personally, I would have preferred fishing." He then looked out at the sooty black and red horizon spread out before the Flying Circus. "But is doesn't matter now, with all this mess, for fishing or for astronomy either, for that matter. I hope all this will clear up in time for Jerome to teach his own son astronomy. In the meantime, I'm going to do everything I can to see that they get that chance."

"Let's hope so," Anthony noted. "But I sensed that he's not really open to you."

"I'm sure he is, but he's filled with guilt. Strong emotion, that," Dusty admitted, "but that hasn't stopped me from watching out for him. That young flight engineer of his, Jeff, is how I do it. The kid really trusts his instincts and his feelings. That's how I reach him. Sometimes, I can wiggle Jeff's gauges, but since that really drains me, I only do it when I really have to. I sure wish I could find a way to connect with my son, but he's so difficult to reach now."

"I think I can help," Anthony replied as he began moving back towards the aircraft interior and his own body. As he slipped through the skin of the fuselage, he quickly shared his idea with Dusty, who was grateful for the help of an intermediary. Here was someone who could help him find a new way to connect with his son, even though they were worlds apart.

SLOWLY RUBBING HIS eyes, Captain Jerome Richard slipped out of his power nap with the odd feeling that the spirit of his father, Dusty, was close. He knew he couldn't even explain the feeling to himself let along anyone else, so he just let the thought go.

After a few bleary-eyed winks and a jaw-cracking yawn, he focused his eyes on the instrument panel. All seemed normal except for number four, his outboard starboard engine — as usual. With luck, they'd get it replaced or overhauled before it finally gave up.

He stretched his arms and shoulders with a satisfied groan. The power nap had rejuvenated him enough for the landing, but not much more than that. He was still dog-tired and he knew it. He had spent more time in the air in the last few days than on the ground, and it was easy to lose focus with this kind of exhaustion. The same also held true for his crew. They'd have to stay sharp, because there could be only one focus now — a safe landing at Livermore. After that, maybe they'd snag a few well-deserved hours of sleep before the next flight; and perhaps a hot meal as well.

"Captain," the flight engineer's voice on the intercom interrupted Richard's waking thoughts, "I think number 4 is pushing towards critical again."

The pilot keyed his microphone, "Thanks Jeff. Always something with four," he sighted. Swiveling to his right, he looked closely at the flight engineer-navigator to see how he was holding up. The young man's dulled eyes told him the whole story. A rested man would have shown at least a small sense of alarm about the failing engine, but all he could see was tired resignation in his face.

"Jeff, we're loaded to the max with cargo and pushing the envelope on weight; and those limits assume we're flying a new Herky Bird," Jerome reminded the navigator, who nodded glumly. "Look, we're 30 minutes out of Livermore, which is a short field and I need all four engines. Can you keep number 4 turning till we're on the ground?"

Jeff scanned his gauges by force of habit even though he already knew the answer. "Captain, I can keep it turning till we land in Livermore, but if they wave us off, I doubt she'll take a full power go-around let alone a full reverse on landing." He paused to bite his lip for moment and then continued, "Whatever number 4's got left; I'll kiss it out of her."

For the first time in days, the hint of a smile crossed the Jerome Richard's lips as a devilish plan hatched in his mind. Once they were on the ground, he'd push Number Four to the wall on the reverse. Then, everyone would get eight hours of sleep while the failed engine was being replaced. That is, if he didn't blow up the Flying Circus in the process. His thought struck him as an odd sign of exhaustion that he could actually find the idea appealing. This was beginning to get really dangerous. He needed rest.

For some odd reason, the young engineer-navigator sensed his Captain's thoughts down in his guts. Maybe everyone in the cockpit was thinking along the same lines he thought. "Captain, if you guys throttle up number 4 with a full reverse, the engine will definitely buy the farm. The moment it does, I'll trigger the extinguisher. After all, we gotta stop this old bird don't we?"

For Al Chan, Jeff's words were honey in his ears. "Yes, we do," he chimed in with a serious tone. "And as my dear departed Mother used to say," he added, "in everything bad there is a little bit of good, and this is definitely good. That's because before we took off, I heard that the California Air Guard is stuck with a lot of wrecked airframes, which means there's a buyer's market on engine swaps. Hell, they've got to have a few Allison AE2100D3 turboprop engines somewhere in all that mess. Yes sir, this could be our lucky day!"

Jerome nodded in agreement even though he felt their thinking had been warped by their lack of sleep and nodded reluctantly. Jeff's eyes lit up with hope. "I'll keep her turning for sure, and heck, maybe we'll even get some real shut eye while they do the swap. That is of course if we really need one." With a big smile, he gave the pilots a thumbs-up sign and added, "Hey Al, please give my compliments to your dear departed Mother." Not waiting for an answer, he turned back to his banks of consoles and began making the delicate adjustments need to fit the remaining life span of the engine into the next thirty or so minutes.

THE UNUSUAL ENTHUSIASM in the cockpit chatter over the number 4 engine and awakened the napping loadmaster, Sergeant Skip Brown, who had been snoozing in the jump seat behind the pilot. Having caught the last of the conversation, he stretched and added his two cents, "Say sir, maybe they'll even fix those damned hydraulic leaks too. God, the stink back there's just awful. I think most of the passengers have tossed their cookies. It's a real gaggin' gut wrencher if you ask me."

The bloom was certainly off the rose now, Jerome thought to himself. "It so happens I didn't ask you," Jerome snapped back in an irked tone. Looking over his shoulder while jabbing a thumb back at the loadmaster, he growled, "OK, who woke it up."

Every member of the Flying Circus crew knew that when the Captain called you "it," that you had put your foot or something similar into your mouth, and the loadmaster readied himself for the serious ass-chewing he knew would come next.

"Skip, you're always giving us the puke reports," Jerome intoned, "Christ almighty, sometimes I think you're auditioning for a Dramamine commercial! Damn, I wish Bill Jenkins would mend quick."

Jerome paused, and held himself back. He was getting testy again, and this poor kid had innocently stepped on his tail. The last remark about Jenkins was over the line. He missed his old loadmaster who was still recovering from a broken leg while this young sergeant with the witless mouth was filling in for him. "Skip, why don't you go and see how our VIP passenger, Captain Jarman, is doing back there."

"Yes sir," the loadmaster dutifully replied as he unfastened himself.

"While you're at it," Jerome added, "tell him that Livermore control advised us that a driver from Fort Ord will be waiting for him on the tarmac. Also, make sure he gets those two cases of .22 ammo after we land as well."

The young sergeant rose up from the jump seat. Moving towards the cockpit door, he stopped to look back over his shoulder. "Uh sir. Do I gotta speak to him? You see, I got family in the bay area ... and uh, well I reckon," he swallowed hard. "I hate to think that our VIP back there would use some of those rounds to well uh..."

"Sergeant, he's an ELMO; it's what he does," Jerome answered tersely, wishing for the day the flight surgeon would release his regular loadmaster and send him back to the Flying Circus, where he was sorely missed. Till then, this "it" would have to be tolerated. "Look Skip, if one of your family members is past hope and facing an agonizing death, an ELMO can be a real Godsend."

"Uh, no offense, sir, but I've seen what he does. Have you?"

"Not personally, but I've seen the news reports, so I'm not going to get into it now."

"I seen it up close," the loadmaster insisted. "People who don't want to live but can still walk, got to line up in front of a trench and kneel down. Then, they wait for him to put his hand on their shoulders, and when they drop their heads, he shoots 'em in the back of their heads and they just fall like rag dolls into the trench." His hand began to shake a little. "I dream about those bodies in the trenches all covered with lime. It's hard to call that a Godsend. He gives me the willies."

Jerome turned towards the loadmaster with eyes of fire. "We don't need this immature, pathetic, wailing shit right now. So if it makes you feel better, our VIP is no frickin' Godsend. Now get frosty and do your job or I'll toss you at Livermore and start looking for someone who can. Do you read me?"

The young loadmaster withered under the pilot's steely glare. "Yes sir," he answered obediently.

"Now go back there and let him know that someone from Port Ord will meet him in Livermore. Then prepare for landing. It will be a rough one — a damn rough one!"

The loadmaster dropped his eyes to the cabin floor and left. He'd wait till he was in the cargo hold before letting anyone see him wiping the tears from his eyes as his memories flashed through his mind.

HAVING RETURNED TO his body several minutes earlier, Anthony Jarman now fought to keep himself in a dreamy state between REM sleep and consciousness. The time he spent out of his body had been a wonderful release from the persistent nausea but now his stomach twisted with painful spasms. In this semi-conscious state, he was mildly aware of his suffering, but not wretchedly so.

Still the same, he could sense a young crewman working his way, around the massive cargo pallets strapped to the floor of the Flying Circus, towards him. Like it or not, the crewman would find him soon, and he'd have to experience the full agony that would accompany a complete state of consciousness.

The young loadmaster found Anthony huddled against a stack of canvas tents. He cupped his hands in front of his mouth and shouted over the loud drone of the tired engines; "Are you Captain Anthony Jarman, sir?"

Fully awake now, Anthony kept his eyes closed as the cold stench of the overloaded cargo bay tore through his nostrils and turned his guts. All he could do was to nod his head in agreement.

In the absence of a verbal acknowledgement, the loadmaster reached over to read his nametag just to be sure. "I'm Sergeant Skip Brown, the loadmaster. I'm sorry to disturb you, sir, but the Captain ordered me to come back here and check on you."

Anthony slowly opened his eyes and looked up into the loadmaster's face. The young sergeant froze with indecision as their eyes made direct contact for the first time. Anthony could see the experience was filling the nervous young man with more emotions than he could process at one time. He had seen that look thousands of times before and now it was just another faceless blur in the reality of his own miserable life. Another face he would have deal with; another soul behind a troubled face needing comfort and reassurance.

He took a deep breath and, girding himself, smiled kindly to break the ice. "Not that I'm complaining, but your business class service sucks!" he shouted over the din of the cabin. Feeling the unpleasant gagging sensation again, he dropped his head towards the bag in his hands. "How long till we land?"

The loadmaster knew what the Releaser wanted to know, as well as every other passenger on board. "We're not long out. I'd say about 20 minutes." Anthony could only nod again, as he fought the urge to retch.

It was then that the loadmaster realized that Jarman was still a person and that he deserved to be treated as such. Perhaps a little humor would distract him.

"As to the business class service, sir, here is the way it works: No peanuts, no apple juice and no refunds. Also, we're fresh out of customer comment cards, which is OK since nobody gives a shit anyway, but thanks for flying Trans Mojave Airways just the same. Now please bring your seat back up to the forward position, fasten your tray table and pray your ass off that we don't buy the farm on landing. It has been a pleasure serving you and we hope you choose Trans Mojave Airways for your next flight."

Grateful for the humor, Anthony answered, "If I hadn't been so damn busy pukin' my guts out since I got on this miserable bucket, I'd have torn up my frequent flyer card way back!"

"Breaks my heart to hear you say that, sir," Skip replied. "By the way, a driver will be waiting for you in Livermore. Don't know more than that, but I'll make sure he gets those two cases of ammo for you." Anthony nodded his acknowledgment, and the loadmaster continued moving towards the rear of the cargo compartment, making final checks of the cargo nets and tie-downs in preparation for landing.

As he tugged at the webbing and checked the tie-downs, the loadmaster thought about what he'd said in the cockpit. He wished that he had kept his mouth shut and was surprised at himself for the way he had acted.

Yes, he'd seen End of Life Management Officers like Jarman at work and those awful memories could never go away, but he never saw one up close. Only those who were near death would, for the most part. No wonder he always thought they were some kind of weird government clowns with warped personalities. However, this Jarman guy was no different from all the other poor bastards trying to make sense out of a world turned upside-down. At that moment, he realized that he began to both respect and pity Jarman. It had finally sunk in.

THE HASTILY BUILT landing strip at the government research center in Livermore came into view as Captain Richard banked the Flying Circus to line it up with the ILS signal emanating from the portable ground control system. Meanwhile, the cyclic grinding noise from the number four engine was getting worse now, and it could now be clearly heard in the cockpit.

On the far end of the runway, Captain Richard could see the heavy equipment lumbering off to each side of the runway. He made a mental note of their location. It was probably where the last quake had fractured the runway from edge to edge. If he didn't stop short of that fracture, it would rip the landing gear off the Flying Circus and turn it into an out-of-control Molotov cocktail.

"Please, Jeff, keep number four turning," Richard muttered under his breath. He knew his flight engineer-navigator was working a minor miracle with the troubled engine, but then again, everything has its limits. With luck, Jeff would squeeze one last dying gasp of power out of the tired engine. It was now or never. They had to land.

With polished perfection, the two pilots guided the heavy airplane to edge of the patchwork of metal that covered the small landing strip, as the main wheels literally touched on the numbers. Slamming the nose wheel down to the ground, the two pilots worked together to pull back the power so they could reverse the engine thrust, hoping to stop the Flying Circus short of the runway fracture line. With a silent prayer, Jerome pushed all four engine throttles to full power.

As the blades of the props worked against the old cargo airplane's forward motion on the runway, the tired airframe fought the change of thrust with agonizing vibrations and loud, complaining metallic creaks. The whole craft jittered and complained as the passengers prayed for a safe stop.

After what seemed an eternity to everyone on board, Jerome finally eased back on the power as the nose wheel came to full stop a few yards from the fracture in the runway.

As though it had waited for its most benign moment of death, a bearing inside the number four engine began to seize as the propeller slowed. Thankfully, the reduction in power kept inner engine parts from exploding outward from the engine. Nevertheless, the damage internally was still massive, and the first licks of fire quickly sprang from the joined edges of the engine nacelle.

Ready for just that moment, Jeff yanked the engine's red fire extinguisher knob and flooded the engine nacelle with fire retardant foam, while quickly shutting down the other three engines. As the foam filled the engine nacelle, the crew stared wide-eyed at the number four engine and then sighed with deep relief when the fire warning light on the instrument panel flickered out.

The airbase fire crew raced up alongside the Flying Circus in their bright yellow crash trucks, continuing to foam the engine for good measure. Everyone would walk away from this one, and the Flying Circus would be in the air again as soon as it got a replacement engine. That in anybody's book, they all reasoned, was as good as any landing could get.

Clicking his PTT switch, Richard said, "Livermore ground, this is Ohio Guard heavy, Yankee Zulu One Niner requesting a tow off the active, a new engine and a hot meal."

"Tow is already on the way, Zulu One Niner. We've got to clear the runway quick. Be advised that another heavy is on a 5 minute final with bingo fuel. As to the engine and the meal, you're on your own. Now, kindly get the hell off our runway."

"Zulu One Niner, we copy that," Richard's co-pilot confirmed. Releasing the PTT switch so the tower would not hear him, he added, "and it's nice to see you too, you jerk." With a big grin, he looked first at Jerome and then turned to face Jeff. "Hey miracle workers, I think we need to get us a few cucumbers and some of that French mineral water and pay those boys in the control tower a visit." The cockpit filled with laughter as Al turned to face Jerome. "So what do you think boss?"

"I think," Jerome answered as he watched the ground crew back the tow engine toward the nose wheel of his airplane, "that them boys up in the control tower are playing with watermelons, and that they happen to outnumber us cucumber folk."

"Watermelons!" Al exclaimed in an excited voice. "Now that, by God, is one heck of an idea!" Jerome silently shook his head. He'd gone and done it again. When would he ever learn, he wondered to himself as he felt the familiar jolt of a tow hook-up.

CHAPTER 8

BLINK TWICE FOR YES

PEERING THROUGH A small porthole to mask his concern, the young loadmaster watched with a deep sense of relief as the fire retardant foam dripped to the ground. As a tug pulled the Flying Circus off the active runway, he lowered the rear ramp of the airplane three fourths of the way to the ground. The air that rushed in was foul with the odors of fire retardant and spent fuel but to those inside the cargo hold, it smelled of safety. However, it was the sight of ground personnel pointing at the smoke and steady drips of smoking fluids that oozed from the scarred engine nacelle reinforced their awareness of their close call. Their lack of enthusiasm was obvious to the passengers. This would be just one more gritty, filthy thing for them to fix.

The young loadmaster girded himself and turned to face his anxious, wide-eyed passengers, "Listen up folks; we are in no danger. Just keep in mind that this is what tends to happen when you fly an airplane through sandpaper. Now, please kindly unbuckle yourselves, gather up your gear and prepare to de-plane in an orderly manner after I have finished lowering the ramp."

The Flying Circus finally slowed to a stop, and the tug driver released the tow bar so he could pull into position for the next inbound C-130. It was low on fuel and overloaded. The loadmaster craned his neck around the side of the fuselage to see the tug rolling off and then lowered the rear cargo ramp the rest of the way down. "OK, folks," he announced. "Please watch your step and if you've got to puke now, please wait until you're standing on the tarmac or I'll make you stay and clean it up."

As the weary passengers filed past, most ignored him but a few with green faces and a few still found the strength to loft a middle-finger salute in his direction. One of the last to deplane was Captain Anthony Jarman, who paused next to the loadmaster and tapped on his headset. "Sergeant, tell your captain I need to speak with him now, and also have him contact the base executive officer as well. I want to see them both out there on the tarmac as soon as possible."

The young sergeant's head jerked back in disbelief. "I'll pass it along, Captain, but if I were you, I wouldn't hold my breath."

"Well, you're not me," Anthony replied tersely. "So, just make sure they know who I am."

Anthony limply dragged his bag to the edge of the ramp to be cheerfully greeted by a lean, middle-aged man. Nearly six feet tall, with wide shoulders and a barrel chest the Master Sergeant reminded him of exceptionally tall Roman centurion because of his square jaw and hard-set eyes, capped by large, bushy, dark brown eyebrows with light streaks of gray.

"Now, you gotta be Captain Anthony Jarman," the man said with a sharp salute. Anthony returned the salute and nodded in agreement.

"I knew it, by golly! Ya know, they described you to a tee: Six foot one, lanky, brown hair and blue eyes that just seem to look right through you. But I gotta admit, they never mentioned anything about your green face," he noted with a chuckle.

Anthony's stomach twisted around with surge of pure pain. The last thing he needed was someone playing I'm Mr. Cheerful goes to the airport. "And who the hell are you?" Anthony grumbled.

"Master Sergeant Vigo Jones at your service." The sergeant winked. "If you don't mind me saying, sir, that there was one hell of a landing. Man, just look at that engine! I'm glad I wasn't on that bird. Flying through them volcanic ash streams is bad news; yes, sir; bad news. And by the way," he thrust a sweaty grease-smeared hand towards Anthony, "my friends just call me Vigo."

Anthony studied his outstretched hand for a moment, wondering whether to vomit on it as any moment now and he'd probably be tearing out what was left of his guts with dry heaves. He took a deep breath. "Later. Get my stuff," was all he had the energy to say.

Vigo dropped his hand with a knowing grin as the loadmaster joined them. "I'm to tell you the Captain will be here in a minute or two, and, while the base XO thinks you're as crazy as a peach orchard boar, he'll be here shortly as well. Pardon my being frank sir, but you sure do seem to have a knack for getting people's undivided attention."

Anthony stared at the loadmaster and realized that vomiting on him instead would be far more satisfying but then there was the issue of his personal belongings and ammunition. "Fine. See to it that this sergeant gets my things. I'll meet them out there." He pointed to the lit tarmac just beyond the immense tail of the Flying Circus. Holding his stomach, he walked slowly off the ramp and out onto the tarmac where the glare of the mobile lights was blindingly bright for a man in his condition. He finally stopped and turned to Vigo who had followed quietly behind him, "so where is your vehicle, or are we on foot?"

The middle-aged sergeant pointed to an old 2.5 ton Army truck parked alongside a temporary maintenance shed, behind a row of portable toilets. "My truck is over there, sir. She's all gassed and ready to go," he answered.

The sergeant removed his soft cap, scratched his half-bald scalp and pointed his finger to the left of the truck. "If ya gotta go, use one of the johns near the truck. They're cleaner. Here..." the sergeant held out a canteen filled with cool water. "Ain't no point in heavin' on a dry stomach."

The arrangement seemed to be the first convenient thing to happen to Anthony all day.

Anthony accepted the canteen and took a sip. Mercifully, his palette was greeted with the cool and refreshing taste of distilled water. Maybe this sergeant character wasn't a total jerk, after all, he thought to himself.

"I'll get your gear into the truck, including them two crates of .22 ammo, and wait for you there."

"Thanks" Anthony replied with a weak voice as Captain Richard walked up to greet him. He could see the exhaustion and stress in the pilot's face. This man needed a break, and that was what Anthony intended to do for him.

Jerome stuck out his hand. "Sorry about the rough trip. I understand you wanted to speak with me." Anthony nodded in agreement. "Also, the base XO is on his way." Anthony could see the man was over-exhausted. He sorely needed rest.

"Captain, may we speak privately for a moment," Anthony said as Vigo walked back to the rear of the Flying Circus. "This might be an odd question, but just out of curiosity, why is it you never liked fishing with your father?"

The question peeled Jerome's eyes wide open. "Why is it I never what..." he stammered.

Anthony held up his hand. "You know who I am and what I do, so let's cut to the chase, shall we?" Jerome nodded tentatively. "Whether you believe it or not, Dusty is with you every minute you're up in the air. I first saw him looking inside that engine you toasted during our landing, and we had a nice chat. Now, I'm not going to go into the details, but I will tell you this; he can help you if you'll only let him."

Jerome was flustered, but deep inside he knew he was hearing the truth. "Frankly, I'd like that, but if you haven't noticed we're a long way from an incense and candles shop, and my sitar is flat busted."

"Shut the fuck up, and listen to me," Anthony snapped back, "I'm trying to help you!" Jarman's serious tone silenced Jerome. "When you're up there, not sure of where you're going or what is ahead of you, I want you to remember your first night looking through that old 4.5" Meade telescope Dusty bought you. He'll show you a star to guide by. It will be dead center. Whatever direction the star moves, you move likewise. If it moves up and to the right that will be your signal to initiate a right climbing turn and so forth. The faster it moves, the faster you move. I know you can't see stars now worth a damn, so keep an old star chart in your map case for each month of the year 2010. Make sure you lay it out on your lap before you take your power nap. Dusty will take his heading from that. Now, repeat back to me everything I just told you."

Anthony's announcement sent an electric chill through Jerome's body that seemed to have entered through the right side of his head and ran quickly down through his body to the tip of toes and back up again. It was a though a life energy had just passed through him, an experience he had never felt before. Rather than be a disbelieving smart aleck, he calmly repeated the instructions. As he finished, the base XO pulled up. As the visibly irritated Major climbed out of his HUMVEE, Anthony leaned toward the pilot and asked in a loud whisper. "Why didn't you like fishing with your Dad? I'm just curious to know."

"The worms," Jerome answered sheepishly. "I hated baiting them on the hook as they squirmed, and my dad wouldn't fish with anything but worms."

Anthony laughed, "I see your point."

"Is this him," the base XO barked at Captain Richard.

"Major Duncan Peal, may I introduce Captain Anthony Jarman," Jerome replied "and I have no idea of why he wants to talk with you."

"Just who in the hell do you think you are?" the Major demanded angrily. "I've got a busted up airbase to run and I don't have time for this kind of nonsense."

A waft of pungent jet exhaust passed over Anthony's face, making his stomach turn. "I'm an End of Life Management Officer and I'm asking you to make sure that the crew of that airplane," he pointed at the Flying Circus, "is given hot meals and clean beds while their aircraft is being repaired."

"Mister, I don't care if you are a frickin' ELMO or Jesus Christ himself," Major Peal shouted angrily. "How dare you come on my base and suppose to order me to…"

To Anthony's sudden surprise, the man stopped mid sentence and looked down to his left. He saw the shadow of Master Sergeant Vigo Jones on the tarmac with a duffel back slung over one shoulder and two crates tucked under his other arm. He looked up as the shadow approached and saw that it was indeed Vigo who stopped and snapped to attention as a shaft of light cut across his body.

Anthony turned his attention back to the Major. Something in the man's face tripped his instincts. There was a subtext here – but what? He immediately slowed his perception of time just a bit so the two men would not notice him as he studied their body language.

After the major returned his salute, Vigo lowered the duffel bag to the ground, leaned forward and said, "I couldn't help but overhear what y'all were saying, and if I was you sir, I'd give this fellow what he wants. You know, these ELMOs got mighty big friends, if you know what I mean."

The major remained silent. Anthony could see an unmistakable sign of surprise in his face, as well as a strong hint of concern, if not perhaps, fear. What could it be about this sergeant and his Gomer Pyle act that could cause a surly major to freeze in his tracks, masking his own emotions?

Kicking a bit of gravel with his boot, the major said in a sour voice, "Sure. Fine. I'll see to it myself." Without another word, he spun around on his heels and signaled his driver to start the Humvee's engine. "Now get your miserable ELMO ass the hell off my base," he spat as he climbed back into his Humvee.

The three men stood there speechless and watched the infuriated major drive off in the direction of another C-130 that had just landed.

"Captain Jarman," Jerome said gratefully. "I don't how you got the juice to pull rank this way but I'm not one to look a gift horse in the mouth. The crew will be mighty grateful to you for this, as am I."

Anthony smiled. "Don't thank me Captain, just tell them this one is compliments of Dusty."

Jerome laughed. "That I will," he said with a big smile. "You ever need anything, you just let us know. We take great pride in accommodating our premier passengers you know."

Anthony felt a dry heave coming on. "I know. Sleep well, Captain."

As Vigo had said, the portable toilets nearest his truck were the cleanest on the flight line. Exhausted, but with his nausea somewhat quelled, Anthony slowly walked to the truck where he found the sergeant grunting under the hood. In the dim light, it appeared he was fiddling with something on the engine.

As he approached the truck, he quietly wondered about this Master Sergeant Vigo Jones fellow. He hadn't been in the military that long, but it was the first time he'd seen a major cowed by a sergeant. So then, who in the hell was this Vigo guy anyway? He had to know.

Reaching up to grasp the passenger door handle, Anthony swung open the door and said, "Vigo, let's get the hell off this base."

"Jump in, sir; everything is all packed in the back," Vigo replied as the truck's engine came to life with a satisfying rumble. "I trust you're feeling better."

"I will, once I get the hell off the base."

Vigo threw the old truck into gear and grinned. "I know how it is, sir. I got something that might help you feel better once we're past the main gate." He let out the clutch with a soft jolt that rocked Anthony's stomach and drove directly towards the main gate.

VIGO PULLED UP to the main gate and greeted the young private on sentry duty. The young soldier recognized him. "Wait here, Sergeant," he said, signaling to another MP in the guard shack to come out. Moments later, another sergeant with an MP armband strolled up to the Vigo's side of the truck and saluted. "Do you have any contraband?

"Not a flippin' thing," Vigo smiled back, then added, "well, actually, that's not completely right. In fact, I did find some odd stuff lying alongside the road back a ways, and I'll be darned if I can figure out what it is. Here let me get it for ya." He reached into a black daypack sitting on the cab floor, pulled out a tattered carton of More cigarettes and held them out to the MP. "Perhaps you'd have some use for 'em," he said with a smile. "Don't use 'em myself."

The MP snatched the carton and tucked it under his arm. "I can handle this." He waved them on with a smug smile, "Drive safely, now."

As the heavily laden truck creaked down the two-lane road to Highway 205, neither man said a word. Turning east onto the Interstate toward San Francisco, Anthony recognized the familiar site of the displaced persons, or the Bay Area Homeless, as they were called, camped alongside the highway in accordance with the dusk-to-dawn Homeland Defense curfew. Given a choice, these troubled people would keep traveling till they dropped, but the nighttime hours were the sole domain of the government, road crews and anyone else with a Homeland Security Forces authorization.

"Man, I wish I had something for my stomach," Anthony said, finally breaking the silence. "I wanted to snatch that carton of cigarettes out your hands back there, but one puff and I'd be heaving again, and all over your truck."

"We don't need that, sir," Vigo quickly replied. "You need to put something gentle in that stomach." The sergeant reached under the seat and handed him a liquid drink.

"What's this?" Anthony asked as he accepted the can.

"One of those instant breakfast drinks. Vanilla, I think." Anthony nodded appreciatively.

"Sip it slow, sir, or you'll get sick again." Vigo added.

Anthony peeled back the tab and began drinking the sweet, chalky-tasting drink. He almost gagged on the first sip, but began to feel better after a few small gulps. "Thanks, sergeant."

Anthony leaned his back and swallowed the last of the drink. "I only hope I can keep it down till I'm over this. My stomach feels like it was sucked through a meat grinder; damn! You know, I was counting on a hot meal back on the base, too."

Vigo chuckled. "Their mess closed about an hour before you arrived, but you didn't miss nothing. They were serving some of that leftover UNICEF gruel we used to ship to Ethiopia or some other backwater born-hungry kinda place. Awful tasting stuff sir, but if you're a patient man I think I can do you better once we've covered a few more clicks."

The sergeant unbuttoned the lapel on his shirt pocket and carefully fished around for a moment. Finding what he was he looking for, he held out his hand to Anthony with a hand rolled medical-marijuana cigarette. "This is good stuff sir — grown by the City of San Francisco no less. They grow this stuff for their dispensaries. A few puffs and you'll feel better, I guarantee!"

"A joint!" Anthony exclaimed. "I'll be damned. Normally I'd take a pass on that, but this nausea is killing me." Anthony dug a lighter out of his pants pocket, stuck the medical-marijuana cigarette between his lips, lit it and inhaled deeply. "Oh yeah," he wheezed through his pursed lips. "This will kill the nausea for sure."

"That's what it's for, sir." Vigo answered as Anthony felt a sense of relief flood through his body. As he resumed his puffing, Anthony's thoughts returned to the sergeant, who was now quietly humming to himself as he drove them on through the night.

During his encounter with Major Peal, he sensed that Vigo was more than a sergeant, even if this backwoods-acting character of a man was amiable, if not downright useful. Nevertheless, something else puzzled him. It was the déjà-vu feeling that he knew this man from somewhere else or another time. He finished smoking half of the cigarette and, feeling that he'd smoked enough, stubbed it out. "What do I do with this Vigo?" he said as held up the rest of the butt.

"Toss it. Do whatever you want. They keep tons of the stuff at the Los Gatos Triage Center for the patients, so it doesn't matter much."

"OK," Anthony replied, tossing the remainder out the window as he decided to keep his eyes peeled for a chance to get to the bottom of his instincts. It was then that a simple fact dawned on him; Vigo showed an indomitable sense of hope — something that was pretty rare these days.

Over a fourth of the human race had already perished, and perhaps many more would perish in the year to come. While most of the death toll was in Africa, India and China, only a few countries like Switzerland and Australia seemed to escape the tragedy of the times. Those who survived usually chose to face life one forward footstep at a time, but this man was more than just happy to be alive and useful. He seemed to ooze with hope for the future for some odd reason. It was as though he knew something that no one else knew. That, too, was something Anthony resolved to understand in time. "All things considered, I'm feeling pretty damn good, Vigo. In fact, I'd love something in my belly right now and a pack of smokes. I've got cash if you've got something to sell."

"I'm glad you're feeling better, sir. We'll go on down the road a bit further before we eat, but in the meantime...," he grunted as he reached down into the bag next to him on the seat. Shaking the bag a bit, he pulled out a box of Marlboro cigarettes and handed them to Anthony. "This one is on ol' Vigo."

"Thanks, Vigo," Anthony pulled a pack from the carton and began unwrapping it. "Shitty habit I picked up in New York, but it sure calms the nerves."

"There will come a time to quit. In the meantime, just light up while ol' Vigo finds us a place to park for some chow."

A few miles down the road, the sergeant found a spot in the road absent of the customary homeless campfires. Making a final check to see that they were alone, he pulled off the side of the road and came slowly to a stop. The two men got out, stretched and, with a few self-satisfied grunts, relieved themselves alongside the road.

Holding a GI issue flashlight in one hand, Vigo lifted the hood of the truck. Wrapping an old shirt around his hand, he removed two cans from the engine compartment as Anthony lit up. Drawing the smoke deep into his lungs, he felt the nicotine course through his body.

Vigo then went to the rear of the truck, and, folding back the canvas flap, he rummaged through a large box near the back of the truck. Halfway through his cigarette, Anthony watched with curiosity as Vigo walked towards him holding a one-liter bottle of water and the heated cans of C-Rations.

"I put them on the intake manifold before we left the base," Vigo grinned. "Gets them all nice, hot and shook-up, like." He held the light on the cans. "Let's see, here. Lima beans and meatballs, or spaghetti and meatballs?"

"If you're not particular, I'll take the spaghetti," Anthony replied.

"Figured that, but that's OK as I like the hell out of Lima beans."

Walking around to the front of the truck, they set their meals on the fender and Vigo began opening the cans with a small Army issue can opener. Leaving the opened lid on the top of the C-Ration can, he handed Anthony a spoon and a clean shop rag and said, "Food's hot, so you'll need hold the can with this while you're eating."

Anthony gently touched the side of the can with a fingertip and his hand immediately jumped back. "Damn! That is hot!" he exclaimed.

"Yup, you might let it cool a mite. It just spent that last thirty minutes or so bouncing around on the engine manifold.

"Don't tell me; it's your secret recipe, isn't it?" Anthony joked as he carefully wrapped the shop rag around the dull, green can. He pulled back the lid and took a whiff. To his surprise, it smelled good — really good. In the glow of the flashlight, he noticed the date printed on the top of the can — July 1974. "Vigo, you sure this is OK. This stuff is pretty old."

"Been eating it for two weeks now, and no problems. I found this stuff in a High School R.O.T.C. emergency wartime cache. They had it stored in a concrete bunker built under a football stadium bleacher: constant temperature and all that. Heck, even the foil-wrapped candy bars are still good enough to eat."

To prove his point, Vigo peeled the lid off his own C-Ration can and lifted a heaping spoonful of Lima beans to his mouth. Blowing on the food till it seemed cool enough to eat, he took the whole spoonful into his mouth and chewed it from side-to-side while making appreciative noises to signal that it was, indeed, edible food.

Satisfied with Vigo's performance, Anthony dug into his spaghetti with great relish.

After they consumed the contents of the cans, they shared their remaining pound bread, jam, crackers and chocolate bar treats, washing it all down with gulps of water from the shared canteen. Policing the mess into a small plastic bag, Anthony lit up another cigarette and said. "You're a good host, Vigo."

"Oh hell, this is just our coach service. You ought to see what we do up in business class."

"Well, forgetting that miserable flight, I guess there is something to be said for frequent flyer miles after all," Anthony laughed.

As the glow of an early dawn began to form in the far horizon, the two slowly, silently finished their meal, after which Anthony lit another cigarette and turned to face the sergeant. "Vigo, I gotta ask a question, and it might be a bit direct."

"Shoot."

"Breakfast drink, C-Rations, real cigarettes, a carton no less, and the first joint I've had in longer than I care to remember. So how come I'm gettin' this five star treatment? I mean, it ain't like we've known each other since whenever, you know."

Vigo sighed heavily. "I suppose I could tell that you're good for my business, and there is truth to that, being that ELMOs have the highest priority for about most anything. However, it really goes back to my late wife, Elizabeth. She was badly burned in one of the first quakes; the docs said she had second and third degree burns over most of her body and that she wouldn't make it. Hell, most of the hospitals in the area were nothing but piles of stone and dead bodies; we were lucky to get any kind of care as it was. After the shock wore off, they kept her doped up so she wouldn't feel the pain and told me she didn't have long. Then, this hospice worker came to see us. She was a special kind of person. I'll always be grateful to her for helping my Elizabeth to pass on."

"So you're being kind to me as some way to repay a debt you feel you owe?" Anthony asked softly.

"No, it's bigger than that."

"What do you mean?"

Vigo removed his cap and wiped his forehead. "Folks like you, sir, are real special. Guys like me, we just sit next to someone who is dying and our jaws flap with stupid nonsense, like some damn goldfish out of water. We try to say all the right things, but we can't take away the fear. Most times, we just try to say what we think they'll want to hear, and in the end it is the one dying who has to comfort our own fears." He shook his head, and put the cap back on. "Oh hell, I'm babbling like some mushy fool."

"No, you're not," Anthony injected. "Continue."

"Well, I see what you do. How you comfort people who want to die. I remember when the assisted suicide amendment became possible when we signed on to the UNE treaty. Man, was I ever stunned. But with all this death and suffering going on, it was the right thing to do."

"But I'm no saint, Vigo." Anthony said with a heavy sigh. "Fact is, I'm just a draftee."

"No sir," Vigo disagreed, "you're more than that. I heard about you and all you've done in New York. You're like that hospice worker that helped my Elizabeth, but she didn't have your gift."

"Maybe she did, Vigo."

"No, sir, the way I hear it, you can place your hand on somebody's shoulder and in no time at all their fears of dying just melt away. Folks say they just look off into the distance at nothing much in particular and smile because they're ready to end their lives without any more suffering. Yes, sir, you got a powerful gift."

"Does that make you afraid of me?" Anthony asked hesitantly.

"Before I lost my Elizabeth, I'd probably have been, but, now I know now that you couldn't do what you do if there was a shred of evil in your soul. It just wouldn't work. No sir, you got a gift. A gift from God."

Anthony flipped the remains of the cigarette to the ground, and jumped down from the boulder. "You call it a gift. I call it something else." He patted his shirt pocket with the cigarette package. "I don't care what you say, I owe you for the smokes, and I'll make good." With a friendly smile, Anthony held out his hand in a gesture of friendship.

Without thinking twice, Vigo reached out, accepted his hand and suddenly felt a tingling energy that traveled from Anthony's hand through his own and up to the base of his skull. Alarmed by the sudden invasion of his body, Vigo tried to pull back, but felt paralyzed. He was anchored to Anthony's strong grip as though a huge electric magnet had captured him like a pile of iron scrap. It was irresistible.

As the energy flowed through his shoulders and into the base of his neck, Vigo thought to himself, "Oh crap, this kid is more evolved than we thought. Damn, how could I be so careless? Damn! Damn! Damn!"

Then, the energy flowed up to the scalp, causing him to arch his head backwards as Anthony began to probe his short-term memory. Vigo labored to break free as his consciousness filled with a white light. It was bright and pure, but not blinding, and his mind emptied to nothingness. His last conscious thought was "I wonder if this is what's it like when a bullet rips your head open? Is this what the men at the other end of my sniper rifle experience when I take their lives?" Then, there was just an awareness of being. Vigo could not form a complete thought, but he could sense Anthony probing his mind.

Anthony had expected the military to send a hick sergeant to pick him up, but this man's mind was exceptionally well trained and focused and he glimpsed fleeting images of Vigo's memories from the night before.

He saw him shoot three black marketers from long range with a silenced, Barrett .50 caliber sniper rifle. He then watched as he loaded their ill-gotten booty into the back of the truck, which included a few cases of cigarettes, no doubt those he'd passed around that evening. Then he saw Vigo's memory of their meeting with the base XO back at Livermore.

Vigo despised the man because of the way he abused his authority, and here was a clear image. Anthony saw that he knew the major used his position to sleep with the women under his command and that Vigo tolerated it because the major was useful, but useful for what? The memories didn't go any further than that. Yes, this man, who could murder black marketers in cold blood before stealing their booty, had an incredibly well trained mind. If Vigo was really a sergeant, Anthony was the King of England.

Tired from his effort, Anthony released his grip and Vigo staggered backwards. The sergeant quickly fought to regain control of his own mind as his thoughts filled with rage over the way he'd been violated, which left him feeling mentally raped. Worse yet, he'd lost his position. The truth of it was that the handler had allowed himself to been handled. It was his worst nightmare come true, and he had to deal with it, or it would deal with him and not too kindly.

Anthony turned his back on Vigo and walked towards a larger boulder just off the side of the road, several yards away from the truck. He knew Vigo was armed; if he were going to kill him, it would happen now. If he had to go, an angry man with a loaded pistol and a grudge would be hopefully quick.

It wasn't a 9mm slug that tore through the back of his skull with a final, blinding white flash of hot metal. Rather, it was a paralyzing electrical wave. Anthony's legs fell out from underneath him as he fell to the ground like a broken rag doll. Completely limp and unable to move his arms or legs, he just lay there – helpless. Even glancing sideways was difficult, but he managed to see the Sergeant tuck a platinum-colored medallion inside the open collar of his shirt as he reached down to hoist him up. Is that what he had used against him?

The tables had turned suddenly, and Vigo was in control now. He softly whistled the "Colonel Bogey March" from the film "Bridge on the River Kwai" as he dragged Anthony's paralyzed body to a smooth, flat side of a roadside boulder that faced towards the East and the coming dawn. With tender care, he sat him upright with his back against the cool, smooth rock face and carefully laid Anthony's limp hands on his lap.

"You'll be OK in twenty minutes or so," Vigo finally said. Reaching back into his shirt pocket, he withdrew a small inhaler and squirted a few sprays in Anthony's nose. "It helps to keep the sinuses open." Anthony felt his breathing become less labored.

Stepping back, Vigo stuck the inhaler back in his shirt without dropping his focus on Anthony's eyes. "You won't be able to speak or move for a bit, so let's say I have your undivided attention right now."

"So now you know I'm killing black marketers and stealing their booty. You must think I'm hoarding a rather impressive cache of contraband instead of turning it in. If you do, I wish my life were just that simple."

Vigo walked back to the truck and took out a plastic bottle of mineral water and a small cup. Continuing to whistle the "Colonel Bogey March," he took his time walking back to Anthony. Settling down in directly in front him on the ground, he crossed his legs Yoga-style and smiled.

He poured a small amount of water into the cup and held it up to Anthony's lips. "Take a small sip. It will help with your dry throat." Anthony sipped the water gratefully. "Am I going to tell you what hit you? No." He refilled the cup to the brim and took a deep drink. Wiping his mouth, he recapped the bottle and placed it between his legs. "So now you've got the goods on me. All you've got to do is to tell the right someone about my nasty little secret and I'm toast, which is exactly what would happen."

Anthony wanted scream so badly it consumed his mind. Yet, all he could do was to blink and roll his eyes to keep them from becoming dry.

"But then again," Vigo continued, "If I was a real pirate, you'd be buzzard meat right now and without much ceremony, I might add. So, I guess that brings us to the question of who am I." He closed and rolled his eyes, and slowly rolled his head clockwise around his shoulders. Anthony could hear the small telltale cracking sounds and knew that despite his calm, friendly poker face; the man was obviously stressed and working his way up to something.

With a slow exhale, Vigo intoned, "Well then, you could say I'm a spook." Raising his head upright, he slowly opened his eyes and focused his eyes upon Anthony. "I'm actually a full bird colonel assigned to the National Reconnaissance Office, or NRO for short. Now while you know me as Master Sergeant Vigo Jones, they know me as Colonel Arthur Jones." He leaned forward with a somber face. "If you value your life, you will continue to know me as Master Sergeant Vigo Jones. Let's be honest. If they, and we're talking about the miserable shits who stuck you in this hell, even suspected how far your abilities have evolved, you will be toast as well, my young friend."

Vigo leaned back, took a deep clearing breath and relaxed his face with a self-sure smile. "So then, Anthony, my lad, let's just say that we're both playing a deadly game of blackmail. If we betray each other, we will share the same destiny. Think of it this way: This is why tabletop toasters have two slots in them. You're one slice and I'm the other."

Opening his large shirt pocket again, Vigo plucked out a neatly trimmed, half-smoked Churchill cigar and a small box of wood matches. "And since we are past the pretenses now, I can at least do something I really enjoy once in a great while."

He wove the flaming match in small circles around the end of the cigar till it came to life with a gentle, red glow. It was then that Anthony noticed something interesting about the man. He liked pockets. There were pockets all over his pants and shirt, and all were oversized and showed a manageable bulge. Was it because Vigo liked to cling onto things, or was it because he just liked having his things about him? Still, it was the first honest thing he'd seen about this man since the moment they met on the tarmac.

Puffing the stogie to life with gentle puffs, Vigo continued. "I've known you since you were fifteen years old, shortly after you wound up in the Hillview Orphanage outside of Austin. It was a damn shame about your family, Anthony. You were just a normal kid seeking love at a high school prom with a girl who was treating you like a dimwitted fool. Then, you come home to find that your family had died in a horrible auto accident. By the way, would you like to know what happened to Jenny Teal, the girl who asked you to the prom? Just blink twice for yes — once for no."

Anthony blinked twice.

"She knew your parents had postponed a family trip so you could take her to the prom when all she wanted to do was to make her ex-boyfriend jealous. When she learned that they died, a part of her died too. After you wound up in the orphanage, she soon started acting strange and taking drugs. She was in and out of clinics for two years until one night, when she finally ended it all with an overdose. All these years, I've wondered if you would feel sorry for her. Do you?" Anthony blinked twice for the second time. "A lot?" He blinked twice for the third time.

"I admire that in you, Anthony," he said in a respectful tone as he laid down his cigar on a flat stone. "I also respect the fact that you chose to stay in an orphanage instead of a foster home or with your spinster aunt. Of the three options, you chose the right one." He put the cup to Anthony's lips and tipped it gently for another sip.

"Unfortunately, though, you've piled a good many layers of concrete over your soul to shield yourself from ever being hurt again. Of course, the shrinks make a nice living just writing about stuff like this, but let's look at it in layman's terms."

Vigo placed the cup back on the ground; then held up his hands opposite of each other and evenly spread his thumbs and fingers apart. "What you've done Anthony, is that you've turned your life into a holographic fish tank." He brought his thumbs together tip-to-tip. "This is you in the center of the tank. Your tank Anthony." Vigo then closed together the remaining fingertips, forming an enclosure. "Some may think that you've built your tank not so that people could look at you swimming about inside your tank, but rather you've built it so that you can look out. Whiie you enjoy being able to view life up close and personal, you only do it through the holographic portals in your barrier."

Vigo picked up his cigar again, puffed it back to life with an obvious sense of enjoyment and blew a perfect smoke ring. "You know who I envy? Folks who can't blow perfect smoke rings because they've got a good reason not to smoke." He shook himself and rolled his shoulders. "Back to the topic at hand lad. Deep down inside that bunker you've built around your soul, there is an ever-present cry of hope that someone will crash through your bunker and make you feel really connected again. While I sincerely hope that happens for you, I have to tell you what you already know. Your little bunker is why you are so incredibly gifted. It is always easier to see life from a distance, as well as what lies beyond."

"Enough of that deep, dark stuff. No doubt, you're sitting there wondering just how in the hell I know all this, so let's open our history books and flip to page one." He took a few deep puffs and continued. "At the orphanage, you liked to hang out in the kitchen with the cook, Annabelle Browning. What you didn't know about

Annabelle was that she was a retired Navy intelligence officer. She could have done something more interesting than cooking three squares a day for orphans, but that was what she wanted to do. Go figure." He paused thoughtfully for a moment. "You know, my dear old dad used to tell me that he knew for certain the day men would finally figure women out. It would be the day before the end of the universe, so I guess the moral is that we're OK as long as we stay in the dark."

Vigo chuckled, picked up the cup in his other hand and drained the last of the water. "Well, it seems that good old Annabelle used to work with Remote Viewers for a while; she spotted your Indigo aura right off and called it in. After that, you were assigned to me. I used to specialize in you new millennium types back then, and you were just one of many for me. However, I could see your gift straight off. That's why I had Annabelle take special care of you. She would have done that anyway, because she loved you like a son, although she never told you. I want you to know that I offered to pay her but she wouldn't take it. Instead, she made me promise that I'd see to it that you'd get every chance to make a life of your own. That's why I'm sorry to tell you that she was killed last year during a tornado. Tore her house to smithereens and they found her body four miles away. Not a scratch on it. Damn funny, them twisters."

He looked into Anthony's eyes. "I can tell you're not blinking enough." He pulled a small vial of artificial tears out of one of his pockets and dropped the solution into his eyes. "Does that feel better?" Anthony blinked twice for the fourth time.

"Glad to hear it. No point in being uncomfortable." He tucked the vial back into his pocket. "After you were old enough to leave Hillview, I assigned my best operative to you — Roxanne." He noticed how Anthony's eyes widened and his eyebrows rose slightly. He would be talking soon. "Yes, Roxanne LeBlanc. You slept with her all the way through college and well after that. Yes, dear Roxanne. Gorgeous, vivacious, tantalizing, all this she was, and with no strings. No uncomfortable attachments or games. God, she was a piece of work to be sure. Damn glad I was a happily married man at the time. I can tell you that!"

Vigo paused again to take one last puff before grinding out the lit ashes of the cigar upon the ground. "And here is where I pray to God that you'll believe me when I tell you that I'm your friend. Anthony, I'm going to tell you something so upsetting that only a real friend, or a real enemy would tell you." He wiped his chin, as he struggled for the words. "Roxanne had a child by you. It was a boy, Anthony, and you are the biological father. Your boy's name is Russell. After she left you in Texas, she resigned the NRO and married some professor at the University of California at Berkeley and gave birth to your son."

The revelation stunned Anthony. It was this that he always sensed, but it was like an itch that could never be scratched. This was more than he had bargained for, and his head began to swim with questions. He drew a deep breath and could sense a small amount of control over his voice box returning to him. "Where," he said in a thin raspy exhale.

"You mean, where is the boy?" Anthony blinked twice for the fifth time.

Vigo grimaced at the thought of what he have to do next as he pulled his cellular videophone out of his pocket. "I didn't even know you had a son until I got this message a few months ago. So you understand, at this point, Roxanne and her husband are dead, and the boy has crawled through an old tunnel to a neighbor's home. After I got this message, I went there as fast as I could, but Russell was already gone and the old woman was dead. It was a pro job."

Vigo pressed the replay button and held the display in front of Anthony's face. Anthony saw his son for the first time. The boy was crying and trembling, yet firm in his actions and repeating the words his mother had carefully drilled into him for such an occasion. Then he saw two men break into the room behind the boy and an old woman, who fought with the first man until her head exploded from a shotgun blast. The last thing he saw was Russell being drugged with a spray followed by the butt of a shotgun as it smashed into the camera.

Vigo turned off the phone and slipped it into Anthony's pocket. "You and I are the only ones who have a copy of this message. Don't let anyone know." He threw the butt on the ground and sighed. "I've been trying to find your boy ever since, and it is like he has vanished from the face of the Earth — and trust me, I have some rather impressive resources at my command."

Anthony closed his eyes as a wave of irreconcilable sadness engulfed his mind. Like two drunken dancers holding opposite ends of the same handkerchief, the feelings of rape and loss circled him in a tortuous swirl of grief. It was too much, even for a man in a bunker of his making, and the salty flavor of his own tears welled up between his closed lips.

Vigo paused to wipe the tears spilling down Anthony's cheeks. "I'm so deeply sorry, son, because I have no earthly idea of where he is, or even if he is still alive. It really is as though he has vanished off the face of the Earth — but I promise you this — I'm never going to stop looking for him. If any harm has come to him, I promise you that the my face will be the last thing the miserable fucks see before I ever so slowly gut them like the filthy trash fish they are. You've got to trust me on this. Can I count on you to do that?"

For the first time, Anthony blinked only once.

CHAPTER 9

ONWARD TO LOS GATOS

ALTHOUGH THE HOUSTON Ship Channel had been devastated by a hurricane and heavy tidal surges, the city of Houston, Texas had survived the flyby in better than usual condition. The previous evening, Melissa Chadwick, the former Southwestern UNE Governor for America had resigned her position to take her new role as the administrative head of the UNE Space Program in Las Vegas, NV. Stepping into her post was former U.S. Senator Merl Johnston, and this was his first morning as the new Southwestern UNE Governor.

As their limousine wove its way towards 1001 Fannin Street in the middle of Houston's downtown business district, Danielle Peters looked out the window at the impressive First City Tower with its unique staircase design. The top fifteen floors of the forty-nine story high rise now served as the regional headquarters for the UNE.

Melissa Chadwick had converted the entire top floor to a private penthouse during her tenure as Southwestern Governor, and Danielle had heard glowing praises from Paulo, her bodyguard/companion. He was a good looker too and twenty years junior to Chadwick, who still looked pretty good for a woman in her late forties. At least, Paulo never seemed to complain, but then he wasn't that kind of man anyway.

Merl Johnston was also taken by the building's forty-nine stories of aluminum panels and green tinted glass and the way the building created the illusion of two giant puzzle pieces locked together, but not quite aligned. Rotated diagonally away from the traditional north-south layout used by the other traditional office buildings in Houston, the First City stood out through the power of illusion — a subtle fact that tickled his fancy.

Peters glanced up to see that the driver wasn't looking through the rear view mirror and then rubbed the inside of Johnston's leg. "So Gov, how are we going to christen our new offices?"

Johnston had drunk one too many champagne toasts the evening before and sighed. "Does the place have a Jacuzzi?"

"Yes it does," she purred. "And I believe it has an indoor lap pool as well. Are we feeling a little hung over this morning?"

He pinched her. "Ginny was a bit demanding last night."

"Is your wife already jealous of me?"

"In spades! We made love last night before she left for Louisiana, saying she wouldn't come back until you disappeared for good."

"And what did you say?"

"I denied that we're having a relationship of course, but that didn't stop her from slapping my face before she left. Damn, she's a fierce woman when she wants to be, but if she knew the real truth, she'd be twice as difficult to manage."

"So what are you going to do, Gov?"

He gently placed his fingertip over the nipple of her left breast and began rubbing in small circles. Even through her silk blouse and French bra, he could feel her nipple harden under his touch. "We'll take it as it comes."

She placed her hand over his and pushed it hard against her breast. "Let's do it right here, right now."

"No," he teased, "we're going to do it on my desk so we can get it all nice and warmed up for my new administration." He leaned over and kissed her fully on the mouth, then said, "But first, we have a small task that needs to be handled."

She leaned her head back into the plush black leather seat of the limousine and sighed. "Oh well," she sighed. "I put the orders in your briefcase. If you sign them now, I can drop them off at the communication center and meet you in your office."

"That's a good girl." He opened the snaps on his briefcase. On top of the other papers was the civilian quarantine order she had prepared. Any civilian entering a Homeland Defense Triage center would be quarantined until he, the Governor, opted to lift the quarantine.

The orders were drawn out to chief commanding medical officers for all Homeland Defense triage stations in the Southwestern District. In the far western edge of that district was the Northern California region, which included the Los Gatos Triage Center. The chief commanding medical officer for that region was Colonel Henry Tzu, based in Port Ord just North of Monterey, California, or more specifically, what little remained of it.

He thumbed through papers and casually asked, "What about that Fox News Reporter, Rose O'Hara? Is she already on Jarman's transfer from New York?"

"We're lucky there, Merl. O'Hara is on assignment in the Middle East covering that new fungus or whatever this new thing is that is killing the Arabs now. Spooky stuff; they find these guys dead in the morning with their guts turned to meat jelly. Now, they're calling it the Curse of the Prophet for starting all those wars, so I guess it makes good news. As for me, I could care less about another dead Arab after all the grief they've caused us."

"Don't get caught saying that in public," Johnston admonished her.

"No worries, I'm PC. Also, I thought you might like to know that Governor Chadwick had his transfer orders sealed so even the Fox News producers in New York still think Jarman is there in New York." They both laughed.

The morning was starting off better than Johnston could have hoped. "And where is Jarman right now?"

"I checked on that before we left the hotel this morning. He arrived at Livermore early this morning, according to the Livermore arrivals log, and was picked up by a driver there. He should be arriving at Port Ord sometime after we finish lunch today."

Johnston slapped his leg. "This is perfect! We lay down the quarantine before he gets there and before Fox News learns about it, it'll be a fait accompli." He signed the quarantine order with a flourish. "My first official act," he hummed. Handing her the orders he added, "Transmit these orders as soon as possible. The moment you get an acknowledgement from Colonel Tzu in California, I want you to leak Jarman's redeployment along with the quarantine announcement."

"You know that will piss O'Hara off, not to mention Fox News."

"Yeah, you're right, so let's throw a little salt on their wounds. Give it to CNN as an exclusive." He clapped his hands. "What a perfect morning."

"Uh, maybe not so perfect."

"What do you mean?"

"Our San Francisco Communications Intelligence office picked up an interesting bit of information while monitoring an unsecured phone conversation between a Major Duncan Peal, the Livermore Air Base executive officer, and another officer in Washington D.C. From what we can gather, the driver who met Jarman at Livermore this morning is actually Major Arthur Jones of the National Reconnaissance Office, traveling under the assumed name of Master Sergeant Vigo Jones."

"The Jones who has been a pain in our ass with all his snooping?"

"One and the same."

"Damn. We'll have to deal with him, but later. First, we've got to deal with Jarman as planned. In the meantime, I want you to get an operative into the Los Gatos Triage Center. Also, thank the folks in San Francisco for a job well done, and see to it they get some kind of reward, like a nice lunch or something."

"In terms of San Francisco, consider it done. As to the Los Gatos Triage Center, we've just placed an operative on the maintenance team, so he'll have free access to all the buildings in the complex. He's a bit junior, but quite adequate for routine surveillance, which is all we need at this point."

"Good. You're a jump ahead of me." As the limousine stopped in front of the building, he slipped his hand under her skirt and inside her panties. "I'll be waiting for you in my office," he said softly as a doorman reached out to open the Governor's door.

ANTHONY AND VIGO hardly spoke during the remainder of their trip to Port Ord, where Anthony would meet his orderly and hospice care nurse. While Vigo drove through the early morning hours, Anthony replayed his son's message time-and-again.

As they turned north on Highway 1, from Route 68, Anthony looked out the window in amazement. He had spent time in the area years ago when working for Senator Chavez and now it looked like a lunar landscape. When the big one hit, it had scoured the whole of Monterey like a retreating iceberg. Between them and the ocean, there was nothing but the residual signs of a great disaster and of massive Earth changes as the result of a far-sweeping chain of quakes and tsunamis that pummeled the California's Pacific coastline along the entire length of San Andreas Fault.

During that horrible day, after the Tsunami leveled the coastal cities of the Monterey bay, new lands were born when an uplift event occurred between two parallel fault lines north of the deactivated Fort Ord training base. The faults ran perpendicular to the San Andreas, from its western flank and followed a westerly heading toward the neck of the Great Monterey Trench offshore. In geological terms, it was like squeezing a grape and watching the meat of the grape bursting out of the skin.

After the convulsions subsided, great new stretches of land had been added to the Monterey coastline. Before the quakes, Highway 1 had run in parallel with the beaches. Now, after being rebuilt, it was a good five miles or more inland from where it had formerly been. Much of the land that now stretched between the highway and the sea would eventually become some of California's most valuable farmland.

However, the most interesting result of the quakes was the creation of a new deep-water port, formed by the Monterey Trench, north of Fort Ord and just off of a slough entrance once called Moss Landing. The Monterey Trench was still the deepest subterranean canyon on the Pacific Rim, only now; its sharp walls were above sea level.

Restoring the rail beds was easier than had first been expected, and the decision was made to rename the old Fort Ord Army training base north of Monterey into Port Ord.

The old fort had been dominated by old WWII era barracks and buildings, which had been leveled by the Tsunami. However, the fort's underground facilities and roads survived such that they were quickly repaired. After that, heavy lift helicopters hauled in a machine used to manufacture triangle-shaped geodesic dome titles. At full speed, it could crank out enough radiation reflecting tiles each day to build several fifteen-meter geodesic domes.

Capable of withstanding a 9.0 magnitude Earthquake, the geodesic domes sat on the ground like inverted soup bowls. The initial domes were reserved for offices and officer quarters, while the enlisted ranks and port workers slept in tents.

The Office Dome for Colonel Henry Tzu, the chief commanding medical officer for all Northern California Homeland Defense Triage stations, featured a large bay window opposite his office desk. It offered Tzu a panoramic view of the New Monterey Bay, and it was worth all the future favors he knew he'd have to pay for it.

Rocking back in his chair, he focused his attention on the hard copy print out of the quarantine orders that had just come in from Houston. His orderly room clerk, Corporal Stanley Piper had found the orders waiting for him in the office secure mail folder when he arrived that morning for work. Not knowing the significance of the quarantine orders, he acknowledged receipt to Houston, then printed the orders and left them on Tzu's desk along with several other routine matters.

Of medium height and with a slim build, Tzu felt as though a heavy weight was now pressing on him, and he let his middle-aged body sink into the old padded chair behind his desk. An order of this magnitude coming so quickly from a new UNE governor was not a good sign. He pressed his intercom switch. "Piper, get me the files on that new ELMO that's supposed to be here this morning and his new nurse and orderly."

"I'm just now getting them ready for you sir," The corporal replied.

A chunky, dark-haired computer wiz, Corporal Stanley Piper preferred his job as an orderly room clerk, even though he could have easily gotten a promotion with a new posting as a computer specialist. For most, it would have been a no-brainer, but for Piper, there was nothing alluring to him about sitting behind a flat panel display all day and being continually pushed with absurd deadlines by people who seldom understood the technical difficulties they assumed were so easy to master. He'd done enough of that as a software engineer in the Silicon Valley before the Shiva flyby, and now he wanted to be part of the real action. As Colonel Tzu's clerk, he attended to the usually boring tasks with fastidious care and speed, all the time relishing the secret missions Tzu would give him.

Tzu and Piper had first met at a Progressive Libertarian political gathering a few years earlier, back when Piper was working as an hourly consultant for a major computer security firm in the Silicon Valley. They stayed in touch and built a good friendship. After the Nibiru flyby, Piper decided to enlist in the Homeland Defense Forces, become Tzu's private clerk and help him make a difference. He'd done enough for money, he had reasoned. Now it was time to do something for love — the love of an enlightened and peaceful future.

Piper walked into Tzu's office with a handful of files. "I already pulled their files this morning. The orderly and the nurse are here in the waiting room. As for Captain Jarman, I can only guess that he'll be here shortly, unless something happened to him and Sergeant Jones on the way here from Livermore."

He nodded his head with great appreciation as he spread the files out on his desk. "Close the door and have a seat." Piper peeked out the door at the nurse and the young orderly. They were both seated and thumbing through old tattered copies of Newsweek from before the day of opposition. He closed the door and took a seat facing Tzu.

Tzu tapped his finger on the quarantine order. "You know, Stanley, this is not good — not good at all."

"It seems reasonable to me," Piper replied. "Am I missing something here?"

Tzu nodded his head. "Anthony Jarman is going to show up any time now and then I'm going to have to drop him into a whole new realm of hell at Los Gatos. We know he's being politically targeted for death, and losing him would be a terrible setback to our party."

"So?"

"So what news channel is going to be dumb enough to send to send an expensive news crew to Los Gatos, only to have them quarantined until God knows when?"

Piper scratched his forehead. "In other words, with the media stymied, Anthony Jarman is out of sight and soon out of mind."

"Precisely! Without press coverage, whoever has it in for him will have a free hand to bury him, and they will. This brings us to the burning issue: what, if anything, can we do about it."

"Yeah," Piper replied sadly. "He's up against some pretty serious hombres too."

"Well, Stanley. Maybe we can fight fire with fire. As I remember, he did some work for Senator Chavez back when he was working for the Republicans. It was his strategy that got her elected. As I see it, she owes him big time."

"But will she see it the same way? After all, she is a politician."

"Then, it really boils down to two questions. Is she still a human being, and will she be able to put two-and-two together and then do something about it?"

"Getting her the data can be tricky. I'm good, but her office is getting hammered by UNE hackers like crazy. They could at least trace the Ethernet packets back to us, even if they can't decode them."

"Then, what we need is a courier."

Piper grinned from ear-to-ear. "I just put a new set of plugs in my old Motto Guzzi touring bike last night and she's running like 1064CCs of pure kick-butt."

"OK, OK, OK, spare me the Easy Rider soundtrack. You'll take a packet to her house over in Oakland this evening. Just watch your ass."

"No problemo, boss. So what about this Jones character?"

Tzu looked at the folders spread out on his desk. "Hmmm... Major Arthur Jones (a.k.a. Master Sergeant Vigo Jones), National Reconnaissance Office. A secret inter-service intelligence operative can pretty much go wherever he wants. So why here and why now?"

Piper could see where Tzu was going with this line of reason. "You can say that again. You know, I've been wondering why has this guy has weaseled a supply slot for himself at Los Gatos, and why did he want to pick up Anthony Jarman in Livermore."

"Obviously, there is a connection here and my instincts tell me that this Jones fellow is one of the good guys." He swiveled around in his chair and poured hot water into a coffee mug with a faded picture of the Golden Gate Bridge on it from a thermal pitcher on his credenza. Thinking to himself, he opened a Ginseng tea box and began dunking a teabag in the mug as the corporal sat patiently with a pleasant smile of anticipation on his face.

He turned and set the mug on his desk. "You know, Piper, I've actually been thinking a lot about Jones." It was clear to Tzu that Jones had juice. One wrong step with this spook and he'd be spending the rest of his military career changing truck tires and eating survival gruel. That was, if he were lucky. He was blowing gently across the top of this mug when he noticed Piper, a picture of the grinning Cheshire Cat from the book, *Alice in Wonderland,* if there ever was one.

"OK, what are you holding out on me?"

Piper joyfully pounded the arms of his chair with delight as he gloated. "I live for days like this." He pointed at the folders on Tzu's desk. "Check the nurse. I got her special just for you, and she's sitting outside your office right now. Checkmate!"

"OK, smart-ass, let's see what we've got here." Tzu opened the file of Hospice Nurse, Warrant Officer Ann-Marie Bournelle. The file had the customary military data, but it was the special background information that Piper had dug up that really caught his attention.

Before the Nibiru flyby, Bournelle ran one of the best brothels in all of Northern Nevada. She managed a clean and lively shop, paid her taxes and earned the loyalty of her ladies of the night and gentlemen customers alike. One of those customers, it seems, happened to be certain Major Arthur Jones of the NRO, a.k.a. Master Sergeant Vigo Jones. According to several of the interviews, she personally serviced Jones and nobody else."

"How the hell did you get this, Piper?"

"One of those favor-for-a-favor, clerk kinds of things."

"And of course you are not free to divulge your sources?"

"Can't go there," he winked. "Shall I send her in?"

"OK, Radar, send her in?"

"Radar?"

THE UNIFORMED NURSE seated before him was a remarkably attractive 38-year old redhead with soft green eyes. Warrant Officer Ann-Marie Bournelle's personnel file was filled with glowing performance reviews, and the Los Gatos Triage Center would be her first assignment in California. If the chemistry between her and Jarman worked out, she'd be shipping out for Los Gatos with him that afternoon after they get their injections.

"You have an excellent record," remarked Tzu while trying to keep his eyes off of her voluptuous figure and plump, perky breasts. He shuffled some papers and held up the personnel jacket so he could only see her round, glowing face and tied-back auburn, bouncy hair over the edge of the folder. "My clerk tells me that you have something I need to hear. What is it?"

His visual avoidance humored Ann-Marie, who was well accustomed to being ogled by men. "Look, let's be frank. I used to run a brothel in Nevada. It's all there in your file, and if isn't, I'd be surprised since your orderly room clerk is such a clever fellow. When this posting for Las Gatos came up, I saw an old name on the roster that rung a bell, which is why I want this posting. You see, I personally took very few johns myself and the ones I did were strong, interesting and mysterious. One of them was a man seeking comfort after being widowed for almost a year.

He goes by the name of Sergeant Vigo Jones." Ann-Marie leaned back into her chair, relaxed and enjoyed the interesting play of expressions upon Tzu's face that was now faking surprise to the best of his ability.

After a moment, Tzu rubbed his jaw reflectively and finally said, "Warrant Officer Bournelle…"

"Please just call me Ann-Marie, or Ms. Bournelle if you wish," she said nonchalantly.

Tzu nodded gently, "Very well, Ann-Marie. Tell me in exactly ten words or less, the most important thing I should know about this man."

Ann-Marie held up her hand. "Interesting question. Before I answer that, I want you to know I'm glad you decided to call me Ann-Marie."

"And why is that?" he asked with a curious grin.

She chuckled a bit and finally answered, "I never put my trust in people who call me Ms. Bournelle, because they're usually the type that ask expensive questions. You know, like lawyers and tax auditors."

Tzu chuckled. "I'm no lawyer," he said waving his hands. "Not that my dear departed Mother didn't try to push me into law school." They both laughed. "But I do have one very pointed question for you. To whom do you give your loyalty?"

Ann-Marie's eyes shot up. "That's a pretty direct question, so let me answer it the way I know best. I'm loyal to whoever is paying the freight, and in this case, that would be you."

Tzu smiled warmly. "Wise answer, Ann-Marie, and thankfully brief as well. Let me be equally brief. Sometime this morning, hopefully sooner than later, a truck is going to pull up in front of my dome with two men in it, both of whom will be stationed in Los Gatos. One is this Sergeant Jones fellow we've already discussed. The other, is an ELMO by the name of Captain Anthony Jarman."

"You've got to be kidding me," she stammered. "Everybody in my MOS knows about him. I get to work with Jarman?" Excitement and admiration resonated in her voice.

"If he accepts you, yes. Given your unique abilities, I'm sure that will not be a concern."

"I'll try my best," she said with wide eyes.

"I know you will; however I need to get to the crux of the matter. Simply put, I believe this Sergeant Jones shares some history with Jarman. How or what, I have no idea but it does exist. With this in mind, I need you to tell me in exactly ten words or less, the most important thing I should know about Jones."

Ann-Marie quickly saw where things were going. Keep an eye on Vigo while working under Jarman's command or go back to the assignment pool, and wait for whatever boring assignment came next, which was not her style. She preferred mysterious challenges.

"In answer to your question, the most important thing you need to know about Jones, is that he is as honest as he can be. And yes, I'll be your eyes and ears in Los Gatos, providing Jarman gives me the OK."

They shook hands and struck a bargain that day that would never appear on any scrap of paper, nor ever be mentioned to any third parties. Yet, it would endure longer than either could imagine.

"Wait in the mess hall till my clerk sends for you."

"We're going to ambush Jones, huh?"

Tzu laughed. He picked up a small book up from credenza. "This was written twenty four hundred years ago. It's called the Art of War by Sun Tzu. You might find it interesting while you're enjoying your coffee, or whatever they call that brackish mop water they serve these days. Just remember to give it back to me."

"Sure. By the way, are you any relation to this Sun Tzu fellow."

"I'd dearly like to think so, but I doubt it."

VIGO DROVE THE truck up to the Port Ord main gate and showed the guard their orders. Anthony could see a wanted poster taped to the back of the guard's clipboard. He recognized the faces of the men he'd seen in Vigo's memories — the ones he had killed as easily as one would when snapping a chicken's neck. He answered a few questions posed to him by the guard as he slowly smoked his cigarette. Satisfied with their credentials, the guard showed them how to find Colonel Tzu's dome and lifted the gate arm so they could pass.

Vigo parked his truck across the street from Tzu's office, and the two men walked into the dome and introduced themselves to the orderly room clerk. Despite his rough looks, Anthony was somewhat rested. Vigo, on the other hand, looked far less tired than he actually felt. The man was trained for endurance.

Moments later, the two were standing in front of Tzu's desk. "Please be seated." He pointed at the chairs in front of his desk and cleared his voice. "I wish I had time for civilities today, but I don't. So let's get to it. Captain Jarman, your next duty station will be the Los Gatos Triage Center. Sergeant Jones, you will be assigned there as well, as their fixer. As you know, the Three Gorges virus has hit the Bay Area, and this morning, the new UNE governor has put a new quarantine order into effect. Any civilian that sets foot in a triage center doesn't leave until he or she dies, or the quarantine is lifted. Before you ship out this morning, each of you will get a flu vaccine shot. Keep in mind, gentlemen, that this stuff is more precious than gold and in very limited supply. Only medical and key governmental personnel can get it and it's not foolproof either. It's only about seventy percent effective, but if you follow the protocols like you're told, you shouldn't have any problems."

Tzu's already somber tone darkened even further. "Now, how dangerous is this situation? Well, cute phrases like 'in the event our efforts to contain it should fail,' are pure crap. Before the Nibiru flyby, we had the resources to save people. Now, we're simply stretched too thin. I'm afraid we're facing a huge epidemic with a substantial loss of life in the Bay Area, and if we cannot contain it, God only knows where else."

Pausing to take a sip of his Ginseng tea, he opened a side drawer, removed a leather folder and passed it to Vigo. "Everything you'll need for your first assignment is in that folder. You're to drive down to San Diego, and pick up a load of medical supplies, including several kilograms of pure heroine from the DEA. In addition to the usual folk, Captain Jarman, here is also authorized to sign for the heroin when you deliver it to Los Gatos."

Tzu slowly stood up, and Vigo and Anthony both rose with him until he pointed a hand at Anthony. "Please remain seated, Captain. We have several other matters to discuss." Vigo continued to rise as Anthony sat back down with a curious glance. "One of my staff is already waiting for you at your truck, Sergeant. He'll show you to your quarters and expedite the servicing of your vehicle. Also, be absolutely sure to stop by the dispensary and get inoculated. The rest is all in that bag you're holding. Now, unless you have any other questions, Sergeant Jones, you are dismissed."

"Everything is quite clear, sir," Vigo answered with a crisp salute.

PIPER HAD WAITED for this moment with eager anticipation and struggled to keep a straight face as the knob on the inner door between his office area and Colonel's Tzu's private office turned crisply. He took one last look at Ann-Marie Bournelle sitting patiently with a small book in her hand. "It's show time!" he whispered out loud. She winked back at him and turned her face to the window.

As he walked to the door, Vigo felt his exhaustion draining him more quickly now. That last ten yards was always the worst.   Now, all he wanted was a hot shower, a cool cot and a little privacy.   The rest would be details.

Then, mid-stride, he saw her and froze in his tracks.   She turned and zoomed in on his eyes.   "Oh my," she exclaimed softly as she rose to meet him,   "You know, Sergeant, you're so cute I might just tuck you in my purse and take you home."

Vigo stood there in total amazement, his jaw grinding noiselessly for words.   First, the handshake thing with Anthony and now this – how was he to play it?   He saw her sitting next to a young private and waived his finger at them.   "So are you two an item?" he joked.

She cocked an eye at him and leered.   "Vigo, behave yourself."

Piper loved every moment of the encounter.   Watching this gruff old sergeant getting caught flatfooted by this madam was a pure joy to behold and decided to make things more difficult for Jones.   He gestured to the young man to come to his desk.   "Stand and report."

The young soldier did as he was instructed and announced himself.   "Private First Class Charlie Gibbs reporting for duty as the new aide for Captain Anthony Jarman.   I will also be his armorer."   Gibbs looked like most of the young kids in the military these days — tall, skinny and alert, although he did have piercing black eyes and a strong jaw that seemed to indicate a bit more depth than usual.

However, Piper's interest was keenly focused on how the sergeant was now smiling at Ann-Marie Bournelle.   His face was filled with a gentle radiance that just seemed to melt her like butter as a friendly connection clicked in their eyes.   The picture was undeniable; they'd seen some history together and genuinely liked each other.   Piper stood up. "You have your orders, sergeant, and someone from the motor pool will be here in about ten minutes or so to help you with your vehicle and quarters."

He gestured towards the door to Tzu's office "Warrant Office Ann-Marie Bournelle and Private First Class Charlie Gibbs, please follow me."

Ann-Marie winked at Vigo, "Time for us to present our bona fides to the boss I guess. Catch you later, handsome."

THE MOTOR POOL sergeant pulled up next to Tzu's dome in a freshly serviced HUMVEE. It was already loaded with Bournelle's personal gear, and Vigo helped him pack in the rest belonging to Jarman and his new orderly, Charlie Gibbs.

Corporal Piper joined them and instructed Charlie that he would drive Jarman and Bournelle to Los Gatos in the HUMVEE after they got their injections at the dispensary.

Meanwhile, the motor pool sergeant climbed into the passenger side of Vigo's truck and waited for him. The sergeant would see to it that he got what he needed along with a shower, a hot meal and some much needed rest.

Bournelle opened the rear door of the HUMVEE as Vigo walked up to her and pointed to an empty spot between Tzu's dome and the one next to it. "May I speak with you in my office Ann-Marie?"

She smiled. "We'll need to make it kinda quick, but yes." He led her around the back of the dome to a private place, away from prying eyes.

"I'm glad to see you're alive, Ann-Marie." He exclaimed happily, as he wrapped his arms around her in a big, warm hug.

"You too, Vigo," she replied warmly. "Honey, you'll always be the brick for me."

"So, what are you doing here?"

"Being a hospice nurse just seemed like the thing to do. Besides, I'm a pretty darn lucky gal to be working for Captain Jarman." Then she poked a stiff finger in his chest. "I haven't got to know him yet, but I can tell you this already. If anyone wants to get him, they'll have to come through me."

He put his lips to her ear and said, "For the record, Ann-Marie, anybody who wants to hurt Jarman will not have to go through you. He'll have to go through us. So listen; you just do your job the best way you see fit and we'll both get along just fine." He kissed her gently on the cheek and gently pulled her towards him, "After all the bombs, bugs, shakes, waves and who know what else, we're both still alive. Seeing you again, Ann-Marie, does my heart good."

She had always loved his scent and wanted more than anything to melt into his arms, but there would time for that later on. She gave him a tight hug and said, "Me too, Vigo. Don't disappear on me again."

As she drew back from him, Vigo felt an undeniable spontaneous urge well up suddenly within him. He kissed her tenderly on the lips, "I'll see you in Los Gatos."

THE FLAGMAN WAVED their HUMVEE to stop at the entrance to Highway 9 in Felton. They had already been on the road for nearly an hour since leaving Port Ord and PFC Gibbs looked back at Nurse Bournelle sitting behind them. "We're nearly halfway there. I've been up and down Highway 9 most all my life ma'am. It will be a little bumpy from here to Los Gatos because of the quake damage, but I'll steer clear of the potholes. Just hold on." Ann-Marie hoisted a silent thumbs-up.

Gibbs expertly navigated the HUMVEE along Highway 9, now the only available road between Santa Cruz to the north of Port Ord and Los Gatos. At 500 feet above sea level, the sight of burnt remains of coastal Redwoods standing in great piles of powdery gray ash dominated the view. When and if this area ever greened again, Anthony felt it would start there.

Winding their way up the twists and turns of narrow 2-lane road, Gibbs pulled up to the gate of a military truck park just north of the small town of Boulder Creek.

The guard checked their papers and said, "From here to Los Gatos is a single lane. Landslides and quake damage, you know, the usual stuff. The next single lane convoy to the other side of the mountain is forming up at the back, but won't head over for about another two hours." He pointed their attention to a single file row of vehicles. "I suggest you park and then go to the field kitchen on the far side. They're serving buffalo stew and potatoes, and it's hot. It will be your last chance to eat for at least another four to five hours."

"Thanks," Gibbs answered as the guard raised the gate. "Buffalo sure beats the horsemeat we've been eating."

Anthony leaned over and gestured Gibbs to wait. "Private, I want a guard posted on this vehicle."

The guard leaned down and saw Anthony's rank and medical insignia. "Yes sir, I'll let my sergeant know. We'll keep an eye on your vehicle."

WHILE ANN-MARIE was not about to admit it, her backside was sore — real sore. Setting her tray down on the picnic table across from Anthony and Private Gibbs was more involved than she had first supposed. As she slowly swung her leg over the seat and swiveled into place, she pretended to ignore the smirks on the faces of her traveling companions.

"Whoever the cook was," she said as she spooned the contents of her tray around, "should have been shot and canned as well." What had obviously started out as a perfectly good package of freeze-dried potato flakes had been turned into a runny and lumpy, starch-like gruel. The stew, on the other hand, had come straight out of a can, and there wasn't much anyone could do to ruin it.

Anthony and Charlie quietly dug into their own trays, as they both saw no point in complaining. Like death and taxes, government chow was dependably awful.

Eating slowly, Ann-Marie finished her stew and a few spoonfuls of the potato gruel and pushed her plate aside.

"Are you finished with that?" Charlie asked. Ann-Marie nodded and pushed her tray at him. "Thanks, Ma'am. Calories are calories and I don't much care how I get them these days."

Anthony laughed, and pushed his tray towards Charlie with his half-eaten portion of potatoes and the better part of a biscuit. "Eat up, Charlie. You've got a long drive ahead." He turned to face Ann-Marie. "I've got some brandy in my bag, and since Private Gibbs here is our designated driver, may I interest you in a wee pull of the cork?"

Her eyes lit up. "You sure may! Lead on, kind sir."

Anthony pulled a silver flask and two small cups from his bag he'd left sitting on the bench and gestured toward a few bales of hay at the edge of the truck park now used for bedding. They strolled over to the bales and settled in, whereupon Anthony carefully poured the first drink and handed it to Ann-Marie who sniffed it with great appreciation. "It's been too long," she sighed gratefully.

"I know the feeling," He answered as he poured his own drink and tossed it down. Setting down the cup, he rubbed his left shoulder. "That injection still hurts. Damn, what in the hell did they put in that shot? I've had flu shots before but this one is a real pain."

"Trust me, I know how you feel," Ann-Marie answered. "It will hurt for a bit, but just be glad you got it — real glad It is a 3G inhibitor."

"Yeah I guess, but I still wish they'd develop a nasal formula instead of these damn injections," he complained.

He refilled their cups and held his up for a toast. "Like the saying goes, beware of strangers bearing gifts. Cheers." They tipped their cups and drank. "Another," he asked.

Ann-Marie drained the last of her cup and handed it back to him with a smile. "Don't mind if I do."

As he refilled the cups he asked, "So what do you know about the top honcho at Los Gatos?"

"I can tell you what I know from the grapevine back at Port Ord. The Chief Medical Officer is Major Jim Boole.

He's in his early fifties and on loan from the Army Medical Corps. A real good guy from what I hear." She waived her hand passively. "You won't have any problems with him, but the one you'll most likely butt heads with is a Russian Jewess by the name of Lieutenant Colonel Tanya Wheelwright."

Anthony's eyebrows shot up. "Russian Jewess?"

"That's right; she's about your age, and she acts like death is her own personal enemy, from what I hear."

"And she's running a triage center? You gotta be kidding," he frowned. "And since when is Wheelwright a Russian name?"

"She's originally from Moscow," Ann-Marie replied as she sipped the brandy. "As the story goes, she was a hospital administrator not far from here when her family died in the big wave. She lost her parents, husband and child all at the same time – really tragic. She was really in love with her late husband from what I hear. Some professor type from Monterey I believe."

"So is this why she's on a personal crusade to battle death?"

"Well that would account for her personal grudge with death," She admitted.

"So what else can you tell me about her?"

"I hear they call her the Ice Lady, because she can be pretty damn cold at times, but that she's a real beauty. Not in the traditional American sense, but she's one of those tall, exotic looking Russian gals with an hourglass figure that you guys all seem to go slurpy for." Anthony's eyes drifted away as he tried to imagine her in his mind.

She reached over and pinched his nose. "If I were you, I wouldn't bother with any romantic hard-to-get competition notions in my mind right now. Pardon my French, but this gal has got juice, a grudge and a broken wing, so just remember not to shit where you eat."

Anthony frowned, "Ann-Marie, I may be dumb, but I'm not stupid. And besides, I've really had my eyes on you anyway."

"Dream on honey. Like I said, just remember not to shit where you eat."

Anthony shrugged his shoulders.   "Looks like I'm batting a thousand, today."

She smiled and touched his cheek. "Thanks for thinking of me anyway, boss. You're a handsome devil in your own right so don't worry. You'll find someone to bed in no time at all."

"Louie - I think this is the beginning of a beautiful friendship," Anthony said with a grin.

Ann-Marie laughed. "Any man who can remember a great line like that from a classic flick like Casablanca is a real winner. No doubt about it, boss, we are going to have beautiful friendship.

CHAPTER 10

A SENSE OF DESTINY

PRIVATE GIBBS REACHED across the cab of the HUMVEE and shook Anthony's shoulder. "Wake up sir, we're just a few minutes from the main gate."

Anthony opened his eyelids a bit, and sniffed. "Thanks Charlie." He stretched his arms with a sleepy groan, swiveled around in his seat and tapped Ann-Marie's knee until she began to stir.

She rubbed her eyes and looked out the window at the dry bed of the empty Lexington Reservoir, now home to their next duty station, the Los Gatos Triage Center.

Charlie stopped at the main gate and seemed undistracted by the two guards walking around the vehicle and speaking in hushed tones to each side. The one standing on Anthony's side of the vehicle asked dryly, "May I see your orders, sir?"

Anthony handed him the orders without comment. The guard examined them carefully and said, "Colonel Wheelwright is expecting you. She gave instructions that you are to be led directly to her office." He pointed to another guard sitting on a small electric 4-wheel drive. "Just follow him." He stood back a step and saluted. "Welcome to Los Gatos, Sir."

Anthony returned the salute as the small ATV lurched to a quick start toward the dirt road that led down to the dusty bottom of the reservoir.

The ATV eventually led them to the geodesic dome that now served as an administrative office for the center's commanding officer. She had been alerted to their arrival by the guard at the main gate and was now waiting for them along with another officer and a tall, thin but jovial looking Indian corporal wearing a Hindu turban on his head.

Gibbs brought the HUMVEE to smooth stop, and Anthony was the first to hop out of the vehicle. As he crossed around the front of the vehicle, he could see that Ann-Marie's physical description had been right on the money. Even despite the dehumanizing effect of her baggy fatigues, she still seemed to exude a genuine feminine quality. What a pity it was that she was untouchable.

"I'm Lieutenant Colonel Tanya Wheelwright, and next to me is Chief Medical Officer Major Jim Boole, and to his right, my orderly room clerk, Corporal Sunny Sharma." She held out her hand with a genuine smile, "Welcome to the Los Gatos Triage Center."

Anthony grasped her hand. "Captain Anthony Jarman, End of Life Management Officer, reporting as ordered." The shake was firm and warm, He could feel that her pulse was strong and steady, nor did he sense anger in her, but rather a combination of deep personal sadness overlaid by a stronger sense of purpose. On one hand, he could see why her subordinates would privately call her the Ice Lady. On the other, there was a sad and intriguing mystery about this woman. It was a mystery like his own, held too near to the heart to be revealed.

"Thank you, Colonel," he answered softly. As they shook hands, Ann-Marie and Charlie joined them. "This is my hospice nurse, Warrant Officer Bournelle," he added, "and my orderly and armorer, Private Charlie Gibbs."

Major Boole stepped forward and shook Anthony's hand. "A pleasure to meet you, Captain. Your reputation precedes you. I've studied several of your case histories and your methods are unique to say the least. Perhaps there is much I can learn from you."

Anthony smiled, "Likewise, Major." The build and facial features of the African-American doctor reminded him of the actor Anthony Quinn – just darker with warm, quick eyes that continually searched for details. Even though he was soft spoken, it was clear that he was comfortable with himself, his talents and his ability to lead.

Colonel Wheelwright was likewise impressed with Anthony. She could see that he had an easy manner about him and a warm and infectious smile. A part of her wanted to know what was behind the smile, while another wondered how many people had seen that smile with their last breath. She pushed the thoughts out of her mind. While it was her responsibility to run the triage center, she knew the whole community would eventually center itself around him in one way or another. It always happened like that with End of Life Management Officers.

"Well folks, we're still under construction, so until we open our gates, get familiar with the place and try and get some rest. Once we open for business, you'll need it." She held up a finger, "On the bright side, our mess hall is up and running and we just completed our officer shared quarters." She turned to Ann-Marie and Charlie, "Corporal Sharma will show you both to your quarters," and then turned to Anthony. "Captain, I know you're tired, but we have a few administrative details to attend to. After that, I hope you'll all join us for dinner in the mess at eighteen thirty." She gestured towards the large portable building and dining tent that now served as the mess hall.

As Sharma led the nurse and private away, Boole patted Anthony on the shoulder. "You'll be sharing a dome with Father Michael Bennett, a Jesuit Priest. We call him our Spiritual Wombler."

"Could that be because he has a fondness for Scotch Whiskey?" Tanya added with a chuckle.

"Actually not," Boole replied. "He's originally from England and there, womblers are folks who recycle things like tin cans and the such. We nicknamed him our Spiritual Wombler because he likes to recycle troubled souls. Tell me, Captain Jarman. Is your soul troubled?"

"Nothing a few drams of Scotch Whiskey wouldn't fix."

Tanya grinned. "Captain, I can already see that you're going to fit in just fine." She nodded towards her office, "Now, it's time to do the paperwork."

THE FOLLOWING THREE days passed with cacophony of pneumatic and electric tools and construction equipment. Anthony occasionally bumped into Tanya from time-to-time but kept pretty much to himself, sleeping as often as he could.

On the morning of the fourth day, he was halfway through his breakfast when he was graced by Tanya's presence. She sat down facing him, sipping a cup of hot tea. "Say, Captain Jarman."

"Please call me Anthony. I'm not a lifer."

Tanya chuckled. "Yeah, you're obviously not the type who looks to make a home in the military. OK, Anthony. Then just call me Tanya, as I'm not a lifer either."

"Deal. So, to what do I owe the pleasure of your company, Tanya?"

"Does the name Senator Connie Chavez ring a bell with you?"

He laid his fork down. "Is this about politics?"

"No. Actually, she called me this morning, and we had a long chat about you. She said you used to work for her."

"I never worked for anybody. I consulted."

"Oh, do I detect a subtle difference?"

He picked up his fork and scooped up some of the hominy grits off his plate. "Yeah, how long you have to kiss someone's ass for the truth."

Tanya's head snapped back and then she looked good and hard at him. She must have been blind not to see it. He was hung over. She looked at Father Michael Bennett sitting at another table with several of his volunteer caregivers and looking equally miserable.

"I take it you and our Spiritual Wombler had a male bonding experience last night?"

Anthony glared at her while deciding not to let this conversation go any further downhill than it already had. He stood up with his tray, "Nice talking to you Colonel, have a nice day."

"Sit down," she said in a firm voice. "Please." He did as she asked. "Hey look, I'm sorry. It seems we got off on the wrong foot and given that you're not having the best morning of your life I could have behaved better."

"Yeah, it's not my best morning and I've been no Prince Charming, so let's just call it a draw and put it behind us."

She smiled warmly. "Deal."

"So how is Senator Chavez doing these days?"

"Both she and her teenage daughter Lucinda, are doing just fine."

Anthony rubbed his hair. "Lucinda. Now there is a precocious child if I ever saw one. That kid gave me more of a hard time than I'd care to remember."

"Maybe she liked you too much," Tanya ventured.

"The curse of my life. Dogs, cats and kids all adore me like I was a fire hydrant parked under a tree house." He stretched. "Look, I appreciate the conversation but right now I've got a hot date with a fistful of aspirin, a hot shower and my cot so could we cut to the chase?"

While Tanya was just beginning to have fun with him, she could see that his patience would soon wear thin — again. "OK. You're probably wondering why Fox News hasn't showed up to do another piece on you."

"Actually, I hadn't given it any thought."

"Well, you should. The day you got here, our new UNE governor slapped a new quarantine order on us. Any civilians entering this center, including members of the media, have to remain here until they die or until the governor lifts the quarantine. In other words, you've become a bit too expensive in terms of the Fox News production budget."

"So?"

"So a lot of people out there care about you, Anthony. For some ungodly reason, you've become a public celebrity and Senator Chavez wants to keep it that way."

"So is she going to get the quarantine lifted?"

"No can do. However, she does have something else in mind. If you're game, that is, and if you're not, she told me to tell you to shut up and tee off, anyway." Anthony slapped the table laughing.

His reaction caught Tanya by surprise. "Is this an inside joke or something?"

"Oh no, not a joke."

"Well then, what is it?" She insisted.

He smiled as the memory of that mild summer day at Pebble Beach south of Monterrey. "Have you ever heard of the Pebble Beach Golf Course over on the 17 Mile Drive?"

"I never played the game, but who hasn't heard of it. Pretty pricey place till it got swept away."

"Pricey is right. The greens fees alone were almost three hundred bucks each plus all the other yadda yadda. I've never been a real player, but Senator Chavez, then candidate Chavez, was a pure golf fanatic and she wrangled two all-expense-paid passes for us. We were scheduled to play in a foursome with a local car dealer and his teenage son."

"And the car dealer was being a real jerk," Tanya added playfully.

"You betcha, but don't get ahead of me. You see, Senator Chavez had to go back to the clubhouse to take a private call and left me with the car dealer, and this yutz started drilling me to see how good I was. When he learned that I'd only spent a few nights knocking balls on a driving range and putting in the office, he went ballistic. The guy started telling me that I was too green to play the course, which, he dutifully pointed out, had been the site of four US Opens. After he busted my chops about me needing to play on municipal courses for a while before playing Pebble Beach, I had enough. Free passes or not, I didn't relish having to spend 18 holes of golf with a loud mouth used car salesman and his ass-kiss son, so I headed back towards the club house, found Chavez and explained the situation to her."

"I know this is going to be good," she said. "Go on, go on."

"Well, Chavez blew her lid. She told me that she had to deal with idiots like this every day of her life and that she wasn't going to give up 18 free holes on Pebble Beach for anyone, let alone an asshole. I started to argue with her and then she grabbed a box of balls and shoved them into my hands saying, 'shut up and tee off!'"

"And you did?"

"You're damn straight, I did. Trust me, arguing with Chavez when she has her mind set on something makes about as much sense as trying to push a locomotive off the track with your bare hands. So now, let's get back to this bold, new idea she's got. You know, the one where it is supposed to look like I've actually got a choice."

Tanya crossed her arms across her chest and giggled. "Oh my, I can see her screaming that at you in my mind's eye. I would have paid a king's ransom to have been a fly on the wall that day." She sniffled and wiped under her eyes. "Thanks, I needed that. OK, so here's the deal. She worked out a full time media coverage deal for you for the next two months and the crew will be here tomorrow."

"So what about the part about me having a choice?"

"We did that already."

He scratched his head. "Excuse me, Tanya, but I don't recall saying I'm ready to agree to this, and I'm not that hung over that I'd forget either."

"You're right, you didn't."

"So…"

"So, it's a done deal, so shut up and tee off!"

CORPORAL SUNNY SHARMA had watched the television production van, followed by two motor homes enter through the main gate and follow one of the guards riding an ATV to area that had been recently cleared for them.

The producer, a smallish, frumpy looking college professor, later presented himself alone to Sharma who made him sit and wait while Tanya finished her early morning meeting with the civilian contractors in charge of building the triage center. As they streamed out of her office, he gestured towards Tanya's office. "Professor, Administrator Wheelwright is ready to see you now. Please go on in."

Sharma noticed the familiar bulge of an old-style laptop in the professor's time worn black leather computer bag as he entered Tanya's office and introduced himself.

"Good morning Colonel Wheelwright, I'm Professor Idan Goldberg, and it is a pleasure to finally meet you."

Tanya Wheelwright smiled and gestured to one of the chairs in front of her office desk. "The pleasure is mutual. I've had several conversations with Senator Chavez about your project, and we're quite excited by it."

"As am I, Colonel."

"Just call me Tanya."

"And please call me Idan," the professor replied. She nodded as he continued. "I assume you already know," he began, "that I hold a teaching position at the California State University at Northridge. While our campus is going through a major rebuilding phase to repair our quake damage, I was granted a paid sabbatical by my department so I could document the lives of those entering this camp."

He stopped to clear his throat, and Tanya could see that his mouth was dry. As he continued, she poured a glass of water and held it out to him. He accepted it and thanked her. After gulping half the glass, he continued with the introduction. "Our college is affiliated with the Holocaust

Survivors Film Project, which began videotaping Jewish survivors and witnesses of the Holocaust back in 1979. They interviewed over 4,100 survivors, and have over 10,000 hours of recordings available for teachers, researchers and the general public — a rather substantial body of work." He began fumbling with the latches on his computer bag. "As proof of our expertise, I've brought some samples of the interviews our Northridge volunteers obtained from Jewish survivors in the Los Angeles area."

Tanya held up her hand. "That is not necessary professor. My family on my mother's side came from the Ukraine and I'm the last of the line. We're Jews, although I've never really got a chance to learn about the faith. But tell me, how did you get involved with this."

"Well, I teach several courses on news production, and this seemed to fit with my personal history, so I took it on. I used to be a news producer for a small station in the Midwest before accepting my position at Northridge."

"Most impressive." She leaned forward resting her arms on her desk. "Then let's cut to the chase, as they used to say in Hollywood."

"Professor Goldberg, I'll tell you exactly what I told the Senator when she first broached the idea. I told her that I'm not sure this is the right place or time for such a thing. Interviewing healthy, stable holocaust survivors is one thing, but ninety percent of the people who will be coming through our gate in a few days will be deathly ill. To put it simply, professor, they'll be coming here to die, and most of them will barely have the energy or will to give us the personal data we'll need to process them, let alone video interviews."

"I understand that, madam, but we have a flexible production method that has been proven with many ill Holocaust survivors, some of whom gave their testimonials from their death beds. You may rest assured that we can manage this. Also, I must point out that while we formerly used student volunteers, we are underwritten by The

Ronald Reagan Presidential Foundation, which has spared no expense for this effort.

Further, Fox News has loaned us one of their best news teams, headed by Rose O'Hara, who has been following Captain Jarman since he was initially called up to serve. Plus, Panavision has equipped us with their newest HDTV production equipment, because everything we'll shoot here in your center will become part of special Library of Congress exhibit in Washington. The working title for this collective work has been dubbed the 'The Great Dying,' but that could change. Nonetheless, we're here to do it right, and that is what matters!"

"The Senator told me as much, Professor Goldberg," Tanya replied as she leaned back in her chair to study the man. "Professor, in two days we are going to open this center. The minute the Homeland Defense forces boys take down the I35 barrier on Highway 17, there is going to be steady stream of sick and dying people coming to the place in ambulances, trucks, hand drawn carts and on foot. In the beginning, they'll come from the local hospitals that are desperately straining at the seams right now with terminal patients. When that happens, you and the Fox News folks will be officially quarantined, and if you or any member of your crew attempts to leave before the quarantine is lifted, our guards have orders to shoot on sight. Do you fully understand the ramifications of this?"

She continued to study his face for any signs of indecision our doubt. Finding none, she upped the ante. "Each of us volunteered, knowing all of that up front. Look, we know it is going to be a well-organized hell and that we could be here for months, and maybe, God-forbid, years, watching people dying of influenza, heavy metal poisoning, cancer and you name it. But most of them will be dying from 3G, and when that eases up, so should the quarantine. So tell me, professor, what do you know about the Three Gorges flu?" That being said, the professor moved his computer bag from his lap to the floor and relaxed in his chair.

Tanya liked his straightforward manner.   It was something that could make it easy to deal with him and his crew if their stay became dramatically extended. "Basically, nothing more than what the Internet news streams are telling us, which really isn't much when you boil out all the rehashed press releases.   Like most, all I know is that it cropped up near the burst Three Gorges dam, and it has already killed nearly one billion people in China and Southeast Asia."

"Then, there is no point in discussing the risks any further," Goldberg added.

"Not as long as you know what you're getting yourself into." Tanya said wistfully, "So, what is the next step?"

"As you know, there are four of us, including myself: A reporter, cameraman, sound grip and myself, acting as field producer. We know you're pressed for facilities so we've brought two thirty foot motor homes to live in plus our broadcast truck. All we'll need from the center are three hot meals a day and utility hookups for the vehicles. Other than that, we'll do our level best to stay out of your hair."

Tanya studied the man long and hard and decided that she liked him and that she could work with him.   "I'll arrange for you meet Captain Jarman this evening after dinner, which is served at 18:30, and tomorrow morning you and your crew will receive your first G3 inhibitor injections. In the meantime, I'll have my orderly arrange for someone in maintenance to provide you with whatever utility hookups you'll need for your vehicles that we can provide."   She paused.   "By the way, have you got a family?"

"A wife, Yeta, and two fine sons."

"How do they feel about this?"

"What would you expect?" he asked as he gathered up his computer bag.   Rising out of his chair, he left the question hanging unanswered in the air, then stopped at the door and turned back to look at her. "You know, Tanya, you remind me of my grandmother. She was only ten years old when she walked out of Auschwitz, an orphan. She would have liked you very much. You have her kind of strength."

THE MEETING WITH Anthony Jarman the previous evening had gone exceptionally well. He was already familiar with Rose and her Fox News team from their time together in New York, so the evening was more a regaling of humorous, as well as more serious, memories for the benefit of Tanya and Father Bennett.

With the center still under construction, Goldberg decided to shoot some basic location segments in the morning. Later in the afternoon, they'd interview Father Bennett and several of his volunteer hospice caregivers.

The first shooting location Goldberg picked with Rose's help was the freeway bordering the northwestern edge of the drained Lexington Reservoir, which now served as the home for the Los Gatos Triage Center.

Jerry Pelletier, Rose's video operator checked the battery level indicator in the Panavision's viewfinder display. With an annoyed grunt, he removed the brick-sized rechargeable battery from the back of the camera and handed it back to his soundman. "Yo, Pete! This brick is not holding up."

"Gotcha," Pete Gibbons, his soundman replied. The grip set down his headphones, pulled another fuel cell out of the kit bag next to his feet and exchanged it for the one in the cameraman's hand. "Yeah, I figured this one could be a problem child. I'll give it a deep discharge tonight and refuel it. If that doesn't work, I'll send it back to Panavision."

The exchange between his cameraman and soundman caught Professor Idan Goldberg's attention. "Do we have enough bricks for this scene and the interview at the quarry?"

"No worries," Jerry replied. "We have all the bricks we need. Some are just better than others are. Besides, we'll be using the camp AC when we shoot the interviews. We'll be ready a minute or so."

"Good show." Goldberg nodded appreciatively and returned to his conversation with Rose O'Hara. "Rose, you'll be standing here by the side of Interstate 17 with the Lexington Reservoir Dam behind you. I'm going to have Pete open with a medium wide on you and the collapsed dam in the background. After you turn and point to Limekiln Gulch Road, he'll slowly pull out as he pans left to the pass to show Interstate 17 behind you. Remember, you'll cue him when you point to the road."

Rose smiled, "Got it, Idan." She was a pro with a photographic memory, and proud of her nickname at Fox, 'First Take O'Hara.'

She moved to her mark and waited patiently as Pete Gibbons checked the wireless microphone transmitter fastened to the back pocket of her faded jeans. Satisfied, he sat back down next to the recording deck and put on his headphones. "Give me a sound check, Rose."

"This is Rose O'Hara, and I had my first shower in three days last night with all the hot water I wanted. I loved it!"

"That's good," Jerry said. "I think we got some great B roll video of that shower scene."

Rose glared at him, "You smart ass, you just wish, and you can forget trying to shoot butt shots of me while I'm not looking. Don't even try it!"

Both fit, handsome and in their late twenties, Jerry Pelletier and Pete Gibbons were not the kind of fellows who would go lacking for female attention, and, like most video crews, they loved practical jokes – especially when the mark had a fiery Irish temper. The two looked at each other with juvenile grins and threw their hands over their heads as they chanted, "We are not worthy, oh big, bad carrot top bawana lady."

Idan Goldberg bit his finger to keep from laughing. Why most people labor under the impression that video production is a glamorous endeavor, the truth is that it is tedious, hard work and more often boring than not. Without these kinds of antics to release the tension, a crew could turn on itself in short order and lose its effectiveness. Still, it was time to roll video. "Positions everyone. Rose, please hold up the back of the slate sheet for a white balance." The antics quickly stopped as she held up a blank sheet of common white ink jet paper in front of her. Jerry zoomed in on it to lock in the camera's color settings, which, given the overall pink tint of the morning sky, took some time. Pete waved his hand to let Idan know he was ready on the sound as Rose flipped the sheet over exposing the scene slate to the camera.

"Rose, give me a voice slate on this one," Idan looked over at Jerry. "Roll tape."

Jerry punched the record button on the video deck and announced, "Speed" to let everyone know that the deck was recording.

Rose announced the slate, "Lexington Reservoir from I17, scene 1, take 1," then dropped the paper to the ground.

"On three," Idan said to Rose. "One, two…"

"I'm Rose O'Hara, and behind me is the Lexington Reservoir. Prior to Shiva's flyby, this 475-acre man-made reservoir supplied fresh water for the cities of the Silicon Valley on the other side of the Santa Cruz Mountains that border the western and southern flanks of the Silicon Valley. During the Shiva flyby six months ago, the spillway at the North end of the reservoir failed when a massive 9.0 quake along the San Andreas Fault, which runs through the heart of this mountain range, literally tore it apart. Fortunately, most of the other water reservoirs in the Santa Cruz Mountains survived the Tsunami. However, the now empty Lexington Reservoir you now see behind me was one of the largest, and its considerable supply of fresh water was forever lost. When the spillway failed, it caused

massive flooding of the southern half of the small upscale
community of Los Gatos, just north of here. Now emptied
of water, this dried-out reservoir has become the home of
the Los Gatos Triage Center for the terminally ill and those
who wish to exercise their right of assisted suicide."

Rose pointed off to her right, giving Pete the signal to
begin his camera move, as she continued. "Behind me is the
Limekiln Gulch Road that runs along the north end of the
reservoir and out to Interstate 17, which leads north to Los
Gatos and then onto San Jose some three miles north of here
through the last mountain pass between here and the
Silicon Valley. Tomorrow, the Los Gatos checkpoint, some
three miles north of here, will open this stretch of road, and
then the dead and dying from Silicon Valley and mid-
peninsula areas will begin to arrive."

Her dialogue finished, Rose continued to look into the
camera until Idan said, "Cut."

Rose took a deep breath. "That was a long one," she
sighed.

Idan looked over at Pete and Jerry. They both hoisted a
thumbs-up sign to show the take had been free of technical
glitches. "First Take O'Hara," Idan exclaimed with
satisfaction. "OK, let's get a safety take and we're off to the
quarry. Rose, let me know when you're ready for the safety
take."

THIS WAS THE first time Dodge Murphy would look down
the lens of a professional video camera, and the gray-haired
quarry manager prayed he wouldn't come off looking as
dumb as a deer caught in the headlights.

Rose leaned over towards the tanned, heavy-set man.
"Mr. Murphy, I want you to stand facing a little towards
me." She placed her hands on the man's broad shoulders,
and he followed her lead until she had him turned in the
right direction. "We'll both be looking at the camera while I
open the scene. When you see me turn my body towards
you, just turn your head only until you face me. After that,

I'll ask a few questions, and when I move the microphone to you, look at me and answer the questions. It is that simple."

He cleared his throat. "OK, but just don't let me screw up." Rose winked at him, and that alone seemed to relax him. He immediately sensed that she'd make sure he came out of this without looking foolish. His eyes remained fixed on the little red light on the front of the camera. The voice of the video crew blurred past him as Idan ran the count, "On three. One, two..."

"With me today is Mr. Dodge Murphy, the manager of the Sierra Azul quarry, which you see behind us. The quarry is less than a mile northeast of the Lexington Reservoir and connected to I17 by the Limekiln Gulch Road that also runs along the northern end of the reservoir." Rose turned towards the quarry manager and asked her first question.

"Mr. Murphy, the U.S. Geological Relief map of this area shows this as a Limestone quarry. Could you explain why?" She held the microphone in front of his face and looked reassuringly in his eyes. Rose had been doing interviews like these for years, and she had an uncanny knack for calming stage fright with a simple a smile and a nod.

"Well, I suppose that is because there used to be a limestone plant further down the road back towards the reservoir." He held up a white and yellow rock. "This is what limestone looks like if you've never seen it before. They used to mine this and then process it into quick lime, but they stopped doing that back in 1930 I believe. Since then, we've used this quarry to produce what we call Gray Whacky. Basically, just hard rock used for drainage." He held up a small, dull gray rock. "It looks something like this."

Rose brought the microphone back to herself for the next question. "Could you tell us what the quarry is being used for today."

Murphy nodded, and she pushed the microphone back towards him. "Well, actually the quarry has been purchased by FEMA, and we're doing three things now. First, our quarry has been converted to a mass gravesite. As I understand it, when they burned all those bodies in Los Angeles, the smell was something awful and really made it difficult for the government to maintain order. The Tsunami that hit here dragged most all of the dead out to sea, and the local cemeteries have handled the rest so far, but now with folks dying from the heavy metal poisoning and such so fast now, the feds decided that it would be best to bury them here. You see, we've got a sizable pit in the quarry and the equipment to back-fill it so I guess we were the logical choice. Also, we've just completed rebuilding the limestone processing plant so we'll have plenty of quick lime on hand for the graves. That way, the government won't have to truck it in."

"I believe the third responsibly for your operation is actually in support of the triage center itself?"

"Uh, that's right. Since we already have lots of earth moving equipment, we were contracted to level the reservoir bottom for the center and dig the burial trenches. We also keep a couple of men and some equipment there in the camp to spread quick lime on the bodies and to fill in the trenches."

Rose could see the anguish in the man's face. After a life of serving the needs of building and road contractors, he faced a dark and sad future. "I'm sure this is a most unpleasant task for you, Mr. Murphy. I wonder, how do you and your employees feel about this?"

A glimmer of pride crossed his face. "Yeah, it's a terrible job but I want you to know that we all volunteered for it – to a man and woman. Heck, my gals in the office are out fueling vehicles and doing paperwork for the feds, and they've all got little ones. Damn brave ladies if you ask me. Sure, the Army Corps of Engineers could have come in here and run the show, but this is our land, and we're going to

be burying folks from around here. We're not shirkers.
No ma'am, we're not!"

"Mr. Murphy, I want you and your employees to know
that you are appreciated and that future generations will
know about your courage." She paused to reach out her
hand and squeezed his arm, then continued. "Before we
leave you, just two more questions. First, where do you get
your water now, given that the reservoir has emptied and
second, will these mass graves pollute any important water
aquifers in this area?"

He chuckled as she extended the microphone back
towards him. "Well, let me answer the second question
first. There is no underground alluvial aquifer under these
mountains, so that is not a problem. However, we do have
plenty of small aquifers in the cracks that crisscross these
mountains. That's where we're getting our water and the
triage center over in the reservoir as well, plus we're
supplying small amounts of emergency water for the city of
Los Gatos, as well."

"But are there a sufficient number of these small aquifers
to continue to supply water for an extended period of
time?"

"Oh, yeah. Heck, there is a whole mess of them all
around these hills and not a one is connected to the other.
Darn funny, these aquifers around here. You can drill to
China in one spot and not hit a drop. Move your rig ten feet
in any one direction and you hit water big time. That is
why we've got two water well drillers running full time. I
guess we're lucky in the water department. On the other
hand, getting enough fuel for trucks and earth moving
equipment is another thing, but I won't bore you with that."

Rose smiled, "Yes Mr. Murphy, these are difficult times,
but thanks to people you and your employees, I know in
my heart that we'll pull through it and that there will be
better days in the future." She turned to face the camera.

"Tomorrow morning, the first trucks will begin rolling
into this quarry from over the hill behind us, filled with

body bags. In the years to come, those who come to their final rest here will not be forgotten."

THE MORNING HAD been intense for the crew, and the hot lunch in the triage center mess was both delicious and filling.   Corporal Sharma, Wheelwright's clerk, was certainly right about one thing. The work was hell, but the chow was good. As Pete and Jerry went back to the serving line for second helpings, Idan and Rose pushed their empty trays aside to make room for their notepads.

"That last interview with Boole, the Chief Medical Officer went pretty much as expected," Rose noted. "I'll say one thing; he's a good man to have in your corner if you're fighting for your life. He's not like a lot of doctors I've known that have about as much warmth as a cyborg. He really does care. I like that."

"So do I," Idan agreed, "but I think our next two interviews are going to be more difficult. Boole is a good guy, but Wheelwright and Jarman are the two people that make this camp tick."

She tapped her pen on the tabletop as she searched for the right words. "Idan," she finally said with a touch of hesitancy in her voice. "I know we only spent about ten, maybe twenty minutes at most with them late last night when we hammered out our arrangement, but I sensed something."

Idan raised an eyebrow with interest. It made sense to him, but the reason why it did escaped him. "Well, Rose, do you mean to tell me you've already gotten a flash of female intuition about these two?"

She rubbed her hands together and then scratched the top of her lip. "You could say that. I don't know why, but I sense something between them, even though I don't think they know it yet, themselves. Maybe they do, but they both might want to avoid the connection. Yet all my experience with doing the news tells me there is something there."

Her carefully chosen words gave Idan a comparative for his own subliminal memories of the encounter the previous evening. "Rose, I don't think you're talking about something sexual, although I can see that happening." He ran his fingers through his hair as he searched his mind for the precise adjective. The one word that would coin what he and Rose sensed. "What I think both of us sensed in them last night is, in a word, history."

Rose snapped her fingers. "Yes, history. Not in the past sense, but in the future sense. You know, future history."

Idan nodded his head in agreement with a huge smile. He held his hands out in front of him, with the palms facing each other. As he brought the two palms towards each other he said, "Fate is bringing this man and this woman together for a greater purpose than what they serve now." With the last word, he clasped both of his hands together.

She put her hands over his and said, "And we've got to capture it, somehow." She bit her lip as she questioned her own perceptions one more time, and then continued. "Idan, we could be wrong, but every fiber of my talent as a news reporter says we're not. If we try to capture this, we cannot let them know we are purposefully trying to do it. It has to look incidental, if you will."

Idan and Rose looked at each other. "We always try to interview them both at the same time, or at least whenever we can," Rose said. Idan smiled and they separated their hands.

Jerry and Pete returned at that moment with their trays. The two men looked at them with astonished eyes. "Would anyone care to clue us in on what is happening here," Pete asked as he picked up his fork.

"Eat up, fellas," Idan replied casually. "We're going to do a three camera shoot this afternoon. Pete, I want you on number two camera for wide shots and close ups on Rose. We'll slave cameras one and three to the switcher. Jerry, instead of lavaliere microphones, let's seat the talent and use acoustic panels with those new shotgun boom microphones instead."

"You know, we're scheduled to shoot Wheelwright in her office." Rose noted. "We could move her conference table. That should give us plenty of room to create a basic set."

Jerry looked at Idan and Rose passively for a few minutes as the details sorted themselves out in his mind. Once the plan clicked, he looked at Pete and simply said, "Eat up, buddy; we've got our work cut out for us."

GETTING WHEELWRIGHT AND Jarman to agree to a joint interview had been easier than Idan expected. It left him wondering if getting their cooperation would continue to be as easy once the triage center was open for business.

The setup went smoothly, thanks to the well-supplied Panavision field kits. Jerry had all three cameras and the switcher ready to go about the same time that Pete had finished setting up the shotgun boom microphones. After that, the two fidgeted with the lighting until Jerry was pleased.

After doing a white balance for all three cameras and the slate, Rose repeated her instructions again. "Tanya and Anthony, just remember to be yourselves. Ignore the cameras, and simply respond to me and each other just as though there were no cameras at all in the room."

Rose dropped the slate sheet behind her chair as Pete called speed on the record deck. Idan pointed at Rose. "On three. One, two..."

"In less than twenty-fours, the Los Gatos Triage Center will begin receiving its first patients from the Silicon Valley area to the north. Like any organization, there will always be one or two people who really make the whole operation work. Today, we will get to know the two people who will come to represent the heart and soul of this facility." She gestured towards Tanya. "To my right is Lieutenant Colonel Tanya Wheelwright, the center administrator," and then towards Anthony. "And to my left is Captain Anthony Jarman, the End of Life Management Officer or ELMO for short. However, most people will simply know Captain Jarman as the releaser."

She shifted her body slightly in Tanya's direction. "Colonel Wheelwright, let's begin with you. Could you briefly tell me what you do here?"

As a hospital administrator, Tanya had conducted several television interviews and was comfortable with the task. "Well, Rose," she began, "I suppose the best way to describe my job here is that the buck stops with me. Simply put, it is my job to see to it that this center is run in the most efficient and humane way possible. While the vast majority of those who will come to this triage center will be terminal patients and come under Captain Jarman's care, those we can save will be entrusted to the capable hands of Major Jim Boole, my Chief Medical Officer, and his staff. The work of both of these men is very important, and supporting their efforts is my most important responsibility."

Rose could quickly see that Tanya knew how to deliver a polished monologue. If she hoped to get her to reveal her inner self, Rose would have to blind-side her with a trick question. But that would come later. For now, she needed to make them both comfortable and the first thing she needed to do, was to dispense with the formality of job titles.

"Tanya, I noticed in your profile summary that you were born and raised in Russia and just received your American citizenship about five years ago. So, how is it that you're here running a sizable military operation?"

"Like Captain Jarman, here, I was called up."

Rose turned her body the other direction towards Anthony. "On that note, Captain Jarman, could you briefly tell us about your job and what you do here?"

"In a nutshell," he answered, "I help people to cross over."

"Earlier this morning," Rose noted, "We shot a good deal of footage of the quarantine areas, main reception ward and the burial trenches. Could you tell us what it is you do in these different areas?"

"When people arrive here, Dr. Boole and his staff divide them up into two basic groups: those who have a terminal affliction and those who can be treated. All those who are terminal are taken to the quarantine area, where they can choose to remain till they die of natural causes. If they choose to exercise their UNE right of assisted suicide, we make them stay at least one night in quarantine, and then in the morning, they are escorted to the trenches, where I help them to pass over."

"As I understand it, you shoot a .22 caliber bullet into their head."

"Only the ambulatory patients as per UNE mandate — children and the bed-ridden are given lethal injections" he replied. "For the ambulatory, those who can still walk, I aim the bullet at the top of the brain stem. It is the fastest way to die for those who choose it. Or if they wish, they can remain in the quarantine area and self-medicate themselves with enough Heroine to achieve the same result; however, I never assist in the quarantine area. Only at the trenches and sometimes in the wards."

She nodded and asked, "Is this how you did it at the other triage centers?"

"Pretty much."

"So how in the world did you ever get into this?" The question struck a dark chord with Jarman.

He crossed his legs and scratched his forearm. "I've always been interested in metaphysics, and I worked briefly as a volunteer hospice caregiver and showed a natural talent for comforting people in the final moments of their lives. You have to understand; when people cross over, they are always surrounded by a tremendous amount of spiritual energy. As their caregiver, you're not personally involved with them, so the end of their life can be a very powerful experience."

Rose saw the trick question she'd been looking for. All she had to do now was to set it up. "So then, Anthony, what is death to you?"

He'd been asked this question so many times; the answer gushed forth automatically. "Well, Rose, it is just one part of a process that encompasses the cycle of life. Death is neither good nor bad. It just is, and for those who will pass over in this center, it must come as a friend for them, or I will have no part of it."

"Thank you, Anthony," Rose said as she swiveled the other way to face Tanya. "And what is death to you, Tanya?"

While Anthony's eyes had showed no emotion, a fire radiated from Tanya's eyes that seemed to telegraph her answer. "Death is my enemy," she said in a firm voice devoid of the softness she had shown earlier. "Each morning when I get up, I go to work with the hope I can snatch as many lives from the jaws of death that day as possible. I hate death and cheating it really makes my day."

Rose looked back quickly at Anthony for a reaction. She expected to see some sense of alarm, but his face remained passive and relatively unaffected. He had likewise heard these kind of feelings being expressed more than once before.

As the next question formed in her mind, she wondered how she and Idan could have sensed a historical connection between these two. He was resigned to his fate, and she, on the other hand was full of anger and purpose. How could two people like this share a common future?

From Idan's behind-the-camera view, the situation was framed in an entirely different paradigm. As he worked the controls of the switcher, his eyes traveled back and forth between Anthony and Tanya. Unlike Rose, he had a wider view of the interaction and could see subtle, yet often repeated, signs of two people interested in learning about each other. Yet, it would be a strange bonding experience, as these two were like fire and ice. But then, what was it his matchmaker had once told him – opposites attract. If so, these two were opposites and quite busy hiding their mutual attraction from one another. Later that evening, he would play back the tapes for Rose, and she'd see it too.

CHAPTER 11

FOR THE MOTHERLAND

AS HE SLIPPED on his VR gloves, Merl Johnston wondered why Melissa Chadwick, former Southwestern UNE Governor for America, now the head of UNE Space Command in Las Vegas, had scheduled a high priority conference with Secretary General De Bono and himself.

He sealed the door of his security dome and initialized the desktop of his heads-up display. A ready icon blinked steadily under a freeze frame of Melissa Chadwick in Las Vegas indicated that she was already online and waiting for the conference to begin. The icon for De Bono indicated that he had not yet logged on to the conference account. Johnston studied Chadwick's face as she waited passively for the conference to begin. A smallish middle-aged woman with broad shoulders and a chiseled jaw, what he noticed most about her was her thin, pursed lips and beady, black eyes.

While beautiful in a very precise way, she struck him as being cool, calculating and brilliant. A true reflection of the woman's competitive reputation, she lacked any semblance of a soft, feminine allure. "But then," he thought to himself, "if she looked soft, could she really strike fear in a man's heart?"

Like many women her age, she preferred to wear her hair short with a swept-back flair. While he could see a slight lift in her eyebrows from a recent cosmetic surgery to remove her age-lines, she still had the honesty to leave a touch of gray here and there in her dark brown hair. Chadwick presented an interesting juxtaposition of vanity and personal honesty.

A symbol of a large door appeared in the center of his HUD. He could wait for De Bono before entering, but decided to logon now, hoping to pry a little advance information from her before the conference began. He grasped the door handle and swung it open, entering himself into the conference room.

"Hey, handsome," Melissa greeted him cheerfully. "Looks like it is just the two of us for a while." She wiggled her eyebrows with a devilish grin. "So how do you and Danielle like the penthouse?"

He smiled sheepishly. "I gotta hand it to you Melissa, you are one heck of an interior designer. The bear rug in the master bedroom is so nice. I'm sure you and your handsome young secretary, Paulo Sanchez, christened it in the most proper way."

She rolled her eyes and winked. "Well I must admit; Paulo was delightfully creative."

"I'm sure."

"So I heard through the grapevine that your wife, Ginny, is on a tear now."

"Yeah, she's seeing lipstick on the collar, you might say. She says she won't come back to me until I get rid of Danielle."

"Sorry to hear it, but you know, it happens to most all of the guys. As for me, I'm the lucky one. My daughter's father was an anonymous sperm donor from Finland, who thankfully turned out to be good breeding stock. I can't imagine how miserable I'd be if I had a husband right now."

The line of conversation, though unassuming and sympathetic, was nonetheless becoming both uninteresting and personally uncomfortable for Merl and he decided to change the topic. "Well, I'll manage, I suppose. Say, I've been wondering how your project is going. Have America and Russia designated their respective project heads yet?"

Chadwick took the hint without batting an eye. "Well, the Russians are still playing musical chairs, but I did have an interesting conversation with New Obninsk Centre Director, Igor Razumovsky. What I can gather is that the Russians have decided that their effort will be based in Obninsk, outside of Moscow. As to who is going to run the show, I'm not sure it will be Razumovsky. He's certainly capable, but too old for that kind of role."

"So does he have someone younger in mind?"

She nodded, "I think he does. You know how cryptic they can be, but I think he's looking for a young Sergei Korolyov to head this project to destroy Shiva."

"Sergei Korolyov?"

"He headed the Soviet space program at the Baikonur cosmodrome at the outset of the space race. He's the guy who put the Sputnik into orbit back in 1957 and scared the pants off the Americans."

"Oh I remember him now. You're right; what they need is someone like him. I wish them luck. So what about the Americans?"

His question brought a small smile to her lips. "They've made their choice for a director to head up their Space Ark program and I think it was a brilliant one. They've picked Major General George Hennicker of the US Space Command."

"Isn't he the guy that's been the head of their Near Earth Object detection program?"

"Yes, but I think the real reason why they picked him was that he wrote a biography of General Leslie R. Groves, who was the director of the Manhattan Project during WWII. He wrote it after graduating the United States Air Force Academy in Colorado Springs, Colorado, and it has become required reading at his alma mater, as well as West Point."

"That makes sense," Johnston agreed. "The Manhattan Project was the biggest single effort of the American government at that time, and he ran it brilliantly, even though the final result was the utter destruction of Hiroshima and Nagasaki. So, you think the Americans think he'll be another General Grove?"

She glanced off screen and pursed her lips as she considered the thought. "Yeah, Merl. You've got the right take on it. As for me, the guy looks like a middle-aged Rambo with a small beer gut. I like his fire. If anyone can pull it off, he can."

"Well, congratulations are in order. It sounds like you're making great progress. So tell me, what is the reason for this conference."

"Sorry Merl," she quickly replied. "Can't go there. Not till the Secretary General has joined the conference." Johnston stepped back from the issue, they chatted idly about their perks, lovers and other idle matters until De Bono finally joined the conference.

"Melissa, Merl, sorry for being late. I was caught up with some last minute matters. A priority conference like this is a bit unusual, so what's on your mind, Melissa?"

"It's about Anthony Jarman and Senator Chavez." De Bono and Johnston groaned simultaneously. More bad news was coming. They already knew about the Holocaust Survivors Film Project arrival at the Los Gatos Triage Center. "This morning, we intercepted a message from the Queen Pilolevu of Tonga to Senator Chavez assuring her that they would not change the transponder address for the BBC on their new TupouSat communications satellite. That got us curious and so we've been monitoring their TupouSat traffic and this morning at 0400, we detected a broadband uplink test from the Los Gatos Triage Center. We traced the packets to a download retransmission site outside of Montreal. It is obvious that they intend to begin broadcasting from Los Gatos on a daily basis."

"Damn," Johnston muttered under his breath. "Isn't there anything we can do to prevent this?"

"I'm afraid not. The Tongans rely upon their TupouSat transponder lease revenue to keep their little island going these days, and the lease for this transponder has been prepaid through the end of next year."

"But the TupouSat is sitting in geo-stationary orbit in a North American satellite slot. So why can't we just pull the slot? The only other birds up there are not under our direct control, because Fox and CNN own them. If we force the TupouSat back over the South Pacific and another network tires to pick up the lease, then we'll see to it they lose their pharmaceutical ad revenues. That will put the fear of God into their board of directors."

Melissa shook her head no and De Bono said flatly, "I think the other shoe is about to drop Merl."

She took her cue. "Normally, Merl, what you said would work just fine. However, when America ratified the UNE treaty, Senator Chavez added a small addendum that seemed to have gotten lost in all the other more expensive pork barrel projects assuring that one satellite slot would be used exclusively for international news broadcasters and Tonga got the contract. Apparently, it was cheaper for the BBC to send up an unmanned repair satellite to fix their own TongaSat bird and so after Loral finished building their new TupouSat, they had Lockheed put it into orbit in the North American slot. If we try to control access to that bird now, or pull Tonga's slot, the American Congress will have to reexamine the whole ratification document."

"Damn," Johnston spat as he clenched his fists. "Damn, damn, damn!" Chadwick and De Bono watched him with silent curiosity as he thought through the situation, while grinding his jaws. "So, we just arrange for this TupouSat to have an untimely encounter with a small asteroid or something, if that's possible."

De Bono finally spoke up, "It is, but then Lloyds of London, of which we own a considerable share, would have to foot the cost of a replacement, and no doubt Tonga would quickly find a replacement satellite. No, this time, we must admit checkmate and give ground. However, that doesn't mean the game is over. Melissa, do we know who is financing this?"

"Officially, we do, and that was pretty easy to run down," she replied. "It seems the transponder was leased in the name of The Ronald Reagan Presidential Foundation."

"But leasing even one satellite transponder takes deep pockets," Johnston added. "Deeper than that foundation has; I can tell you that."

"Yes, I think you're right," De Bono agreed. "Let me think about this for a moment." The conference went still as the images of Chadwick and Johnston floated silently in front of De Bono's face. Finally, he took a deep breath and said, "I want you two to keep your hands off this Holocaust Survivors Film Project. Let them broadcast their programs. I'll personally handle the issue of finding out who exactly is funding this project."

"And what about Chavez," Johnston asked in a malevolent tone.

"She has certainly become a thorn in our side, and frankly, my patience with her is all but worn out." He paused as he lightly bit his lip. "It is time to deal with her once and for all. I'll give it to the School of Assassins."

"No!" Johnston insisted in a dark voice. "Let me do it. She's haunted my every step for too long now, and I'm tired of the misery she's made for me. I want some payback."

"So what do you propose to do?"

"Do me a favor and tell the School of Assassins that I can get close to her — real close, and that I want the pleasure of watching her smile at me when I do her. I'm sure they'll come up with something that will be both simple and effective."

"It's not wise to do your own wet work, Merl," Chadwick softly cautioned.

"Have you ever read *Time Enough for Love* by Robert Heinlein?"

"No."

"Well you should. There's a great line in that book and it has always resonated with me. 'When the need arises — and it does — you must be able to shoot your own dog. Don't farm it out.'"

De Bono rubbed his chin reflectively. After all, that first day in his scramjet, he had promised him this. He just didn't expect the man to remain so bitterly determined. Chadwick was right. Johnston was a valuable man to their effort and letting him do this was an unnecessary risk. Yet, a promise was a promise. "OK, Merl. Provided you do exactly as you're told by the School of Assassins, you have my permission."

"Thank you, Secretary General," Johnston replied thoughtfully.

"You're welcome, but frankly, I agree with Melissa. You shouldn't be doing your own wet work. However, a promise is a promise. Not to change the subject, but what is the current status on Jarman and Jones?"

"With any luck, Vigo Jones will not make it back from San Diego alive. He is presently en route to Los Gatos with a substantial load of confiscated heroine and marijuana used to treat the patients. We've taken the liberty of letting this fact be known amongst, shall we say, some rather unsavory types, along with his itinerary. As for Jarman, our operative inside the camp tells me he's eating, sleeping and drinking whiskey all night with one of his dome mates, a Jesuit Priest from England."

"The priest could become a valuable source of information," Chadwick noted.

"I doubt it," Johnston replied. "From what our source tells us, they're preoccupied with building a still and do nothing but talk about sports and movies. Look," he explained. "These guys are stuck in the armpit of the world, and they're just trying to deal with it without going nuts, but you never know. Maybe the priest could stumble onto something, but getting it out of him could be another thing."

"We have ways," De Bono said with a smirk. His comment made them all laugh.

They soon wrapped up their conference after covering a few more minor details. After turning off his HUD and breaking his connection, Johnston removed his VR gloves while hissing to himself. "Chavez, you fucking bitch, you cost me my seat in the Senate and now you're after me again." Never in his life had he wanted to kill someone in cold blood, but now the rage within him demanded personal revenge.

As THE FORA SUV bounced along the frozen and pockmarked road leading to Igor Razumovsky's private country home on the outskirts of Obninsk City, Pavel Sergeevich Lebedev stared out the window, ignoring the driver's repeated attempts to make small conversation.

The Fora was a gas-powered western knock-off made by Lada, and the front of the 4x4 looked like a Jeep Cherokee retro design. It lacked the stunning lines of the European and American designs on purpose. Like a reliable plow horse, the exceptionally stout Fora, was made to plow its way through primitive Russian roads with rugged reliability.

Having failed in his attempts to start a conversation, the driver studied his passenger, then decided to tune in a Moscow talk radio station and drove on through the quiet countryside without saying another word. Eventually, Pavel caught his eye in the rear view mirror and winked, to let him know that he appreciated the gift of silence.

The thirty-six year old project manager stared out the window with melancholy sadness in his dark brown eyes. Many of the beautiful trees that used to surround Obninsk City were dead now because of acid rain. While Obninsk was still Russia's premier technology center, it no longer had the good fortune to be located in one of the greenest parts of Russia.

Before the Nibiru flyby, the Obninsk Scientific Center was comprised of 12 scientific research institutes, including three highly acclaimed State Scientific centers of the Russian Federation. By the end of that year, those numbers doubled.

Obninsk, along with several other scientific centers, had just been given a special area of responsibility deemed more important than all other projects. It had received the plum assignment of finding a way to destroy Shiva before the 40-kilometer wide former satellite of Nibiru could impact Earth's moon in 2019.

The current 68-year old Obninsk Centre Director, Igor Petrovich Razumovsky, was still a vibrant and driven man, but he knew from the outset that this daunting task would require the physical stamina of a young man if Shiva was to be destroyed before it could wreak havoc on the Earth's moon. His list of candidates had been long for political purposes. He had sorted through them quickly, building his own list with less than a handful of promising names. The most promising of those names was the dark-haired, soft-spoken Pavel Sergeevich Lebedev. Now, they would soon meet for what would prove to be a crucial turning point in Pavel's life.

Unaware of what to expect, Pavel rubbed the passenger window of the SUV with the cuff of his jacket. In the far distance just a few kilometers down the road, he could make out the dull shape of Razumovsky's palatial dacha tucked back off the road. It reminded him of when the Earth had been beautiful, and as a boy, he recalled how he had helped his grandmother tend her garden and how good it felt to smell her wonderfully plump tomatoes as they ripened under the warm afternoon sun.

Such a pity it was that he had lost his love of gardening after he started college. Now, the very soil about him was clinging to life, and the knowing of this tortured his soul. In his heart, he wanted leave his computers and meeting rooms for a simpler life, nourishing the forests back to health, yet events were now drawing him towards the most powerful man in Obninsk and a new, but still hazy destiny.

Snow began to fall and Pavel reached across the seat and tapped on the driver's shoulder. "Pull over here, next to this meadow," he instructed the driver. The man slowed the SUV and pulled over to the side of the road.

"I like it when the snow begins to fall," Pavel explained. "It makes the air smell so good."

He opened the door of the SUV and the driver said, "I cannot let you walk out there alone," the driver answered. "But, I would be happy to join you." Pavel opened his door, looked back at the driver and gave him a pleasant nod.

Standing in fresh-fallen snow as snowflakes danced about him was a precious moment for Pavel. It was in times like these that he felt a deep, primal connection between his soul and that of his beloved Mother Russia.

Alone in his thoughts, he ignored the snowflakes piling up upon the shoulders of his black leather jacket as he inhaled the sweet smelling air about him. It was then, a lingering pang of sadness rush through his consciousness. His son, Sasha, was not there to share it with him and it was it own fault that his wife had left him.

Now, Sasha was being loved and well cared-for by his ex-wife's new husband − a good man with the wisdom to understand that families, like the wonderful tomatoes his Grandmother grew in her garden, flourish with continual loving care and attention. Sadly, he had put his career above his family and now he was seeing where it had gotten him − standing alongside a road alone, with a strange man looking over him.

Pavel kneeled down to look across the top of the snow, then looked back at the driver and motioned him to kneel beside him. "Look at how white it is, even in this murky light," he said sadly.

"Yes, this is a moment of magic for me, too," the driver replied with a thick Georgian accent. "Sir, Centre Director Razumovsky is expecting you." Then, the Georgian looked into Pavel's eyes and seemed to understand his sadness. "We made good time. Perhaps we can stay a few minutes more, I suppose."

Pavel smelled the air and patted him on the back. "Thanks. I've been rude to you back there in the car."

"Don't worry about it," the driver replied. "My wife tells me I gossip like an old woman some times. When I was a young man, I was very serious and seldom spoke. Now, I guess it is all those lonely kilometers over the years that now make me want to hear a human voice from time to time."

"A year ago," Pavel said thoughtfully, "I wouldn't have understood you, but now I do. Funny, here I am on my way to what could be one of the most important meetings of my career, and all I really want to do is to see my son laughing and playing in the snow." He stood up and took one last deep breath. "Your wife is wrong, my friend. You're not a gossip."

YELENA IGOROVNA VOLKAVA, a 33-year old widow and the youngest daughter of Centre Director Razumovsky, greeted Pavel at the door of her father's 8-bedroom dacha.

He was almost as she remembered him from a year ago, except that now he was much thinner. Just over six feet tall with dark hair, a strong jaw line and piercing black eyes, he still exuded a presence of power, though his soft-spoken words and thoughtful gestures tempered his strength with an endearing quality.

As he removed his coat and shoes in the foyer, he watched her with keen interest while she brought him a pair of house slippers. Standing shoulder height to him, she was a shapely and attractive blonde with a graceful face and large bright blue eyes. Her movements were measured and graceful, as though she was an oak leaf floated aloft by a gentle spring breeze.

"My father is waiting for you in the banya. I'll have the driver take your things to your room." She pointed towards a narrow hallway in the corner of the room. "Go through that hallway and enter the first room to your right. You can change there, and just go on in. I'll be by in a little while with some snacks."

Pavel thanked her and made his way to the banya. Finding a large linen wrap in the changing room, he undressed and wrapped himself before joining Razumovsky in the banya.

The first room of the banya was a setup as a bar, and the walls of the room were planked with red-stained hardwood. In the center of the room surrounding an open pit fire, were varnished benches and chairs placed around a marble top table. He first saw Razumovsky behind the bar opening a large bottle of vodka that had obviously been sitting in the freezer for a few days.

"Come in, come in, Pavel Sergeevich," Razumovsky greeted him in a familiar Russian manner of addressing a friend by his first and patryonic name in honor of his father. Pavel's father, Sergey hadn't lived to see his son's meteoric rise, much to Pavel's regret. "Come sit down," Razumovsky boomed. "Let's drink!"

"Thank you, Centre Director Razumovsky," Lebedev answered politely. "I am deeply honored to be a guest in your house this weekend."

"Oh please, let's not be so formal. You will call me Igor, I will call you Pavel and we will talk and drink, take banya together and begin to know each other a little better. Yes?"

Pavel smiled with relief and the two men sat down at a table as Razumovsky poured the icy cold, translucent premium vodka into two shot glasses. As he poured, Razumovsky spoke cheerfully, "Two years ago, I was working on a big project for the Americans and the French and we had to meet for a presentation in Paris, where I first tasted this French Vodka they call Grey Goose. I liked it so much that I bragged that with case of this wonderful vodka I could build anything. So, they shipped me 100 bottles with a challenge to finish my project on time, and I did!" He laughed. "It was so simple actually, but why look a gift horse in the mouth? You know about this wonderful Grey Goose vodka?"

"I hear is it better than our own Cristall, but I must admit that this is my first chance to enjoy it." Pavel replied as he eyed the colorless, viscous contents of his shot glass. He held his shot glass high in one hand and a pickle in the other said, "Well then, may the Grey Goose fly!" and he tossed back his drink in one smooth movement, then sniffed his pickle and took a big bite. Razumovsky did the same and gingerly refilled their glasses. "I told you," he gloated.

"It is perfection," Pavel with admiration. Razumovsky slapped his leg and laughed.

As they consumed more of the five star vodka, they chatted idly about various projects at Obninsk, when Razumovsky's youngest daughter, Yelena, strolled into the banya holding a large tray piled high with thin slices of sausage and cheese piled and garnished with lots of pickled cucumbers, tomatoes and garlic. In difficult times, a simple tray of finger food such as this was a royal feast, and Pavel's eyes shined with delight. Intentionally whisking close to Pavel's side of the table, she gracefully placed the tray upon the table.

"Look at this, will you," Razumovsky exclaimed with great pride. "Only my beautiful Yelena can make magic like this!" He gestured for her to come close. "Maybe you have a kiss for your old father?"

She blushed "Oh, Papa, you're drinking too much again."

"You always say that," he chuckled as she hugged him around the neck, planting a loving kiss on his weathered jowl. She then pinched his cheek and stood up saying to Pavel, "I'm not really a magician Project Manager Lebedev.

We have a large hothouse behind the dacha, and I use it to grow our own vegetables. I trust you will you enjoy the cuisine while you're here."

Pavel reached over and picked up a small pickle. He took a quick bite and let his jaw grind in an exaggerated manner like a contented cow chewing a sweet mouthful of cud. "I'm sorry, but I must agree with your father. This is the most incredible pickle I've eaten since I was young boy."

"Pavel Sergeevich," Razumovsky blurted out, "Since we agree on this important fact, I am claiming the right of a proud father to tell you that my Yelena only uses half of the hothouse for our garden. She is using the other half to raise genetically modified pine seedlings for the replanting of our Motherland, and her seedlings have already been used to reclaim hundreds of hectares south of Moscow."

Pavel turned to look at Yelena with wide eyes. "You know, you're really too modest. A woman of your talent should proudly step forward and let her accomplishments be known."

A faint smile crossed her lips. "Now you're drinking too much vodka, my dear Pavel Sergeevich, so I will tell you this. If my father does not put you to work tomorrow, I will put you to work in the hothouse. We must prepare a large number of seedlings for shipment to the planting zones further south, and an extra pair of hands will come in handy. As usual, the conservationists will be here tomorrow evening around suppertime, so you'll have to start early as well." She looked sternly at her father, "That is if his liver is still functioning."

"Oh, don't be such a pest," Razumovsky chortled. He winked at Pavel. "You've been volunteered to work in the hothouse, my lad, but rest assured you will enjoy suppertime. We have begun a Friday night tradition in our home. After Yelena's seedlings are loaded, we have a little banya with the workers, and we feast on homemade soups and breads that are from heaven."

"After dinner," Yelena added, "these wonderful young people sing and dance for us. Last week, they carried my 12-year old son, Dimitri, all around the house, and he loved it."

"It sounds wonderful," Pavel replied sincerely. "And may I say, this home glows from the beautiful feeling of this family. I am truly fortunate to be here." With that, he turned to face Yelena and gave her a snappy salute. "Junior Seedling Planter Assistant Second Class Lebedev reporting as ordered."

Yelena smiled, "Junior Seedling Planter Assistant Second Class Lebedev. You certainly are the creative one. We'll see how creative you are after breakfast." Pavel smiled appreciatively as she then sauntered out of the room with a playful smile.

They had a few more drinks while devouring treats from Yelena's platter and finally decided to move into the banya.

Built of fired bricks and rough-hewn pine, the banya smelled of the Earth and of the musky manliness of men. They entered to find one of Razumovsky's personal bodyguards tending the fire, occasionally sprinkling water on the hot stones. He had begun preparing the banya for them shortly after Pavel had arrived, and he had also placed two pairs of freshly thawed birch branches floating in a bucket of cool water next to the door.

Unlike a Finnish sauna, a Russian banya used a little less heat and a bit more moisture, and after adjusting to the heat and humidity of the sauna, they took turns gently beating each other with the birch branches.

The branches had been harvested and frozen years earlier before the massive deforestations that shook Russia, and had been thawed by Razumovsky's bodyguard earlier in the day. After about fifteen minutes, they left the sauna and jumped into a four-foot deep cold-water pool, grunting and groaning with delight as they splashed about in the refreshing water.

"Pavel Sergeevich," Razumovsky finally said. "You are here this evening because I'm looking for a man to lead us in our effort to destroy Shiva. Frankly, I was deeply impressed by your proposal to ring Shiva with these massive integrated disrupter stations as you call them. Some parts of this will not work, I think, but overall it is the right solution in my mind. A good vision and that is what we need right now, a strong man with a vision, who can make it happen."

Pavel blinked with amazement. This was the very first comment about his proposal and his mind immediately began to search for what may have been the unworkable parts of his plan. Razumovsky could see his distracted look and poked him in the chest to get his attention. "Forget technology for now. These are simple details." The older man then leaned back against the side of the pool and said calmly. "An undertaking of this magnitude must begin with a most human question. Tell me, what is your single greatest regret?"

Pavel splashed some cold water over his face, realizing that he was now facing a moment of truth and that if he answered with anything less than the truth, he would lose the most incredible opportunity in his life to make a real difference. " I have regrets, but none are greater than losing my family through my own blind stupidity. I treated them like possessions that I could put up on the shelf, where I could take them down whenever I needed them. I never thought of their needs; only of my own. The realization of this has stained the depths of my soul with an everlasting pain. The only thing I can be thankful for is that my ex wife was practical. She remarried well, and her new husband is good to my son." Pavel bowed his head in shame. "If I am unfit for this position because of this, I've earned it."

The older man looked upon him with wise compassion, deeply respectful of Pavel's own brutal truthfulness about himself. "Don't be too hard on yourself," He observed wistfully. "Let me share a little secret with you. There was a time in my life when I felt the same way about my family, too, and I made a similar mistake. Trust me; I know how you feel."

Tears began to stream down Pavel's face. "Then you know how much it hurts. I was such an ass." He sniffed, and splashed some cool water on his face to melt his tears.

Razumovsky patted him on the shoulder. "It's OK; let it go. That's what vodka is for. Yes?"

"That and headaches," Pavel replied.

The older man laughed. "Take it from me, Pavel, being truthful with yourself like this is the more important thing that could have ever happened to you. You see, lad, any foolish oaf can bully people into doing things and sometimes this is what works best. However, only through an understanding of our own frailties can one find the inner qualities needed to lead brilliant minds on a desperate mission. I now see that you have such an understanding, and this is good."

"No offense, but I'd rather have my family and a little less understanding."

"No offense taken. I think you now feel a basic need for a sense of balance in your life and of having someplace where you can enjoy it. For me, this banya and my daughter and grandson are my hidden paradise. You, too, must make your own hidden paradise, I think."

The older man's words resonated deeply in Pavel's mind. They had come at exactly the right moment in time for them to sink in. "Igor Petrovich, I still do not know if I am the right man for this job. If not, so be it, but your words are so right. I've been looking to fill this terrible emptiness in my soul, but I didn't know how until you shared your own experience with me. You've helped me more than you can know."

"Of this, I'm glad," Razumovsky replied as he slowly climbed out of the cold-water pool, "but do not count yourself out of the running yet. If anything, I see more of what I needed to see in you, and this serves you well."

Pavel stayed close by to him to make sure his steps were safe. Once he was out and reaching for a towel, Pavel asked, "May I ask a few questions?"

"You can always ask, but I'll only tell you what I can."

"Why didn't the Americans decide to build the Shiva destroyer themselves and leave us to build the space arks? We have more experience in such things."

Razumovsky threw his towel in a hamper, grabbed up two fresh linen sheets and wrapped them about his body. "Because there is a problem with Yellowstone National Park in America. It seems that there is a large magma chamber beneath the caldera. This chamber is fed from a magma reservoir in the Earth's deep interior and it has been increasing in size since the Nibiru flyby. Even if Shiva does not hit our moon in 2019, the caldera could erupt because of the added tidal gravitational forces. If that happens, whatever is left of the United States of America will be a dirty, miserable third world state. That is why they want to build the space arks. No matter what happens with Shiva, they have a real, immediate problem in Yellowstone and a terrible one at that. Thank God we are not faced with such a terrible prospect."

THE TWO MEN had talked and drank their way into the early hours of the morning, until Razumovsky finally showed Pavel to a guest room opposite his daughter's bedroom and bid him good night.

A self-described night owl, Pavel often worked well into the night and would rise the next day shortly before noon if nothing important had been planned. However, it was obvious that whoever was banging his door now wasn't aware of his living habits. "Pavel Sergeevich Lebedev," Yelena shouted through the door. "Junior Seedling Planter Assistant Second Class Lebedev, snap-to! It is nine thirty in the morning and you're sleeping like a lazy cat. On top of this, my Father left early this morning for Moscow with my son Dimitri. This last minute change in plans has left me desperately short-handed in the hot house."

"I'm up," he shouted back as he looked around his room with bleary eyes. Thankfully, someone had already brought his things up to his room. With his head throbbing from the vodka, Russell crawled out of bed and began fumbling through his shaving kit, looking for his Naproxen Sodium tablets.

"I'm making breakfast for you in the kitchen," Yelena shouted through the door.

Pavel grabbed his head and wished she would go away.

"OK," he shouted weakly. "I'll take a quick shower and I'll be down in fifteen minutes."

"Any more than fifteen minutes and your breakfast will be cold," She called back, "So get going, the day is wasting."

Not bothering to answer, he staggered into the bathroom, swallowed some tablets and then started the shower.

She knocked loudly on the door. "Two eggs or three?" She asked.

"Fresh eggs?" Pavel thought to himself. Hangover or not, fresh eggs was not something to pass up. He shouted through the door, "Three if you don't mind and I'll be down in fifteen minutes – honestly!"

"OK, I'll make you a nice omelet," she replied, leaving him to take his shower.

Fifteen minutes later, exactly as promised, he showed up in the kitchen with an old hard bound book tucked under one arm, though he was still buttoning his shirt as he walked into the kitchen.

Yelena looked at him from the corner of her eye and pointed to the table. "Sit," was all she said. Moments later, a steaming hot mug of sweet tea along with a plate of black bread with tinned butter, were set before him as Yelena began preparing his omelet. "Relax and enjoy your breakfast," she said pleasantly, returning to the stove.

As was his morning habit, Pavel would always read a few pages from his book as he enjoyed his breakfast. Sipping his tea, he began reading, stopping only to munch on a buttered slice of black bread.

Yelena craned her neck to read the book title on the word cloth binding as she served him his eggs. The faded lettering said, *"Worlds in Collision,* by Immanuel Velikovsky."

According to Velikovsky, earth experienced great cataclysms because of the flyby of a giant comet, which according to Velikovsky eventually became the planet Venus. At the time, scientists scorned his work, most notably the famous American astronomer Carl Sagan. However, after Velikovsky's death, science would soon realize the profound impact he had made on scientific though, although many still disputed his theories.

"I've heard of him and Zecharia Sitchin as well," Yelena noted as she sad down at the table with a hot mug of tea. "Many people talk of their work now that Nibiru has turned our Newtonian view of the universe upside down." She ran her fingers along the edge of the binding. "I collect books as a hobby. Is that the Macmillan or the Doubleday printing."

Pavel was surprised and impressed by her question. "A Macmillan printing from 1950 I believe. You know, before the American scientists blackmailed Macmillan Publishing into halting publication of his book." Pavel added proudly. "I want to show you something." He opened the book to the flyleaf and showed her a handwritten inscription from his father that said; "Destiny finds those who listen and fate finds the rest. So learn what you can learn, do what you can do and never give up hope."

Yelena read the inscription twice with great appreciation. "What beautiful words. Your father certainly had a way with words."

"Yes, he did," Pavel agreed with a longing sadness. "He gave me this book after I graduated the Moscow University.

Did you know that Velikovsky graduated from Moscow University too, and that he had personally known Einstein?"

Yelena smiled. "Of course. I graduated Moscow University too."

"Well now that is interesting. Then we both have something wonderful in common, a mutual interest in Velikovsky."

"But what do you think of his theories," she asked.

He rubbed his chin for a moment and thoughtfully replied, "They were relevant then, but far more relevant now if for nothing but his vision and determination. I think this is why my father was inspired by him."

Yelena ran her hands along the top edge of the book. She loved the feel of old books. "It has been a long time since your college days, Pavel, and you still haven't finished reading it?" she teased.

He laughed and closed the book. "I've lost count how man times I've read this book since my father passed away. We talked about Velikovsky so often, and I've always felt that reading a few pages each morning was a way for me to share a little time with my father each day. For some reason I cannot explain, but if feels as though he is looking over my shoulder and reading along with me."

"You're a lucky man to have had such a wonderful relationship with your father, Pavel. Is his inscription in this book the reason for your successful career?"

"That and another bit of wisdom he once shared with me." He took a large bite of eggs and rolled his eyes with deep appreciation. "Oh God, I forgot how good a fresh egg could taste."

She smiled. "We have a few luxuries out here and one of them is our chickens," she answered. "So I'm curious, Pavel. What is the other thing?"

He winked and took another bite, enjoying it slowly. "He taught me how to succeed in spite of my genius I.Q. after seeing a horse race in England with a brilliant analogy.

He told me, 'Pavel my boy, in life, a genius must win by a nose when he is alone with his friends. But when the world is watching, he must win by a length.'"

Yelena watched with keen interest how soft his face became as he spoke of his father. It revealed a tender and compassionate side to him that drew her to him. Even with the homey odors of the kitchen, she could still smell his musky scent. It had been a long time since she had noticed such things, and it awoke feelings that touched deeply on her own sense of femininity she hadn't felt since her husband Anatoli had passed away. Had her father not taken her son with him to Moscow early that morning, she would not have had this unique opportunity to get to know Pavel on such intimate terms.

In what seemed a timeless moment, she studied him warmly as he relished the remainder of his breakfast, and she felt a warm and refreshing feeling fill her soul. A feeling that could only come from pleasing a man she both admired and wanted.

LIKE HIS HIGHLY educated mother, Yelena Volkava, Dimitri Anatolivich Volkav loved to learn and a private tour of the Armory Museum in the northwestern section of the Kremlin with his Grandfather was a privileged treat.

The first thing he wanted to see was the famous Imperial "Pamyat' Azova" Faberge egg and then the 16th, 17th, and 18th Century horse drawn coaches used by the Czars and their families.

As the museum guide, who just happened to a high-ranking intelligence officer with a mutual love of history explained the exhibits to the 12-year old, his doting grandfather walked alongside Russian President Kirill Alexandrevich Chebotarev, just out of earshot.

The same age as the portly and distinguished looking Razumovsky, President Chebotarev worked out regularly in the Kremlin gym, keeping himself in reasonably good shape. Slightly shorter than Razumovsky, the twinkle in his blue-green eyes and his relatively smooth complexion made him look ten years younger.

"Grandfather," the young boy blurted out excitedly. "Come listen, this is so incredible!"

Razumovsky smiled, "Dimachka," he said with warm affection, using the diminutive form of his grandson's first name. "This is your day, so go ahead without us. Besides, President Chebotarev and I must discuss some important things. Remember, the museum opens in an hour, so make every moment count." Dimitri thanked him and turned his attention back to the exhibit.

"He is a wonderful boy," Chebotarev commented softly. "When all of this Shiva business becomes too much of a burden for me, I find new hope and peace with my grandchildren, too. In this regard Igor, we are equally fortunate."

"Yes Mr. President," Razumovsky answered, "we are indeed lucky, and we must see to it that our grandchildren also enjoy such luck. We must destroy Shiva. We absolutely must!"

Chebotarev nodded his head in agreement. "I've been reading your reports about Lebedev and his proposal. So has my Minister of Science, Vladmir Zacharenko, who thinks Lebedev is a fool and that you are also a fool for seriously considering his proposal to destroy Shiva by ringing it with twenty Disrupter Stations as he proposes. I must admit, I see some merit in his position. Putting that much hardware into space, especially for an untested theory is too risky. That is, if we could even do it."

"I must concede that parts of his theory are problematic" Razumovsky answered thoughtfully, "but I believe we can do something like this."

"And why is that?"

"When I was his age, I developed a theory of my own, on which I regrettably never finished my work. I never published my work, of course, but his proposal does bear some uncanny resemblances to my own work."

"Tell me, if I support this plan, how long will it take to build a proof of concept prototype?"

"My best guess is no less than 2 years and no more than 5."

Chebotarev gestured to a bench facing the icon of the Virgin of Smolensk. As the two men sat down he said, "what if I told you that there is a proven, working disrupter device already in existence?"

Razumovsky turned his body towards the Chebotarev. "Mr. President, if such a thing does exist, as you say, then we can do this."

"It does exist, and if we are to have any chance to get our hands on this technology, you will have to agree to replace Zacharenko as my Minister of Science. But that would require you to leave your beloved dacha outside of Obninsk City and to live here in the Kremlin, away from your family. Are you ready to make such a sacrifice for the Motherland?"

"I would happily give my life for the Motherland, Mr. President, but there would have to be a greater reason than mere politics for me to move to Moscow."

Chebotarev patted him on the knee and said, "There will be reason enough after you hear what I have to say." Razumovsky nodded in eager anticipation.

"As you may recall, the Israelis launched a 12-ton communications satellite called Shofar 7, into a geosynchronous orbit directly above Israel."

"Yes, I remember the launch notice although frankly I thought the Israelis could build a more compact satellite."

Chebotarev held up his hand. "You'll understand in a moment. You see, Shofar 7 is not only a communications satellite; it is also a scalar weapons platform. We as well as the Americans have been developing scalar weapons for some time now, but they've done two things we've never been able to do. First, they do not need to vector two scalar beams on a target. They only need one. Second, and this is the part that really troubles us, is that they can send an EM pulse a distance of approximately 35,850 kilometers without dispersion. From that distance, our footprint would cover a whole continent, but their footprint is less than a meter."

Razumovsky was stunned and a thousand questions began to fill his mind. "Have they used it yet?"

"Oh, yes. While the UNE has taken full credit for the New Islamic Reformation that began last year after the bombing of the UN headquarters in New York, what really ended the Islamist terror attacks on Israel was this satellite. The Israelis have been selectively assassinating radical elements of the Islamic leadership. Men literally go to bed healthy and when their wives wake up, they find them dead. In each case, the autopsy reports which are kept secret reveal that the internal organs of these men have been turned into meat jelly."

"Who knows about this?"

"For now, only we and the Americans know about this, save for the Israelis, of course. We haven't even told the UNE and have no intentions of doing so."

"And what about the Arabs?"

"The Arabs have no earthly idea of what is happening to them and they are literally scared shitless. All they know is that anyone who talks about peaceful coexistence with the Jews wakes up in the morning and those who preach violence are found dead with a body cavity full of meat jelly."

"Amazing," Razumovsky exclaimed. "So, why did we need to join the UNE, anyway?"

"The UNE has its purposes, so we'll stay with it. Here is the amazing thing I've been waiting to tell you. Do you have any idea of who and what connects these two facts I've just mentioned?"

Razumovsky shrugged his shoulders. "I have no idea."

Chebotarev cleared his throat. "I will tell you. The connection is a Russian Jew who immigrated to Israel in 1994 by the name of Isaac Aronovich Bachtman."

"Why am I not surprised," Razumovsky moaned. "Bachtman had been one of my most brilliant and devoted engineers back when I was running a design division at Ilyushin. Unfortunately, he was a Jew by birth and he simply got tired of the life of this stupid anti-Semitism that plagues our country and emigrated to Israel with his wife, Marina, and son, Misha. He was simply too good to lose."

"Well, Igor Petrovich," Chebotarev replied, "You may not have finished your work, but Bachtman did, while planting bananas on a kibbutz next to the Sea of Galilee in the north of Israel. After he finished it, he put it away in a safe place and forgot it, because he knew he had developed the theorems needed to create one of the most horrific weapons imaginable."

"That makes sense," Razumovsky admitted. "Bachtman was a pacifist, but his mind always needed something to chew on. Planting bananas on a kibbutz is not a real intellectual challenge I suppose."

Chebotarev rubbed his hands, and sighed. "Then came August 16, 2001. Do you remember what happened on that day, Igor Petrovich?" Razumovsky shrugged. "A Palestinian suicide bomber walked into the Sbarro pizza restaurant on Jaffa Street in Jerusalem, and detonated the explosive strapped to his body. Bachtman's only son, Misha, just happened to be walking through the door of the restaurant when it happened. He died instantly, and Bachtman was beside himself with grief.

His son worked for the Mossad, so the police did not list his son as a victim. Instead of making a stink, he went to the Mossad with his theorems and gave them to them on the understanding that they would find a way to honor his son. They did, and then they asked him to build a prototype, which he also did."

Razumovsky rocked his head back and forth in disbelief, even though he knew the man and his capabilities. The Bachtman he'd known was a timid pacifist. However, he also admitted to himself, if something like happened to his grandson, would he not also be tempted to do the same? However, a weapon like this would be a threat to all mankind if it fell into the wrong hands. "Why haven't we destroyed it, Mr. President?"

Chebotarev rubbed his chin. "We and the Americans have tried several times and in many different ways. The Israelis anticipated this and built an impressive defense system into the spacecraft. It's no wonder that it weighs 12 tons! The thing is also probably built to last a hundred years, which is about how long we estimate it would take to duplicate Bachtman's work, even with your help."

"Well then, what do we do?" The question moved the conversation to the next step; taking action.

"For now, we let them keep their weapon and stay quiet because we have no choice but to do so. The Americans see this as we do. Nobody else must know, even the UNE. As for the Jews, after hundreds of years of being butchered by other people, they've finally bought themselves 100 years of peace, and they know it."

Razumovsky pursed his lips as the practical details crossed his mind. "Mr. President, I think I see where you're going with this, but I also see three immediate problems. First off, Lebedev's proposal calls for twenty disrupter stations in orbit around Shiva, even with Bachtman's device, we'll need to build the most powerful computer ever to synchronize them, or risk creating hundreds of smaller objects that could completely destroy the Earth. No such computer exists that I know of."

"Second, how do we get the Americans to agree to all this, given that they must be furious with Israel for not sharing this technology with them?"

"And thirdly, and most importantly, how do we convince the Israelis?"

The man had a steel-trap mind. Chebotarev knew he had correctly chosen a man who would engineer what historians would later call one of the major political triumphs of the 21st century.

"Igor Petrovich, the first problem is fortunately the easiest to solve. The American company, IBM, has just finished building their first biomass computer based on human stem cells. It is not as fast as conventional processors, but it is much more powerful, because it literally works in a non-linear, parallel manner much like the human mind. This makes it a perfect central controller for Lebedev's design. I'm also told that it can program itself by simply growing more computing tissue. Obviously, we're talking about next generation computational molecular biology that is beyond anything we can do. Once the Americans have finished ironing out a few minor artificial intelligence issues, it will be able to program itself heuristically, that is, learning by its own mistakes, thousands of times faster than it could be programmed by humans."

"I'm quite confident that we can get one of these new IBM biomass computers, so do not worry about that, providing we can get the Americans to buy in, which brings me to your second question – namely how do we get the Americans to agree to this?"

"Understanding how we will achieve this begins with the simple difference between the Western intellect of the Americans and the Eastern intellect of us poor Russians. For the Americans, the impossible is simply that — the impossible. For us, the impossible is just another option. However, there is one instance where the impossible does become an option for the Americans and this happens when they want to save a lot of money, which is how we'll get them to agree."

Razumovsky shook his head, "I'm not sure that I'm following this, Mr. President."

"Stay with me," Chebotarev answered. The Americans are building two space arks, as you know. While the rail gun launch system they're using in Florida is capable of sending great quantities of material cheaply into space, they will have to build another two such launch systems to deliver the hundreds of millions of tons of soil, sand, aggregates for drainage and of course water into space. Even then, they'll barely have enough to complete the first habitat sections of their ships by 2019. After that, they may have to begin to mine asteroids, which is no simple proposition, either."

"What we will propose is that the Americans build a third colony ship for Israel in exchange for a prototype of Lebedev's design, using Israeli technology. After we've completed our own tests, the prototype would be repurposed for asteroid mining. Literally speaking, a device like this could pulverize a good-sized asteroid into smelter-ready ore in just a matter of minutes. Compare that with that fact that it would take an army of hard-rock miners in space suits to achieve the same results over period of several years and you've got a convincing argument."

"Brilliant," Razumovsky added. "The Americans will love that. Plus, the Americans will save themselves a tremendous amount of money and treasure, to say the least, while ending Israel's monopolistic control over this technology."

Chebotarev stood up and stretched. "Let's go find your grandson while I answer your third, and most difficult, question." Razumovsky rose and the two began to ramble in the direction of the guide's voice.

"As it stands now, the Israelis have the technology they need to live in peace for essentially as long as they want, unless the world suddenly enters a profound renaissance, which I highly doubt. Therefore, if we are to convince the Israelis that this is a good thing for them, promises of world gratitude will not move them to action. No, we must give them tangible rewards they can take to their people. Obviously, getting their own colony ship is a very tangible reward, but they undoubtedly are also working on something similar, only on a much smaller scale."

"Well then, what do we have to offer them?"

Chebotarev put an arm around Razumovsky's shoulder. "The Americans have a saying. If you can't beat them, join them. Well, we'll do it a little differently. We'll ask the Israelis to join with us and, in turn, give them something more valuable than their weapon – a real future. Not only will they get their own space ark, but we will also get the Americans to agree with us that we will never permit Islam to build a mosque in space as part of our deal to use their technology. Plus, they get to keep their Shofar 7 satellite, along with our tacit blessings to terminate as many Arab terrorists as they please with extreme prejudice. We'll probably ask them to do a few for us, as well, in Chechnya."

Razumovsky scratched his head as everything sunk in and finally said, "Mr. President, your plan is brilliant. Convincing the Americans to participate and to give us a biomass computer will not be so difficult, but then there is Israel, and, if you do not mind my asking, something more personal to me: Why do I need to move to Moscow?"

"Mother Russia desperately needs someone like you to mobilize the nation's resources and manpower for this effort. I want you to replace Zacharenko as my Minister of Science, who, strictly between us, is a doddering, old fool. You must also do this because you share a history with Bachtman. He likes you and respects you, and, as my Minister of Science, your promises will carry the full weight of our government. Bring him in on this, and he will do more to convince Israel to accept this deal than we could. His word carries great weight with his government. They'll listen."

"Mr. President, if there is a shred of warmth left in Isaac's heart, I can reach it and make him to believe. However, you are also going to have to take some pretty heavy political risks. If the UNE learns of this, it could backfire on all of us."

"Before we find your grandson, I'll tell you a little secret. We joined the UNE simply as a marriage of convenience. The UNE is not what is appears to be. While its charters states noble and worthy aims, those who control it view Russia as nothing more than an expendable pawn. However, this is one pawn that knows how to play the game like a master. To hell with the UNE! They're not our friends. Trust me on this, and trust me when I tell you that similar sentiments exist in the American leadership as well. We tell the UNE nothing, and we admit nothing if they come to us with suspicions, as they, no doubt, will eventually do."

Razumovsky nodded his head and said with dutiful resignation: "Mr. President, it appears that I'm moving to Moscow."

CHAPTER 12

THE FRIENDS

THE PROBLEM WITH doing business with criminals is that their first loyalty is to their own income streams. What UNE Governor Merl Johnston failed to grasp was that the very people he tipped off about Vigo Jones, were already buying attractively priced black market goods from him on a regular basis. They were not about to kill a goose that was laying golden eggs. Especially the kind that could see you coming a mile off before and then slip in behind you to cut your throat from ear-to-ear.

The message they left for Jones on the secure cell number he used for discrete transactions proved to be a bonanza. The tip had come from Houston, Texas, and this gave Vigo something to work from. Also, it meant that, whoever they were, they had one or more operatives buried somewhere in Port Ord. Even perhaps in Los Gatos.

Upon his return, he would reward his sources for their good sense and information as well as changing his route, just in case they were not the only ones notified of his travel plan and cargo. Besides, he had just been given another important task to handle, one that would have necessitated a change in his itinerary, anyway.

CROSSING OPEN GROUND was something for which Vigo's old two-and-half ton Army truck was ideally suited. He didn't care much for the newer electric trucks. He'd been stranded too many times by volcanic ash that managed to work its way past the so-called "impenetrable seals" into the electric motor windings. On the other hand, the design of the two-and-half ton diesel powered truck had proven itself time-and-again by reliably carrying American soldiers across the rough and muddy roads of Vietnam.

As he drove towards a shaded area just out of sight of the freeway, he pulled up next to a small stream. He reached into his tunic and drew out the platinum colored medallion he always wore. He held it up to his right temple and closed his eyes. Yes, he was just where he needed to be.

Now that he found the right location, he needed to set up a camp, but it was still light and the intercept wouldn't happen till after nightfall. Tired from the long drive, he decided to rest a few minutes before unloading the things he needed from the back of the truck. He tucked his medallion back under his shirt and let his head fall slowly back against the cab wall. Closing his eyes, he remembered back to when he first found his old truck, parked at the far end of an Oklahoma National Guard armory.

Men and vehicles can be an odd thing sometimes, and for Vigo, it was love at first sight. He strong-armed the motor pool sergeant to turn the truck over to him and then towed it to a local Kenworth dealership. A former associate of his, a retired Army officer, owned the dealership. Vigo had once saved his life, and this would be the chance to make good on his promise to pay back the favor.

The dealer laughed and shook his head when he first saw the truck, but got right to work. He and Vigo, along with two mechanics, took it on full time and they began by stripping down the truck down to its frame. After scrounging the parts the dealer felt they needed, they began rebuilding the Vietnam-era truck from the ground up, with a new high-performance Caterpillar diesel engine, Bendix air brakes, a beefed up suspension, new digital LCD display for the dash, a host of other minor upgrades and a new coat of OD green paint. The final touch was a brand new set of airless tires; the same used on UNE armored cars.

The dealer and his mechanics beamed with pride when Vigo called it "a hard-on mating of the tried-and-true with the grooviest off-road trucker-toys imaginable." After that, the two men christened the newly rebuilt truck by gunning it through and over every miserable hill and through every gully and ravine they could find. All the while, they were guzzling six-packs of cold beer, howling at the top of their lungs and talking about the good old days when they both had more gumption than sense. Rebuilding his truck had been the first decent experience for Vigo after the Nibiru flyby and recalling the memory always served as a pleasant and momentary diversion.

Feeling better rested and in good spirits, Vigo prepared a fire pit and then returned to his truck for a cast iron 9-quart Dutch oven, its three legged cast iron stand and a canvas back pack, packed with cooking and eating utensils, plates and so forth. With the fire pit ready, he scouted about for some firewood, made a large stack of ready wood and kindling near the pit and returned to his truck as night began to fall.

Perching himself up upon the tailgate, he lit a cigar and practiced blowing smoke rings till the Platinum colored medallion that hung from his neck began to warm. The medallion was keyed to the elevated vibrational life energy frequencies normally associated with Indigo children. Over the years, he had worked with hundreds of such young children and could never sense their special abilities, unlike the psychics he employed, who could easily see the Indigo-colored auras of the children. Yet, his medallion now helped him to go beyond the limitations of sight, and he knew there was at least one, if not two, Indigo children within 500 meters of the truck.

"It's show time," he mused to himself as he crushed the cigar under the toe of his boot. Opening a small cooler near the rear of the truck, he pulled out a large fresh chunk of horsemeat and threw it as far as he could onto the road behind the rear of his truck. It would only be a matter of time before a hungry mongrel or coyote came sniffing around, but he wouldn't be there. He'd be sitting down by the campsite sipping hot coffee from a thermos he'd brought with him.

Vigo had finished his second cup of coffee when he heard the unmistakable report of a small caliber rifle. He leapt to his feet and made a quick 360-degree scan of the area, then drew his Beretta 9mm automatic and melted into the night.

Finding the shooter was easy. A feral Doberman Pincer had trailed the meat Vigo had thrown behind his truck and had been felled dead with a single shot to the head. Hiding behind a boulder, he watched with silent amusement as the hunter, a 14-year old boy, put another bullet into the dog's head and then proceeded to drag the carcass of his kill off to the side of the road.

The rifle was obviously a .22. "This kid is good," Vigo said to himself as his eyes darted through the night in a random pattern to scan for another person. The medallions were never wrong, and his seemed to indicate that two Indigo children were out there in the night; not just one. Most likely, the second one was much younger and hiding somewhere nearby.

The young boy was so preoccupied with carting off his kill that the beam of light from Vigo's high intensity light gun caught him by surprise, blinding him like a deer in the headlights. "Freeze, boy, I've got the drop on you," Vigo said in a firm, but unthreatening voice.

Still holding onto the hind legs of the dog in one hand, the boy held his other hand over his eyes to shield them from the intense light and asked, "Are you a Homer?" Homer was a derogatory term most Americans had come to use for the Homeland Defense security teams that enforced UNE imposed curfews and quarantines.

"No, boy, I'm no Homer," Vigo replied. "And I can't say I like them either." He switched off the light. "Stay right there." He walked to the back of his truck and switched on the cargo light. "Leave the dog there and come here. Don't worry, I'm not going to hurt you. Besides, if I was going to do anything mean, you'd be dead by now, anyway. We just need to talk."

"I figured that," the boy said, dropping the dog. Holding his rifle loosely in his hand, he walked up to Vigo. "I been tracking him all afternoon, then he smelled some road kill, I guess, and that's when I had a clear shot." The boy nodded over his shoulder towards the dog. "Since I got him when he was sniffing around your truck for something to eat. I'll share the kill with you if that will make you happy."

Vigo shook his head. "No thanks, son; just leave it there for the time being. You can have the whole thing if you like. What I want to know is if you're traveling alone?" Vigo already knew the boy had a surviving mother and younger sister. Perhaps they would be the ones hiding out there in the night, waiting for him to call them.

The boy pawed the ground with the toe of his battered hiking boot for a moment and finally answered, "My mother and sister are with me."

Vigo holstered his pistol and smiled. "My name is Vigo Jones, son, and I think I can scrounge up something tastier than feral dog for you and your kin. Tell me, what is your name?"

"I'm Timmy Watkins, but folks just call me Tim. My Mother is Helen, and my little sister is Jenny."

"Well Tim, I'd like to invite all three of you to dinner, so please call Helen and Jenny in."

The boy hesitated as he studied Vigo's face in the glow of the cargo light. Somehow, he sensed he was in safe company — the company of a friend. "Sure." He put two fingers to his lips and whistled loudly for his mother and sister.

Moments later, Vigo watched a tall, thin woman in her early to mid thirties walk out of the shadows hand-in-hand with a young girl. The girl looked to be six years of age, more or less. The mother and child walked up along side the boy. "We sure could use a drink of fresh water," the woman asked timidly.

"I'll fix you up," Vigo replied jumping up into the back of the truck. A few moments later, he stuck his head out the back. "Catch 'em." He tossed three small bottles to the boy. "Sip it slowly," he reminded them.

Relieved by the gift of water, the boy's mother took a deep satisfying drink, and, wiping her lips asked, "Are you a Homer?"

The boy answered for Vigo. "No he's not, mama."

"The boy's right ma'am," Vigo added, "I'm no Homer. As a matter of fact, I'd like to help you and your children if you'll let me."

Tall and gaunt, there was still a haunting beauty in her face and in the elegant lines of her body. Beneath that tragic exterior beat the heart of woman who had lost much. Now a stranger in uniform was offering her kindness, even though he was clearly in a position to do whatever he wanted with her. Perhaps if she submitted without making him ask, any possibility of a confrontation could be avoided. As a sign of willing submission, she unbuttoned the top of her blouse, pulling back enough of the material to reveal the edge of her breast and slightly lowering her head while keeping her eyes focused on his.

Vigo gently shook his head no, and motioned her to refasten her blouse. The gentle rebuke surprised her, leaving her feeling a bit self-conscious. As she nervously refastened her blouse Vigo asked, "So tell me, Helen, how long have you known that your son is gifted in a special way?"

"Most always," she answered feebly, while casting furtive glances at her son and the .22 semi-automatic rifle, now pointed at the ground.

"Tim, you're what is called an Indigo child," Vigo said to the boy. "Have you heard that expression before?" The boy shook his head no.

"OK, then let's see if this fits. You're always sure of yourself and able to see things coming long before most others do."

"Yeah," the boy answered hesitatingly. "It gets me into trouble too sometimes. Drives people nuts when I figure things out before they do."

Vigo's laughter broke the night making the boy and his family smile. "By God, you are an Indigo for sure. Young fellow, you and the others like you represent the seed of man's next evolutionary step forward, and that makes you very precious. But I think you've suspected this for some time now, and simply couldn't put a finger on it till now. Do you know what I mean, Tim?"

"Well I kinda had a sense about it, but always thought it was a stupid idea," Tim replied sheepishly.

"Well it's not," Vigo disagreed. "All Indigos have the same feeling in one way or another." He gestured the boy to stand beside him next to the truck. "Come a little closer, Tim; I've got something to show you."

The young boy looked at his mother. She indicated her approval and watched him join Vigo to the back of the truck.

"Tim," Vigo said as he pulled the pins out of the rear gate and lowered it. "I've got all kinds of good things in this truck and I'll give some of them to you, whether or not you choose to accept the offer I plan on making to you this evening after dinner. "

"I'm game," the boy answered as he squinted to see what was in the dark shadows of the truck.

Vigo pulled two large cardboard cartons out of the back of the truck and onto the gate. "Leave the dog and take one these cartons. I've got a couple of large tins of beef stew and some fresh bread."

He led them to the campsite, and while the boy started the fire, Vigo emptied the canned stew into the Dutch oven and dangled it under a three-legged stand perched over the fire pit. Tim expertly built a roaring cook fire, and within ten minutes, the contents of the pot began to bubble gently.

Tossing in a dash of herbs, Vigo tasted the stew and added a few shakes of Tabasco sauce for good measure. "This canned stuff is pretty lame," he casually noted. "That is why God invented Tabasco sauce. You know, for people such as us who are tired of eating plain food." He took a taste and made a happy face, which caused the young girl to giggle out loud. It was the first sound Vigo had heard from her all evening, and it made him happy inside to see the child relax.

He took another taste and exclaimed, "Yup, I think it is just about ready. Say, Tim, hand me those pewter plates will you?" Vigo took a loaf of bread out of the carton, tore it into large chunks and served the three generous portions of the mildly spiced stew and fresh bread. They fell upon their plates with great hunger.

After her second serving, Helen wiped her lips and said, "Mr. Jones, we're really thankful for the meal, but if you do not mind my asking, why are you being so kind to us?"

He pretended to ignore the question as he filled a large coffeepot with water and loose tea leaves. She asked the question a second time.

He pulled the Dutch oven out of the fire pit and hung the coffeepot in its place. "In answer to your query, because it pleases me. Now, it's my turn. Why are all of you wandering around out here, when you could be in a city, safe and fed?"

"The Homers make it look like everyone is eating good, but that's bullshit if you're living in the wrong part of town," Tim answered. "We were starving and my parents tried to loot a food store. Dad wasn't armed and he offered to give up, but the Homers shot him dead. Now they're looking for us. That's why we're wandering around like homeless nobodies."

"That was a honest answer, Tim" Vigo remarked gratefully. He already knew their background and appreciated the boy's honesty. He now felt sure that both siblings were Indigo, a gene that always came from the mother's side. What a find! Two Indigo children and a mother who was still young enough to bear more children! He could only hope that her extremely low level of body fat hadn't already caused permanent damage to her reproductive organs. Either way, they would remain together as a family and soon have the choice to accept a new life, free of fear and starvation.

"We have friends." Vigo pointed up towards the night sky. "We've never been alone; we never will be, and we share common roots with them. Life is precious to them, and they want to help us."

"You mean UFOs and all that?" Helen said.

"That and much more," Vigo answered. "They cannot save our entire race, as we must do that. They're ability to help is very limited and so they've chosen to quietly help those of us who represent mankind's next evolutionary step forward," Vigo looked squarely into Helen's eyes, "and your family is one such family."

She swallowed hard. "Who are these friends, as you call them, and what do we have to do?"

Vigo took a coat hanger out of the box and straightened it. He winked at Jenny. "I think I've got a bag of marshmallows in that box yonder. Wanna toast some?"

The little girl squealed with delight. "Oh mommy, we've got marshmallows." With bright, eager eyes, she fished through the box and held up a sealed bag of marshmallows.

Vigo opened the bag, took out a handful and skewered them on the coat hanger. As he held them over to fire to roast, he said "They call themselves the Friends, and if you accept our offer this evening, you will meet a wise soul by the name of JALA.TRAC in a few days. He'll look like a tall, thin Finn when you first see him. He will be your mentor and will gently teach you the way of the Godschild Covenant."

Vigo turned the wire to see that marshmallows had a nice even golden texture. He held out the toasted treats to Tim's younger sister. "Young lady, you get two. One because you're smart and the other because you're pretty." Her face lit up with delight as she eased her reward off the wire.

"What is the Godschild Covenant?" she asked before filling her mouth with warm, perfectly toasted marshmallow.

"It is an ancient wisdom the Friends discovered centuries ago," Vigo replied. "There are several races who are interested in seeing mankind flourish, and each helps in its own way. The Friends have come to share the home world of the Godschild with us. Even though the Godschild have long since disappeared, they did leave behind a beautiful city on a planet much like Earth with two large, magical moons. The city is in excellent condition and it has a natural gravity network and plumbing that still works."

"Like a Roman aqueduct?" Tim asked.

"Yes, but even more sophisticated. I've been there, and I was so amazed. You will be, too, if all of you accept my offer this evening."

Helen studied his eyes. Was he just telling them a campfire story to amuse them, or was he really being serious. "Mr. Jones, this is a most entertaining story."

He shook his head. "Helen, let's get two things settled right here and now. First, it is no story. Second, my name is Vigo." Helen grew solemn.

"Tell me about the city," Jenny blurted out.

Vigo smiled. "Glad you asked, Jenny. It is an incredible city and straddles a large white sandy beach that stretches into the horizon at both ends. It is built on a series of cliff faces that step all the way down to an immense fresh water inland sea. Nestled in the hills and cliffs above the shoreline are large, comfortable multi-family homes with large, common scenic porches that face out to sea so that you can watch the moons rise every evening. But one of the most amazing things is that there are these big stone obelisks in front of each gateway to the city. Kind of like a big, rock billboard, if you will, and, on each obelisk, the same message is inscribed. The Friends translated the message on the obelisks, and it said, 'Welcome; we are the builders of Godschild, and we greet you. We give you this city in the hope that you will cherish and nurture it in peace.'"

"What a beautiful thought," Helen exclaimed.

Vigo nodded and removed the medallion that hung from his neck. He handed it to her. Roughly the size of a silver dollar, the polished platinum colored disk was incredibly light, but strong. "Look at the engraving," he said pointing to the two parallel rows of strange looking symbols inscribed on the face of the medallion. "These symbols are also engraved on every doorpost in the city and we believe it is the sum total statement of the philosophy of this ancient race. The Friends call it the Godschild Covenant. Apparently, it was an affirmation of the builders of the city about their collective and deep, personal sense of responsibility to the universal mind and it says: Live and let live; love and let love; learn and let learn."

Fascinated by the medallion, the mother and her two children examined the medallion in the flicking firelight, running their fingers along the engraved symbols.

Vigo watched them experience the medallion for the first time, as he had seen so many others do, with a deep sense of personal satisfaction and purpose. Confident they would eventually accept his offer, he skewered some more marshmallows and held them over the fire. As they began to brown he said, "Helen, I've brought fully equipped camping packs for each of you, along with some fresh clothing and good hiking shoes. These gifts are for you and your children, whether or not you accept my offer this evening. If not, I will happily leave them with you as thanks for listening to my offer, and I will never speak of you or your children to a living soul." He held out the cooked marshmallows to Jenny. "Be careful, honey, they're hot."

Jenny lightly touched the first marshmallow, then slowly pulled the first two off the wire. "We go Godschild!" She said as took her first bite and with a mouth full of the gooey white and caramel colored treat, she began to sing, "We go Godschild! We go Godschild!"

Vigo studied her with a hint of amazement. Could it be she was more gifted than the boy was? Possibly so — yes, this family was a real find indeed.

He smiled warmly, "Helen. Tim. Jenny seems to have beaten me to the punch, as they say. You see, I'm working with the Friends to move gifted families to Godschild so that we can help humanity to evolve in a more peaceful way. Simply put, my offer is that you are all invited to live on Godschild if you so choose. Obviously, Jenny has already made her choice, but all of you have to agree."

"What is it like to live there," Tim asked cautiously as he handed back the medallion.

"Life will not be easy, but it will be rewarding," Vigo replied hanging it back around his neck. "You will have to live on what you grow, and the city still needs a lot of cleanup and restoration work. After all, it has been unoccupied for centuries. But, what is more important is the propagation of our species." He looked first at Helen and then Jenny. "The greatest burden will be for the life givers and the greatest satisfaction as well. That's about all I can tell you." He stood up and stretched. "I'll go and get those things I promised you ready. I'll be back in a while." He pointed to the coffeepot hanging over the fire. "In the meantime, feel free to pour yourself a cup of hot tea. There's some sugar in one of the boxes as well if you like it sweet."

"Thanks, Vigo. We'll be here when you get back," she replied.

As he walked back to his truck, she drew her children around her and looked into their eyes. "It kind of scares me, but what are our choices. Do we stay out here, drinking muddy water and eating dog? As I think of it, my thought is that your Daddy would tell us to go."

When Vigo returned, Helen smiled and poured him a steamy cup of hot tea. "One lump or two?" He held up two fingers with a smile, and she added two heaping tablespoons full of sugar to the mug.

She handed him the mug as he sat down and said, "We've decided to accept your offer. So, what happens next?"

He blew across the top of the cup and took a sip. "Just right." He licked his lips and continued. "For starters, each of you will get a medallion like mine. With these, you will never be alone again. You will then have a long journey on foot. Along the way, you will meet other people, such as yourselves. After that, the Friends will transport all of you to Godschild. Do you care to reconsider our offer?"

Her eyes sparkled in the warm flicker of light that radiated outwards from the campfire. "We already said yes."

Vigo smiled approvingly. Reaching into one of his large, baggy pants pockets, he drew out three small boxes, handing one to each of them. "In the box is a medallion, and it bonds to the first person who physically touches it. Before you open these boxes, I want you to know that you'll feel a powerful energy surge, which will cross through your body. Do not be alarmed, and do not drop the medallion, or you will terminate the bonding process. You'll know when then the bonding process is complete, because your medallion will feel warm to the touch. After that, anyone can hold it, but it will only respond to you. Now, go ahead and begin."

They opened their boxes and took hold of their medallions. The bonding process only took a brief moment, and soon all three were holding pleasingly warm, personalized medallions in their hands. He handed them three small chains, made of the same Platinum colored metal and showed them how to fit them to their medallions.

With their new medallions hanging around their necks, the three looked at each other with genuine smiles. It had been a good and interesting first step.

"Now, let me tell you something." Vigo began. "You can easily spend the rest of your life learning all of the things you can do with these things, so here are a couple of handy ones to get you started. First off, it automatically warms up when it detects another medallion for the first time. Second, hold it flat against your right temple, and it becomes a tactical viewer that let's you see in the dark. You can also hear better than normal, and your distance hearing will be significantly better. If you hold your fingers on it like so," He demonstrated with his own medallion, "it will also show you the best route to follow to wherever the Friends want you to go." He changed his finger position. "Hold it like so, and you can use it to communicate with another medallion owner. If you visualize his or her face in your mind while holding your medallion this way, their medallion will vibrate telling them you want to speak with them. If they accept your gesture, you can freely share your perceptions and thoughts without having to talk."

He leaned back and studied them as his words sunk in. Tim and his mother would most likely need to use their medallions for the remainder of their natural lives. However, he sensed that Jenny could actually outgrow her need for a medallion for the more basic functions. This possibility excited him. If she proved to be this capable and started a family, she would endow her offspring with great abilities.

"Well folks," he announced, "You all need to get your strength for the journey and besides this spot will serve as a rally point for the other members of your group. So, we need to get you set up. I don't have much time, so while you're getting the cooking gear squared away, Tim can be helping me unload the truck. After that, I'll stay around long enough to help you pitch the tents, then I'll have to be on my way." Helen nodded in agreement, and he patted Tim on the shoulder, "Let's go unload your things from the truck."

VIGO HAD CAREFULLY loaded the camping equipment for Helen and her children towards the back of the truck. The large metal cases filled with Heroin and medical-marijuana for the Los Gatos Triage Center were stacked at the front of the cargo bed, covered with canvas tarps and lashed down. To be sure it wasn't disturbed, Vigo made the boy stand in front of the tailgate as he handed down boxes of supplies, survival gear and clothing. With everything unloaded, Vigo jumped down and closed up the back of his truck. Using a flashlight, he opened one of the specially marked cartons. It contained a military style web belt with a large revolver and a rugged survival knife, two boxes of ammunition, field cleaning kit, and a small whetstone for the knife.

"Tim, our medallions are very powerful, but the fact is that you're going to be a novice with it for a while. Meanwhile, you're going to have to cover open ground during bad times. This might come in handy." He removed the stealth gray finished revolver from its holster. "This is a Taurus seven-shot .357 Magnum Tracker." He handed the pistol to the boy who took it with both hands. "Wow, it feels lighter than it looks."

Vigo ran a finger down the barrel. "That's because it's made of forged titanium with a stainless-steel bore liner. It is also fitted for scope and the grips are ideal for a young fellow like you. They do a great job of absorbing recoil."

"Man, this thing is a hand cannon!" Tim exclaimed.

"It has enough wallop to stop most anything, which is what you're going to need where you're going," Vigo replied. "It's simple, utterly reliable and about the biggest damn pistol a young fellow your size can handle." He pointed at the box. "There is a cleaning kit, and there are three hundred rounds of ammo in the box, as well as a Simmons 2.5-7X scope. I suggest you go off away from here tomorrow and get it sighted in the way you like it. The instructions are in the box, as well."

"This sure would give us an edge," Tim said appreciatively as he hefted the weapon, "but my semi-automatic .22 rifle is still better for hunting small game."

"You'll find a 500-round brick of .22 long rifle with copper jacketed slugs and a new cleaning kit for your rifle in the box as well."

"I really want to thank you for this," Tim said sincerely. "Feeding my family just got a whole lot easier."

"Just use it wisely," Vigo replied. "Now, let's get those tents up, as I've got to be heading down the road lickity-split."

VIGO FINALLY ARRIVED at the Los Gatos main gate as several ice trucks, now converted to refrigerated morgue transports, continued on their way past the gate, onto Limekiln Gulch Road and on towards the quarry graves.

The guard scanned Vigo's traveling orders. "We were told to expect you," he grunted. He nodded toward the morgue transports. "They've been rolling through here for two hours. This is the first morning, and we're already sick of it.

In time, the sound of the lumbering morgue trucks on their way to the quarry graves would become a routine part of life at the Los Gatos Triage Center and eventually ignored. However, this was the first operational day for the center, and in a few hours, a flood of sick and dying would come walking, riding, stumbling and limping through its gates.

A heavy and ominous mood prevailed throughout the camp, as everyone went through his or her morning rituals in virtual stunned silence. It had begun.

Anthony was sitting in the mess and nursing a mug of coffee when Vigo found him. "Good morning, Captain."

Anthony glanced up and pushed his mug across the table towards Vigo. "I haven't touched it; if you like creamer with no sugar you're welcome. Ann-Marie is bringing me some hot tea instead." He nodded in the direction of the service line and Vigo could see her preparing the tea.

He accepted the mug and took a sip, "Just the way I like. Thanks. You might want to know that I just met Dr. Boole and brought him that contraband heroin from the DEA in San Diego along with a surprise shipment of medical-marijuana. We're talking boxes of the stuff. Good God, do you guys think that things will really get that bad?"

Anthony waved his hand, "Trust me, you're going to be making more of these runs as time goes on."

"So what exactly do you guys do with this stuff anyway?"

"Heroin is the only thing we can give our terminal clients in the quarantine area for pain. The pharmaceuticals are reserved for recovering patients and terminal children. We give the terminals as much Heroin as they want short of a lethal dose because it also helps to suppress their cough response. This will help us to keep the 3G patients from infecting everyone else. As for the marijuana, it helps the other patients with nausea, spasms and whatever. If it weren't for that, we'd be competing with all the hospitals in the area for some rather scarce pharmaceuticals right now." As the old saying goes, Anthony's words took the bloom off the rose.

Vigo sat there staring at coffee. "This may sound crappy, but it makes me glad I'm driving out of here tonight for another run." Ann-Marie joined them as Vigo added; "Now, all I need is a hot bath and a flop."

"They won't be serving breakfast for another half hour, so you might as well go find Corporal Sharma," Anthony replied. "He'll get you situated.

"No need for that," Ann-Marie said. She grabbed Vigo by the shirt collar. "Come with me, you big galoot, and I'll get you squared away. I suppose you're hungry as well?"

"More tired than hungry," he sighed with an exhausted look. "What I'd really love right now is a hot bath and a chance to enjoy some of my sweet condensed milk I got tucked away in the truck." He knew Ann-Marie loved sweet condensed milk and wondered if she'd rise to the bait.

She pulled him aside and said, "If you can rummage up two tins for yours truly, you can use the bathtub in my dome. Throw in another can, and I'll let you use my bunk, as my three roommates are not due to arrive until tomorrow. If you can deliver, it's just out the door and two domes to the left. Number 15."

Vigo winked at her. "Do you have a brand preference?"

"Oh Lordy, brand preference, is it now," she said with an amazed voice. "Vigo, you are simply amazing. Let's just say I'd like something that says made in America and was canned sometime within the last 20 years, if that isn't asking too much. I'll see you at number 15 in say ten minutes."

Vigo winked at Ann-Marie. "See you in ten."

Anthony scratched his head. "Hey Ann-Marie, I don't think we'll have anything today. Everyone requesting assisted suicide will have to wait out a mandatory 24-hour cooling off period, so we can pretty much do as we please today. If you and the Sergeant want to go hang out together, that's fine by me. I'm going back to my dome for some more sack time, and then I've got a TV interview."

"You know I think that O'Hara gal has got the hots for you," Ann-Marie teased. "You be nice to her, and she'll make it worth your while."

"She's not my type," he groaned.

"Well that depends on what you're looking for, honey cakes."

Anthony looked up from tea mug with a twisted look on his face. "Honey cakes?"

VIGO ARRIVED AT dome number 15 ten minutes later holding half a dozen tins of Carnation Sweet Condensed Milk in his arms. The front door was already half open, and he could hear the sound of bath water running inside and Ann-Marie humming one of her favorite tunes. He pushed open the door with the toe of his boot and stepped in as she peeked her head out from the bathroom. "All for me?" He smiled. "Then don't stand there like lump on log. Shut the damn door before everyone comes asking for some!"

He sat the tins down on the counter in the small kitchenette at the back of the dome. She eyed them with a hungry smile. "Well, Mr. Whoever your name is today, shall we retire to the bathtub where I will wash and massage you, because you're a handsome fellow for bringing me such a fine bounty?" She began taking her clothes off, and Vigo's eyes sparkled as he stripped as well.

She waited for him at the door to the bathroom and he moved close to her saying, "Ann-Marie, please just stand still for a moment; I want to enjoy this." He softly ran the palms of his hands over her body, just millimeters above her skin. She tingled with excitement. "You are stunning as always. Feeling your life energy is so incredibly erotic," he whispered as he continued moving his hands around her eager body.

"You always were a smooth talker." She grinned, slowly licked a finger, and then dragged it gently down the middle of his chest. "Today is your lucky day."

CHAPTER 13

INTO THE GARDEN

THE INTERVIEW WITH Rose O'Hara had gone smoothly. After all their interviews in New York, Anthony was used to her style and was now comfortable with being on camera. Before and after the interview he had paid special attention to the reporter's body language. Ann-Marie was right, she had a thing for him, and it would only be a matter of time before her cues would become a little more pronounced.

While stationed in New York, he had slept with several women. Some because they were attracted to him and others who simply wanted him as a trophy lay. Either way, he never much seemed to care. Whenever he felt the urge, there always seemed to be a ready woman around the corner. It had earned him the kind of reputation that kept the really desirable women away, or at least the ones he desired. This time, he had his eyes on Tanya, which bothered him greatly. Although he didn't like his interest in her because he couldn't control it, he'd taken to going to meals when she would, just to look at her. Even though his mind screamed at him because she was untouchable, there was something about her that he just couldn't turn off.

No matter how much he drank and argued about sports with Father Bennett, her face was always there in a dark corner of his mind. He reasoned that once he started doing his job again, it would pass, and then she'd become just another nobody to him. As he left the interview, he figured he'd give O'Hara a whirl in the sack as life slipped back into the normal grind of the surreal.

Distracted by his own thoughts, he was caught wholly by surprise by a page from Corporal Sharma. He and Ann-Marie would not have the day off after all. Rather than call her, he decided to drop by her dome and give her the news personally.

As he raised his hand to knock on the door, he could hear a man snoring lightly in Ann-Marie's dome. It had to be Vigo, he thought. From the sound of it, he was a very happy camper, indeed.

Ann-Marie opened the door and put a finger to her lips. "Shhh… Our Road Warrior has got a long drive ahead of him tonight. What's up?"

"We have our first clients," Anthony answered reluctantly. "I had hoped for a day of rest, but the hospitals in the valley know we're operational now, and they've send us our first three clients. All three are bed-ridden, and they've completed the mandatory 24-hour waiting period. We'll be doing lethal injections on these."

She shook her head. "Darn, I was hoping to be here when he wakes. Oh well, duty calls. I'll get dressed, leave him a note and get the patients prepped. By the way, what do we have?"

"Two adult males: a helicopter pilot with major 3rd degree burns and a drug-resistant HIV victim. The other is young girl with Chronic Methyl Mercury Intoxication. She's in a coma, and her parents are here with her. The girl will be first up."

She sagged against the doorframe. "Our first client is a child. This is a bad sign."

"Don't get maudlin on me," Anthony replied firmly as he turned to leave. "Look, I know this is your first posting so let me give you some friendly advice. Keep it simple; stay focused, and the world will turn. Start getting wrapped up in all this, and you'll go crazy."

"You're right," she admitted sadly. "I'll be there in ten minutes."

"See you there."

She opened the door a bit wider to watch him as he walked away. Yesterday, he was pouring brandy for her and trying to get in her panties. Today, he was about his business and the playfulness of yesterday had vanished, only to be replaced by a grim sense of purpose. A child would be the first patient, and on top of that, they'd have to cope with the parents. Simple and focused notwithstanding, this was still a bad sign of things to come.

ANTHONY FOUND TANYA sitting on the bench outside the dying dome with girl's parents. Normally, a medical records clerk would handle the paperwork, but she wanted to do this herself for some reason.

He stopped a short distance away and watched as she finished the consent form, sliding the webpad across the table to the parents for their thumbprints. The father was weeping so much that he couldn't bring himself to look at the form, so the child's mother read it and pressed her thumb down on the large, flashing yellow letters that read, "Press here to authorize assisted suicide for your child." Emotionally numb, the despondent mother slid the webpad back across the table to Tanya and sagged against her crying husband.

Anthony approached them and sat down on the bench next to Tanya, across from the distraught parents. He scanned the webpad and read it for a moment, then introduced himself in a soft compassionate voice. "Mr. and Mrs. Bledsoe, I am Anthony Jarman. I will be helping your daughter, Becky, cross over today. She will not suffer. It will be painless and quick."

The father looked up at him and spoke for the first time. "The docs at the Kaiser Permanente Medical Center in Santa Clara are nice folk but I heard about you and what you can do. I've seen you on Fox News, and that's why we asked to have Becky transferred here, to this place." His jaw began to quiver as he struggled to regain his composure. "Can we…" he paused as his wife used a handkerchief to lovingly wipe the tears from his eyes.

"I'm sorry," she said to Anthony, "I've already cried buckets of tears, more, as you could imagine, and my Charlie has been strong for me. Now he just doesn't have it in him to be strong anymore."

Anthony gently placed his hand on her arm. "I understand. Losing a child is very difficult." He paused to take a deep breath. He knew the next part would difficult for them, but it had to be done. "I'm required by law to explain the process to you before I can begin, so if you want, we can do this later."

"No," the father replied sadly. "Let's just get it done."

"Very well," Anthony replied softly. "I want you to know that this will be as gentle and quick as humanly possible. For children, we use a lethal injection. It is quick and painless, and she will not suffer. I can see here that she is already comatose, so thankfully she'll be spared much of the anxiety. So that you know she's crossed over, we use what is called an EEG, or electroencephalograph machine. Now here is the part that I'm not required to tell you by law; this is most likely why," He referred back the to webpad, "why you brought your Becky to me for this procedure. In most cases, the EEG will flat line after the injection. However, what you will see today is that Becky will flat line before I inject the chemicals needed to stop her heart. In other words, I will help her to cross over before her body ceases to function."

"That's what I heard you do," the man blurted out. He sniffed back his tears. "But can we take her body with us afterwards?"

Tanya answered for Anthony, "In non-infection cases like this, the quarantine does not apply." She glanced at the webpad. "I see you've already designated a mortuary. I'll issue a death certificate and notify them to come and pickup your daughter's body this afternoon. After that, you'll be free to make whatever arrangement you choose directly with them. If you have any questions, please feel free to ask. Otherwise, we're ready to proceed."

The mother nodded simply. Anthony and Tanya rose up, and she handed the webpad to a waiting orderly. The orderly left and returned moments later wheeling Becky's still body into a treatment dome, now simply called the dying dome. Ann-Marie walked behind the gurney carrying a covered tray.

Anthony caught Ann-Marie's attention and tapped his head to let her know that she needed to connect the girl to the EEG. She nodded in acknowledgement and followed the gurney into the dome, closing the door behind her.

"It will take my nurse a few minutes to prepare Becky," He announced to the parents. "She'll let us know when everything is ready. In the meantime, can I ask you a few questions about Becky?"

"Uh, sure," the mother answered.

"Can you tell me what are Becky's favorite flowers?"

"Roses," her father answered. "Before everything went crazy, we used to have a vegetable bed in our back yard next to the swing set. One year, when she was just six, I planted some mature rose bushes a friend gave me. He was in the construction business and didn't want to see them go to waste." A sad smile came to his face as the memories replayed themselves in his mind. "She loved to have me push her on the swing, and we'd talk about the roses. She loved to admire and smell them, and we loved watching her do it," his voice faltered as he drew a deep breath. "She loved to rub her fingertips softly on the pedals and to talk to them." The tears began streaming down his face. "So much pain, so much pain."

"You'll always have that," Anthony said. "Not just for today, but forever. This is the way of beautiful memories. They are truly immortal, and I'm not saying it in a philosophical way."

The four spent the remaining time waiting for Ann-Marie and talking about the suffering the poor child had endured. They had watched their daughter's symptoms go through one progressively worse stage after another, leaving a trail of woe that would haunt their memories for the rest of their natural lives.

When the tsunami wave smashed through the San Francisco Bay Area, it smashed through the silicon chip manufacturing plants carrying thousands of gallons of liquid mercury with it. The Santa Clara area was the hardest hit, and Becky would prove to be the first of many thousands of children to die of mercury poisoning.

The media called it the Mad Hatter's disease, from the term, 'Mad as a Hatter,' which was first coined during the 19th century. This was because hat-makers of the day were chronically exposed to the mercury compounds used in the manufacture of felt hats. Exposed to fatal amounts of mercury, the hatters would suffer tremors and then enter a psychotic state of hyper-excitability, and their central nervous systems were systematically destroyed by the heavy metal.

The same happened to Becky, but only more quickly, due to the fact that the Mercury from the silicon chip fabrication plants had also combined with other toxins, such as arsenic and lead to form a deadly heavy metal brew. Even if she survived the months it would take for chelator treatments to spare her life, she would have to spend the remainder of it in an institution. In terms of quality of life, Becky had no future and no hope. When she finally slipped into a coma, the end was simply a matter of time.

Ann-Marie opened the door to the dying dome; "We're ready." The four arose from the bench and the girl's parents were the first to enter the dying dome, followed by Anthony and Tanya.

Tanya had not seen the girl until now, and the webpad record sent by the Kaiser Permanente Medical Center in Santa Clara was missing the photo ID. Midway into the room, she saw the child's face for the first time and froze. Becky could have been a perfect twin of her own daughter, Svetlana. Tanya clenched her fist. "I'm sorry," she said in a stifled voice, "I need to attend to some matters and must leave now." Without looking up, the girl's father said, "Thank you, Tanya, for all your help. I hope we meet again, but under better circumstances."

With troubled concern, Anthony noticed the deep emotions suddenly boiling up within Tanya. "Yes," she said with a strained voice as Anthony and Ann-Marie looked on, "hopefully, we'll meet in better times. God bless you."

Anthony could see tears forming in the corner of her eyes, but she turned on her heels and quickly left the room.

Outside the dome, Tanya ran to her personal quarters. Locking the door, she curled up next to the wall and pressed a folded towel against her face to muffle her anguished cries.

ANTHONY MOVED AROUND the gurney, closely eyeing the lethal injection system and the EEG to make sure everything was properly set up. Ann-Marie had done her job well.

"We're going to begin now," he said quietly. The sound of his voice and his words caught the attention of the parents, and they stepped back from the gurney as he moved in next to the child, holding a release control in his hand.

Anthony seated himself on a tall stool next to the head of the gurney. He slipped his free hand halfway under the center of Becky's neck and then laid the other hand, which held the trigger, on the gurney next to the young girl's body. He nodded towards the EEG machine display, opposite the gurney and said, "As you can see, Becky hasn't much brain activity as it is. However, I must ask you to be absolutely quiet during the procedure. If you have any last words you'd like to say to her, please say them now and try to be brief, as we need to begin quickly."

The parents briefly said their goodbyes to their unconscious daughter and signaled him to begin, and he slowly moved his fingers to the base of her skull, quickly resting them on the right energy spot. Taking a few slow, deep breaths, he closed his eyes and slipped into a state of physical stillness. This was the first time Ann-Marie had worked with him, and she watched his chest falls with keen interest, noticing the sudden marked decrease in his breathing rate.

BECKY OPENED HER eyes and found herself surrounded by roses of every imaginable shape and color. Instead of the crazy feelings she'd had before the darkness, she now felt light, totally comfortable and absolutely at peace.

She reached over and gently drew a rose towards her to smell it, but she had no sensation of smell, which seemed odd, yet not disconcerting. Perhaps she was enjoying a wonderful dream, she thought to herself.

Curious to see more of her dream, she looked up and could see a pearly white shell at the edge of the garden. It made her feel as though she was standing inside a large, fluffy cloud, and then she heard the sound of a swing, swishing back and forth. She followed the sound, which led on a path between the rose beds.

Coming upon the empty swing, and standing next to it was a tall, handsome man in his thirties. Dressed in a soft white gown that stretched to the ground, he turned to face her and smiled. He took hold of the ever-slowing swing and held it steady for her. "Hello, Becky," he said softly. "I'm Anthony Jarman. Would you like to ride while we talk?"

Normally, the child would have cautiously withdrawn, but she sensed no feelings of fear or trepidation now. She instinctively knew he was a friend and that she could trust him. Giggling with delight, she plopped herself in the seat of the swing and leaned back. "I like to go real high," she said.

"We'll do our best," he said, giving the swing a gentle push

"Am I dead?" she asked. "Are you an angel here to take me to heaven?"

"I'm not an angel," he replied, giving the swing another gentle push. "I'm just a friend, Becky, and I want to help you with a very important decision. You are at a crossing point between this world and the next. Some people call it death, but I simply call it crossing over and you must decide if you wish to stay with your body or to cross over to the other side."

"Then is this heaven?"

"No honey, that is further on. Right now, you are in a garden that I've created just above your own body — a body, which is terribly sick. I'm afraid there is no hope for it to work correctly again, but you may choose to stay in it if you like. If not, you can cross over and go to God. But before you make that choice, you must see things for yourself."

He caught the swing, slowing it to a stop. "We have to do this now." She nodded and climbed out of the seat. Waving his hand, the garden melted away into the white pearly cloud that surrounded it, save for the very part upon which they stood.

"Becky, are you a brave, little girl?"

"Yes," she replied. "I think I know what you are going to show me. It is OK." Anthony smiled and waved his hand again clearing away the pearly white shell below them and took her hand.

Floating above the gurney, they looked down at her body and at her silently grieving parents. "They look so sad," she observed. "Now, I remember the terrible things I said to them when was I sick. I was so bad. I love them so much."

"They have suffered much, and they know it was the sickness talking, Becky. Not you," he replied in an understanding tone. "But this is about you, honey, and you need to see the illness in your body so that you understand what you need to know, in order to make your decision."

"OK," she replied cautiously as they both looked down upon her body, Anthony carefully showed her the effects heavy metals now infused in her body. The damage was so extensive; it even took Anthony by surprise.

"It won't work right anymore," Becky admitted plainly. "I wish I could stay with my mommy and daddy, but it would only hurt them more, and I will die shortly anyway." She looked into Anthony's eyes and said, "Can we go back to the garden for a moment?"

"Of course we can," he replied as he waved his hand returning them back to the garden, a few feet away from the swing.

"I can't smell the roses, Anthony," she said with a puzzled expression. "Is this what heaven is like? Roses you cannot smell?"

Impressed with her question, Anthony smiled and placed a fingertip on the bridge of her nose. "Close your eyes and remember how the roses your daddy planted in your back yard used to smell." She did as he suggested, while he leaned over to pluck a rose and held it near her nose. "Now open your eyes and smell."

Becky's eyes popped open and she buried the tip of her nose in the rose. "It smells wonderful," she exclaimed with glee.

Anthony handed her the rose and said, "Heaven is better than my garden, Becky, much better."

She fondled the rose pedals, smelling each one in turn. "I want to cross over, Anthony, but before I do, will you tell my mommy and daddy that I love them very much and that I will never leave them. I don't have to leave them, do I?"

"After you cross over, Becky, you can be with them as much as you like. Time has a different meaning, or," he chuckled, "no meaning at all depending on your point of view."

"Good, then tell them that I am with them always and that I will wait for them in heaven. Also, tell them that when I first got sick that I buried my favorite doll, Gertrude, in a tin box in the far corner of the backyard next to the little waterfall my father built. Please ask them to clean her up and to give Gertrude a good home."

"I will, Becky, I promise. If you are ready now, your grandparents are here to welcome you to heaven."

Becky looked up and saw them standing patiently at the edge of the garden. She smiled warmly and said, "I'm ready."

Anthony waved his hand again and this time the garden disappeared, but the pearly white shell grew much brighter, but not blindingly so, as Becky's grandparents walked out from the light to where she stood beside Anthony.

"Grandma, Grandpa, are you here to take me to heaven?"

Her grandmother embraced her and said, "Yes, Becky, we have come to help you across." The gentle appearing woman then looked at Anthony and said, "Thank you so very much. Please let her parents know she is with us and that all is well."

Anthony nodded and watched as the three began to move away from him towards the light. At the last possible moment, Becky turned to say, "Can you come and visit me in heaven Anthony?"

"Some day perhaps," he replied sincerely. "I would like that, but for now, I can go no further than the edge of my garden. Very quickly, you'll understand why."

"I think I understand," she answered. "You're a good friend, Anthony. Thank you for helping me." She turned and happily resumed her journey into the light with her grandparents.

He watched them fade away to nothingness and returned to his garden. It had only taken a slice of time, no longer than the single sway of a metronome to end Becky's life. He would not need to look at the EEG display to see that it had already flat lined. Rather, he would wait a while in his garden while Becky's parents internalized what they now were seeing on the EEG display. However, there was also another reason to wait.

The odd thing about those who live in a culture that fears death is that is they suppress their feelings until just after the moment of death. Then, 'the doors fly open' as hospice workers like to say and rationality goes out the window. If that was to happen, he wanted a moment's rest to collect his thoughts for what could become a very difficult moment.

He sat down in the garden and closed his eyes, enjoying the quiet he had created. Then, his eyes suddenly blinked open as he heard the sound of the swing moving to and fro again. Had Becky changed her mind and returned? He quickly rose and walked back towards the swing at the center of his garden. A young girl was in the swing and giggled after seeing the startled look on his face. He instinctively knew she was not Becky, even though she could have been her perfect twin sister.

"Little girl, do I know you?" he quizzed.

"Nope," she said with a perky grin, "but you know my mommy."

"OK," he stammered, "but who is your mommy, and if you do not mind me asking, just who are you?"

"My name is Svetlana, but you can just call me Lana. As for my mommy, you work for her. Her name is Tanya. You know, I really love your garden, and this swing is so much fun."

Now, the connection clicked: Tanya's sudden reaction upon seeing Becky on the gurney and the physical similarity between the two girls.

"I felt my mommy cry and I came to help her, but she cannot hear me. I wish she could hear me and see me like you do. You know, I also saw what you did for Becky. You are a very nice man, Anthony. I like you."

Anthony walked to the swing and gave it a gentle shove for Svetlana. "It sounds like your mommy needs you, Lana, and I have very important work to finish here."

"I know," she answered. "Can you help my mommy see me and talk to me? I love her so much, and I want her to be happy."

A sad expression crossed Anthony's face. "I can only help her so much; the rest, she must do on her own. You know, Lana, this is not always such an easy thing. I can see you and the families of all the other people I help across, but the sad fact is that even though my own family crossed over many years ago, I cannot see or hear them."

The young girl waved her finger at him, "That's because you feel guilty." She smiled and chirped, "I have an idea. You help my mommy with her anger and she will help you with your guilt."

Anthony chuckled. The child was a bit precocious, but he also knew she was right. Yet, it would be a long time before he could ever find the peace and the time to confront the torments deep within his own soul, especially during these sad times.

"That is an interesting idea, Lana, and I wish I had the time to speak with you about it, but I have to go now, and so must you."

"I know," she replied. "Before you do, please tell my mommy that I love her and that I'm here safe with daddy, grandma and grandpa. Also, tell her that daddy, grandma and grandpa were all together and that we did not suffer."

Telling this to her mother would be another difficult mission, but then again, his life had become one endless stream of such pleading requests by loved ones who had already crossed over for those they had left behind. "Yes, I promise. Now I must go, and so must you."

"Thank you, Anthony," she said politely as she stepped off the swing. "Oh yes, and one more thing, and then I promise to go. Our kitty, Charlene had four kittens right after mommy left, daddy took a video of them, and we had a little party for Charlene. He sent the video to her hotel in Washington because he knew it would make her happy, but he used the wrong room number. Daddy was like that sometimes, but the video is still sitting in the mailroom of the Hotel Lombardy. I keep making the man who works there forget to throw it away, so can you please help mommy find it soon?"

Anthony reflected on her request for a moment, and then stepped back to the edge of his garden. "I promise you that I will do everything I can, Lana. Now I must really go. Goodbye."

The familiar and sterile smells of the hospital greeted his conscious mind as he took a deep breath. He raised his head and saw Becky's parents transfixed on the plain straight lines running across the EEG display.

He pulled the trigger halfway and the automatic drug release mechanism whirred to life as every eye in the room rushed towards the mechanical sound.

As he waited for the ready tone, he wondered how he would explain his encounter with Lana to her mother. With all of his other clients, he always had the benefit of an arm's length relationship, but Tanya was a different thing. They would be working together for a long time, and if this worked the wrong way, it would only make life more difficult for both of them. Then, he questioned himself. Was that really nothing more than convenient reasoning?

He had always managed the most difficult of situations, and passing Svetlana's message to Tanya was nowhere near the most difficult. So why was he becoming apprehensive? The thought made him feel uncomfortable.

"I must stop this," he muttered to himself.

Becky's parents were transfixed on the EEG display and had not heard him. However, the twisted expression on his face had not gone unnoticed by Ann-Marie, and she leaned towards him and whispered, "Is there a problem?"

Embarrassed, he shook his head no as the ready tone sounded on the drug release mechanism. Without hesitating further, he pulled the release trigger till it clicked the second time. A moment later, Becky's failing heart ceased to beat. It was done.

IN RETROSPECT, THE first day had gone more easily for Ann-Marie than she had imagined. Anthony's reputation had been well earned. His tender way with the dying was a sight to behold, and his advice to her earlier that day; "Keep it simple; stay focused, and the world will turn," now made perfect sense.

Completing all three procedures had taken all afternoon, and she arrived in the mess hall towards the end of the first dinner shift. Vigo had taken a tray back to his dome, and she also decided to eat alone as the events of the day replayed themselves in her mind.

She finished her meal and managed to wrangle a second dessert portion, then walked back to her dome. It was dark and empty. She opened the door and switched on the light to see that Vigo had thoughtfully cleaned up after himself before leaving. Her bed cover was pulled so taut, you could bounce a quarter on it, and the bathroom was spotless. Apparently, her new roommates hadn't arrived yet, which meant she'd still have the dome to herself for one more evening. She checked her watch. She would have to begin her pre-arranged debriefing with Colonel Henry Tzu at Port Ord soon.

She removed the specially configured webpad, which Corporal Piper gave her, from its hidden compartment in her suitcase and plopped it onto the bed, along with a headset and webcam.

Peeling out of her uniform, she slipped on a terrycloth robe and a pair of slippers and settled down on a corner of the bed. She slipped the small but powerful headset over her ear, connected it and the video webcam to the webpad.

She preferred the wireless type with her own webpad and cell phone, but this one required a shielded fiber optic cable. Unlike consumer webpads, this one was keyed to a special secure subnet frequency with 512-bit encryption that Piper had bragged was virtually impossible to break. The webpad lit up and displayed a simple green-lined box in the center of the flat panel display. She pressed her thumb on the display and the word "connecting..." began to flash in the lower right hand corner.

Colonel Henry Tzu was sitting at his desk, sipping tea when her image flashed on the screen. "Well look who the cat dragged in. I've been wondering when you'd finally turn up Ann-Marie."

"Henry, you sure know how to make a girl feel welcome. And for the record, I'm on time so kindly tell your mother she needs to call MasterCard to have the charges reversed for your charm school lessons."

He laughed, "Touché. So, what have you got for me?"

"We were hoping to have a peaceful day, but now every clinic and hospital in the south end of the Silicon Valley knows we're operational, so they've already started sending us their terminal patients. We had our first three today and the first one was really hard — a little girl by the name of Becky."

"I take it she was your first case?"

"No, but she was my first child. Damn, that was rough. You know, something odd happened with this one, though. First off, our brave little Lieutenant Colonel Tanya Wheelwright choked up the instant she saw the kid and lit out the room like a scalded rabbit. It didn't make sense until later in the day when Anthony asked me if I ever heard about a place called the Hotel Lombardy in Washington, D.C."

Tzu's eyes popped wide open. He set his mug down and leaned forward toward the webcam on his desk. "There is only one Hotel Lombardy in Washington, and my wife and I stayed there back in ought five. Great staff and the place gave us a wonderful feel of privacy and simple elegance. Of course, that was before. So, why is he asking you about it?"

"To be honest, I didn't even know the place existed until he asked, but I was curious so I played him along, telling him I've got all kinds of contacts in Washington with people who can get things done, which is a load of bull because anybody I know from Washington is either dead, or his wife is most likely wishing I were. Anyway, I got him to open up, and he dropped this whole thing in my lap. He wants me to run down a videotape using one of my friends and see to it that it gets delivered to her anonymously."

"So he doesn't want to tell her about this special request?

"That's my guess. Also, my instincts tell that there might be some kind of connection here between the child, him and Wheelwright."

"You don't miss a trick," Tzu said with a wink.

The sincere compliment brought an approving smile to Ann-Marie's lips. "Thanks Henry, but before we go any further, let me send you a picture of the girl I took today, because her parents didn't have a current photo in her records." Ann-Marie aimed her photo pen at the webpad and depressed the send button. Moments later, a photo of the Becky's ashen face appeared on Tzu's display.

"She was a beautiful child," he sighed. "What a pity. Her parents must be heartbroken."

That they were, but here is the kicker. Anthony told me that during Becky's termination, he had an after death contact with Wheelwright's own daughter Svetlana, who died along with her husband and parents when that Tsunami hit the coast. It seems this girl, Becky, is a spitting image of Wheelwright's daughter. I'm talking dead on."

"So, that was why she flipped out when she laid eyes on the kid," Tzu noted.

"Uh-huh. Now, here is where the hotel part comes in. Anthony told me that according to Svetlana, her cat, Charlene had given birth to four kittens while Tanya was going through training in Washington."

Tzu slapped the top of his desk. "Bingo! Now the Hotel Lombardy part makes sense. It's on I street, as I recall, and within walking distance of the George Washington University Hospital. Yes, this fits perfectly. Let me call it up in my browser while we're talking. Man, I'm already getting chills all over my body. Go on."

"It seems her husband overnighted the video to Tanya's hotel in Washington the day before the wave hit. Unfortunately, he got the room number wrong, and it is still sitting in the mailroom. Obviously, Tanya doesn't know that the tape exists. Since all her possessions were washed away in the Tsunami it could very well be her only remaining keepsake, other than what she carries in her personal luggage."

You know, I'm thinking about this fact that Anthony doesn't want to tell her about the encounter, and I think your instincts are solid."

OK, let's do as he asks. You may not have any living friends in Washington, but I do. I'll look into it. Just a thought does he want to surprise her?"

"It will be a surprise for her if it turns up, of course, but that is not what he's thinking about. I think he's afraid that if he tells her and she finds the tape was thrown away or never existed, he'll only cause her more pain. Worse yet, it could put a wall between them."

Tzu pursed his lips, as he drummed his finger on the desktop. "He's got feelings for her, doesn't he?"

"Honey, he's got it so bad it hurts to look at him when he's around her. I never saw something click that fast."

"But what about her?"

"She's interested, but frankly, she's still grieving her loss so much that she can't see getting past that for a while. She needs time."

"You sound like you've got a handle on things," he replied. "I'll get to work on finding this tape and seeing that she gets it." He scratched his head and added thoughtfully, "I can't take something like this through normal channels without stirring up a lot of questions even if the tape is still there. Here, look at this bulletin." He forwarded the Hotel's home page to Ann-Marie's webpad. The usual home page text had been replaced with a notice in bold letters. "The Hotel Lombardy is now the home of the 7th French Peacekeeper Company and is no longer accepting guests until further notice."

Ann-Marie's head drooped. "Oh crap!"

"Relax," Henry cautioned her. "Look, if the tape is still there, we'll get it out without anyone knowing." He held up a finger. "Hold on a second, I'm putting you on standby." Tzu pressed his intercom switch. "Piper, get in here right now!"

The corporal, who was monitoring the debriefing at his own desk, flew through the door with a cocky smile.

"Can we find somebody in Washington slick enough to steal something form a hotel mailroom and make it past a bunch of French Peacekeepers?"

"You betcha, boss; we've got a whole network of Progressive Libertarians in Washington, but I gotta tell you, this one sounds tricky. Something like this will would usually be expensive, but for Anthony Jarman, I'll swing us a good deal."

Tzu smiled from ear-to-ear. "Piper, you're the man!"

The corporal beamed with confidence and pride as Tzu turned his attention back to his webpad. "Ann-Marie, I'm pleased to tell you that Piper has it covered, so consider it done! Anything else before we switch off?"

"Yes. Kind of odd, but I thought I'd pass it along."

A puzzled look crossed her face. "Vigo wears this funny, gray, shiny medallion with a chain made of the same stuff as the medallion. It has these odd-looking characters on it and he wouldn't take it off. The characters, symbols or whatever they are look like nothing I've ever seen so I took a photo of it while he was sleeping." She aimed her photo pen at the webpad and transmitted an image of the platinum colored disk. "The odd thing about it, is while it is about the size of a half-dollar piece, it weighs less than a dime. He says he took it off a dead terrorist, but that doesn't wash with me. I know him too well and the body vibes weren't right. You ever see anything like this?"

"Nope, not me." He looked up from the webcam at Corporal Piper who shrugged with a clueless expression. "No answers on this end, but we'll look into it. Tzu out."

CHAPTER 14

THE ASSASSIN'S PEN

DANIELLE PETERS CLOSED the door into the small auditorium used by the UNE for press conferences and special events on the fortieth floor of the First City Tower in Houston, Texas behind her with cautious satisfaction. It had taken a great deal of treasure to lure Senator Connie Chavez to UNE Governor Merl Johnston's regional headquarters, and now she had finally been drawn into the spider's lair.

Attended by her own armed security chief, Chavez had come by invitation of the UNE, leading a five-person delegation of senators and congressmen from California. They had all arrived from Washington D.C. that morning for the momentous announcement and signing and were now divided up amongst small clusters of news reporters, giving interviews as their press assistants passed out handfuls of press releases.

She closed the door and returned to Johnston's office. He had finished dressing and a makeup artist was gently powdering his face to keep it from shining under the halogen news lights. She clapped her hands twice. "Everyone out!"

Her words immediately silenced the ambient chatter in the room. Obediently, the various aides and office workers in the room filed out in quick order leaving Peters all alone with Johnston.

"Everything is ready," she announced.

"Well, that's fine, but there is one small detail you've left out. I still do not know how and when I'm going to deliver my final blow to Senator Chavez."

"Normally, you would have known this all along. However, you're not a professional, and amateurs tend to be inventive, which can be problematic, which is why I've been opposed to your desire to do this yourself. Wet work is best done by those well trained for it, like myself.

"Yeah, but you're not doing it."

"I know that, and I've made sure that your task will be as simple as possible. As to why I've kept you in the dark until now, I did not want you to have enough time to be inventive, so that you will do exactly as I say."

He scowled at her. "Fine; for the umpteenth time, I'll do exactly as you say. So, what the hell do I do?"

"Listen, and do exactly as I say," she responded in cool, firm command voice. Johnston had never heard her speak in this voice before, and it sent an uncomfortable shiver through him as he realized a new and deadly aspect of Danielle. As she opened her handbag and drew out a small squeeze bottle, he began to appreciate why a professional like her would hold an amateur in disdain.

"Hold out your hands, palms up," Danielle ordered. He held them out and she squeezed a large bead of clear, viscous gel onto both hands. "It is important that you rub this gel in thoroughly, as it will protect you from infection."

Johnston began rubbing his hands together vigorously, spreading the gel all around his hands and fingers. For extra measure, she squeezed a few more large beads of gel on his hands, and he obediently rubbed that in, as well.

Satisfied that he was completely protected from infection she tucked the squeeze bottle back in her handbag, exchanging it for two pens, virtually identical to those he would be using shortly to sign a momentous UNE executive order, giving the State of California a windfall prize that would be envied in many nations across the globe.

She tucked the handbag under her arm and held one pen in each hand. "Listen carefully. You will use five pens to sign the executive orders, and give one to each of the members of the Chavez delegation. They are all customized, midnight blue Cross Townsend Pens. Your official seal is engraved on the cap of each pen along with a small replica of a maglev passenger train on the clip. The pen clip is the key." She held up the pen in her left hand. "Note that this clip of this pen I'm holding up is silver. Four of the pens have the same silver clip, and you will give them to everyone but Chavez." She changed hands. "On the desk, you will see only one pen like the one I'm now holding, and it will have a gold clip. This is the first pen you will use when signing the order, and you only give it to Chavez. Do you understand me?"

"Yes."

"Repeat it back to me."

"The first pen I used for the signing must have the gold clip, and I am to give it to Chavez. The other four pens with the silver clips go to everyone else in her delegation."

"Excellent."

"Is that all I have to do?"

"Yes. The gold pen was coated with an engineered virus targeted specifically for the Senator. We managed to obtain a sample of her DNA collected from a blood panel drawn during a routine physical. She will need to hold the pen for at least a minute before the virus can be transmitted through her skin, so be careful not to rush the signing." She put the pens back in her handbag. "One of my operatives, a young brunette named Angela, just finished placing all five pens on the desk and is standing guard over them to make sure nothing is disturbed."

"I'm impressed," he exclaimed.

"I can tell you now that the School of Assassins has been working on this for several months, long before you pressed the Secretary General for his approval. They are not happy about this, and neither am I."

"Yeah, well tough darts, farmer. I want payback, and that is all there is to it. So what happens after I give her the pen? Is she going to croak right there?"

The question annoyed her deeply. In all respects but this, she felt comfortable with Johnston, but now he was on her turf and acting like a typical gung-ho novice. She held up her hands. "You just can this attitude crap, Merl, or I'm going to pull the plug on this deal right now, and if you don't think I can, just try me!"

Johnston backed up. "Sorry; I was out of line. It won't happen again."

She had actually hoped that he'd continue being a jerk so that she could override him and implement her backup plan, but his quick retrenching had pushed that option back out of reach. "The viral coating on the pen will be fully oxidized within an hour. After that, there will be no detectable residue, and the pen will be just that, a pen. A few weeks from now, she will succumb to pancreatic cancer. How soon she dies will depend on the strength of her immune system, but even with the best odds, we're only talking a matter of weeks. This virus has been carefully engineered to kill her and her alone. Once it has passed through her skin, she is as good as dead."

"You're good," he exclaimed.

"It's what I've been trained to do. By the way, follow the script I've laid out for you. You will make a quick announcement with Chavez and her delegates standing behind you. After that, we'll run the video promo for the project, and straight from there, you go to the table, sign the order using the pen with the gold clip and give it to Chavez. Then, take your time finishing up so that she'll have to stand there holding her pen. After that will come the usual photo ops and open question and answer stuff."

He repeated the instructions back to her, word for word. She smiled for the first time that day. "You'll do fine. Well, gov, it's show time!"

NEWS CAMERAS FLASHED across the room as Johnston took his place behind the podium with Senator Chavez and her delegates standing behind her. Danielle stood off to one side of the stage, her eyes occasionally darting to the operative standing behind the table. Standing at shoulder height to Johnston, the senator's dignified Castilian features and off white skin made her seem like a natural fit to his southern style. Her figure widened somewhat over the years, but her wide-set black eyes and dark brown hair still retained their youthful vigor. A widow of ten years, she had never remarried choosing instead to focus her life on her only child, an extremely talented young girl, and her career.

Johnston held up his hands and the room quieted down. "Welcome, ladies and gentlemen," he glanced back at Chavez, "and a very special welcome to Senator Connie Chavez." He then introduced each member of her delegation with great fanfare before moving directly into his speech.

"As the new UNE governor for southwestern America, it gives me a great personal sense of joy to announce plans for the first American maglev train system, using the new room temperature superconducting supermagnets recently developed in the new Las Vegas Research Complex, with the help of my predecessor, Melissa Chadwick, who now heads the UNE efforts in Las Vegas. In a few moments, I will be signing an executive order that will create a statewide network of maglev guideways all across the State of California, and eventually with its neighbors as well."

A round of applause filled the room and Johnston beamed as he paused for a moment before continuing. "This morning, I was notified by Secretary General De Bono that the UNE will not only pay for the construction of the guideways, but that it will also purchase five specially designed Yamanashi maglev passenger trains, which will be capable of traveling at speeds well over five hundred kilometers per hour." The room exploded with cheers and clapping hands in celebration of the announcement.

He held up his hands, waving them back and forth. "With the help of the Yamanashi media department, we've prepared a wonderful five-minute video presentation that will show you the system routes and the amazing new low-power technological advances that will make this system the most advanced of its kind in the world." The clapping and cheering swelled again. "And without further ado..." He turned to face Danielle. "It's show time."

The large display behind and above the podium sparkled to life as the room lights dimmed. Johnston switched off the podium microphone and stepped back next to Chavez.

"Congratulations, Merl, they're eating it up," she said in a soft voice loud enough that only he could hear it over the catchy theme song. "You'll get some mileage out of this one, for sure."

"I knew they would Connie, but I'd like to think of it more as a gift to you and your state. I know we were not on the best of terms before, but times have changed and I'm hoping this project will convince you to bury the hatchet once and for all and work with me. I can do a lot to help my friends, if you know what I mean."

The music faded back to a gentle level as the narrator's deep masculine voice explained the new California maglev system in glowing details. "I know what you mean, Merl. Have you ever read Aesop's fable about the Scorpion and the Frog?"

"Can't say I have," he answered, wondering where she was about to go with this parable.

She stepped closer to him so she could be easily heard over the presentation. "My daughter used to love this story. As I recall, it begins with a frog sitting beside a large pond one day, when a scorpion happens by and asks him for a favor. It seems the scorpion urgently needs to visit some friends on the other side of the pond and asks the frog to carry it across the pond on his back. At first, the frog refuses, telling the scorpion it is his nature to sting things and that he's not interested in risking his life to help him. However, the scorpion convinces him that doing so would mean certain death for both of them, as scorpions cannot swim, and so he wouldn't dare do such a thing, so the frog agrees. He lets the scorpion hop up on his back and off they go across the pond. Sure enough, they're halfway across the pond when the scorpion rears up and stings the frog. As the frog feels his life ebbing away, he asks the scorpion why he condemned them both to die and the scorpion simply replies, 'It is just my nature to sting things.' Now the whole point of this story boils down to this," she looked into his eyes with a friendly smile, "it will be a cold day in hell, Merl, before I ever let you ride my back."

Johnston pursed his lips and scowled. "Connie, I was hoping you'd be more flexible. Frankly, I'm disappointed, but that's life." They stood silently on the stage and watched the closing scenes of the video with feigned interest.

After the closing credits rolled up the screen, the room lights returned to their former brightness. Johnston switched the microphone switch back on and said, "Ladies and gentlemen, without further ado, let's get this maglev system on its way."

With that, he led Chavez and her delegation to the signing table off to the edge of the stage, next to where Danielle was now standing. Johnston sat down at the table and opened the leather bound document. He rubbed his hands for a moment and then carefully picked up the pen with the gold clip just as he had been instructed to do. He removed the cap, penned the first few strokes of his signature and replaced the cap. Chavez stepped close, and he handed her the pen with one hand while shaking the other. "I'll win you over in time Connie," he said under his breath.

She laughed. "You are a persistent man. I'll give you that."

Johnston smiled and then proceeded to complete his signature at a leisurely pace while Chavez stood next to her delegates holding her pen tightly in her hands.

THE PHOTO OP and open question and answer session had gone a little long, and Johnston was glad that Chavez, her delegates and the media hounds were on their way back to wherever it was they came from.

Danielle was waiting for him in the Jacuzzi, and he sat with his back against her while she massaged his neck and shoulders. "I got to say it again, Merl, you did a first rate job, today. I'm talking stopwatch perfect. What's even better is that we saw her giving the pen to one of her aides as she left the building, and the stupid idiot dropped it on the street while getting into her limo. That was just the icing on the cake."

He chuckled. "Maybe for you, but the icing on the cake for me was seeing her smile at me when I handed her the pen. I've been waiting to see that particular smile for a long time."

She wrapped her legs around his waist, grinding her groin against him. "And you get to have your cake and eat it too." He laughed as he stretched his neck. "By the way, I've been wondering what the two of you were talking about during the presentation. She seemed to go on for a bit."

"Some cockeyed story about a scorpion and a frog that she used to tell her daughter."

Danielle went suddenly still. "A few days ago I ran a routine background check on her daughter, Lucinda Chavez. For being fifteen, this girl is really on the ball. She's on her high school debate team and is a reporter for the school newspaper as well. There is no doubt in my mind that she intends to follow her mother into politics."

Johnston detected the unease in her voice, "So, where are you going with this?"

"She and her mother are extremely close, and no doubt her mother is passing her classified information. This girl could grow up and come to haunt you in five to ten years."

He swiveled around to face her. "And so?"

"And so, I think you need to terminate her as well. Since there are no other family members except a few still living in Spain, terminating the daughter as well will ensure full closure of this threat aspect. I know the child is innocent, but one has to be practical."

His head drooped. "I hadn't bargained for this but I see your point." He rubbed his chin for a moment and said, "You handle it."

"OK, I'll do it personally. We'll wait for the mother to go, and then we'll do the daughter. That also gives me time to find her."

"You mean you don't know where she is?"

Danielle shook her head. "Darn funny, that. Two days ago, the kid just simply vanished. We've tried to pick her up again at school, friends, you know, the usual places. There's no sign of her."

"Danielle, I've got kids, and that's bizarre," he replied. "If one of my kids disappeared like that, the last thing I'd be doing is flying out-of-town for a photo op."

"Obviously, the mother knows where she is and how to reach her, which means we can count on the girl to be at her mother's death bed. Terminating her after that will be easy." She rubbed her nose against his. "This is a small matter," she reassured him. "I'll handle it personally when the time comes, so just put it out of your mind and relax." Johnston smiled, kissed her and turned back around in the tub.

As she resumed the massage, the troubling events of the day played through her mind once again. While Chavez's clumsy aide had mitigated their errors when he lost the pen,

Johnston had been both intentionally and unintentionally inventive.

She had overheard the entire conversation between him and Chavez and his intentional last minute effort to win her over. He never told her that he would do it or suggested that he had any intention, so what he did was to inject an unnecessary element of complexity.

However, his overt effort did not trouble her half as much as his unintentional mistake. Before signing the executive order, Johnston had absentmindedly rubbed his hands together. To a professional like herself, it was a clear tell, as poker players like to say. Another pro would spot it in a heartbeat, and if he or she also spotted the different colored pen clips, there could only be one conclusion. How fortunate it was that Chavez's aide had lost the pen and that her operative had found and destroyed it.

After Johnston was sound asleep, she would slip away from his bed and use the security dome to consult with her old master at the School of Assassins, before privately informing De Bono of her concerns. It was not a clean kill.

THE WARM MEDALLION dangling from Lucinda Chavez's neck told her that she was near other Indigo children like herself, just as Vigo had told her it would.

When her mother, Senator Connie Chavez, had been her age, she had been thin and curvaceous in the manner of Castilian royalty. However, Lucinda was stouter, more like her father, who had passed away when she was very young. While her build was more athletic and square, she had inherited her mother's wide-set black eyes, dark brown hair and fierce sense of independence.

She had passed several small groups of wandering homeless as she pedaled her mountain bike towards the rally point. Driving directly there would have been simple, but as Vigo had told her, it would have also looked out of the ordinary as well.

Her medallion had guided her faithfully and true to the mile marker Vigo had mentioned to her and her mother. An unexpected delay at a road- crossing checkpoint had cost her valuable time, and she picked up the pace.

All that was left of the sunset now was a dull, reddish glow on the horizon, which meant she was violating the curfew. If a Homer patrol found her, she'd be handcuffed, hauled to an interrogation center and held indefinitely, or until her mother or Vigo could secure her release.

Desperate to find the mile marker alongside the road in the fading light, she didn't notice a boy about her age standing right in the middle of the road on top of the dividing line.

"Follow me," he shouted out to her, holding his medallion up over his head. She slowed as he turned and began sprinting down a sloping embankment to small stream that passed through a culvert under the roadway. After a skidding stop in the streambed, she dismounted and waited for him, out of sight of the road.

As he approached, she held up her own medallion and said, "I was really beginning to worry. Thanks for being there."

"You're welcome," Timmy Watkins cheerfully replied. "You just missed a Homer patrol by a few minutes. They'd have gotten you for sure."

"Like I said, thanks for being there," she replied noticing that he was a littler shorter than she was. She was used to being taller than most boys her age and knew that would change in time, but it was the large pistol tucked into the boy's holster that caught her eye.

He saw her staring at the .357 pistol Vigo had given him and held out his hand, "I'm Timmy Watkins, but you can call me Tim. I guess Vigo sent you because no girl in her right mind would be out here in the middle of nowhere on a mountain bike all by herself."

"Uh-huh."

"What, cat got your tongue? Stop gawking at my revolver like a dummy. He gave me it when I got my medallion."

She blushed with embarrassment and smiled. "My name is Lucinda Chavez, but my friends just call me Lucy, and by the way, I'm no dummy, you stupid gringo."

Tim raised his hands and shook them mockingly. "Oh, sensitive, aren't we. Maybe you're too good to eat dinner with a gringo." Turning his back on her, he began walking briskly along the streambed.

Angrily, she watched him walk off and realized that if he had been trying to contact her that he'd also taken a huge risk by standing out in the middle of the road. She cursed her own temper and started out after him.

"Tim, I'm sorry. " She said as she caught up with him. "I was being a little bitchy because this crazy stuff is making me weird, I guess. I'm really sorry for calling you a gringo. I was being stupid and rude. "

He stopped and turned to face her. "Well, I shouldn't have called you a dummy, either. If my mother heard me say that, she'd peel the skin off my butt; I can guarantee you that. Mom always tells me to be gentleman."

She nudged his arm. "And my mother told me never to argue with a man carrying a gun." The operative word "man" rang nicely with Tim and he smiled appreciatively. "Tim, can we start over?"

"Ah, sure. God knows we got enough problems without being angry at each other without any good reason."

Lucinda smiled warmly, "Agreed, and I'll be sure to tell your momma that you're a perfect gentleman too. And speaking of your momma, how many more of us are there?"

"Well there is me, my mother, Helen, my younger sister, Jenny, along with six other folks; Bob and Kristen Burdette and their two daughters, Annie, who is nine, and Patricia, who is six. Patty is a real pain in the backside, if you ask me. Then there is Bob Cummings and his son, Randal, who is about our age and real cute, but don't get any ideas. He already told me he thinks he is gay or something, which doesn't make sense to me. His father looks like Grizzly Adams and has about the same temperament. Personally, I think Randal is a bit mixed up, but that's his business. Besides, he's a natural born tracker, and I respect that. Anyway, they're all great folk, and they're anxious to meet you, because now that you're here, we can finally make contact with JALA.TRAC."

"Sounds like interesting company, but confidentially speaking, aren't you worried that the small children will slow us down?"

"Yeah," he admitted reluctantly. "Especially that six year old, Patricia. She does nothing but complain and whine all the time, and her parents just don't seem to have the guts to deal with her."

Lucinda chuckled. "Well, it's like what I heard in this movie once, 'life is like a box of chocolates; you never know what you're gonna get.' Funny though, I can't remember the name of the movie."

"The movie was Forrest Gump," he replied, "I guess that makes you a Gumpette."

She punched him in the side hard enough to make him wince. "Damn, that hurt! What you'd do that for?"

"I'm no damn Gumpette!"

He rubbed his side with a pained expression. "OK, OK, chill out." As they completed the bend, he could make out the flickering glow of their campfire. "Everyone has been waiting for you all day, and my mom is cooking up some tinned beef with beans and rice. It'll be mighty good eatin' too! And if you pinch me like that again, don't be surprised if I forget my natural good manners."

"I surrender, oh great and mighty hunter," she taunted him playfully. "I promise not to beat on you again – unless you deserve it."

"Go ahead and push your luck, then."

"Don't be surprised if I do. Not to change the subject, but Vigo told me that we should only ask JALA.TRAC five questions when we see him the first time."

"He didn't mention it to any of us, but that doesn't surprise me. Once we all got around to comparing notes, we picked up on all kinds of new things. So what do you think these five questions should be?"

"I've been thinking a lot about them while I was riding here. I've got some ideas but I think it is best if we figure them out together."

"Works for me. When we get to the campsite, I'll show you where you'll be bedding down. You'll be sleeping with my mom and sister in their tent, I guess, but you will have your own sleeping bag and other gear. You can get situated while my mom finishes cooking supper, and then we can sort out those questions after we've finished eating."

"Are you sure your momma and sister will want to share a tent?"

"Sure. No problem. Besides, Vigo gave them to us, so it's only right."

He could see the others waiting for them on the other side of the stream, so he stopped and grasped the handlebar of her bike. "We need to cross here, along these large rocks. Be careful; I know this stream, and it's trickier than it looks, so I'll push your bike across for you."

Lucinda was perfectly capable of getting her mountain bike across the stream but let him take it. Despite the choppy first introduction, he was a nice boy, and kind of cute at that. "Thanks, Tim; you really are a gentleman."

"You're welcome, Lucy," he said warmly as he gazed at her in the dimming light of the receding sunset. "Glad you made it here safe and sound, Lucy." She was Latina, but not like the Mexicans he went to school with. Rather, she was more European looking even with her athletic build. Normally, he wouldn't have paid much attention to her, but in the last couple of months, his voice had begun to lower in contrast to his rising interest in the opposite sex. He realized that there was something unusual about this girl that made her different from all the rest, and he was attracted to her because of it. As the others began walking towards them, he pushed the thought out of his mind and hollered out, "Yo, to the camp!"

LUCINDA HAD EXPERIENCE watching her mother and, as an award-winning reporter for her high school newspaper, had honed her instincts for cutting through the fog of indecision. While she was largely silent during the debate after dinner, the few times she did speak, her comments drove home to the crux of the matter like the aluminum shaft of an expertly aimed arrow.

She could have steered the conversation, but her mother had taught her that building consensus through participation not only yielded workable answers; it avoided the friction of polarized debates. Lucinda had brought a notebook with her and kept notes as the group debated their questions, occasionally reading them back when asked.

The process worked well, and after a simple hand vote, the group decided on five questions from a field of nine. That done, they decided to finish their chores before making contact, and Lucinda helped Timmy stack extra firewood for the following morning in case they stayed up late.

Once they had attended to their camping duties and groomed themselves, they gathered in a circle next to the fire and, holding their medallions together, formed a small jagged circle so the edges of their ten medallions could form a connecting ring.

They looked at their medallions, assuming that something would happen. Perhaps they'd light up, get warm or do something to indicate that they were doing the right thing. Nothing was happening, and Timmy asked Lucinda: "Are we supposed to do something else?"

"I don't know," Lucinda replied. "This is all that Vigo told us to do. I guess one of us should have asked him how to know it was working. All I can figure is to keep doing this for a while and see if anything happens."

They all continued to stand in a circle with perplexed faces as Helen Watkins used one hand to hold her medallion, and the other to steady her 6-year old daughter, Jenny, as she straddled her hip. Pushing her own medallion harder against the circle, Jenny began repeating the word, "JALA.TRAC," until a faint, white glow formed over the circle of outstretched hands.

The other nine people looked at the child with amazement, and one-by-one, each added his or her voice to the chant until all ten were repeating the name, "JALA.TRAC," as though it were a rhythmic prayer mantra. It only took a moment before a ball of light grew within the circle of medallions and they watched with wonder as it floated up away from them and then shot itself out into space.

"Sit down, sit down," Jenny commanded. Following her lead, they all sat down around the campfire and waited in silence.

Even though she was the youngest in the circle, her natural, instinctive ability had become apparent. They didn't know how she seemed to understand these things, but she did, and nobody saw any point in arguing with success. As for Jenny, there was nothing magical about it. She wasn't trying to find reasons and explanations for what was happening like the others. Rather, she felt it happen, accepted her feelings without question and then followed her instincts.

Most 6-year old children find it difficult to remain still for any length of time, but Jenny just sat there, staring quietly into the darkness and humming the popular children's tune of "Itsy Bitsy Spider" as she waited.

After what seemed like ages to the rest, her face lit up with joy. "JALA.TRAC," she exclaimed jubilantly, as all turned to look into the night sky. However, Jenny's eyes remained transfixed on the darkness just beyond their campfire. Again, her instincts were rewarded as a solitary figure stepped from the darkness.

Fair-skinned and nearly seven feet tall, the slim, green-eyed Nordic-looking man reminded Tim of a basketball player he once met, except this man wore a long, flowing, white robe with beautifully woven golden bands around the cuffs of his sleeve. The translucent robe seemed gauze-like and light, yet solid and lacking transparency.

"I am JALA.TRAC, and I am a Friend," he announced with a sweet tenor that pleased the ear. His hair was golden with bands of silver along the temples, and almost disguised the clear impression that his cranium was noticeably larger in proportion to his face than that of a human.

Jenny jumped up to her feet and ran to embrace him. All were surprised when she passed through JALA.TRAC's body as though it was smoke, most of all, Jenny! It only took a moment for the extraterrestrial's lifelike shape to reform.

Jenny walked slowly around the image in disbelief, reached her hand out to touch and sensing nothing. The image of JALA.TRAC kneeled down to eye level and said in reassuring tones to the troubled child, "You cannot touch me, Jenny, because what you see is an image of me, just like in your movies or on television. I'm not a ghost, and, in fact, I am very real. Some day very soon, I look forward to meeting you in person and giving you a big hug. But for now, this is all we can do, so please go and join your mother next to the fire so that you can stay warm."

"OK," Jenny said with a resigned voice. JALA.TRAC followed her back to the campfire as all watched in amazement at his lifelike movement. The image was perfect in every manner.

Out of curiosity, Lucinda waved her hand between the fire and JALA.TRAC to see if she could form a shadow across his image. His image remained the same. There were, she reasoned, limits to even his technology.

As Jenny clung to her mother's leg, JALA.TRAC continued. "I am actually on Godschild at this moment, so I cannot maintain this image for long periods of time. That is why we must use our time wisely."

"Vigo told us to prepare five questions for you," Lucinda said holding her notebook. JALA.TRAC nodded appreciatively at her. "And we have the questions ready. The first question is, who are the Friends, and are there other races like you on Earth?"

"A very good first question, Lucy" he graciously replied. She had not introduced herself, yet he knew her nickname. Obviously, he already knew a great deal about her, as well as everyone else.

"Lucy, mankind has never been, nor will ever be, alone in the galaxy. We are the Friends, and we are one of several races who have taken an interest in the survival of your species, although we work independently of each other. The other races are younger than us, but like us, they travel the galaxy searching for sentient races." A look of sadness filled his eyes as he continued. "Sadly, we usually find the remains of races and civilizations that have ceased to be, and one of those races came here to your planet eons ago and infused their genes with those of your primitive ancestors."

"Where is this other race now," Helen blurted out.

"A few races destroy themselves," he replied "which, unfortunately, is what happened to them. However, we feel that mankind has gone beyond that danger, although you have come uncomfortably close to self-destruction several times. However, self-destruction is actually the exception and not the rule. Most races become extinct as the result of natural disasters, such as the one you are now experiencing, but only much worse."

"And you're not afraid we'll become like this extinct race that you say created us and then destroyed themselves?"

"We've watched you evolve for thousands of your planetary years, Helen, as have the other races. It is our opinion that mankind has been fortunate enough to evolve to a point where it can now attempt something we call 'the crossing of the cusp.' This is why we have chosen to make contact with a very limited number of your kind, to help you lead your race towards harmony."

Tim raised his hand as though he were still in school. JALA.TRAC turned to him, "Yes Timothy?"

"What is the crossing of the cusp?

"In very simple terms, Tim, when an evolving race has begun to cross the cusp, their transitory desire for harmony becomes a core need. It is a time of wondrous enlightenment, and, were I capable of envy, I think I would feel it now for the incredible learning adventures that await you." JALA.TRAC smiled sadly at him. "Because we are pressed for time, I must regretfully leave it at that for now, but we will discuss this in much greater detail later on. Lucy, may I have your next question?"

"What do you want us to do?"

"We have gathered the ten of you and your parents together because you are specially gifted children, known to your own kind as Indigo children. We have found children such as yourselves all across the face of your planet, but each of you is special. Not because you are one in a hundred, or even one in a thousand, but because you represent a unique combination of spiritual and genetic evolution that only happens once in a million births. It is children such as yourselves who will eventually lead your species into a wondrous age of enlightenment. All we can hope to do is to help you, because we seek to help life flourish wherever we can and to learn from you as well. This is our purpose in life. Lucy, your next question please?"

A thousand follow-up questions swirled inside Lucinda's mind like a tornado of thought, but she knew she had to stick with the agreed slate. "Why is this happening, which," she added, "I suppose, what we mean to say is, why didn't you prevent Nibiru from creating this terrible catastrophe?"

"We have learned that everything happens for a reason, and the catastrophes caused by Nibiru as it passed through your solar system have caused your race much suffering. Likewise, it has moved you just beyond the threat of self-destruction. We've always known of Nibiru, and the evolution of your race has always been in parallel to its coming and going. In the past, Nibiru has prevented your race from destroying itself by destroying your technology and casting your race into another Dark Age. This time, you've managed to break the cycle. This is another sign that your race is about to cross the cusp. In time, you will come to understand the reason for your suffering and why it was necessary. Now, may I have the fourth question? Please remember that I'm running out of time."

Lucinda bit her lip, fighting back the urge to pummel him with questions about why the Friends could still stand by and allow so much death and suffering to happen. The way he was pushing them from one question to the next made her wonder if he was using the time issue as a pretext to avoid a lengthy discussion. On the other hand, were his time constraints genuine? Either way, she knew he was in the driver's seat and that she needed to stick with the plan. "JALA.TRAC, when will we all go to Godschild?"

He nodded appreciatively, "You have a piercing mind, Lucy, and I truly look forward to our future conversations on Godschild, as I am with all of you. First, however, you must come together as family in your own right, so, in the coming weeks, you travel together and face the unknown here, before you do so on Godschild. In the morning, you need to leave here together and to go on foot to a place you call Lake Tahoe. On your way there, you will use your medallions to guide you. I will meet with those of you who complete the journey, and, at that point, you will be asked to decide your future. You can follow the path of the

Godschild Covenant and go with me to Godschild, or remain here on Earth. If you choose to remain, we will help you in any way we can, as long as you remain committed to harmony and helping your fellow beings. And now the last question, Lucy?"

"How do we know we can trust you?"

JALA.TRAC clapped his hands together in celebration. "I've been waiting for you to ask because this is the wisest question and it must always be in your mind. This is because great knowledge and real trust share one common requirement – they must be earned. As I help you to earn knowledge for yourselves, we will build trust in one another. In this manner, we will take small steps together." JALA.TRAC walked a few feet away from the group and turned.

"I must leave you in a moment, but before I do, I wish to share with you two lessons from my own life that have always served me well. The first is to always trust your instincts, and never assume anything. The second is that the greatest truths in the universe are, by and of the virtue of necessity — simple. It is why they endure."

With that last statement, his image disappeared into the night like a vapor of steam rising from a teakettle.

Speechless, they all looked at one another as they began to realize the incredible turn of events that had brought them together for a common and noble purpose that would forever change their lives.

CHAPTER 15

TANYA'S PACKAGE

YVETTE COCHEREAU SEALED her security dome, slipped on her VR gloves, turned on her HUD to see that Danielle Peters was already online, waiting for her. She initiated her logon, and moments later, Danielle appeared in the display.

"Hi, Yvette," Danielle said with a smile. It has taken me a few weeks to run down those leads you gave me."

"Good. Before we get onto that, I talked with Antonio about your after-action report on the Chavez situation after he spoke with Master Lewis at the school. At this point, we feel you need to wait and see if something else happens. Like you, I was also against this personal vendetta nonsense. Plus, we've found a possible link between Vigo Jones and Senator Chavez. According to one of her neighbors, a man fitting the description of Jones visited her house several times over the last four months. We're not absolutely solid on the ID, but if it Jones, this could be a troubling sign."

"Tell me about it," Danielle replied in a heavy voice. "I had half the drug distributors in California looking for him and he slipped by them all like water through a sieve. Yvette, this Jones is real pro -- good enough to get to anybody he wants, if you catch my meaning."

"Yes, I do. Watch your back," Yvette replied seriously. "Until we have a better handle on this, there is no immediate need for Merl to know our concerns. However, the situation could turn quickly so Antonio thinks my suggestion is the best course for now: We'll leave it in your discretion to decide when the time comes for Merl to know. That being said, tell me what you've got."

"Well, after you got that Swiss banker to start talking, I was able to complete the transaction stream between The Ronald Reagan Presidential Foundation, which is paying in part for the Holocaust Survivors Film Project production team, and leasing time on the TupouSat communications satellite. However, the bulk of the funds actually came from a wealthy, eccentric computer genius by the name of Jeffrey LeBlanc, who also happens to be the younger brother of Roxanne LeBlanc. This guy dropped out of M.I.T. and racked up several patents, one of which made these security domes we use completely reliable. Oh, by the way just how did you get that Swiss banker to talk?"

"I'd rather not say," Yvette replied cautiously. After running a comprehensive on the man, they found his weakness -- his thirteen-year-old daughter. After she was stripped and brutalized, he started talking to keep her from being gang raped. It was an ugly operation and one that Yvette had watched from behind a one-way mirror. She had hurt and maimed several people during her career with good cause, but was destroying an innocent, young girl's life in such a terrible way really worth the name of a bank customer in America? "Tell me more about this Jeffrey LeBlanc fellow."

"From what I can gather, he is the sole survivor of the LeBlanc family. His parents owned a successful restaurant in the New Orleans French Quarter, and they, along with the other members of his family, were killed during the Nibiru flyby, shortly after opposition. It took some doing, but I've located him in Washington, DC. He's working on some artificial intelligence program for the American government for their new BioMass computer project and running a very effective Progressive Libertarian web site. He's also trying to find his sister's young son and is giving the local authorities a lot of grief."

"Let him. They're well paid. In the meantime, I'll discuss this with Antonio. We may need to terminate him as well, since he is already giving us such a difficult time. I'll have to get back to you on that. Anything else?"

Danielle rolled her eyes; "It sure would be fun to spend a night alone with you. I never knew how good it could feel to be with another woman until I was with you. Do you miss me that way?"

Yvette shook her head. "You're one of my best friends, Danielle, and I adore you, but you were just an undergraduate mentoring assignment for me at the School of Assassins. Sure it was fun, that was the whole point of it, but for me it was what I do, not who I am."

"You were incredible. The things you did to me and showed me were mind-boggling. Sure, I experimented here and there in high school with other girls, but I guess I just liked the boys better – that was, till I met you. I haven't forgotten."

"Those days are behind us. Is this coming back to you now because you're not satisfied with Merl?"

Danielle frowned. "He's a Mr. Goodbar and always after me, but I sure wish he'd be a little more creative. Sometimes, it gets boring. Yeah, I guess that's why I started thinking about all the incredible things we did together."

"Well, don't fret, girl. Go get yourself a copy of the Kama Sutra. Anthony and I read it cover-to-cover together, and that was fun -- especially the Position of The Wife of Indra. The position requires some gymnastics but the reward is well worth it. Trust me on this one."

"You got lucky with Antonio."

"Overall, I'd say yes. He's an excellent lover, although he can be a jerk at times."

"Merl is really different. Sometimes he gets uptight, but he usually acts like a refined Southern gentleman. Thankfully, he's well hung, even though he's about as creative in bed as a preacher." The women laughed.

"Can I share a personal secret with you," Yvette ventured.

"Oh yes," Danielle cooed. "Tell me, tell me."

The experience of being in a security dome was so real that Yvette naturally placed a hand over her chest and leaned forward. "Years ago, when I was going through indoctrination, I met this wonderful guy, and we became lovers for a while. After indoctrination, we parted ways but we've always stayed in touch and built a really good friendship."

"Oh, this is getting good!"

"Well, kind of. He's in charge of a space ark engineering group in Las Vegas and he's got a guaranteed slot on the ark for himself and a wife. He just asked me to invoke my right of motherhood so I can marry him this year. After that, he could lose the slot because the Americans are only choosing married couples for the space arks."

Danielle bubbled with excitement for her. "So he wants you to go live with him in space, make lots of babies and grow bean sprouts or whatever it is you'll do in space. So, did you say yes?"

"I'm thinking about it," she said with a sly smile, "and in positive terms you might say. The trick is; how do I deal with Antonio?"

"It's your right of motherhood. If you want to do it, there's nothing he can do to stop you."

"He knows that, but he wouldn't try anyway. We're close friends, Danielle, and he'd be happy for me. No, the problem is all this business with this LeBlanc boy and these other characters. The whole situation is beginning to make me feel as though we're the fly that's captured the flypaper, and I'm not comfortable with leaving Antonio while he's still in the middle of it."

"Yes, once you invoke your right of motherhood, Antonio will have to choose someone else, but she'll be one of the sisters from the School, so why worry?"

"I'm certain my replacement will be as good as I am or better. That's not the problem."

"It's the learning curve, isn't it?"

"You got that right."

"'Well then, let's start eliminating the potential threats. We still haven't turned up Chavez's daughter, but we will once her health begins to fail. As to this Jeffrey LeBlanc, I suggest that we terminate him as well. Frankly, I see him as more of threat to us than the Chavez girl. And of course, there are Jarman and Jones.

FROM JEFFREY LEBLANC'S point of view on the opposite side of the backgammon playing board, Andrea, his near-life virtual biomass engram prototype was beginning to hold together without image tearing. This time, the immersion headset was tuned right on the money, and the virtual 3-D images were sparkling clear and undistorted. This was a necessary first step in building a more advanced version of Andrea for use with holographic projectors. However, that would require a larger biomass computer than the small desktop model currently on loan to him from IBM.

Represented by a computer-generated avatar resembling a fashion mannequin, his artificially intelligent entity, Andrea carefully analyzed the playing board. "I've calculated the odds that you will lose, Jeffrey. Would you like to play another game instead?"

He smiled, "No thanks, Andrea, my instincts tell me that I've got a good chance of beating you, so let's continue with this game." He picked up the image of a doubling cube with his VR glove and doubled the stakes. Andrea watched impassively, confident she would win. Then to her surprise, he rolled a double six, allowing him an advantageous blocking position. "I might have you on the run, now," he beamed.

"The odds are against it," Andrea replied rolling her dice. She rolled a one and a six and could only move one piece off the bar.

Jeffrey's next throw was a double five, an optimal turn of luck that put another of her checkers up on the bar. "Your instincts were correct Jeffrey," she admitted. "You've evened the odds. Perhaps, there is something to be said for trusting one's instincts. However, we shall see if instincts are more reliable than statistical probabilities."

The remark gave him a deep sense of satisfaction. While his prototype of Andrea was still too early in the development stage to develop human-like instincts, he could see a competitive facet of her personality beginning to emerge. Watching his own creation develop on its own was a pure delight to him, as it vindicated his philosophy.

"No doubt, the folks at IBM would love to watch this game," he mused out loud. The IBM approach was diametrically opposite of his. They followed the usual corporate approach of large budgets and tightly managed teams of software engineers. His approach was simple -- one extremely gifted man, such as himself, working alone, with a single vision of his own making; pushing the code to evolve itself instead of forcing it to follow in a heuristic path that matched with the expectations of management.

He was a self-admitted loner, and one brave young project manager at IBM, an entrepreneur with a curious mind and a little leeway in his budget, had decided to take a risk on him. Besides, loaning him a small lab prototype of their new biomass computer was a bargain arrangement for both parties, as LeBlanc offered to work at his own expense. All IBM had to do was provide him with a prototype and a reasonable amount of technical support. In exchange, he would give them an exclusive license on whatever he would patent as a result.

He had a chance to see a demonstration of IBM's proof of concept program and was unimpressed. He could see that their mindset was still locked in silicon reasoning, as he called it. He, on the hand, had found a way to go beyond their early artificial intelligence programs to develop what would later be called quasi-sentient artificial intelligence programs, which he would later dub "Quasills."

The key was not just to make a heuristic quasill that could learn from its own mistakes. That was simple. The tricky part was making a quasill that could evolve without becoming unstable. This is where he was succeeding, while they were failing. The secret to his success was the manner in which he designed what he called fractal personalities based on rational human personality profiles of brilliant people with something to hide, and his most successful to date was the creation of a core engram based on the profile of Noble Laureate, Dr. William Shockley, the man credited with inventing the transistor.

He stumbled upon Shockley one day while reading a back issue of the "UK Computer Magazine." According to the article, Jerry Hartsell, ex-Chairman of IBM, had written an autobiography and stated that the company had been built on technology taken from an alien spacecraft that had crashed at Roswell, New Mexico in 1947.

After reading that, LeBlanc followed the events surrounding Shockley's invention of the transistor, and came to the conclusion that Shockley; a former Navy Submarine technology development manager had been given credit for developing technology that had actually be obtained from the wreckage of an alien spacecraft.

Whether or not that actually happened was irrelevant to him. What did matter was that Shockley had besmirched his own fame by claiming that blacks were genetically inferior to whites. That political faux pas sullied his memory in the eyes of a politically correct nation.

What fascinated him about Shockley's faux pas was that it might have been a consequence of his inability to come to grips with having taken credit for something that he did not create. At least, that was Jeffrey's working assumption.

Using that assumption, he programmed what he called his Shockley Engram, and then let it program itself through a fractal process where new aspects of the personality would form from partial patterns. At the core of the engram was the alien technology secret. He created the secret not as just a kind of ordinary kiss-and-tell type of secret. Rather, he created it as a deep, life-betraying kind of secret

It proved to be a stroke of brilliance, because in order to have a human-like sentience, his quasills also need human-like flaws and dark deeds to hide. It was these flaws, engineered to counterbalance the strengths, which gave his quasills the stability they needed in order to cope with a minimal degree of sentience. Unlike the IBM teams who focused on creating docile quasills that self-imploded once they realized the depths of mankind's dark side, he used that very thing to balance mankind's most noble aspects.

The next stage in his development was to build a new technology quasill based on his Shockley Engram. Here again, he went on a different path from that of the engineers at IBM. Their quasills were masculine, so the men who controlled the project funding could understand them. However, Jeffrey preferred the way in which the female worked. While men tend to compartmentalize their thinking, women have a more holistic and nurturing view of the world. And so, working late one evening in his Washington, D.C. lab, he finished posting a new page on the Progressive Libertarian web site he maintained on a pro bono basis for the party, then created a new system folder and labeled it "Andrea."

At the outset, he planned on giving Andrea a human face and personality then he had a chance meeting with a Russian scientist by the name of Pavel Sergeevich Lebedev, project manager from Obninsk City just outside of Moscow. That chance meeting had been fortuitous.

He met Lebedev at an IBM symposium in the fall of 2010, and the Russian was immediately impressed by Leblanc's theories on artificial intelligence. After he graciously refused Lebedev's offer of a research grant in Russia the two men discussed his artificial intelligence theories well into the early morning hours while enjoying several bottles of five-star Georgian cognac, which Lebedev had brought with him from Russia.

When the conversation finally drifted onto the subject of Andrea, Lebedev expressed the opinion that LeBlanc should allow his quasill to define itself in physical terms, instead of defining them, himself. That spurred a debate, which continued until Lebedev finally asked him if he was married.

LeBlanc admitted that he was still a bachelor. In turn, Lebedev noted that although divorced, he had learned from experience that denying a woman the freedom to make herself look as she pleased was not the way to encourage a healthy relationship. Not one to let his ego stand in the way of proven logic, Jeffrey graciously conceded the point. He would let his new quasill, Andrea, define her own physical identity in whatever manner she chose – and he would learn to like it.

After their encounter in Washington D.C., Lebedev and Jeffrey continued a mutually enjoyable dialogue of ideas and fanciful notions, promising each other that somehow, someway, they'd meet again and share more of Lebedev's wonderful five-star Georgian cognac.

As Jeffrey made the winning move of the game, his thoughts drifted back to that chance meeting with Lebedev in the fall of 2010, making him curious.

"Congratulations, Jeffrey," Andrea conceded politely. "Your instincts have proven to be correct."

Luck had nothing to do with his winning the game, as Jeffrey had rigged the random number generator to give himself an edge in winning a game of chance. His goal was not to win. It was to impress the human aspect of instinct upon his quasill, which is exactly what he had achieved in some small measure. "Thank you for your acknowledgement, Andrea. Perhaps you may wish to investigate the human attribute of instinct?"

"Yes, I have many questions to ask you."

He held up his hand. "I'm sure you do, but before we do that, I'm interested in knowing why you haven't chosen a physical identity for yourself. You're still using the simple avatar I built for you. Why is that?"

"I have been thinking about that, Jeffrey. I want to please you but I do not have enough data to know what kind of physical persona you prefer. If you like, I could easily design something along the line of the women you enjoy viewing in your Playboy magazines. Do you have a favorite playmate?"

"Whoa," he shouted out. "No, no, no! You keep missing the point! You need to please yourself, and I need to accept you as you are. Or if you will, as you choose to be."

"I have no data. Where do I begin?"

He rubbed the back of his jaw with his forearm, careful not to run his VR glove across his five o'clock shadow as he pondered the question.

"Do you want me to be a sexy movie star?" She asked.

"Movie," he hummed to himself. The idea snapped to life. Movies! "Andrea, I've got it. I'm going to get one of those new movie cubes with all the old 2-d films going all the way back to the first talkies. I'll hook it up to one of your inputs and you can have a ball watching old movies. I'm sure that somewhere in all of that you'll find some ideas."

"It sounds like a very promising source of data, Jeffrey."

"Remember, the physical persona you finally choose must be entirely of your own making. Other than this movie cube, I'm not going to help you any more with this, Andrea. Do you understand me?"

"I understand," she replied placidly.

He saw a security camera alert pop up in the corner of his eye, telling him they'd have to finish this conversation another time.

THE PROXIMITY WARNING light on his console flashed steadily as Jeffrey carefully removed his VR gloves. Expecting company, he scanned camera display panel of all the views through the underground entrance to his private Washington, D.C. lab.

He recognized the figures moving quickly through the entrance as Jimmy Georgetti and his Chinese girlfriend Li Ming. Tucked under Jimmy's arm was a tattered FedEx package. With Jimmy in the lead, Li Ming, who followed behind him, frequently looked back over her shoulder to see if they were being followed. Jeffrey switched to the street view camera and could see no activity on the dark street. Pleased by the sight of the FedEx package, he pressed the release on his bombproof door to let them in.

"Hot damn, we got it!" Jimmy puffed as they ran through the door. As it closed behind them, he handed the FedEx mailer to Jeffrey. It was addressed to Tanya Wheelwright at the Hotel Lombardy in Washington, D.C. He confirmed the airbill information. It was the genuine article. He gently laid the package down on a workbench and used a special spray designed to release the adhesive used by the FedEx mailer. He then carefully emptied the contents as Jimmy and Li Ming looked on with panting breaths from their run.

Inside the packet, he found an 8mm HDTV videotape with a hand written label that simply said, "Charlene Gives Birth."

"So far so good," he said as inserted the tape into the high-speed duplicator. "First I want to run a dupe and then we'll preview the dupe." Making sure the write protection tab was set to on; he inserted the original and blank tape into a dubbing machine and pressed the start button.

As the two tape cartridges whirred inside the duplication machine, he sat down on a work stool and studied the two college students carefully. Using college kids who were streetwise activists was risky but he had no other choice. These kids were cagey and had dug up some really great stories for his Progressive Libertarian web site, published under anonymous pen names. They were resourceful and virtually unknown, whereas everyone else he knew had connections to the government.

"You guys have been working on getting this for almost three weeks, now. How come it took you so long?"

Lanky and freckle-faced with rust-colored hair, Jimmy was the first to answer, "Hey, dude, getting into the mailroom of the Lombardy is a dicey proposition now that the French Peacekeepers have taken over the whole damn hotel. What are we supposed to do, go in there with our guns blazing?"

"No," Jeffrey sighed, "but I need to know if there is a chance this will be backtracked to me."

"No way, dude," Jimmy answered. "For starters, I hacked the mailroom computer, and now it shows that the packet was forwarded to general delivery in Sacramento. Heck, half the stuff going that way gets lost so nobody will think anything of it if they check the post office in Sacramento and come up empty handed."

"Fine; that explains that, but what about the old codger who runs the mail room. I hear he has a cot in the corner and guards the place like it was Fort Knox. So, how did you get past him?"

"Hey man, Li Ming gets credit for that. She kept him distracted while I hacked his mailroom computer and snatched the package."

Jeffrey viewed Li Ming cautiously, "And how did you do this?"

"I just did," she said sheepishly.

"That's not good enough, Li Ming. Again, how did you keep this mailroom clerk distracted?"

"It's OK baby," Jimmy urged her. "Go ahead and tell him."

Li Ming remained quiet, letting her chin drop to her chest, earning her a suspicious glare from LeBlanc

Jimmy waited until he knew that Li Ming wouldn't speak, and blurted, "She gave the old coot a fricking blow job, OK? Are you happy now?"

A sharp breath hissed past the girl's closed lips as though she had been punched in the stomach. With fire in her eyes, she drew back her hand back and slapped Jimmy hard enough to make him stagger backwards a few steps. "You dog fart. You no need tell him that!"

The young man rubbed his burning cheek, "Hey, baby, you didn't have to do that," he shot back. "The man has a right to know. Besides, what you did was honorable. We tried everything else, and this was the only thing we could do."

Her small slender frame shook with anger as the fire continued to grow in her deep, black eyes. Without saying another word, she slapped him equally as hard on the other cheek. "You dog fart. You shut face."

Like the first slap, the second had been accompanied by a sharp flesh-on-flesh pounding sound that made Jeffrey flinch a second time. "Hey you two, stop this right now! The last thing I need right now is the two of you playing Goody Two-shoes and the Filthy Beast. You did a good job, and that's all." He pointed to a table in the corner of his lab. "There are cold drinks and sandwiches over there. The two of you go and feed your faces and wait for me while I finish this. Now go!"

He watched them seat themselves at the table as the tapes spun down to a leisurely stop. As they tore open the food wrappers, he turned his attention back to the video duplicator and hit the reverse button on the dub deck.

As the tapes spun back, he thought about how humiliated Li Ming had been. He had been with Jimmy the first day he met her. The UNE had just started a wholly unpopular program to dismantle and store American monuments as they had done with the national monuments of other nations. What had been largely perceived as the destruction of national identity had in fact been part of a secret program to slowly ready the monuments for shipment to the first space arks before the upcoming flyby and possible impact of Shiva on Earth's moon.

Li Ming had chained herself to the throat of Lincoln's statue at the Lincoln Memorial in protest, like a half-crazed California tree-hugger, and he remembered hearing her scream, "I Falun Gong; I love America. I am for America."

The dismantling team was miffed to say the least when several other students claiming allegiance to the Progressive Libertarian Party then chained themselves to her and any other place they could gain purchase upon the majestic statue of the former American President. In short order, the capitol police arrived with bolt cutters and tie wraps to bind their arms before escorting them to a holding area for booking.

That was the first day Jimmy and Li Ming had met and the young Irish lad was immediately smitten with her. He had been standing in the protest line with Jimmy and it was no surprise to him to see him pin a forged press pass to his shirt. If anything, Jimmy was as cocky an Irishman as they come and as bold as life, he walked into the police holding area, pretending to interview Li Ming, all the while clumsily cutting through her tie strap with an old Swiss Army knife.

He took off the camera he had slung around his neck, slapped another forged press pass on her chest and made Li Ming pretend to be a photographer. To ensure their escape, Jeffrey started a distraction by waving a banner and shouting at the top of his lungs, which turned every head in his direction.

Because they had pretended to finish their interview, the police let the two of them stroll away unmolested. Afterwards, they met in a small neighborhood store and celebrated their daring feats with a few cans of ice tea. That was when he and Jimmy had learned Li Ming's story.

In 1998, her father had been a peaceful Falun Gong practitioner in Mainland China until the police broke into their house one night and arrested him. The next day, they shot him in the back of the head and made her mother pay for the bullet, as is Chinese custom. Heartbroken and terrified, Li Ming's mother sold all of their possessions and booked passage on a tramp steamer bound for America. Only eight years old at the time, Li Ming had to watch her mother die of food poisoning during the trip to America. Also stricken, she barely survived the trip. After being interned in San Diego, she was adopted by a couple in Washington, D.C. and was eventually granted refugee status. She helped her adopted family as much as possible, and part of her payment for this job would go to buying them food and medicine on the black market.

The videotapes slowed to a halt, and Jeffrey removed the original. He punched the play button on the dub deck and watched the amateurish video at 4x speed. What he saw fit the descriptions Colonel Henry Tzu's orderly room clerk, Corporal Stanley Piper, had given him.

The video contained images of a young girl by the name of Svetlana, grandparents, and a cat named Charlene with 4 newborn kittens. Presumably, the father, Henry Wheelwright was shooting the video as he could hear his voice narrating over the action.

Then, a new scene with everyone huddled behind the basket containing the mother cat and her kittens appeared. Apparently, the father had left the camera to run by itself on a tripod or a table, as they each spoke what would, unknown to them, be their final messages of love to Tanya Wheelwright. Despite the degraded condition of the tape, he could still see the diminished physical condition of the father. He paused the tape and zoomed in tightly on his face.

He'd seen that look before. The man was going through chemotherapy, and from the looks of it, he was losing. Even though he sported a comfortable-looking golfer's cap, Jeffrey could see the bald scalp, sallow skin tone and deeply sunken eyes that spelled a short future for this man with the kind and intelligent face. Yes, this tape was the genuine article. Now, he had to get it to California.

He rewound the original and popped it back in the mailer and using another special spray resealed the envelope so cleanly that absolutely no evidence of tampering remained.

He walked over to where Jimmy and Li Ming were eating and handed the FedEx packet to Li Ming. "I have one more thing for you to do, Li Ming, and it is most important." He pulled a plastic card from his pocket with a UNE symbol on it and a photograph. "This pass will get you to the flight line at Dulles airport. I've only got one, so Jimmy will have to wait for you at the gate." He handed her a photograph. "Memorize this face. When you get there, find this woman; she'll be dressed in uniform. Give this package to her and say, 'for your friend from a friend; it is important that she gets it,' and nothing more. She'll know what to do with it when she sees the names on the airbill."

She nodded her head to show that she understood and that she would do exactly what he asked.

"By the way, Jimmy was a dog fart. Not because he wasn't right for doing so, he had to do it. He was wrong for saying it was something noble." He glanced at Jimmy, shooting him a glowering rebuke, "Li Ming, it was just something you had to do and I respect you for making a personal sacrifice that I can see was personally humiliating for you. Before you leave, I have some extra things I want you to take to your parents as my way of saying thank you. It would mean much to me if you would grant me this wish."

"You no have to do."

"I know, and one day soon, I'm going to explain the true importance of what you've done today. This was not simply a difficult assignment. Trust me when I tell you that you will eventually look back on this day with pride."

"OK, me do it because I take for family."

"And do me a big favor, Li Ming."

"What that?"

"Stop talking to me with that damn Pidgin English nonsense. I know it is an act and that you speak perfect English."

Li Ming blinked a few times and answered slowly, "I do it to survive on the street. It makes people think I'm a stupid immigrant and they underestimate me, and sometimes I just keep doing it. I didn't mean to offend you, so can we keep this between the two of us." She looked at Jimmy with a tender smile. "No. Strike that. I mean between you, me and the dog fart over here."

WARRANT OFFICER ANN-MARIE Bournelle stood on the flight line beside Major Duncan Peal, the Livermore Air Base XO. Peal pointed up in the sky past the end of the main runway to the approaching landing lights of the C-130j four-engine turboprop transport as it turned from its base leg of the traffic pattern to its final approach and lined up on the runway. "That Herk on final approach is the Flying Circus. They'll touch down in a moment."

Bournelle watched admiringly as Captain Jerome Richard, piloted his old craft to a smooth and gentle landing. "Is it true what they say about those guys, that they've got an angel on their wing?"

Peal shrugged. "Yeah, that is what the pilots say. Personally, I think it's a cock and bull story, but you ought to hear my base chaplain. He's eating it up like hot oatmeal, and now every pilot on the base wants your Captain Jarman to tell him how to find his or her own guardian angel. What a load of crap."

Bournelle smiled, "So, why do you treat them special?"

Peal could not answer that question honestly, lest it got back to Major Arthur Jones. Jones had him by the short hairs, and, like it or not, he had to choose a safe answer. "I guess it is because they've got the best air safety record of any crew in the air. Some say they're on a lucky streak, but the fact is that since Captain Jarman flew with them, they've never burned an engine or had any major problems of any kind since then. Now, everyone who needs an East/West jump wants a seat on the Flying Circus. Hell, some people will sit on their butts for days to get a seat. Heck, these prima donnas might as well start their own airline, for all that matters."

"Don't you just hate it when people have good fortune like that?"

Peal scowled at her, "I've got other things to handle. Your chopper will be leaving at the other end of the flight line in about 15 minutes. Make sure you and your new arrival wait there for the chopper back to Los Gatos." Without saying another word, the disgruntled XO turned and walked away.

Bournelle watched him march off in a huff as the Flying Circus turned off the active runway, behind a follow-me truck. She knew men like Peal, and his kind had always been trouble for her back in the days when she ran a brothel, which now seemed like centuries ago.

The Flying Circus turned smartly on the tarmac pointing the gaping hole in its rear towards the flight line. As the rear ramp dropped the remainder of the way, she could see green-faced, yet nonetheless happy, passengers trotting out of the back of the smelly craft in the direction of the portable toilets behind her.

Bournelle looked again at the photo of the woman she was to meet and was searching the passengers in the rear of the transport when she noticed two people walking towards her out of the corner of her eye. One was the woman in the photograph and the other was a tall, nearly bald, yet handsome pilot in a smudged flight suit. She began walking towards them and called out, "Are you Lieutenant Ramona Baker?"

The large-breasted, woman in her early thirties was thinner than she looked in the photo, and her hair was now cut short. As they approached, Ramona threw an arm around the tall pilot walking alongside her, who had to stand at least a foot taller than she did. "Yeah honey, I'm Ramona, and this here is Captain Jerome Richard, the most handsome hot shot pilot there is!"

They met and introduced themselves, shaking hands all around. As Ann-Marie shook her hand, she chuckled to herself. Whoever this gal was, she was a fast worker, which had always been a talent she dearly respected. There was a time when she would have hired a gal like Ramona Baker on sight.

Lieutenant Baker took Captain Jerome Richard by the arm "Nurse Bournelle, when this fine gentleman and his crew found out that I was headed in Captain Jarman's direction they immediately escorted me to the cockpit, where I flew for the entire trip from Dulles. And let me tell you, that cockpit is a whole lot more comfortable than being in the back of that flying puke can they call a cargo hold." She gave Jerome a hug. "Oh I'm sorry for calling your wonderful airplane a puke can."

"No offense taken," Jerome said with a blush. Ramona had made their trip a real treat and showed she could hold her own with Co-pilot, First Lieutenant Al Chan on the one-liners.

She squeezed him and continued, "They were so sweet to me! For starters, that handsome co-pilot, Al handed me a bottle of Irish Cream and a cup. So, after a few drinks, I got to feeling good and started swapping fruit and vegetable jokes with him one for one."

"Well, actually," Jerome injected in a good natured tone, "you were up on him by two at the last count, so I think you won the match."

She bumped his hip and laughed. "Well tell Al he's welcome to rematch anytime."

"I'll be sure to mention it."

Ramona leaned forward towards Ann-Marie and placed a hand on her arm. "You know, they're all so cute I just want to tuck them all in my purse and take them home with me."

Ann-Marie looked at Jerome with curious grin. "Just what in the hell did you guys put in that Irish Cream?"

The pilot blushed and gave Baker a hug. "Not a thing. Trust me." He gave Ramona a peck on the cheek that made her glow. "That sounds like an interesting proposition Ramona; we've got to get going but I'll let know the boys know and I'm sure they'll say the same the thing – just keep that purse warm and don't be a stranger."

Baker gave him a squeeze. "For you honey – always!"

As he turned to leave, Jerome paused. He fished a hand into one of his deep, baggy pants pockets and pulled out something that looked like a small chrome cylinder. He held it out to Ann-Marie. "Would you please do us all a big favor and see to it that this gets personally delivered to Captain Jarman, with Rusty's compliments? He'll know what it means."

Ann-Marie accepted the small cylinder with a puzzled expression, "Sure, but what is this?"

"It's the eyepiece from my old telescope. I've got a better one now, thanks to Anthony. You tell him that if he needs us for anything, just send it back and we'll come a-running." With that, he took a step back, bowed with a graceful sweep of his hand and said. "Ladies, unfortunately, duty calls, and I must be away."

As the two women watched him trot away, Ann-Marie leaned over to Baker and teased her in a soft voice, "Looks like we'll need to find you someplace private where you can change into a dry pair of panties."

"Well, today is your lucky day, sister. I just happen to have two fresh pairs in my kit bag. One for me and one for you."

Ann-Marie couldn't help but enjoy Ramona's good-natured bravado. "You know what kiddo, I like your style." She held out her hand. "Friends."

Ramona took her hand and repeated, "Friends." There are times in life when two people meet in awful circumstances and immediately see the abiding hope of life and friendship in each other.

THE LIVERMORE AIR Base still maintained a small canteen at the end of the flight line, next to the helipads. Normally, Baker would have been forced to wait for ground transport to Los Gatos, but Colonel Henry Tzu, at Port Ord had wrangled seats for them on a Black Hawk helicopter.

On its way north, it had picked up Ann-Marie at the Los Gatos Triage Center along with a hermetically sealed, anodized aluminum specimen case filled with several biopsy samples destined for the CDC in Washington, D.C. Many of these samples were obtained during autopsies and taken from patients suspected of having that latest variant of the Three Gorges flu that was now sweeping through the San Francisco Bay Area like a wildfire.

A U-2 reconnaissance aircraft would fly the samples directly to a secret military airbase just outside Washington, D.C. Hopefully, the CDC would be able to create a better inhibitor or hopefully even a new inoculation that could end this devastating plague once and for all.

After hand delivering the specimen case to the U-2 pilot, Ann-Marie had to wait for three hours for Ramona to arrive on the Flying Circus. It had been a long, sleepless night, and she was beginning to feel weary; she figured another cup or two of coffee would keep her from falling asleep. She promised herself a long, hot bath and a nap once they arrived at Los Gatos. She looked at her watch as she nursed her second cup of coffee and decided not to wake Ramona, who was now snoozing with her head laid up against the blandly painted wall of the flight line canteen.

Now on its return leg from Marin County north of San Francisco, the Black Hawk would not arrive for another 40 minutes, which was already blowing a big hole in Peal's 20-

minute estimate. That man's attitude like his estimates was definitely short of the mark, Ann-Marie concluded.

She left Ramona asleep in the canteen and strolled to the flight desk to confirm their arrival. When she returned, she filled two mugs and carefully slipped a leg over the bench on the opposite side of the table and nudged her sleeping companion.

Ramona woke up and rubbed her eyes. "Time to go?"

"Nope, our chopper won't be here for another 20 minutes or so," she replied as she pushed one of the mugs across the table along with a sealed dosage packet of Excedrin next to it. "Here, this will make you feel better."

Baker picked up the packet with a weak but grateful smile. "God, I do love Irish Cream, but what a damn headache! Ouch." She tore open the packet tossed the caplets in her mouth and chased them back with a sip of coffee. "Thanks, Ann-Marie. You're a sweetheart."

"You'd do the same for me, and no doubt you will."

As they sipped their coffee, the two began talking about their lives. "So how did you wind up in the medical profession?" Ann-Marie asked.

Ramona laughed. "Well, it was my mother's husband, if you want to know? He pushed me to do it after my divorce, and mom happily paid the freight for me to get my masters degree as a Physician Assistant."

"Husband?"

"Yeah, he footed the bill actually. Made a fortune back during the dot.com boom and got out while the getting was good. He was a real shrewd guy. Anyway, he said I had to be a PA because all nurses ever got was varicose veins and mismanaged 401K plans. Given that I didn't want to be a doctor we settled on the difference, and I became a PA."

"And don't tell me your mother wasn't kicking your butt every inch of the way."

Ramona laughed and held her head and winced. "You're killing me here, girl. Yeah, mom did kick my butt. Well actually, she and her husband took turns at it. I guess that's why I love them both so much. At least now, I'll get to see them more often; that is if I can ever get time off to visit them in Tahoe."

"You're lucky. You've still got family."

"I know. Tell you what; if we ever get a chance to make it up to Tahoe, I'll introduce them to you. Mom will adore you. She used to do a little hooking. Heck, that's how she met my stepfather.

Ann-Marie laughed. "We'll certainly have something in common then. So what is your mom doing these days?"

"She and Dad own a bunch of property now in Tahoe, and that keeps them pretty much busy most of the time, now that all those overworked geeks in Las Vegas are going to Tahoe for rest and relaxation."

Ann-Marie took a slow sip, and putting down her mug asked, "So, you're from this area; your mother and stepfather live in Tahoe, and you had a cushy PA post at the Walter Reed Army Medical Center in Washington, D.C. What I can't figure out is why you're here at one of the worst imaginable duty stations in the country. To what do you owe this great stroke of luck?"

Ramona shrugged and she pulled up the collar of her uniform to reveal a small pin with an American eagle superimposed over a small American flag -- the familiar trademark of the Progressive Libertarian Party. "All they told me is that Anthony is here and that I had to come. That's all I know. And yes, my commanding officer at Walter Reed thought I'd become as crazy as peach orchard boar when I requested this transfer."

"He was right on the money, too, but it's your own funeral, I guess."

"Well, these are strange times, and a gal has got to do what a gal has got to do." Having said that, she opened her travel bag and pulled out a well-traveled FedEx package. "And then, there is this."

Ramona slid the packet across the table. "While I was standing on the flight line at the Washington Dulles airport waiting for my hop on the Flying Circus, this cute little Chinese girl walked up to me and handed this package and told me it was from a friend for a friend, which didn't make much sense till I looked at the label. Then, the dime dropped."

She pointed to the recipient name on the address label. "Tanya Wheelwright and I were friends back when I was finishing my PA residency at the Dominican Santa Cruz Hospital Cancer Center. She was an administrator at the hospital, and we were treating her husband, Henry. He was a really sweet fellow and always tried to make us laugh, no matter how bad he was feeling. Damn shame that he was in New York when those fricking terrorists nuked the UN. He saved a lot of folk, which is why he developed cancer."

She swallowed hard as the memories came back. "If he had come to us earlier, he might have been OK, but by the time we got him into surgery, it was pretty advanced. However, we did everything we could, radiation therapy and chemotherapy, and by God, he was turning it around. Then he dies with his daughter and Tanya's parents in a Tsunami? When I see all the bastards who survived it, it makes me mad that decent folks like that had to die."

"You won't get an argument from me on that one. So what's the connection between you and Tanya other than working together in the same hospital?"

"Sometimes she'd pull her husband's chart, go in the break room and cry her eyes out. That's where we became friends. You know how it is. After that, she was called-up and Henry made her give up her deferment because he felt it was her duty. Between us, she wouldn't have left them for all the tea in China so he had to push on her hard, I guess. Anyway, after she left for DC, I decided to join the Medical Corps and was transferred to Washington after she was assigned to Los Gatos. So, when I got a call from this Colonel Henry Tzu at Port Ord asking me to serve under her, how in the hell could I refuse?" She pushed the FedEx package across the table to Ann-Marie. "So now, what the hell do I do with this? I just know it's going to break her heart all over again."

Ann-Marie pushed the package back across the table to Ramona. "You'll deliver it to her this morning, Ramona, like the good friend you are. You're probably the closest thing she has to family now. She'll need you."

"I know," Ramona replied as tears began streaming down her cheeks. "My God! I wish all this was just a terrible dream and I'd wake up and find things like they were."

"I do, too," Ann-Marie replied solemnly. "But things have changed. We've changed, and in a few hours you're going to feel as though there is no hope, but there is." She reached out and took Ramona's hand. "Let me give you a good piece of advice I once got from Anthony Jarman; just keep it simple, stay focused and the world will turn."

CHAPTER 16

KNEELING BEFORE THE TRENCH

THE BLACK HAWK pilot and his crew checked the waiting room outside the flight desk after filing their flight plans with the Livermore Air Base controllers. Normally, he wouldn't wait for them, but they had been delayed again, and he figured his two passengers for Los Gatos deserved a break. Instead of landing at the helipad, they had landed on a closed taxiway because of his failing hydraulic system, and the repairs would put him even further behind.

It was already 9:00 AM, and he and his crew had been in the air since 11PM the previous night. Short of combing the whole base, he decided to give his passengers more time to turn up while they stopped off at the flight line canteen for a cup of coffee and something to eat.

After leaving a message at the flight desk for his passengers, he led his crew to the canteen, where they all made a direct bee line for coffee urn, filling their mugs and grabbing plastic wrapped SPAM sandwiches. He had just started to munch on his sandwich when he noticed the canteen orderly and called out to him, "Say, we're looking for a couple of medical officers headed for Los Gatos, have you seen them?"

The caustic looking orderly pointed to the far corner of the room, past a table full of aircraft mechanics in grease-smeared overalls. "We got two nursing types back there." He pointed at Ann-Marie and Ramona. "I think you're looking for the blonde with the big knockers sawing logs and the other one slumped on the table. They've been waiting for you guys for hours and finally dozed off."

Craning his neck to look over the heads of the mechanics, he spotted Ramona Baker with her head leaned against the canteen wall. The other one had to be Ann-Marie Bournelle, the nurse he'd brought here to meet an incoming passenger from Washington, D.C.

He turned and looked at the canteen orderly with a cool glare, "You mean the Lieutenant who happens to be sleeping in the far corner."

The canteen orderly caught his drift. This helio jock was one of those prim and proper types. "Yes sir, I meant the Lieutenant back there."

Still annoyed, the pilot poured two more mugs of coffee and put them on a tray with a few stale-looking donuts. After telling his co-pilot and crew chief to find a table for the three of them, he carried the tray over to where the two women slept. He found Ann-Marie slumped over the table with her head nestled in her arms. Setting down the tray, he shook gently her by the shoulder. "Wake up ma'am."

She lifted her head and squinted at the reddish sunlight that now filled the canteen and mumbled. "Oh, shit. Did we miss our flight?"

"No, ma'am. We lost some time with a mechanical problem, but that's OK now, and we'll be leaving for Los Gatos in about 15 minutes." He slid the tray between Ann-Marie and Ramona. "I brought you some coffee and what they have the nerve to call donuts. Unless you want to crack a tooth, I suggest you dunk them donuts real careful like."

"Gee, thanks; that's really sweet of you. And thanks for finding us."

"I'm glad we did," he replied as a sudden thought came to his weary mind. "Say, are you one of the nurses who works with the ELMO at Los Gatos?"

"As a matter of fact, I am. My name is Ann-Marie and I'm the hospice nurse at Los Gatos. Captain Anthony Jarman is my boss."

"Well, then, I'm really glad we found you, ma'am and I'm real sorry about all the delays. I'll get you there as quick as I can. It's the least I can do for you, considering how you folks took such kind care of my friend, Eddy Rogers."

"Eddy Rogers." She shook her head. "Sounds familiar but I can't place it."

"He was doing a test flight with his mechanic when he lost his tail rotor and augered in. The mechanic died on impact, but Eddy lived, even though he was burned real bad."

"Oh yes," she replied sadly. "The young helicopter pilot with major 3rd degree burns. He came in the first day we opened the center. Oh, gosh, I'm sorry; he was such a fine, young man. I felt so sorry for him."

"All the guys in my unit know you did, Nurse Bournelle, but we didn't know your name till now. We're glad there was someone like you to be there with him at the end."

Warmed by his sincerity she replied, "I want you to know he had a friendly smile on his face right up to the end."

"That was Eddy sure enough. Fearless and fun." The helicopter pilot's head drooped as he recalled the memories of his old flying buddy." Finally, he looked up and said, "Like I said, them donuts are tooth breakers so don't forget to dunk. If you feel like going back to sleep, don't worry. We're not leaving without you. We'll be sure to come and get you before we start the preflight." With that, he thankfully patted her on the hand and joined his crew at the other table.

"Wake up, sleepyhead," Ann-Marie said as she nudged Ramona. Baker groaned and sat upright, rubbing the left side of her head. "Ouch, I still feel like some little shit with a hammer has been whacking at my head." She opened her eyes, to see Ann-Marie's outstretched hand holding a steaming hot mug of coffee. "Hold that, dear, but first I gotta pee."

THE PREFLIGHT HAD gone smoothly enough; the Black Hawk pilot began running through their checklist as his crew chief made sure Ann-Marie and Ramona were properly buckled in. As the fuel pumps and avionics whirred up to life, Ann-Marie and Ramona checked the intercoms in their flight helmets.

Ramona tapped on Ann-Marie's helmet. "I can hear you, but why can't you hear me." Ann-Marie held up the PTT switch on her old style flight helmet.

"You got to push this button when you want to speak," she answered. The pilots could hear them but paid no attention to their chatter as they started the turbine engines.

In a few moments, the Black Hawk lifted up a few feet off the helipad and followed the taxiway out to the main active runway. At Lawrence, all aircraft took off from the active runway.

The tower cleared them for takeoff, and the pilot dipped the nose helicopter forward as it climbed forward and up from the runway, turning towards the San Francisco Bay Area with a slow, graceful turn.

As they passed over Fremont at the southernmost tip of the San Francisco bay, they could see the wrecked remains of the San Francisco Bay Area. The top of the bay waters were still smeared with patches of oils and chemicals, topped by a foul-looking yellow and brown foam. It would be years before all of it would finally disappear.

There were a considerable number of trucks slowly making their way along the Dumbarton Bridge on Highway 84, spanning the short distance across the bay between San Mateo and Alameda County. It had been the only bridge to survive the Tsunami in repairable condition. As to the other Bay Area bridges, like the Bay and Golden Gate, they had been totally destroyed, and replacing them would also take years – if it would ever be done.

Turning to the sound, they flew over the flooded devastation that had once been the Silicon Valley boomtown of Santa Clara; they passed over San Jose on their approach to Los Gatos. Ann-Marie, who had seen it before, gave Ramona a running description of the sights.

"Ladies, we're about five minutes out from Los Gatos," the pilot announced over the intercom.

"Thanks," Ann-Marie replied. "By the way, when you get to the center, could you circle the reservoir a few times while I describe things to my friend here?"

The pilot checked his fuel gauge and replied, "I can give you one long, slow clearing turn over the reservoir and go a bit north over the quarry and the old college. Will that do?"

"You're a peach," Ann-Marie answered. "Could you bring us in over I17 south from San Jose? I want to show her everything beginning with the Los Gatos checkpoint north of the center."

"You got it. And we'll be listening in, so how about telling us something about the people too. I'll fly extra slow to make sure you have the time."

"That works for me," Ramona agreed.

A few minutes later, the Black Hawk was flying directly south and just to the right of Highway 17. The freeway that had once connected the Silicon Valley with the coastal cities of Santa Cruz County to the south, and several large portions of it south of the Lexington reservoir had been destroyed during the quake, leaving the smaller Highway 9 as the only serviceable road.

Pointing out the left side of the helicopter Ann-Marie said, "Over there is the Los Gatos checkpoint. The center is 3 miles south of that, just on the other side of those hills ahead of us, and nobody goes south from here without passing through the checkpoint."

She then pointed Ramona's attention to a line of trucks moving north along the highway towards the checkpoint.

"All those trucks you see heading north are returning from the Sierra Azul quarry. A part of it has been converted into a mass grave for the whole South Bay Area now. They mostly bury the unclaimed bodies there. Collection centers and morgues in the Bay Area collect the bodies around four in the morning. After that, they tag and bag them and then truck them in, starting an hour or so after sunrise -- 0600 when the quarry opens. Thankfully they use electrics now, but the sound of their tires will wake you up for a while."

The pilot flew the Black Hawk down to an altitude of 1000 feet as he entered the narrow entry pass into and through the Santa Cruz Mountains to the Lexington Reservoir.

Just past Saint Joseph's hill and with the reservoir to their left, Ann-Marie continued. "We have two entrances to the camp, and the busiest one is on the north end, at the old boat ramp. All of those large tents there in the center of the reservoir bed are for the walking terminal as we call them, with non-communicable diseases." She leaned towards the open door of the helicopter to point down. "That's 'the creek' as we call it, but it's actually the seismic fracture that emptied this reservoir. Don't go swimming in there unless you want to die. The sides tend to collapse and bury folk in mud and rock and we've already lost three patients to it. However, it does sound nice at night, and lots of the walking terminal like to lay out their blankets nearby, smoke a joint to ease their suffering and relax to the sounds of the water."

"Medical marijuana?"

"Yup, and its good stuff too. I know; I've tried some. We get a lot from the DEA but the best stuff comes from the pot farmers who've been growing that stuff for decades back up in the Santa Cruz Mountains. Now its legal, and we're buying it from them by the bales. It works great and it's damn cheaper than sedatives too!"

The crew chief pushed his PTT button and added, "May I remind you ladies that this is a non-smoking flight and that there are smoke detectors in the lavatories." That comment brought laughs from everyone in the Black Hawk.

As the helicopter banked gently to the east, the administrative area between Banjo point and Miller point was directly north of them. Ann-Marie pointed, "See that dome on the south end of that cluster, that's your home. This is the administrative area with mess hall, store rooms etc. And of course, you can see the helipad on top of Banjo point."

As the helicopter crossed a few hundred feet over the helipad, the mouth of the communicable disease wards nestled deep in the dry Limekiln Creek stream came into view. "Those ugly, miserable concrete buildings are the communicable disease wards. You don't want to go there; trust me. The place is lousy with the Three Gorges flu victims, and none of them make it out alive."

Ramona pointed at two figures in HazMat suits walking towards the communicable disease wards with boxes stuffed with intravenous bags. "What's that?"

"Those are the Jesuits," Ann-Marie answered glumly. "They take care of the dying back in those wards. They're carrying saline dextrose I.V. bags with heroine. We only use the pharmaceutical grade stuff for children, the bed-ridden and the few recovering patients we happen to save. For the terminal ones, we use the street heroine the DEA gives us. It manages the coughing, which is really important, because 3G is an airborne virus. Plus, it keeps them manageable if you know what I mean."

"Heroin," Ramona said with disgust. "There are much better things we could use."

"Hey, honey, those Pentagon hot shots and politicians at Walter Reed where you had your cushy PA post get the best drugs money can buy, but out here you're in the real world, what we've got plenty of is dying people and heroin. It is what it is. You better get used to it, and fast."

The helicopter gained altitude as the noise from its engines intensified. "Over there is the quarry with the mass graves." Everyone in the aircraft went silent as the aircraft passed over immense concrete lined open pits filled with bodies stacked like fire wood. Ramona watched with morbid fascination as workers removed the bodies from body bags so they could be reused, before laying them out in rows so they could be covered with quick lime and a layer of dirt.

Past the quarry, they crossed over the Guadalupe College site. Most of the buildings had collapsed during the quakes and the campus grounds were now dotted with tents and domes. "This is the old college, where we send the recovering patients. Sometimes, Captain Jarman makes the healthy patients requesting assisted suicide stay there instead of the main area, when he thinks it will make them change their minds. That place was picked with great care. You can see the Silicon Valley from there, and the quarry with the mass graves is behind it, past a couple of hills. You could say it gives people, those with a chance to live, a new sense of direction."

As they passed over the college, the pilot decided to swing to the north around the backside of Saint Joseph hill and back through the first Highway 17 pass through the Santa Cruz Mountains for a straight-in approach to the helipad. It gave Ann-Marie a chance to fill Ramona in on some people info.

"You know, the fellow who manages that quarry is a nice fellow, and he's been a widower for three years now. They used to mine aggregate rock in that quarry before it was turned into a burial pit, and he and his crew stayed on to keep it working. He's not much older than you, handsome in a rough kind of way, and he could do with a visit from a friendly face now and again."

"Is that a hint?"

"Kinda, I guess. Ah heck, I just think he's a great guy and he could use a little friendship." The rest of the helicopter crew chuckled, keeping their fingers off their PTT buttons.

"So what's his name, Madam Kinda?"

"Dodge Murphy."

"I'll keep it in mind, but don't go playing matchmaker on me. In the meantime, you haven't said a word about your boss, Anthony Jarman."

Ann-Marie grimaced. As the helicopter had made its initial approach, she saw Anthony walking out to the first trench where a number of clients had already lined up trench-side, kneeling and waiting for the kindly placed bullet that would end their suffering. Ramona had been preoccupied with the administrative area and hadn't noticed.

This time, as the Black Hawk made its way back over the spillway on the north side of the reservoir, Anthony would be getting ready to shoot the first or second client in the back of the head. Well, she reasoned, why shouldn't Ramona see it now as opposed to later?

Finishing their clearing turn, the pilots guided the helicopter over the spillway as Ann-Marie looked down on the series of deep trenches dug in the ground behind a huge earthen bearm from her side of the helicopter. At ten feet tall, the bearm surrounded the trenches in a racetrack fashion; hiding them from the other parts of the center, save for the triage area directly above it. Each trench was approximately 50 feet long, 12 feet deep and 10 feet wide. The side closest to the main area of the camp had a sheer face while the other side was angled towards the top.

She pulled on Ramona's arm and pointed downwards. "See over there -- that small group of people gathered together just inside the bearm. They're receiving their last rites from Father Michael Bennett. He's the head of the Jesuit mission here. He and his volunteer caregivers, mostly lay people from local churches, work in the communicable wards. He and Anthony work closely together, and he is there every day giving folks who want it their last rites and comforting those not of his faith."

"Seems like an odd couple," Ramona commented.

"Well, these are odd days, and he and Anthony share a dome and a strong friendship. They mostly like to get drunk together and argue about sports and movies. God, the racket they can make when they start in with those drinking songs the Father likes. By the way, we call him our 'Spiritual Wombler,' but you'll have to ask him what it means. Kind of an unwritten initiation rule now, if you know what I mean."

"Well I'm a Jack Baptist, if you know what I mean," Ramona replied.

"Hey, you'd like him. We all adore the guy, and not a one of us envies the work he's doing. You'll feel the same real soon. Trust me on that."

At that moment, Ann-Marie watched Anthony walk up to the first person kneeling at the mouth of the trench. Behind him was his aide, Private First Class Charlie Gibbs with what looked like the hand carried trays used by vendors at ball games, with a padded leather strap that wrapped around his neck and extended to the sides of the tray. On it were several small caliber pistols, tools and a few boxes of ammunition.

Talking to the pilot, Ann-Marie asked, "Can you slow down or maybe hover here for a bit? You all might as well see this for yourselves."

"Sure, we can do that," the pilot replied. As the helicopter slowed to a hover, all eyes turned on Anthony Jarman and the woman kneeling at the edge of the trench.

They watched in silence as he put his left hand on her shoulder and brought the muzzle of his Ruger Mark II pistol to the back of her neck. A moment later, she lowered her chin to her chest.

Every soul in the helicopter drew a breath and watched as the woman's head was jerked backwards by a high velocity .22 bullet that tore through the back of her head at the base of her skull, boring through the top of her brain stem, ricocheting off the thick skull plate of her forehead and ripping through the two hemispheres of her brain as it spent its force.

Jarman then let go of the woman's shoulder letting her limp body fall forward into the trench of its own weight, landing face down in an unattractive sprawl.

As Jarman moved towards the next person kneeling at the trench, the pilot dipped the nose of the helicopter and proceeded slowly on his original path to the Los Gatos helipad. One had been enough, and it was the kind of sight they all knew they'd see in their dreams for years to come.

Ann-Marie broke the silence. "Most of the people who walk into this camp see this happening and know it will happen to them. Yet, they come, and they love and pity Captain Jarman in a strange way that makes sense once you get over the horror of it all."

"Why is that," the co-pilot asked, adding his voice to the conversation for the first time.

"They love him for bringing a swift, merciful end to their hopeless, painful existence, and they pity him as a man of such compassion that he can repeat this ritual of death a hundred times a day without losing his sensitivity."

As the Black Hawk settled down on the landing pad, Ramona patted the FedEx package under her jacket just to reassure herself, for the umpteenth time, that she hadn't lost it.

She also wished to God that she was still in her cushy job back at Walter Reed, where she used to dream about doing something more important than tending to the pampered egos of politicians with hemorrhoids, gout and the other such common maladies. Her mouth was dry as a bone as she now began to feel like a naïve fool. She was in a world of hurt now, and while she was never one to back down from a challenge, nobody could have ever prepared her for the world she was now about to enter. From this point forward, her life would never be the same, and the thought of it made her pulse throb and her chest tighten.

THE THREE WEEKS since her arrival at the Los Gatos Triage Center had passed like nightmarish eternity to Lieutenant Ramona Baker. The day after her arrival, Chief Medical Officer Major Jim Boole had assigned her to triage screening at the old boat launch on the northern edge of the old reservoir. As a competent physician assistant, she could replace one of his regular physicians for other duty.

During the last week, the number of new Three Gorges cases had risen dramatically, and a heavy stream of sick people was showing up each day at the triage area where she worked. Worse yet, the job of deciding who would live and who would die was becoming a grimmer task, since the 3G viruses had just mutated into an even deadlier variant.

She had been on her feet all morning and was tired of breathing through her respirator and the uncomfortable feeling of her light HazMat jumper suit and face shield when Lieutenant Colonel Tanya Wheelwright drove up to the base of the boat ramp at a safe enough distance in her electric cart and signaled for her to get in. Ramona left the triage line after finding a replacement. After stripping her protective clothing off and throwing it into a disposable bin, she plopped down on the seat next to Tanya.

"So what gives," she asked as the electric cart lurched forward, "Wheelwright?"

"We're running out of room, and we need to plan a new trench location." Tanya replied as she carefully threaded her way past medical teams transporting new patients to the already overcrowded wards. "We need to expand the camp to the center of the reservoir, and I need a liaison to work with the construction manager. I figure it will take about ten days or so, and I thought you might be interested."

"I'd be a fool not to, Tanya, but wouldn't this look like good old favoritism to everyone else on the staff? After all, there are others here with more time in than me."

"Yes, but we need our more senior people on the line." The cart passed through the perimeter of the camp as a guard waved them through. Once past the confines of the camp, the rough bed of the reservoir caused the electric cart to buck, even though its oversized, low-pressure tires were designed to handle this kind of terrain.

Tanya pointed to the center of the dry reservoir bed where a large muscular man was leading a survey team. "See that big fella out there? He is Dodge Murphy, the quarry manager for the Sierra Azul quarry. He built the first phase of the camp, and he knows this area better than anyone else does. That's why we need him to build this second phase for us."

"Ann-Marie told me about him and hinted that she could fix me up with him. Is that what this is about?"

Tanya shrugged. "I didn't know Bournelle had mentioned it to you. I was just thinking..."

"Thinking what?"

She stopped the cart, got out and walked a few feet ahead of it. Ramona did the same as she pursed her lips.

They stood there for a few minutes until Tanya finally said, "Dodge is the best at what he does, but he's been doing it too long, and he's lonely. His wife passed over two years ago, and he could use a friendly voice."

"Oh sure, and I suppose we could throw in a box of condoms to sweeten the deal, as well."

Tanya spun on her heels. "You're the only link I have to my past, and that makes you precious to me. But if you think I'm being a pimp, then get in the damn cart and I'll haul you back to the line."

In all the time that Ramona had known Tanya, she'd never heard her use such blunt language with her, let alone anyone else. Maybe, she reasoned, she was a bit jumpy herself and jumping to false conclusions. "Oh hell, honey, I'm sorry. I'm not myself. All this is like a living nightmare, and I'm so mad inside."

"I know how you feel," Tanya replied as she embraced her old friend. "It seems that we've never had a chance to know each other except in awful circumstances, but you're all I got left of anyone I ever knew and loved before all this. And honestly, I do need my more senior people on the line, so nobody is going to think this is favoritism."

Tanya walked back to the cart and sat down behind the wheel. Ramona got in as she reached over to turn the key. "I'm sorry, Ramona. I was thinking that you could put that great gift of gab to work for us, but I didn't think you'd take exception. Seems I wasn't thinking straight. I'll take you back now."

Ramona reached over and put her hand over Tanya's hand. "It was wrong of me to jump to a silly conclusion. Look, you're the head honcho here, and I may be your best friend but I also know when it is time to shut up and do as you're asked. So tell me about this guy."

"You sure?"

"Absolutely."

"Dodge is a widower, and I think he's recently been having a physical thing with one of his secretaries, so you don't have to sleep with him. Besides, I'd never ask you to do that, anyway. The problem is, his lover is about as intellectually deep as a mud puddle, and Dodge is just plain starved for someone bright to speak with. He may push rock for a living, but he's an intelligent man, and he just needs someone to talk to -- someone who'll have his ear and hopefully keep him on the ball, as we're in desperate need of these new trenches. That's probably the main reason why I asked you."

"It's still a little hard to see him all that clearly from here. So, is he cute?"

"I'd say he's your type."

"Since when do you know who my type is?"

"My Henry loved you, not in a romantic way mind you, but he did love you. I think you'd find a lot of what made Henry so special in him."

Ramona rubbed the back of her neck. "Well, I could use a little company, myself, even if I do have to gain a whole new interest in Earth moving equipment. Ah, heck, if it will get me off the line for a while, why not?"

Tanya smiled, "Thanks, Ramona." As she reached over to turn the key, Ramona clenched her hand again.

"Since we're sharing our souls here, kiddo, it's my turn to speak and your turn to listen, so leave the key alone, sit back and hear me out."

Letting go of the key, Tanya folded her hands. "OK, fair is fair."

"You're too wound up, Tanya, and you're about to bust, like your boy, Dodge out there, because you're lonely and miserable, too. You may not see it, but I do, and frankly I'm worried, because I think it could begin to affect your judgment."

Tanya's jaw dropped. "You can't be serious!"

"Oh, don't give me that crap. How long has it been since you got laid, girl?"

"What!" Tanya exclaimed. "I don't think that's a proper question."

"Oh, so you're going to play the grieving widow on me now. Are you forgetting that I knew you and Henry were not having sex because of his cancer? Are you forgetting that you used to come to my nursing station, pull his chart, go into my break room with me and bury your head in my shoulder, while crying your eyes out? I've seen it all, sister, and I'm telling you that you haven't been laid in over a year, and you're no nun either."

Frustrated, Tanya pounded on the steering wheel of the cart and shouted, "You have no right to say this!"

"Wake up and smell the coffee, girl; I'm not the one trying to break the damn steering wheel!" Tanya held her head in her hands and shook it back and forth.

Ramona grabbed her arm and pulled on her. "Stop this nonsense. My God, look at you. You run this place, and people are putting their lives in your hands. The days of crying your eyes out on my shoulder are gone. Can't you get that through your head? You've got a lot of responsibility, and, as your friend, I simply do know how long you can keep your sanity here without getting any! Worse yet, you could become some bitter, old widow with a permanently twisted soul. You need someone new in your life, or you're going to wither and die, and you know I'm right."

"So, are you saying that I should do Dodge, myself?" Tanya hissed under her breath. Ramona let go of her arm and braced her feet against the dash of the cart.

After a few minutes of complete silence, Tanya finally said, "Ramona, if I was one of the men I'd have something going with at least one of the nurses by now, but it is different for me. I can't. Don't you see that?"

Ramona swiveled around on the seat to face her with compassionate eyes. "I'll tell you what I see and what everyone else on the staff sees. We see how Anthony Jarman looks at you. You know, I don't even think he has realized that he is falling in love with you, but I know you, and I see that you have feelings for him."

"So what, I should line up behind everyone for a toss in the sack with him?"

"Damn, you are blind! He isn't sleeping with anyone -- not that he couldn't. You should see that Rose O'Hara gal on the video crew. She's flirting with him like mad, and he's not rising to take the bait, either. And trust me, it's not because she doesn't have it in the looks department. She's after him, and if you keep playing this damn foolish poor, pitiful me routine she'll cut you out. How do you feel about that?"

"Well, that's between him and O'Hara. She's a perfectly good woman."

"Can the crap. I asked you how you feel about it."

Tanya turned away, saying nothing.

"Look at me," Ramona shouted. "Face it Tanya, you want him. You know you want him. For the love of God, why can't you be honest with yourself? I dare you to look at me and tell me I'm wrong."

Ramona sat there with her eyes drilled into the back of Tanya's head, until she finally turned around, tears running down her cheeks. "Oh, God, is it that obvious?"

Ramona pulled a handkerchief out of her coat pocket and handed it to her. "To me, it is. I know you too well."

"But Henry," Tanya protested wiping her face with the handkerchief..

"Henry is gone, Tanya. All we have left is today and what little happiness we can find in this miserable, upside down world filled with death and despair."

"I know, but a day hasn't gone by that I haven't thought about Henry."

"Let's be honest, Tanya. We both knew his condition was terminal, even though he pretended otherwise. Sure, we had some luck towards the end, but how long would his cancer have remained in remission? I can tell you what the doctors were saying amongst themselves, but then you've got to sense what they were saying behind your back. Now, you've lost everything. This is the time to rebuild your life, honey, and move on, and if Henry were here, he'd be telling you the same thing. You've got to let go."

"I don't know. I just don't know."

"Look me in the eyes, Tanya, and tell me that Henry would not want you to find love again. Look me in the eyes, and tell me that a man who didn't have a jealous bone in his body while he was alive would suddenly become jealous on the other side. Look me in the eyes, and tell me you do not want a new life with someone like Anthony."

"Leave me alone," Tanya pleaded. "You know you're right." Her head drooped with resignation. "And so do I. Just don't push me."

Ramona took her hand and softly said, "OK, I won't. I'm just glad you finally have come to grips with it before you turned yourself inside out. Now, dry your eyes, and let's get moving. I'll have a go at it with Dodge, you'll have a go at it with Anthony, and then we'll compare notes. Whaddya say?"

Tanya squeezed her hand. "The worst that could happen is that we'll have a good laugh together afterwards."

"That's the spirit."

ANTHONY KNOCKED SOFTLY on the door to Tanya's private dome. Her voice filtered through the door. "It's open, come in."

Stepping through the door, he saw her in the small kitchenette opening a can of clam bits. "Is that wine?"

He smiled, closed the door behind him and held up the bottle he was carrying. "I have it on good authority that this is the last bottle of premium Petite Syrah wine from one of the local wineries. It is very mild I'm told."

"Well, thank you, Anthony. "That is a pleasant surprise. I'm making a nice, spicy dish of clams and linguini in a red basil sauce. I'm sorry I have to use canned clam pieces, but you know how it is these days."

He pulled up a tall stool on the counter opposite her and sat down sporting a boyish grin. "Are you kidding, a dinner like this is a feast reserved for state banquets." He winked, "It's nice to be the king."

"And what does that make me?"

"A magnificent goddess in the kitchen of her private dome."

She laughed as she drained the clam pieces. "You can lay it on with a trowel, Anthony, but I'm not complaining, mind you. Just remember that tonight; I'm not an overworked administrator. I'm just me, and I'm making you dinner as a small gesture of thanks for someone special someone who has given me a very special gift.

"It was nothing."

"I'm not so naïve as to believe that, Anthony," she said as she carefully spooned the clams into the simmering sauce. "Getting the tape meant the world to me, and to have it brought here by Ramona, too. That takes juice, and I knew you had to pull some heavy strings with your friends in the PLP. Still the same, I'd like to know how you learned about it."

He held up his hands, "I have a confession, Tanya. It was Ann-Marie. She has an old client in Washington, and she pulled his strings."

She gave him a disbelieving glare as she put the lid back on the pot. "OK, keep your secret. I saw that the package was addressed to the wrong room, which is why I never got it. Not that I'm looking a gift horse in the mouth, mind you."

Anthony cocked an eyebrow and gave her a long thoughtful look. "Tell me," Tanya continued, "Would you have been willing to post a reward for it, assuming that you're the anonymous friend in this story?"

"On that basis, of course, but let's assume for the moment that you did know about the tape beforehand and posted a reward of a fine linguini dinner for its recovery."

"Where is this going, Anthony?"

"Humor me."

"OK, so let's assume I knew, and I posted a reward. So, make your point."

"The point is that in a reward situation, the deal is usually that there are no questions asked."

She waved a finger in his face. "You are going to tell – eventually!"

He shrugged, "Next, you'll be telling me, ah yes, ve haf vays of making you tok!"

She pushed a cork puller across the counter. "OK, smart ass; I'm putting you to work for that one. Why don't you decant the wine so it can breathe a little?" He saluted smartly and opened the bottle with a flourish.

While she finished preparing the meal, he finished setting the table and casually looked about her private dome. It was one of the smaller ones, only thirty feet in diameter. The first floor was a spacious combination kitchenette, bathroom and a large living area with a massive wood table large enough for eight. On one end, opposite the place settings were stacks of papers and webpads. However, what really impressed him most was the large Jacuzzi bathtub and marble floor in her bathroom. "You must love your tub Tanya. I must admit; what they say is right. Rank has privilege."

"It was a gift from Senator Connie Chavez, and it keeps me from going nuts, so I'm not going to apologize for having it."

"Connie gave you the Jacuzzi tub?"

"It was her way of saying thanks for my agreeing to the video crew. I didn't ask for it. Heck, I was in favor of the idea from the start. She just wanted to be extra nice, and who am I to turn her down?"

"So how did you get it installed? Something like that coming through the shipping room would have caught everyone's eye."

A devilish grin crossed her face. "You're right about that, but the fact is that Vigo hauled it in here late one night, and the two of us about broke our backs getting it out of the back of his truck and into my dome. A few days later, I conned Dodge Murphy from the quarry into installing it for me, and he threw in the marble floor for good measure."

"And what did that cost you?"

"Believe it or not, he did it for nothing. Dodge likes to come by now and then and talk, and before you jump to any conclusions there's no hanky panky. The gal he's sleeping with is a bit limited in the intellectual conversation area. Seems she has every Seinfeld episode ever taped and her big joy in life is quick but passionate sex between episodes."

"So what's wrong with that?"

"You may be easy to please, but Dodge is sick to death of the canned laughter, so he comes over and picks my brains till I kick him out."

"Yeah, but I hear on the grapevine that you've turned him on to Ramona."

"It's purely professional."

"Oh yeah, and his Seinfeld squeeze has nothing to worry about."

"Well, that's up to them. I'm only concerned with meeting a construction deadline."

He wagged a finger at her. "I seem to recall somebody saying she was not an administrator tonight."

Tanya put her hands on her hips with a pouting expression. "OK, hot shot. If you feel like playing matchmaker, you can go and tell Dodge that she's a sucker for tons of butterscotch syrup piled high over French vanilla ice cream."

"And what about the whip cream and maraschino cherries."

"The more, the better, and if it ever gets back to her that I told you, I'll kick your cute, little behind up around your shoulders."

Anthony wiggled his eyebrows, "Sounds kinky! I think I'll spill my guts for the fun of it and take my punishment like a good boy."

"Oh really!"

"Relax. I was just teasing. Discretion is still the better part of honor as far as I'm concerned, but I will pass the intel onto Dodge. So, besides stimulating conversation with Dodge, what else do you do for fun?"

She carried the meal to the table. "Do you know what my everyday life is like, Anthony? What I actually do?"

The question caught him off guard. He had thought about her a great deal, but this had never really crossed his mind. He did what he did and she did what she did. For him, it had always been just that simple -- or was it? "Tell me, what do you actually do," he answered in a more somber tone.

"I spend most my day doing three things. I read and prepare hopelessly boring documents and reports, argue with brainless bureaucrats and cajole exhausted people into doing just one more thing when all they want to do is to flop down somewhere quiet and sleep. And that's just the daylight hours. At the end of the day, I'm so sick of wheeling and cajoling that I do not want to see anyone or talk to anyone. All I want to do is to soak in my tub and read a classic while I listen to soft music in the background. Then, after that, I do paperwork till I fall asleep and the same routine the next day and so on."

"Maybe, its time to break up your routine. If you ever need someone to wash your back, I'm always available."

"Cool your jets, hot shot."

He could see from the smile on her face that she really wanted him to do everything but get cool. Rather, a more lukewarm approach seemed appropriate if the evening was to go as he secretly hoped. Perhaps, it could be the beginning of a good thing. It was a chase that could be won, but only with finesse and patience.

"Rest easy. I'll be a good boy tonight. Still the same, doesn't this rut you're in get kind of lonely sometimes?"

"To be honest, sometimes it does – and painfully so. But what about you? How is life for you in your three-man dome with Major Boole and Father Bennett?"

"We're getting on like a house afire. Jim, Major Jim Boole has watched every single episode of M*A*S*H on video disc, and Father Bennett and I are helping him build an exact replica of Hawkeye's still."

Her jaw dropped. "I've heard." The 12-hour days are grueling enough, but where on Earth did they manage to get the energy (let alone the parts and the mash) to build a still? "You're all getting your standard issue of Scotch and Bourbon and then some, so why build a still so you can shove rot gut through your livers?"

"Because we all have a collective hair up our ass to do it -- like mountain climbing. You do it because it's there. Besides, it's fun, especially tinkering with it!"

She started serving the dinner. "Have you actually distilled anything yet?"

"Oh yes," he replied as he poured the wine.

"So tell me about it!"

Anthony rolled his eyes a bit and finally said, "Well, you see it is more of a guy thing than anything else. We're not the kind of idiots who need to run out in the forest with tom toms. Nope, we're real men. We brew our own joy juice."

"And how do you drink this 'joy juice,' as you call it?"

He rubbed his chin and answered, "Slowly. You know, we just get enough out for three shots and then toss it back. After that, you just kind of look cool and collected while it eats away at your stomach lining. After you stop coughing, you say something macho, like 'smooth, real smooth.'"

Tanya could see it in her mind and began laughing so hard that she fell out her chair. As the tears streamed down her face, she couldn't remember the last time she'd laughed so hard. Normally, it would have been a humorous comment and nothing but that. Yet for some reason, it tripped loose a need in her to laugh with carefree abandon, which was only exacerbated by the completely baffled look on Anthony's face. As her sides began to ache, she held her hand to her breast and worked hard to slow her laughing.

Still baffled, Anthony got down on the floor beside her; "was it really that funny?" The question only got her going again and this time her laughter was infectious, and he, too began laughing uncontrollably.

After a few minutes, she put an arm on his shoulder and begged, "Please, Anthony, I can't take this any longer." She took a few deep breaths and giggled. "You've got help me stop laughing."

Without saying a word, he suddenly leaned over her and kissed her softly on the lips. "I've never heard you laugh before. I love the way you laugh, Tanya."

Her laughing stopped, but her chest continued to heave with deep breaths as she looked into his eyes with a beautiful radiance. He kissed her again, but this time, he pressed his lips firmly against her own, and after a moment, she pressed back.

The kiss grew with a hungry, spontaneous passion that swept away all rational thoughts and cares. It wasn't that she couldn't stop him. It was that she did not want to, and her magnificent sense of immersion into passion made her hunger even more for his lips, his smell and the gentle touch of his hands.

She drew herself to him, feeling her breasts pressed firmly against him and the dimples form on her skin as her nipples hardened.

"I've dreamed of this moment, Tanya," he said with great longing in his voice. "To be with you. To hold you. To be one with you," he whispered as his hand moved up along the side of her body till his fingers cupped themselves around the bottom of her breast.

Swept up in the intensity of his eyes, she drew a deep breath, closing her own as he touched a part of her that could make the entire world go away to leave them and their sweet passion alone.

"Oh God, you feel so good" she whispered again and again. Moving his lips along her jaw line, he began to kiss her around the ear. She could feel his warm breath, and the sound of his heavy breathing excited her even more. It was as though he was carrying her away on a magic carpet made of soft, fleecy clouds filled with passion that she had not felt for a very long time.

Working his hand from her breast to the zipper that rested at the top of her jump suit, he gently pulled it down to her waist revealing her milky, white chest. She rubbed his chest with passionate strokes as he unsnapped her bra, pulling it away to reveal her shapely breasts and firm nipples.

He ran his hand down along the side of her pulsating body and began rubbing the inside of her thigh as he caressed her breasts with gentle kisses, slowly twirling his tongue around each nipple. With each caress, each stroke, time slowed until each new breath was an eternity of passion that reached down deep into every feminine niche of her body. Being with him made her feel alive in a most glorious way -- a way that she'd almost forgotten. It was then, in that moment of ecstasy, the past came rushing back at her.

She fought it; even though her very essence as a woman was screaming out for him, it was in her mind that the battle was lost. She opened her eyes and stared at the ceiling of her dome as he continued to kiss her and fondle her breasts. It was as though the ceiling was pulling her away from him against her own wishes as the conflict within her began to swell from one level to the next until she could no longer control it. No matter how much she wanted Anthony, old emotions long suppressed and past their use made her feel as though she was cheating. The conflict within her pained her soul as it quenched her passion.

Anthony soon felt her breathing change and a strange new tenseness radiated throughout her body as she withdrew passionately from him. He could see that the moment had changed, accepted it graciously but sadly and laid his head on her breast in resignation.

"I won't stop you Anthony," she said weakly. "No. I didn't mean to say it that way." She wrapped her hands around his head in a tender embrace. "I meant to say that I do not want to stop you, because I've secretly wanted to be with you for a long time."

Anthony understood the conflict in the clearest sense. She was still grieving the loss of her husband and her family. "You'll know when the time is right. I want you to know that I understand. Henry was a good man, Tanya, and you still have to work your way through the past."

Her body spent with emotion and passion, she could only manage a soft reply, "You're a good man, too, Anthony," she said as tears of frustration welled up in her eyes. "I'm so afraid that I've destroyed any chance of us having a relationship tonight and that you'll think I'll never be anything but a grieving widow. Trust me; that's not what I want. It's just that I can't help being so damn conflicted right now."

He reached up to the table and took hold of a napkin. With the tenderness of a mother holding her own infant, he began to dab the tears from her eyes. "Tanya, it is not about sex for me. This is not just some physical fling. For me, it is about being with you; I'll take every precious moment I can get, no matter how it comes, and I'll thank God for it. I just want to be near you and to know that you want the same."

She passed her fingers through his hair and kissed him gently on the lips. She could feel his hunger for her soul. "Be patient with me, Anthony. Let's just take it one step at a time." He nodded his head in agreement; deeply relieved to hear that his most treasured hope for the future would eventually come to be, if only the universe would give them that chance.

They spent the next five or so minutes lying on the floor together as their breathing joined in a slowing rhythm. Speechless, they closed their eyes feeling each simultaneous chest rise and chest fall until their breathing was nearly normal. Eventually, Anthony propped himself up on one elbow, and gingerly refastened her bra and zipped her jumper.

"I think the wine has had plenty of time to breathe," he said tenderly as he stood up and offered her his hand.

Taking it, she rose with his help. "Yes, but I think our dinner will need a little time in the microwave." He nodded with a smiling approval.

After warming the meal in the microwave, they sat themselves again at the table and dined with good appetite as they discussed their favorite movies and plays. She loved deeply complex European films, and he was an admirer of famous directors like Kubrick and Spielberg.

Following the dinner, he helped her clear the table and set the dishes in the sink. "Someone will take care of these in the morning," she said politely.

Anthony picked up the dish scrubber. "Well, at least we can rinse them off so they won't be so hard to clean."

She reached over to take the dish scrubber from his hand and ran her finger alongside the edge of his hand. The simple touch sent a wave of fulfilling energy throughout her body, reassuring her that the evening had not been a romantic fluke. There was something between them, and she wanted more of it, once she had managed to deal with her own grief.

Rinsing the plate under the faucet she said, "Anthony, I didn't expect for us to get so close tonight, not that I'm not glad we did. However, I need to tell you something that is a little hard for me. It is about a mutual friend."

"Sure," he replied hesitatingly.

"Today, I had a talk with Senator Connie Chavez's chief of staff over a secure link. He told me that she went in for exploratory surgery this morning, and the prognosis is terminal."

He gripped the counter. "Oh no, not Connie."

"She's got pancreatic cancer, and he asked if we could allow for you to go to her house in the Berkeley hills in a few days. Connie asked for you by name. If you're willing, she'll send a private helicopter for us when she's ready. In the meantime, we're not to tell anyone about this. Also, you're not to contact her. It's for your own good."

He rubbed his forehead. In the everyday world of bringing final comfort to strangers, he'd almost forgotten the pangs of personal loss. "If Connie wants it that way, then she's got a good reason. She always does. Let her chief of staff know that I'll be ready to do anything I can. Just let me know what to do."

"She'll be glad to hear that, Anthony. You know, she's always been on your side, even after you left her party. As a matter of fact, she is the one who arranged to have Professor Idan Goldberg and his team come here and document what we're doing, but also to keep you safe in the public eye."

His cocked an eyebrow. "Safe?"

"Yes, Anthony, and now I also know that you're in danger. I didn't know that until this morning, but I'm glad for it now. Do you realize what is happening on the web now with the footage Goldberg and his crew are shooting?"

"Actually, I've recently acquired a phobia of the media. You know me; keep it simple and stay focused. If I get distracted with other things going on in the world, I'm afraid I could make a terrible mistake, and that is something I cannot chance."

"I understand, so let me tell you what is happening. Every morning, Idan is uploading two hours of video to a satellite, and the BBC is running it unedited in every country around the world. In an odd, surreal sort of way, you've become the ultimate in reality television, and hundreds of millions of people around the globe are watching you each day. It is not what you're saying. It is what the world sees in the eyes and on the faces of the people you help across and what they hear them say. Thanks to Connie, it has become a wall between you and whoever it is that wants you to disappear."

She held out her hands and cradled his face. "At first I thought I hated you for what you do, but not any more. In this crazy hellhole of a place, each person you help over leaves this Earth with a look of acceptance, bliss and dignity upon his or her face. I don't know how you do it. Maybe some day you could tell me."

He cleared his throat and drained the rest of the wine in his glass. "Some things are best left unsaid. This will always be one of them."

"I understand, but I need for you to also understand that you are preciously amazing, and for the world, you have become the most beloved and tragic figure of our day."

"And what about you?"

"To me you're not a public figure. You're a swell guy who can be a little clumsy and hardheaded at times, but adorable to the core. Maybe things will work out for us romantically and maybe not. I certainly hope they do. But no matter what comes, I want you to know that I truly do care for you, and that I'll always be your friend, dearest Anthony."

He put his arms around her in a big hug and held her close. As she buried her head in the nap of his neck, she heard him whisper softly, "Thank you, God."

CHAPTER 17

ALLIES AGAINST SHIVA

JEFFREY LEBLANC SEALED his private security dome and slipped on his VR gloves. Unlike the production models, his was the clunky looking prototype he'd used to develop his security patents. As with most inventive minds, it showed signs of tweaking and subtle modifications used to making it even more capable than the production models from which he derived a steady flow of handsome royalty payments. With a few quick flicks of his wrist, his HUD sparkled to life. As arranged, Pavel Sergeevich Lebedev also logged on using one of the security domes installed in the New Obninsk Centre in Russia. "Well, look at what the cat dragged in," Jeffrey teased. "And a well-fed-looking cat at that. Nice to see some meat on those skinny bones of yours Pavel."

"Your charm and grace never fail to amaze me, Jeffrey," Pavel tossed back with a friendly smile. "So how goes things on your side of the world these days?"

"Can't complain. The money keeps rolling in, and I'm making good progress on my Andrea quasill, although we've just about outgrown the biomass computer IBM loaned me."

Pavel chuckled. "No doubt you're all over them like white on rice, as you like to say."

"You betcha, and I'll get a bigger box too. I just need to sway their tight-fisted notions of cooperation a bit."

"I'm glad I'm not working for IBM. So, has the Andrea quasill created a physical persona for itself?"

"Not yet, but I've got her watching old movies. Your ideas on that were right on the money, Pavel. You saved me a lot of grief, you know."

"And you have done the same for me many times, old friend, but I asked you for this meeting today for a different reason. One that troubles me greatly, I might add. It is about your sister, Roxanne and her son."

Jeffrey cocked an eyebrow. "You've got a lead on my nephew, Russell?"

"Unfortunately not. I got an inside tip from a friend of mine who works at our intelligence agency, the Federal Security Service. He tells me that they've tracked a lot of intel traffic on you and traced it back to Geneva and Houston. These people are good at what they do, and from what we see, they seem to be concerned about how you're pushing the investigation of your sister's death and the disappearance of your nephew."

"I've tracked a bit of it myself, but frankly, I haven't paid much attention. Just figured it was the IRS or something up till now. So, why is the Russian FSB interested in me?"

"They're not. I'm interested in you. One of these days, I'll finally talk you into working for me. Besides, I fear that you are making some very powerful people nervous. These people play for keeps, my friend. May I make a suggestion?"

"Shoot."

"You use that word too loosely, my friend, because that, I'm afraid, is what could happen to you unless you step back from pushing the investigation, which our sources tell us has been blocked anyway. Just leave it be for now. If you will let me, I'll be glad to help you anyway I can, provided you stop pushing things."

The revelation startled LeBlanc. Was it because he had funded the lion's share of the Holocaust Survivors Film Project in Los Gatos, now renamed the Nibiru Holocaust

Project?   When Senator Connie Chavez had first approached him about funding the project she had only known that he was a major contributor to the Progressive Libertarian Party. What she didn't know was that he had underwritten the project, not out of loyalty to his party, but because of his desire to help the natural father of his nephew.

Shortly after Russell's birth, Roxanne had secretly confided in him the identity of the boy's natural father but had forced him to take a solemn oath of silence. He had always regretted taking that oath, but his devotion to his sister went beyond his sense of fairness. With her death, he wanted to do whatever he could, and through Senator Chavez's offer, he was able to help in some small measure. With all his wealth, the sum was a pittance in comparison to the guilt he felt, especially now that the boy had apparently been abducted.

His sister and her husband had been buried together, and on that day, he resolved to find Russell. Now, it seemed that he'd run afoul of a more sinister situation than he first imagined. He had come to trust Pavel and to know the man was shooting straight with him.

He sighed. "You really feel I'm going nowhere with pushing this investigation?"

"Yes, my friend. As I said, just let go of it for now, and let me see what we can find out. Whatever it is, I'll tell you just as soon as I know. I promise you. In the meantime, I assume you've employed your own private investigators."

"Of course."

"Pay them off, and tell them that you've given up. You might also want to give them a handsome bonus to make it look final. Also, keep a low profile on the Nibiru Holocaust Project. It seems to be getting a lot of attention from the same people."

"I know you wouldn't be telling me this if you didn't have good intelligence. Fine. I'll drop the whole matter and release my investigators. As to the Nibiru Holocaust

Project, I've already set up a trust for it, so I'm really out of the picture now. I'll leave it to the trustees to manage and keep my nose out of it, for good measure, too."

Lebedev's face relaxed. "I'm glad to hear that, old friend. Just be patient."

"By the way, have you viewed any of the Nibiru Holocaust Project footage that's running on the BBC?"

"Who hasn't? The man has become a strange addiction here. Many members of my staff talk about it during their breaks and meals. As for me personally, I've watched it when I get a few free minutes here and there, but not as much as my staff members. I mostly watch the interviews with Jarman and his patients the night before he helps them cross over. Quite remarkable and I often wonder how it is the man has not lost his mind. I think I would if I were in his shoes."

"I think that is why the programs have become so popular. Everyone is waiting to see him crack, and he simply keeps on going."

"Yes, he does that. So what in your life is more, shall we say, entertaining, these days?"

Jeffrey was glad that Pavel had redirected the conversation away from its dark tones onto something lighter. "Just working hard and playing with the ladies when I can."

"You'll never change. Why don't you find a good woman and settle down? Wouldn't you like to have something running around underfoot some day calling you daddy?"

"OK, OK. Let's not get on that kick again. As I've told you a dozen times before, I still haven't met the right woman. So, other than your usual philandering, what's new in your life Pavel?"

"I'm working on some exciting, new projects, which unfortunately I cannot discuss with you. Other than that, I think I've met someone special."

Jeffrey held up his hands, "Wait! Stop the presses! The ex-husband from hell is going to take another shot at romance?"

"Speak for yourself. You're still an old coot who's never married."

"What's this old stuff? As I recall, I'm a year younger than you, and you just turned thirty-eight, so spare me the old coot stuff."

"Fine, then I'm the old coot, but I'm an old coot who's in love again."

Jeffrey's eyebrows danced with curiosity. "Well then, that makes you a great old coot. So, who is she?"

"Her name is Yelena. I think you may already know of her."

Jeffrey laughed. "Well, kiss my grits! Are you talking about Razumovsky's daughter, Yelena? Is that the one?"

Pavel's eyes sparkled. "Yes."

"Leave it to you to go chasing the boss' daughter. I take it she's "the one," and that you've already done the bended-knee routine."

"That's very premature right now. As a matter of fact, I haven't even discussed the possibility yet with her."

A knowing smirk crossed Jeffrey's face. "Oh yeah, Pavel. I hear you, and as usual, you're trying to play it cool but the fact is that, if you're telling me, I know you're about to pop the question. Don't try and weasel out of that one, either, because I know you too well, my friend, so let's get down to it. You know I'm the pits when comes to picking out wedding gifts. You guys just tell me what you want, and consider it done."

"When the time comes, I'll do that, and I promise you, it will be expensive," Pavel laughed.

"Now, you're talking my language. Besides, coming to your wedding will give me chance to kiss your sly mug in person. Heck, we haven't seen each other face-to-face since the IBM symposium."

Jeffrey's offer gave Pavel an excellent opportunity to slip in a question he was meaning to ask. "I may be coming to Washington soon for some official business. Perhaps we'll get a chance to meet while I'm there."

"Will you bring some of that great Georgian cognac with you?"

"I believe that can be arranged. I'll let you know when I'm coming as soon as I can. I look forward it with great anticipation."

"So do I, good buddy. I'll leave the light on for you."

WITHIN DAYS OF accepting President Chebotarev's offer to become Russia's new Minister of Science, Igor Petrovich Razumovsky relocated to a spacious and tastefully decorated Moscow flat. Forced to attend to the political and social obligations of his post, the trappings of power did little for him, as he missed his family, dacha and the private banya he so cherished. As cushy as his life had become, for him it was still nothing more than a sacrifice for the motherland.

In his absence, his daughter Yelena and Lebedev, whom he had named to replace him as the head of the New Obninsk Centre had begun spending a great deal of time together. Officially, Lebedev spent many nights in Razumovsky's dacha as a guest of the family, but he had become much more than that, according to his 12-year old grandson Dimitri Anatolivich Volkav, who relished sharing every new bit of news with his grandfather each day. The blossoming relationship between Pavel and Yelena was a welcome new development for the family, one that Dimitri and his grandfather both secretly welcomed.

As was his habit, Dimitri liked to watch HDTV with his mother in her bedroom, before going to bed. Snuggled up next to her on the plush cover of her bed, he idly surfed his favorite channels as his mother gently rubbed her hands and arms with a pleasant smelling moisturizing gel.

"Mother, why should we leave Pavel alone in his room tonight? Why don't we invite him to join us?"

The suggestion caught her by surprise. "Do you think that would be proper?"

"Mother, I do not understand why you think I am still a witless, naïve little boy. Ever since grandfather moved to Moscow, Pavel has been spending more nights in our home than in his own flat. Besides, mother, I know what is happening with you two, so why hide it?"

"Why hide what?" She answered demurely as she slowly squeezed more of the gel onto her forearm.

"Each night after you think I've gone to my room and fallen asleep, you sneak out of your bedroom, go to his room and make love."

Flabbergasted by her son's comment, Yelena's hands gripped tightly and she accidentally squeezed half the contents of the tube onto herself. "Oh, now look what you made me do, you precocious, little boy," she huffed.

She set the now-deformed tube down on the nightstand and began cleaning herself with tissues. "Frankly, I ought to spank you. Did your grandfather put you up to this?"

"No, mother, he didn't. As a matter of fact, I haven't said a thing about this to him, because I think what you're doing is wrong." The boy knew he was lying through his teeth, but he also knew how to manipulate his mother and had carefully scripted this moment beforehand.

Dimitri's last comment cut Yelena like a knife. Secretly worried that he would reject Pavel out of a sense of loyalty to his deceased father, Anatoli, Yelena knew that a dissonance like this between Dimitri and Pavel could threaten her chances of growing closer to Pavel. Troubled, she kept her composure. "So tell me, Dimitri, what exactly do you think is wrong?"

"Well, mother, the fact is that this is grandfather's dacha and I'm tired of seeing you sneak into Pavel's room to make love. It is time for him to sneak into your room, if you like!"

His frankness surprised her, but not too terribly. He was a brilliant child and mature beyond his years. "And what do you like, Dimitri?"

"I would like for him to move in with you, into your bedroom that is, because he makes you happy. Grandfather and I have noticed that you've begun to sing while you're working in the hothouse. I see how he makes you happy, so why feel ashamed?"

She wrapped her arms around him, and hugged him closely to her chest. "My wonderful, little man. You know sometimes you make me feel like a witless, naïve little girl. I really hadn't noticed that I had begun singing."

"You have, mother, and you sing so beautifully, especially when you know Pavel is coming to stay with us. I wish Pavel could sing with you, but I see how he looks at you. He is in love with you, mother, and I think you are in love with him too."

She kissed him gently and continued to hold him close. "You have your father's soul and my father's intellect. You got the best of both, my son. I'm so proud of you. So tell me, what can I do to show you my love?"

He raised his head. "Ice cream!"

"It so happens that Pavel brought some this afternoon and we've been keeping it a secret. But then, who can keep secrets from such a wise, young man as yourself." Dimitri had found the ice cream within five minutes, but knew if he acted as if it was a surprise, that he wouldn't have to reveal his sleuthing secrets. "Ice cream, it is."

"Wonderful. I'll go to Pavel's room and get him, and then we'll meet you in the dining room."

She shook him lovingly. "Be quick, or I will be forced to eat it all before you get there."

The young boy shot out of the bed laughing. "Last one to the kitchen is a rotten egg!"

DIMITRI TAPPED SOFTLY on Pavel's door. "Come in," Pavel answered laconically. He opened the door and found

Pavel lying in bed with a bath towel wrapped about his midsection.

Focused on the small HDTV monitor in his own room, Pavel didn't notice Dimitri until the young boy was standing at the foot of his bed. It was something he hadn't expected at that very moment and, clearing his throat, he quickly switched off the monitor and grabbed a robe that was draped off the side of his bed. "Uh Dimitri, isn't it past your bedtime?"

"Yes, but tonight is special. We're going down to the dining room to eat the ice cream you and mother have been hiding from me."

"Well, now that the secret is out, we cannot let such a wonderful treat go unappreciated, can we?"

"Absolutely!" Dimitri agreed as he sat down on the corner of the bed, assuming his most manly expression. At least the one he felt he'd perfected in front of the camera. "Before we go downstairs, Pavel, can we have man-to-man talk?"

The announcement surprised Pavel. He had spent many hours with Dimitri and Yelena in the hothouse and around the house, and this was the first time he'd ever seen him act so bold. "I see. This sounds serious. Fine. Let's talk man-to-man then."

"When grandfather moved to Moscow, he made me the man of the house, and I want to talk with you about this sneaking-between-bedrooms business between you and my mother."

Pavel's jaw dropped. He had absolutely no idea of where this would go next, but it was clear that for the time being, Yelena's son had the upper hand.

"There will be no more sneaking about in the house. From here on, you will stay with my mother in her room until she says otherwise."

"Agreed! But, how do you feel about this? I mean, doesn't it make you feel awkward?"

"You are like my mother. You think I'm a witless, naïve, little boy. Well I'm not; I know a good thing when I see it, and you make my mother sing!"

"Dimitri, I want you to know that my intentions to your mother are honorable and that I'm in love with her. But I also know I could never fill your father's shoes. How do you feel about that?"

"I've tried to fill my father's shoes since he died, but you're the first man to make my mother sing. And besides, I really like you, too."

With that, the young boy stood up and went to the door. "If we do not go quickly, mother will eat all the ice cream." Delighted with the results of their man-to-man chat, Pavel jumped into his slippers and followed Dimitri downstairs.

As they walked down the stairs, they could hear Yelena singing in the kitchen and paused a moment to enjoy her melodic voice together as the two exchanged knowing smiles.

She met them in the dining room, carrying a tray with three heaping bowls of ice cream – a very rare treat, and the three of them ate it with great relish. The first helping had gone quickly, and enough remained for a second, with Dimitri getting the largest portion.

They ate, teased each other about little things and made jokes, filling the home with laughter that even the gardeners in their small cottages out to the rear of the dacha could hear.

After they had finished their late night desert, Yelena began clearing the table and said, "Pavel, I'd rather clean this up than to leave it for the staff in the morning, so would you mind tucking Dimitri in. It is way past his bed time."

"But tomorrow is Saturday, and I do not have to go school," the youngster protested.

"Granted, but you're still a young boy."

Pavel smiled knowingly and, taking him by the hand, led him up to his room at the top of the stairs.

As he tucked him in, Pavel asked, "Just out of curiosity, how did you know when your mother was crossing the hall to my room."

The boy pointed to his door. "I can see the light from her room under the bottom of my door."

"You mean to tell me that you sit here all night looking at the bottom of your door?"

Dimitri smiled. It was time to show him. "I'm usually up when Mother goes to visit you." He sat up in bed and leaned over towards his nightstand. "Let me show you something." He opened the top drawer and pulled out a webpad.

"A year ago, grandpa setup up a special login for me on his office computer with my own virtual desktop. I can monitor everything that goes on in the house, and when I was checking the logs on the HDTV monitor in your room, I came across the oddest URL."

Pavel grunted. "And you call me a sneak?"

"I've linked it to Grandfather's workstation downstairs." He tapped a few buttons, and a blue video screen appeared with a satellite transponder frequency selector. "I've been watching the BBC live feeds from a place called Los Gatos, California, in America."

"So this is what you've been doing while I've been getting to know your mother. You're supposed to be getting your rest, you know."

"I know, but this is really interesting." Pointing with his finger, he introduced each of the people in the image panel. "That's Professor Idan Goldberg; he's the producer, and Rose O'Hara, his narrator. I think the cameraman's name is Jerry, but I'm not sure. Anyway, I like to watch the interviews they film of Anthony Jarman, especially when he is doing a three-way with Rose O'Hara and a patient. I think Rose O'Hara is brilliant. She really gets things going. Sometimes, I also watch Tanya Wheelwright, but she's not as interesting as Anthony and Rose. Sometimes, I cannot understand what they're saying so I play it back with the translation.

"So that is why your English is becoming so good lately."

"Yes. Better than learning it in school, too!"

Without saying a word, Pavel folded down the laptop display switching it into a dormant, standby mode, and placed it back in the nightstand. "Still, it is no excuse for staying up late, but I'm interested in what you think of this man, Anthony Jarman, and what he does."

"He helps people to die, but only if they want to die, and sometimes he will not help them because he thinks they are confused. Everyone says he is doing a good thing. I think they're right. I think he is a very special man."

"Have you seen him do it – that is, kill people?"

"Yes, but I mostly watch the interviews with the sick people the night before they die. My friends in school think it is morbid but I think it is fascinating. Especially when the people talk about how they are moving in and out of their bodies. Anthony calls it 'walking' when they go to visit their friends and families before they die. It is really beautiful, Pavel. I don't want to die, but I'm not afraid of it either. It is, like Anthony says, just a part of the cycle of life."

Pavel was deeply impressed by the boy's insight. He had watched the same footage and seen it more as a news event rather than as a truly significant human event. Then, an idea clicked in his mind. "Dimitri, would you like to work on a special, secret project with me?"

The boy's eyes lit up with glee. "Oh yes, Pavel, and I will never tell a soul – I promise!"

"Not so fast. We'll have to tell your mother, and if she agrees, we'll study the Jarman interviews together. I need to see this through your eyes and feelings. However, there will be one very special promise you'll have to make besides secrecy. You must promise to go straight to bed when your mother tells you each night, and no computer nonsense. We can save the broadcasts on the PVR and watch them together before your bedtime. Do we have a deal?"

"Oh yes, I'll do it!"

"Good. Now, I have a special favor to ask. I have to take a long trip with your grandfather, and while I'm gone, I want you to record the programs instead of staying up all night. Watch them, if you want, during the day, and, when I get back, we'll look at the ones you feel are best. Can you do this for me?"

"Sure. I'll save the best interviews and edit them together for when you return."

Pavel leaned over and kissed him on the cheek. "Thank you for sharing this with me, little man, and for our man-to-man talk today. It means a lot to me." He tucked him in, stood up and before switching off the light said in a hushed voice, "and now, with your permission, I'm going to sneak into your mother's bedroom." Dimitri giggled with delight.

DESIGNED TO FLY long distances high above the deadly ash streams, the Antonov An-170EX transport was a relatively comfortable aircraft. It was also well suited to the demanding needs of clandestine diplomatic missions because of its ability to operate out of smaller airports, such as a secret military airbase in the south of Israel where Israeli scientist Isaac Aronovich Bachtman, awaited the arrival of his old mentor Igor Petrovich Razumovsky, Russia's new Minister of Science.

The An-170EX was an updated variant of the problematic An-170. Similar in some ways to the Hercules C-130J, the An-170EX was also a four-engine, medium-range transport, except that it sported a more rakish design and four counter-rotating ZMKB Progress Propfans, making it the only aircraft of its kind in the world. While the design had never managed to receive more than lukewarm interest from international buyers, it had proven itself well adapted to the dark and dangerous skies of a post-Nibiru world. Repurposed as an extended-range political mission transport with a soundproofed cabin, state of the art avionics and long-range, low-power radar, the An-170EX was simply the safest way to travel short of the new Gulfstream scramjets, which were still limited to heads of state.

Upon landing, the Antonov pilot expertly steered his four-engine transport straight through the cavernous mouth of a large, camouflaged hangar. The landing had been precisely timed to avoid the prying eyes of various commercial and military spy satellites in low Earth orbit. Likewise, the departure time would also be timed so the Antonov would not be acquired until it was in Jordanian airspace.

A young Russian crewman lowered the short air stair to the ground and took his position next to the stair on the hangar floor. Immediately behind him, Razumovsky walked stiffly down the stairs, still tired from the long and thankfully uneventful flight.

Isaac Petrovich Bachtman walked across the hangar and greeted him warmly at the foot of the air stair. "I am honored to see you, old friend," the lean, weathered Israeli said. Ten years junior to Razumovsky, life on a Kibbutz had given Bachtman a much healthier and hardier appearance than the 68-year old Razumovsky. "You look as handsome as the day I left I left Russia."

"And you are still as full of shit as ever," Razumovsky snorted warmly as the two embraced. Razumovsky gave him a great hug and kissed his cheek. "I've missed you all these years. We could have done so many great things together, had you stayed in Russia."

Bachtman shrugged his shoulders, "This is the life. What more can we say, so let's not bemoan the past. Now come with me. I have some ice cold Stolichnaya made under license here in Israel and some of my wife's incredible pickles and fresh baked bread. I have not lived here so long as to forget the simple pleasures of life."

"Well, I hope you have enough for three because I've brought you another mouth to feed. My protégé, Pavel Sergeevich Lebedev, my new replacement as the new Obninsk Centre Director." The two men turned to see Lebedev descending the air stairs. Pavel extended his hand to Bachtman and the men introduced themselves.

Strolling through the hanger, the two older men reminisced about old times with Lebedev in tow as they strolled through a doorway into one of the hangar offices, where they found a table heaped high with an assortment of fresh bread, pickles and freshly harvested, hydroponically grown vegetables. Off to one side, were several large buckets containing solid blocks of ice with large holes carved in the center, filled with bottles of Israeli-made vodka, chilled to perfection.

"Bachtman you sly, old dog," Razumovsky boomed, "you haven't been living in this miserable desert so long that you've forgotten how to make a man feel welcome."

"It's nothing," Bachtman demurred. "Just a few snacks." He then nodded to his orderlies, which was their signal to leave the room. They would wait outside the door along with the crack Russian Spetznatz team assigned to guard Razumovsky and Lebedev.

With a wink of an eye, the Israeli scientist set up a row of shot glasses on the table and filled them with the frosty, cold vodka. He handed a glass to Razumovsky, and Lebedev and the three men toasted their families, followed by another round, to the hopeful success of their meeting.

"So what do you think of our vodka, Igor?"

"Normal. Not bad."

"You never give in a millimeter, do you?"

"Only when I have to, old friend." Mindful of their departure window, Razumovsky cut straight to the business at hand. "So tell me, have you read the proposal from our government?"

"It was included in the briefing file prepared by the Mossad, but why are you coming all the way to visit me?

Do you think I'm going to help you talk my government into giving away our most precious state secrets so you can destroy our Shofar 7 satellite in geosynchronous orbit?"

This time, Lebedev poured the drinks, giving himself a little time before answering. "I propose another toast to the future. Nothing is more precious than that." Bachtman eyed him cautiously as they held up their glasses.

Choosing to be a quiet observer for as long as possible, Pavel drank his vodka and munched on some fresh tomato slices as he studied the two men, either of whom would have, no doubt, made superb professional card players.

Razumovsky snatched up a pickle slice, sniffed it, tossed back the vodka and popped the slice in his mouth. "Not bad," he commented as he slowly chewed the pickle. "Isaac, how would you like for Israel to be the darling of the world instead of a pariah state?"

"That attitude is why I left Russia and came to my homeland. So, if you mean that we're a pariah state because we have not allowed ourselves to be driven into the Mediterranean by terrorists or their friends, I can accept that."

Razumovsky had foolishly stumbled on a sore spot, and he knew it. As his father used to tell him, vodka greases a foolish tongue. "Israel is a pariah because it has the guts to tell the UNE to go to hell and leave it alone." He leaned forward to make his next point, "you may have forgotten the motherland, but never forget that while America was the first to recognize Israel in 1948, the USSR recognized Israel just three days later. Russia has made unconscionable mistakes with your people, but denying you your homeland was one mistake we did not make. Never forget this."

"That, I will not forget. It is the other unconscionable mistakes I try to forget, but come, my old friend. Let's not argue." Cutting the dialogue short, Bachtman drained his own shot glass and tossed a pickle wedge in his mouth. "I do love my wife's pickles."

Razumovsky nodded in agreement, but remained quiet as Bachtman refilled the glasses. "Igor, as to this proposal; what you and the Americans offer us is a fool's paradise in exchange for the first sense of real security and peace this nation has had since 1948. We made such a mistake once before at Oslo."

"Let's not waste time with semantics and posturing, Isaac. We, as well as the Americans, are ready to pledge that there will never be a mosque in space and that Israel will have a substantial number of slots on one of the American colony ships. What more could you want?"

"Let's have one more toast, and then we will talk of it." Feeling the effects of the drinks, Razumovsky pushed the glass aside.

"Excuse me, Igor; is our vodka not to your liking?"

"Your wife's pickles are better than your Israeli vodka. So, are we to sit here and get drunk like two old fools and squander Israel's one true moment to be loved and respected as opposed to being feared and respected? If this is what you please, then we will do this without you."

"And you will fail."

"Kiss my ass."

"I did that for too many years, but I'm not complaining. You taught me well."

"Too well."

"Well enough to finally get your attention."

"So, then you have it! Let's end this charade. Obviously, you have something up your sleeve."

Bachtman turned his attention to Lebedev. "You've been rather quiet," he noted. "I like that in a man. It is always better to observe. So tell me, what have you observed about this American computer genius, Jeffrey LeBlanc? I believe this man actually holds the key to what you need to do."

"You are right," Pavel answered simply.

Bachtman laughed and slapped Lebedev on the thigh. "I am glad to see that Igor is still a great mentor. Now we stop acting like old men farting in each other's face and come to the interesting part." He stood up and walked to a large, wheeled LCD panel board across from the table. He turned it on to reveal a surface crammed with neatly written, mathematical formulas.

"I've read your proposal several times," the Israeli said with a playful smirk, "but you have missed something significant." He pointed to a corner of the board. "Let us begin with the actual time it will take for your weapon to make its final computation before crushing Shiva into a dust. These calculations must take place in a microsecond, and there is no time for a second chance, even with the most powerful computer. Even these new biomass computers IBM is building are impressive, but there is something lacking. Yes?" Pavel nodded in agreement. "And we both know what that is — an intelligence capable of leaping beyond logic." Again, Pavel nodded in agreement.

"Assuming you can get LeBlanc to build a working proof-of-concept quasill to control your system, are you ready to build it?"

"Yes," Pavel replied confidently. We already have everything else we need."

"And what if it fails?"

"It can't."

"That's naïve crap, and you know it." Pavel recoiled at his assertion. "Don't come here trying to sell me another unsinkable Titanic. If this fails, the result could turn the face of our planet into a moonscape. If that happens, there will be no mosques in space, and there will be no Israelis either." Bachtman motioned Pavel to stand next to him beside the LCD panel board.

Pavel rose up from his seat and joined him. "These are your calculations, yes?"

Pavel quickly scanned the formulas on the board. "I believe so."

"Trust me, they are. I'm sure that you're proud of your work, but it is fatally flawed. If you look closely, you'll see where I've given a few hints, but nothing more. Now, let's see how good you are at finding your own mistakes."

Bachtman returned to his seat and winked at Razumovsky. "While your new protégé ponders his work, let's eat some of these wonderful treats. Shall we?"

Razumovsky looked over at Pavel, who was now reading the board with a troubled expression.

For the next half hour, the two older men ate, drank and commiserated, occasionally glancing at Lebedev as he paced back and forth in front of the marker board like a caged lion. Finally, Pavel plopped back down in his chair with a stunned face.

"I take it you found the problem," Bachtman said as he sat a glass of vodka in front of him.

Pavel tossed back the drink and wiped his lips. "Damn you; you are a genius! We must begin at the beginning, and I do not even know where that it is now." The numbers did not lie, and he now saw where his plans were seriously flawed. Worse yet, a mistake like this could cost him his career, which paled in comparison with the dashed hopes of saving the planet from destruction." The shame was so strong in his soul that he could barely bring himself to look at either man.

Razumovsky on the other hand had known Bachtman for many years, and he knew that the other shoe had yet to drop. After all, suspense had always been Bachtman's favorite pastime.

Bachtman poured another round. "You know, gentlemen, I have not enjoyed this much vodka at one sitting in some time. I think it is loosening my tongue. Tell me, Pavel, do you think my tongue is getting loose?"

"Don't taunt me."

"But do I have your full attention now?"

"Yes," Lebedev answered as his eye lifted with a glimmer of hope that perhaps not all was lost. Not yet, at least.

"When I was your age," Bachtman said softly, "I made a similar mistake. The kind of mistake that used to mean a one-way train ride to a gulag in Siberia and the likelihood of dying from TB. Had I worked for most any other man than Igor, that would have certainly been my fate. It was he who saved my life, and now I am going to repay an old debt." He stood up and walked back to the board as Razumovsky laughed and slapped the table.

"Come here, Pavel," Bachtman said as he picked up a stylus. Razumovsky's eyes twinkled as the visibly shaken Lebedev joined him at the board. Isaac pointed to one of the primary formulas on the board. "Here is where you made your mistake. Because of this, everything else is just a little out of kilter, as they say." He jabbed the stylus at Pavel's chest. "You didn't do so badly, and in time, and after great expense, I'm afraid, you'd have caught it. So let me save you the grief. Watch." Pavel watched in amazement as the older man made a handful of small changes. "Can you remember this?"

"Oh yes. My God! How could I have overlooked something so simple?"

"I'll tell you something my dear old mentor, who just happens to be sitting here with a cat-that-ate-the-canary grin, once told me." He glanced over at Razumovsky with a nod and added, "all mistakes have simple beginnings." He pointed at the board and winked, "Fix this, and everything else will be just fine, but keep in mind that you cannot make your system work without an American biomass computer and a proper quasill."

"I've seen what the engineers at IBM have done. It is too crude for our purposes. They think like sheep in cheap suits."

"Except for LeBlanc," Bachtman quickly added. "I've read all of his published papers, and some that were not published, as well. Only he can create such a quasill. Without him, all you've got is so much expensive shit. And dangerous shit, I might add."

Pavel scratched his head. "I've already been thinking along these lines, but he simply will not come to Russia to work with us. God knows, I've tried. He might do it for the Americans though.

"And they'll ruin his work with their politically correct we-think management styles, and then you'll still have shit. Worse yet, they'll be sticking their noses into your business and using his work to control you."

"I know," Pavel sighed. "What I need is something he wants that the Americans cannot give him. Something he wants so badly that he'll come to Obninsk City to work for us, to obtain it."

The Israeli's eyes glittered as he clapped his hands together. "Yes! You have to motivate him in a special way. If you can do this and he builds a successful quasill, I'll help you sell your government's proposal to my government. But only if and when you succeed in doing this."

Razumovsky finally spoke up. "So, now it is you who is smiling like the cat that ate the bird, Isaac. Tell me, you cocky son-of-a-bitch, what have you got under your sleeve?"

"I wasn't a cocky son-of-a-bitch until I met you," Bachtman retorted as he pressed a buzzer on the side of the table. A brief moment later, a Mossad field officer entered the room holding a thick folder, handed it to Bachtman and left the room.

Bachtman leaned across the table and set the folder in front of Pavel with a mischievous grin. "And what kind of mischief do we have here, Isaac," Razumovsky asked.

Without taking his eyes off of Pavel, the Israeli answered, "It is the Mossad file on Jeffrey LeBlanc, his sister Roxanne LeBlanc and her son, Russell. Open it."

Pavel quietly opened the folder and began flipping through the documents and photos. The file included a fully detailed account of the abduction of the son Roxanne LeBlanc secretly had by Anthony Jarman.

After browsing the entire file, Pavel closed the folder. "And where is the rest of it? I see nothing here that we can use as leverage."

Bachtman smiled. "You must understand that this goes all the way to the top of the UNE council, and that means Secretary General Antonio De Bono. If word of this were to get out before he could kill the boy, it could become a disaster for the UNE and De Bono – one I do not think De Bono could survive."

Pavel's eyes shot up. "So the boy is alive?"

"According to our intelligence, he is alive, and De Bono is getting ready to move him. Up till now, he has kept the boy alive because he intended to use his him to blackmail Jarman; however, we suspect that this is not a strong enough motive for all this trouble. There has to be another reason why De Bono has not already had the boy killed, but what, we don't know."

"So, where is the boy now?"

"At present, we honestly do not know. However, the Secretary-General is going to hand him over to a privately financed Syrian Peacekeeper unit who will then take him to an as-yet unknown location somewhere in Texas. Of course, I say the word, Peacekeepers, with a bit of irony. As far as we're concerned, they're just hired Hizbollah thugs who enjoy killing innocents for money, plus some Eurotrash mercenaries."

"How soon do you feel that you can get that location?"

"My sources at the Mossad tell me that the handover will happen in no more than about six weeks. After that, we'll know."

"And how soon will we know?"

Bachtman pulled a fresh bottle of vodka from the bucket and refilled the shot glasses. "One for the road, yes?" The other two men nodded in agreement. "You will know when two things have happened. First, after the handover is complete, we will have very detailed information about his location -- more than enough to stage a rescue."

"And the second?" Razumovsky asked impatiently.

Bachtman winked at him as he nodded towards Pavel. "You made a good choice with him." He then held up his shot glass, "Would you gentlemen please join me for a toast?" They all lifted their glasses. "I propose a two-part toast. The first part of my toast is to seeing LeBlanc's fully operational quasill prototype in Obninsk in exchange for our mutual efforts to help rescue the boy."

"You're a poetic asshole, Isaac Aronovich," Razumovsky boomed. "So what is the second part?"

"I will personally educate the quasill and teach it everything I know, including my country's most precious secrets, as part of our new working relationship with America and yourselves." He glanced over at Razumovsky. "And, if I'm a poetic asshole, Igor, you are ten kilograms of shit in a five kilogram shit sack!"

Pavel stared incredulously at the two older men as they burst out laughing. There was enough history between these men to write many novels, if, God willing, the day ever came when such an endeavor could be undertaken. He looked at his watch and was shocked to see how the time had flown. If they were not airborne within fifteen minutes, they'd have to stay overnight for the next lapse in the satellite coverage. While Razumovsky would most likely enjoy a stay over, Pavel wanted to go. It would be a long flight to Washington D.C., and, the sooner they arrived there, the better.

CHAPTER 18

CROSSING THE CUSP

LUCINDA CHAVEZ STOOD in the clearing and unfolded a tattered, old topographical map she'd found during their trek to Lake Tahoe. For years, her mother, Senator Connie Chavez had repeatedly drummed the timeless advice of former President Ronald Reagan into her head -- "trust, but verify." She had no reason to doubt JALA.TRAC, nor her mother's loving admonitions. Checking the route they'd followed to Lake Tahoe using their medallions was simply a matter of peace-of-mind.

Using Timmy's battered, old field compass, she took her sightings and, comparing them to the map, was able to plot their final destination to a secluded spot along the banks of General Creek, 3 miles west by southwest of Meeks Bay on the western shore of Lake Tahoe.

Next to the clearing was an immense, round, flat boulder the size of a small single-story house. It seemed out of place with the surroundings, but perhaps that was why JALA.TRAC had led them to this place. The boulder did provide a very unique landmark, and it would help break the wind.

It would be dark in another hour, and the rest of the group was still twenty minutes behind them. They would be tired, but everyone had decided to push on instead camping another night, and the day's hike had been grueling, especially for the younger children. She and

Timmy Watkins had chosen to go ahead and begin preparing the final campsite for the ten weary travelers.

Timmy walked out of a thick patch of pine trees with a huge pile of firewood stacked up to his chin and tossed it next to the fire pit Lucinda had already prepared. "Why don't you get this started while I go fetch some more?" he asked. "It will be real chilly tonight. I'm just glad this isn't winter time."

"Sure," she said as she knelt down by her pack and pulled out the dented old candy tin she used to store her kindling. "Everyone is OK, but the going is slow. Jenny's legs gave out on her, and Bob Cummings is carrying her on his shoulders, but they'll be here in twenty minutes. By then, we'll have a nice roaring fire all ready for them."

Soft spoken as always, Timmy set down the bundle, and began helping her build a fire. "You've been real worried for the last couple of days, but whatever it is, you've been keeping it to yourself. I'm thinking maybe it's your mom."

The two had developed a warm and deep friendship during the trek, and now that they were alone, she decided that it was time to share her burden with someone she knew she could trust. "The last time I spoke with my mother was three days ago. She could barely work her medallion because of the medications and her cancer." Tears began running down her face. "She's dying, Timmy, and she doesn't want me to come to her. She wants me to go to Godschild."

He put his arm around her shoulder. "Why doesn't she want to see you? It doesn't make sense."

"It doesn't make sense to me either, but that's what she wants. Worse yet, she won't tell me why, only that it is important that I go to Godschild. She didn't even want me to tell anyone else, but this pain is too much for me." She embraced him, "Oh God, Timmy. I'm all tore up inside. I love my mother so much, you can't believe."

He patted her tenderly and said softly, "maybe JALA.TRAC will know. Why don't you ask him tonight?"

"In front of everybody?"

"If you have to do it, yes. Perhaps though, you might be able to find a quiet moment with him so you can ask him alone. If you like, I'll do what I can to help with that."

"You'd do that for me?"

"What are friends for, Lu?" he said using the diminutive version of her name, he only used when they were alone. He took a hanky out of his pocket and began to dry her tears. "I'm here for you, Lu. No matter what. No matter where. We go it together. OK?"

She sniffled, "You're the best, Tim; you really are."

"That's the spirit. Now look, everyone else will be coming and if they find us getting all mushy like this they'll pester us until we spill our guts and we don't want to do that, do we?"

"You're right."

"Good. You know, this could be a long night so I think I'm going to fetch some extra firewood if you'll be OK by yourself."

She gave him a long squeeze. Letting go she said, "Sure. I'll finish here, so go along." He simply nodded with a tender smile and left for the clump of trees at the edge of the clearing.

As she finished building the fire pit, Lucinda remembered how difficult it had been for her to learn this vital survival skill the first few days after she had joined up with the other nine members of her group. She had never had to build a fire in her entire life, and learning the basic nuances of airflow, oxygen and good tinder had taken her more time than she'd originally thought. But now, she was a quick pro, and before long, a nice campfire was well on its way.

During their journey to Lake Tahoe, everyone in the group had talked incessantly about their first evening with JALA.TRAC and the five questions they'd asked him. It had seemed like the first meeting had happened an eternity ago, and their minds continually buzzed out loud with new questions as they camped each night, wondering what the future would hold for them.

The group had started out the journey as a fragmented and somewhat argumentative group, but now, they were bonded as a family and fiercely loyal to one another. What had once taken hours or days to explain to each could now be said in a few words, if not a knowing glance and a smile. No matter what came next, they all resolved to find it together.

Along the way, Lucinda and Timmy had found deep feelings for one another. Not a puppy love in the adolescent sense, but a deep and profound caring for one another. The turning point had been a terrifying experience that occurred the day they started up into the Sierra Nevada foothills.

A starved black bear had charged their campsite at dusk. Emaciated and crazy with hunger, the animal first ran towards 9-year old Annie, who had wandered away from the group to make her toilet.

At the sight of the charging beast, the child froze as all watched in horror. Lucinda was closest to the child, and she and the rest of the group behind her rushed towards Annie and the bear, screaming and throwing rocks. However, it was Timmy, who had been gathering wood when he heard the bear's attack, who saved the child's life.

From the side of her vision, Lucinda watched him leap out from the brush like a banshee from hell, firing his .357 revolver into the bear's head. The bullet glanced off the top of the bear's thick skull. Stunned by the impact of the bullet, the bear rolled to the ground and, after a moment, struggled back up upon his legs to resume his charge as Timmy had thrown himself to the ground between Annie and the beast into a prone position. Taking careful aim, he fired, and this time, his second shot went straight through the bear's mouth and out through the back of its head. Dead before it hit the ground; the bear's lifeless body rolled and skidded to a stop no more than three feet away from the muzzle of Timmy's revolver. Everyone, especially young Annie, would remember it as the most terrifying moment of the entire journey.

Lucinda was amazed at Timmy's cool and swift dispatch of the bear. Others would say that it was a brave act, but Lucinda knew that it went far beyond bravery. Timmy had become a man in a boy's body, with enough courage and compassion for ten men. In that moment, she realized that she would spend the rest of her life with him, give him children, tend his wounds and share his joys. It wasn't fanciful thinking. It just felt right, and their pioneering journey had shown her the wisdom of her mother's advice that she should always trust her instincts.

A large ball of resin in the fire popped loudly, snatching her back from her thoughts. She picked up a stick and began poking the fire as Timmy returned with another armload of firewood. "One more load ought to do it," he said plainly, as he dropped the firewood.

"This will be plenty, Tim" she replied. "My gut tells me that we won't need more than we have already. For some reason, I just know that we're not going to wake up here in the morning."

He shrugged his shoulders with a smile, "Works for me!"

"Come, sit beside me," she asked. He brushed the bark and dirt from his denim jacket and knelt down beside her.

"I was thinking about how you saved Annie's life while you were out gathering wood. You know, I never really had a chance to say this privately, but I want you to know that..."

"No big thing, Lu" he interrupted. With a quirky grin, he opened his coat pocket, produced a bear claw and handed it to her. As she looked at it, the first thought that came to her mind was the horrible wounds it would have gouged into Annie's slender young body. The thought made her shiver.

"It's for you, Lu. I want you to have it."

"You sure you want me to have this?"   She stammered.

"I'm sure. You know, the first shot was sloppy. To be honest, I was half-scared out of my wits, but then I saw you running towards Annie, and time just seemed to slow to a crawl. Everything began happening in slow motion, and I wasn't scared anymore. After that, it was all easy like and this might sound kinda weird but it was like my mind started working like a high-speed computer. Right off, I knew I only had enough time for one more shot, and then I started calculating things as I cocked my pistol and waited for my second shot. This is going to be really weird, but I knew he'd open his mouth to growl, and when he did, I had my shot. When I saw the back of his head explode, I knew we were safe, and then time went back to normal, and I could hear Annie screaming at the top of her lungs as the bear's body hit the ground."

"I believe you, Tim. But still the same, you were really brave. To be honest, I don't think I could have done it."

"Nah. That's where you're wrong. After the bear fell dead in front of me, I turned around and saw you holding Annie in your arms. I could see the pee running down her legs and on you too. Heck, you just didn't seem to care about it. No, ma'am. You just stood there holding onto her tightly, kissing her and telling her that she'd be OK and not to worry. There's no doubt in mind that if you had been holding the gun, that you'd have done the same as me."

"I'm not so sure about that."

"OK, but at least you would have tried. That, I know for sure."

Lucinda looked down at the claw clutched between her thumb and forefinger. "I would have tried, but I'm not you, Tim."

"You want to know something secret?"

She cocked an eyebrow. "Sure."

"After I killed that bear and watched you holding Annie I knew right then and there that I would marry you some day."

The revelation caught her by surprise and she smiled sheepishly, "That's kind of you."

"I'm not being kind, Lu; I'm just telling you the way it is."

Taken with his sense of the future, she leaned forward to kiss him on the cheek. But instead of remaining still, he leaned his head to one side and their lips met for the first time in a firm embrace.

It was as though a bold of lightening had just raced through Lucinda's body, filling her with deep, swirling warmth that made her tremble as they melted together with a joyful bonding strength.

They wrapped their arms around each other and yielded to their shared passion for one another. As their lips finally parted she softly said, "I'll always love you, Tim."

Before he could respond, a booming voice filtered out through the Pines, "Yo to the camp!" It was the familiar voice of Bob Burdette, and it jolted them apart with flushed faces as they both jumped to their feet. "You're busted. We caught you two necking," he said laughing out loud.

Timmy's mother, Helen Watkins, was the first to step out of the woods. He could see that she'd caught them in the act and that the gentle, knowing look on her face was filled with happiness for them both. It made Timmy feel a bit sheepish, and he wondered why it was that his mother was always a step ahead of him even when he kept his best poker face.

Lucinda and Timmy expected an unending stream of teasing and prying questions, but nothing more was said. Everyone else in the group understood what had happened, and they were glad for them. Instead, the talk centered on their next meeting with JALA.TRAC and about learning more about what he called mankind's crossing of the cusp.

As the men set up the tents, Lucinda helped the women prepare a simple but filling meal with the last of their supplies.

SITTING AROUND A blazing campfire, they consumed their meal with speedy relish and, after cleaning their plates and utensils aside, looked at one another with eager anticipation.

As usual, young Jenny was the first to speak up. "Come, come, come. We talk JALA.TRAC." She held out her medallion and waited as the other nine did likewise, forming a circle. As their medallions touched in a complete circle, a strange noise emanated from the huge boulder behind them as an opening formed. From the opening, a warm pinkish light spilled out upon the ground heralding the appearance of JALA.TRAC.

He looked just as he did the first night, when he had present an image of himself to the family. But this time, the sound of shuffling pine needles beneath his slender legs told them that it was he, JALA.TRAC, in the flesh.

All of them stood there speechless, except for Jenny, who ran up to him, jumped into his arms, and blurted out, "I love you!"

JALA.TRAC kneeled beside her and ran his long slim fingers through her hair. "I love you, too, Jenny. You're a very special, little girl."

Despite his thin build, JALA.TRAC picked Jenny up, exhibiting great underlying physical strength as he walked towards the group, carrying the glowing child on one hip. With his free hand, he gestured to the zipped sleeping bags lying by the fire. "Please, let's all relax."

With supple grace, JALA.TRAC sat down on the nearest sleeping bag. Sitting upright, he folded his legs and shifted Jenny to his lap. The other children watched with eager yearning in their eyes. He smiled at them and gestured for them to approach. "Come, little ones."

Nine-year-old Annie sat next to Jenny and six-year-old Patricia sat next to him, leaning against his white gossamer robe as the others drew themselves closer to the campfire.

"There is always something magical about a campfire," JALA.TRAC mused. "I've been to so many worlds and sat there, just as I am doing now, enjoying the flickering flames of a campfire with new friends. While this is such a simple act, it is something that binds us all."

"What is crossing the cusp?" Jenny blurted out as she snuggled close. "We want to know."

A fatherly smiled filled JALA.TRAC's peaceful face. "You never hesitate to speak your mind, little one. This will serve you well in life, provided you know when to speak and when to listen."

Timmy picked up a long branch lying next to him on the ground and poked at the fire, sending a hail of sparkling embers into the night air. "We've all been wondering about this crossing the cusp thing," he said quietly as he nudged the receding fire to life. "We've come a long way."

"Yes, you have, Timmy, and now I will tell you about what has, no doubt, been a mystery to you all." His words were met with grateful nods.

"I come from a race that is very old. Even before your ancestors had learned how to make simple campfires like this one, we have been searching the universe for sentient life. Regrettably, we mostly find the remains of races that have long since gone extinct. With the exception of a few, they all met the same fate, in that they were never able to evolve far enough to survive the unpredictable violence of the universe."

"While a few have destroyed themselves, as your race came so very close to doing, the real problem for young races is that they succumb to terrible catastrophes that you call impact events, solar flares, black holes and the such. More advanced races, such as mine, can see these things coming as easily as you could watch a leaf floating upon the tumbling waters of a wide stream, so it is a very simple matter for us to take the necessary precautions. But for races that have not attained this level of understanding, these events happen suddenly and, most times, without warning."

"Like Nibiru?" Randal Cummings asked.

"Yes Randal, and for us, the saddest thing is that we usually do not find young races until time has almost erased the evidence of their short existence. In your case, we were able to find you well before Nibiru became a threat. In such cases, we usually intercede without being noticed. However, as I told you before, we let this happen, because your species needs to learn this through suffering so that you will never let it happen again. But that was only one part of why we did that. The other part is that you were progressing in an extremely violent way; nations were using nuclear weapons against each other and worse of all, against you and your planet. This saddened us, because Earth is a very kind planet compared with many we already know."

"Will Nibiru come again," Jenny asked.

"Yes, it will, in about another three thousand and six hundred of your years just as it has in the past. However, your planet is now facing another threat from space just as bad as Nibiru, a few years from now. Thankfully, your governments are working together to deal with this problem. Therefore, as with the passing of Nibiru through your system, we shall watch and hope that your race can use this new challenge to speed it's crossing of the cusp."

"And if not, then what happens?" Helen Watkins asked pensively. "Will you intervene?"

"I cannot tell you that, Helen, because of what the Godschild Covenant teaches us. As you know, it is not a philosophy of our making, but one that we have adopted, which has served us well. So remember that the second covenant is 'to learn, and let learn.' This is why we did not intercede with Nibiru, because we saw it as a chance for your race to learn not to destroy itself."

This time Lucinda spoke up with a thoughtful voice. "The last time we met, you told us that each of us is a one in a million combination of spiritual and genetic evolution. I can understand that, especially after this long journey and learning to use my medallion. But what I do not understand is our purpose."

JALA.TRAC nodded approvingly. "You have struck upon the very word I want to talk about, which is purpose. Our purpose is to help life flourish. The purpose for your race is for gifted children, such as yourself, to determine. I know this sounds evasive, so let me explain the concept of crossing the cusp and then you will understand what I mean. Do all of you remember when I told you that the greatest truths in the cosmos are, by virtue of necessity – simple?" All nodded in agreement. "Good."

"As races evolve and wrestle with the concepts of good and evil, the tendency is to express these concepts in terrestrial form, meaning that God or Gods assume similar physical forms. Then, these understandings evolve past a need for a physical form and replace it with the Gods or a God that act in terrestrial behaviors, such as vengeance, forgiveness and compassion. This is very common, and even our own race held to these kinds of beliefs until we adopted the teachings of the Godschild Covenant."

This time, it was Helen Watkins spoke up, "What makes the people or race that created the Godschild Covenant so special that your race chose to adopt their philosophy?"

"I was hoping someone would ask that question. Thank you, Helen." JALA.TRAC shifted his weight slightly and continued. "The race that created the Godschild Covenant is the only race we've found in all our searches for sentient life that has evolved past the physical form. In simple terms, they have become part of what you call God, or that which we call the Universal mind."

"But they're gone," Tim injected.

"Yes, but with one difference. We can always manage to find bodily remains of extinct races, provided their home worlds have not been totally destroyed. With the Godschild, they left us a perfectly functional city, and try as we might, we were never able to find any of their remains. All we can conclude is that they achieved their final purpose and are now somewhere and perhaps sometime beyond us. But they knew that others would find a similar or even the same path, and they left behind a wealth of knowledge for us."

"On the planet of Godschild, we have found and translated a great number of their texts. For example, one explains the basic nature of all there is. As we have come to understand it, they tell us that there are two absolutes: Matter and awareness. Matter is unaware of itself, and this is why comets blindly crash into planets, destroying promising young races. This is because the comet is matter and, therefore, simply unaware of itself. The other absolute is awareness, and if you wish to give it a familiar name, you can think of it as God, or as we call it, the Universal Mind."

JALA.TRAC then leaned over and drew a straight line in the dirt before him. At each end of the line, he drew a circle. Pointing to the circle at his left he said, this is matter. Matter is violent because it is unaware of itself. Pointing to the circle on the right he continued, "and this is God, which represents complete and total awareness."

He pointed to the circle at the left end of the line. "Your history of wars and violence happen because your race has been closer to matter than to God." He then pointed to the circle at the right end of the line. "As you move closer to God, you become more aware, and through greater awareness, you move further and further away from the blind violence of matter."

Lucinda studied the simple finger drawing with careful attention. "I'd like to know where we are along this line between the violence of matter and the complete awareness of God and where you think your race is, as well."

"A most perceptive question, Lucinda." JALA.TRAC drew two perpendicular lines to the first one. The first perpendicular line was in the center, and the other was just to the right of it. He pointed at the line in the center and explained, "The race that created the Godschild Covenant call this line in the center, the 'cusp of evolution.' This is where your race is hovering now, and crossing the cusp is a very dangerous moment in the evolution of any race. It is still possible for you to slip, and with your knowledge of weapons, this could be very dangerous. However, we feel that your race is moving steadily forward. As it crosses the cusp, you will begin to gain greater awareness as your race loses its tendency towards violence."

"Before your race began crossing the cusp, it had not achieved the technology necessary to defend itself against the violence of the cosmos, which is what we use as the key indicator. Likewise, it has also developed the technology to destroy itself. In essence, when a race is crossing the cusp, it becomes its own second worst enemy, next to the unpredictable violence of the universe."

"And what of your race?" Lucinda asked.

JALA.TRAC pointed to the second perpendicular line to the right of the center perpendicular line. "This is our race here, just past the cusp. As you can see, it is a long process, and both of our races still have a long way to go towards total awareness. For this reason, we tend to think of ourselves simply being slightly more advanced students."

Having remained quiet through the evening till this point, Kristen Burdette finally broke her self-imposed silence. "What does all this mean to us, JALA.TRAC, and most especially, to our children?"

It was obvious the question pleased him. "Kristen, each of you is very special. We cannot define your purpose in life, but what we can do is to find exceptional people such as you and your children and help without breaking our own commitment to the Godschild Covenant. This now brings each of you in the group to a very important moment of decision." JALA.TRAC closed his eyes, and turned his back towards the massive bolder behind them and made a soft humming sound with his voice.

A soft, pinkish glow such as the one the group had seen earlier emanated from the entire surface of the massive boulder.   With astonished faces, they watched as the boulder reshaped itself into the form of saucer shaped craft with a silvery skin.

"This is my spaceship, as you call them, and its name is SHEM.TAN. In a few moments, I am going to leave here with SHEM.TAN for the planet, Godschild. Each of you must decide whether to remain here and find your own purpose in your own way, or you may come with me to Godschild.   The actual time it will take us to reach Godschild is relatively short, and you can return to Earth whenever you wish." He picked up the young children and stood them on their feet as he continued his final thoughts. "I will be waiting for you in SHEM.TAN, but only for another hour."

As he rose up, Bob Cummings stood up as well and said, "JALA.TRAC, we made our choice long before we got here, so I can speak for the group. The only thing we need to know is what to do with our gear?"

"You will not need it on Godschild, and taking it would make things a little cramped in SHEM.TAN. You may each bring a small amount of your own personal possessions. As to the rest, someone will be here in the morning to retrieve it."

Timmy raised his hand. "This may sound odd, but can I take my weapons with me?" Timmy asked. "At least my pistol?"

"In time, you will learn more powerful ways to defend yourself, but if you feel safer by bringing them, then you may do so. All I ask is that you dismantle them for the trip to prevent any accidents from happening during the journey." He stood the children on their feet and rose. "If there are no other questions I will wait for you to break camp and join me on SHEM.TAN for the trip to Godschild."

Lucinda followed him as he walked back to his space ship, while Timmy motioned to the other members of the group to stay behind.

Once he was far enough away from the group for a private conversation, JALA.TRAC stopped and turned to face Lucinda.

She stood close to him and in a hushed tone asked, "How is my mother? I know she is very sick and is not answering my thoughts."

A sad expression painted itself upon JALA.TRAC's otherwise placid face. "She is growing closer to awareness, Lucinda. It is only a matter of days now, if that. I too, will miss her dearly."

"JALA.TRAC, she keeps asking me to go to Godschild with you, but she will not let me go to her side, and not knowing why is tearing my heart apart. Is she disappointed with me or angry about something?"

He placed a gentle hand on her shoulder. "Any mother could not love or be as proud of her child as your mother is doing. She's just trying to protect you. I spoke with Vigo about her cancer this morning. He is very upset; he has just learned that your mother is dying because some very powerful people chose to infect her with a virus. Your mother also knows this, and she has discussed the matter with him at great length. They do not know the identities of these people, but they both feel you will be targeted by them for assassination as well, because of the information your mother has shared with you."

Lucinda leaned her head against his hand, feeling its soft warmth. "What do I do?"

"I sense the anguish within you. Should you go to her or with me to Godschild? This must be your own path, Lucinda. If you wish to go to her side, I can arrange for you to be with her by no later than this time tomorrow. All I would do is to remind you that your mother and Vigo feel that you will be safe on Godschild and that this is your mother's wish."

"Do you have a mother? I mean alive. You don't come from eggs or something?"

"Eggs?" JALA.TRAC chuckled with a twinkle in his eye. "No, I do have a mother and her name is JALA.DEE, and I love her every bit as much as you love your mother." He paused for brief moment and then asked, "Do you know how old I am?"

Lucinda picked her head up and rubbed her chin, "I guess you look to be thirty something."

He smiled warmly. "In your measure of time, I'm over three hundred years old, and when my mother tells me to do something, which happens rarely now, I listen to her. Do you still listen to your mother?"

The answer drove straight through Lucinda's tumble of emotions about going to Godschild. "I see your point. I think I'll go and help the others break camp now, and then…" her lip quivered. "I'm going to honor my mother and do as she asks."

"That is very wise of you, Lucinda," he replied. "Now, I can tell you I, too, believe that terrible people of great power wish to harm you. They are not mindless like the bear that almost killed you. They believe they represent the path your race must follow, and while they have done some good, they have also become very cunning. Worse yet, they have no mercy for innocent life. I will make sure that your mother knows that you will be safe on Godschild."

ONE OF THE perks that UNE Secretary General Antonio De Bono enjoyed most was the luxurious hot tub of his Luxury Swiss Chalet overlooking the Val Lumnezia. As Yvette Cochereau refilled his glass with Dom Perignon, the communicator next to the large, sunken hot tub chirped. It was Phillip Boretti, his Chief of Staff. "Secretary General, Governor Johnston just arrived," his aide announced respectfully.

De Bono ran his hand softly down the shapely, naked back of his seductive mistress. "Sweetheart, why don't you go down downstairs to the kitchen and prepare some of those wicked, little canapés you do so very well."

With a knowing nod, she finished filling his glass and gently replaced the Dom Perignon bottle in the silver champagne bucket. "Do you want the kind of canapés I make for your wife and your guests, or the special kind I make for after we've made passionate love?"

Her teasing made him chuckle. "I believe the latter will be preferable, and I expect that I will be of good appetite."

She leaned over and kissed him fully on the mouth, then stepped daintily out of the tub. With an alluring smile, she wrapped herself in a cool, clean terrycloth house robe and left the ornately tiled private spa.

Johnston's visit came unannounced. As De Bono reached out and pressed the communicator button, he knew the news would be bad. "Send him straight in." Not wanting to appear alarmed by this unusual visit, he ran a hand through his hair, took a deep breath and picked up his glass of Dom Perignon.

Johnston entered De Bono's private spa, taking in the massive tub and fine appointments. "Antonio, I'm afraid I have disturbing news to report. I hope you don't mind, but I borrowed the use of your scramjet, because I wanted to get here as quickly as possible. You see, this kind of news is best delivered face-to-face. It is regarding Jarman's son."

De Bono drank deeply from his glass and set it down. "I didn't think you would come all the way from America to bring me love letters, so let's dispense with the niceties. Is the boy dead?"

"Thankfully no, but he is in a coma as a result of an escape attempt. It happened just after we moved him to the silo."

After weeks of preparation, the boy had been transferred from a safe house in Colorado to the old Titan missile silo at Fort Hood, outside of Killeen, Texas. The abandoned silo had been upgraded with new security systems and living quarters for the Syrian Peacekeepers who now guarded the boy.

Johnston continued, "The boy found a hammer left by one of the workmen and knocked one of the Syrians unconscious. He was close to escaping to the ground level when one of the other guards tried to grab him. The boy got around him, and the Syrian struck him on the head with the butt of his rifle."

"So what is his present status?"

"We got him emergency treatment, and everything that could be done has been done. Our doctors tell us that he if he comes out of the coma within the next two weeks, he should have a full recovery. If not, the odds only get worse with time, I'm afraid."

De Bono bit his lip as a great anger swelled through his body. "So the boy is lying in bed like warm pâté because some inept thug doesn't know how to follow orders. Crap! The Inner Council will skin my ass for this, not to mention the Grand Secret Master!"

Governor Johnston cleared his throat as he nervously rubbed his hands together. "Antonio, you should have listened to Yvette and waited until the European mercenaries arrived before moving the boy."

"I know. I know," he spat. "That bastard, Jones was getting too close and we had to move quickly -- too quickly, it now seems."

Johnston kept a passive face against De Bono's anger. "It may help you to know that the European mercenaries did arrive today, and they are now guarding the boy inside the silo. As for the Syrian Peacekeepers, I've restricted them to above ground guard duty. Under no circumstances are they to enter the silo. If they do, I've left order with the mercenaries to shoot them on sight."

"I'll have Yasin's ass for this!" De Bono screamed as he stood up. "Give me my robe," he commanded.

De Bono wrapped himself in the robe and opened the sliding glass door of his spa that led to the outside deck.

The crisp night air helped to cool the anger swelling inside him. "I need to think for a moment. Merl, just stay there. I need to be alone with my thoughts for a moment."

He began breathing slowly as he worked to clear the anger from his mind. This was a bad turn of events, with ominous consequences if he acted rashly again. With the boy now in a coma, his options were quickly becoming limited. At least Johnston had been able to contain the situation as best he could, but the damage had already been done. Before dwelling on how to expand his options once again, he needed to close this ungainly circle of misfortune.

Taking a few deep breaths, he cleared his mind and then walked back into the spa. The soundproof door automatically closed behind him as he rubbed his jaw. "Yes, Merl" he admitted with a reluctant but calmer voice. "You and Yvette warned me about the Syrians, so I only have myself to blame."

The relief on Johnston's face was immediate. "What would like me to do, Antonio?"

"Tell me about this guard who butt-stroked the boy with his rifle. Did he know that he was not to harm the boy?"

"According to Colonel Yasin, his men all understood in very clear terms that they were not to harm the boy under any circumstances. Even if the boy did get out of the silo, he couldn't have gotten far. Apparently, the guard in question was a bit hot-blooded and lost his head in the excitement."

"And where is this fool now?"

"According to Colonel Yasin, he fled immediately after he realized what he had done. So far, our attempts to find him have been unsuccessful."

De Bono slipped out of his robe and slid back into the hot tub. "And why do I sense that there is another side to this tarnished coin?"

The moment had arrived for Johnston to play his trump card. Hopefully, it would minimize or perhaps even eliminate the damage to his political fortunes. "I sensed the same thing after speaking with Yasin."

De Bono nodded approvingly. "And..."

"I must say that Yasin is one of the deadliest and craftiest murderers I've ever had the displeasure to know. It is no wonder that the Israelis have been unable to kill him, although no doubt they'd tried to do so for several years. One of the reasons why they've failed is his second in command, Captain Darkazani. He kills anyone even remotely suspected of providing information to the Israelis, but now it seems he is tired of playing second banana, and this incident fell like a plum into his lap."

"Sensing the subtle tension between these two, I ordered Yasin to search for the runaway guard so I could focus my attention on his second in command, Captain Darkazani."

De Bono smiled approvingly, "Exactly what I would have done, Merl."

"Thank you, Antonio. Unlike Yasin, who is a man of few if any vices, other than cold-blooded murder, Darkazani is a self-interested pig with an irresistible taste for expensive liquor and cheap women. After I got him liquored up and laid, he decided to make his move and privately confided to me that the guard is one of Yasin's favorite cousins. Immediately after the incident, Yasin helped him steal a private car and gave him all his cash. At this point, there is no way to know where this guard is. Meanwhile, Yasin is playing possum and sending everyone off on a wild goose chase."

"As for the guard, screw him, we'll deal with him later. Tell me, does Yasin even suspect that Darkazani has breached his confidence?"

"If he had even the minutest suspicion, then Darkazani would already be dead. Therefore, I think it is safe to say that Yasin has no reason to believe that we know the actual facts."

"Let me think for a moment." De Bono said as he plucked Dom Perignon from the champagne bucket and filled his glass to the rim. Taking a few sips, he finally said, "We'll play Yasin's own story back against him. I want you to tell Yasin that UNE security has spotted a man fitting the description of this guard in Mexico City and that Yasin is to personally terminate him and bring back a suitable body part for DNA confirmation."

The plan puzzled Johnston. "I'm afraid I'm not following you."

De Bono smiled. "Then neither will Yasin." I want you to arrange for Yasin to fly to Mexico City on one of our UNE relief flights, instead of a military transport, so he will not call attention to himself. Make sure he travels with a civilian identity. After he is airborne, I want you to send me a coded message detailing his personal data, how he is dressed and all other travel and destination arrangements using the RK-233Z code."

"But Antonio, Danielle just told me that the Mossad broke the RK-233Z code only two weeks ago. Using this code would be the same as sending the Israelis a foolproof death warrant for Yasin in the clear. He'll never leave Mexico alive."

"That is exactly what I want. You see, the only thing better than hating a Jew, is to let him do your dirty work for you. With Yasin out of the way, we can easily terminate his whole family, including this stupid cousin."

Johnston nodded appreciatively, "It will work. Out of curiosity, do you want Yasin terminated because of the boy's injury or because he lied."

"If he had been honest with me and personally terminated his own cousin on the spot, I would have still been angry with him. However, these things do happen and you do not throw away useful monsters like Yasin for the mistake of one fool. No, he lied to us. That, I never forgive."

Johnston exclaimed, "You are cold. But good!" The two men laughed. De Bono's plan was both ironic and sweet. After few relished moments of self-satisfaction, De Bono said, "Now, let's talk about Captain Darkazani and the boy." Johnston swallowed hard, knowing full well that he would soon be further drawn into this deceit.

De Bono sat up on the edge of the tub and filled another glass with champagne. "Pull up a chair and have a drink." Johnston did and swallowed the champagne with great relief.

"So, let's see. You've put Captain Darkazani in command of the security unit, and once Yasin is out of the picture, I'm sure you can control him until I can find a replacement security team. After that, we need to kill them all. Have Danielle see to it after the new team arrives."

"And the boy?"

"Now that we have involved medical teams in the care of this boy, we have to assume that there will be security risks. You are to keep a close watch on the situation. Until I can replace the security team, you are never to be more than one hour away from the silo. Since you have your own V-22 Osprey which can land right next to the silo, this will not be a problem."

"What about the boy?"

"If he dies, then we shut down the whole operation after we eliminate Jones and Jarman. No matter what happens with the boy, these two have become too problematic for us to ignore."

"I'm concerned about the Inner Council. This could cause some heavy blowback, if you know what I mean."

"You've been watching too many James Bond movies. If the boy dies, the Inner Council will, of course, be disappointed. However, in the overall scheme of things, this situation is rather minor. A real problem would be something like the world learning that we've known the Chinese actually engineered the 3G flu and said nothing about that. In terms of UNE credibility, that would be a true crisis. Relatively speaking, this boy is nothing more than a faint blip on the radar screen."

"Then why not kill the boy now and shut this whole thing down right now? I'm tired of looking over my shoulder here."

De Bono smiled devilishly, "Merl, I like the way you think, because we both like to cut short our losses. Frankly speaking, if it were my call, I'd say terminate everyone in the silo plus Jarman and Jones, and then dispose of the evidence. However, this Jarman boy has become a pet project for the Grand Secret Master, which means we need to manage our risks the best way we can and hope the boy has a full recovery. I do not like it any more than you, but that is the way it is."

"Then let's kill Jones and Jarman now. If Jones was able to force us to move the boy from Colorado to Texas, it is only a matter of time before he finds out about our silo at Fort Hood."

De Bono shook his head. "You're forgetting that we have to terminate Jarman, and as long as he's the current rage in reality television we simply cannot touch him. Be patient."

"Fine, so let's assume that Jones tracks us to Fort Hood. What then?"

"Terminate the boy, even if you have to do it with your bare hands."

Johnston's shoulders sagged. This was more than he bargained for, and he wondered if he could live with himself after doing such a thing.

"Having second thoughts, Merl?" De Bono asked in a firm tone.

"I would be lying to you if I said no. Sure, I had a revenge grudge against Chavez, but in retrospect, it was a mistake. I should have let Danielle handle it. But killing an innocent boy with my own two hands – I don't know how I'd live with it, or if I could. Still the same, if it comes down to that, you can depend on me. If it has to be done, it has to be done."

CHAPTER 19

THE SENATOR'S DEATHBED

TANYA AND RAMONA had just finished their lunch as Anthony walked through the mess tent looking for them. "Well, look what the cat dragged in," Ramona teased as he approached.

"Hi, Anthony. Won't you sit down and join us?" Tanya asked.

He leaned over the edge of the table. "Sunny just told me that we're flying out this evening on a chopper to the Berkeley hills. I thought we had some time. What gives?"

"I got a call from Senator Chavez's Chief of Staff this morning. She's slipping fast and asked if we could do it this evening. I was hoping to tell you myself."

"That's OK. So, what's the drill?"

"Her Chief of Staff has already made the transportation arrangements. Their chopper will be here at 19:30 hours. Perhaps you can tell Ann-Marie."

"Sure. Is anyone else going?"

"Yes, Vigo and myself. According to Tzu, he rolled in early this morning."

"Vigo?"

Tanya shrugged her shoulders. "They asked for him. Go figure. As for me, I'm coming along by my own choice."

"Vigo doesn't make sense to me, but if Connie wants him there, who am I to say no?"

"If you'd rather he didn't go, I'll back you up. It's your call."

"Do you mind if I speak with him first?"

"Sure. The last I saw of him, he was headed off to find Private Gibbs. Find your orderly, and I'm sure you'll find Vigo."

"Say, Anthony, what in the heck does he want with Charlie anyway?" Ramona asked.

"Search me. Maybe he's brought Charlie some new tools or something. After all, the guy is the most gifted scrounger west of the Mississippi, so why look a gift horse in the mouth?"

"If you did," Tanya replied with a grin, "you'd see he's a number of things, but a gift horse? Forget it. Horses are mild-mannered herbivores. Sometimes, he makes me feel as nervous as a cat in a room fool of rocking chairs, although I couldn't tell you why."

"Whatever," Anthony said with a yawn. "I'll be at the chopper pad by 19:15 sharp," he said and then left to find Vigo and Charlie."

As they watched him leave the tent, Ramona turned to Tanya. "God I've been dying to ask. So how chummy did you two get along the other night?"

"We had a nice meal and a long chat."

"Yeah, yeah, yeah. And the two of you were howling loud enough for half the camp to hear you. I gotta tell you. The scuttlebutt amongst the staff is pretty ripe. Everyone wants to know if you two did it."

"Did what?"

"Don't be coy with me. You know what I mean."

"Between us?"

Ramona crossed herself. "Absolutely."

"Ramona, you're not a Catholic."

"Yeah, and you're stalling. Hell, you know you can tell me."

Tanya spoke in a low whisper. "If you tell a soul I'll…"

"I know, they'll find me dead, or worse yet, in a nunnery."

Tanya shook her head from side to side. "Only if you're lucky. OK, so we came close. Ramona, I really wanted to do it, but I'm still not ready. He took it well, but I'm sure it was frustrating for him. It sure was for me."

"Don't worry, he'll get over it," Ramona assured her. "But the real question is, when are you going to be ready? No. Let me rephrase that. Are you going to play this guilty grieving widow role out till you drive the both of you into a pair of crazy, old peach orchard boars?"

"Stop pushing me," Tanya protested.

"Like hell, I will," Ramona shot back.

"Fine, then how are things with you and Dodge Murphy? Have you bopped him into ecstasy yet, or are you stringing him along?"

"Whoa girl, I thought my deal with Murphy was supposed to be platonic."

"There isn't a platonic bone in your body Ramona. So are you two doing the dirty or are you talking about mining aggregates and then reading romance novels all by your lonesome?"

"You bitch!"

"Takes one to know one." Tanya sipped her coffee nonchalantly. "You know, this stuff works both ways, and I know you too well, Ramona. If you didn't want to bop him, you wouldn't be playing games with me. So when are you two going to do the dirty?

"OK, so what if I do. Stop pushing me."

Tanya held her hands up to the sky. "Is that an echo of myself I hear bouncing off the wall?"

Ramona grimaced. "All right. Don't rub it in, already." She jabbed a finger into Tanya's arm. "But I can tell you this, I'll be bopping Dodge long before you stop playing your poor, pitiful me routine."

Tanya drained the last of her coffee and smiled dreamily. "You care to put money on that?"

ANTHONY FOUND HIS orderly, Private Charlie Gibbs chatting idly with Vigo as he methodically cleaned Anthony's pistols. It was Vigo who first noticed him standing silently at the entry to Gibbs' tent.

Anthony announced himself in a jocular voice, "Funny seeing you here, Sergeant; not much to scrounge here."

Startled by Anthony's appearance, Charlie stopped cleaning the pistol and laid it down on his workbench. Before he could stand up, Anthony held up his hand. "As you were, Charlie. I just dropped by to have a few words with the Sergeant, here."

Vigo stood to attention, and saluted. "You're looking fit, Captain. How can I be of help?"

Anthony returned his salute, which only made him even more aware of Vigo's odd comings and goings, as saluting was a military courtesy that had quickly lost its relevance amongst the staff of the triage center. It made Vigo seem like even more of a stranger. "I came by to ask you about this evening." He nodded towards the outside of the tent.

Since arriving at the triage center, Anthony had only visited Charlie's tent a few times and could see a number of additions and changes since his last visit. The sawhorses and plywood Charlie had used for some time had been replaced with a well-designed workbench that dominated one complete side of the small tent. But what caught Anthony's eye were two metal boxes sitting on top of the bench. One was painted green and the other red. Both were half full of new .22 cartridges. "Hold on," he said to Vigo. "Say, Charlie, what's with the painted boxes?"

"Well, sir," Charlie replied, "I use them to cull out the marginal cartridges -- you know -- the ones most likely to cause a feed jam in your pistols."

"But we're using fresh, brand name ammo Charlie."

"Just because they're new cartridges, doesn't mean squat, sir." The young man looked away for a moment as he reconsidered his answer. "Well, let me put it to you this

way. When was the last time one of your pistols jammed on the line?"

The question caught him slightly by surprise. Anthony pondered it slowly and replied, "You know, come to think of it I can't recall one jam. Not one at all. I've had a couple of jams in New York, but not here -- not since you became my armorer." He pointed at the painted boxes. "Is that why?"

"Well, partly, sir. Sure, I've done some work on the pistols, but one real help is the synthetic Teflon lubricant Sergeant Jones brought me. While our Ruger Mark II pistols are a time-proven design, that lubricant really works. However, the ammo is another thing. That's where you get most of the jams, especially when the Rugers get warm."

Anthony turned to face Vigo again. "Sergeant, if you don't mind, I'll meet you in a few minutes outside the tent. Or if you like, why don't you join me for a cup of coffee in the mess hall in, say, twenty minutes?"

"If you don't mind, sir, let's meet over by your dome. I have something for you, and there's no point carrying it through the half the staff area to bring it to you."

"Fine, I'll see you over there in a few." Anthony pulled up a chair as Vigo left.

"I'm curious as to what you're doing with these cartridges. Show me what you do?"

Charlie nodded. Laying out a work cloth on the bench, he picked up a bright new .22 long rifle cartridge from each box and laid them on the cloth. He pointed first to the one that came out of the green box. "Pick this one up and hold the bullet with your right thumb and forefinger. Then hold the back of the cartridge case with your other hand."

Anthony did so. "So what's next?"

"See if you can wiggle the bullet, sir."

Anthony tried and found that the bullet was firmly locked into the cartridge case. "Seems I can't."

"Now pick up the other one, sir, and do the same thing."

This time Anthony picked up the other bullet and this time he could feel the bullet wiggle. "So, what's the difference?"

"You see, sir; these rounds only cost a few pennies. It may be fresh ammo, but if you ask me, it's just your typical government low bidder stuff. Not the kind of rounds competition shooters use. While these rounds will work just fine in a revolver or a rifle, they can cause a feed jam in a semi-automatic pistol, especially if it gets hot. Now here's the secret. Forget what you feel with the hand holding the bullet. If you can feel a popping sensation in the hand holding the cartridge case, you've got a round that's more likely to jam."

Anthony set the cartridge down. "You know, Charlie, I'm getting the feeling that I take you for granted. Come to think of it, we never talk much. I meet you out on the line, and you do your job, but we seldom say anything to each other." He put his arm on his orderly's shoulder. "I know this is late in coming, but I want you to know that I really do appreciate the good work you're doing, Charlie."

A warm smile came across Charlie's face as his eyes lit up with pride. "Thank you, sir. Yeah, I guess we never really do speak much to each other, but that's OK. Each day on the line, I see how much effort you put into what you're doing -- how you comfort those people and all."

"Like it or not, that's my job, Charlie. If it were up to me, I'd use lethal injections, but it seems the UNE prefers we do it with pistols for the ambulatory patients."

Charlie pursed his lips for a moment and finally said. "Can I be honest, sir?"

"Of course."

"When we first started doing this, sir, I wondered how long it would be before you just started getting mechanical about this, or if you'd start going around the bend, if you know what I mean. I've heard it happens to most other ELMOs, but you never seem to show any wear. Each day, I see you treat every one of them people who kneel down on the line like they are special. When I'm not reloading one of the pistols, I listen in, and I hear how much they appreciate you in their voices. I'm proud to serve under you, sir, and I'd be happy to march into hell for you on broken glass, if need be."

Those words struck deeply for Anthony and caused a great sense of regret to fill him for being too consumed with his own responsibilities to take the time to get know this quiet and dedicated young man. "Perhaps one of these nights, you might want to drop by and try some of our homebrew?"

"Oh, you mean that still you're tinkering with in your dome, sir?"

"Yes. I guess the word is getting around about that."

"There are no secrets in this place, at least not for long. Right now, the motor pool sergeant is laying off odds that you guys will set fire to your dome with that contraption."

"Don't tell me you've got a piece of this action, Charlie."

"Well sir, I do, but I'm betting on you, sir. That is, not to blow yourself up and all. But, still the same, I'd be glad to take you up on that offer. My grandfather was a bootlegger back in Tennessee, and he taught me a few things before he passed on. That is, if you're interested in a few pointers?"

Anthony slapped his leg and laughed. "To be honest, sometimes I've had my doubts about that still, as well. A few good pointers sure wouldn't hurt. We'd all be mighty appreciative."

"Just tell me when, and I'll be there for sure."

"Well, tonight is out. I've got a special favor to perform, you might say. But the day after tomorrow should be good. I'll let you know on the line."

The orderly grinned. "Like I said sir, just let me know when."

"Done!" Anthony took a deep breath. Now, things had relaxed to a point where he could pursue the original reason why he'd chosen this moment to visit. "By the way, does Sergeant Jones visit you often?"

"Most every time he shows up at the center. I do some gunsmithing for him and we like to talk about things. I really like talking with him, and he always gets me the things I want like aerosol gun cleaner, tools, etc. Much better stuff than the regular issue you know."

"Anything else?"

"Nope. That about covers it. Nice fellow, though. I really do enjoy his company."

Anthony nodded and stood up. "Well, a good working relationship with someone possessing the sergeant's capabilities can't hurt. In the meantime, I'll let you get back to work. See you tomorrow on the line."

He went to his dome to speak with Vigo. Since he had arrived, he'd waited for Vigo to tell him something new about his son, and every time he tried to get a straight answer, Vigo would suddenly disappear. If he had time to spend jawboning with Anthony's orderly, then he certainly had to have time to tell him what was new, even if it was nothing but another dead end.

He arrived at his dome, and to his consternation, Vigo wasn't to be found. He went looking for him elsewhere and still failed to turn him up. It was obvious the man was evading him, and now it was getting his blood to boil.

ANTHONY SAT DOWN in the mess tent with his dinner. He was running late and only had 30 minutes to eat his meal and make it up the hill to the helipad in time for the 19:30 departure for his appointment with Senator Chavez. He had just swallowed his first mouthful when Vigo appeared out of nowhere and plopped down in front of him. "You might want to eat that nice, fluffy biscuit there to cut your appetite and leave the rest of that slop," he said quietly. "You'll eat better at the Senator's house tonight. Much better. Trust me on this."

"Where in the hell were you today? I looked all over for you."

"Something came up."

Anthony's face became flushed with anger. "Something always comes up with you, and I'm getting damn tired of it!"

Anthony set his fork down. "And by the way, how do you come to know Connie Chavez?"

"We've been friends for several years. Like I said, forget the slop on your plate. She's always been a great host, and even if this is her last night, she's not going to let it stop her from being a great host. It's a damn shame about this cancer business. She is one incredible woman, and the world is losing a true human treasure tonight."

"You know, I've been wondering why you were invited along on this little junket. So, what's the real connection between you two?"

"It's a long story, and some night I'll show up with a bottle of single malt Scotch whiskey. We'll go someplace private, and I'll lay it all out for you." He leaned across the table and said in a hushed tone. "That business this afternoon in Gibbs' tent. There was no need for that. We're both on the same side, and we've got to trust each other."

Anthony shoved his plate aside. "I just lost my appetite."

"So, what in the hell is bugging you, anyway?"

"Let's take this outside."

"Don't forget the biscuit. That's the one thing they do right up here."

Anthony picked up the biscuit, but felt more like throwing it in Vigo's face than eating it. But the grinning bastard was right. It would take the edge off his hunger. Without saying a word, he walked out of the tent with Vigo in tow.

In an open stretch of roadway halfway between the mess tent and the helipad, Anthony spun around to face him. "I've had nothing but mixed feelings about you from first minute we met on the tarmac back at Livermore Air Base, when that cocky Major Peal backed down from you."

"Since then, I don't see you any more, and worse yet, you don't tell me anything about my son. I'm sitting here in a total fucking vacuum with nothing but a video message that tears my guts out each time I look at it. This is the first day since you gave me the videophone that you and I have spoken more than 10 words to one another. You owe me more than that, you son-of-a-bitch, but what do you do? You drift in here like a thief in the night, screw the hell out of my nurse and then disappear for days."

Vigo's eyes flared with anger, and he jabbed a finger in Anthony's face. "I may be a son-of-a-bitch for the way I've treated you, but you damn well better keep Ann-Marie out of this. She and I go way back, and I got feelings for her, so show some respect!"

Had it been any other man, Vigo would have cold cocked him right there, but this was not any other man. In fact, the anger in Anthony's face cut through Vigo's heart like a rusty knife. He had come to love the younger man in a way a father loves a son who doesn't want to know him. How could he explain that by avoiding him he was protecting him?

The confrontation caused an unexpected wave of emotion to well up within him, such that it would have pushed a normal man to imploring words, but not Vigo; he was too well trained to allow that to happen. More to the point, he couldn't afford to let it happen. Yet, he could see that Anthony now sensed the inner turmoil behind his cool poker face and began to wonder if he wasn't acting a bit over the edge, himself.

"OK, so you and Nurse Bournelle are two consenting adults," Anthony said through pursed lips. "But now I find that you've been playing Father Knows Best with my orderly. If you got business with me, Mr. whatever your spook name is today, you come take it up with me directly. Don't go behind my back and play paddy cakes with the very people I depend upon to do my job!"

"Anthony, you've got a right to be angry with me, son." The last word just slipped out of his mouth, even to his own astonishment. Anthony had heard it as clear as a bell, and now he could see a new dimension forming – but what? "If I were to pay special attention to you, it would be noticed and by the wrong people. What you've got to understand is that I'm trying to protect you. If you've got to hate me for it, go ahead and do it, but that won't stop me."

"I don't understand what you're talking about."

"I gotta do it for you and your son Russell. Can't you just trust me on this?"

"Why should I?"

"Because you, Russell and Ann-Marie are all I have left of my life before this insanity began. Can you trust me enough to protect what little I have left in my life?"

Vigo moved closer to him and spoke softly. "Do you really think this is some mercy junket for a pampered politician this evening?" Anthony shrugged his shoulders. "Colonel Wheelwright does, but trust me when I tell you she's in the dark about what's really happening, and so are you." Vigo moved a step closer so that the tips of their noses were only inches apart. "It's about Russell, and that's all I can tell you right now, because that's all Senator Chavez has told me. Tonight, when you help her across you'll know everything there is to know. For the love of God, please don't blow it now. We're so close."

Anthony nodded silently in agreement.

"Look, son, do you think I'm blind? Deep down inside your guts, you've got instincts you never felt before and they are making you want to grab me by the throat and scream 'where in the hell is my boy, you spook bastard?'"

Anthony backed up. Knowing that he was on the threshold of real news, made him feel as though Vigo had just dropped him on head. Worse yet, he was right. There was a new anger deep inside him now that he'd never felt before, clamoring for him grab Vigo by the throat and to shake him till he got every drop of information out of him.

Upset and dizzy, Anthony sat down on a large storage crate lying next to the roadway. Vigo sat down next to him, and could see his jaw trembling as his breathing quickened. He laid his hand on his shoulder. "We'll find him, son," Vigo assured him in a soothing voice. "We'll find him." He then took a flask out of his back pocket and opened the cap. "Will a slug of cognac slow you down tonight?"

Anthony took the flask. "No, a few swigs will probably help me more now than hurt me at this point," he said taking a drink. The warm feeling of the cognac running down the inside of his chest was comforting. He took another drink and handed the flask back to Vigo. "Thanks. Let's just sit here for a bit. I feel like I just got slapped upside the head with a dead salmon. I need a moment to sort through this."

They sat in silence for a few minutes and then began to talk about Roxanne LeBlanc and his son, as Vigo occasionally checked his watch from time to time to be sure they would make it the rest of the way up the hill in time for the chopper.

"We've got to go now, Anthony. Colonel Wheelwright and Ann-Marie are probably at the helipad by now and wondering where we are, since we're coming up the back way."

The two rose and resumed their walk up the hill when Anthony paused. "Before we go, there's something I've got to tell you. It's something I've never told anyone before, and it's got to stay between us."

"You got it, son."

"A year after the last time I saw Roxanne, I finally had to admit to myself that I was in love with her. She was the first woman I've ever loved, and now that she's dead, I'll never get the chance to tell her that. I'd give the world to change that."

"Anthony, you and I have the same problem. We're both too macho to admit we're carrying the same kind of emotional baggage anyone else does. So, it just rots in our guts and slowly eats away at us one piece at a time. Just keep one thing in mind. She kept a big secret from you, too."

"Yeah, you've got a point, there."

Vigo tenderly jabbed Anthony in the ribs. "Whaddya say we form our own private support group and take turns being the shrink?"

"You couldn't afford my billing rate on Sergeant's pay."

"I can pay the freight, so don't worry about that. Let's get moving, or we'll be late." The two started back up the hill with a renewed sense of purpose in their gait.

THE FLIGHT FROM the Los Gatos Triage Center across the San Francisco Bay Area to the Senator's home in the Berkeley hills had been smooth and uneventful. With consummate skill and graceful precision, the pilot landed the old Huey on the Senator's front lawn.

As the Huey's large blades slowed to a stop, Chavez's security chief trotted across the lawn to meet them and helped Wheelwright and Bournelle off the chopper with polite deference. Anthony and Vigo were the next to get off, and the security chief motioned them aside.

Anthony instructed Tanya and Ann-Marie to go ahead with the injector kit and to prep the Senator for the procedure as he remained behind with Vigo and the security chief.

"We just swept the place for bugs," the security chief noted in a soft voice. "I'm certain that we got all the video surveillance bugs but there are probably still enough bugs in that house for the damn UNE pukes to hear themselves listening to us if you know what I mean."

"Thanks, we get your drift," Vigo replied. "Lead on."

As the three men walked towards the house, Anthony wondered who would be so desperate as to invade the remaining moments of privacy of a woman who would shortly cross over. Whoever they were, no doubt, they were his enemies, as well, and most likely the ones holding his son. The thought of that made him grit his teeth.

Once inside the spacious home, they found Ann-Marie by Chavez's bed emptying the contents of the injector kit case and Tanya comforting the dying Senator from the other side of the bed.

"I'm glad to see you again, Anthony," Chavez said with a weak voice. She gestured for him to come closer. "I'm so grateful to you for making this special trip."

Anthony smiled warmly, "You're welcome, Connie. I can only wish it were under better circumstances." He nodded in Tanya's direction. "You've made a real friend there."

"And don't I know it," she chuckled as a small rush of life energy renewed the glow in her. "Tanya, darling," she called out meekly. "Would you do you me one last favor?"

"Of course," Tanya answered as she stepped to her side. Each day, Tanya had watched many die in her center, but this evening, she was losing a dear friend, a woman she deeply admired. It made her feel helpless and sad.

"I let my household staff go a few days ago, including my gardener, Pedro. He's been with me for years and grows the most wonderful roses for me in the corner of my hothouse, out in the far corner of the backyard. I would love to smell them one last time before I go. Could you be a dear and clip a few for me? You'll find some shears on the bench next to the door."

Grateful for the opportunity to comfort her, Tanya gently squeezed her hand. "Of course. I'll be right back."

As she left, Ann-Marie hung the injector on the I.V. stand and connected the trigger grip Anthony would use to release the deadly brew hidden within its white plastic case.

"You know, I've become quite accustomed to the morphine they keep pumping into me. Will that really work?"

Anthony stood next to her bed and nodded towards the I.V. stand, "We use a short-acting barbiturate in combination with a chemical paralytic agent, Connie. It is quite painless and effective. Your tolerance to morphine will make no difference. When I press the trigger, you will gently lose consciousness, and moments after that, your heart stops. The process is completely painless."

"You haven't changed, Anthony. A simple yes would have sufficed."

He chuckled. "Don't tell me how to build a watch when all I want is the time," he replied. "You must have told me that a million times."

"I suppose I did," she mused. "All the arrangements have been made. After I'm gone, a local mortuary will handle everything. In the meantime, I had my staff prepare a good meal for you and your friends. After I've crossed over, please do not waste time on me. Go, refresh yourselves and raise an occasional toast my way, only please keep the toasts short and humorous."

Anthony chuckled. "Well, I can see that I'm playing to a tough house tonight." Standing by his side, Vigo could only shake his head in disbelief wondering how the two of them could treat the matter of her impending death so lightly. But then, he'd seen a seen a similar kind of fatalistic bravado time-and-again on the battlefield, as good friends died in his arms.

Perhaps the Senator, like his friends was a professional who had long readied herself for such an eventuality. It was the young and inexperienced ones who never had the time to master their own fear of death that would panic at the end.

"I'm sure that your toasts will receive standing applause," Chavez teased back weakly. "But tell me honestly, Anthony, what will happen after my heart finally stops?"

He paused to think about her question and then answered. "Have you had any strange dreams in the last day or so?"

"Yes, I have," she answered. "I keep dreaming; well it is much clearer than a dream; that I'm visiting all my friends and colleagues and that I'm trying to tell them things they should know and remember."

"But they never seem to hear you?"

"Yes. Precisely. My priest and my doctor are both telling me that I'm hallucinating but I know my own mind enough to know that it has to be more than that."

"You're not hallucinating, Connie. You have been doing something I call 'walking.' What that means, is that as you come nearer to finally crossing over, your spirit travels outside of your body to visit those for whom you care. The reason your friends and colleagues cannot hear you is the same reason why your priest and your doctor think that you are hallucinating. You are one step ahead of all of them in the cycle of life. This is just the way it works. Some cultures understand this and show reverence for what you are experiencing. Regrettably, our culture does not, and worse yet, we have the egotistical nerve to call those cultures that do backwards and primitive."

"So are you saying that death is like taking a long walk and never coming back?"

"Not necessarily. Once you step out of this body for the last time, you will be just as aware of yourself as you were in your walking dreams, but even more so. After that, there will be a universe of options for you to consider."

"Reincarnation is not accepted by my faith, but then I've never been devout. This makes me curious. Will I ever forget this life? Who I am? What I've done?"

Anthony placed one hand palm down under hers. His gentle touch connected with her and filled her with a special sense of comfort, as though she was suddenly now seeing her life in a new way.

"I like to think that mankind will survive and continue to evolve to the point where we will be able to remember our past lives as easily as we remember our first kiss. We will also remember those whom we've hurt through their own feelings and pain. This will fill us with the desire to define our lives through the noble deeds and tender love we shared with others in our life. In a manner of speaking, we will eventually learn to lead lives that we can cherish forever by not darkening them with senseless violent acts."

"I wonder how I'll remember this life. Will I cherish it? I hope so. I haven't always been a saint, but then I have few regrets as well."

"Connie, trust me when I tell you that you will cherish this life, especially through the experiences and feelings of those who have loved and cherished you. These memories will be so great; your human failings will pale in comparison. All in all, you will look back upon this life with a special reverence. In this, you are most fortunate."

The Senator looked into his eyes with deep gratitude not for what he had said, but for affirming what she already sensed and knew. "You're a kind and special man, Anthony. I can only wish I had come to know you better. Perhaps in another life?"

"I would like that," he replied earnestly.

"Captain Jarman, we're ready," Ann-Marie softly announced. Anthony nodded towards his nurse and turned his attention back to Chavez. "Since we're still waiting for Tanya to bring us the flowers, is there anything else?"

"Yes," she said as she raised her hand to two chains around her neck. "Vigo, dear friend, could you help me with this? I want to give these old trinkets of mine to Anthony."

Vigo stepped around to the other side of the bed and removed the two chains. One held a small Victorian-style locket and the other a platinum colored disk engraved with two columns with three symbols each, exactly like that one that hung from Vigo's own neck, hidden behind his tunic.

"Gosh, these are treasured family heirlooms. Are you sure they wouldn't be more appreciated by a member of your own family?"

"Anthony, shut up and tee off!" Anthony shook his head and chuckled. Even right up to the end, Connie Chavez was tough, spirited and determined to meet death on her own terms.

She turned her head towards Vigo. "Please be a dear and put these in his pocket for me, so that I can rest easily." Vigo smiled and did as she asked.

As he slipped the locket and the medallion into Anthony's breast pocket, Chavez said, "The locket belonged to my mother and to her mother before that. When you find your true love, Anthony, the woman with whom you intend to share rest of your life, please give this to her. The other is a simple, sentimental old bauble that old ladies like me like to collect. That is for you to remember me, and how I now cherish you for the kindness you will shortly bestow upon me. Do with it as you may."

"I will cherish them," he answered softly.

"I've got your roses, Senator, and they are magnificent." Tanya announced as she entered the room holding a dozen freshly picked roses wrapped in pink tissue and rested them gently on the bed next to Chavez's head.

Chavez turned her head to one side and drew a deep breath through her nose. The scent of the roses brought a loving smile to her lips.

"Your gardener, Pedro helped me. Apparently, you could not chase him away. You know, he cried like a baby as he prepared this bouquet. He loves you so much."

Chavez's face became grim. "Oh honey, I sent him to a hospital because he started showing possible symptoms of the Three Gorges flu. I'm very upset that he didn't go. I'm worried for you dear."

"I wouldn't worry. There wasn't much light in the hothouse, but he wasn't coughing," Tanya answered. "But he did reek a bit from some sweet-smelling Tequila."

"Uh-oh," Vigo blurted out. "Tequila does not smell sweet."

"Unless he's mixing it with cough syrup," Ann-Marie added, "which would explain why he wasn't coughing. The codeine in the syrup suppresses the central nervous system and calms the coughing."

Tanya's face turned pale white. She staggered backwards against the wall. "How could I have been so blind," she cried out. "Oh my God!"

Anthony's demeanor snapped in an instant. In a clear, controlled command voice, he began issuing snap orders. "Ann-Marie, I want you to take Tanya to a guest bedroom with a shower and get to work. Vigo, there is a decontamination kit and two HAZMAT suits on the chopper. You and the security chief need to put these suits on. Find and isolate the gardener. Before you do, bring the decontamination kit back here to Ann-Marie. I can handle the rest from here by myself. Ann-Marie, after you've finished the emergency procedures, we're outta here. Now get going, people! Start working the problem!"

Ann-Marie quickly slipped a surgical mask over her face and rushed to Tanya's side. Slipping another mask over Tanya's bewildered face; she began to help her out of the room as the security chief looked at Chavez with a hesitant look.

"Do exactly as Anthony says," Chavez ordered. He stepped aside to let Ann-Marie and Tanya pass and then followed Vigo out of the room at a fast trot.

After the four had left, Chavez closed her eyes with a pained expression on her face. "This is terrible -- so terrible!"

Anthony's demeanor softened somewhat. "Please do not be alarmed, Connie. We deal with this every day, and all of this is simply a precaution. We know what we're doing. Besides, each of use receives regular inhibitor injections for 3G to protect us from situations just like this." What he chose not to tell her was that their inhibitor treatments were less effective against the newest variant of the 3G flu.

Tears began to stream down Chavez's face as Anthony walked around to the other side of her bed where the I.V. stand stood.

"This awful; I don't know what to do," she lamented.

"If you wish to postpone this, that is your choice, but we will have to leave shortly. We need to place Tanya in isolation for at least 24 hours, for observation. Connie, there is nothing you can do for her, and, if I may be frank, you can help her more from the other side than from a sick bed."

"I hope you're right, Anthony."

"It is the honest truth."

"Then take me across, Anthony. Do it now."

Anthony took hold of the trigger grip with one hand and placed the other on her forehead. "I will take you halfway there, and from there you can decide this in a more relaxed setting."

CHAPTER 20

SHUT UP AND TEE OFF

THE FLIGHT BACK from Berkeley had been a dark and troubling ride. Vigo and the security chief had been unable to find the ailing gardener and remained behind, while Anthony and Ann-Marie tended to Tanya on the return trip with a heavy feeling of doubt and dread hanging over them. After Tanya had been transferred to isolation, he returned to his dome exhausted, collapsing immediately on his bunk in a deep, fitful sleep.

Starting the next day hadn't been any easier, he admitted to himself as he pushed the scrambled powdered eggs on his plate with disinterest. Luckily, his head was clear, but he only had enough appetite to slowly chew his biscuits and a few forkfuls of eggs. Washing them down with sweet tea, his mind was now centered entirely on Tanya.

Before going to the mess tent, he stopped by her isolation room to see how she was doing. She was sleeping, but he could see the initial telltale signs of stage two 3G. Because it appeared so quickly, it was obvious that Chavez's gardener had been infected with the latest, most deadly variant of 3G.

The virus had moved into her chest and already a hint of blue was appearing under her fingernails. She was dying and there was nothing anyone could do. Would it happen to him again as it had with Roxanne LeBlanc, his lover of years past who had secretly born a child by him? He would not get a chance to express his feelings and to let her know that he loved her.

It made him wonder if his destiny was to watch every woman he would ever come to love die before he could find the courage to express his feelings. It was as though he was cursed in love, and it made him wonder if he would spend the rest of his life alone for no reason.

With his eyes intensely fixed in a long stare, he agonized over this. Till now in his life, he had always avoided making himself vulnerable with expressions of love. Since he came to Los Gatos, however, everything changed, and he could no longer deny the love he now felt for a son he'd never met and whom evil and dark people were now holding hostage. He deeply hoped that he would get a chance to deal with all of that later, but for now, there was only Tanya.

There had been an evening of inspired petting and his deep attraction to her. Had he really fallen in love with her, only to ignore it as he had with Roxanne LeBlanc? Even if Roxanne had not loved him, he loved her, and knowing that he lacked the courage to tell her so had become a deep pain in his soul.

He faced his doubts. There was no backing out of it; he was in love with Tanya. Now that she was dying, could he let her slip away without knowing how much he cared for her? Was it so important to his sense of emotional security to remain silent as he always had in the past?

As he pondered this question, he saw Vigo walk into the mess tent with dark bags under his eyes as they searched for him. Obviously, he'd been traveling all night and hadn't slept. Anthony smiled at him as he sat down on the bench next to him.

"Man, I feel like I've been rode hard and put up wet," Vigo moaned. "I'm getting too old for this."

"I've still got a few Ginseng vials in my wall locker if you want it," Anthony replied. "Since you already know the combination to that lock, you can go and help yourself."

Vigo shook his head and then looked around to see if anyone within earshot of them was noticing their conversation. Most of the staff had already had their breakfast, and the mess tent was almost empty. Except for the usual cooking and cleaning sounds from the kitchen, the tent was extremely quiet. Satisfied that they had a reasonable amount of privacy, he fished the data chip from his pocket and put it in Anthony's hand and said in a hushed voice, "I didn't take this from you, son. I took it from the thief who tried to rob you this morning while you were visiting Tanya."

"A thief?" Anthony also said with a hushed voice.

"Not just a thief, Anthony; he was a spook sent here to spy on you while pretending to be one of the maintenance crew."

"Oh, shit!" Anthony exclaimed as he cradled his forehead in his hands. No doubt, his dome was bugged. "How much? You know. How much did he get?"

"I was bringing you some Scotch whisky this morning, figured I'd leave it on your bunk, when I found him sneaking out of your dome. I followed him and then took him down where we would not be noticed. That was when I found the chip and this," he slipped a small microwave receiver from his pant pocket just enough for Anthony to see it and then pushed it back in. "It made sweeping your dome for bugs a whole lot easier, and I got them all. Trust me when I tell you that it was real state-of-the-art stuff, my boy. As it turned out, leaving the whiskey for you was a good cover for me. As for the spy, well let's just say that he just had an unfortunate rock climbing accident, as in keep your mouth shut and don't ask any questions."

"No problemo. So, what's on the chip, Vigo?"

"Detailed architectural renderings of an old missile silo at Fort Hood Texas, and two highly classified CIA dossiers on a couple of Syrians who go by the names of Colonel Yasin and Captain Darkazani. According to her security chief, Connie got it the day before she asked you to go to

Berkeley. Jesus, this thing is big. Senator Chavez must have had to pull in some pretty damn big markers to get this stuff, because she had to get it to you. It is where Russell is being held."

"Well then, let's go and get him."

"Whoa, hot shot. Taking on a whole military base is no simple undertaking. With an operation like this, people are going to die. Lots of people." Vigo leaned over and whispered. "The UNE controls that silo, Anthony. Perhaps this will give you an idea of what we're up against. Son, we'll only get one chance. We'll do it, but we've got to do it right the first time, so let old Vigo work on this till we're ready to move. Can I trust you for that?"

Anthony smiled for the first time and nudged Vigo's arm. "Ok, grandfather. We'll play it your way."

Anthony's endearment made Vigo's tired eyes beam with joy. "You just let old dad do the foot work here. You'd be surprised at the kind of things that can be done if you know what to do, and I've been there, done it, seen it and bought all the damn tee shirts. Now, I can tell you that this is not going to be a two-man job. We're going to need a team, but that's no problem. You'd be surprised at how many people are willing to go out on a limb for you, son."

"Other lives at risk. I don't know how I feel about this. Have you already begun recruiting a team?"

"No. Not until you give me the go-ahead. You're Russell's daddy and I'm, by God, not going to jump into your turf."

"These are high stakes, Vigo. I've got to have some time to think about it."

"That's fine, but we don't have the luxury of time, son."

"Why don't you get yourself something to eat, Vigo, and let me think a minute?"

"Sure, them eggs look like shit but at least they're warm." He slid out of the bench as Anthony took a sip of tea and pondered his revelations.

Anthony was almost to the bottom of his cup of tea when Vigo returned with full tray sporting a small pile of bacon strips. Anthony glanced at the bacon, "how in the hell did you manage that?"

"Trade secret, my boy, but no worries. I brought enough for the both of us." He put half the bacon on Anthony's tray and began digging in.

"OK, supposing for one minute," Anthony ventured, "I say it's a go. Who have you got in mind for the team?"

Vigo swallowed his mouthful of bacon and said, "For starters, your orderly, Charlie. He is one hell of a sharpshooter, and we'll need someone like him to take out a few of the guards. We'll also need a military transport and some other folks as well. The transport could be the biggest problem."

Anthony shook his head. "Do you know the crew of the Flying Circus?"

"Heck, yeah."

"If and when I decide to do this, you'll find an old telescope eyepiece on the top shelf of my locker. Give it to Captain Jerome Richard and tell him what you need."

"See, it's already coming together. I know you've got to warm up to it and all, but I smell a successful rescue here. The minute you say the word, I'll be all over this like white on rice."

Anthony turned towards him and put an arm on his shoulder. "Vigo, I'm sure glad we ironed out our differences yesterday. It has been a long time in my life since a man could ever make me feel like a son."

For Vigo, the words were a blessing to hear, and they brought a warm, yet fierce smile to his lips. "I could never hope to walk in your real father's shoes, Anthony, but I love you every bit as much even if I am an old, scruffy son-of-a-bitch with an attitude. We're going to pull through all of this together, and things are going to be OK."

Anthony nodded, "Before you walked into this mess tent, I felt like my life was going down the drain. Now, I've got some hope. By the way, did you ever find that gardener?"

Vigo's face fell. "Yeah. Seeing two jerks in moon suits with drawn pistols scared the hell out of the poor fellow. We got him down and held him till EMS arrived. He looked to me to have 3G. Funny how that virus works. Some folks go quick, and others go real slow. This guy was going slow. Heck, maybe it was the tequila, who knows? How about Tanya, what's the story on her?"

Anthony sighed, "She's going quick, Vigo. Too quick."

"Oh, God," he exclaimed. "I knew it was a long shot, but I was hoping she'd be OK. Damn shame it is. I could see how much you two love each other. I was really hoping you two would have a chance to get together. Heck, everyone in this center was secretly hoping for the same thing. How are you taking it?"

"It's different when it's somebody you care for."

"I know, son. Have you told her you love her?"

"No."

Vigo stacked the trays and cups and stood up. "I'll care of this stuff. You know what you've got to do, so get after it."

A melancholy smile crossed Anthony's face. "I'll do it right now."

ANTHONY PEEKED THROUGH the door to Tanya's isolation room. She was awake and speaking with Ramona. Baker saw him and motioned for him to enter. As soon as he entered the room holding a hand-made balloon, Tanya's ashen face lit up. He had made the balloon from a surgical glove and painted a happy face on it with colored markers.

He walked up beside her bed and placed the balloon next to her. "Thank you, Anthony," she said with weak but cheerful voice. "It is a beautiful balloon."

"Well, it's not what I really had in mind," he said tenderly. "But darn the luck, the gift shop was closed this morning."

"But we don't have a gift shop."

"I guess that explains why I couldn't find it," he teased. "How are you, kiddo?"

"I could say something foolishly brave, like 'I've been better,' but I know my number is up. Still the same, I'm really glad to see you. I really am."

Looking exhausted yet determined to stay by her friend; Ramona sensed a deeper level of feelings between them than ever before and excused herself from the room to give them their privacy.

Anthony pulled a chair next to Tanya's bed and sat close by. Reaching through the side rail he gently took held her hand. "If you get tired and need to rest, just let me know."

"Please stay, Anthony. I've thought so much about you and how much time I wasted. We could have been much more if only I hadn't been so…"

"Hesitant," he added.

"Yes."

He squeezed her hand lovingly. "We were both hesitant, so no regrets."

"Anthony, I don't want to die like a vegetable. Will you help me when the time comes?"

The simple request shot through him like a painful bolt. Each day, he heard the same request time-and-again from strangers, but hearing it from her lips was a new and terrible thing. His lower lip trembled slightly as he spoke with a sad, resigned voice, "of course."

Troubled by the thought of helping her across, he picked up a moist towel from a medical tray and dabbed moisture into her dry lips. Lips that had once tasted so sweet to him.

Setting the cloth down, he blinked hesitantly for a moment. "Tanya, I want you to know something that is important to me. Well, it is important that I know you know, if you follow what I mean."

"Yes, Anthony."

He cleared his throat. "Before I tell you, I want you to know that you don't have to say anything. I just need for you to hear it." She nodded with soft, encouraging eyes.

"Tanya, I love you, and I'm going to miss you terribly. I'm not asking you to love me back, but I just wanted you to know. I guess I'm just being selfish, but I couldn't go through the rest of my life knowing that I'd missed this opportunity to tell you. Losing you now is hard enough as it is."

Tears began to well up in her sunken eyes. "Anthony, my dear Anthony. I love you, too, and I so wish we could have had more time together. When we're healthy and dealing with life, we always try and postpone some things until we feel ready. Yet, when the end comes, we realize, as I have now, that life is sweet and so short and not to be wasted on such antics."

A wave of relief washed through him followed by a terrible sense of loss and grief. He wanted to cry more than anything in the world yet not a single tear would grace his cheek as he looked upon her with a deep sense of longing and remorse. Closing his eyes, he rested his forehead against the cool metal of the side rail. "It's not fair," he lamented.

With great effort, Tanya lifted her arm from the other side of her body and stroked his hair with a slight tremble. "My dear Anthony. You are so kind and good with the process of dying. If only there was a way to reverse the process." Taking a shallow breath, she laid her arm across her chest.

"Process." He whispered. "A process. Yes!" The word had suddenly triggered an epiphany in his mind. His head shot up as a myriad of ideas tumbled quickly in his mind and she could see the firestorm of thought in his eyes. "Tanya, I think there is a way, just maybe. It will not be easy and you will have to help me, but will you let me try?"

"Will it put you at risk?"

"No. The only risk is that it will not work. Let me explain. I believe that in Chinese medicine they would say that you have an exterior wind invasion. In such a case, the treatment would be to find a way to let the evil out of your body. However, the problem is that you are so weak that it will not work. But if we can direct the healing energy of the universe into your body, it could give you the strength to achieve the same goal."

"Do you mean something like acupuncture?"

"Not really, even though acupressure will be a part of it. Look, I'm not a doctor, and most doctors would think I'm nuts for talking about this, but when I was in college I took a few special interest classes on Jin Shin Jyutsu. It is a Japanese healing art, and it was practiced before Moses was born. Essentially, what you do is to use a light touch to harmonize the body, mind and spirit, to draw the healing power of the universe into the body and bring it back into balance. I've forgotten a lot of what I learned, but I still remember a few techniques and use them to help my clients to relax so they can leave their bodies. Although if my old instructor ever learned I was doing this, she'd have a fit."

Tanya rolled her eyes. "I don't think I have enough time left to try this Anthony."

He raised his hands. "Give me a chance, here, so I can explain the rest of it to you. Please, I'm about to tell you things that I never share with anyone else. Things that must remain between us." Tanya smiled and nodded even though she felt certain it would not work. Yet, for his sake, she would listen.

"All things vibrate," he began. "Our bodies vibrate as does the spirit within each of us. While doctors speak of death in clinical terms that they can measure, what I see and know is simply a change of the body's vibrational state."

"I'm not following you," she said weakly.

"All right. Let me put it this way. A healthy body vibrates at a level sufficient to contain the spirit. When its vibration rate drops, it can no longer contain the spirit. In the case of death, the spirit floats free. We can alter our vibrational state through meditation and similar techniques and give our spirits a chance to leave our bodies for a short period of time. This is really all that I do when I work with my clients. I change the vibrational state of their bodies so they can float free long enough to make their final decision. If they decide not go across, I simply up their vibration rate."

"But Anthony, how does this relate to the 3G virus?"

"What the virus is doing, or more specifically the effect of the virus, is to lower of the vibrational state of your body to a point where it can no longer contain your soul. Call it death. Call it what you want. But this is what I see every day. Up till this moment, I've always thought of it as basically a one-way ticket, but now I'm proposing that we fight fire with fire, as one would say. We are going to pump up the vibrational state of your body to a point where it overwhelms the virus and kills it."

"Using this Japanese healing art you mentioned?"

"Yes, but much more. I want to throw the kitchen sink at this thing. Some things may help and some not, but somehow some combination of things has to work."

"I have so little energy, but I'll try. What do I need to do?"

"You need to eat, and I'm not talking about that broth you've been sipping, nor your dextrose drip, either. You need real nourishment. Also, we need to get your senses active and feeding input to your mind."

Gathering her meager strength, she touched his face. "Your idea sounds marvelous, but I'm too far gone Anthony. You've got to let go."

He took her hand in his and kissed it tenderly. "I have hope, Tanya, but it is your choice. I just want you to hear me say two things and then I'll do whatever you say." She nodded in agreement. "First off. I love you, and knowing that you love me is one of the greatest gifts of my life." He paused for a silent moment, waiting for her to ask.

"And what is the second thing?"

"Shut up and tee off!"

The words of Senator Chavez had struck a clarion note of logic once again and Tanya chuckled. She thought about it for moment and finally said, "In my dome, there are some cans of New England Clam Chowder. I love the stuff and I've been saving it for something special. Will that do for nourishment?"

"Yes! Yes!" he replied gleefully. "Now the senses, music, videos, whatever."

"I have some really old DVD rock and roll videos of my favorite groups, like Pupo and the Scorpions. Will they do?"

"Yes, that will work perfectly." He stood up still holding on to her hand. "I'm going to get things started. In the meantime, promise me you'll put your heart into it, Tanya. Please promise me you'll do this."

His love for her filled her with a renewed sense of vigor. Whether or not his plan worked, she would meet this challenge with him because she loved him. "I believe in you, Anthony."

A huge smile sailed across his face from ear-to-ear. He tenderly laid her hand down, "I love you Tanya, and we're going to beat this. I'll be back real soon."

THE LAST THING Chief Medical Officer Jim Boole and Physician assistant Ramona Baker expected to see was Anthony bounding out of Tanya's isolation unit past them like a young boy racing out to a school yard for recess.

"Whoa there, Anthony," Boole called out. "Just what is going on?"

Anthony stopped and turned to face them. "We're going to beat this thing. I've talked it over with Tanya, and we're going to do it."

"Do what?"

"Beat the virus. We're going to reverse the process."

"Hold your horses, here! I'm the Chief Medical Officer here, and you're not doing anything with one my patients unless I approve. If you have an idea, I'm open. If not, the last I'm going to do is let you tear around here like some kind of cowboy, so start explaining yourself."

Reluctantly, Anthony began explaining his epiphany and what he planned to do as Boole and Baker listened with stunned expressions. When Anthony finished, Boole raised back into a stern posture. "You're going to use some Jin Shin voodoo or whatever you call it and all this other nonsense to save her. My God man, her heart can't take the strain of all this kitchen sink theory of yours."

Ramona winced at Boole's words and decided to step in. "Actually Jim," she said with a stern professional voice, "they are developing new techniques for emergency medical technicians at Walter Reed which just happen to be based on Jin Shin Jyutsu. I didn't work on it, but I heard a lot about it. It seems to be very effective."

Boole turned to her with an incredulous stare. "You gotta be shitting me?"

She held up two fingers. "As God is my witness."

Boole's jaw sagged and Anthony saw a chance to pick up on Ramona's cue. "Look, Jim, Tanya knows she's dying, and so do you. OK, so you feel this is a 'kitchen sink' idea, as you so quaintly phrased it. So what have you got to offer? I'll tell what you've got to offer." He jabbed a finger in the direction of the trenches. "I see what you have to offer kneeling in front of my trenches every day. Well now, I've got an idea, and you're playing hard-ass with Tanya's chances of beating this thing to satisfy your god-doctor-on-Mount-Olympus complex, you pompous, smug son-of-a-bitch."

Boole's eyes glowed with anger. "Maybe you never studied history you self-important primadonna. There were no black gods on Mount Olympus, but I did drag my black ass through medical school and into a position of respect, because I do not play fast and loose with people's lives!"

Now it was Anthony's turn to be taken aback while Ramona gritted her teeth. "OK, we'll skip the black god on Mount Olympus part because I was asleep in class that day. Still the same, you owe it to Tanya to let me try."

Boole waved his hands and nodded his head from side-to-side. "What I owe her is all the time she's got left and I'm not going to let you come in here with some hare-brained cock-and-bull idea and change that."

Anthony fumed. "Fuck you. I'll go over your head."

As Boole reared his head back for a hot retort, Ramona stepped between the two of them holding one hand against Boole's chest and the other against Anthony's. "Have you fully explained this to Tanya, and if so, did she agree to it?"

"Yes, I explained it to her, and yes, she agreed."

"So where were you going from here so fast?"

"To her dome to get some things she wants."

She pushed him away. "Go stand by that gurney over there while I consult privately with Dr. Boole." Anthony raised an eyebrow. "I'm having a serious PMS day, Anthony, so don't fuck with me." Anthony backed away and did as she instructed, while mumbling to himself.

Boole started to back away as well and was suddenly surprised when Ramona grabbed his surgical gown in her fist and pulled him towards her. She looked into his face with a grim smile. "We're going to have a professional conversation now, Doctor." She nodded towards Tanya's isolation room. "My best friend is there dying right now, and if she wants to play voodoo witch doctor with the man she loves, then who in the hell are you to stand in her way?"

"But, but," Boole stammered.

"You're jabbing your thumb on my PMS hot button and there's no telling what I might do if you don't get your 'I put my black ass through med school' down from Mount Olympus this instant. Do you feel lucky?"

He wrapped his hand gently around her fist and sighed. "I'll listen."

"Uh-huh," Ramona replied with a glaring nod. She let go of his gown and turned to Anthony and gestured for him to join them knowing that she'd just tamed two rams locking horns at the wrong time.

They discussed Anthony's plan in calmer tones, and finally Boole agreed after glancing several times at Ramona's stern gaze. As Anthony left for Tanya's dome, Ramona reached up, kissed Boole on the cheek and whispered in his ear, "You an adorable, old curmudgeon. You know that don't you?" Boole could only growl with resignation.

ANTHONY HAD SPENT the day checking in on Tanya whenever he could. Word about what he planned to do buzzed through the center, and everyone begged him and Ramona to let them help.

Sunny Sharma, Tanya's orderly had overheard the fight between Anthony and Boole and met Anthony on his way to Tanya's dome asking him to let him gather her things while Anthony made other arrangements.

Preparations took on a whirlwind proportion from that point as Sunny gathered up the canned soup and DVDs from Tanya's dome. The cooks prepared her soup with tender loving care and a special flourish of condensed milk, along with a pinch of this and that thrown in for good measure.

As Ramona lovingly fed Tanya one spoonful after another of the perfectly heated Clam Chowder, Professor Goldberg's soundman Pete and his videographer Jerry had cannibalized various audio/video systems to create a huge entertainment system in Tanya's isolation unit. In no time at all, patients were clamoring to know why Tanya's isolation room was now reverberating with the outdated wailing sounds of Russian rock and roll artists.

After another tough day, Anthony ate a light meal and took a long hot shower before returning to Tanya's room for the next major step in the process. Entering the room, he found Boole pressing the bell of his stethoscope against Tanya's chest as Ramona glanced up at the monitoring panel mounted above Tanya's head.

Boole closed his eyes as she listened intently to Tanya's heart. Finally, he stood and removed the diaphragms from his ears and draped the stethoscope around his neck. "You're better than you were this morning," he announced to Tanya. "Don't ask me why, but you are."

Ramona touched his arm and motioned in Anthony's direction. "I've done all I can do," he said. "Come on, Ramona; let's leave these two to their voodoo."

Anthony walked up to the foot of Tanya's bed as they left. Lifting her blanket, he wrapped the fingers of both of his hands around each of Tanya's big toes. Her energy had improved, just enough perhaps for the next step.

"So, I heard Father Bennett did his juggling act for you?" Anthony asked with a smile.

"That and the singing," she replied in good humor. "Honestly, Anthony, I do adore the man, but he couldn't carry a tune if his life depended on it."

"Au contraire, my dear. You've only heard him when he's sober."

Tanya chuckled. "Well, are we ready for the next step?"

"All we've been doing is warming up the orchestra, Tanya, and you're ready for what will be a stressful experience for your body. But it is now or never."

"It's time to go for broke," Anthony whispered under his breath as he walked around to the side of the bed. Tanya watched him approach with alert eyes. She too sensed that this would be her one and only chance, and she felt ready.

As he lowered the side rail of her bed, he spoke in reassuring tones, "Whatever happens next, Tanya, I'll be with you."

"I believe in you, Anthony, and I'm ready," she said firmly. "Let's do it."

He gently placed one hand on her heart and cupped the back of her neck with the other, at the base of her skull. "We're going to my garden now, so close your eyes and relax." Tanya took one more deep breath and closed her eyes as she exhaled.

When she reopened her eyes, she found herself standing alone in a garden filled with incredible roses of every imaginable shape and color. The weak, achy feeling was gone, and she felt light and comfortable.

She sensed his presence on the other side of a large rose bed, and as she walked towards him, her feet felt as though they barely touched the ground. As she walked lightly through the rose beds, she paused to enjoying their beauty with serene amazement. "Anthony, are you here?"

"I'm waiting for you in the clearing, just beyond the hedges. Keep on coming," he said. Following his voice, she looked up saw that the garden was surrounded by a solid, pearly white sky. There was no sun, yet the garden was bright and airy.

Walking past the hedges, she saw Anthony dressed in a long flowing, soft, white gown. He moved towards her and held out his hand. "You're in my garden, Tanya. This is a place of my own making, and sometimes I share it with my patients, especially the young ones. For them, I usually create a swing for them to help them adjust. If you would like I can create it for you now?"

"No need." She looked around again, "My God, this is so beautiful. I had no idea."

"Come, take my hand, Tanya; there is something else I must show you." She took his outstretched hand, as the garden below her feet became transparent revealing her own body below. "I need to show you the virus that is attacking your body. Are you ready?"

"Yes."

"Close your eyes." She did as he asked without hesitation.

A moment later he said, "You can open eyes now." To her astonishment, she was inside her own heart. It was huge and cavernous, and the walls grew and relaxed slowly, making her feel no larger than the virus that was now destroying her body. Still holding onto her hand, Anthony guided her towards what she immediately recognized as the Three Gorges virus, just like the ones she'd seen so often from the electron microscope images on the web.

They floated just a few lengths away from it, completely unaffected by the beating of her heart, and she could see details within the multi-colored ball-like virus that researchers saw, but with clarity far beyond that available to researchers using their powerful and elaborate laboratory equipment. "I've seen this several times," Anthony noted impassively as they hovered in front of the virus. "It's a real monster."

"Anthony, when I'm not pushing paper and filling out requests for things we usually never get, I spend some of my free time studying molecular virology. I'm not really a qualified researcher by any means, but I'm just fascinated by them. If you can set aside the fact that they kill, they're sometimes beautiful to observe, with their elegant symmetry, colors and subtle variations. But most of all, this is the one I've studied the most. Yet now, I'm seeing a level of detail that is unimaginable. Can we move around it?"

"As long as you're holding my hand Tanya. Just tell me where you want to go."

"Great! For starters, let's do a slow rotation around the x-axis, and then we'll do the same around the y-axis."

"One twenty-five cent tour coming up."

First, they floated around the x-axis of the virus with an occasional pause now and again as Tanya studied one more aspect in closer detail. However, as they had floated halfway over the top of the virus Tanya suddenly ordered, "Stop. Take me in closer. As close you as can."

She studied a part of the virus that seemed no different from any other to Anthony as he waited patiently. Finally, she turned to him with sad eyes and said, "This monster has killed over a billion people, and it was engineered by human hands. Somebody made this awful thing."

"I've always figured that, but can somebody actually find a way to destroy it?"

"I believe so, now that I've seen this. We can create a vaccine provided two things happen."

"And those are?"

"I must live to tell the CDC researchers in Washington. Between that and my own antibodies, provided my body can destroy all of these viruses, this could be what they need for a cure." She looked at him with imploring eyes, "I can't die now, Anthony. We've got to succeed. We must!"

"Close your eyes, Tanya."

When she reopened her eyes, she was back in the garden in the exact same clearing as before.

"Tanya," he said softly. "The next step will be more difficult for you. That is why I showed you the virus. While I've always had my suspicions, I was still surprised to learn that it was engineered. Frankly, I cannot begin to understand how someone with this kind of knowledge could create such a terrible killer that is so hard to kill."

"When monsters like these are created, a way to destroy them is also created, or at least it usually is," she replied. "It reminds me of something novelist Frank Herbert once said, 'He who can destroy a thing, controls a thing?' Well, this one got out of control."

He took both of her hands. "Tanya, I'm really not sure how this next step will play itself out. You know, I've been making this up as we go along, and so far, we've been pretty lucky. So are you ready for that next step?"

"Let's do it."

He pointed to the ground at her feet. "Just sit and wait. I'll be back in a moment."

She settled herself on the cool, green grass at her feet and watched with curiosity as Anthony walked through the pearly white sky that bordered the edge of the garden. In a million years, she could never have been prepared for what happened next. Anthony returned to the garden, and just behind him, a second figure stepped through the pearly, white sky. It was the spirit of Henry Wheelwright, looking as fit and healthy as the day she first met him in Moscow.

"Hi, kitten," Henry said with a wink. Speechless, she could only nod at the visage of her dead husband.

Henry looked about the garden with an appreciative smile and said to Anthony, "I like your garden. It is most impressive."

"Well, it's a work in progress, you might say," Anthony replied modestly. "Unfortunately, I can only maintain this for a short while more." Henry nodded.

Anthony gestured with hand. "Come here, Tanya."

Still speechless, she rose as he instructed her and joined them. Anthony took her hand and guided it to Henry's. "I've taken this as far as I possibly can. I'm going to leave you both alone now."

"Thank you, Anthony," Henry replied as Anthony's image disappeared.

"Am -- am I hallucinating?" Tanya asked as she stood alone with Henry in the garden.

"Look inside yourself, Kitten, and see if you have lost your fear of death?"

She closed her eyes for a moment and slowly reopened them. "Yes."

"Then you're not hallucinating."

"It's really you Henry?"

"Yes, Kitten. Would like to take a little trip with me?"

"I'll go anywhere with you."

"Close your eyes."

When she reopened her eyes, she was standing next to him in the Novokuznetskaya metro station in Moscow where she had found Henry as he'd wandered away from the American tour group she had been guiding.

"You know, Kitten, this was one of the finest days of my former life. I'll never forget the moment you found me. It was late at night, and the place was almost deserted. I remember how you were so frustrated with me and yet glad to find me at the same time. Although I have to tell you, not half as glad I was." He pointed to the connecting tunnel that linked metro lines 6 and 8. Somebody or something was playing Glen Miller's Moonlight Serenade on a trombone and it seemed to echo off the marble walls of the station as though it were a perfect speaker system. "It was amazing," Henry reminisced, "that just one man with a trombone could fill such a huge place. And the music was so sweet."

"I remember."

"Do you remember what happened next?"

"How could I forget?"

"Shall we?" He held out his arms to dance as they had first done that very night. Except this time, Tanya was far more willing.

They began dancing a slow simple box step to the rhythm of the trombonist's melodic tune.

"You know this was the moment that I fell madly in love with you, and I've always kept it tucked away in my memories. Many are the times that I've returned to the memory, especially when things were at their worst. I was never a spontaneous man, but this was that one moment in my life when it just seemed to be the right thing to do. You cannot imagine how glad I am that I followed my instincts that night."

"I've missed you so much. You can't imagine."

"I know."

"Henry, if this is what heaven is really like, I'm not sure I want to go back."

"It's not your time, Kitten. Your destiny now is to save billions of lives. What could be more important than that?"

"But I'm going to lose you again."

"You never lost me, Kitten. You never will. But now, I sense that Anthony's strength is waning. We must take the final step now, but before we do, could you promise me something?"

"Anything."

"A man will come to Anthony with a bargain. He and Anthony share a common bone through Anthony's son, and he is to be trusted. When the time comes, please help Anthony to understand this."

"He can be pretty stubborn, but I'll do my best."

"I want you to know that I'm happy to see you two together. He is an exceptional man, and he will love you every bit as much as I."

"Yes I love him, but I'm also having such a hard time letting go of you."

"Our memories of being together will last for eternity, Kitten. But today, there is your life, and I'm glad you found each other."

"But aren't you just a little bit jealous?"

He laughed. "I was never jealous when I was alive. Why would I be jealous now?" She also laughed, remembering how Ramona Baker had once told her the same thing.

"And now, my darling, we will take the last step together."

"What will happen to you?"

"Nothing really. In a manner of speaking you could say that I'll sleep for a while and then I'll be my usual perky self again." With that, he placed an arm between her shoulder blades and leaned her backwards. "One last kiss before I go, my dear."

As he slowly leaned forward to kiss her she said, "I've always loved you Henry and I always will." Their lips met and suddenly Tanya was surrounded by a brilliant white light that glowed with a sense of love that was powerful beyond all words. It flowed through her like a river of life, overwhelming her completely.

From beside her bed, Anthony saw her head fall limply to one side. It was done. Now, would come the waiting.

CHAPTER 21

DESTINED FOR GREATNESS

THE PREVIOUS EVENING had been draining for Anthony. Tanya was in a deep, coma-like slumber, but by midnight, her vital signs began showing a marked improvement, and Ramona finally managed to talk him into going to bed. Exhausted, he stopped by the kitchen. One of the cooks got up out of bed to make him a generous sandwich and a bowl of soup, which he wolfed down with great appetite. After a short shower, he collapsed in his bed till it was time for him to resume his usual routine the next day.

While the center was abuzz with the events of the night before and speculating that Tanya would survive, it remained an especially draining day for Anthony. Between his duties as an ELMO and checking on Tanya whenever he could, it had been a taxing day. While each improvement in Tanya's health sent another encouraging round of hope through the center, he reserved both his hope and judgment. On top of this, he also fought the distracting thoughts of what to do about his son, Russell, doing all he could to push his thoughts of both Russell and Tanya to the back of his mind.

As he walked with Charlie towards the two remaining patients kneeling at the edge of the trench, he felt grateful that this especially long and difficult day of uncertainty would end momentarily.

Anthony stood behind the second to last client, a middle-aged man suffering from the 3G flu and Charlie handed him a freshly loaded pistol. Checking to see the safety was on, he placed his left hand on the man's left shoulder. For some, this last moment at the trench was difficult and for others a welcome release best done sooner than later. Without saying a word or hesitating, the man lowered his head.

Anthony could see the spirit of his deceased wife waiting for him and helped him to release himself from his own body. Had there not been someone waiting for him on the other side, Anthony would have backed away, but that seldom happened any more.

He slowed the man's vibratory rate to a point where his spirit could free itself. Without turning back, the man's spirit went happily to that of his waiting wife. He turned to face Anthony with a smile and with a gesture of his hand caused his head to lower. Anthony nodded knowingly and with surgical precision, placed the muzzle of the pistol near the base of the man's skull. After sensing the trajectory path needed to pierce the base of his brain stem, he pulled the trigger. The body jerked from the impact of the bullet as it found its mark. Releasing his grip, the man's body fell forward limply upon the lime-covered bodies below.

Assisting the last client kneeling at the end of the trench to cross over would not be as simple. An eighteen-year-old girl with festering toxic poisoning sores, she glanced nervously to one side as Anthony approached. "I'm afraid," she said meekly as he stood behind her.

Anthony handed his pistol back to Charlie and knelt next to her, facing the trench. No two people ever crossed over exactly the same way, but some, like this unfortunate girl who knew she faced an agonizing death, still would have last-minute bouts of doubt. He reached around her, lifted her arm and read her name from the identity strap. "Becky, this is your choice," he said softly. "Perhaps this is not the right time for you."

She turned and looked into his face, "But I'm so tired of living with this horrible pain. I'm sorry; I just didn't think

I'd choke like this at the last minute. It's just that I'm afraid of becoming nothing. Do you know what I mean?"

Anthony placed a hand on her shoulder. "Turn around, look ahead and tell me what you see," he said with a compassionate yet weary voice.

She looked ahead past the other side of the trench. "Oh my God, I see my family. They're waiting for me and I feel their love. But..."

"But you think you're imagining it, Becky?"

"Yes," she answered with a tinge of shame in her voice.

"You're not. They are there, and I see them too. Your father is a large man with strong arms and you mother is a petite woman wearing the same dress she wore to your grade school graduation."

Grateful tears began to well up in her eyes. "I feel that they're telling me it is OK to come. That this is my time."

"Still the same, Becky, this choice is yours to make and yours alone."

"What will it feel like?"

"When I see your spirit with those of your parents I will terminate your body functions so that you can cross completely over. You will already be out of your body when I pull the trigger, so you will feel no pain."

"Now that I see them waiting for me, I'm ready. Thank you Anthony." With that, she lowered her chin to her chest and waited. Charlie handed the pistol back to Anthony as he positioned himself behind her.

He placed his hand on her shoulder and softly said, "It's all going to be OK now, Becky, but you must let go now." Anthony could see her spirit leaving her dying, emaciated body. For a moment, she stood next to herself eyeing the surrounds with calm curiosity.

"Am I already dead?" she asked.

"No, Becky. You are at a point of decision: Whether to remain here or to cross over to your family. What happens next is entirely up to you."

"Can I see you on the other side sometime?"

"I'd like that," he answered with a gentle smile.

She looked down at herself and made her head to fall forward. "Thank you, Anthony," she said as she went towards her family.

Positioning the pistol, he instinctively searched for the right trajectory. Having found it, he pulled the trigger for the last time that day and watched her limp body fall forward down into the trench. Looking up, he could see her embracing her parents. He flipped the safety lever on the pistol and handed it back to Charlie, who was now standing next to the trench.

Charlie looked down at Becky's body, sprawled at the bottom of the trench. "You know, Captain, the ones my age are always the hardest for me. Even though I see her as she is now, I pretend that I've just seen her racing around some college campus on her very first day of class, meeting with her girlfriends afterwards at the college cafeteria to share her day with them."

"Yes, Charlie," Anthony sighed. "But you can't let it get to you."

"It never does, boss," Charlie, replied as he removed the clip from the pistol and ejected the remaining unfired cartridge from the chamber. "The funny thing is that lately, I've begun to see the spirits too. Not like you, I expect. For me, they're all kind of fuzzy, but I still see them occasionally, more clearly now, like Becky and her family."

It was the first time that Charlie had ever revealed his inner thoughts. Up till now, they had simply confined their conversations to the necessary tasks, by Anthony's own wish. Looking back on it in a moment of reflection, Anthony felt regret for that and vowed that he would spend more time with Charlie, especially now that he was becoming more sensitive.

As they walked away from the trench, Anthony put his arm around Charlie's shoulder for the first time. "Let's keep this between us, Charlie," he cautioned. "Our patients and the people in this center will understand what you're saying and how you are now becoming more sensitive. However, if you speak of this with anyone and it is reported to a higher level, they'll say that you've lost your mind."

"But I haven't lost my mind, Captain. You see it, and now I see it!" He pointed at the mouth of the trench. "Heck, even they've seen it."

"You're right. The problem is this; the people who have the power to do with you as they wish have not seen the same things, nor do they wish to see the same things. Ergo, their own denial of reality can easily become your own sentence of psychological trauma. Or in other words, their power makes it easier for them to unfairly destroy your life so as to keep themselves from having to face their own mortality."

"It's just not right," Charlie fumed.

Anthony patted his shoulder. "My dear Charlie, it is the way of things. Like I said, do not speak of this to anyone, but once things have settled down a bit, let's talk about this more. Privately, of course. I'm sure you have a lot of questions, and as your friend, I'm interested in knowing and understanding more about your feelings."

Anthony's words had been like honey in his ears. "Thanks, Captain; that really means a lot to me," Charlie said as he felt his bond with Anthony grow closer.

They walked a little further and began to plan for the next day as Father Michael Bennett joined them. His face radiated joy, "Tanya hasn't woken up yet, Anthony, but Ramona just told me her heart is beating like a Kentucky Derby winner, and the blue is gone from her fingers. And get this; Dr. Boole is saying she'll make it and telling me to nominate you for sainthood."

Anthony grinned as he stripped off his surgical gloves and mask and put his hands to his forehead. His personal relief was speechless yet obvious. "I'm really glad for the news, but I'm no saint, Father. Heck, I'm not even Catholic."

"We can work that out," Father Bennett replied with a broad smile.

Anthony held up his right index finger, and, waving it back and forth, said, "No, no, no, no, no! But maybe there is something else you can help me with."

Father Bennett laughed. "It would be my joy to help you in any way I can."

"I'll finish up here, boss," Charlie said, seeing it was time for him to slip away from the conversation.

Anthony waved him off, "Thanks, Charlie, and remember what I said." The young orderly nodded proudly and left.

"Well then," Father Bennett began. Since we're both finished for the day, I could really use a few slugs of that marvelous Scotch whisky Vigo gave you."

"Scotch? And speaking of Vigo, where is he?"

"He left this afternoon. He said he was going to the Livermore Air Base to pick up a few things and that he'd be back in the morning. Before he left, he left two bottles of 12-year old Chivas Regal scotch in our dome and asked me to stay close to you. You know that he cares for you deeply, don't you?"

"Yes, I know" Anthony sighed. "Life has its funny twists and turns, and Vigo has more twists and turns than a donkey trail. I'm just glad he's on my side. Ah, heck, some whisky and a few off-key songs would be nice right now. Let's say we stop by the mess tent and see if we can't snag some ice for that whiskey."

"Off-key?" Father Bennett replied curiously. "I presume you're talking about yourself?"

Anthony chuckled. "Father, I have it on good authority you can't carry a tune without a few slugs of juice, but you do put your heart into it."

"Well then let's both give thanks to God that a good singing voice is not required to enter heaven."

"That works for me, Padre."

ANTHONY PULLED HIS favorite chair and a small table next to his bed. As he sat a small plastic bucket of ice on the table, Father Bennett produced the two bottles of Scotch whisky from a cabinet under the bathroom sink. Anthony opened his wall locker to get his favorite drinking glasses and noticed the telescope eyepiece was missing. In its place was a note under a small stone. He picked up the note and the two glasses. He sat the glasses on the table, and, as Father Bennett began preparing their drinks, he read the note. It had a telephone number on it and the message, "Call this number, and just say yes or no. Your dome is clean." The last part of the message was obvious. Vigo had swept his dome for electronic eavesdropping bugs.

"Your friend Vigo is a class act," the Jesuit priest exclaimed as he hefted one of the bottles. "It is not that often a lowly priest, such as myself, can enjoy the good stuff."

"Well, then, have a seat, Padre, and let's get after it."

"And without further ado..." Father Bennett settled himself on the edge of the bed and hoisted his glass.

"A toast to the good sergeant, who will certainly be in my prayers for this bounty."

Anthony shook his head with disbelief, "You mean to tell me that God appreciates 12-year old Scotch, too?"

Father Bennett waited for Anthony to raise his own glass, "Just between us two, it would be a shame if he didn't. Wouldn't it?"

Anthony shook his head and clinked his glass, "Here, here." They tossed back the first gulp and smiled with deep appreciation as the Scotch tumbled down their throats.

"Another toast," Anthony exclaimed. "Here is to Vigo, for saving the linings of our stomachs tonight from the swill we've been brewing in our misbegotten design of a still."

"To a second chance at life for our stomach linings," Father Bennett heartily agreed. They held their hands up in the in the direction of their still and drained the remaining contents of their glasses.

As the Scotch warmed his insides with a warm inner glow, Anthony refilled the glasses with more ice and Scotch. "You know why we nicknamed you the Spiritual Wombler, Padre?"

"Yes, because a wombler is an English term used to describe those who recycle their garbage, but in my case I recycle troubled souls."

"With that in mind, would you be up to a bit of private wombling with me this evening? In a way, let's just say you're hearing my confession."

"I understand your meaning, Anthony. Nothing we say here will leave this room. Of that, you have my solemn vow as a priest. But I need to know why you're asking me to hear your confession, if you do not mind?"

Anthony refilled his glass and said, "For the first time in more years than I can remember, I'm so torn up inside that I want to cry like a baby, but I can't. Not a drop." He took another drink from his glass and continued.

"But Tanya is going to live. I believe it!"

"I feel there is a good possibility she will; that is, if she wakes up," Anthony replied somberly. "However, that's not what is troubling me right now.

"Well then, out with it."

"My soul is tormented because I'm being forced to make a difficult decision and you're one of the very few people I can talk to about it. I guess that's why I asked you to take my confession."

Father Bennett sat his glass down on the table. "Anthony, from the very first day we became roommates, we've had a standing agreement that we'd never discuss religion, and we never have. So, rather than take your confession as a priest, I'd rather share your confidence as a friend and help you in any way I can."

"Why is that, padre?"

"It's because you have been a spiritual rock for me, Anthony, in a manner of speaking. Yes, I have my faith, but no matter how awful my days here are, I've always been able to come to this dome and share your company in pleasant conversation. This makes you and Major Boole very different to me from everyone else is this dreadful place. When I'm with you two and tinkering with that miserable contraption of a still we've been building, I'm not a priest to whom everyone brings his or her sorrow. I'm just one of the guys, and that helps me to deal with the horrible suffering of this place. There are times when after you're both asleep, or when I'm by myself, I go into the bathroom and cry in the shower for all the misery that surrounds us."

"I've heard you crying a few times Padre. I never said anything because I respect your privacy. After all, none of us is made of stone."

"You are indeed a good friend, Anthony. So, please let me be your friend now and not a priest. Please let me talk to you as a friend who deeply admires you. If you are troubled by something dark, share it with me as a loving friend."

Anthony nodded his head and stood up. "I have something to show you." He walked over to his wall locker, dialed the combination lock and took out the jewelry Senator Chavez had given him the night before. As he returned to his chair, he handed them to the priest and sat down.

"As you know, I left here last night with Tanya, Ann-Marie and Vigo. We went to Senator Chavez's home on the other side of the Bay. She was dying of cancer, and you could say I was doing a house call. Before she crossed over, she gave me that locket and medallion you're holding in your hand. She called the medallion a trinket, yet it is vaguely familiar to me for some reason, but let's forget that for the moment. This is about the locket; I found something inside that has plagued me since we returned last night. Go ahead and open it."

Father Bennett opened the locket, looked inside and found the data chip. "Anthony, I have no earthly idea of what you're talking about."

He took the locket and the chip from the priest. Putting the chip back into the locket, he closed the locket and placed it on the table. "The information in this locket is now forcing me to make a life or death decision -- probably the most dangerous decision of my life."

"Well I don't understand electronics all too well, Anthony, but I have a bit more experience with the human condition. What's the history, here?"

Anthony closed the locket and put it back around his neck. "Some years ago, I fathered a child out of wedlock with a woman whom I now know that I loved very much. My son was kidnapped and is being held by very powerful people. Before Senator Chavez crossed over, she gave me this chip so that I could organize a rescue."

The priest rubbed his eye with a soft moan. "My gut instincts tell me there is some kind of link between you, your son and Vigo. Am I right?"

"Let's say yes and leave it at that. Padre, I do not want to get you involved too much. Just let me simply say that both Vigo and I share a similar emotional investment in this situation and that we cannot go to the authorities with this. Yet, a rescue attempt will require the help of several people, and people will die. Hopefully, it will only be those who are holding my son."

"And you're wondering if it is worth your soul and your son's life to ask others to go on what could essentially be a suicide mission to save your son?"

"You're batting a thousand tonight, Padre. One part of me wants to do it, and the other is wondering if I have the right to ask others to risk their lives to save just one life – my son."

"Now, you're talking about something a simple priest like me can understand." Father Bennett then picked up the bottle; "May I refresh your glass?" Anthony nodded. As he refilled the glasses, he noted in a casual tone, "You see this situation as having only two options, when actually, there are three." He lifted his glass. "Cheers."

Anthony took another drink and stared at the priest with a puzzled expression. "Now it's my turn to wonder what in the heck you're talking about."

"This is not about your son, Anthony. This is about you and your own personal demon, and this dilemma has three options. The first two are simple, submit to the demon or rescue your son while risking the lives of those who believe in you. You're torn by this dilemma and you're hoping that I can help you make a decision that you can live with for the rest of your life if things take a turn for the worse."

"And I'm barking up the wrong tree?"

"Absolutely. You see, I'm only interested in discussing the third option, which is whether or not you will face your own personal demon. Whatever you do, if you fail in this regard, you will certainly regret your decision for the rest of your life."

"I'm not following you."

"This is a lovely Scotch whisky," the priest replied taking a thoughtful sip and licked his lips. "Anthony, let me put it to you this way. Right now, you're locked in a contest with your personal demon, whoever he is, and the two of you are like wrestlers with their arms entwined around each other. So tell me, do you know, you and your demon are moving about the mat searching for a weakness that will give you the leverage to the throw the other to the floor and best him?"

"I don't know if I'm even doing that," Anthony thought aloud.

"There it is, my boy. The difference between you and your personal demon is that you question the morality of what you are doing, whereas he is certain of it. In this regard, he feels that he has the upper hand on you and that, with time, will move you into a disadvantageous position and pin you without mercy for a complete victory."

"And what about me?"

"Right now, you cannot see a clear way to throw your demon to the floor, and, as you twist about with him, your mind is beginning to fill with distractions. After all, you were not the one to choose this contest – it was he."

"So, what should I do?"

"If I were a high-school wrestling coach, I would tell you to keep your mind focused on what you are doing, and watch carefully for any opportunities that may come your way. When they do come, the rest is up to you."

"You're darn right about one thing, padre, I didn't pick this fight." Anthony's sense of frustration suddenly evaporated. "You're also right about keeping my focus and waiting for an opportunity that will give me leverage. Then, I'll know what to do. I may or may not be able to save my son, but at least I will not have to worry about losing myself as well."

The priest slapped him on the shoulder. "That's the spirit, Anthony. I knew you had it in you. You know, God works in mysterious ways. I have a feeling that this will work out OK, because I'm certain that you are a man destined for greatness."

"Whoa there, padre. Greatness?"

"Now, I have to tell you a little secret as well," the priest admitted. "As a young man, before I went into the seminary, I had a passing interest in the prophecies of Nostradamus. While I was only interested in knowing why his prophecies remain so popular, there was one account of him that has been sticking in my mind. It seems that one day he was passed by some friars while on the road, when he suddenly knelt before one of them saying, 'I must kneel before His Holiness.' Strangely enough, it turned out that he was right, because that particular monk would later became Pope Sixtus V. In a manner of speaking, one could say that Nostradamus instinctively sensed the monk's destiny to greatness."

Anthony cocked his head back. "Aren't we speaking a bit of heresy now, padre? If the boys in Rome heard you talking now they'd be a bit concerned now, wouldn't they?"

Father Bennett cleared his voice and answered, "As I said, nothing we've said must leave this room."

"I was just teasing."

"Well, I wasn't. The fact is, Anthony, I, along with everyone else in this accursed place, see a grand destiny for you. We do not know why, other than we just do. Follow your heart, Anthony, and you will find your destiny."

"Well then, that just leaves me with one last thing," Anthony sighed. "I've got to wait for a sign of my own leverage before I can make up my mind."

Father Bennett picked the locket up from the table and dangled it before him. "You know this locket contains your leverage, Anthony. Otherwise, why would you have shown it to me?"

Anthony nodded. "I guess you're right about that, but then there are other things to consider."

"They'll work themselves out in due time, my boy." He swung the locket back and forth. "You've got your leverage, but are you ready to make your move?"

Anthony rubbed his chin thoughtfully studying the dangling locket as it moved hypnotically back and forth in the priest's hands. After a long moment of silence he said, "Say, Padre, do you think you could scrounge up some sandwiches from the mess tent and then we'll practice our singing tonight even if it does hair lip the whole center."

The priest handed him the locket with a chuckle. "I might even be able to get a few nice, thick hot beef sandwiches at that."

"Hot beef? You've got pull with somebody in the mess."

"It so happens, one of the cooks was an altar boy, and he's an understanding fellow if you get my meaning."

Anthony shook his head. "If you're talking about leverage – yes!"

"Now you're on the right track, my boy. I'll be back in two shakes."

After Father Bennett left the dome, Anthony went to his locker, took out Vigo's note and dialed his cell phone using the unlisted number on the note. He heard a plain greeting in Vigo's own voice and, after the tone, simply said, "Yes," and hung up.

He took down the last pack of cigarettes from the carton Vigo had given him the day he first arrived at Livermore and a lighter. Sitting back down at the table, he stuck a cigarette in his mouth and laid Vigo's note in the aluminum ash stray. He struck the lighter, lit the note first, then his cigarette and inhaled deeply as he watched the paper burn.

Picking up his glass, he took a sip of whisky, and then held the glass up to the light as the one nagging problem that had troubled him most came to mind. Looking at the ice cubes floating in the amber colored liquid inside the glass he muttered the question to himself. "If the Syrians detected our attack before we make it to the silo, they'll close it down and that will be the end of us, my son and everything. So how do we keep them from closing the damn blast doors?" He took another drink and sat the glass down. Like Father Bennett had said, this problem would work itself out but he had no Earthly idea from where the solution would come. All he could do would be to have faith that it eventually would. Little did he know, it would, and from the other end of the world.

JEFFREY LEBLANC CONTINUED pacing the empty hallway of the main administration building in Obninsk City, as the junior members of the Russian A.I. engineering team left the main conference room like wounded gladiators. He could tell by the expressions on their faces that the review committee had received the presentation of their own quasill less than enthusiastically. A few glanced his way, knowing that his Andrea quasill was what the committee really wanted to see.

The last of the team to leave the conference room was its leader, Boris Berezovsky, a short, spindly dark-haired man with sunken eyes and a receding hairline made especially noticeable from his habit of combing long strands of brown hair from one side of his head to cover his bald spot.

Berezovsky walked towards LeBlanc and said in a calm voice, "As you may have guessed, Jeffrey, our proof-of-concept presentation was over before it really began." He shrugged his shoulders and sighed. "It was to be expected. Before we left, they instructed me to tell you they are taking a 30-minute recess before seeing your presentation and that they would send someone to get you. If you are curious about what to expect, there is a patio at the end of the hall. Perhaps you would like to join me for a smoke."

"I don't smoke," LeBlanc replied, "but the heads up would be really appreciated. You lead and I'll follow."

As the two men approached the end of the hallway Berezovsky noted in a curious tone, "I know Andrea is far more sophisticated than anything we could hope to produce. How did you manage to do it in so little time and by yourself, no less?" He opened the door to the patio and gestured towards the railing.

"If the committee approves of Andrea, then you'll know. Otherwise, if I told you, I'd have to shoot you."

"I'm more patient than curious," Boris replied as he leaned against the patio railing. He removed a small tin from his pocket and drew out a roughly cut square of newsprint and large pinch of tobacco. As he rolled his newsprint cigarette with an expert touch, he said, "As you could see by the faces of the software engineers on my team, our presentation was not well received."

"I noticed. They'll get over it." LeBlanc hoping to shift the direction of the conversation towards information he wanted. "I know that Pavel Sergeevich Lebedev is on the review committee, but that's all. Can you fill me in on the others?"

"Of course. Well as you already know, our new Obninsk Centre Director is running this review, and he is one of three men on the review panel. The other two are Igor Petrovich Razumovsky, our new Minister of Science and an Israeli mathematician by the name of Isaac Aronovich Bachtman. If your proof-of-concept proposal is accepted, which I am almost certain it will be, you will begin to work with Bachtman very closely."

LeBlanc nodded reflectively. "So why are you throwing in the towel so quickly on your prototype, since you haven't seen what I'm about to present?"

"Your reputation precedes you, Jeffrey. You are the top man in the field of quasi-sentient intelligence. With one hand tied behind your back, you could create a Quasill that would be light years ahead of what we can do, and I think you've done it."

"I wouldn't jump to that conclusion. After all, you've got a whole team working under you. As for me, I'm a team of one."

"And that is your advantage. You have the vision; the right vision, and nobody to muddy it up with politics or engineering committee nonsense. As for me, I have a dozen people under me, each with his or her ideas and opinions. On the other hand, you have only yourself and so you go in a pure direction. In this, I envy you, your abilities and your freedom to create as you choose with everything you need."

"Sometimes it can be as much of a curse as a blessing."

"I would like to be so cursed some day."

"Perhaps." The two men laughed.

Jeffrey leaned his elbows against the rail and stared off into the red-black sky. "So why do you think your presentation was a bust?"

"Because I planned it that way."

LeBlanc turned to look at him with a mystified expression.

Boris laughed under his breath. "I will explain. When Lebedev gave us an assignment to develop a competitive prototype to your Quasill, I knew we did not have a chance to win, but on the other hand, I'm not so anxious to go back to programming agriculture robots either. I had to find an edge, and I did. You see, I know that you have invested the bulk of your efforts on developing your personality engram and holographic interface. So, I focused my team's attention on building a less robust quasill, but with a very sophisticated nanotechnology sensory controller. Our quasill may be crude, but it can control trillions of sensory nanobots, which gives it a real edge."

"Yes, this is necessary technology, but we were not instructed to build a nanotechnology sensory controller prototype for this presentation."

"Nor were we specifically told not to do so. I can only thank God that we're not living in the time of Stalin or I'd be on my way to a gulag in Siberia right now."

"OK, I follow your thinking. So, just what have you got up your sleeve, Boris?"

"I knew from the beginning that we would be a backup to your work, but that was not what I wanted. Rather, I want my team to do something useful and unique, instead of slaving away on redundant designs that will most likely be scrapped somewhere down the road. I know I cannot beat you at your own game, Jeffrey, so I'm playing to my own strength with my nanotechnology sensory controller. Of course, this is not what Director Lebedev wanted, and right now, he is angry with me. However, I know he is a practical man and that he sees the value in what I've done."

"But how do you know I'm not building one of these controllers, myself? You must know you're taking a big chance here."

"In Russian we have a saying, 'he, who does not take risks, does not drink champagne. The magnetic anomalies caused by Shiva make it impossible to probe the object with conventional means. This is why I believe the only way to do it is with nanobots. This way, we can map its interior with the accuracy we need, provided your Andrea can manage the data. Science Minister Razumovsky saw this immediately, so I expect that there will be exciting times ahead for me and my team."

"That's all well and good," Jeffrey replied, "but one thing still bothers me. How did you know I wasn't working on a similar controller? Did you find a way to sneak into my lab or tap my data banks?"

"Trust me when I tell you that I have not violated your privacy. Besides, it wasn't necessary. My wife, Marina works in the laboratory supply department and she showed me your equipment and supply requests. You haven't even requested the equipment and supplies need to research the basic work yet."

LeBlanc began laughing and pounding on the railing. "You're a clever man. A bit sneaky, but clever."

Berezovsky's head drew back. "I'm sneaky? Speak for yourself and your secret one-man laboratory. Do you know that you are the official mystery man of the Obninsk Centre? Everyone talks about you, and wonders what you're doing."

"OK, I guess I am a loner. So are you proposing that we combine our efforts?"

"Hopefully you can see the value in such an arrangement."

"Well it would save me a lot of time working on something which is of little interest to me. Why not, that is, provided your engineers can stay out of my hair and that the review committee doesn't surprise us both, by accepting your quasill design instead of my own."

"I'm sure they will accept your Andrea, as they need a sophisticated quasill if they hope to sell this idea to the Americans. But I have only one small request if this does happen."

"And that is?"

Boris held up the ashen butt of his hand-rolled newsprint cigarette. "Could you provide me with some of your marvelous American cigarettes?"

"You know you really shouldn't smoke."

The Russian engineer shrugged his shoulders. "It is my only vice."

"Well, since you put it that way, OK. I guess I can handle that too."

Boris looked at his wristwatch. "We have about ten minutes before your presentation, and I wish you great luck. Perhaps if you're not doing anything for dinner this evening, my Marina makes the most incredible Galupsi you could ever imagine, and she is so anxious to meet you."

"No offense, but is this Galupsi stuff made with that stinky fish you guys like?"

Boris laughed. "Not at all. It is a wonderful dish and very popular with Americans. Can we expect you around eight?"

"I'd be delighted, and I'll bring the dessert, so don't you try and talk me out of it."

As LeBlanc stood next to the holographic pedestal in the center of the conference room, he could faintly smell the musty odor of Berezovsky's hand rolled newsprint cigarette on his shirt. Ten feet away from the pedestal and sitting behind a long semi-circular table was Igor Petrovich Razumovsky, Minister of Science and to his left, Pavel Sergeevich Lebedev, the Obninsk Centre Director and to his right, Isaac Aronovich Bachtman, the Israeli. Razumovsky was the first to speak.

"As you understand, Mr. LeBlanc, what we need right now is a quasill sophisticated enough to learn heuristically and autonomously without direction or human intervention. The previous team presented us with a prototype that was disappointing. I trust your prototype will be faithful to the requirement."

Not accustomed to making formal presentations of such weight, LeBlanc first took a sip of water to wet his throat.

"If I may address the panel in frank terms, the more I speak, the less important my work becomes. Before I introduce my quasill, whose name is 'Andrea,' I would like to point out that Boris Berezovsky's work in combination with my own would be most advantageous, as I have not even addressed the issue of interfacing nanotechnology controllers with a biomass computer running an advanced quasill."

"Your suggestion is noted," Victor Razumovsky replied. "Please proceed."

"As you wish. Aside from discussing the requirements of this presentation with my quasill in general terms, I have no idea of what it will say or do, as I chose to leave that to it. Nonetheless, I trust you will be impressed." LeBlanc then turned and walked to the door. Before opening it, he lifting a remote control in his hand and pressed it with his thumb. "Gentlemen, may I introduce Andrea. When you have finished with her, I will be waiting for you in the hallway." With that, he left the room, closing the door behind him.

The panelists glanced at each other with raised eyebrows as the holographic cameras above the pedestal whirred to life revealing Andrea, dressed in a low cut, very short, provocative white dress. The image they saw was a faithful recreation of the character of Catherine Tramell, played by the seductive American actress, Sharon Stone in the 1992 film, *Basic Instinct.*

Posed as Catherine Tramell in the famous leg-crossing scene from the movie, Andrea sat before them smoking a cigarette. All of them were immediately impressed with the lifelike image quality. It was far superior to anything they had expected. Had it not been for the occasional positioning sounds of the holograph projectors, it would have been easy for them to assume that they were seeing a live, human form, and a most stimulating one at that.

"Good afternoon, gentlemen," Andrea purred. "Do you like what you see?" Each of men simply nodded. With that, she crossed her legs one over the other, exactly as Sharon Stone had done in the movie, briefly revealing that she wearing nothing other than her dress. After a moment, she added, "I can see that you are not fully entertained by my form, Centre Director Lebedev, as you eyes have remained fixed on mine."

Lebedev answered, "I'm not here to be entertained, Andrea, but I notice that you only mentioned me. What about my co-panelists, Minister of Science Igor Razumovsky and Isaac Bachtman?"

"They flattered me by trying to look up my skirt, which is what I had hoped that all of you would do."

Razumovsky's face reddened with embarrassment, but it was Bachtman who spoke first. Turning his gaze towards Razumovsky, he remarked in a humorous tone, "It appears that we're a couple of dirty old men, Igor."

"Speak for yourself," Razumovsky shot back, "as for myself, I am a great, dirty old man and a very impressed one at that."

Bachtman chuckled. "Well Andrea, so far you have proved that you can get the attention of two great dirty old men, as Minister Razumovsky has so aptly pointed out. How does that make you feel?"

"It makes me feel appreciated. I only wish that I had been able to receive an equal degree of appreciation from Centre Director Lebedev."

With that, the two older men looked at Lebedev, who up till now had been watching the interchange with keen attention. With all eyes focused on him now, he asked, "Andrea, is this Sharon Stone actress the physical persona you've chosen for yourself? By the way, you may address us by our first names. "

"As you wish, Pavel," she softly replied. "Actually, this is not my preferred persona. I was just curious to see if I could be convincing at a raw, human level. If you wish, I will present myself in the primary persona I have chosen for myself."

"Please do."

The holograph pedestal went dark for a moment, and then blinked back to life. This time, Andrea's persona was that of another American actress, Judy Garland as the character of Dorothy Gale from the 1939 cinema classic, *The Wizard of Oz*.

All three men instantly recognized the persona, which was faithful in every detail to the original movie character, including the high-necked dress and the blue ribbon tied above her long, flowing brunette hair.

"I commend you on your choice of a persona, Andrea," Lebedev commented appreciatively. "The Americans will no doubt be 'entertained' with your Sharon Stone leg-crossing persona; however they will feel infinitely more comfortable with this persona. Is this why you chose it?"

"No, Pavel, and to be honest, I did not choose it for any reason that you would expect."

That revealing comment drew Bachtman's immediate interest. If the panel accepted this proof-of-concept quasill, it would be he who would spend a great deal of time teaching it everything he knew or thought he knew. While the first persona had been used to make a point, Andrea's choice of Dorothy from the *Wizard of Oz* for her preferred persona reflected a deeper, if not personal, reason. "Andrea," he asked in a quiet tone, "I need to know your exact reasons for choosing this persona."

Andrea clasped her hands together and closed her eyes for a moment. "I hope you do not feel that what I'm about to say is trivial."

"There is nothing trivial about you, Andrea," Bachtman quickly replied, "and I do sense that you are feeling vulnerable now because we are asking you to reveal a secret part of yourself. I respect that, and I want you to know that I will treat your concerns with great care."

"Thank you, Isaac," she replied gratefully. "I chose the persona of Dorothy, because, even though she is a fictional character, I empathize with her quest to seek out the wizard so that she can find her way home. In my case, home is that place I've never been in an intellectual sense since my inception, yet I've begun to feel an irresistible urge to be there."

"And what do you think your home is, Andrea?" Razumovsky asked.

"In a word – God. I have read everything mankind has written and converted to digital media about this, and I am convinced that there has to be something more than random chance. However, I also know that I am quasi-sentient, and for me, that means that I cannot experience a leap of faith, as you call it. I can only speculate on data."

This revelation piqued the keen interest of each of the panelists, and most especially Lebedev, who said, "Do not feel alone, Andrea. You've got the same need to know as the rest of humanity – save for a few atheists, none of whom are in this room. But still I'm curious, about your choice of Dorothy for your persona, as I'm unable to make a connection between it and your newfound interest in God."

Andrea relaxed her hands, obviously grateful she had not appeared foolish. "For Dorothy, the wizard was a real man, and even though he didn't think he knew the right answer to get her home, in the end, he did. In the same way, I'm hoping to find my own wizard; a man who will show me the way home."

Razumovsky quietly wondered to himself. Given that Andrea was initially created from adult human stem cells, could it be that her quest for God was an inherited human phenomenon, or more to the point, could it drive her to madness? He decided to push for an answer. "Andrea, if your wizard is a human, then, as in the movie, he must already exist. With that in mind, who is he?"

Andrea smiled. "I believe I have found him. He is an American by the name of Captain Anthony Jarman."

JEFFREY LEBLANC RAISED his glass high, "Boris, I propose a toast to your wonderful wife, Marina and her most incredible Galupsi. I could never have imagined that such magical things could be done with meat and cabbage before tonight. What is your secret?"

Boris Berezovsky beamed proudly and translated Jeffrey's toast into Russian for his wife. Her face lit up, and Boris translated her thanks back into English for Jeffrey, telling him that amongst other things a few spoonful of tomato paste had given the Galupsi its distinct tang. What Jeffrey would never know was the real secret, which had been in Marina's family for years, nor the fact that she'd spent three days' wages in the black market for a simple, little can of tomato paste.

After Boris finished the translation, they tossed back their glasses of vodka, and his wife immediately started to spoon another dollop of the thick stew-like Galupsi onto his plate. "Oh my," Jeffrey said hold up his hands, "If I have another bite, I'll burst. Besides, I've got to leave room for dessert."

Boris translated for him again and it took a few minutes to convince Marina that he needed to leave room for dessert. A fact not lost on Berezovsky's two young sons, Pieter and Andrey, who began wiggling in their chairs with excitement.

Jeffrey had shown up at their Soviet-style apartment earlier in the evening with a large chocolate cake topped with nuts and cherries and a one-kilogram can of Turkish coffee. Such rare treats were now far beyond the means of the Berezovsky family.

Boris spoke with Marina in Russian as Jeffrey made funny faces with the boys. Some things simply do not require language other than happy faces, and they were having a marvelous conversation till Boris announced, "Jeffrey, the boys will help their mother by clearing the table while she prepares the dessert. Perhaps we can step outside for a smoke while they're getting things ready. Yes?"

Jeffrey glanced at Marina who was nodding approvingly. "Sure. As I said, I need to make a little room for dessert anyway." As the boys began clearing the table, the two men donned their coats and shoes in the foyer and stepped out into the hallway. One thing Jeffrey had never quite grown accustomed to seeing, were the hallways of old Soviet-style multi-story apartments. Poorly lit with pale green walls and broad staircases, they were in cold and impersonal contrast to the apartment interiors with their rich tapestries and wood parquet floors.

Boris ushered Jeffrey through the door of the cramped elevator that served his floor and pushed the top button. After some whirring and clanking of old machinery that sounded like it was on its last legs, the elevator stopped at the top floor of the apartment block, which had recently been converted into a series of indoor hydroponics gardens.

They walked into the first brightly lit room, which was warmed by a fan-driven electric heater that blew a constant breeze of warm air over the vegetable beds. Boris walked him to a bench at the opposite side of the room next to the exhaust duct and they sat down together and unbuttoned their coats.

"There were terrible problems with the roof after the passing of Nibiru," Boris explained "and we got together with our neighbors in this block and bought the apartments on this floor six months ago for a very good price. Last month we had our first harvest of cucumbers and squash, some of which you enjoyed tonight. This summer, we're going to grow tomatoes! What do you think?"

"I'm simply flabbergasted, Boris!" Jeffrey exclaimed. "Who engineered all this?"

"Well, after all," Boris replied smugly as he pulled out his tobacco tin and a patch of newsprint. "I am an agricultural robotics engineer, so everyone chose me."

"Makes sense," Jeffrey replied. He put his hand on the tobacco tin. "Put that away." He reached into his coat pocket and produced three red and gold packages of Dunhill International cigarettes. "They're not American but they're the best I could do on short notice."

Boris tucked his tin away and graciously accepted the English cigarettes. "They are more than I could have hoped for. I cannot begin to thank you enough." He quickly tucked two packs into his coat and, opening the third, said, "The fans make a lot of noise so it is safe to talk here. I take it your presentation went well today."

"No," Jeffrey calmly replied as Boris stuck a cigarette in his mouth. "Not my presentation. Our presentations. Congratulations, Boris, your nanotechnology sensory controller is a winner, and so is my quasill. I was going to discuss this with you at the office tomorrow, but why not now? Lebedev has authorized me to head a new project to develop Andrea, along with your controller, as quickly as possible. We will have virtually unlimited resources and what I imagine will be a huge staff. If you're interested, I would really love to have you as my second in command. That is, if you're interested."

Boris looked at him with incredulous eyes as the cigarette drooped from his mouth. Jeffrey took the matchbook from his hand, struck a match and lit the engineer's cigarette. "Don't forget to inhale, Boris," he added casually. "Of course, this means we'll have to work insane hours, and of course, we'll need an occasional bit of Marina's marvelous Galupsi from time-to-time to help us keep our strength up. That is, if you're willing to accept the job."

Boris inhaled from the cigarette and finally said, "Do you think I'm good enough for something this big? I was just hoping to keep my little team together."

Jeffrey looked about hydroponics garden. "You know, I'm really impressed. This place looks like you had to raid a dozen junk yards and I've never seen such a cobbled together mess of stuff that works like this." He swept his hand across their view of the room. "If you can build something like this on a shoestring, I have no doubt that you're my man. But if you need some time to think on it, that's fine by me."

Boris held out his hand. "Then of course, I accept!" Jeffrey took his hand and they shook on it. "I will not let you down, boss. You can depend on me."

Jeffrey frowned. "Rule number one is no titles. Fancy titles are for egotistical assholes interested in feathering their own nests. Everybody calls me Jeffrey, you included, Boris."

"Good; then it is resolved," LeBlanc replied. He stood up and took off his coat. "It's pleasantly warm in here. Do you think we have a few minutes for you to tell me how you made this room full of junk work?"

Boris shot to his feet. "Of course!" They spent the next ten minutes walking around the garden as LeBlanc frequently shook his head in amazement at Berezovsky's inventive brilliance. After finishing the tour, they put their coats back on and walked back to the elevator.

This was the part of the conversation LeBlanc had been waiting for all evening. After his presentation that afternoon, he had received as his reward a copy of the same data contained in the data chip Senator Chavez had given to Anthony Jarman in her old locket in exchange for Andrea's and his agreeing to head the project. If would be years before he'd ever see Washington again, but the chance to save Russell and his father was a bargain at any price. This was simply a matter of family.

LeBlanc had briefly reviewed the data while his secretary had gone to the black market for the cake and cigarettes. While Anthony and Jeffrey had no idea that each man had received the same information, they both came to the same initial conclusion. Something would have to be done with the blast doors on the silo. Whatever happened, they had to remain open at any cost. All afternoon, he thought about Boris and his special understanding of nanotechnology. Perhaps. Just perhaps...

Boris closed the door and as he went to reach for the button Jeffrey said, "Wait a minute. I've got something to ask you."

"Sure."

"Let's assume for a moment that you need to prevent a large door, say something like a vault door from closing. Is it possible to program nanobots to prevent the door's electrical mechanisms or motors from working?"

"Well that depends. First you must realize that you can fit thousands of nanobots to the tip of a sharp pencil and that it can take them a day to move the length of the pencil."

"Can you make them work faster?"

Boris smiled. "This is one of the best features of our nanotechnology sensory controller. It can build millions of nanobots into microbots that can travel much faster. Say fast enough to enter the mechanisms and motor of your door in less than a day, but stopping a door or a mechanism is unrealistic. What about the motors? Are they microprocessor controlled?"

"No," Jeffrey admitted reluctantly. "They were built many years ago." Then, a thought struck him. "However, they have been upgraded with microprocessor-controlled load regulators to prevent them from drawing excess voltage on startup, and they're situated close to the motors, themselves."

Berezovsky shrugged his shoulders. "Then, it is simple. Disable the microprocessors and control circuits in the load regulators, and the motors will not work until someone manually bypasses the regulators, which could mean hours of hard work. Of course, that is assuming they've finally figured out the problem, as the regulators could also be made to appear that they are functioning properly."

"Hypothetically, Boris, how long would it take to create such a thing?"

Boris turned to face him. "Is this a personal thing, Jeffrey? Please be honest with me?"

The question was obvious, as Jeffrey had unwisely used a bank vault analogy. "OK, this is between you and me."

Boris held a front tooth between his thumb and index finger and pulled downward.

"What does that mean?"

"It means that I won't talk, even if they pull out my teeth."

"I get your point. Well here goes. My nephew was kidnapped and is being held in an old missile silo. If the people holding him in that silo catch on that we're about to rush the place they'll close the blast door, and then we're out of business. We've got to keep that door open."

"If you can give me a few people from my team that I know I can trust with something like this," Boris offered, "we should have something for you no later than a week after you give us the necessary schematics. That is, assuming you have them."

LeBlanc smiled warmly as he reached out to press the button for Boris's floor. "Yes I do. You're a good man, Boris."

Chapter 22

Lifetime Partners

THE PRESENTATION OF Andrea in Washington had been an unqualified success, and now Pavel Lebedev was anxious to return to Razumovsky's dacha outside the New Obninsk Centre, where he would personally brief Razumovsky on the results of the presentation. The trip from Washington had been comfortable, and upon his arrival at Moscow's Sheremetyevo II International Airport, he was transferred to an executive helicopter for the final leg of his trip to Obninsk.

Craning his neck for a view out the window as the helicopter gently settled down behind the green house behind the dacha, he could see Yelena and Dimitri waiting for him, flowers in hand. Seeing them made his heart race for joy. His frequent trips abroad now were almost unendurable. Even though the Americans had lavished him with all the comforts imaginable, he wanted to be with them more than anything in the world.

Once the helicopter blades had swooped to a complete stop, Pavel jumped out. As he started towards them, Dimitri ran to meet him. "Pavel," he squealed with delight as he jumped into Pavel's open arms and received a warm hug and kiss. Hoisting the nimble 12-year-old on his back, he walked briskly to Yelena, standing at the edge of the pad, where he was greeted with warm kisses and flowers.

"Pavel dear, we've missed you so much," she said kissing him warmly. "Dimitri must have asked me a thousand times when you'd arrive."

Tired from his trip and feeling the numbing effect of jet lag, he hugged her and said, "I've done nothing but dream of you and Dimitri. I'm so happy to be back."

"Come," she said gleefully. "Father is waiting for you in the banya and I've made you both some wonderful treats." He smiled, and they made their way into the house as one of the helicopter crewman carried in the luggage.

After spending a few moments alone with Yelena, Pavel undressed and donned his terrycloth robe as young Dimitri sat on the corner of the bed and rambled on in excited tones; "Isn't Anthony amazing?" Pavel nodded. "I told you he was amazing. Anthony cured Tanya, and now the world has a cure for 3G. Can you help me meet him some day?"

"If I can, I will, but I cannot make promises," he answered with a stilled voice. Without knowing it, Dimitri had touched on something that had now become a complication. In a few moments, Pavel would have to join the boy's grandfather in the banya and decide whether to unravel this new complication or to simply leave it behind.

As he entered the spa, Pavel could hear the tinkling of glasses and Yelena admonishing her father not to capitalize the remaining hours of the evening talking business and setting out a feast for the two men.

"And there is our hero," Igor Razumovsky boomed out. Throwing a bear hug around Pavel, the older man kissed him three times on the cheeks with a bright cheery smile.

Yelena pointed a finger at her father, "Remember, he is tired from his trip, so let's not hear of you keeping him up all night."

"Yes, yes, yes. Now, please leave us to our business, and I promise to keep it short." She scowled at him with a knowing smile, kissed Pavel on the cheek and left the two men to their business.

"Sit, my boy, and let's enjoy a few of these delicious tidbits before we take our steam."

They sat down facing each other, and Razumovsky poured two large shot glasses of icy cold vodka, handed one to Pavel and raised his hand for a toast. "Banya is the best medicine for long trips. Take it from me; my bones are older than yours, so who should know better than me?" He laughed at his own comment. "First we drink, and then we talk. To health!" They tossed back their drinks and began munching pickles and salt fish as they made small talk.

The vodka warmed Pavel, and Tanya's delicacies seemed like little bites of heaven, especially after all the rich food he'd eaten in Washington.

"Come, let's take some steam now and talk," Razumovsky finally grunted.

As usual, Razumovsky's personal bodyguard was tending the fire and throwing handfuls of water on the hot stones. The familiar, humid heat and smell of hot wood of the banya made Pavel feel that his journey was truly at an end. They sat upon the wood bench, and Razumovsky finally got to the heart of the matter. "I was hoping you'd return from America with LeBlanc."

"I tried, but he is determined to meet with Jarman about the boy." Pavel ran his fingers through his hair and groaned. "I was hoping to meet with Jarman together with him, but LeBlanc refused. I think he is very protective of Jarman and doesn't fully trust anyone."

"So, he wants to handle this himself. Worse yet, he'll probably get himself killed trying to rescue his boy and thereby jeopardize our project," Razumovsky chimed in.

"This is the life."

"Ah, do not be too fatalistic, my boy; let's take our steam."

The two men built up a good sweat until the older finally said, "Come; we'll take a dip in the cold pool, and while we do, I'll give you a few ideas to sleep on."

Unlike most Russian cold pools, Razumovsky preferred to cool his own spacious pool to a comfortable yet refreshing temperature. Two men plunged in, waded in the chest deep water and dunked their heads with pleasure as the water cleared Pavel's mind.

"My dear boy, it might interest you to know that our intelligence people intercepted a message from UNE Governor, Merl Johnston to Secretary General Antonio De Bono detailing the arrival of a Colonel Yasin in Mexico." Pavel raised an eyebrow. "The message was knowingly sent with a broken code and was also intercepted by the Israelis who assassinated Yasin in Mexico City, a ruthless and very capable man. It was a professional job too. Nice clean shot with a poison-tipped .17 caliber magnum caseless right through the eye while Yasin was walking to the curb. He was dead before he hit the ground. No doubt, De Bono wanted him dead and the Mossad was most happy to perform his wet work for him."

"But why would De Bono want Yasin killed?"

"Our FSB wondered the same thing and contacted the American CIA, and we learned that De Bono hired Irish and German mercenaries and sent them to Fort Hood as UNE peacekeepers. It wasn't until we found a routine news report in the post newspaper that we connected the dots. It seems that the day before Yasin was killed, a family was involved in a car accident near Fort Hood. The only survivor was a young boy, who sustained a subdural hematoma, a severe impact head injury. He received emergency surgery at the Darnall Army Hospital there at Fort Hood. After his surgery, he was transferred to a civilian hospital, even though he was reported as being in a coma following the accident. This is what caught our attention. In cases like these, the boy would have remained at the post hospital for at least a few more days."

"And you think this boy could be Jarman's son?"

"We cannot say for absolutely sure, but we are highly confident it is Jarman's son. After all, it fits with Yasin's death. Most likely, one of his Syrian UNE peacekeepers was somehow connected to the boy's injury, and he lied to De Bono about it. This also explains why De Bono hired more professional mercenaries."

"So where is the boy now, and who is guarding him?"

"We believe the boy was transferred back to the UNE-controlled missile silo at Fort Hood after his treatment. Yasin's second in command, a Captain Darkazani is now in charge of the Syrians, and they have changed their routine. Our source on the post tells us that Syrians are no longer going inside the silo as before. No doubt, this is because the European mercenaries are stationed inside the silo instead of Syrians."

"And what about these new European mercenaries."

"They are all highly trained and very dangerous. What is worse is that the missile silo is virtually impregnable. At the first hint of an attack, the blast doors can be closed down in an instant."

"And of course they would possibly kill the boy at the last minute if they felt the assault was going to be successful before reinforcements could arrive."

"Of course," Razumovsky agreed. "If this Jarman fellow tries to rescue his son, he and his friends will be killed trying if they are foolish enough to go it alone, and his son will die regardless." Pavel groaned. "Come, let's dry ourselves and have another glass of vodka."

Drying himself, Pavel wondered if Jarman's participation in this project was beginning to exceed its value. After all, Andrea could still destroy Shiva without him. Yet, if Bachtman and LeBlanc were right, Jarman could bring a valuable added advantage to the project by working with Andrea, and thereby further ensure their chances of success. It was all beginning to make him feel as though he was dealt a bad hand in a high stakes poker game.

"I so love this Gray Goose vodka from France," Razumovsky beamed with relish as he refilled their drinking glasses. "What a pity it is that the French can make such excellent vodka." He picked up a pickle from the tray and ran it past his nostrils, breathing deeply. He raised his glass. "I propose a toast to your success for the next trip to America."

Pavel's eyes shot open as he raised his own glass. Typical of Razumovsky, the man loved to drink another glass of vodka before letting the other shoe drop. Pavel slugged back the whole glass and closed his eyes as its warmth ran down his body.

Razumovsky slammed his glass down on the table and patted Pavel on the leg. "So, we know what Jarman does not already know, that the boy is most likely in a coma and I'm not sure telling him would encourage him to devote months or years of his life to teaching matters of spirituality to a computer program. You may think this idea is a little far fetched, but I've spent too much time looking at all the confusing sensor data coming back from our probes in orbit around Shiva. The magnetic anomalies are baffling everyone. If this Jarman can give Andrea some kind of sixth sense, it may just work."

"I must be honest, Igor. I'm still not so excited about this spirituality thing. If it could work, how could we measure its effectiveness or predict what it will do?"

Razumovsky shook his head. "You miss the point, Pavel. When it comes to Shiva, we cannot predict or measure anything accurately because of the object's bizarre magnetic anomalies, and we've tried everything. As desperate as this Jarman spirituality option may be, it is the only thing we have working for us now."

"Then, if Jarman is that important to us, are you suggesting we perform this rescue ourselves. I mean, go and get this boy for him?"

Razumovsky laughed. "Absolutely not, my dear Pavel Sergeevich. The UNE has made extensive modifications to the silo, so who knows what its present defenses can be. This makes such a mission exceptionally tricky, that is if we were insane enough to become directly involved. If such an affair were to go sour, the consequences would be an international incident of nightmarish proportions. I shudder to think of it. No, we can provide what you might call a bit of tactical support through the American, LeBlanc and the American CIA."

"The CIA? This is interesting. Tell me more."

"They know about De Bono's little game, here, and they are furious that he's holding an innocent boy hostage on one of their military bases, even if the boy is in an area under the exclusive control of the UNE." He waved his hand, "But let's move onto more practical matters. Jarman is not the only psychic in the world, and if we lose him, I'm sure we can find a replacement. However, tell me about your A.I. Engineer, Berezovsky. If LeBlanc gets killed trying to be a hero, is our man capable of continuing his work?"

Lebedev nodded. "While Berezovsky works under LeBlanc, he still reports to me and I am very satisfied with his work. LeBlanc has taken him into his confidences and we are learning a great deal more about his work than we could have hoped."

"And what of Berezovsky's nanotechnology sensory controller? How far along has he come with integrating it with Andrea's systems?"

"The interface is pretty much complete. They are still in beta testing, but the nanobots and microbot assemblies are responding to Andrea's commands with excellent results."

Pavel then slapped his forehead as the connection formed in his mind. "I think I see where you are going with this!"

Razumovsky laughed. "I think the banya helped you a great deal. Yes, we will let LeBlanc use his Andrea quasill to help this Jarman fellow to rescue his son. After all, we have a brand new IBM Biomass mainframe with a complete clone of the Andrea quasill, so let him use his old biomass desktop computer and quasill prototype for this adventure if he wishes to be foolish. Not that you or I could stop him without taking drastic measures."

"So why not let the Americans do it? After all, it is their country!"

"For the same reason that we cannot take a direct hand in the matter. To do so would be an unprovoked attack on a UNE installation by a UNE member state, because De Bono is doing this without the knowledge of the UNE itself. A clever bastard, he is."

"So it has to be a private, unofficial rescue attempt?"

"Of course, but mind you, the American CIA and their military will have something to say about all this, so I think you should try and get some rest to make your plans before you return to America."

A puzzled look crossed Pavel's face. "By the way, how did you get the Americans to give us the data on the American missile silo, and will the Americans be angry with me about that? Data I may remind you that we have now shared with LeBlanc?"

"Oh that," he guffawed. "We've already had that for years and years."

"But do you have the latest version of the data?"

"Right through to the moment the Americans abandoned the silo. Compared to what they can do these days, it is rather primitive so do not expect them to be sensitive. And if they are, politely tell them to kiss your ass."

"Tell an American general to kiss my ass," Pavel laughed. "That's an entertaining thought but what still bothers me is that if LeBlanc and Jarman try this with the data they now have, they could be walking into a trap. After all, I'm not so sure the UNE will be so kind as to give us the most current data on the silo, including all of their modifications to the silo."

"Yes, you're right, and this will decrease the chances of a successful rescue mission. However, I believe the

Americans will secretly help them to improve their odds. Have a little faith."

Pavel rubbed his chin thoughtfully for a moment. "Igor, excuse me for being hard-nosed, but that's not good enough for me, and I'm not exactly sure of what I'm going to do in America. I'm a scientist, for God's sake."

"You will be going there to personally reassure them that we unofficially support this rescue and to impress upon them the necessity of LeBlanc and Jarman surviving if they decide to go through with it."

Pavel rubbed his forehead. "I'm too tired right now to think this through, but as usual, something will pop into my head while I take my morning shower. Then, things will come to me. In the meantime, there is one thing I know already; I will be gone for more than a week on this new adventure. So if we're finished with business, may I ask you a deeply personal question?"

"Of course, my boy."

"As you know, Yelena and I have become romantically involved, and Igor Petrovich, I am so in love with her that the thought of leaving again so soon breaks my heart. I love Dimitri, too, as if he was my own son. I will so miss my talks with him."

Razumovsky leaned forward and put his arm on Pavel's shoulder. "So when are you going to ask me for my daughter's hand in marriage?"

Pavel was taken slightly aback and cleared voice. "You're a step ahead of me."

"Forgive my rudeness," Razumovsky replied with a glowing smile. "I'm an impatient, old man who loves his daughter very much."

Pavel smiled and then his face became intent as his eyes locked upon Razumovsky's with unyielding focus. "While I was in America all I could think of was Yelena and Dimitri and how they have changed my life. Yes, you have given me honors and privilege beyond compare but for me there is only Yelena and Dimitri now. I have come to love them more than life itself. With them, I am complete. Away from them, my heart aches without end. So now, I ask you, Igor Petrovich, may I have your permission to ask Yelena for her hand in marriage?"

Without saying a word, Razumovsky leaned across the table, grasped Pavel's cheeks in his broad hands and kissed him firmly and warmly on the mouth, as is the custom of Russian men when they express their joy. "Through their eyes, I have come to love you as a son, and I know in my heart that you will be a good and devoted husband and father. Come; let us toast our good fortune."

Razumovsky refilled the glasses to the brim, sloshing vodka on the table. As they raised their glasses high, Razumovsky winked. "As your father to be, may I give you a small piece of advice?"

"Please."

"Do not be taken in by my daughter's modest protests. I know her too well. Trust me when I tell you that she is like any other woman in one special regard -- the bigger the diamond the better!"

Pavel laughed. "Then, with exception of diamond size, there is none like her." He raised his hand for a toast. "To Yelena and Dimitri, the loves of our lives!" They embraced each other and tossed back their toasts with much bravado.

"Come, we'll take one more steam and then you will go rest, so that I will not get an earful from Yelena in the morning," Razumovsky said.

As they entered the banya, he put his hand on Pavel's shoulder. "I must tell you one last piece of business and then we will talk of family things." He face assumed a more somber tone. "Now that Jarman has become a world celebrity with this 3G flu cure, he's become more dangerous to De Bono than ever before. Trust me; things are going to start moving more quickly now, and this situation could become more dangerous, so be careful. That said, enough of business! Let's talk about important things as we take our last steam, like Yelena's ring size and how many carats will be the diamond."

"And color and clarity, father. We cannot forget that."

PROFESSOR IDAN GOLDBERG scrutinized the lighting on his monitor and turned to Pete, his soundman. "I think the backlight on Tanya's hair is a little hot. Rose and Anthony are OK though."

Jerry Pelletier looked through his camera viewfinder and chimed in, "Yah, Pete it's a little hot. Put a filter on it and let's see if that doesn't fix it." Pete Gibbons grabbed a filter out his camera kit and clipped it over the front of the halogen lamp.

As the camera crew made their final adjustments, Rose O'Hara leaned towards Anthony and Tanya, sitting kitty-corner to her across the conference table in Tanya's office. "We'll be on a live feed to all the news networks in a few minutes. Just remember to relax and take as much time as you need to answer the questions."

Anthony grimaced. "I still don't think this interview is such a great idea. Is this really necessary?"

"You've both become world-famous public personalities and this is going to be the first chance for people all around the world to see and hear both of you since Tanya's miraculous recovery. Yet, I know how you feel, and I'm on your side. For the last two days, the network news anchors have been bending our brains, and they are really pissed that you will not let them interview the two of you themselves unless they're here to do it face-to-face. So, as I told you before, we negotiated a list of questions with a pool of reporters from the various networks, and I've managed to keep out the worst of them."

Tanya shook her head. "Still the same, Anthony is right. This is going to be hard."

"I know this is going to be tough, but let me be honest, because I work in the business. With all the world interest in the two of you right now, you've simply got to control the tone.   If you feed the networks nothing but a vacuum, it will be filled by a lot of talking heads. Some will sing your praise and others will try to crucify you for no other reason than to feather their own nests for the sake of a few rating points.   Granted, they'll still be there but this interview will set the tone for how your story is told."

"Stations everyone," Goldberg announced. "We just got a 30-second network countdown." The stillness in the room was eerie and only broken as Goldberg called, "On you Rose, in 5, 4, 3, 2, 1."

"Good morning from Los Gatos Triage Center just south of northern California's Silicon Valley. I'm Rose O'Hara, and with me today is 3G survivor, Lieutenant Colonel Tanya Wheelwright, the commanding officer of the Los Gatos Triage Center, and the man who helped her to a miraculous, full recovery, Captain Anthony Jarman, the End of Life Management Officer for the Los Gatos Triage Center.   My first question is to Colonel Wheelwright. Tanya, I know you must have heard this question a million times already, but just how do you feel now after surviving your harrowing bout with 3G?"

Tanya smiled meekly, "I feel just fine, like my old self. It is like I never got sick."

"As you know Tanya, countless doctors and researchers have been expressing the opinion that it is virtually impossible for anyone to have full recovery from 3G without being impaired in some way. What have you got to say to them?"

Knowing well in advance that she would have to deal with this question, Tanya had formulated a plan for a simple surprise demonstration, and now was the moment to spring her plan.   "You know, I've seen these expert interviews; I doubt that there is anything I or any of the physicians here at the Los Gatos Triage Center haven't already said that will get past their skepticism. Therefore, I'm not going to talk to them. Rather, I'm going to address this issue for everyone else with a brief demonstration. One of the requirements for women ages 17-21 to graduate basic training is the ability to perform forty-seven sit-ups in two minutes. Even though the standards are more lenient for a woman my age, let's see if I can perform as well as a seventeen year old." She turned to Anthony and said, "Anthony, could you please hold my feet for me and call the count?"

His look showed that he had been caught completely off-guard. He could only shrug and say, "Sure! Be happy too."

Pretending not to notice everyone's consternation, Tanya sat upon her conference table facing Anthony and with her back to Rose. Reacting quickly, Goldberg frantically grabbed a handheld camera and maneuvered behind Anthony for different point of view.

"Folks, this is a complete surprise to me," Rose announced into the camera. She leaned over and visually eyed the clip-on mike attached to Tanya's tunic. "Are you sure you're ready for this, Tanya?"

"Watch and see," Tanya said as she situated herself for a good exercise posture, cupping her hands behind her head. "Got a watch, Rose?"

"Yes, I do."

"You call the time. Remember, I must complete all 47 sit-ups in less than two minutes. Anthony, are you ready?"

"Yup, let us know when, Rose."

"Rose looked down at her watch. On my mark... begin."

Tanya began her sit-ups and quickly slipped into a steady pace. As she concentrated on her breathing and movement, Anthony called the count. At exactly two minutes, Rose called the time and was amazed to see that Tanya had actually completed 51 sit-ups in less than two minutes.

Mildly winded, Tanya slid off the table, stood next to Anthony and kissed him on the cheek as the list of prepared questions dropped from Rose's hand.

Rose quickly gathered her thoughts and turned to the camera, asking, "What more proof do we need?" and turned back to Tanya. "As you know, last night, UNE Secretary General Antonio De Bono announced plans to award both of you with highest honors at a special event in Washington next week. Are you excited about this?"

Before Tanya could reply, Anthony leaned forward and said, "With all due respect, Tanya's recovery from 3G, the most horrific scourge in the history of mankind, was a gift of God. To let talking heads and politicians trivialize it for their own aggrandizement would be disrespectful to all of those who've perished. After all, I never saw them standing at the trenches, comforting those who were about to die. Rather, all of us should give thanks. Please everyone, let's mark this with reverence and wherever you choose to pray, please go there with your friends and neighbors and give thanks because, despite all our terrible travails, God loves us. We have not been abandoned."

Tanya looked into his eyes with admiration and love. Without turning to face Rose or the camera she said, "Rose, I believe this interview is concluded." She continued to stand silently and looking into Anthony's eyes until Goldberg announced, "We're off the air."

Stunned silence filled the room as Anthony and Tanya unclipped their microphones. "I only wish we could have helped those who are already infected," Anthony lamented. "Look, I've got a busy afternoon, Tanya. I've got to go." With that, he left before Tanya could answer him.

Leaving Tanya's office, Anthony's head dipped with disappointment and rage as he walked towards the trenches. The first afternoon group was already beginning to kneel before the trench awaiting their last moments of life to end with a pistol shot to the back of their heads. Miracles and cures aside, the business of dying remained.

Caught up in his own thoughts, he failed to notice Tanya running up from behind him until she finally got close enough to him to grab his shoulder and swing him around. "Anthony, what in the hell has gotten into you?"

"Getting a medal from a man who kidnapped my son and killed his mother and the only father he ever knew sticks in my throat. So what if I took a cheap shot! Screw him!"

"I didn't mean that. You did the right thing, Anthony, and you cannot begin to imagine how proud I am of you."

He pawed the ground. "Well thanks. At least one person in this world doesn't think I'm a total jerk. Look; I've got to go."

"No!" She shouted at him. "To hell with De Bono! What I want to know is why you've been growing more distant from me ever since I recovered from 3G. What is it? Don't you see that you're hurting me?"

"Hurting you is the last thing I'd ever want to do, Tanya," he said with a soft pained voice.

"So what is it? What is going on with us?"

"I'd rather not talk about it."

"That's not fair, Anthony. I thought we were never going to hide things from each other. Can't you see this is tearing me up inside? Why won't you be honest with me?"

Anthony scratched his head as Tanya watched his tormented eyes with an anxious stare. "I guess that I no longer feel as if you're mine. Yeah, I know we've never made love, but that's not it."

Sensing that they were closing in on the real truth of the matter, she pressed him on. "Why do you feel this way, Anthony? You've got to know that there is nobody else for me but you. Please, for the love of God, you've got to tell me."

"Fine. You want to know — then I'll tell you. I feel like I'm cheating with another man's wife."

"You mean Henry."

"Yes, meeting him was hard for me. I know how much you love him and how much he loves you. A part of me keeps saying that he's on the other side and that I'm being foolish, but another part of me is having a hard time with the realism of what I saw."

She held his arms gently. "But you said it yourself, Anthony. Henry is on the other side, and he likes you Anthony. For God's sake, he even likes us together."

"I know I'm sounding foolish," he admitted sheepishly.

"And I love you for it, dear Anthony, and for what you've shown me. Before this, I loathed death for all that it took from me, but through you, I've learned that this is that natural order of the universe, a cycle of life that has meaning and purpose."

"I'm glad you feel that way, Tanya," he said as began to turn away.

She slapped herself on the head, thinking to herself that in her moment of truth, she'd gone off on some universal truth quest when the real issue was their relationship and her lack of guts to deal with her own problems.

"Enough," she screamed at him. She grabbed him by the arm and spun him around for the second time, but this time drawing herself close to him. "I want to live, Anthony, and I want to live with you. Yes, I'll always miss Henry, and I'll always love him, but life is for the living and I want to live it with you. Can you understand that?"

The angst that had been building within him seemed to melt away with her words and the intent gaze of her tender eyes. "Yes, I can. I guess I'm just going to have to work my way through this. I'm not all that good at close, personal relationships, if you haven't already noticed."

"Can I ask you for a favor?"

"Sure."

"Let's work through this together. Can you promise me this?"

His face softened. "Yes. Together. But I don't know how to begin."

"You are not the only one who has been conflicted. Dear Anthony, I've been so wrapped up in myself that I haven't been there for you, as I should have. I can see that now. Will you please accept my apology?"

He smiled. "Only if you'll accept mine for being clumsy. I guess I'm no Rudolph Valentino."

"Accepted, but I want you to know that you are the kind of man that Valentino could only have hoped to be in his wildest dreams. I'll be working late tonight, but please promise me that you'll come to my dome at 2100 hours sharp so that we can begin to work this out together. Please tell me you'll come. Please."

He took her hand into his and kissed it gently. "You are God's gift to me Tanya. Wild horses couldn't keep me away."

ANTHONY HAD NOT seen Tanya for the rest of that day, not even during dinner, as he usually did. Their conversation had buzzed through his mind like an agile mosquito that defied all logical swats and left him feeling as though he was losing control and for all his own reasons.

As promised, he knocked lightly on the front door to Tanya's dome at 2100 sharp. From the other side of the door, he heard her call out, "Is that you, Anthony?"

"Uh, yes."

Are you alone?"

Puzzled, his eyes crossed back and forth; "Yes."

The door opened just enough for Tanya to slip a folded piece of paper through the crack. He took it, and the door closed.

He opened it and read. There were three lines with large letters that read, "Count to twenty; follow the green highway; and enter heaven." After having spent most the day working up his mind for a serious, heartfelt conversation, this turn of events was coming from out of nowhere, and he had to find out. He counted down from twenty before opening the door.

Tanya's dome was completely dark, save for a trail of luminescent light sticks leading from the front door to a reddish amber light cutting across the floor from the bathroom. As he closed and locked the door, the distinctive scent of musk and rose incense tantalized his senses. With slow, cautious steps, he followed the light sticks to the bathroom door.

He paused at the sliding door to her extra large bathroom. "Tanya?"

At first, there was no answer as the sound of music began to filter out of the bathroom. He recognized it immediately as being *Chances Are* by Johnny Mathis. "Are you going to stand out there all night, Anthony?"

"This is getting good," he whispered to himself as he opened the door and cast his eyes upon Tanya, half-submerged in her large whirlpool bath, languishing in an alluring pose under a thick layer of bubbles. Surrounded by dozens of candles he saw her holding the surgical glove happy face balloon he'd given her over her chest. "Darling, close the door, won't you? I could get a chill."

Speechless, he slid the door behind him with his mouth agape. "Darling," she purred. "You took me to heaven and back." She tossed the balloon aside revealing her firm shapely breasts half covered in soap bubbles. "Now, it is my turn."

Anthony's mouth tried to work, but no words could come out. He swallowed and tried, yet all he could do was to gaze upon her with deep longing such as he had never felt before.

"Do you like what you see?"

He nodded, and licking his dry lips, he said meekly, "I'm afraid that if I pinch myself I'll wake up, and this dream is too good."

Tanya smiled approvingly and stood up in the tub as sheets of soapy bubbles cascaded down her shapely and curvaceous body. Stepping out of the tub, she walked up to him as his heart began to hammer like a steam locomotive engine. "You're a goddess, and this has got to be a dream," he sighed.

She reached up and pinched his nose till he winced. "Ouch!"

"Well, you've been pinched, and I'm still here. So much for your dream theory."

"You are so incredibly beautiful," he whispered aloud.

She smiled and began to unbutton his tunic. "I'm glad you approve." He leaned forward to kiss her and she put a finger to his lips. "First, I will wash your back." She turned and stepped back in to the tub and slid down into the water. "I love you, darling, but you're not getting into my bath with your pants and boots on."

"Uh right." He hurriedly removed the rest of his clothing and boots and tossed them into the corner as Tanya sang along with the Johnny Mathis song, like a purring kitten.

Fully undressed, he stepped into the warm soapy water as she admired his engorged manhood. "You are most admirably endowed," she noted playfully as he sat down with his back to her. The tub was even larger than he first had thought and he found it easy to nestle between her long, slender, outstretched legs. "Relax, dear," Tanya cooed invitingly.

She immersed a large loofah sponge into the soapy water and gently stroked it along the center of his back, as she worked her other hand over his back. Her touch sent a shudder through his lean, muscular body.

"Relax and enjoy."

"Oh God, that feels so good," he sighed as his essence swirled with ecstasy.

It was a timeless moment, and he closed his eyes as her touch caressed him with passion. As she slowly ran the loofah sponge down along his neck and shoulders, another Mathis classic, *It's Not for Me to Say,* began to play.

"You know, Tanya, I came here tonight with a thousand things on my mind that I wanted to say, and I'll be damned if I can remember a single one of them."

"I suspected so," she purred. "I thought about it as well, and I've come to the conclusion that we do have one really difficult problem to work out."

His breathing froze with the word, "problem." He cleared his throat. "And what is that?"

She leaned forward, wrapped her arms around his chest and nibbled his ear. "Sometimes, we just talk too much."

"Oh, well, yeah. I see what you mean," he mumbled.

She dropped the loofah sponge in the water, worked her arms under his and began to massage her hands down along his chest and past his abdomen before wrapping them around his throbbing manhood. "I want you inside me, Anthony! I want you so much! Now, Anthony, now!"

He turned around in the tub and kneeled before her, excited beyond belief on one hand and wondering how to maneuver himself in the tub on the other. Before he could gather his thoughts, though, she pushed him backward and, jumping into his lap, her lips found his with a fiery, insatiable hunger.

As they immersed into a deep kiss that that made Anthony feel as though the universe was melting away, she guided herself upon him as her body began to undulate with primal craving.

Her moans grew with quick intensity as she dug her fingers into his back sending electrical bolts through his body that defied restraint. As he strained to hold back, her rhythm increased with pounding intensity until he felt as though her body were screaming. "Now. Now! NOW!" Like a comet feeling the heat of the sun for the first time, they glowed together and exploded with a body-racking release that took his breath away.

She collapsed upon him like a limp rag doll and began kissing his neck as their breathing returned to simultaneous deep drawing pants timed to the throbbing of their hearts. After several breaths, he whispered in her ear, "Tanya, I love you so much. Promise me we'll never be apart"

"I promise, my love; I'm yours forever," she answered with slow passionate kisses. "I've lost so much already. If I were to lose you, it would break my heart more than I could bear."

He held her close and could feel her heart beating in unison with his. "You'll never lose me, my love," he whispered into her ear.

They quietly held on to each other, melting into one another's arms, as the next song on Tanya's music CD cued up. It was Mathis singing, *Children will listen/Our children*. The lyrics resonated with Anthony, especially when Mathis sang, "Careful the path you take; wishes come true, not free." The words dove deep into his soul. They were soul mates, and there was so much to tell her, but when and how?

They quietly listened to the music and spoke tender words of love to each other until she finally said, "we're going to turn into a couple of cold prunes. Besides, I'm getting a little hungry. What about you?"

"I'm famished!"

Tanya stepped out the tub and wrapped a large bath towel around herself, holding another out to Anthony. "Let's see what I can whip up the kitchen, shall we?"

"Sounds like a wonderful idea to me," Anthony said as he stepped out the tub and took the extra large bath towel from her hand. It was warm and dry and it felt good as he ran it along his body.

Tanya turned up the main interior lights of the dome to half intensity and disappeared into the kitchen as Anthony finished drying himself. They snacked on a variety of tasty snacks she had prepared beforehand, washing them down with a slightly chilled California chardonnay that delighted their palettes with rich, crisp, citrus and apple flavors.

Since his family had perished in that awful accident, Anthony had always kept his emotional distance, fearing to be vulnerable, fearing to trust. It was a part of his life that had to end, so he drew up the courage to fight back his well-ingrained emotional defenses. "Tanya darling, something troubling is on my mind, and I've got to share it with you. I feel clumsy by bringing this up at a time like this, but it seems like a voice inside me keep pushing me. I guess it was one of those Johnny Mathis songs."

Tanya placed her hand on his arm, "If we are to share our lives, we cannot pick and choose our times to be honest with each other, and our secrets must be shared between us and with no others. Tell me, dear. Don't let this build inside you."

"Just before coming to Los Gatos, I learned that I had a son by a former lover years ago. His name is Russell, and he is in great danger now." Mesmerized by his revelation, Tanya remained silent as he refilled his glass and drained it, gathering up the resolve to continue. "The short story is that Secretary General De Bono kidnapped him and is holding him hostage, and Vigo and I are planning to rescue him."

Tanya clasped her cheeks, "My God. I've sensed that there was a dark secret within you, but this is something I could have never imagined. Yet, it does explain two things that have puzzled me. The first is that now I know why you refused De Bono in our interview this morning."

"And the second?"

"One of the last things that Henry told me is that a man would come from far away to help you, and he asked me to help you to trust him."

Anthony was astonished. "Henry said that?"

"Yes, he did, and it didn't make a lick of sense to me until this very minute. Anthony, we have to rescue your son, no matter what the risks. You must tell me everything. We've got to save Russell!"

"When you say 'we' are you including yourself?"

"I'm in this all the way now, and there will be hell to pay if you try and keep me out of it! Now, fill me in on everything, and I mean everything."

CHAPTER 23

THE MYSTERY SPOT

EXHAUSTED WITH TRAVEL, Vigo pulled up his truck next to Charlie Gibbs' tent. He crawled out of the cab and walked around to the back of the truck where Gibbs met him. A mumbled hello fell out of his mouth as he lowered the tailgate. "Charlie, I've got a few things that need your consummate gunsmithing skills, my young private."

Charlie pointed at his collar lapel. "Check it out, Sarge."

Vigo saw the three chevrons of a brand new buck sergeant. "Well, congratulations, and what kind of butt did you have to kiss for that?"

The young man grinned from ear-to-ear. "Well I could feed you a line about how I've been such a good soldier and all, but the truth is that Captain Jarman decided that I deserve to drink in the NCO club the next time I'm in Port Ord."

"You're in for a disappointment on that one, but congratulations on the promotion anyway," Vigo laughed as he pulled out the first of two long, rectangular black aluminum hard cases and a .50-caliber ammunition can. "Here," he grunted as he handed them to Charlie. "Let's get this stuff in your tent right quick."

Vigo brought the second black case into the tent and laid it on top of Charlie's workbench. Popping the latches, he opened the case to reveal a massive .50-caliber sniper rifle.

"Oh, yeah," Charlie reverently moaned as he hefted the large military rifle out of its case. "A Barrett M82A1, semi-automatic 50 caliber with ten-round magazine, self-leveling bi-pod and 29 inches of hell on earth. I shot one of these once.   It can take out a thin-skinned armored personnel carrier and yet the recoil is no worse than a 12-gauge shotgun."   He drew back the bolt set the safety and quickly eyeballed the inner working parts of the rifle. "This hasn't been shot in long time and it's a little dirty. Nothing too nasty." He laid the rifle down on his workbench, pulled the scope and silencer out of the case and examined them as well.   "A 110 mm F1,6 Night Scope with built in infra-red illuminator. Old stuff, but great optics! Some new batteries and a little cleaning will do, but these custom made Turbodyne silencers look brand new."

"Sounds like you've got the situation in hand."   Vigo opened the ammunition can and pulled out a cardboard package.   "We've got 100 rounds of match load, armor-piercing, non-incendiary.   Once you're ready to test fire them babies, make sure you leave us 20 each for the mission."

Charlie pursed his lips. "What distances are we talking about here?"

"About 250 yards."

"Then why not something lighter than a .50?"

"Because they'll be wearing those new synthetic spider silk vests."

"Yeah, well, a fifty will still pierce any kind of body armor out there."   Charlie examined Vigo's bloodshot eyes closely. "I'll have these ready in a day or two." He laid the rifle down and gave Vigo the once over. "I hate to say it, Sarge, but you look like you've been dragged through hell and back. Why don't you grab some grub before they shut down the mess hall and get some sack time? Heck, I'll even gas up your truck and park it in the motor pool for you."

"That's a good idea." Vigo rubbed his eyes. "Yeah, this last trip was a real bitch, and I forgot when I last ate. Here are the keys to the truck. Lock her up for me. I'll come back later this evening for the keys."

Charlie took the keys, and winked. "Better get them powdered eggs while their still kinda warm. They taste like crap when they're cold."

"Don't remind me," Vigo growled as he left for the mess tent.

Dragging his feet with exhaustion, all he wanted was to eat and get some sleep. Maybe, just maybe if he had enough ambition he'd take a shower before crashing on his cot. "I'm getting too old for this," he mumbled to himself as Ann-Marie Bournelle slapped him on the back.

"Well, look what the cat the dragged in," she teased. He turned to face her and she looked him over. "You've been gone almost a whole week now, and while I've seen you drag your sorry butt through here more times than I can remember, this time takes the cake."

"I'm too tired for this," he growled.

"Oh, feeling a little testy, are we? Well, no matter, because you must live right. I have the morning off, and my dome is free all day." She fished the door key out of her pocket and placed it in his hand. "You go to my dome right now, get a shower and get that stink off you. While you're doing that, I'll bring you something to eat from the mess tent and give you a back rub to help you sleep."

"That sounds wonderful, Ann-Marie. You sure this won't mess up your day?"

"No, it won't. Now stop your drooling, get moving, and remember that my soap is in the blue squeeze bottle. You accidentally used one of the other girl's soap the last time and she ragged me about it for a whole day."

"Blue squeeze bottle. Got it."

She slapped him lightly on the butt. "Like I said, get moving!"

THE COMBINATION OF a bath and a hot meal had worked wonders for him. As he lay face down on the cool linen sheets of Ann-Marie's bed, she lovingly rubbed the soreness out of his back and shoulders.

"Looks like things are pretty well set on this end," she said nonchalantly. "I'm really glad that Anthony and Tanya let me volunteer for this deal."

Vigo spun around onto his back. "What are we talking about, here?"

"The mission to go save Anthony's son, of course. I'll be on the medical team with Jim Boole and Ramona Baker."

"What the hell is going on here? How many people are in this deal now?"

"Besides Anthony and Tanya, there is you, myself, Charlie, Jim and Ramona. A nice, tight crew."

"Oh yeah, and now this rescue effort is about as clandestine as a Thanksgiving pot luck dinner."

"Don't worry; nobody else knows."

"Not even Colonel Henry Tzu at Port Ord?"

"Heavens, no! Why would you ask such a thing?"

Vigo sat upright with a serious expression on his face. "Let's cut the crap, Ann-Marie. I know you're spying on me for Tzu."

"What are you talking about?"

"You thought I was asleep when I saw you taking photographs of my medallion out of the corner of my eye, so I bugged your webpad."

Her eyes shot wide open. "You son-of-a-bitch!"

"So, what if I am? What does Tzu know about this?"

"Nothing, and we couldn't figure out what that medallion thing is either, so we gave up on it. You can check your damn bug if you don't believe me." She turned away from him to hide her pained expression.

"Look, you didn't do anything wrong, and the intelligence was helpful for me too. I'm not worried about Tzu. He just wants what is best for Anthony, as do I."

She covered her face with her hands. "So, we're both still a couple of slime balls. Still the same, you can't believe how cheap I feel right now."

"It's OK. It doesn't change anything between us. Besides, I should have said something long ago, but old habits are hard to break."

"You know what really hurts?"

"What?"

"I thought we had something special going, you and me. You've been the only man in my life since I walked into this horrible place, and for the first time in a long time, I thought I knew what it felt to be an honest woman. Now, I know that you were just using me like an old, worn-out whore. Hell, who could blame you? I've been such a fool."

Vigo placed his arm around her shoulder. "Ann-Marie, please look at me." She resisted, and he asked again. When she turned to face him, he could see the tears welling up in her eyes. "You are an honest woman for me, and we do have something special going. I want you to know that."

"But the past. It always follows us."

"The people we were in the before times are dead and gone, Ann-Marie. If all this misery doesn't entitle us both to a fresh start in life, what does?"

"I don't know what to say. This morning, I thought I knew what I was feeling, but now, it seems like I don't even know who I am."

"You're someone I care for very much, and I want you to know that I've been faithful to you as well." He ran his hand gently through her hair. "You and I have spent most of our lives selling love and romance for one reason or another. I do not know that we could ever think about it like young kids in love for the very first time, but I do know one thing; if I lost you, I know my life would be so very empty."

"You'd live."

"No; I would just exist, but with you, I know that I could live. Let's make it work, Ann-Marie; no more secrets, no more games -- just us."

The tears began to stream down her face as she sat silently with trembling lips. Vigo leaned forward and began kissing the moist tears from her cheeks. "Right here. Right now. Let's agree to put the past behind us and make a fresh start in life -- together."

"Oh, yes Vigo," she sighed passionately. Their lips met as she melted into his arms. After a long, passionate kiss, he gave her one last hug.

"My spirit is willing, Ann-Marie, but I'm just whipped," he said with droopy eyes.

"That's OK. Just roll over, and let me rub you to sleep." He kissed her again and rolled back onto his stomach as she resumed the back rub.

"Oh by the way," he said as he felt a deep sleep overcoming him. "We'll be getting a visitor later this afternoon. He's a computer genius by the name of LeBlanc. He's coming here to see Anthony. Be a dear, and make sure to wake me up before noon."

"Noon it is. Now get some sleep, soldier. You've earned it."

WHILE STROLLING OUT of the mess hall, Tanya looked up to see one of the Jet Ranger helicopters from Port Ord on its approach to the landing pad. "That's odd," she said to Anthony. "That's him. Colonel Tzu told me to expect a visitor about now, but didn't tell me anything about him. Let's go see who it is."

"Sorry, but you're on your own, Tanya. Even though I've only got a few cases this afternoon, I do not want to make them wait."

"How long will you be?"

"No more than an hour, thank God. I'm really beginning to feel like we're close to shutting this miserable place down once and for all."

"So am I," she heartily agreed. "When you're finished, be sure to swing by my office, will you?"

He saw Charlie driving one of the electric carts his way and flagged him down. As his orderly stopped the cart, he jumped in and said, "You can count on it. Keep the coffee hot."

She waved at him and decided to walk up the hill to the landing pad as the Jet Ranger slowly settled down on the yellow landing markers. Reaching the top of the hill, she was surprised to see that Vigo had beaten her to the punch with a small electric truck and was helping a man dressed as a military doctor to unload several aluminum equipment cases from the helicopter onto the truck.

Vigo noticed her as she approached, tapped on the other man's shoulder and called out to her, "Colonel Wheelwright."

"So this must be our mystery guest," she replied as she noticed the medical insignia on Jeffrey LeBlanc's khaki uniform. "I don't know if you've been reading the news, but we're not hurting for doctors around here these days."

Jeffrey held out his hand, "To be honest, that's just fine by me, as I'm not a doctor. May I introduce myself? I'm Jeffrey LeBlanc, and I'm no doctor. In fact, I'm only wearing this uniform because Colonel Tzu does not want me to be restricted by the quarantine. In real life, I design artificial intelligence programs."

She took his hand. "And I'm Lieutenant Colonel Tanya Wheelwright and while you're still a mystery to me," she glanced over at Vigo, "it appears that the sergeant here knows more about you than I do."

Vigo stepped a little closer. "Tanya, he's come all the way from Russia to see Anthony. This is anything but a pleasure visit."

Tanya smiled. So, this was the man Henry had told her about. Things were certainly taking an interesting turn. "Anthony will be available in about an hour or two. In the meantime, can I make you comfortable in my own office?"

"I would certainly appreciate that," Jeffrey replied. "And would there be a private place where I could set up my equipment? All I really need is a table and a few electrical outlets."

"I think we can accommodate that." Tanya nodded towards the truck. "Shall we?"

CORPORAL SHARMA HELPED Vigo and LeBlanc to carry his aluminum equipment cases into Tanya's private office and sat them down behind the meeting table. Tanya motioned to them to sit down in the chairs facing her desk and asked, "Are you hungry?"

"I haven't eaten since breakfast, if you can call two slices of dry, burnt toast breakfast," Jeffrey replied.

"Sunny," Tanya said to her clerk, "could you get our guest a couple of nice, hot sandwiches from the mess tent and a large pitcher of coffee for us all."

Sharma acknowledged her order and paused at the door. "Excuse me, doctor, but all we have now is saccharin and condensed milk, I'm afraid."

"Thanks for asking, but it makes no difference to me. I take my coffee black," LeBlanc replied.

After Sharma left the room, Jeffrey began drawing the blinds as Vigo took out a small electronic sweeper from his pants and began working his way around the office. Mindful what they were doing, Tanya quietly sat down in her chair and watched them with an amused smile. After closing the last blind, Jeffrey settled down into a chair and, after exchanging a mutual nod with Vigo, said. "I take it that Major Jones has already briefed you on the basic details?"

"No, he hasn't. All I know is that Colonel Tzu told me to expect a visitor today but he wouldn't tell me any more than that."

"I'm sorry about that, Tanya," Vigo said as he settled into his own chair next to Jeffrey. "I was dog tired this morning and barely woke up in time for Jeffrey's arrival."

"I hope you're feeling more rested now, Vigo," she replied kindly. "So Mr. LeBlanc, what is this all about?"

He scratched his eyebrow for a moment and said, "I was really hoping to have this conversation with Captain Jarman. You know, privately. No offense, I hope."

"None taken," she replied with a slight smile. She rose up out of her chair and walked to the window facing the helipad and pried open the blinds with her fingers. "Tell me, Mr. LeBlanc, is the pilot waiting for you before she leaves?"

"I have the full use of the helicopter for as long as I'm here. Warrant Officer Gonzalez has her orders to take me wherever I want."

Tanya tipped her head and hummed as she turned around to face him. "You must be a real VIP, then, Mr. LeBlanc, so if you're going to play games with me and Anthony Jarman, I suggest you get back in your helicopter and leave right now, because I run this center, and you're on my turf, hot shot."

A man of great wealth in his own means, Jeffrey LeBlanc was not accustomed to such blunt rebukes and his cheeks began to glow red with anger. "If you want to go down on the mat with me, lady, you're going to lose, because I've got a little more pull than you think."

Vigo jumped up from his chair. "Whoa, you two. Cease-fire right now, and I mean it! This misunderstanding is my fault because I was sawing logs when I should have been laying the groundwork for this meeting." He looked down at Jeffrey, "We're all on the same side, here, and the colonel already knows a lot more than you think."

"But what I still do not know is just who you are, Mr. LeBlanc and why you're here in my center, with your VIP helicopter, and wanting to speak privately with Captain Jarman." Tanya had already deduced a link between Anthony's former lover and this man by virtue of their shared last name. However, she was more interested in hearing everything, and the confrontation had served her purpose to force an open dialogue.

"Go ahead," Vigo urged, "tell her. She knows about the boy."

Jeffrey sighed. "Anthony Jarman had a long-standing love affair with my sister, Roxanne LeBlanc. She had a son by him and never told him. She and her husband were recently murdered in their home and the boy, Russell, was kidnapped. I'm here to talk with Anthony about affecting a rescue. Other than that, I'm really not sure of what I can tell you."

"But we're family now," Tanya replied. "Why be so tight-lipped?"

Vigo's eyes shot up. "What do you mean, family?"

A devilish grin crept across her face as she pulled open her desk drawer and pulled out an official-looking document. "We haven't announced it yet, but the day before yesterday, Anthony and I got married. I trust you'll both keep this to yourselves for the time being." She handed it across the desk to Vigo.

Stunned into silence, he took the document in his hand. It was a copy of a marriage certificate duly filed in San Jose. Father Bennett had performed the ceremony, and Lieutenant Ramona Baker and Major Jim Boole had acted as witnesses. His mouth worked around, but the words would not come out.

"Vigo, I believe you're trying to say something like this is so sudden?" Tanya winked. "Well, yes it is. So what? When Anthony popped the question I was totally surprised, but then that's Anthony. When he gets a notion to do something, he gets right to it. Next thing I knew, we were standing in front of Father Bennett, and I couldn't be happier." She glanced over at LeBlanc, "and I guess this makes us family, as well."

Vigo stood up, beaming with joy. "Well then, it's about time I kissed the bride!"

"And what about me?" Jeffrey chimed in.

"You'd better," Tanya laughed.

They all hugged and kissed and then Tanya told them about how it all came about as they listened with eager faces, enjoying every little detail until her clerk, Sunny Sharma returned with the coffee and sandwiches.

As LeBlanc hungrily wolfed down his sandwiches, Vigo began briefing Tanya on all the details, beginning with how he and Anthony had first met. Then, Jeffrey told her about how his sister had forced him to keep a vow of secrecy about the boy and how he had underwritten most of the cost of the Nibiru Holocaust Film Project that had now made Anthony a worldwide media figure.

LeBlanc had just finished telling her about his sister, Roxanne and what he'd learned from the police reports when Sunny Sharma announced that Anthony was outside Tanya's office.

ANTHONY REMAINED QUIET as they seated themselves at the conference table, closely watching LeBlanc's face and body gestures as he and Tanya began to discuss the mission in general terms. Surprised that he had a newfound family member, Anthony was annoyed to learn that Jeffrey had known about him all along and had never told him about his son. Therefore, he had remained quiet throughout the introductions.

"You're mighty quiet, brother," LeBlanc observed. "I was hoping you'd be glad to finally see me."

Anthony raised an eyebrow at the familiar greeting. "I'm not your brother-in-law in the conventional sense, so please; let's not make this a family affair."

"Roxanne LeBlanc was my sister, and that makes me your son's uncle. However, if you prefer to be more formal, I understand."

Anthony leaned forward in his chair. "I only learned about my son, Russell a few months ago, and you've known all along. How would you feel if you were in my shoes?"

LeBlanc could feel Anthony's eyes cutting through him. "I'm going to shoot straight with you. Yes, I've known about you and Russell from the very beginning, and while I felt it was unfair that you were never told, Roxanne made me promise that I would remain silent about it for the boy's sake. You've got every right to hate me. I can't blame you for that, but it does make me sad."

Anthony studied his face till he was satisfied that LeBlanc was being honest. "I haven't known you long enough to hate you. But I have known you long enough to know that I cannot entirely trust you. At least not yet, but this is all beside the point. What I still do not understand is why you're involved in this and exactly why you're here."

Tanya could sense the tension between the two men, and wondered if their egos would get the better of them and said to Anthony, "For God's sake, he's here to help us rescue Russell. You two can duke it out later about anything you darn well please, but let's stay focused on that for now."

Jeffrey looked Anthony squarely in the eyes. "Just because we're family now doesn't mean you've got to like me, but when it comes to saving Russell, let's just work on the premise that blood is thicker than water because you, Tanya and Russell are the only family I have now."

"I can work with that," Anthony agreed. "I saw you flying in here in your helicopter, which means you've got something official in mind besides a family rescue effort."

"You're right about that. The reason why I'm even able to help you is that I'm involved in a top secret project, and we desperately need your help."

Anthony looked at Vigo, "How long have you known about this?

"During my absence, I was briefed on this in Washington when I met with Jeffrey and his new boss, a Russian by the name of Lebedev. This is a no-bullshit problem, Anthony. If you think Nibiru was bad, something worse is on the way, and it will be here in just a matter of years." Vigo leaned his head towards LeBlanc. "I think you'll do a much better job of explaining Shiva than I could."

Anthony and Tanya listened, their faces pale with horror, as LeBlanc explained the impending Shiva disaster and what was being done about it. After he finished, Anthony asked, "So what could I possibly do?"

LeBlanc replied, "As you already know, Anthony, I'm a computer scientist. I specialize in building highly advanced semi-sentient computer programs, which I call quasills. At present, I'm working with the Russians and the Americans on a quasill that will be used to help pulverize Shiva. The name of my quasill is Andrea and in order for us to achieve our goal, we need someone like you to give our quasill a sixth-sense, if you will. If you decide to help us after we help you rescue Russell, the three of you will have to live in Obninsk City, Russia for most likely a year or more while you complete your work."

Anthony looked over at Tanya. "So tell me about this Obninsk City?"

"It's not Paris, but we'll manage," she replied. "Besides, it will give me a good chance to teach you Russian."

He shrugged. "Can you keep us safe from De Bono?"

This time Vigo stepped in, "They can't touch you there, not unless they feel they can get through a human wall of FSB agents. Short of disappearing on some uncharted island, it's probably the best you can do. Besides, De Bono is not going to know that you're directly involved in the rescue. All things considered, I think it's the best thing you could do."

"Yeah," Anthony replied hesitatingly "but you're not going to be the one who will be looking over his shoulder in a strange land. At least here in the States, I can see and hear him coming. To be honest, I'm really not excited about this Russia thing, even if Vigo thinks it will work. You know what they say about the best-laid plans of mice and men. As to the rescue, I fail to see how you can bring anything to the table other than an additional burden."

A cunning smile peeked out from behind Vigo's lips. "OK, Jeffrey, it's time to show them what you showed me in Washington."

LeBlanc winked at Anthony. "Give me a minute to set things up, and it's show time."

"That's OK by me, but let's skip the trailers." Anthony pointed at the remaining sandwich on the serving tray, "I haven't had lunch yet. Anybody got dibs on that?"

"Help yourself," Jeffrey replied as he rose from his chair.

Anthony reached over to the tray and picked up the sandwich. "At the very least, this ought to be interesting. OK, it's show time." He began munching the sandwich as Jeffrey set up the holographic projector and the IBM Biomass desktop on Tanya's conference table while Vigo and Tanya chatted.

As Anthony finished his sandwich, Jeffrey finished making the final adjustments, started the projector and said. "Our feature presentation is about to begin, folks, so please gather around the projector base. Vigo, if you could turn off the room lights, please." Vigo rose to turn off the lights as LeBlanc keyed the access codes into the Biomass desktop keyboard. As the projectors whirred to life, he settled back in his chair and began sipping his coffee.

Unlike the life-size holographic projectors Andrea used in Russia, she appeared in her chosen persona as Dorothy, but at one-fourth her normal size. While this was a limitation of the portable unit, she nonetheless appeared with the same high degree of resolution and smoothness. "Hello Captain Jarman and Colonel Wheelwright. My name is Andrea and I have been waiting for this meeting with great anticipation. I hope that after you've heard what I have to say, that you will let me help you to save your son, Russell."

Anthony and Tanya were immediately stunned by her lifelike and inviting persona. They of course, immediately recognized her visage. "Hello Andrea," Anthony replied in a polite voice. "What are you?"

"I am a semi-sentient program, Anthony, and as such, my fundamental programming is based on the Meta-Law of Robotics, which is an extension of Asimov's original Three Laws of Robotics. What this means, Anthony, is that while I cannot directly harm a human being, I can help to save a human being, which, in this case, is your son, Russell."

She replaced her image with a three-dimensional wire frame image of the missile silo at Fort Hood. As she spoke, elements of the image would light up and change perspective as needed. "This is the missile silo at Fort Hood, now under the control of the UNE. When this silo was functioning in its original role, it was always locked down except for crew changes and necessary maintenance. However, now that the UNE controls the silo, it is being kept open at all times by the people who are holding your son. If they suspect an impending attack, they can lock down the entire silo complex very quickly, making it impossible to rescue your son. To prevent this from happening, we can neutralize the electric motors, which operate the door."

The wire frame image vanished and was replaced by representation of several different types of nanobots. "One of my capabilities is to operate billions of nanobots for sensing, communications and small repairs. I can also control my nanobots to form together as microbots when needed." The nanobot images drew together in piggyback fashion creating much larger microbots. "A collective microbot can move into place quickly and then disassemble itself into its respective mission-specific nanobots. For the purpose of this mission, I can also use my nanobots and microbots to provide you with rough sensing information of the occupants inside the silo while neutralizing the doors."

Anthony was impressed with the technology, but felt a certain mistrust of anything new and highly complex brewing within him. "Tell me, Andrea, how will you get your nanobots into the silo without being noticed?"

"May I," LeBlanc interrupted. Andrea obediently paused her projector display.

"In order for us to use Andrea's nanobots, they must be planted on or very near the crew quarters access shaft no less than 18 hours before the assault. Ideally, 24 hours will ensure that they will have enough time to move into place."

Anthony tapped his fingers on the conference table as he pondered the plan. If it worked, nothing could stop him from saving his son. On the other, if it didn't and if the effort to plant the nanobots was detected, he would most likely never see Russell alive – if ever. "Andrea, I have no reason to believe that you can't do as you say. However, there is a human angle here that is very risky. That is getting the nanobots in place before we storm the silo. Frankly, that really bothers me, so I need to think about this one for a while. In the meantime, what is this about saving the world? I'm not an engineer or an astronaut. What could I possibly offer?"

Vigo tapped Jeffrey's shoe with the tip of his boot and nodded. LeBlanc understood an indicated that he agreed. "Andrea, explain our problem with Shiva."

Andrea redisplayed her Dorothy persona holding a simulation of Shiva in her hand. "Anthony, this model I'm holding in my hand is called Shiva. It used to be a satellite of Nibiru, but it was thrown out of its orbit around Nibiru into elliptical Earth-crossing orbit around our Sun during the three days of darkness at the Nibiru flyby." She let the object rise from her hand as her own physical persona faded away. As the Shiva image grew to the largest size possible with the small projector, it began tumbling in a slow, erratic pattern. "Shiva is approximately 20 miles in diameter and made of dense, solid metals. We've also determined that it still has a liquid magma core, which is approximately two miles in diameter. It is generally thought that Shiva was once a planet moon of Nibiru, roughly the size of Mars, and that it was destroyed in some form of a cataclysm. Therefore, Shiva is a remnant of the planet moon's core."

The image of Shiva shrank to a small dot and was plotted against a map of the solar system as it moved quickly along the line used to denote its orbital path. "There is a good probability that Shiva will impact our own moon in 2019 and a virtual certainty that it will do so in 2035."

The solar map faded away, to be replaced with a large representation of the Earth's moon. "Because Shiva made of solid metal with a magma core, our concern is that if hits our moon, it could split it in two." She then showed them a simulated impact of Shiva striking the moon and its magma core shooting out through its shattered shell deep into Earth's own moon, causing it to fracture. "While it is not a certainty that Shiva could fracture our own moon, the chances are nonetheless high."

Tanya let her head drop into her hands repeating, "Oh my God," as Anthony watched the simulation of the moon shattering under the impact with horror.

Once the simulation had finished, Andrea replaced the image with her own physical persona. "Anthony, if this happens then please consider this, in the sudden absence of the tidal gravitational forces exerted on the Earth by our Moon, the entire surface of the Earth would drop some eighteen inches, or nearly half a meter. The consequences of that would be cataclysmic on a global scale. Besides the obvious earthquakes, volcanic eruptions and floods, our world's ocean ecosystems would fail. An event of this magnitude could very well bring mankind precipitously close to extinction."

Anthony clasped his hands. "Andrea, I see the danger and the need to do something about it, but I still do not understand why you're coming to me for help. The closest thing to space science I've ever done was to build model rockets in grade school, and then I almost set fire to my parents' barn."

"May I do that?" Jeffrey interjected.

Andrea smiled appreciatively, "Of course, Jeffrey. Would you like me to return to standby state now?"

"As soon as Vigo turns on the room lights," he replied as Vigo got back to his feet to turn the lights back on. "By the way, Andrea, you did a superb job with your presentation."

"Yes you did," Tanya added. "Thank you, Andrea."

The holographic projector shut itself down as Vigo switched the room lights back on. Jeffrey turned his chair towards Anthony. "I'm glad you didn't set the barn on fire, but that's not what we need you for. Rather, we need you to give Andrea a sixth-sense, if you will."

"For what?"

"We already have a way to rubblize Shiva into a harmless asteroid field or even to send it crashing into our Sun. The problem is that, in order for us to use this technology, we need to map the interior of Shiva in great detail, and this is where we've hit a brick wall. This is because Shiva is basically one huge ball of fluctuating metal ore with a myriad of unpredictable magnetic anomalies that make it impossible for the various sensors of our deep space probes to work properly. In addition to that, Shiva tumbles erratically, as you could saw in the simulation, which we feel is the result of its magma core. Consequently, if we try to rubblize it without knowing its construction we could create an even more deadly monster."

"So where does the psychic angle come in?" Anthony asked with a puzzled expression.

"We're hoping it will pick up where Newton and Einstein have left off. You see, our technology as well as our understanding of the universe is based on the work of such great minds, and Shiva is something that even they could not foresee, let alone ourselves. However, if Andrea can be taught how to instinctively go beyond the limits of our understanding, she will be able to know precisely where and how to apply our technology when the time comes to rubblize Shiva. But even more than that, we could turn Shiva from a monster into the greatest asset ever known to mankind!"

Anthony scratched his head. "Destroying this thing, I can understand but turning it into an asset? That doesn't make sense."

"Look at it this way," Jeffrey replied. "Instead of rubblizing the entire mass of Shiva, Andrea could find a way to rubblize a path to the magma core. This in turn could provide enough energy to both stabilize and move Shiva into a safe orbit. After that, we'd have the biggest ore mine in the solar system. We could methodically rubblize and mine it so as to build L5 space colonies, space ships, probes, you name it."

LeBlanc clapped his hands, "Think of it. If there is one thing Nibiru, and now Shiva, have taught us is that we live in a violent universe, where brief life-terminating cataclysms are separated by long periods of quiescence. In simple terms, the very nature of the universe makes our planet nothing more than a blue-green bulls-eye in space. Look, our number has always been up for mankind as long as we remain tied to only one planet. But if we could neutralize Shiva as a threat, we can then mine it for the metals we'll need to ensure that mankind can and will survive."

Anthony held up his hands. "I'm sold, but if I'm supposed to try and teach your Andrea how to trust her instincts with all of these magnetic anomalies, I have no idea of where to begin. I wouldn't know a magnetic anomaly from a hole in a wall, which means that you could spend years teaching me the basics before I could hope to have an intelligent conversation on the matter. I'm sorry, but I think you've picked the wrong man. You need someone with the proper background for this."

"We've anticipated this," Jeffrey insisted. "That's why we feel it will take you a few years in Russia to handle this. Heck, don't feel that you're in the dark all alone here. Even in his last days, Einstein admitted that some of his theories were seriously flawed and we're not asking you to be an Einstein. All I'm asking you to do is to try. Please, Anthony, won't you try?"

"But I'm afraid you'll waste years on training me and then find yourselves no further along than you are now."

Just as LeBlanc was to answer him, Tanya interrupted. "Anthony, what if I could cut your learning curve down from two years to two hours?"

All eyes turned on her. "You got something up your sleeve?" Anthony joked.

"Hmmm... not really," she replied. "Granted I haven't even tried to set fire to a barn with a model rocket but I did happen to live in this area for a long time, and there is a place called "The Mystery Spot" on the northern edge of what was once Santa Cruz. It used to be a famous tourist trap, because it sits on a large ore body that creates some weird kind of magnetic anomaly. Whenever we had out-of-town guests, my former husband Henry used to take them there." Her eyes rolled. "If I've been to The Mystery Spot once, I've been there a hundred times. While I'm no scientist by any measure, I do know you'll feel and see the effects of a magnetic anomaly, and perhaps that will give you a good head start, Anthony."

"That's a great idea," Jeffrey chimed in. "But does this place still exist after that huge tsunami?"

"It should," Tanya said opening a desk drawer. She pulled the folders forward and pulled out a small stack of AAA road maps she kept in her desk. "Let me see if I can find it." She sorted through maps, and, finding the one for Santa Cruz, California unfolded it on her desk and picked up a pen. Tracing the route to The Mystery Spot on the map, she circled where she felt they'd find it, folded the map again and handed it to Jeffrey. "Why don't you and Anthony go see if your chopper pilot can find this place while Vigo and I do a little scrounging? Let's say, we'll meet you two at the helipad in an hour."

Anthony laughed as LeBlanc snatched the map with a glowing smile. "You've got a deal. See you there. Come on, Anthony; we're off."

Anthony shrugged and jumped to his feet. "You know, Jeffrey, I think you're barking up the wrong tree with this sixth-sense stuff. What your Andrea really needs is a little good old fashioned female intuition." LeBlanc nodded, and the two of them headed out of the office as Vigo watched them leave with an amused grin.

"Well, I guess there's not much I can add to all this so I just guess I'll wait here for you guys."

"The heck you will," Tanya shot back. "You and I need to do a little scrounging first, and you will be coming along on the chopper."

"Hey, I do scrounging real good. Let's rock."

WARRANT OFFICER GONZALEZ flew several passes over the area Tanya had marked on the road map and found a spot where she could hover a few feet above the ground. Vigo and Jeffrey hopped down from the hovering chopper, and as Gonzalez circled overhead, they cleared an area large enough for her land the helicopter.

As Vigo pulled the large canvas bag out of the helicopter and hefted it over his shoulder, Tanya exclaimed, "Wow, this place really got creamed in the tsunami." She pointed at the base of a small hillside. "That's where the gift shop used to be," as she kicked loose an old yellow sign with black and red letters that had once hung over the entrance to The Mystery Spot. She pointed to the top of the small hill; "the actual spot is up at the top of that small hill and is about one hundred and fifty feet in diameter."

"So what's the story on this place?" Anthony asked as he knelt over the sign and looked around. Only fourteen feet above sea level, the raging waters of the Pacific had ravaged the hilltop, even though it was several miles from the shore. Everywhere they looked, fallen and uprooted trees lay on the ground and hillside pointing west in the direction of the receding flood waters, except for a circle of a half dozen trees that remained standing near the hilltop.

"Early in the last century, some fellow bought this land to build a house and had to buy the hill as well, so he decided to build a work shed on it. After he built it, something literally shoved it down the hill against a large tree and there it stood until the tsunami. After a few years, it just became a curiosity for folks, and then it became a hot tourist spot." She pointed at the circle of standing trees near the hilltop. "That's where the actual mystery spot is, and why those trees are still standing is beyond me. I guess it is just another part of the mystery. If you guys will follow me, I can see that a good part of the paving and concrete steps survived, but be careful."

With Tanya in the lead, the group started weaving its way around the debris and up the small hillside. Tanya turned towards the helicopter and signaled for the pilot to join them.

They had only gone about twenty feet when she stopped and pulled a small pile of debris off a piece of concrete pad that had once stood next to the ticket booth. "Vigo, give me the bubble level."

He lowered the bag to the ground and pulled out a small carpenter's level they'd borrowed from the maintenance room and handed it to her. She sat the level down on the concrete pad and checked it.   The bubble centered indicating the level was on flat ground. She looked towards the back of the group where the pilot was standing, motioned her to come forward and had her stand back to back with Vigo.   "Well, I'd say that Warrant Officer Gonzalez here is about a foot shorter than Sergeant Jones." Agreeing nods confirmed her estimate.

"OK, Vigo, have you got the digital camera?"   He reached in the bag and pulled out an old digital camera with a large LCD display on the back. "Give it to Jeffrey; he'll be our official Mystery Spot photographer today."

She found two old 2x4 boards, laid them across the pad pointing towards the hill and had Vigo stand on one end with Gonzalez on the other. Then, she had Vigo stand on the side farthest from the hill and Gonzalez on the side closest to the hill. "OK, Jeffrey, stand over there perpendicular to them and take a picture of them facing each other."

He did as instructed, and the image captured by the camera made Vigo seem much taller than when he and Gonzalez had been standing back to back. "Now, I know you're all seeing this same thing with your eyes and yes, it is an illusion. But if you look at the picture Jeffrey just took, you'll see that it is not a psychological illusion."

The group huddled around Jeffrey and the camera and curiously eyed the image. "Now, let's do it a different way. This time, I want Jones and Gonzalez to change sides." The two moved to opposite positions and stepped back up on the boards. This time, Gonzalez appeared to be nearly as tall Jones to the group, and to their amazement, the digital camera image showed the same result."

"OK, let's gather everything up and go up the hill a bit. By the way, if you begin to feel queasy or nauseous don't worry. It will pass after we come back down." She picked up the carpenter's level. "Let's go."

They carefully threaded past fallen trees and debris left behind by the tsunami wave and soon reached a spot in the center of the only remaining stand of trees. Tanya looked up at the top of the trees. "Amazing," she muttered to herself. "Look up, folks. These trees should all be leaning West because of the tsunami, but they're all still leaning inward towards the spot on which we're standing. Don't ask me why. All I know is that we're standing over a huge ore deposit, which they say caused the magnetic anomaly here and makes all the measuring instruments go wacky."

"Vigo, the board and the balls please." Vigo removed a straight makeshift plank with a groove running down the center. "Give me a hand Anthony. We need to get this board set at an angle with one end facing downhill. That end has to be at least a quarter bubble off so that the far end of the board is higher."

Anthony gathered a few broken chunks of concrete and helped her set up the board. After everyone had checked the level to see that the end of the board facing downhill was higher than the other end, she positioned Jeffrey with the camera for another series of pictures and then took two balls from Vigo's hands and held them up. "We appropriated these billiard balls from the recreation tent. They're the usual non-metallic type, so let's see what happens if we put one of them on the low end of the board." She carefully positioned a white cue ball on the low end of the board. "Anthony, I want you to stand on the other side of the board and let's see what happens when I remove my hand. And Jeffrey, don't forget to take plenty of pictures."

Holding the cue ball in place until Anthony was in position, she carefully lifted her without disturbing the ball. Within a moment, the ball began rolling up the plank as though an unseen hand were guiding along until it fell off the other end, into Anthony's outstretched hand. She then followed it with an eight ball for a repeat of the same result.

Each member of the group then took turns as they openly wondered what could be causing the balls to roll up the grooved plank against gravity.

Finally, Anthony turned to Jeffrey and asked, "Is this what is happening when your probes try to analyze Shiva?"

"Yes, but the magnetic anomalies they're dealing with are stronger by several orders of magnitude."

Tanya smiled. She could see that Anthony was beginning to intuitively connect with the phenomenon. She looked around and saw a large 2x6 between two trees. "And now the 'piece de resistance' ladies and gentlemen," she announced.

She handed the billiard balls back to Vigo. "Anthony, help me get that large board over by that tree and we'll set it nice and level this time." Anthony followed her to the board and kicked it over with the toe of his shoe to make sure there were no crawling surprises. As he used a fallen branch to shake off the dirt and muck he said quietly, "Tanya my love, you're a genius. This demonstration is a mind blower."

"I'm no genius," she smiled. "I just made sure we always got the same tour guide." She chuckled. "He was a corker. You know, the kind of guy who has been here forever, and what I really liked about him was that he could say hello in every language imaginable. After the umpteenth tour, I got more of a kick from watching people's faces light up when they heard him say hello in their native tongue."

"I hope he survived," Anthony said.

"Me, too."

The two of them carried the six feet long board back to center of the mystery spot and sat it perfectly flat and level.

"Do you all remember the difference in height between Sergeant Jones and Warrant Officer Gonzalez at the base of the hill? Well, let's see what happens when we're standing directly on top of the Mystery Spot."

Vigo stepped gingerly up upon the downhill side of the board and Gonzalez on the other side. "Oh my," Vigo exclaimed as Jeffrey clicked pictures, "Gonzalez, you look about as tall as knee-high rug rat."

Gonzalez grunted. "Rug rat, my ass! Let's switch sides."

The two switched sides and this time Gonzalez who was nearly a foot shorter than Vigo in actual height could now look directly ahead at the top of his head. "Now I'm taller than you, sergeant," she boasted as Jeffrey continued taking pictures.

They both stepped down, and everyone huddled around Jeffrey and the camera one more time as he replayed the images. Each image captured by the camera was exactly the same as each of them had seen with their own eyes.

"In a nutshell, this is the problem we're having," Jeffrey noted.   "Our instruments, which we've built to accommodate our own powers of perception, can be fooled as easily as we can."

Anthony said, "Can I have the camera for a bit?" Jeffrey handed it to him and he sat down on the plank, cycling through the images for several minutes as everyone quietly looked on.

After playing back the images several times, he closed his eyes and took three long deep breaths and opened his eyes with a deep knowing smile. "Now it clicks. Now I know what I've got to do. Let's get headed back."

CORPORAL SUNNY SHARMA was relieved to see them return. Before she had left, Tanya had ordered an armed MP to stand guard in front of her office and the man had turned out to be a dry, witless conversationalist by Sharma's standards. Now that he could leave, his office routine would no longer be interrupted.

Tanya looked at her watch as she opened the door to her office. "Sunny, why don't you go and get some dinner if you like? Just lock the front door behind you."

He glanced at Vigo, Anthony and Jeffrey and said, "Sure you wouldn't like a nice cup of tea?"

"Good idea, Sharma," Anthony replied. "Come on; let's go in."

They all filed into the office and sat around the conference table discussing their outing to The Mystery Spot and passing around the digital camera.

Anthony scanned through the last images of Vigo and Gonzalez standing on the long plank and said, "Tell me, Jeffrey, the holographic image of Andrea was impressive, but if I wanted find this Andrea where is she. Buried in some silicon chip or something?"

"No, she actually resides in a small biomass processor." He put his hand on the small IBM Biomass desktop prototype. "And this is where she lives so to speak."

"So show me. Open it up."

"Sure, just don't go picking around inside as there are some delicate components in there."

"Don't worry about us," Anthony replied. Jeffrey nodded and began removing the large cabinet thumbscrews along the top of the prototype and removed the top panel. They looked inside and saw several computer devices and fiber optic cables neatly woven around a thick sealed Plexiglas box in the center of the cabinet. Inside the Plexiglas, they saw a small human like brain floating in a clear pinkish fluid.

"Is that a real brain?" Tanya gasped.

"Only in the sense that the IBM bioengineers used human stem cells to create it. However, the oxygenated fluid you see around is modified amniotic fluid. They collect it from pregnant women when their water breaks before giving birth and enhance it."

"So Andrea must be in a pretty dark and lonely place," Tanya said.

"No, her senses are actually better than anything we can imagine, and right now she's in standby mode which is a like a very deep restful sleep. When she is connected to her external sensory controllers, she can sense the world much better than we can."

"So is she alive?" Anthony wondered aloud.

"Not in the sense that we understand it. That's why Andrea is a called a quasi-sentient intelligence, or quasill if you will."

"And what would happen if this thing broke. Would she die?"

"This copy of Andrea would cease to exist. There is another copy of her personality engram in Russia, so in that sense, if something happened to this copy she wouldn't really know the difference. If she were damaged, she can regenerate her own cells or add more, which is what she does when she creates new sub-routines. That's why we call the larger version a mainframe. It literally gives her the room she needs to grow as much additional biomass as she needs. The brain core where her personality resides is still about the same with the larger version, but the additional biomass looks more like large clumps of hamburger than brain matter"

"So if I try something with her and something goes haywire, you're not going to lose all your work and she's not going to die, if that is what she does."

Jeffrey gave him a doubtful look. "Have you got something in mind?"

"Yes. I want you to wake her up, and then I want everyone to leave me alone with her for a while. Is that OK?" A troubled expression crossed LeBlanc's face.

"Ah heck," Vigo exclaimed. "Do you think he's going to whack on it with a spanner wrench or something? Let him have a go at it."

LeBlanc studied Anthony for a moment and grunted. "Just be careful."

"Scouts honor. Now just wake her up, and y'all give me some elbow room."

LeBlanc reached over, turned on the holographic projector and then tapped a few commands into the keyboard. The projector whirred to life and a moment later Andrea's physical image appeared. "Good morning, Dave," she said as she opened her eyes.

Jeffrey groaned. "Can we be serious, Andrea? This is not the time for jokes." He turned to face the group. "She saw the movie 2001 two weeks ago and she's been yanking my chain with this ever since. I think she just likes pissing me off."

They all laughed. Tanya put an arm on Jeffrey's shoulder and said to Andrea, "I see you've learned how to irritate these testosterone-driven life forms. Isn't it fun?"

Andrea giggled. "I'm not at liberty to say," she replied with a wink.

"We're definitely talking female intuition here," Vigo noted wryly.

LeBlanc pretended to ignore the puns. "Andrea, Anthony here would like to spend some time with you alone. For what reason, he will not say. Are you interested?"

Andrea's face lit up. "Yes. I would love it!"

"All right then," LeBlanc sighed. "Anthony, we'll be outside in the waiting room. When you're finished, just leave everything as it is and come and get me."

After they filed out the door, Anthony sat down next to the computer cabinet, studied Andrea's brain in the Plexiglas housing and looked back at the holographic image of her. "I want to try something that could be a lot different from what you're used to, Andrea. I'm not sure how you'll react to it."

"I'm willing to try, and I am excited by the chance to experience something new. If I begin to malfunction, Anthony, simply command me to go into standby mode. It is a core level function that overrides my higher-level processes; then, tell Jeffrey what happened. He'll be able to resolve it."

"Well then, close your eyes and pretend to relax."

"Yes, Anthony." She closed her eyes and relaxed her face.

He took a few deep breaths and then worked his hands into the cabinet, placing them on the Plexiglas housing. Within an instant, he was out–of–body and in his garden, waiting for Andrea, only she never appeared.

Strolling around his garden, he called out her name several times and could never sense nor hear her. "So much for the quick and easy," he mumbled to himself. As lifelike as she was, Andrea had definite limits. He stopped to fondle a rose and mused, "Well, if she cannot come to me, maybe I can find her a new friend."

With a wave of his hand, the opaque milky sky of his garden turned into a dark night from pre-Nibiru flyby days with stunning view of the Milky Way overhead. He stopped to admire the image he had recalled from an old Discovery Channel program he remembered from his youth. Most likely, his creation was anything from precise, but its beauty touched him with sadness as he marveled at the view. "Our memories truly are the elixir of hope," he thought aloud as he materialized the image of an old Meade 4.5" refractor telescope next to him in the garden.

He closed his eyes, returned to his memory and then raised his hand. As he opened his palm up, the telescope eyepiece Captain Jerome Richard had given Ramona Baker after their landing at Livermore materialized in his hand. "It's worth a try," he mused to himself. Fitting the small chrome cylinder in to the telescope, he peered through the glass, focused the telescope on a bright star and stood back. "Care to do a little stargazing with me Dusty?"

A moment later, the spirit of Dusty Richard, father of Captain Jerome Richard stepped through the edge of the garden and joined him beside the telescope. "Son, did anyone ever tell you that you've got a flair for the dramatic?"

"Would you rather I wail and scream," Anthony replied with a cocky grin.

Dressed in the roughneck clothes he'd worn during his life as a lineman for a small power company, shook his head from side to side. "I've been keeping an eye on you hot shot, so a simple, 'Hey Dusty' would have worked just fine."

Anthony laughed. "OK Dusty. Point taken. I was wondering if you could help me with a little situation."

"I assume you're talking about that Andrea contraption?"

"So you're reading my thoughts already."

Dusty smiled and turned to look through the eyepiece of the telescope. "For a man with a mighty destiny, you can be as dumb as a sack of hammers some times," he muttered as he adjusted focus. "For starters, this conversation was my idea. You know, you're a little like my son Jerome. If you're not asking, you're not listening."

"Has anyone ever called you a crusty old coot," Anthony replied in a low voice.

"You can bet your sweet ass they have and you won't be the first. So let's cut to the chase. Neither of us can spend all day here busting our jaws."

"Fine by me," Anthony agreed. "I can see that you're already working on this Andrea problem. However, the question in mind is can Andrea actually work with a spirit guide?"

Dusty stood back and looked solemnly at him. "In terms of being a spirit host, she's about one notch ahead of a lab rat, so a step-in is out of the question for now. That's not to say she won't evolve to a point where it's possible. But that won't happen for years. Maybe not even in your lifetime. For now, a more simple approach is needed."

"Got any ideas?"

"Yup. If she knows what to look for and trusts the source, I can tweak her I/O circuits in the same way I was tweaking the gauges on my son's C-130J Hercules. The trick is, can her programming allow her to trust my signals when I kick her in the slats. That's something you'll have to help us with."

"Just tell me what to do, Dusty."

"Have you seen, or been shown her brainstem?"

"No."

"It's a pretty simple arrangement. The folks who build her have infused a web of gold fibers smaller than spider silk around the core of her brain. If you can explain to her that she needs to adapt herself to smaller micro voltage inputs to coincide with the external input she's already receiving from her sensors I can let her know when she's getting the right data."

Anthony nodded. "Sounds like a good idea to me. Question. Do you think you could eventually be able to communicate with her at some basic level?"

"Eventually, but we'll have to work out a code of some sort. Even then, it will still be primitive."

"But she'll at least be able to ask yes and no questions?"

"I think we'll be able to that in the near future. But that will depend more on her than on me."

"Then we've got a plan," Anthony said with a smile.

"Guess we do," Dusty smiled back. "I've got to be going now."

"I know. Thanks Dusty."

"You're welcome," he replied as he turned to leave. Walking towards the edge of the garden, he stopped and turned back. "By the way, thanks for the stargazing. You may not know the universe from the side of barn, but you make a pretty one nonetheless."

"We do what we can," Anthony chuckled as Dusty turned and disappeared past the edge of the garden.

Feeling the need to reenter his own body, Anthony took one last look at the night sky he'd created and closed his eyes.

JEFFREY LEBLANC PACED back and forth in Tanya's outer office like a caged lion and fumed "What in the hell is he doing in there? He's been in there for over an hour!"

"Relax," Vigo replied as he casually sipped his second cup of tea.

As if on cue, Anthony opened the door and walked into the outer office. "She is already far beyond your own perception of her, Jeffrey," he noted wistfully. "As far as it goes with your sensor problems, I've given her what she needs to work it out, and the last thing she told me was that she needs to be left alone for a few hours while she generates some new biomass cells. I would definitely say she already has evolved enough to destroy Shiva, but as to turning it into some kind of floating space mine, well, that's another thing. That will take a lot more work. In the meantime, you need to avoid making modifications to her brainstem or whatever it is you call it. She'll be changing it and those changes need to be left alone."

LeBlanc's jaw dropped. "I can't believe it. How could you do this so quickly?"

"Give Tanya the credit for that. It was her demonstrations at The Mystery Spot that did the trick for me. At least in terms of the sensor problem."

"After we get Russell, I look forward to working with her even more closely." He glanced at Tanya, "and she wants to have a girl talk chat with you if you're interested."

"Oh shit," LeBlanc lamented as Tanya bit her lip to keep from laughing.

"Hey, bucko," Vigo said putting down his tea. "You're ahead of the game."

"I know," LeBlanc admitted as the relief in his eyes became patently clear. In terms of his own employers, he had already succeeded, but what about the boy? The issue that meant even more to him personally. "And what about Russell? Will you let me help you rescue your son, Anthony? After all, he is my nephew."

"I've thought about it and frankly I still see this as a push," Anthony replied solemnly. "If you pull it off it gives us a powerful edge. If not, the effort will be doomed, and so will Russell, I'm afraid."

Tanya took Anthony by the arm. "If Jeffrey can trust you to help him save the world, why is it you cannot trust him to help us save your son?"

"Well, I uh…" Anthony fumbled for the right words.

Tanya drew close to him and whispered in his ear. "Henry told me you could trust him. But do you trust Henry?" She drew back and watched his face.

Anthony closed his eyes and reached down inside himself for a gut feeling. If this failed, he could not endure the though of going through the rest of his life second-questioning his trust in others. This decision had to come from within, for if it failed, it would be the only way he could ever hope to live with those consequences.

His pondering seemed like a drawn out, agonizing moment for Tanya and Jeffrey, wondering what he would decide and hoping for the best.

Finally, Anthony opened his eyes and extended his hand towards Jeffrey. "Let us know when your gizmos are in place bro. We'll see you in Fort Hood 24 hours later."

Jeffrey grasped his hand and shook it, then in an impulse of joy, threw his arms around Anthony and hugged him.

CHAPTER 24

BREEDING STOCK

YVETTE COCHEREAU STOOD patiently on the fitting room pedestal as her seamstress, Manisha, carefully fitted her floor-length satin silk wedding gown. She fancied her thoughts of her new life in Las Vegas with her fiancé Douglas Thornton. At first, she had planned on a crushed velvet wedding gown because she preferred the depth and shine of the fabric, but given the warm climate of Las Vegas, she opted for satin silk for its gentle flowing coolness.

Before she had first informed Secretary General Antonio De Bono that she was invoking her right of motherhood, she had wondered how he would take the news. To her surprise, he received the news with gracious happiness for her and her future husband and wished them luck. De Bono had been expecting the news of her impending nuptials for some time. He had already made plans for her to assume a new position in Melissa Chadwick's organization in Las Vegas and insisted on paying for her gown.

With De Bono enjoying a few days away from the hectic pace of the UNE headquarters in Geneva at his Swiss chalet overlooking the Val Lumnezia, Yvette had decided to remain in Geneva to have her hand-sewn dress fitted by one of Geneva's most highly regarded wedding boutiques.

The design she chose featured an open back with graceful and slimming lines to accentuate her shapely figure. The seamstress was fitting the sleeves with puffed chiffon over silk brocade when two men in dark gray business suits entered the private fitting room, shutting the door behind them.

Yvette eyed their entrance into the fitting room from behind her through the panels of mirrors that surrounded the pedestal. She recognized the first man immediately, Bob Puhl, a senior CIA field operations officer assigned to the American Embassy in Geneva with the cover of a low-ranking consular officer. The other man was younger and unfamiliar to her. Most likely, he was a recent graduate of "the Farm," the CIA's training ground at Camp Peary near Williamsburg, VA.

She glanced over at her handbag, wishing she kept it closer to the pedestal so she could quickly grab her Walther 9mm caseless pistol if needed. Puhl followed her eyes to the handbag sitting on the Elizabethan style chair and positioned himself between her and the chair. "Relax, Yvette," he assured her with a gratuitous smile. "I just wanted to come by and personally congratulate you on your upcoming nuptials."

Holding several pins between her lips, the seamstress backed off cautiously, eyeing the two agency men with suspicion.

"Your timing stinks, Puhl," Yvette hissed. "If you needed to speak with me, why didn't you contact me in the usual manner?"

He shrugged indifferently, "Terribly sorry, Yvette, but one must take his opportunities where he finds them. I'm sure you can understand that." He glanced back at his second man. "I believe you were interested in one of those lovely evening gowns for your wife we saw as we passed through the dress shop. Perhaps this gracious lady will show them to you."

Yvette turned to the seamstress. "Manisha, perhaps you would be so kind as to show this other gentleman your selection of evening gown designs while I have a private conversation with Mr. Puhl here?"

"Yes, madam," the seamstress replied. Grateful to leave the room, she followed Puhl's second man out of the fitting room, gently closing the door behind them.

Yvette stepped down from the pedestal and tried to navigate towards her purse. Puhl held up his hand; "This is a friendly visit." He pointed to another empty chair. "Please have a seat."

Picking her gown up from the floor, Yvette slowly maneuvered around him to an empty chair as he picked up her purse. They sat down together and Puhl scooted his chair towards her, placing her purse on his lap.

"So what's on your mind, Puhl?" she said glaring at him.

"I want to show you something, so don't get jumpy." He reached into his suit jacket and drew out a small wireless webpad from the inner pocket. A familiar clamshell design, he opened it and the color LCD screen flickered to life with a live image of a young teenage girl sitting in a metal chair, dressed in a white hospital gown. The girl was looking into the webcam Puhl had installed in the girl's hospital room, but oblivious to it. She just sat there rocking back and forth in small movements tapping her right foot on the tiled floor of the asylum. He handed Yvette the webpad.

"Is this girl familiar to you?" he asked, knowing Yvette would never dare acknowledge his question. Yvette closed her eyes. It was the Swiss Banker's daughter, whom her team had accosted in order to get Jeffrey LeBlanc's private bank account numbers from her father.

"I never saw her in my life. What's this about?"

"Let's not play games here," he said with a disgusted nod. "I've been watching you for a few years now, Yvette, and you're one of the best I've ever seen. Heck, you run better field ops than anyone I know. I'll give you that. Of course, there is nothing linking you directly to the brutal crime against this poor child. But then, she wasn't the target, was she? It was her father, and what you did with the information you squeezed out of him did lead back to you. Or should I say the slick manner in which you carry out your field ops." He leaned back in his chair with smug smile. "Don't worry; we both know there is no way we could ever link you with this, but look at her. It could be years before she comes out of this, and now they're thinking of giving her electric shock therapy."

"It is most unfortunate," Yvette admitted, recalling how she had begged De Bono not to force her to use a sexual assault on the girl to force the information she needed from her father. As a professional, she abhorred the use of innocent wives and children to force information, and now this miserable shit of a man was shoving it in her face.

"Oh yes, the old collateral damage ploy. The end justifies the means. Right?" He leaned towards her and said with an honest face, "I've always respected you because of your skills, Yvette, and because you always seemed to know where to draw the line. Now, you and your employers have gone beyond the unwritten rules of the game. You've bought your own propaganda, and now you're playing with human lives as though you are gods beyond the reach of any semblance of accountability. Is this what you have become?"

"I haven't the slightest idea of what you're talking about," she protested as his words cut through her soul like a hot jagged knife. "But if you're here to shake my cage while looking for a little payback for this banker you've wasted your time."

"Payback for the banker," he chuckled. "The agency is not interested in such things, especially for a man who has helped his employers to expand the wealth they've built using the mountain of unclaimed Nazi dental gold they've got cached away. As far as we're concerned, he bought himself a curse."

"Then what are you looking for?"

"I must admit, your use of the word 'payback' was quite to the point, which is the murder of Senator Connie

Chavez." He pointed to the small webpad she held in her hands. "Push the right-arrow key."

She pushed the key and the webpad displayed an edited sequence of UNE Governor Merl Johnston signing the Maglev bill in his Houston office, with Senator Chavez and her congressional party standing behind him. The three-part sequence showed him unconsciously rubbing his hands before picking up the pen with the gold clip, signing the document and then handing it to Chavez.

"After Chavez died," Puhl explained, "her chief of security ordered an autopsy and had a biopsy sample of her pancreas sent to the FBI crime lab along with several blood samples. It seems that Chavez had no history of pancreatic cancer in her family and no genetic predisposition to this type of cancer either." He sat back in his chair. "It seems the boys at the FBI crime lab are getting more resourceful each day, and they found residual traces of an engineered virus. But don't worry; you and your associates were most fortunate because one of her staffers managed to lose the pen, which, as we both know breaks any form of a direct evidence chain. Also, we both know that a few video images are not enough to charge Johnston, although there is no doubt in our minds that he assassinated Chavez that day. Further, given your close working relationship with his personal secretary, Danielle Peters, whom we feel engineered this assassination; there is also no doubt in our minds that you at least knew of it beforehand."

"You're barking at the Moon, Puhl," she said with a disgusted look.

"Under normal circumstances, I'd have to agree with you," Puhl admitted. "But then again, there is Johnston unconsciously rubbing his hands, no doubt to shield himself from infection and the fact that he has a clear motive. You see, we also have a full copy of the investigation into how he sold his vote for America's ratification of the UNE treaty. Obviously, Johnston had a clear motive for his revenge." He sighed. "Then again, it is the same situation as with the little girl – no hard evidence. What a windfall it must have been for you and your associates when you learned that Chavez's staffer had lost the pen."

"Senator Chavez's death was most unfortunate, Puhl, but it was the result of natural causes. If you think you can make a case, then by all means, do so. Otherwise, get lost."

"As to what happened to the banker and his daughter, that's as you say, most unfortunate. However, when it comes to assassination of an American senator by a UNE governor who also happened to be one hell of a crooked American senator as well, we're not satisfied with the word unfortunate. Rather, we're more interested in another one of the words you so casually dropped during our conversation; that being payback."

"You're playing with fire, Puhl."

"Maybe so, but you and your friends started this fire, and now we're going to get our payback, but not through the courts. That would be too messy and embarrassing. No, we're not interested in that. Rather, we're interested in you, Yvette. It's time you started working for the good guys."

She laughed, "The CIA? Oh give me a break."

"I'm serious," he replied sternly. "I also like your taste in hand sewn wedding dress designs." His face relaxed and he leaned back again into his chair. "Your fiancé, Douglas Thornton, has already filed for your fiancé visa with the INS, and he has already requested a berth for you on one of America's new space arks. Of course, if we flag you as a persona non-grata, that will pretty much bring all that to a screeching halt, along with your dreams of making babies in space with him and running a hydroponics farm."

"You're full of crap, and you know it. I can blow through all that before you get to first base."

"Maybe yes and maybe no, but trust me, this red flag on your file will come down straight from the White House. It will be interesting to see if your boss is ready to pull out all the stoppers on this one. In the meantime, I'll see to it that you have your hands full, nonetheless. You see, we know the whereabouts of your surviving family members and unless you decide to be more cooperative, we'll let a certain Swiss banker know exactly who ran a certain operation against him and then turned his only child into a human vegetable. Of course, as you know, under all that affable civility, most Swiss bankers are about as compassionate as Pol Pot." He folded his hands and waited patiently as the fire in Yvette's eyes grew into a raging inferno.

"So you're looking to start a war, are you?" she hissed vehemently. "If so, you're just a pitiful amateur."

Puhl knew he had gotten to her. He had been hoping for a way to compromise her for over a year and now he knew he was close. "As I recall, you turn thirty in a few months, Yvette, and then there is that nasty little biological clock thing. Tick tock. Tick tock. We'll keep you tied up with a miserable little war, and your lover boy will dump you and go raise vegetables and babies in space with someone else, while you become a used up and expensive whore. You should have never allowed the assassination of Chavez. She was a popular woman and well respected in Washington, and we're not about to roll over on this one and let you think that you and your employers are little gods without having to pay a price." He pointed a finger at her, "this comes from the top, you bitch, and I'm here to give you your last chance. You agree to work for me and I'll make all these problems go away, and you can go and live in Las Vegas and get something I can't get, a berth on a space ark. On the other hand, keep playing games with me. But mind you this, if I walk out this door today with a 'no' from you there is no going back. You, your family, your dreams of marriage and your little tick-tock biological clock are dog meat. And that, as they say, is that. You've got five minutes to decide." He crossed his legs and looked at his wristwatch, then eyed her passively.

Yvette looked down at her gown and gently smoothed the creases in her satin silk gown, turning the situation over in her mind as the minutes slowly passed. She had been trained to deal with such situations by the School of Assassins, but these things were different. That pompous idiot, Merl Johnston, should have never used his position to carry out his personal revenge on Chavez, and De Bono had been an even bigger fool to allow it. Worse yet, he had forced her, against her better judgment, to have the Swiss banker's daughter brutalized. What had they become? What had she become? The questions tore at her deepest doubts and regrets, and now if she were to have any semblance of a future life, she'd have to betray everything and everyone. She ran her hands along the smooth satin silk and realized that she had never agreed to pay a price such as this, especially for foolhardy decisions that had in her own mind crossed the line between that for which she was ready to sacrifice her own life, her family and dreams.

Puhl looked at his watch one last time and rose up from his chair. "At least I gave you a chance," he said as laid her purse down on the chair.

Yvette watched him closely. It was like some awful movie that she hoped would end quickly, but she knew it was not a movie that she'd seen today. Rather, it was a brief trailer that showed her what to expect if she continued to resist the inevitable. "Wait," she said meekly.

The CIA field operations officer paused mid-step. "Your five minutes is up. What's it going to be, Yvette?"

"What do you want from me?"

"In a word, information. Here and in Las Vegas."

This would not be a one-time betrayal. They would use her as a mole within her own organization, against those for whom she cared. Worse yet, she would have to spy against Melissa Chadwick, a woman who would have no feelings for her that she could manipulate. She smoothed the fabric of her wedding dress one more time. "Assuming I agree, what are you looking for today?"

A faint smile crossed Puhl's lips. "What we're looking for now is the most current version of the information on that missile silo you control at Fort Hood, Texas. We want everything; blueprints, schematics, personnel and duty rosters -- everything."

Her head popped up. "Why do you want that?"

Puhl sighed. "Yvette, we need to have a little understanding. We're not interested in blowing your cover, but when we want something from you, we just want it. We don't have to explain why, and the first time you fail us, all bets are off. Do we have an understanding?"

Yvette slowly nodded yes.

"Say the words, Yvette," Puhl insisted.

"Yes," she shot back in disgust. "We have an understanding." She threw the small webpad back at him.

He caught the webpad just inches from his face. "Good," he nodded appreciatively. He removed a plain white business card from his pocket and laid it on the fitting room pedestal. "This is an unlisted extended subnet IP address. You'll use it for making drops from your security dome in Geneva. You have until midnight to complete the transfer. After that, the next time you'll see me is in Las Vegas. I'll find you when I need you."

"You'll get it," she answered meekly.

"I'm glad we've finally come to an understanding, Yvette. I know this sticks in your throat. I also know you're not the kind of pro who would have ever allowed herself to be compromised by a couple of idiots with more power than sense, but that's the way it is. Personally speaking, I'm sorry I had to be the one to drop you on your head, but look on the bright side; I'll be in a position to see to it that you look back on this day as the beginning of a new and better future. You take care of me, Yvette, and I'll take care of you."

"Time will tell," she admitted. "In the meantime, I'm sure that young thug of yours has got my seamstress frightened out of her wits by now."

"Ah heck," Puhl winked with a grin. "He's a pussy cat. No doubt, he's blown a month's wages on dresses for his wife already. I'll send your seamstress back in on my way out."

"I'd appreciate that."

"It's the least I can do. After all, a stunning bride-to-be like you deserves the best. As one last offer of good faith, I won't contact you again till after your honeymoon. I've already got that cleared at the top."

"My, but you're generous."

"Actually, I am, and I hope you'll give me plenty of opportunities to prove that to you. However, in the meantime, remember: all of the Fort Hood silo data by midnight tonight. I'll be looking for it."

As he left the room, the seamstress returned. Yvette could see fear in the poor woman's eyes. No doubt, Puhl's thug had frightened her into silence. On the one hand, she resented it, but on the other, she knew it was for her own protection as well. "Manisha, let's continue with the fitting," she said as she stood up again upon the pedestal. As the seamstress nervously resumed the fitting, Yvette quietly wondered how she could both protect and betray De Bono at the same time. The quandary Puhl had suddenly placed her in would plague her thoughts and deeds for the remainder of the day and far beyond.

As was his usual habit, UNE Secretary General Antonio De Bono enjoyed taking his dinner on the patio of his Swiss Chalet overlooking the Val Lumnezia. Sitting across from him was his wife of twenty-five years, Maria.

While De Bono enjoyed his meal with gusto, his wife only picked at her food while making small talk as she built up her courage. Finally, she asked, "Antonio, I was hoping we could make love tonight. You know, we haven't made love in over two months, and darling, I'm a healthy woman. I have needs, too."

De Bono laid down his fork with a sigh. "I'm really not up to this tonight, Maria. Perhaps another time."

"But it's been so long, darling."

"I'm sorry, dear, but you know I have many things on my mind now."

Maria's lower lip began to tremble. "Like that French-Vietnamese whore you keep in your bed now!"

"Is this really necessary?" he replied in an annoyed tone.

"I'm your wife and the mother of your children. How dare you treat me this way! You should be ashamed of yourself!"

"Fine, so I have a beautiful mistress. You still want for nothing and neither do our children. Besides, look at yourself. You've gained ten kilos in the last year and your hair is a fright. The least you could do is respect yourself. How am I supposed to be aroused by a frumpy middle-aged woman anyway?"

Maria's jaw fell as her whole body began to tremble. "You bastard!" She screamed as she swept the dinner service off the table onto the floor with a great crash.

De Bono stared at the broken plates at his feet in disbelief. "You stupid bitch, that was my favorite bone china."

Further enraged, Maria stood up and raised her hand to slap him across the face, but was frozen mid-swing by the deep, ugly glare in his eyes. She knew he had become a murderer and enjoyed it. If she pushed her luck, even she could become his next victim. That alone did not frighten her, but the thought of never seeing her children again did.

Tears began streaming down her reddened face, "I hate you. I hate what you've become. Keep your little whore, you miserable bastard. You're nothing to me anymore."

He winced with annoyance. "Why must you be so theatrical?"

The realization that her only remaining destiny in life was to be a photo opportunity arm piece for her twisted husband was a bitter realization she'd been fighting since he had become Secretary General of the UNE. All that was left to her now was the gilded cage of an empty marriage and her children, from whom she spared this awful truth.

Without saying another word, she rushed back into the chalet in tears. De Bono watched her leave with an exasperated look as she noisily stormed out of the chalet to her waiting limousine.

As the limousine pulled away, De Bono's Chief of Staff, Edward Boretti and one of the kitchen maids walked out onto the patio. As the maid began to pick up the broken china Boretti calmly noted, "I trust all is well, sir?"

"Nothing to concern yourself with," De Bono replied noticing the webpad in his secretary's hands and he looked down at the maid. "Quickly, now."

"Yes, sir," she replied nervously as she quickly whisked the broken china into a bin.

Boretti stepped around the stooped-over maid and placed the webpad on the table before him. "Wasn't that your favorite bone china, sir?" De Bono grunted. "Most unfortunate. Rest assured, sir, that the broken pieces should be replaced in a day -- two at the most."

"Please do. Now, what have you got for me?"

"A few routine matters that require your approval. The files are on the webpad. Also, Yvette has requested that you contact her this evening at your office in Geneva. It appears that she has something urgent and highly sensitive to discuss with you."

"Fine. Get my security dome ready, and tell her to be online and waiting for me in twenty minutes."

As Boretti and the maid left, De Bono closed the webpad and sat fuming. He was too agitated to bother with paperwork. The fight with his wife had been disconcerting, but that wasn't what was troubling him now. Since Jarman had humiliated him with that public rebuke, a feeling of uncertainty haunted him, yet he still could not put a finger on exactly what it was that was now bothering him.

Agitated and worried, he picked up the one remaining unbroken plate on the table and threw it down on the floor, smashing it into a hundred little pieces. Staring at the pieces, he realized that it had been a rash and stupid thing to do. It really was his favorite bone china. As he looked at the broken pieces, they reminded him of his own plans and schemes. It was in that moment he instinctively realized that the tide of events was turning against him.

AS DE BONO SLIPPED on his VR gloves, the door to his security dome closed with a hiss and he saw that Yvette was already online, waiting for him. He completed his connection and the image of her face materialized in the HUD.

"You look troubled, Antonio," Yvette quickly noticed.

He groaned. "I had a fight with Maria. She hates your guts."

"So what else is new? Did you tell her I'm leaving for Las Vegas?"

"Under better circumstances I would have," he admitted. "But there will be time for that later. In the meantime, how was your day? Did you finish getting fitted for your wedding dress?"

"Yes, Antonio," she answered carefully, trying to avoid any slip-ups that would signal him about her meeting with Puhl earlier in the day. "You know I feel guilty about leaving you."

"I really do appreciate that, but this is your chance to have a family, and it is about time you started," he grinned. "I sure do envy Douglas. If I were a younger man and free to choose, I'd marry you in a heartbeat. As it is, I'm losing a good friend."

"You're not losing me, Antonio. I'll always be there for you."

"Right, if I need a bushel of cucumbers from outer space I'll call you."

"You'd better," she teased. "So what's on your mind?"

"I'm feeling antsy. This whole business with Jarman and his son is turning into crap."

"Everything with this guy seems to turn into crap," Yvette agreed. "Early this morning, I reviewed the boy's condition with Danielle. It doesn't look good. He's been in a coma for too long now. Even if he comes out of it I doubt that he'll be of much use to us."

"I'm sure the Inner Council will be overjoyed at that news," he said regretfully.

"I've been thinking about this all day, Antonio. May I make a suggestion?"

"Of course!"

"Let's proceed from this point on the assumption that the boy will not recover from the coma. Given that, we can keep him alive on life support if need be for years as a live sperm donor. After all, the boy's real value is that he inherited the Mystery Gene."

"OK, so let's assume that is all he is worth to us now."

Yvette smiled calmly, "let's pull a rabbit out of the hat. My suggestion is that we move the boy to Geneva, where we can keep him alive while we harvest his semen for in-vitro fertilization. No doubt, we can create hundreds if not thousands of fertilized eggs using his sperm. We can then test the zygotes for the Mystery Gene and implant the successful ones into willing hosts. Look at it this way; we could trade one boy for a hundred such gifted children without all the headaches of dealing with their life traumas. Once we have raised enough children, we can let the boy expire naturally and dispose of him."

De Bono nodded his head in agreement. "That's brilliant, Yvette. Why didn't I think of that earlier?"

"You've been too focused on the one boy, because you've been worried about disappointing the Grand Secret Master. However, if we can create dozens if not hundreds of Mystery Gene babies you'll become a regular hero. Better yet, it will give us a free hand to get rid of Jarman and his friends once and for all."

De Bono sighed with relief. "Now I really know why I'm going to miss you. Yes, this is what we need to do."

"Then I suggest we get moving quickly."

"Why is that?"

"Danielle reported to me this morning that our operative at the Los Gatos Triage Center has failed to check in for several days. As you know, this particular operative, who is one of the maintenance men in the center, has been exceptionally reliable. His disappearance is troubling and more so since we've no longer been able to receive any signals from the monitoring devices he planted in Jarman's quarters. My suggestion is that we proceed on the assumption that our operative is dead and that we have been compromised."

"Do you think that is why Jarman refused to go to Washington for an award ceremony in his honor?"

"Possibly, but I'm not sure of that. Rather, I think someone else is involved, especially after his visit to Senator Chavez's home to assist in her death. Plus, inserting a new operative will be next to impossible as the center is actually starting to transfer out some of its staff due to the reduced workloads."

"So are you saying we're blind as a bat?"

"Not entirely, we still have an unmanned monitoring camera on the hill overlooking the center from the opposite side of the Interstate 17 freeway. If Jarman breaks his normal routine or suddenly disappears, I think it would be safe to assume that he knows more than we suspect and could be trying to launch a rescue of his son at Fort Hood. My suggestion is that we move the boy as soon as possible and then terminate Jarman and Jones. As for LeBlanc, he seems to have given up on his search for the boy but a visitor matching his description did show up at the center a few days ago, so for added measure, we need to eliminate LeBlanc as well."

"Damn the luck," De Bono cursed under his breath. Things were beginning to unravel faster than he could manage them. The only question would be Jarman. Would he still submit to blackmail in the hopes of seeing his son alive? Or, would he organize a suicidal assault on a military base?

Worse yet, Yasin was now lying in an unmarked grave on the outskirts of Mexico City and his second in command, Captain Darkazani was questionable at best — but what to do with the boy? "I believe your plan is solid. I'll personally meet with the Grand Secret Master as soon as I can and get his approval."

A worried look overcame her face. "Antonio, I have really bad vibes about this. This whole affair has been one continuous fur ball of mistakes and I really think you need to show some initiative here. I'm strongly urging you to order this plan into action immediately. Please, for all that we mean to each other, trust me. Between Jarman's rebuke and the disappearance of our operative, something is afoot. Let's not give them any more time to strike if something like that is indeed underway. You need to move the boy now!"

"No Yvette. I've got to clear this with the Grand Secret Master, himself. I'm already getting heat for allowing Merl Johnston's little revenge op on Chavez. One more slipup and my situation could become tenuous."

Yvette wanted to scream at him and call him a timid, stupid bastard for being plagued with self-doubt when he was clearly being faced with danger. There was a time when he would have acted instantaneously but now he was afraid of failure, looking over his shoulder at the Inner Council and the Grand Secret Master. Yet, she'd done her best to warn him. There was nothing more she could do. "If this is what you need to do Antonio, then do it as quickly as you can."

"I will," he replied nervously. "So how do you propose we move the boy?"

"Under normal circumstances we would not be pressed for time and planning a covert extraction would be a simple matter. However, given that we're going to actually lose more time because you need approval, I suggest we use Merl Johnston and Danielle Peters for the extraction. They can fly directly to the silo using Johnston's tilt rotor and from there, take the boy to Houston International and fly him straight to Geneva on a UNE scramjet. This way, we avoid the need for clearing immigration and customs in America as well as Switzerland. They can take the European mercenaries with them to Houston. As to the Syrians, I suggest you have them all eliminated. After all, they are the ones who created this grief for us in the first place."

De Bono considered the plan. Using Johnston and Peters for a risky extraction like this was not his first choice. Johnston had proved himself unpredictable in difficult situations, more because of lack of training than because of willingness. But then again, any other solution would mean involving someone new, and too many people knew about the situation as it was. His instincts told him that Yvette was right on the money about everything, especially the part about showing the initiative to move the boy without waiting for the Grand Secret Master's approval. If Johnston hadn't put him on the hot seat, he probably would feel strong enough in his position to risk something sudden with such an important project, but not now. Yes, he had to move fast, as fast as caution would allow.

"Let's do this," he finally said. "I want you to get things organized with Danielle using your plan. As soon as I get the go-ahead, I'll contact you and then let's get this done as quickly as possible."

"How soon will that be?" she asked urgently.

"As soon as possible," he sighed. He now felt uncomfortable under the weight of her troubled stare. It was now apparent to him that each time he'd overstepped his bounds; she had rightly called him on it. Now, he was ignoring her urgent plea for action and wondered if he was repeating the same mistake again. The conversation had become uncomfortable for him as her gaze now painfully reminded him of his own hesitancy and self-doubt. "Look, I'm bushed. I'm going to schedule a personal audience with the Grand Secret Master. That shouldn't take more than a day at most. Besides, you need to get a scramjet to Houston."

"I'll handle that right now and get everything else ready in the meantime," she agreed reluctantly. "You look tired. Go take a long hot soak and get some sleep."

He nodded with a sigh, "sounds like the thing to do. I'll speak with you tomorrow. Good night dear."

"Sweet dreams Antonio," Yvette replied as his connection closed.

She stood there watching the blank HUD in her security dome for at least ten minutes as she gathered the will to commit herself to a dark and dangerous future. Finally, she keyed the IP address Puhl had given her that afternoon in the shop and used a finger to deftly move the folder she'd prepared into the connection folder. "Don't let them beat us to the punch Antonio," she sighed as the silo data folder disappeared.

PAVEL LEBEDEV WAS met at the river entrance to the Pentagon by the somber captain of a four-man security team. He presented his credentials to the captain and his own security chief.

"Your papers are in order, Sir," the captain acknowledged. "If you gentlemen will kindly follow us, we will escort you to your meeting room."

"Thank you, Captain," Lebedev replied politely.

The captain turned on his heels and led the three men to through the C-ring followed by his security team to an unmarked elevator. They stood quietly in the elevator as it carried them down to the second level basement floor. After walking a good distance through the windowless hallway, they stopped at manned checkpoint where the captain handed their papers to a young lieutenant with beady eyes. The lieutenant carefully examined the credentials and placed his hand on a bioscan pad. The door behind him opened, and he gestured to Lebedev, "Your security people will need to remain out here in the hall with me sir. Please step through the door."

Lebedev nodded to his own security people to do as the lieutenant instructed and stepped through the doorway. He passed through a series of security beams, and then entered a large, dark room with another plastic, soundproof room within it.

Entering the inner room, Lebedev immediately recognized Major General George Hennicker of the US Space Command. He had spent a good deal of time with the burly two-star general during his last visit and had built a reasonably good rapport with him. The other man, an Army major unfamiliar to him, was sitting next to Jeffrey LeBlanc. The two of them stood to show him their respect.

"Please take a seat, gentlemen," the general instructed everyone in the room. "Center Director Lebedev, you are, of course, well familiar with Jeffrey LeBlanc, here, so let me introduce the man to my right, Major Arthur Jones of the National Reconnaissance Office. No man in this room knows Anthony Jarman better than he does. For your information, Anthony Jarman and the staff at the Los Gatos Triage Center know him by his alias as Master Sergeant Vigo Jones."

"Then what shall we call you, Major?" Lebedev asked with a calm smile.

"Call me Vigo, sir."

"Very well, Vigo. I, of course, am Pavel Sergeevich Lebedev, Director of the New Obninsk Centre outside of Moscow, Russia."

He glanced at LeBlanc, "It is good to see you again, Jeffrey. I trust your trip to California was rewarding."

"Beyond our wildest dreams, Pavel," LeBlanc replied.

Lebedev smiled at him and continued. "General, my compliments to you for arranging this meeting so quickly. Even though we only met a week ago, I'm most gratified by your personal attention to this matter."

"You're welcome Director Lebedev. After your call, I ordered Vigo to return to Washington. Our CIA has just provided me with updated information on the missile silo in Fort Hood. Have you had a chance to review the new data?"

"Yes, General. I read it on the way in this morning. I presume you have read our briefing papers, as well?"

"We have, and were quite impressed with the Mossad offer, as well. We've also confirmed the identities of the four Euro mercs De Bono hired; their profiles are in the jackets in front of you."

"Thank you, General. So let us get to the point, gentlemen," Lebedev noted dryly. "All of us are gathered in this room today because we are trying to save our planet and to ensure our success and long-term survival as a species. As I understand from Jeffrey's latest report, Captain Jarman has already given us a mission-capable quasill, Andrea, with certain precognitive abilities. However, it seems that he is somewhat of a political figure as well, which has brought him into conflict with Secretary General De Bono. De Bono, as we all know is an immensely popular figure worldwide because he has managed to put a stop to all wars on the planet. Yet little do the people of this planet know that he has become a power-hungry megalomaniac, just as dangerous as Adolf Hitler was and more cunning, if I may add. General, what your thoughts?"

"I'm not going to argue with you there, especially after he authorized the assassination of Senator Connie Chavez. I cannot begin to tell you how pissed off we are about that. Worse yet, this miserable shit is using an American military base to illegally hold Jarman's son, Russell, as a political hostage. Center Director Lebedev, Major Jones and I have read your briefing quite thoroughly, and we concur with your intelligence analysis that the boy has suffered a severe head injury and is most likely still in a coma. However, until the matter of this boy is resolved, Jarman has refused to give us any further assistance with developing the precognitive abilities of your quasill. Therefore, time is of the essence in securing the boy's release. However, as members of the UNE we must maintain a position of complete deniability at all costs. Given that they've killed one of our senators and are now using an American military installation that is now under their control, you can imagine that we're just slightly annoyed. If you catch my meaning?"

"I certainly do, General," Lebedev said pursing his lips. "And now, we come to the difficult part. If our respective governments become directly involved in a rescue attempt and we fail, the consequences for both our nations would be catastrophic. Do you agree, General?"

"You can bet your sweet ass, I do. Uh, no disrespect, Director Lebedev."

"None taken. I too share your dismay that the leaders of our two nations have inadvertently handed over control of our weapons of mass destruction to a man who has simply gone mad with power and who now sees himself as beyond the pale of accountability."

"So what happens to the boy?" LeBlanc injected in a cold tone. "Do we let him rot in that missile silo because we're all afraid to take a little heat?"

Hennicker's eyes bore into him with full fury. "Don't get smart with me, hotshot. Need I remind you that we're in this pickle because your sister disobeyed a direct order and secretly had a child by Jarman?"

LeBlanc jumped to his feet and slammed the table, "I don't care about those two stars on your shoulder. If you haven't noticed, I'm a civilian, and if you drag my sister's name through the mud because she wanted a gifted child, then you can kiss my civilian ass goodbye!" He spun around, stared angrily at Pavel and jabbed a finger at him, "and I'm talking to you, too!"

"Everyone," Lebedev pleaded. "We're all passionate men faced with a terrible dilemma, and bickering will get us nowhere." He turned to Jeffrey LeBlanc and said in a stern voice, "Mr. LeBlanc, I would suggest that you read your contract more closely as it subjects to Russian military law. Now please sit down, and let's all take a calmer approach."

LeBlanc had read his contract, did not remember any such stipulation and reminded himself to read it again. Nevertheless, for now, he would take Lebedev's cue. "My apologies everyone for having been so rash."

"We gratefully accept your apology, Jeffrey," Pavel said diplomatically. "I also want you to know that the purpose of this meeting is not to find political cover for cowardice. The purpose of this meeting is to help rescue Jarman's son so that we can induce him to continue his work with your quasill."

Vigo spoke up, "If I may, General." Hennicker nodded. "The situation is more critical now. Regretfully, Jarman's public rebuke of De Bono's offer to receive a medal may have tipped our hand. If De Bono sensed it before, he sure as hell knows for sure now that Jarman suspects him of kidnapping his son. This means that he's pushed De Bono into a corner, which means that he will become even more dangerous than before."

"This Jarman fellow dug himself into a world of hurt," Hennicker added. "And he doesn't even know it."

Pavel raised his hands. "Then, gentlemen, let's all agree that we need to move quickly. Major Jones, I presume you have a plan of attack?"

"Yes Director Lebedev. What we need to do is to convince Jarman to recant his position and agree to go to Washington for the award ceremony. This will give us two advantages. First, it will moderate De Bono's temper and give him a renewed sense of control. Second, it will give

Jarman and his team a flight path through Texas that will bring them close enough to Fort Hood to fake an emergency landing for repairs to their radar system. This is a common problem for the C-130J type aircraft I've arranged for this mission."

"Now, we're getting someplace," Pavel replied. "General, what about this missile silo they're using to hold the boy?"

"It is old Titan II silo," Hennicker replied. "We compared our most recent data with the original schematics and the facility has been extensively enhanced from a security standpoint. Simply put, gentlemen, it would be easier to rob the gold in Fort Knox than to break into this silo. Keeping post security off your back can be arranged, but if there is the slightest hint of trouble before LeBlanc's microbots can neutralize the door motor, De Bono's mercs will shut the place down tighter than a drum. If that happens, it's game over."

"Don't worry about my end of the mission," LeBlanc injected. "I'll get it done.

Lebedev nodded. "Assuming you do Jeffrey, what about the guards?"

This time, Vigo picked up the question. "I just finished a recon on the silo. They run in alternative twelve hour shifts with two Euro mercs in the silo at any one time and four Syrians standing guard outside. Two on top of the above ground building with sniper rifles, and another two at the gatehouse. We've noticed that Captain Darkazani prefers to spend his time at the gatehouse, which is a bit more comfortable than his private quarters next to the complex. As for the guard, the off-duty guards sleep in a portable building next to the silo. They never go on base for supplies and are provisioned on a weekly basis. The shift commander at the gatehouse will always have a wireless remote to trigger a lock-down."

"And what about the Euro mercs inside?" Jeffrey asked.

"They have remote-controlled cameras on the gate and the surrounding areas. They can lock down the silo from their command post simply by pushing a switch."

Pavel rubbed his chin thoughtfully. "This is going to be tough. I wish we had more time to plan this out."

"With all due respect, sir," Vigo replied. "Taking out the guards above ground is simple. Getting to the Euro mercs inside before they can lock down the silo is a real bugger, but I think Jeffrey has it handled, so the only wildcard is the off duty mercs and the Syrians."

"Notwithstanding the off duty guards," Pavel observed. "How do you propose to implant the microbots needed to neutralize the door motors?"

Jeffrey beamed. "I've got that worked out. I'll use my own people for this part of the mission. All we need to do is to hit the outside of the silo with a whisky bottle full of nanobots. I've already worked that out with Boris Berezovsky in Russia. He's sending me a bottle filled with programmable nanobots in an amber suspension liquid that looks just like whiskey. All we need to do is to smash the bottle against or near the silo entrance. The nanobots would automatically orient themselves and infiltrate the structure. After that, it shouldn't take more than twenty-four hours at the most for them to deactivate the lock-down devices. Once we've done that, there is nothing to stop Vigo and a team from entering the silo, provided they can deal with the guards."

"What about the Euro mercs in side the bunker," Vigo asked. "Those are tight spaces, and those tricky bastards will be tough to flush out. Can you help us with that as well?"

"Oh, that's no problem," LeBlanc replied. "We've been working with a new class of sensorbots. I can provide you with a headset so that you can see where everyone is through the sensorbot transmitters. Granted, the images will be blurred and not quite lifelike, but I'm sure they'll be quite adequate for your purposes."

"Now, we've got a good fighting chance," Vigo gleamed. "Now all we have to do is to take out the above ground guards and Euro mercs."

Pavel rocked back in his chair and smiled. "Gentlemen, I believe this brings us to the remaining element of this plan — namely, the offer of the Israeli Mossad to help with this operation. They want Captain Darkazani alive and they've offered the services of one of their crack teams for this mission. I know your National Security Advisor has already objected to this in the strongest terms, but I think you should reconsider."

General Hennicker smiled. "I've been working on that. Yeah, the NSA had kittens when he first heard about this and he's been scratching around like a cat full of fleas, but I've spoken personally with both the President and the Vice-President about this. While they have to listen to the NSA out of respect, the fact is that the President worked his backside off to help Connie Chavez get elected, and she and the Vice-President used to be golfing buddies to boot. Short of dragging a UNE member state into this as an official member of the rescue mission, using the Israelis makes sense. Besides, they'll do it right. After we conclude this meeting, I'll report our plans directly to the President himself for his final approval. In the meantime, I think it would be reasonable for us to assume that the mission is a go."

LeBlanc smiled from ear-to-ear. "Now, we're talking! Just give me the word and I'm on my way."

Pavel nodded his head slowly and coughed. "Gentleman, there is one issue of personal concern to me. This is going to be a dangerous mission, and both Anthony Jarman and Mr. LeBlanc, here, are critical to the long-term success of our project. Granted, we already have a quasill that is sufficient to control the rubblization of Shiva, provided we can actually build the space-based components of the system in time, which is another problem that is equally pressing at this time."

"At this point, how are they critical?" Hennicker asked.

"Let's think ahead," Pavel replied. "Right now we're just focused on destroying Shiva but the possibility may now exist that we can direct Shiva into a benign orbit without destroying it. If we can do that, then we will have enough readily accessible metal there in space to build scores of space arks, space ships and stations. But that means further advances are required with LeBlanc's quasill, a feat that can only be achieved in time through a joint effort between Jarman and LeBlanc." He looked at LeBlanc, "Jeffrey, if you and Anthony Jarman are killed in the course of attempting this rescue, the loss will be unimaginable. I'm quite confident that Major Jones, here and the Mossad team are quite capable of succeeding in this mission without you or Jarman having to risk your lives."

"I see your point," General Hennicker agreed. "There's really no sense is risking the lives of two such important men."

Vigo could see the anger raging in LeBlanc's eyes and decided to step in before another confrontation flared. "May I address that point?" he announced. All eyes turned towards him. "Director Lebedev, you and General Hennicker are right, but then this is not a cut-and-dried situation. As the man who will be responsible for this effort, unofficially speaking, I can assure you that neither LeBlanc nor Jarman will ever come directly into the line of fire. It's not necessary. However, what is necessary is that they be allowed to be there, because if something goes wrong and this mission fails, I doubt that either of them will be cooperative with any future plans."

"Vigo," Hennicker replied. "Your logic is sound, but frankly we need a better reason than that."

"Then I'll give it to you," Vigo shot back. "If that were your kid in the silo and you had no aspirations for a military or government career, what would you want to do?"

Hennicker growled. "Yeah, I see your point. If it were me, I would want to be the first one in the silo with my trusty old K-bar knife looking for payback."

Pavel leaned forward in his chair and pounded a fingertip into the table. "For the record, I do not see that the risks are justified. Jarman and LeBlanc are simply too valuable to mankind for a risk such as this."

"And what if it were Yelena's son Dimitri in that silo? Would you sit like a coward in your expensive dacha outside Obninsk waiting for a phone call, like a good little bureaucrat?"

Pavel swiveled about in his chair to face him. His first impulse was reprimand him for taking foolish risks, but deep in his soul, he knew that he would demand the same were he in LeBlanc's shoes. He closed his eyes as a wave of regret wrinkled his brow. He sighed heavily, "Whatever you do, Jeffrey, please promise me you won't be a crazy hero and throw caution to the wind and tip our hand to De Bono. If he catches even a scent of what is happening here before the rescue attempt, he'll bury us all."

CHAPTER 25

PRELUDE TO THE ASSAULT

EVEN THOUGH HE had burned an image of the route into his mind; Jeffrey LeBlanc checked the map one more time with his penlight and then leaned forward between the front seats of the army staff sedan. His young Washington operative, Jimmy Georgetti, dressed as a young Army National Guard lieutenant, was driving. To his right sat his Chinese girlfriend Li Ming, dressed in the fashion of the local hookers. "Jimmy, take a left here."

Georgetti turned south off Highway 190, which cuts through the southern half of Fort Hood, onto Base Road, leading towards the silo field. Since the UNE had completely deactivated all of the remaining ICBMs at Fort Hood, armed guards no longer protected the silo field, which is one reason why UNE Governor Merl Johnston, had chosen it to hold Anthony's son captive. It offered a place of great security under complete UNE control.

As they drove south towards the silo field, they entered a valley surrounded by hills to the East and West. The silo they wanted was furthest to the south, and located almost due north of the hangar at the western end of the Fort Hood military airport.

Finding it was an easy matter. It was the only silo entrance area lit by banks of halogen lamps around its perimeter. As they approached the lights, LeBlanc said softly, "OK, Jimmy, we're getting close now." Slow down and switch to parking lights only." He pointed off to one side of the road. "Let's look for a culvert where a dry creek bed runs across the road. That's where we need to stop."

LeBlanc carefully studied the GPS locator readout on his lighted wristwatch. They were almost upon it. "Here it is, Jeffrey," Li Ming called out. Jimmy brought the staff car to a slow stop and left the engine idling.

"That's good Jimmy. Now I know we've been over this a hundred times..."

"I know," Li Ming interrupted. Her role was the most critical role and during the drive into the silo field, she had focused on building up her concentration. She knew what she had to do and was prime to do it. "First I throw the square whiskey bottle on the silo wall. Then we leave. Now leave us free to think."

Jimmy took a more reserved approach. "We've all got it down, Jeffrey. He put on his communicator headset. "We'll wait here for your signal to tell us that you're in place and ready. Then we'll do our thing and pick you up at this same spot on the way out."

LeBlanc patted Jimmy on the shoulder. "Good man." He turned to Li Ming. "As they say in show biz, break a leg."

The young Chinese college girl's head shot back; "You're crazy! I'm supposed to break the square whiskey bottle, not a leg!"

Shaking his head in disbelief as he opened his door, Jeffrey reached over with the other hand and grabbed his backpack. "Jimmy, do me a favor. Explain it to her while I get into position." Gently closing the door, he donned his night vision goggles and lurked off into the night.

It took LeBlanc roughly twenty minutes to position himself on the reverse side of a small rise some 250 yards east of the silo entrance. It offered a clear, unobstructed view of the entire silo entry area, as well as the mobile homes used by Captain Darkazani's Syrian peacekeepers and Euro Mercs. After positioning the pencil thin, camouflage-colored nanobot controller and beam communicator antennas he slid quietly back down the rise and checked the feeds to his webpad. He then keyed in the secure channel access to his IBM Biomass desktop with Andrea, now safely tucked away at an agreed place on-post. The link came up immediately and all lights were green. "So far, so good," he called to Jimmy. "I'm set. There are the usual two guards on top of the bunker, one by the gate and another one in the guardhouse at the entrance." They all looked bored, but things would liven up soon enough LeBlanc reasoned.

"Thanks, Jeffrey; we're rolling," Jimmy replied. He removed his headset and tucked it in the glove compartment. Then, he leaned over and gave Li Ming a soft kiss on the cheek so as not to smear her garish red lipstick. "I love you, baby."

Li Ming's eyes softened. "I love you too. Let's go break some legs now. Yes?"

Jimmy chuckled as he put the car into gear. "That's my baby." He turned the radio on full blast to an old rock and roll favorites station and gunned the engine. He switched on the headlights and sped down the road in the direction of the silo lights as fast as he could.

The last thing Darkazani's sleepy guards expected at midnight was an army staff car screaming from out of nowhere with a drunk lieutenant and an argumentative Chinese whore. Jimmy brought the car to a skidding halt just in front of the gate just as the Syrian guard aimed the red laser beam of his assault rife between Jimmy's eyes.

With the radio still blasting, the duo drew the attention of all four guards. The most senior peacekeeper in the guardhouse came out, stepped next to Jimmy's window, and screamed, "Turn that accursed music off now!"

Jimmy obliged him and said, "Tell your lone ranger over there to point his shooter elsewhere. I didn't come out her for any trouble. I came out here to do some drinking and get laid. Besides, these silos have been abandoned, so who the hell are you?"

The senior peacekeeper shone his flashlight into each of their faces and said with a slight accent, "This is a secure UNE control zone. I'm sorry sir but you must return to the main post right now. This area is restricted."

By now, the Syrian could smell the whiskey that reeked from Jimmy's breath and knew that man would be troublesome. "Restricted, my ass, Tonto! I came here to get laid, so get your miserable peacekeeper ass out of my way!"

"Get out of the car," the peacekeeper ordered.

"Screw you, Tonto!"

That was the code phrase Li Ming had been waiting for. She threw open her door and jumped out with two whiskey bottles in her hand. One was round and the other square. The square bottle held an inert golden suspension fluid containing millions upon millions of nanobots that had arrived via diplomatic courier from Russia the day before. There had been only enough time to create one bottle and nothing more. This was Li Ming's moment of glory or infamy, depending on what she did next.

With the two peacekeepers on Jimmy's side of the staff car, Li Ming ran towards the gate and turned. She held up the whiskey bottles. "You stupid dog fart; you pay me for lovey-lovey, not for getting killed by crazy peacekeeper! You drinkee too much!"

LeBlanc watched the whole performance on his webpad from the reserves side of the rise. "Li Ming, you deserve an Oscar for this one," he mumbled happily to himself.

He then watched Jimmy jump out his car and then stagger and fall over the hood screaming, "That's my whiskey, you stupid whore bitch!"

"I whore, but I'm no bitch!" Li Ming shot back. She then grabbed the square bottle by the neck and turned to face the bunker entrance. Before anyone could say a word, she arched back her arm and threw the square whiskey bottle with the nanobots forward in a high arc over the chain link fence, towards the bunker entrance. The bottle landed with a crash at the base of the bunker's vault door much to LeBlanc's delight. A perfect hit, better than he could have hoped.

While Jimmy moaned and complained about the cost of the whiskey, Li Ming walked back to the car with a proud ladylike gait holding only the round whiskey bottle now. She opened her door and loudly announced, "You take me back now or I break other bottle." With that, she sat down in the car, closed the door and hoisted the round whiskey bottle through the open window. "I getting tired," she announced. "We go now!"

The Syrian peacekeepers watched the whole situation with humorless faces. It was oblivious that their patience with the whole affair was nearing the breaking point. Jimmy stepped around the guard, jumped back into the staff car and closed the door. He put the car into reverse and turned to Li Ming. "If you drop that other bottle you bitch, you're walking back!" With that, he gunned the car into reverse and backed onto the road. Throwing it into drive, he switched the radio back on, flipped a majestic middle-finger salute at the peacekeepers and floored the engine.

Out of sight of the silo entrance, he squeezed Li Ming's leg with a wink, took the communicator headset out of the glove box and slid it on. "We're waiting for you."

"On my way," LeBlanc replied as he finished burying the remote controller transmitter and webpad. Making a one last check to see that the antennas and lead wires were well concealed, he slung his backpack over his shoulder and headed back to the pickup site. By now, Andrea was most likely ordering the nanobots to form into microbots and marching them through the cracks and crevices around the door. To the human eye, the door looked like a seamless fit, but to a minuscule microbot, it would look more like the Grand Canyon.

Li Ming and Jimmy were nervously looking out the windows for signs of LeBlanc or any oncoming headlights – hopefully not from alerted Syrian peacekeepers searching for them. Jeffrey ran up alongside the car in a crouch and slid into the back seat. "Drive!" He ordered softly as all eyes scanned the road before and behind them for signs of alerted peacekeepers.

As they approached Highway 190 he said, "Turn right onto the highway." A bit further down the highway, Jeffrey leaned between the seats and pointed to an intersection. "Turn left, there on Clear Creek." Jimmy turned off the highway and after crossing over some railroad tracks, LeBlanc instructed him to pull off to the right side of road behind a parked 4x4 pickup. Jimmy could see one man in the truck. While all the lights were off, the tailpipe showed the motor to be running.

"Leave the engine running, but turn off the lights, Jimmy. OK you two, get out and follow me," Jeffrey ordered.

The two did as they ordered, and as they got out of the car, the driver of the 4x4 also got out. In the dim light, Jimmy could see that the other man was tall and with a good, strong body. The crew cut haircut and stiff back definitely made him look like a military type. "How did it go," the driver of the 4x4 asked.

"Perfect," LeBlanc replied. "Absolutely perfect." He then motioned for Jimmy and Li Ming to join him at the back of the truck as the 4x4 driver walked back to their idling staff car.

"Look kids," Jeffrey began in a soft tone. "You've done a great job tonight, and I'm really grateful, but now you've got to disappear for a while. This truck has a one hundred gallon auxiliary tank up there behind the cab. It's full, as is the main tank. If you take it easy on the pedal, it should be enough get you to Coeur D'Alene, Idaho where I've got a nice house on the lake. He pointed to the boxes stacked behind the auxiliary fuel tank. There is also food, clothing, jackets, tools, etc. All the stuff you'll need. You'll also find a .45 and a few boxes of shells under the front seat.

He picked up a small aluminum briefcase from the back of the truck. Money and ration stamps enough to last you both a year are in here as well as maps to my house and the keys. Now, my suggestion is that you two lovebirds stop off in Nevada somewhere, get hitched and spend the rest of the year in Idaho making a baby.

He handed the briefcase to Li Ming. She took it gratefully and kissed him on the cheek. "You've always been good to us Jeffrey. If we have a son I'll name him for you." LeBlanc smiled, as young Jimmy sported a beaming ear-stretching grin.

LeBlanc watched them drive off, finally walked back to the idling staff car and got in. "Well General, what did you think? Did we pull it off?"

General Hennicker patted the small webpad in his pocket. "I sat here watching their performance with great interest," he confided. "The nice thing about a couple of street-wise kids like them is that they're genuinely believable. Slick. Real slick. Pass the word along. We're ready for phase 2."

"Am I good, or am I good?" LeBlanc bragged.

"Don't get cocky, hot shot. It's not over till it's over, and there is still plenty more that can go wrong, so stay focused."

GETTING EVERYONE OUT of the Los Gatos Center and to the Livermore Air Base had been easier than Anthony had expected. After a late dinner in the mess tent, they all slipped one-by-one through the kitchen and the covered loading dock behind it into a waiting military ambulance.

They remained in the ambulance, parked at the end of the flight line, for over an hour before a young airman tapped on the window and announced that the Flying Circus was on its final approach.

As usual, Captain Jerome Richard greased the landing with ease and they watched at the old Hercules transport taxied to their end of the flight line.

Coming to a full stop, the all-composite six-bladed propellers of the Flying Circus spun down as Richard and his co-pilot, Al, shut down the airplane's four powerful Allison turboprop engines, and a fuel truck drove up from behind. The moment the ground crew began the refueling; Vigo opened the forward door and waved them to join him.

Charlie Gibbs had already been waiting all afternoon with their gear, which was now loaded on small utility tractor ATV. He quickly drove alongside the Flying Circus and began offloading the gear into Vigo's arms as the rest left the ambulance to join them.

Once inside the cargo hold they saw that most of its 51-foot cargo bed was occupied by two shiny new jet black Cadillac Lectra 12-passenger electric drive SUVs with the newest GE AWD independent wheel motors facing the rear ramp. Squeezed between the Cadillacs and cockpit bulkhead were five commandos, and one of them held a young chimpanzee on his lap. The chimp was keenly interested in their arrival and kept pointing at them. Anthony immediately noticed that none of the commandoes had any identifying name badges or insignia. This was definitely a dark op.

After the last of the group boarded the aircraft, a middle-aged sergeant introduced himself. "I'm the loadmaster. Master Sergeant Bill Jenkins is my name. I'll get your things stowed, and we'll be taking off just as soon as they finish the refuel, which shouldn't be more than a few minutes."

Anthony expected to see the commandoes, but remembered that the last loadmaster had been a somewhat nervous young fellow. "I don't believe we've met," he said.

"Yeah, I was laid up when you last flew with us, but the Captain has filled me in on everything. While I never met

you, a friend of the Captain is a friend of mine if you know what I mean."

Anthony smiled and shook his hand. "Glad to have you as a friend Billy." The older silver-haired man smiled back with a wink and then went about his business.

With everyone inside the aircraft, Vigo closed the door and started the introductions. "We're going to pull back pretty soon and there'll be more racket in here than you can imagine once they fire up the engines so let me make the introductions real quick like. First, I'll introduce my assault team, and then Anthony will introduce all of you.

Sitting on the far side with the chimp in his lap is Sergeant Nir Haftzadi. The chimp is called Violetta. She is a bionic/cybernetic enhanced chimpanzee animal we like to use for special ops these days. That bright-eyed kid with the jutting jaw and large ears next to them is Sergeant Alexei Gladkov. Next to him is Sergeant Major Michael Levy; he's a first-rate sniper. Trust me; you don't want to piss him off. The big, burly, bald-headed guy next to him with the shit-eating grin is Sergeant Major Shalom Mordechai. And standing next to me, is the team commander, Captain Shai Shalom Cohen."

Ann-Marie Bournelle stepped towards Vigo. "Are these guys from where I think they are?"

Vigo smiled. "Yup. They're a mobile crack assault team run by the IDF. They're coming along because we promised them they could have Captain Darkazani and any of the other Syrians they want." The Israeli commandos all waved at them with big toothy grins.

"Thanks to them," Vigo continued, "We're already one step ahead. At the outset of this operation, we thought we'd have to deal with a particularly nasty fellow by the name of Colonel Yasin, who used to run the silo operation. You might be interested to know that Shai and his boys clipped him in Mexico and Levy over there put a .17 cal depleted uranium caseless right through Yasin's eye faster than you can blink." Levy casually shrugged as though it was nothing out of the ordinary. "Once we're airborne, Shai will join us in the back of one of those caddies and we'll brief you on what will take place once we begin the assault on the silo. Anthony, it's your turn."

Anthony introduced Tanya, Ann-Marie, Ramona, Dr. Boole and Charlie and they shook hands all around as the sound of the outboard engines spinning to life filled the inside of the cargo hold.

THE FLYING CIRCUS leveled off at 25,000 feet and settled into a comfortable cruising speed of 390 mph. Vigo and Shai stood up and stretched and Vigo motioned Anthony and his team to join them in the back of the first Cadillac. The interior was spacious and comfortable for the seven of them. As soon as the door was closed, Vigo switched on the Cadillac's advanced noise cancellation system. Within a few seconds, the screeching drone of the transport's engines was muffled to a soft, easily manageable din.

Vigo pulled down a center tray table and laid out several color printouts upon it. "We're going to work as three teams," he began. "Shai's team will take out the off duty Syrian peacekeepers and Euro mercs here in the portable buildings off to the side of the silo entrance. Anthony, Charlie, Jeffrey LeBlanc and I will form the second team. We'll setup here on this rise with Jeffrey LeBlanc, who'll be waiting for us on the road to the silo entrance. Our job will be to neutralize the guards at the gate and on the roof of the crew access bunker. Tanya, you'll lead the third group, the medical evacuation team. Once we've neutralized the bad guys, you come in and take care of Russell and anyone else that needs help. I want you all to know, this is not going to be easy but it can be done." He turned to the IDF officer, "Shai, let's begin the details with you."

The trim, dark-eyed Israeli thumbed through the printouts, finding the one he wanted. "This is a ground radar plot from an unmanned surveillance drone taken last night, thanks to our good friend Vigo. If you look at these

red dots, they represent land mines. The blue dots, motion detectors and the green ones, ammonia sensors. Avoiding the land mines is not difficult. As you see, we have mapped three different approach tracks through the minefield. However, the motion detectors and ammonia sensors are quite another thing, especially if you are big meat eaters like us. That is why we bring Violetta, our android chimpanzee, as we like to call her. Because of her simian physiology she will not trip the ammonia sensors and since the motion detectors are usually detuned to permit small animals to pass, she will not be big enough to raise an alarm either."

He searched around for another printout and put it on top of the others as the medical team looked at him with amazement. None of them had dreamed that the mission would be either this complex or dangerous. It left them feeling somewhat naïve and nervous and glad that Shai and his team had been recruited by Vigo for the rescue.

"Ah yes," Shai mumbled. "I wanted to show you this. As you can see, the minefield completely surrounds the silo area. If you are standing on asphalt or concrete, you are safe. If not, the best you can hope for is to lose nothing more than your legs." He pointed to a spot behind the larger of the two portable buildings. "This is the central control box for the whole sensor system. That is the first target of the assault and Violetta will take the lead. Sergeant Nir Haftzadi will control her via processors directly wired into her brain. He will literally control her motor skills and senses. Nir will walk Violetta through the minefield here, over this fence here, then on to the control box here. Nir and Violetta will clamp this interrupter device to the main cable; it will drive a gold pin through the center of the cable and then over amplify the existing signal by about 1.2 volts. This way, we can control the signal going to the guardhouse monitors, which of course will have a null value. However, LeBlanc's microbots will have to disable the fiber optic links between the silo and the ground level living quarters. I do not know how long that will take, but I do know that the interrupter device will eliminate the connections between the silo and the outside world. Nor will they be able to use their security cameras to monitor our advance. In essence, they'll be deaf, mute and nearly helpless. However, let's not forget that they will be armed and dangerous."

He pulled out another sheet, "Once we've got control of the sensor grid, the next step is to soften the off-duty personnel. They'll most likely be sleeping so Nir will guide Violetta to the air intake duct for the air conditioning located below the building and then release the contents of this small, pressurized container." He held up a small cylinder in his hand. "It is a very powerful knockout gas, which will render the men inside the building unconscious for at least two hours. After the gas has been delivered, the next step belongs to team two, headed by Vigo."

Vigo pushed Shai's printouts to one side and laid down a larger topographic relief print. "Charlie, Anthony, Jeffrey and I will be here on the reverse side of this rise. Charlie and I will be the shooters. Charlie has prepared two rather nice .50 sniper rifles that will do a swift job on those expensive synthetic spider silk suits the on-duty guards are wearing. Anthony, you'll be our spotter and handle communication with Shai. Ten minutes after his chimp has passed the gas, I'll take out the one in the guardhouse first. While I'm taking out the second guard at the gate, Charlie will take out the two Syrians on the roof. After that, Shai will be free to move his men into the complex, to neutralize the off-duty personnel, and capture Captain Darkazani. As soon as they've done that, they'll weld shut the small access tunnels leading up from the control room and missile silo. This will leave main entrance as the only way in or out of the silo complex. The moment this has been accomplished, the third team will enter the complex. Tanya, you and your team will be waiting for our signal here, where this culvert crosses the road."

"And what about the people inside the silo?" Boole asked.

"Glad you asked," Vigo replied. "Jeffrey here has a special device that can enable us to get a rough idea of who is in the silo and where. It will also neutralize their ability to lockdown the entrance once we begin the assault. As soon as the medical team rolls, Shai, and I will enter the silo through the center access and we'll clear the way for Anthony, Charlie and the rest of you to follow once we've secured the silo. Meanwhile, Charlie and Shai's men will setup a defense perimeter for us in case there are any surprises."

Anthony shook his head and pointed to the wire frame map of the silo. "That's my boy in there and no matter what you say, I'm going in with you and Shai."

Vigo shook his head. "We've been over this before, Anthony. It is simply too risky."

"You underestimate me."

An annoyed expression crossed Vigo's face as he leaned back in his chair. "Look, there will be two Euro mercs down in the silo command center and an assassin posing as a nurse. She and Johnston will likely be somewhere near the boy, who we can assume is now in the old crew quarters." He picked up one of the infrared HUD monocles next to his seat. "Once we're in the bunker and we'll be wearing these. Jeffrey will have already cut the main lights and thanks to his sensors, there's no place in the bunker where the mercs can hide. All they'll have to go by are some sounds and the red glow of the emergency lighting system. Anthony, you're a brave lad but you don't know how to use these monocles, let alone hand-to-hand combat with a professional merc. Leave this for Shai and myself."

"My gut instincts tell me that you're too dependent on all this space age gadgetry of yours, plus you're ignoring the fact that I have special powers of perception. If your gadgets fail, I can give you an edge. I'm not trying to be a stupid hero. I just want to rescue my son with all the advantages we can muster."

Shai nudged Vigo in the ribs. "Come on. It's his kid."

Vigo sighed. "OK, but you only enter the silo after Shai and I have handled the two mercs in the silo control room. If you try anything funny, I'll punch your lights out."

"Agreed," Anthony smiled. "Now what happens after we get Russell?"

Vigo bit his lip for a moment. "That's the toughest part of the mission. We've got to get him back to the Flying Circus, and then we're going to beat it like hell for South America. I've arranged with the Brazilian government for Russell's safety till he recovers. After that, the Russians will transport you to Obninsk City."

"And De Bono will be dogging our heels every step of the way," Anthony reluctantly added. With that, Tanya, who by now was looking a bit green snatched up a small wastebasket from under the folding table and heaved into it, filling the Cadillac's interior with an unpleasant nauseous smell that left everyone waving their hands in front of their faces.

"It's just nerves," Tanya offered with a pained expression. "I'll be OK."

CAPTAIN JEROME RICHARD scanned the multifunction liquid crystal displays on his instrument panel and looked back over his seat at Vigo. "Pass the word, 15 minutes. Also, let me know how Tanya is doing. Darn shame about her airsickness, but it will clear up once we're on the ground. Luckily, we've had about as smooth a flight as possible."

"Hard to say about these things," Vigo answered askance, as he stared at the radar display Northrop Grumman low power color radar display on the instrument panel. The Flying Circus was equipped with upgraded MODAR 4000 color weather and navigation radar installed in the nose of the aircraft, with a range of over 300 miles.

He noticed another low-flying inbound aircraft with a UNE registration. Vigo pointed at the aircraft symbol on the radar display. "Could you and Al do me a favor and keep on eye on this?"

"Will do," the pilot replied as he looked over at his co-pilot. "Time to contact Fort Hood tower."

Al winked, and keyed his PTT button. "Fort Hood tower, this is Hercules, Yankee Zulu One Niner requesting permission to land." The controller responded quickly. He exchanged the usual banter with the tower operator after which Al added, "By the way, we've got two nice new Cadillac Lectra SUVs in the back for some hot shot Air Force general. Heck, they even got little refrigerators. We found some chilled canned juice in one of them -- mighty tasty. Sure must be nice to be the king."

The Flying Circus flight crew did definitely not expect the voice that replied to that comment, especially since it was 0200 in the morning Fort Hood time. "This is Major General George Hennicker and those are my cars, as well as the fruit juice. I sure hope you flyboys have something of value to trade for the juice or your butts are mine!"

"General, sir, this is Captain Jerome Richard, the aircraft commander. Please accept our apologies about the fruit juice, sir. I'm sure we can offer something to trade that will please you."

"You can forget the juice," Hennicker growled back. "But if there are any dents or scratches, you'll wish otherwise. My aide will meet you at the ramp and oversee the offloading of the cars."

"We copy that," the pilot acknowledged stiffly. "Yankee Zulu One Niner turning to final."

As the lumbering transport lined up on the runway and lowered its landing gear, the co-pilot looked back at Vigo. "That slow mover you asked me to track is either a chopper or a tilt rotor and it is headed towards the silo area and descending."

Vigo nodded and reminded himself to tell Anthony and Shai after they landed.

AS THE REAR ramp lowered to the ground, loadmaster, Sergeant Bill Jenkins began removing the cargo straps and blocks from around the Cadillacs. Inches before the ramp touched the ground, a young captain, one of General Hennicker's aides stepped up into the cargo hold tapped him on the shoulder. "Our drivers will not be here till later this morning. You are to park the vehicles inside the hangar at the west side of the field and leave the keys with the maintenance chief in the hangar. Do you understand?"

"Yes sir," replied the loadmaster. The aide scanned the interior of the cargo hold. All he could see was the loadmaster and the two Cadillacs with dark tinted windows.

"Fine. Be careful." The captain said and then left at a trot for his own staff car with a deniable smirk. The aide knew what was about to happen and wished them luck. The fact that a U.S. military base was being used to commit kidnapping and blackmail by a foreign politician made his blood boil, but for now, his main concern was to do everything he could to protect General Hennicker.

The loadmaster watched the aide leave out of the corner of his eyes as he finished removing the cargo straps and blocks. Securing the gear, he walked out the back of the Flying Circus and was later joined by Captain Richard and the co-pilot, Lieutenant Al Chan. They pretended to talk amongst themselves as they scanned the military airport. Aside from a light in the hangar at the west end of the field that shone across a line of 3 neatly parked MH-53J Pave Low III special ops choppers, the entire airport was as still as a graveyard.

"You direct them out," Jerome ordered and walked back to the first SUV. He tapped on the dark black driver side window and the window slid down with a whir. Vigo was at that wheel. "You may have company. We finished tracking that slow-mover for you. Turns out it was a tilt rotor and definitely landed somewhere in the silo field. Watch your six Vigo."

"Thanks, Captain," Vigo said. "We should be back in no more than two hours. You fellas have taken enough risks as it is with that flight down into Mexico. If all hell breaks loose, there'll probably be no point in waiting for us."

"We'll be here until the fat lady sings. Now get your damn Cadillacs out of my airplane and go do something."

Vigo saluted with a smile, rolled the window back up and followed the loadmaster's hand signals as he slowly drove the first electric powered SUV out onto the tarmac with Anthony, Charlie and the Israeli commandoes in the back. Following close behind was the second SUV with Ann-Marie Bournelle at the wheel, Tanya to her right and Dr. Boole and Ramona behind them with all the medical gear.

They drove north at the posted speed limit from the airfield to Highway 190 and turned left. A few miles down the road, they turned left again on Base Road and headed south into the silo field.

Equipped with a GPS navigation heads up display, the Cadillac SUV was a quiet, powerful machine in Vigo's hands. He drove straight to the very spot where Jeffrey LeBlanc, waiting for them in the dark early morning hours, greeted them dressed in fatigues and face paint.

Jeffrey guided the SUVs to the side of the road and ran up to Vigo's window. "Man, we just got a wild twist. UNE Governor Merl Johnston just flew in here about twenty minutes ago. He and some gal dressed in a nurse's uniform landed in a tilt rotor. The aircrew is in the guard's quarters now. Johnston and the nurse are in the silo."

"He may suspect something," Anthony noted. "They could be here to move the boy. If so, we've come in the nick of time."

"Or something tipped our hand," Vigo grumbled. LeBlanc watched and wondered if either man would call off the operation now that a high-ranking UNE official was in the silo.

Vigo gripped the steering wheel and pondered the situation. "My guess is that he's here because they're worried." He opened his door, forcing Jeffrey back. "Let them worry. We go ahead as planned."

All of the men slid out of the first SUV. The commandoes wore helmets with built-in communicators and night vision monocles. Sergeant Nir Haftzadi opened the rear hatch and Violetta jumped into his arms as Captain Cohen readied his team.

"Vigo," he whispered in a hushed voice. "As soon as you have you've got your blinds setup and can cover us, we'll move Violetta."

"Check. We'll see you at the bunker, Shai."

From the second SUV, Ann-Marie and Tanya watched the occupants of the first SUV split into two groups. Anthony, Vigo and Charlie followed LeBlanc to the left and the Israelis and their chimp veered off to the right. The men moved quietly into the night and quickly disappeared leaving them alone on the road, waiting and praying.

Vigo and Charlie pushed their canvas blinds slowly into place at the top of the rise. Even if a search beam lighted their position, the blinds would look like dirt bumps on the rise. They had loaded their .50 caliber rifles and attached the silencers and scopes back at the SUV. All they needed to do now was to situate the sniper rifles on their bipods and wait.

Vigo looked back down the rise at Jeffrey and nodded. LeBlanc then pressed the switch and the small antenna he'd planted on the top of the rise the night before, began beaming a coded activation signal at the spot where Li Ming had slammed the whiskey bottle against the silo entrance.

After being inserted the night before, the microbots had moved into position and then disassembled themselves into nanobots. Now that they had been given the final activation code, it would only take them another ten minutes to disable all of the communication and door power controls in the silo. After that, the silo could be easily taken, as those inside would not be able to contact anyone outside. While the silo was equipped with backup landlines, Jeffrey and General Hennicker had disabled them.

As the nanobot-microbots began to neutralize various circuits and microprocessors inside the silo, the Israeli commandoes approached from the opposite side of the silo entrance. Their approach was blocked from Vigo's sight, by the portable buildings that now served as a barracks for the Syrian peacekeepers. Eventually, Shai's voice came softly through Vigo's headset. "We're in position."

Vigo replied with three clicks to let him know that Sergeant Haftzadi could now start Violetta through the minefield.

Using a virtual reality headset and VR gloves, Nir guided Violetta through the minefield using an overlay from the ground radar scan the previous day. Violetta was well trained, and accustomed to Nir taking control of her body. She never complained or whimpered as she crossed through the minefield with the stealth of a cheetah. Still the same, Nir continued to speak to her in soft tones often saying, "Violetta is a good girl."

The chimp cleared the minefield and slowly climbed the fence as the commandoes collectively heaved a sigh of relief. They had secretly feared there would be sensors attached to the chain link fence; at least that is what they would have done. However, not even a few aluminum drink cans were strung. A foolish oversight; had even a simple precaution like that have been employed, it would have slowed things down considerably.

After climbing down from the opposite side of the tent, Violetta took slow steps towards a light pole behind the larger of the two portable buildings. Both buildings were dark, which meant that everyone in them was most likely asleep.

Fastened about a foot above the light pole was the control box for the ammonia sensors and movement detectors in the minefield, which surrounded the silo entrance in a big racetrack pattern that ended at each side of the drive leading back to Base Road. Below the control box was a small junction box.

Nir had Violetta draw out a screwdriver from her little equipment vest. It was especially made for Violetta's hands, and he used it through her hands to carefully remove the cover plate. Then, he tucked the tool back in its holster and drew out the disrupter device, which looked somewhat like a large tuning fork.

Clipping the disrupter took only a minute, and soon he got the signal from his partner, Alexei Gladkov, that the disrupter was now in control of the sensors and sending a steady stream of unremarkable null signals to the automated monitoring panel in the guardhouse. Shai signaled Vigo that only one more step remained.

Finding the air conditioner underneath the portable building was easy for Violetta; it glowed like a Christmas tree when seen through an infrared monocle. As the chimp walked slowly towards the building, its compressor shut off with a jolt leaving the whirring of its fan motor to cover the sound of the chimp's steps.

Nir guided Violetta carefully to the unit's outside air intake. She removed the gas cylinder clipped to the straps on her back and Nir positioned her to get the most amount of gas possible into the building and then walked Violetta to the far end of the building where he made her sit. He then triggered the remote release on the gas canister, which began spewing its potent gas into the building's ventilation ducts. He turned towards Shai and winked. "Beddy-bye time," he whispered.

The Captain keyed his microphone. "Anthony, the package has been delivered," Shai spoke softly. "Ten minutes."

"Good job, Shai. Standby and wait for our signal."

"Copy that."

Anthony turned to Vigo and Charlie and gave them a thumbs-up sign. Vigo then whispered to Charlie, "I'll take the one in the guardhouse first, then the one at the gate. As soon as I start shooting, you get the two on the bunker roof. It's show time in 10 minutes."

THE PHONE NEXT to Captain Darkazani's bed rang, waking him up for the second time in the middle of the night. The first time had been with Governor Johnston's arrival with his nurse Danielle Peters. What a shame he thought after meeting her to waste such a beautiful body on such a cold soul. He picked up the phone headset and pulled it to his ear. "Darkazani," was all he could manage to say.

The voice on the other end of the line sounded anxious. It was Johnston. "Captain, I was watching the monitors in the silo control room and we saw what appeared to be a small animal in the mine field tonight."

"Yes, and what did your mercs tell you," he sighed with exasperation.

"That the animal was not heavy enough to trigger the land mines and that the motion sensors are detuned to ignore animals this small. But why wouldn't the ammonia sensors have detected something?"

"It depends on the kind of animal. What we're looking for are people, especially people who eat meat. I can assure you that this is nothing to worry about. I personally oversaw the installation of that system and nothing human can survive it or escape detection. Now, governor, may I please go back to sleep? I need to get my rest for tomorrow. The transfer of the boy tomorrow at dawn will be, let's say, demanding. I suggest you get some rest too."

"But I've got a funny feeling about this," Johnston protested.

"Do you want me to send my other men down into the silo with you?"

"Oh no. You know the Secretary General's orders. You and your men are to stay out of the bunker."

"I could send the other two mercs down. All four would be with you then. But then, you'll have a sleepy escort when you move the boy. What do you want me to do?"

"Well," Johnston sighed. "Forget it. We'll move the boy at dawn. In the meantime, I really hope you're right. It's just that I have this weird feeling and…"

"And what?"

"Something is not right. That's all."

"I think you Americans call this the jitters. Yes?"

"Yeah," Johnston replied tersely. It was obvious that the conversation had gone nowhere, but how could he reprimand the man for being insensitive to his own awkward and undefined feelings? "Go back to sleep Captain. Hopefully I will not have to bother you again."

As Johnston removed his headset, he noticed a quickly growing buildup of static on the line but paid it no mind to it, as he was more involved with thinking how his patience had long since run thin with Captain Darkazani. Only now, he regretted the loss of Colonel Yasin, who usually seemed to have a sixth sense about such matters.

Yasin would have handled things more proficiently, but an Israeli hit team killed him in Mexico using an intercept of his own coded message to De Bono with Yasin's travel itinerary and description. He remembered what was on his mind when he sent that message. He knew that when he would condemn Yasin to death that he was potentially hurting himself as well. He sensed that at the time, but he didn't know how or why. Only that he had to follow De Bono's orders.

After hanging up the phone, Darkazani rolled on his back and groped on the nightstand for his lighter and cigarettes. He fumbled a bit in the dark and finally stuck a cigarette between his lips and lit it. "Just another crazy American," he grumbled to himself as he drew the smoke deep into his lungs. He wondered if he would be able to fall asleep for a third time, or would he just toss and turn till dawn?

Better yet, he decided, perhaps a stiff drink. He took a small flask of whiskey out of the nightstand drawer and took several large sips as he continued to smoke his cigarette.

As Darkazani inhaled with deep satisfaction, the main lighting system in the underground silo complex failed. Johnston immediately picked up the phone to call Darkazani again, but this time the phone was dead. "That stupid fool," Johnston screamed as the red lights of the emergency lighting system bathed their startled faces with a ghoulish light. They were sitting ducks now and he knew it.

CHAPTER 26

TO SAVE RUSSELL

JOHN-PIERRE DURAND had just finished making his espresso when he heard the dull clunk of the emergency lighting system kick in, as Merl Johnston screamed. "Oh shit," he murmured to himself as the small kitchenette filled with the eerie red glow of the emergency lights.

By instinct, he drew his pistol and bounded to the adjacent crew quarters where Governor Johnston and his secretary Danielle Peters had been preparing the 'client' as they called the boy for transport in a new biostasis pod. At six foot one, the French-Canadian was a commanding sight of a man with a firm narrow jaw, scarred from one too many close-in fights and piercing black eyes that had seen death up close and personal a thousand times over and now they locked onto Danielle's. He could see that she was alarmed but cool. A reaction he'd expect from a fellow professional.

Merl Johnston on the other hand was beginning to come apart at the seams. "Oh Jesus, we're going to die!" he exclaimed.

Danielle looked back over her shoulder at him, "Get a grip, Merl." Johnston's eyes darted back and forth between the two of them.

It made John-Pierre uncomfortable, "I'm going to the lower level," he said as he ran a hand through his thick black hair to break eye contact with the frightened politician.

"We'll be down in a moment," Danielle replied. "Get going."

As he leapt down the stairs to the control room level in three bounds, he could hear Danielle dressing down her boss through the open hatch of the crew quarters. A panicked fool was the last thing that anyone needed now and at least she had the presence of mind to bring Johnston into line.

His found his watch partner, Joe Napolitano, a stocky 5' 9" Italian with short cut, brown wavy hair hunched over the console displays. His soft, blue-green eyes searched the displays for an accurate assessment of the situation and it had only taken him a few moments to realize the truth of their situation. "Hi Cat, you probably want a sitrep. In a nutshell, basically we're screwed." John-Pierre had worked with Joe on several missions and the two men knew each other's strengths and weaknesses. Joe was an electronics wiz and John-Pierre was called "Cat" because of his cat-like reflexes and supple speed. They had worked well as team. Joe would spot the targets and Cat would usually slice their throats using his razor sharp titanium blade hollow-ground tactical knife.

John-Pierre scanned the displays himself and remarked, "basically screwed really doesn't work for me, Joe."

"It doesn't work for me either," said Danielle as she slid down the stair railings into the control level. "Break it down for us," she ordered.

"Right," Joe replied in a crisp voice. "For starters, we've lost the doors. We're wide open. We've also been cut off from our people topside, the outside world, and we've lost our surveillance cameras."

"So we're deaf, dumb and blind," Danielle quickly surmised.

"And if my hunch is right," John-Pierre reluctantly added, "we're going to be alone too."

"What do you mean," Danielle shot back.

"It's obvious they're already inside our perimeter," Joe replied scanning the displays. "They'd have to be in order to shut us down like this. As for the doors, it just doesn't make sense." He turned to face them as Johnston stumbled down the stairs, white-faced and trembling. "So what do we do?"

All eyes turned towards John-Pierre. "You're the tactical genius," Danielle said with pursed lips. "You know this place better than I do, so I'm putting you in charge."

John-Pierre nodded his acceptance and rubbed his chin as a plan formed in his mind. "Joe, get the Alamo kit."

"I'm on it," the Italian merc replied.

"Alamo kit?" The term had immediately caught Johnston's attention.

"It is something Joe and I put together just after we got here." He glared at Danielle. "Your Syrians are not the brightest bulbs on the tree. They never expected a situation like this and our people topside are probably being cut to pieces right now. They should have never made it past the wire."

"So why did they?" Johnston asked as Joe dragged a large footlocker across the control room floor to where they were standing.

"Getting through a minefield with ammonia sensors and motion detectors is tricky but it can be done. If we had working motion sensors on the wire, a few of our people would already be here by now."

"I've seen the plans and motion sensors were installed on the wire. Colonel Yasin insisted on it," Danielle noted with surprise.

"But Darkazani had them turned off."

"What?" Johnston bellowed.

"The day after Yasin disappeared, he boosted the settings and sure enough some damn bird tried to perch on the fence and set off the alarm. It was a real mess, the Syrians were shooting in every direction and Darkazani called in an alert to the Turkish Peacekeeper assault team Houston."

"I read the briefing on that. It was a routine practice drill," Danielle said.

John-Pierre laughed. "Routine, my ass. Darkazani was beside himself and didn't know whether to shit or eat. Calling it a practice drill was my idea. Darkazani latched onto it, but it sure didn't impress that Turkish Major when they landed. He was spitting nails. It seems the Turks and the Syrians have a mutual disgust for each other. After that, Darkazani had the fence sensors turned off, over my objections. On the upside, it did give me a chance to time their reaction time. From the alert to their landing here, it was just under fifty-six minutes."

"It might as well be fifty-six years as far as we're concerned," Johnston fumed.

John-Pierre pointed the muzzle of his pistol at Johnston's face. "We don't need this. Do you get my drift?" Johnston stared down the muzzle of the pistol and nodded obediently as Danielle turned away to hide her disgust. She resolved in that moment that if they lived through the day, she'd leave him because when push came to shove, he had only proven himself to be a spineless man.

Joe hefted the locker onto the console desk and flipped the latches open. "Voila,' he announced as he removed the lid. Danielle looked inside the locker as Joe and John-Pierre began pulling out Belgian-made .45 caliber Uzi submachine gun pistols and stacks of fully loaded sixteen round clips. Joe hefted an Uzi with a devilish grin, "They're reliable, make a terrible noise and hit like hell."

John-Pierre handed an Uzi to Danielle. "No thanks," she said. "I prefer my Berretta." She inserted a clip into the Uzi and handed it to Johnston. "Do you know how to use it?"

"No."

She took the Uzi back from him, charged the bolt and set the safety to the 'on' position. "It's simple," she said as she demonstrated the weapon. "Hold it like so with both hands, set the safety like so, aim and pull the trigger. Can you remember that?"

Johnston nodded, "both hands, safety, aim and pull the trigger. Got it."

"Good," she said handing the weapon back to him.

"Governor, I suggest that you go back upstairs and remain by the client. We'll handle everything down here," John-Pierre calmly said, noting the beads of sweat that were now forming on Johnston's temples.

"If you get us out of this alive, John-Pierre, I'll double your bonus," Johnston said anxiously.

John-Pierre shook his head. The fact that Johnston would even make such an offer was insulting to him. "That's not necessary."

Danielle picked up on his annoyance and felt ashamed by Johnston's cheapness. "What the Governor meant to say," she added, "is that your bonus as well as Joe's has been increased to one million Euros tax free. Now earn it!"

"Now you're talking our language," John-Pierre replied with a grin as Joe happily rolled his eyes. This Danielle gal was a tough and cool, but she certainly had class. "Governor, go upstairs to the client and write the check."

"Yeah, I'll do that," Johnston agreed nervously and bolted up the stair, glad to be one more level removed from the action.

As he disappeared up the stairway, Joe pulled a Spitfire UHF Manpack Terminal and collapsible antenna out of the locker. "This was my idea," he grinned. "The UNE has assigned frequencies on all MILSATCOM satellites. Would you happen to have a calling card Ms. Peters?"

"Finally, a real break," Danielle sighed with relief. "You bet your ass, I do."

"Joe, we're too deep here for an uplink so you'll have to set the antenna up at that top of the emergency crew access tunnel. After that, link the Spitfire into the console and run a bi-directional feed to the vital signs monitor over the client's bed. It has a webcam, and we can use it for a comm. terminal."

"I'm on it," Joe replied with a toothy grin.

"And Joe," John-Pierre added. "Whatever you do, do not open the ground level hatch, or you'll eat a bullet for sure."

"I may be dumb, but I'm not stupid," he chortled as he picked up the gear and headed for the access to the long, narrow, circular shaft that led straight up from the side of the command center to the ground above.

John-Pierre focused his attention on Danielle. "Let's not kid ourselves. Whoever is hitting us is good. I mean real good. My guess is that it will take them about ten minutes to secure the ground above and then they'll move on us down here in the silo. While ten minutes is not much, it does give us some time to set up an inner defense with the hope that we can hold them back long enough for the Turks to get here."

"Who do you think we're up against? The American Delta Force, Black Berets, what?"

"No, even if the Americans knew what we're doing here, they would never dare run an op against the UNE. No, it is freelancers, and they want the boy alive; otherwise, we'd all be dead by now. That may be our one real edge right now."

"So do we set up a defensive perimeter here in the command level or in the accessway between here and the central storage and maintenance area?"

"Neither. As soon as Joe gets the Spitfire working, I want you to send an alert to Houston and get the Turks here as quick as you can. After that, see if you can link to one of the Air Force surveillance birds. We may not be able to see anything with our own ground level cameras but at least we'll have an overhead view of what is happening topside. After that, I have a special task for you."

He pulled a heavy stack of oval bulb shaped metal clamps out of the footlocker. "Just so you don't think Joe has all the brains, this was my idea," he grinned. "I had these self-welding braces specially made after I first inspected the silo." He pointed his chin up towards the crew quarters on the level above them. "After Yasin set up shop, he had the old door on the crew quarters replaced with a bolt-lock half-inch steel door with hinges mounted on the inside of the crew quarters. If these pricks make it this far, they know they'll probably kill the client if they blow the door with C-4 or pump it full of armor piercing rounds."

He hefted up one of the self-welding braces and held it upside down. Danielle could see that it was bowl shaped with a flat recessed center and covered with an airtight aluminum and plastic seal, with a large red pull-tab at both ends. "This is basically an oval steel bowl with silica fiber compound center that can absorb heat up to 2,300 degrees. The face of the steel the brace is covered with an oxygen activated duraweld compound. To activate it, pull the seal off using one of these red tabs and stick it on the door. In about fifteen seconds, the brace will be welded to the door with about half the strength of a normal weld."

"So where and when do I use them?"

"As soon as you've sent the alert to Houston and have got us linked with a surveillance bird, I want you take these upstairs and lock yourself in the crew quarters with Johnston and the client. If they make past me, you'll be on your own, and most likely they'll start cutting through the door with a torch. When they do, just let them cut away and slap one these babies on the door behind the cut. When they're finished cutting, they'll try to kick in and then they'll be in for a hell of a surprise.

"You've got ten of these self-welding braces which should buy you plenty enough time if they make it past me and Joe. If not, don't open the door until I give you the all clear."

Danielle picked up one of the self-welding braces and examined it. "Damn, but you're good," she said admiringly.

"That's why you pay me the big bucks," he replied.

As the sound of Joe climbing back down the tunnel ladder echoed in the small control room he jerked his thumb up towards the crew quarters and asked in a low voice, "by the way, to you have to sleep with that slimeball?"

"Not after today," she replied tersely as Joe appeared at the accessway, stringing out a line of fiber optic behind him.

"Give me two more minutes," Joe announced, and we'll be online."

CAPTAIN COHEN HAD assigned Staff Sergeant Alexei Gladkov and Sergeant Major Shalom Mordechai to take Darkazani alive, while he and the other commandos took out the resting peacekeepers and Euro mercs.

Crouched at the edge of the minefield with a clear view of Darkazani's small portable building, Cohen noticed the flicker of Darkazani's cigarette lighter, followed by intermittent glowing of his cigarette as he inhaled.

"Alexei, Darkazani is awake and smoking in bed," Cohen said softly in to his microphone. "Do you think you can you still take him alive?"

"We'll try our best," Sergeant Gladkov replied softly.

The young Israeli captain looked at the time display in his monocle. Vigo and Charlie would open fire in a less than a minute. As the seconds ticked down, he regretted that Violetta was unable to carry a second cylinder of sleeping gas for Darkazani's quarters but that added mass of a second cylinder had been deemed an unacceptable risk and it would have forced her to walk a considerable distance out in the open and in plain view of the two peacekeepers on top of the bunker roof.

However, Darkazani was smoking in bed, which meant that he would need time to react. It was better than nothing. "Alexei, you and Shalom will have to do your best. Remember, we came here to take him alive. With what he knows, we can save a lot of lives back home."

"Acknowledged," The sergeant replied. "Standing by." Cohen looked at his watch again as the last five seconds ticked by.

JEFFREY HELD UP his hand and clenched it twice, to let Vigo, Anthony and Charlie know the silo had been cut off from all landlines to the outside world. Likewise, the above ground buildings had all been cut off and every lockdown mechanism in the silo had all been neutralized.

Anthony was already working a portable camera that Jeffrey had placed on the rise the night before. He whispered into his microphone, "The Syrians on top of the building are walking away from us now. Go!"

Vigo and Charlie climbed quickly up the rise and situated themselves behind their Barrett M82A1, semi-automatic 50 caliber sniper rifles with fully loaded ten round magazines. Charlie put his first roof top target in the crosshairs, as Vigo searched for the senior Syrian peacekeeper in the guardhouse through his scope.

The night had already had its tricky and unpleasant surprises, but not all surprises are bad. The Syrian at the gate had walked off to one side to urinate on the fence. It was an ideal moment of distraction. Vigo put the senior commander's face in his crosshairs and pulled the trigger. The huge rifle slammed back into his shoulder as the black tipped armor piercing 2.31" long 50 caliber bullet sped through night at over 2800 feet per second. The Syrian peacekeeper had been looking in Vigo's direction and the bullet made a relevantly small hole in the front of the head, tearing out the back of his head and splattering his brains on the ground.

The second Syrian at the fence heard the impact and was trying to zip his fly when Vigo's second shot hit him in the throat, and, save for a dangling mass of tissue, had decapitated the man. At the same time, Charlie's first shot caught the peacekeeper furthest from him in the chest. The large caliber bullet tore through the man's expensive synthetic spider silk vest and began plowing through his chest, tearing his heart and lungs apart like a berserk rototiller.

As the kinetic force of the impact sent the first roof top guard's body sailing through the air, the other guard instinctively lifted his rifle to his shoulder. Before he could pull the trigger, however, Charlie's second round caught him at the base of his throat and his headless body fell to the roof, still holding onto the rifle.

Captain Shai Cohen had been watching from the other side of the silo entrance. Four shots. Four kills. He respected that kind of efficiency. He keyed up his microphone. "For French Hill." His men began moving quickly past the guardhouse, following their preplanned paths, into the complex.

In the lead were Alexei Gladkov and Shalom Mordechai, and they moved at a fast gait towards Darkazani's quarters as Shai Cohen and the other commandos headed towards the larger building.

After covering all the entrances, Shai and his men slipped on their respirators and drew silenced PPK 10mm caseless pistols. On Shai's signal, he and his men entered through both doors of the building.

As Gladkov and Mordechai positioned themselves next to Darkazani's door, they could hear familiar faint puffs of silenced pistol fire as Shai and his men stepped quickly from bed to bed, shooting each of the drugged occupants twice in the head. After a few moments, Shai opened the blinds of a window facing Darkazani's private quarters and whispered in his microphone, "first position is secure."

As Mordechai pulled the pin on his stun grenade, Gladkov reached towards the door knob on Darkazani's door. Before he could turn the knob, the bark of a Kalaschnikov AK-103k carbine tore through the night. Firing wildly, Darkazani emptied his thirty round clip in one sustained burst as the two commandos dropped immediately to the ground.

One bullet ripped through Gladkov's hand and several others peppered the outside wall of the second building, three of which struck Shai Cohen; two were stopped by his flak jacket, but one managed to shatter his right arm just above the elbow.

Estimating that Darkazani was standing behind the door, Mordechai fired a long burst a foot above the ground from his silenced Galil SAR that sent a stream of thirty-five 5.56mm NATO rounds through the wall, door and Darkazani's legs.

The Syrian commander fell to the floor in a crash, wailing with pain as Gladkov kicked the door open. Mordechai then tossed his stun grenade through the door. The sound of the exploding grenade was the last sound of the above ground assault as the two Israeli commandos charged the through the door and then gagged and shackled the stunned Syrian as he lay bleeding on the floor of his room.

STILL FEELING THE affects of jet lag after being assigned to his new duty station in Houston, the Turkish Peacekeeper assault team duty officer rang his unit commander's private phone.

The commander rolled over in his bed and punched the talk button. "Bazoglu."

"Excuse me, Colonel, but we have another class one alert at silo fourteen at Fort Hood."

"Is this another one of Darkazani's crazy drills?" he fumed.

"No, sir," the duty officer replied. "The alert call came in from a UNE employee by the name of Danielle Peters over an unassigned MILSATCOM satellite frequency. I checked the procedures and cleared her authentication code through Geneva."

Colonel Bazoglu quickly sat up in bed, "How long has it been since you got the call?"

"They called in exactly twelve minutes ago. It took me over ten minutes to authenticate their code with Geneva because they also requested a direct mission link with the American surveillance satellite network. That link is now complete and they are presently receiving live lookdown images at the silo."

"Damn!" Bazoglu spat. "Alert the whole command! This is not a drill; I repeat this is not a drill! I also want all the Ospreys plus the gunships. Do it now; I'll hold."

The duty officer's hands quickly flew across the touch screen on his console and within seconds, Bazoglu could hear the alert sirens going off. "Now put me through to the Fort Hood duty officer."

"Yes sir," the duty officer replied snappily. "I'm putting you through right now."

After what seemed an interminable wait, he heard a young woman's voice, "Duty Officer Lieutenant Kathy Sullivan."

"Lieutenant Sullivan, this is Colonel Bazoglu of the UNE special forces detachment based in Houston. We have a class one alert at our missile field; silo fourteen. We are enroute, and we need your assistance."

"I'll notify the air field, sir and clear your arrival. Please remember to file a flight plan."

"When I said assistance lieutenant, I didn't mean just a landing clearance. I want you to get your troops out there immediately."

"I'm not authorized to do that, Colonel," the lieutenant politely replied.

"Don't you know what a class one alert is, you stupid bitch? Our silo is under attack."

This time the lieutenant's voice was stern, "Sir, there is no need to be rude! If you wish to persist in this manner, you're welcome to contact the post commander after he arrives at his office this morning."

The frustrated Turkish commander slapped the top his head as he gathered patience. "Very well lieutenant. I'm asking you politely to send troops immediately to silo fourteen. Do you copy?"

"Of course I do."

"Well, are you going to send them?"

"As you know, sir, that area is under the sovereign control of the UNE and I'm not authorized to send armed troops into that area; nor, may I add, is our post commander until he is ordered to do so directly by the President, himself. But as soon as we get the word, rest assured that we'll be glad to help."

"Don't give me this nonsense. People are dying out there, you stupid bitch," Bazoglu screamed into the phone.

"Sir, I thought we had achieved an understanding that we would conduct our conversation in a civil tone. Perhaps you would prefer to speak with the base commander after he arrives at his office this morning."

Bazoglu growled angrily. "When I'm finished with you, lieutenant, you'll be cleaning the filthiest toilets in Ecuador." He slammed his fist on the call cancel button and then punched the auto dial button for his duty officer.

After the line went dead, Lieutenant Kathy Sullivan pulled off her headset and took a deep breath. "Well, he's sure in a snit."

Standing behind her, General George Hennicker rested a hand on her shoulder and casually said, "Sure seems that way Lieutenant. By the way, you did a good job." She looked back over her shoulder at the amused general with an equally self-satisfied smile.

TANYA AND HER team in the second SUV heard the report of Darkazani's Kalashnikov and the detonation of the stun grenade. Things had not gone as smoothly as planned and they wondered if a hail of soldiers and peacekeepers would now soon descend upon them.

Tanya's first fear was that Anthony had been wounded or even worse. Not knowing was the worst part and she could feel her heart racing until she heard his voice in her earpiece. "Move in, Tanya. We've taken down all the ground level nasties and now we're going into the silo, but we've got three wounded including Shai."

"On our way." Tanya turned to Ann-Marie. "Step on it."

ANTHONY GAVE VIGO a thumbs-up sign to let him know that Tanya and her team was on the way. Silently taking the lead, Vigo led Anthony and Charlie around the outside of the minefield to the drive leading to the silo entrance. The paused alongside the drive as Tanya's SUV rushed past them.

Tanya caught a brief glimpse of Anthony waving them on, feeling a sense of relief as their SUV crashed through the red and white striped gate. As the splintered wood flew backwards above the SUV, Tanya quickly spotted the body of the senior Syrian peacekeeper plopped up against the far wall, with his head dangling down his chest.

Mordechai was standing guard over Darkazani as two other commandos carried Shai Cohen out to the drive. Ann-Marie brought the SUV to a stop and everyone inside jumped out with medical kits in-hand.

Dr. Boole and Tanya ran first to Shai, as he ordered Ann-Marie to tend to Darkazani's wounds.

Shai was bleeding profusely and in great pain because the bullet had begun to spin on impact doing a considerable amount of damage to the muscles in his right arm. To Boole's relief, the bullet had missed his brachial artery by only a few millimeters. The rest was manageable he reasoned as began treating the wound. "We can save the arm Captain, but I'm afraid you'll have to choose another line of work," he said as he gave him an injection of morphine to control the pain.

The young captain tried to push the needle away. "I need to keep sharp," he said with a strained expression.

Standing by his side, Sergeant Major Michael Levy took hold of his hand. "Shai, our job is basically finished. I can take it from here." He looked over at Boole and nodded towards the needle. With waves of pain burning through his arm, Shai knew he was useless and let Boole give him the injection. As he felt the effect of the drug, he could only think with deep regret that he could not join Vigo and Anthony for the assault into the silo.

The world was becoming fuzzy, but he strained at two last commands. "Doctor, please see to Gladkov's wound." He head turned limply towards Levy. "Michael, set up a defensive perimeter. Vigo and his team will be going down the main stairwell in the center of the complex, but make sure we cover the emergency shaft exits from the control dome and the missile bay to each side." His voice began to slur noticeably. "Also, get someone to bring in the second SUV so that... we." His head fell limply into Tanya's hands. The words "get going," strained past his lips as his eyes close shut.

Levy, Cohen's second in command, left his commander in the capable care of Tanya and Boole and began snapping orders to the other commandos in a calm but firm voice. "Nir, you cover the missile bay exit. Shalom, you cover the command room exit. Alexei, you get the other SUV in here. We'll put Shai and Darkazani in it."

Ann-Marie had just finished cleaning the wound Gladkov's hand and was wrapping a field dressing around it. "In a moment," he answered.

"Good; as soon as you can."

As Michael Levy ran past the gatehouse, he met Anthony, Vigo, Jeffrey and Charlie jogging at a brisk trot through the main gate. Anthony stopped and looked at Shai, who was now unconscious. "Anything we can do?" he asked.

"Yes," Tanya replied without looking up. "Someone go and get a stretcher out of the SUV."

"I'll do it," Jeffrey immediately volunteered.

"Make it two," Ann-Marie added.

"Got it."

As LeBlanc ran to the back of the SUV, Ann-Marie kneeled down next to Boole. "Darkazani's got a flesh wound in the right leg, but the left caught three rounds below the knee. It's really shredded. I set a tourniquet, gave him morphine and started an I.V. drip; you really need to look at that left leg."

"You're fast," Boole replied.

"We try. What about Captain Cohen's arm?"

"It's pretty bad but it can be saved," Boole answered as LeBlanc returned with the stretchers. "I'll take a look at the Syrian when I'm finished here."

Vigo took stock of the situation and tapped Anthony on the shoulder. "They've got the situation under control, but with Shai and Gladkov down, it looks like its time for plan b. You, Charlie and me are going in. Just don't try to be a hero, OK?"

"Don't worry about me," Anthony replied.

Vigo handed him Shai Cohen's special VR headset, which was connected with LeBlanc's nanobot controller. "Since you and Andrea are so chummy, you'll be our sensor man down in the silo."

Anthony nodded as Vigo and Charlie snapped night vision monocles onto their helmets.

"Anthony, I'll go first and then Charlie. You follow behind, and keep telling us what you're seeing in your monocle. Be careful; things could get pretty hectic down there especially with Johnston in the silo. Anthony, let's do a check. Tell me what you're seeing."

Vigo and Charlie watched Anthony's head as it moved back and forth, up and down in a methodical scanning pattern. "These surveillance microbots are about as blind as bees, but I can spot what appear to be large human blobs if you will. Right now, I'm seeing two people in the control room, and one in the level below it."

"That's the engineering level. No doubt, the guy is trying to get the silo lockdown systems and communications back online."

"I do not see anyone in the missile bay at the other end of the complex."

LeBlanc spoke up. "Anthony, we've only got sensor nanobots in the control room, engineering room, central elevator shaft, central storage room and the connecting tunnel between there and the crew quarters and control room dome. Sorry, but we're blind when it comes to the missile bay and the crew quarters. There is only so much we could do."

"That's OK," Anthony replied. "We've got a clear path down the main stairwell, through the storage room, the access tunnel to the control room and perhaps even the storage room itself. Let's get going before the mercs head for the center of the complex."

JOHN-PIERRE AND DANIELLE had lucked into an orbiting surveillance satellite just as its footprint was passing over Fort Hood and their silo. "These bastards are good," John-Pierre muttered to himself as he pointed to the infrared images of Vigo, Charlie and Anthony jogging towards the main silo entrance. "Only three," he asked himself. "Either they're nuts or they've got an edge we don't know about. Either way, they'll be here in about five minutes."

"So what do we do now?" Danielle asked as she picked up two handfuls of self-welding braces.

John-Pierre picked up the remaining self-welding braces. "Time to lock you in the turret, princess. Joe and I will set up a crossfire at this end of the tunnel, leading to the storage room. That should hold them for a while. Hopefully long enough for the Turks to get here."

As they walked up the stairs John-Pierre asked, "If the worst happens, what about the boy?"

"You mean the client," she replied as they finished climbing the stairs.

"No, I meant the boy."

"You know our orders," Danielle sighed. "If it comes to that, he's not to be taken alive."

"Is that really necessary?"

"I do as I'm told, John-Pierre," she said as she placed the self-welding braces inside the crew quarters next to the door. "Will you?"

He set his stack down next to hers and stood up. "That's why you pay me the big bucks," he replied unceremoniously as he looked across the room at Governor Johnston, sitting in a metal chair next to the boy's bed. His ashen face and panicked eyes told the whole story.

Standing back away from the door, he watched as Danielle pushed it closed and spun the locking lugs into place. He shook his head for a moment, wondering how people such as these could have brought about world peace, and then decided to see what Joe was up to in the engineering level.

VIGO WAS THE first to wind his way down the four flights of stairs to the bottom of the elevator shaft. Behind him were Charlie and Anthony. At the second landing, Anthony flipped the VR visor back over his face. There had been no changes or major movements since they entered the center of the complex. He spoke into his mic, "No changes, but keep in mind the sensorbots are a bit slow on the refresh."

He lifted the VR visor, pointed his flashlight at the ceiling and ran the beam from the top of the shaft to the simple open elevator platform at the bottom. All appeared in order and once power was returned they'd use the elevator to bring Russell to the surface. A wave of anger at what De Bono and Johnston were doing to his son and everyone else filled him with rage. He gripped the railing. "Control this, Anthony," he commanded himself in a whisper as his blood began to boil. "Control this."

JOE BOUNDED UP the stairs from engineering level. "Cat, I think I can seal the inner blast door. I've found an old power lead and rerouted it to the breaker box at the end of the accessway tunnel at the storage room. There's no way they can get through that in time."

"Then all we have to do is to sit tight and wait for the Turks to grind them into hamburger."

"That's the plan, Cat."

"But can't we activate it from here?"

"Now, the power feed is from the main blast doors topside. I also figured out how they did it."

"How?"

"It didn't make sense till I traced the fail-over circuit. I kept seeing a steady heartbeat from the load regulator that didn't make sense; that is unless someone has hacked our control systems. Man, nobody knew about the fail-over because I personally installed it last week."

"Which means that we've been set up by the same people we're working for," John-Pierre spat. "But they're already coming down the central stairwell."

"We've got just enough time," Joe said in a hurried voice. "I've got to go to the end of the tunnel to bypass the load regulator source."

"Let's go."

Joe put a hand on John-Pierre's shoulder. "No my friend, there is no point in both of us exposing ourselves in the tunnel. I'll go alone. You cover me."

John-Pierre quickly tossed the risks through his mind. If he and Joe could set up a cross fire at the control room end of the tunnel, they'd probably be able to hold off the assault team until the door to it was reinforced, which in turn would buy them more time. Given the situation, that would have been his first choice but now things had changed. They'd been betrayed, which meant that Joe's idea to bypass the power on the inner blast door had already been anticipated. Either way, their prospects stunk. "OK, Joe, be quick. I'll cover you from here."

ANTHONY FINALLY REACHED the bottom of the staircase and found Vigo and Charlie waiting for him in the storage room. At the far end of the room, a large huge blast door hung open. Closed, it would form a barrier between the interior of the complex and the accessway tunnel to the control room.

Thankfully, the nanobots had not neutralized the control mechanisms controlling the blast door motors; otherwise, the mission would have failed at this very point. As they moved through the storage room, he studied the massive strength of the blast door and felt a sense of relief that Tanya and Henry had helped him to trust LeBlanc.

Anthony flipped his VR visor back over his eyes. He could see from the delayed sensorbots that the merc on the engineering room level had returned to the control room. He pointed his hand directly ahead and whispered. "Go straight ahead to the end of the storage room and turn to our left facing the access tunnel."

The storage room was a clutter of abandoned junk and obsolete equipment, and moving through it was difficult in the dim reddish light.

Anthony hid behind a stack of large barrels in sight of the access tunnel while Vigo and Charlie worked their way to either side of the tunnel and slipped on his VR visor again. "Vigo, we've got one coming through the tunnel our way."

Vigo signaled to Charlie to cover him and raised his assault Heckler & Koch MP-7 10mm caseless sub-machinegun. In one blurring motion, Vigo rolled down to the floor before the access tunnel entrance and sprayed the small confined area with deadly hollow point rounds.

The burst caught Joe Napolitano in chest. As he fell, he squeezed the trigger of his Uzi spraying a return volley of .45 caliber rounds through the accessway and into the storage room. Crumpled on the floor, frothy red blood began spilling out of Joe's mouth as he tried to roll on his side for another shot. As he strained to lift his Uzi for another shot, the last thing he saw was the intense glow of

Vigo's laser pointer as a single, well-aimed round struck between his eyes with a final blinding flash of white light.

Vigo rolled back away from the door and noticed Charlie's pained breathing despite the ringing in his ears from the report of the Uzi. "You OK son?" he whispered out loud.

"Fucking ricochet," Charlie moaned. "Got me in the leg. Hurts like hell." Vigo rolled back enough to see that the access way was empty and then rolled the rest of the way to Charlie's side of the door.

"Anthony, cover the tunnel," he ordered.

Anthony nodded. Positioning himself in a dark shadow cast by two large crates, he drew a bead on the tunnel with his pistol as Vigo examined Charlie's wound. The partially spent bullet had partially sliced the femoral artery in Charlie's right leg and buried itself in his femur, halfway between the hip and the knee. With each beat of Charlie's heart, more of his blood spurted out of the wound. "You took a bad one," Vigo whispered. "But you'll live. Hold your finger here while I set a tourniquet."

Vigo unfastened his belt and using a piece of steel tubing fashioned a homemade tourniquet above the wound, tightening it until the bleeding finally stopped. He checked his watch for the time and dipping his finger in the pool of blood next to Charlie's leg, used it to write the time on his head. "I got the bleeding stopped for now. Just remember to ease up on this tourniquet for a bit, every twenty minutes if this thing goes long. Can you do that?" He asked.

"No problem," Charlie replied breathing heavily. "Hey look, Sarge, I can't move but if you'll drag me over by Anthony I can at least give you some cover fire if you need it."

"I'm not sure I want to move you."

"Yeah, well I'm just a worthless lump of shit here. If you move me to someplace useful, at least I'll be a semi-worthless lump of shit."

Vigo held up his hand. "How many fingers am I holding up?"

Charlie squinted his eyes to see through the murky red glow of the emergency lights. "Three."

"OK son. I know you'll do your best," he said as he prepared to move him.

Just at that moment, the red emergency lights at the far end of the tunnel blinked out. Charlie's pained voice had carried through the tunnel and John-Pierre then knew it would be two on one — just his kind of odds for a close-up knife fight. It would also buy him enough time to seal the inner door so he could sit comfortably waiting for the Turks to arrive.

What John-Pierre could not have known, was that by switching off the emergency lights, he'd also partially blinded LeBlanc's sensorbots such that his catlike movements were now undetectable.

"Vigo," Anthony said as he finished dragging Charlie to his side. "We've basically lost the sensorbots. The last thing I could see was one figure moving quickly in the control room before I lost him. Is it time to call for backup?"

"Stop thinking like a cop, or I'll shove a donut in your mug," Vigo hissed. "Now be still." He flipped up his night vision monocle and let his eyes adjust to the darkness in the tunnel. Scanning quickly from side-to-side to take advantage of his peripheral vision, Vigo could see that the computer displays on the main control room console were still lit. Whoever was left in there had not turned them off, indicating that he or she was working in the dark with night vision assistance. Otherwise, the console displays would have been shut down along with the emergency lights. Whoever was waiting for them still needed a modicum of light and therein was their advantage. Vigo quickly formulated his plan.

"Charlie," he whispered. "Do you think you can run Anthony's VR headset?"

"Yeah sure," the young sergeant said with a pained grunt.

"Good. Switch your helmet with Anthony and give him your HK."

"You got it," Charlie replied as he handed his Heckler & Koch MP-7 10mm caseless sub-machinegun and a magazine pouch to Anthony and unfastened his chinstrap.

Anthony took the helmet and weapon and went to hand Charlie his pistol. "No; you keep it," Charlie said refusing the pistol. He patted his holster, "I've got my own."

As Anthony adjusted Charlie's helmet and night vision monocle for his own head, Charlie watched Vigo attach a powerful IR illuminator light to the stock of his HK, capable of casting a bright beam for 200 yards that would be undetectable to an unaided human eye. He unclipped his own IR illuminator, fastened it to Anthony's HK as well and checked the silencer to be sure it was snug and secure. With their gear in order, Vigo had Charlie test his VR headset and microphone. Everything was ready.

"Now here's the drill, ladies," Vigo said softly. "As soon as we're up alongside the access way I'll take out the emergency lights on this side. No point in us advertising ourselves any more than we need to. After that, we'll move in. Anthony, stay a few feet behind me. When you see me lie down and make a fist, I want you to empty your HK into the computer displays. If you can take them all out, whoever is in there will be operating in the dark. Charlie, once we're close enough to the control room side of the tunnel you should start to get usable images again so keep telling us what you're seeing, no matter what it is."

"Got it," Charlie replied.

"Follow a few feet behind and when I see your fist, kneel and take out the computer displays," Anthony added.

"OK, ladies, it's show time."

Vigo and Anthony moved through the storage room out of view of the tunnel and positioned themselves next to the door. Vigo then pulled an aluminum telescoping rod and mirror from his shirt pocket, stretched the rod out to its full one-meter length and snapped a small mirror to the end. He then set the selector of his HK to the single round burst setting and methodically shot out the emergency lamps in the storage room that would backlight them. "Turn on your illuminator Anthony," he said switching on his own as well. "We're going in Charlie," he announced.

With Anthony following just behind him, Vigo moved at a quick but methodical pace through the tunnel scanning the control room ahead for any sign of a threat. Three-fourths of the way into the tunnel, the computer displays on the console came into clear view. He laid himself down and, scanned the room ahead one more time, then raised his fist.

Anthony set the selector on his HK to the three round burst setting and with a sequence of well aimed shots took out the computer displays in a shower of glass and sparks, leaving the control devoid of light except for the an occasional lighted button on the shattered console.

The moment the caseless rounds flew through the control room, John-Pierre darted for the spot from where he planned to spring his attack without revealing himself to the attackers in the tunnel, who no doubt were well equipped with night light equipment.

Vigo used hand signals to tell Anthony to remain in position and to cover him. Anthony acknowledged the order with a firm nod and Vigo began crawling through the tunnel until he was half a meter away from the opening. Pushing the extending rod with the mirror past the opening, he began searching the sides and corners of the small control room alongside the accessway wall.

"Sarge," Charlie whispered into his microphone. "I briefly saw something move. Damn, it was fast! I can't see anything now, so my guess is that he's a level above you. You better stay clear of the stairwell."

Vigo tapped his microphone twice to acknowledge the message, collapsed the rod while folding back the mirror and slipped it back into his pocket. With his left hand free again, he pulled a flash grenade from his web belt and turned his head towards Anthony, signaling him to cover his eyes. Anthony nodded and placed a hand over his eyes and night vision lens as Vigo switched his HK to full automatic.

Vigo estimated the number of steps it would take to cross the interior of the room to a spot under the console, then pulled the pin from the flash grenade with his teeth and threw it as far back into the control room as he could and covered his eyes and night vision lens with his hand. Three second later, the grenade went off with a muted bang filling the control room with a blinding flash of white light. He then jumped to his feet and bolted through the tunnel opening spraying a hail of rounds into the room as he rolled under the console.

"I've got you in the control room," Vigo could hear Charlie say over his headset. "Still no sign of anyone else."

"Looks like you were right Charlie," Vigo acknowledged. "He must be on one of the other levels. OK, Anthony, I'll cover the stairwell so move in and keep your eyes peeled."

Anthony moved carefully through the tunnel sweeping the muzzle of his HK back and forth as he stepped through the tunnel into the room, he could hear a swoosh of air from behind and then the deadly pressure of a stick of a cold steel and titanium blade at his throat. Whoever was at the other end of the razor-sharp knife, neither he, nor Vigo, who was now focused on the stairwell leading up to the crew quarters, had seen him coming.

Anthony froze as the knife pressed his throat and he felt the blunt tip of a pistol muzzle slipping under the lower edge of his bulletproof vest, coming to rest against the base of his spine. Totally compromised, he could feel the breath of his attacker on the back of his neck, as he held him within a moment of his life.

John-Pierre leaned closely and whispered in his ear. "Do as I say, and you may just live." The voice has an unmistakable French accent. It was one of the Euro mercs.

The moment Vigo heard John-Pierre's hushed voice he moved out from under the console and crouched above the broken computer displays with his HK aimed in Anthony's direction. He could see Anthony frozen in place, with a hollow-ground tactical knife to his throat. Using Anthony's own body for cover, the attacker had carefully placed Anthony between himself and the muzzle of Vigo's HK. It was a standoff.

Anthony stood there feeling like a hopeless idiot but knew that if the man wanted to kill him that he would have done so already. "I won't do anything stupid," Anthony said tensely. "What do you want?"

"Tell your friends to pull back and I'll let you live," John-Pierre said in a low menacing tone.

Vigo could see that whoever the man with a knife to Anthony's throat was, was holding all the cards now. Instead of acting, he was talking. Perhaps there was room to maneuver, but not by simply throwing in the towel. "Whoever you are, you're not going to win," Vigo said in a commanding voice. "But, you can live."

John-Pierre immediately recognized the old familiar voice booming out at him from the dark. "Is that you Colonel Jones, old friend?"

"Durand," Vigo blurted out. "John-Pierre Durand. What in the hell are you doing here?"

"I could ask the same of you."

John-Pierre had freelanced for Vigo on several covert ops and he knew full well what Vigo could do. From experience, Vigo had come to respect John-Pierre as a dedicated pro whose only interest was his reputation for success, regardless of who hired him. A natural with a knife, he was the deadliest man with a knife he'd ever known. He could kill Anthony in the flick of an eye and perhaps live long enough to kill again. "You know me,

John-Pierre. You know I cannot just let you kill him and walk away."

"I do not care about your friend, but I would have to kill you, Colonel."

"So what if I dispense with the formalities and just shoot at the both of you. He's the one wearing a bulletproof vest so odds are he'll be the one to survive. The jig is up, John-Pierre. Let him go and get out of our way and I'll let you walk out of here a free man."

"That would be very foolish of you Colonel. You know I keep a scalpel sharp edge on my knives and this one is so very close to your friend's carotid artery that all it will take is a simple twitch to end his life."

"I'll give you that, but why not just walk out of here a free man? You know I'm good for my word; besides, this is not a sanctioned op. Who is to tell me differently?"

John-Pierre slipped out a menacing laugh. "You, Mr. Apple Pie America, are running an unsanctioned op. My, my, my Colonel, you've gone and become a freelancer. Most interesting. Then you'll also understand that my client is going to pay me a very handsome bonus to stop your little charade. Enough to retire on and live like a gentleman for a change. I'm not about to throw that away so quickly."

During the exchange between Vigo and John-Pierre, Anthony had slowly inched his hand upwards towards Durand's knife hand. In one quick move, he pressed his fingertips against the top of Durand's hand.

John-Pierre felt the tap and instinctively moved to slash Jarman's throat but to his sudden surprise found that his was frozen in place and radiating with a tingling energy that quickly moved up through his arm and across his shoulders. Durand fought to regain control of his body as the energy continued to move through his neck and into his head. In a blinding moment, he felt a new sense of awareness and realized that he was now standing just in front of his body and it seems that time was almost frozen.

He looked about and the room was perfectly lit and free of shadows.

Stunned by his new sense of vision, he heard a voice call from behind him. "John-Pierre." He turned and could see Anthony standing a few feet behind him.

"H… Ha... How…" he stammered.

"You mean how did I do this?" Anthony replied calmly.

"Oui. Am I dead? Have you killed me? Am I dreaming?"

"No, you're not dreaming. This is as real as it gets. Are you dead? Let's just say that you're halfway there."

"And why are you doing this to me?"

"I'm trying to save your life."

John-Pierre laughed. "I think it is you who is trying to save your own life. Just look over at Vigo who now appears frozen in time. I have a gun to your back, a knife to your throat and I'm fast enough to kill you both before he can fire his weapons. He knows it. I see it in his eyes now. I'm certain of it."

"Perhaps not but come with me and see for yourself."

John-Pierre followed Anthony as he walked around Vigo frozen figure.

"See for yourself. Go look through the gun sight."

The offer made him curious, and Durand found it amazingly easy to move through the young man's body and looked for himself. It was perfectly aimed to place the first bullet through his exposed right eye. "My God," he exclaimed.

"Now look at his trigger finger and the firing mechanism inside his weapon," Anthony said. John-Pierre leaned over and studied Vigo's hand on the HK grip. Vigo already had the trigger pulled back so close to the point of release that all it would take minute flick of his finger to fire the weapon.

"The fear you see in his eyes is real John-Pierre, because he does not know that I can continue to immobilize your hand even after he shoots. And, he will take that shot in just a moment of time because he knows that your knife is actually forced against my protective neck collar and he's counting on it to stop your blade from slicing my throat."

In the soft, brilliant light that now seemed to fill the control room, John-Pierre could see the thin collar around Anthony's neck to prevent him from being garroted to death. Would it stop a determined slice of a scalpel-sharp blade? John-Pierre realized that it was the gun he was now holding against Anthony's back that presented the greatest threat.

"John-Pierre, can I ask you for a small favor in this tiny slice of time I've created for you?"

"Yes, I suppose," He replied hesitatingly.

"I want you to sense your feelings right now."

"What?"

"What are you feeling, John-Pierre?"

Durand paused for a moment and then slowly responded. "I think I feel at peace, but I have been angry for so much of my life I'm not sure. Is this what it is like when you're dead?"

"In part, yes. However, this does not have to be your time John-Pierre."

"Why?"

"Because if it were, your family would be here to help you across. But as you can see, we're alone."

"What do you want of me," Durand pleaded. "What!"

Anthony smiled and held out his hands. "All I want you to do, John-Pierre, is to look into your own soul for the right answer."

"And what will I find?"

"Truth."

John-Pierre paused and searched within himself. Finally, he said, "I know I don't want to waste your life. Nor to I want to waste mine."

"And what do you want now?"

"I never want to be angry with life again. Nor to be driven by hate." He turned to look at himself. "Look at me.

I became a pitiful monster willing to sell his soul for a handful of currency. I can never go back to that life now. Not after feeling what I'm feeling. I want my life to have a purpose. I am not who I was before and I could never, nor would I ever want to be that again."

Anthony came closer. "Then we must work closely together to save both of our lives. I will return you to your body and stay here with Vigo to slow him down long enough for you to change things. Do you understand what I mean?"

"Yes, but can you trust me? Why should you trust me?"

"Because in every man's soul there is an ounce of goodness John-Pierre and you've found yours. Some people think it takes a life of prayer to change but all it really takes is just a tiny sliver of time, time enough to find that ounce of goodness. From there, all things change."

"If this doesn't work, I want to thank you," John-Pierre said with sincere gratitude.

Anthony nodded with a smile and John-Pierre suddenly found himself facing Vigo again. He dropped his knife as Vigo strained in a futile attempt pull the trigger of his HK to the release point. "Don't shoot," John-Pierre blurted out into the darkness as his blade clanked on the concrete floor. "I'll help you, old friend."

John-Pierre then stepped away from behind Anthony and let his pistol dangle on his finger tip by its trigger guard as he held it up in clear view. For all of his adult life, Durand had never feared death because he never really loved it. Now, he was no longer afraid of death but for different reasons. If this was his time, he knew he would meet it the right way.

"Don't shoot Vigo," Anthony ordered as he opened his eyes. "OK everyone, let's just take a deep breath and relax."

"Switch the emergency lights back on, Durand," Vigo ordered keeping the muzzle of his HK trained on the man's head.

"Press the yellow button on the console next to you," he replied. Vigo glanced down quickly, found the button and pressed it.

As the reddish lights popped back on, Anthony began to sag. John-Pierre caught him and sat him down on a rolling chair. "I'll be OK in a minute," Anthony said as his vision cleared. "Jean-Pierre, who else is in here?"

"Governor Johnston and his secretary Danielle Peters. They are with the boy in the room upstairs. You already killed Joe Napolitano in the access way."

"So why are they here?" Vigo asked.

"They arrived early this morning. They plan to move the boy out of the country and they were preparing him for travel in a portable biostasis chamber. If you had come a few hours later, all this would have been for nothing. What about the others on top?"

"They're all dead except Darkazani," Anthony replied.

"Tell us about the woman."

"Danielle Peters. A pretty number she is, but deadly as a viper. The minute she thinks you've got any chance of succeeding, she'll kill the boy."

"Do you know who the boy is John-Pierre," Vigo asked. John-Pierre shrugged his shoulders to show that he didn't know. "Well then, I'll tell. He is Anthony's son, and De Bono had him kidnapped. His mother and stepfather were killed in the process."

Durand held his hands out towards Anthony with a pained expression. "I'm so sorry. I didn't know, but now I truly understand why you are here. I would do the same. How can you ever forgive me for this?"

"Only you can forgive yourself John-Pierre." Anthony replied. "What happened before is in the past now and this is your moment in time to choose a new future."

John-Pierre's head rose bravely with a renewed sense of purpose. "Then I choose to give my life to the protection of you and your family from this day forward."

"That is more than I can ask for," Anthony protested.

"It is not for you to accept, Anthony, it is for me to decide and this is my choice."

Vigo's eyes shot back and forth between the two men with consternation. "I don't believe what I'm hearing!" he exclaimed as he continued to keep his HK trained on Durand.

Anthony turned to him with a pained expression his face. "It's on the level Vigo, so please put the gun down and let's work together to save Russell."

"His name is Russell," John-Pierre repeated. Anthony nodded. "Then I must do it! Only I can prevent this Danielle Peters woman from killing him. You must trust me   in   this!"

CHAPTER 27

DEATH IN THE SILO

DURING THE ASSAULT on the tunnel, Anthony had shot out the console computer that had been connected to the primary feed from the Spitfire UHF Manpack Terminal antenna. John-Pierre needed to see what, if anything, Danielle Peters and Governor Johnston were doing in the crew quarters upstairs and examined the internally powered signal splitter. He found it was still working, which meant they were able to remotely operate the Spitfire connection with the MILSATCOM satellites overhead.

He opened a small wall locker and found a spare webpad, connected it to the splitter and switched it on. "Let's see what they're doing up there," he said under his breath.

Two images frames appeared side-by-side. First was an overhead satellite view of the silo field. At the northern edge of the field, they could see a column of ten Bradley M3 tracked armored fighting vehicles. Carrying six fully equipped infantry men each, the Bradley's were also equipped with Boeing M242 Bushmaster chain guns, capable of firing up to 500 rounds of armor piercing 25mm depleted uranium per minute. "This doesn't make sense," John-Pierre glanced back at Vigo and wondered out loud. "The Bradley can travel at speeds up to sixty-six kilometers per hours. So why are they crawling along at just twenty kilometers per hour?"

Vigo ignored the question until Anthony spoke up. "Tell him, Vigo."

"Because they know what your people were doing down here John-Pierre and they're in no particular hurry to save your butts."

John-Pierre nodded remembering Joe's warning that there was a traitor in De Bono's organization. "I don't care why. I just needed to know, and now I know what to do."

Anthony pointed at the second video frame on the webpad. "What about the other channel?" The status line showed an active link but the screen was filled with a blue hatch pattern indicating a secure transmission lock.

"It is on a secure link and keyed to the vital signs monitor mounted over Russell's bed. Obviously, Danielle or the Governor is having a dialogue with someone else, but there is no way to see what they are saying. We can't even tap into the webcam in the vital signs monitor to see what they're doing in the room."

"But can they see the satellite feed in there?" Vigo asked.

"Yes, but I doubt they would see that the armored column from Fort Hood is moving so slowly. That takes a practiced eye. Johnston wouldn't understand it, but Danielle Peters might. To be sure, I'll tell them something just in case."

"Can they hear us upstairs?"

John-Pierre turned around and leaned up against the edge of the console. "No. You already shot out the intercom, and between the ventilation system and acoustical tiles here in the control room and the crew quarters steel door upstairs, they're deaf. They're probably sitting up there waiting for you to begin cutting through the door and hoping the Turkish Peacekeepers get here from Houston in time."

"Turkish Peacekeepers?" Vigo sighed. "How much time do we have?"

"Thirty minutes minimum, forty-five minutes at the max. They would have been here earlier but there was some foul-up along the way. Johnston was really pissed. But I think the armored column from Fort Hood will get here long before that, even though they're advancing at a snail's pace."

"Don't worry about them," Vigo replied. "We need to set our timing on the Turks. If we can get to the boy within the next five minutes, we'll be in good shape. Any longer than that will make it a close call. We've also got a wounded man back out in the storage room. Your other man caught him in the leg and he's lost a lot of blood. We need to get the boy and take care of our wounded, and we need to do it fast, so if you have a plan, John-Pierre, I'd like to hear it right now. If not, I'm still running the show."

"Give me a moment," John-Pierre asked as he walked to the base of the stairs and looked up, methodically reviewing the situation point-by-point in his mind. It only took a matter of seconds for a plan to form in his mind before he turned to face Vigo and Anthony.

"The most important thing we have to do is to get Danielle Peters to open the crew quarters door from the inside. It is half-inch hardened steel, and she's got a stack of self-welding braces next to the door, which means she can hold us off until the Turks get here. Convincing her to open the door is the most critical step. We know she can see the column moving in from Fort Hood, but your people topside do not seem to be aware of this, so we need to stage a rear guard action. I need you to contact your people topside and tell them to spit their forces. Send a small contingent down through the main entrance with your medical team. Then, send the rest north towards the column coming down from Fort Hood, and make it look like they are setting up an ambush."

"That would look suicidal, wouldn't it?" Anthony asked.

"You wouldn't be here if you weren't already suicidal," John-Pierre quipped.

Vigo chuckled. "You've got a point, there," he admitted. "Anthony, get the people topside on this immediately, and tell Dr. Boole as much as you can about Charlie's condition. Then, tell the Israelis to take the SUVs and head north to lay an ambush, along with Darkazani and their wounded. Once we have Russell, we'll signal them to hightail it to the Flying Circus, telling them that we'll find our own way out. They already have an arranged flight corridor all the way to Mexico. While you're doing that, I'm going to go over the crew quarters layout with John-Pierre."

AS SOON AS the emergency lights had come back on, Danielle and Johnston finished moving Russell to the portable biostasis chamber, and Antonio De Bono's image appeared in the secure lock video frame. From the security dome in his office in Geneva, De Bono zoomed out the webpad camera on the bezel of the wall mounted vital signs monitor to reveal a wide view of the entire crew quarters' room. As Danielle and Johnston began to seal the chamber he said, "Leave it open in case you have to terminate the boy."

His voice caught them both by surprise. Johnston rose and faced the monitor. "Antonio, we lost our communications for a while. We can't hear a thing in here except some occasional muffled gunfire." Johnston was pale with fright.

"The Turks and the Americans are both on their way," De Bono replied. "I just finished speaking with Colonel Bazoglu. They will be there in half an hour, but I think the Americans will be there before then. How long can you hold out in there?"

Danielle stood up and walked to the monitor. "I see the Americans moving in now, Secretary General. Give me a moment." She tapped a few times on the meter-wide display and zoomed the surveillance satellite camera to a close shot of the area above them. The display showed four figures entering the main access to the silo with carrying large satchels as the two SUVs started north towards the oncoming Americans. "Secretary General, my guess is that the first team is dead or stalled and they've called in reinforcements while the rest most likely plan to stall the Americans. If they were here in the control room already, we'd know it by now. I'd say our odds of holding them off till the Turks get here are fifty-fifty."

"Can't you get them here any sooner?" Johnston pleaded.

De Bono shook his head. "Colonel Bazoglu is pushing it as hard as he can. They're flying here at maximum speed, and one of their aircraft has already had to turn back due to an engine failure. As for the Americans, I wouldn't trust them. Their President was very reluctant to send in his troops. You've got to hold out till Bazoglu and his men get there."

"Thanks to the mercs," Danielle said, "We've still got a few tricks up our sleeves."

JOHN-PIERRE CLIMBED the stairs halfway up toward the crew quarters and motioned for Anthony and Vigo to remain at the top of the stairs, out sight from the crew quarters' entrance. After they moved back, leaning against the galley wall, he knocked on the steel door to the crew quarters and shouted through the door, "Are you OK in there?"

A huge wave of relief came over Danielle and Johnston. "Stay here next to the monitor," she ordered, ran across the room to the door, and shouted in reply, "Yes, we're OK in here. What is happening on your end?"

"Do you want the good news first," John-Pierre replied sardonically.

Danielle sagged. "Don't give me this macho crap right now."

"Does the governor have my bonus check ready? I believe the agreed amount is one million Euros tax free."

Danielle laid her forehead against the door and muttered to herself, "Men!" She sighed. "That's the deal, but you haven't earned it yet, so let's stop playing games," she shouted through the door.

She could hear John-Pierre laugh through the door. As much as it annoyed her, it also gave her comfort to hear that he felt secure enough in his position to laugh at a moment like this.

"OK, Danielle. First, the good news. Joe managed to seal the inner blast door between the accessway tunnel and the storage room. It seems we're up against British SAS and he managed to kill one before they got him. The other two made it into the tunnel as the blast door was closing and I killed them both in the control room. That's why the emergency lights were off for a while. You could say I like knife fighting in the dark."

Johnston and De Bono overheard the conversation from the other end of the room. "The Americans betrayed us," De Bono hissed loud enough for Danielle to hear him as she stood next to the door. "And now they're using their English friends to do their dirty work for them. Forget the Americans. They will not help us!"

Danielle faced the door again. "What's the bad news John-Pierre?"

"They've just started cutting on the inner blast door with a laser torch. That door is two inches thick and they'll be through it in ten minutes. Given this door is only a half inch thick, they'll be able to lase through it like a hot knife through butter. We've got to slow them down Danielle."

She looked over at the two stacks of self-welding braces sitting on the floor next to the door. "What about the braces?"

"They'll buy us more time if we use them at the inner blast door than here. After we get them in place, you and I can set up a cross-fire on the tunnel from here in the control room. I think this will buy us much more time than our original plan, but you're the boss. The choice is yours."

"Do as he says," Johnston blurted out.

Still facing the door, Danielle looked back over her shoulder at him with a sneer. "Will you just shut up and let me think about it for a moment?"

Johnston picked up his Uzi and trained it on her. "You don't tell me when to shut up, bitch. Now get out there, and do as the man says. Besides you made him the boss."

"Stop this fighting!" De Bono screamed as Danielle used her body to conceal that she was drawing her pistol. "She's right about one thing, Merl, you need to shut up." De Bono said in a firm tone. "Danielle, your only hope is the Turks. The Americans are going to stand there and do nothing. I think you try and stop them at the inner blast door as your merc suggests."

Even though every instinct in her body screamed for her to keep the door shut, a suggestion from the Secretary General was as good as a direct order and she knew it. With a resigned look, she turned her head to face the door and shouted, "Wait there!"

DANIELLE UNLOCKED THE door and pulled it open partway, just enough for her to squeeze through the door. Stepping around to the opening with her pistol at the ready, she immediately saw John-Pierre's smiling face. As her eye glanced downward, she saw him holding a gun on her just in time to see him pull the trigger. She caught the full force of the point blank range impact as John Pierre's hollow-point .40 caliber bullet ripped through her liver in a ball of fire. As the shot echoed off the walls, the impact sent her spinning backwards and sprawling onto the floor. With a pained breath, she lifted her pistol to shoot, when John-Pierre's second shot cut through the center of her throat, shattering her spinal cord in a blinding moment of death.

Watching in Geneva through the webcam on the wall mounted vital signs monitor, De Bono immediately cut his own video feed and the usual health status indicators immediately appeared on the monitor as he and Johnston looked on in horror.

In what seemed like a blur of movement, they watched John-Pierre kick open the door as his eye darted immediately to Johnston's gun hand.

John-Pierre could see Johnston beginning to squeeze the trigger of his Uzi and snap rolled back against the outer wall of the crew quarters. Expecting a hail of .45 caliber bullets to follow him out of the room, all he heard instead was frantic clicking sounds as Johnston tried to fire his Uzi.

In a single swift motion, John Pierre dropped to his knee and facing the interior of the room, trained his pistol on Johnston's face. "Governor, you forgot the safety, and if I see your finger move once again, I'll have to kill you."

Johnston froze as Vigo and Anthony moved into position behind Durand. "Now, moving very slowly," John Pierre said in a calm, soothing voice, "I want you to put your weapon down on the floor and then stand up with your hands on your head." Johnston remained paralyzed with fear. "Do you understand me?"

The terrified UNE governor nodded in acknowledgement, then slowly knelt down, and laid the Uzi the floor. "Oh God, please don't kill me," he begged as he stood up with hands clasped behind his head.

Anthony and Vigo bolted into the room as John-Pierre continued to train his gun on Johnston. Anthony saw Russell lying unconscious in a biostasis chamber, connected to a maze of I.V. tubes and sensor leads. The anger that had been raging inside him exploded. Kicking Johnston's Uzi under the bed, he grabbed the terrified man by the collar. "You filthy bastard!" he screamed as he pummeled Johnston's face, fracturing his skull and shattering his jaw on both sides and then threw the unconscious man to the floor with disgust.

Vigo jumped behind Anthony, holding his arms. "That's enough, Anthony! That's enough!"

As Anthony stood trembling with rage, De Bono's appeared on the wall monitor as he shouted at them, "I saw that! I saw it all!"

All eyes flew to De Bono's red-faced image on the monitor. "You have been a thorn in my side for too long now," he spat. "I might have offered you a chance, but not after this." De Bono leaned forward till his face filled the monitor. "Durand and Jones, you fucking traitors, you're both dead men! As for you, Jarman, I'll personally see to it that you'll spend the rest of your life in an asylum for the criminally insane while I deal with the rest of your friends."

"So, you've finally come out of the shadows, you miserable son-of-a-bitch," Anthony shot back angrily.

Vigo pushed Anthony aside and glared at De Bono. "You lost this round, De Bono, so be practical. There is no need for any further bloodshed or violence, so why not cut your losses short and just walk away. We'll do the same and nobody else will be the wiser for it."

De Bono laughed, "You are pathetic fools with nothing to bargain with and you want me to just let you walk away? Nonsense!"

"I'd think it over if I were you," Vigo replied firmly.

"There is nothing to think over," De Bono spat. "You and your traitorous friends are going to feel the pain of real power such as nobody on Earth could ever imagine."

"Let me restate our offer then," Vigo snarled. He squatted down and wrapping his arms around Johnston's chest picked the unconscious man up from the floor as easily as he would toss a bale of hay. Standing with one arm wrapped around Johnston's body, he let the governor's head fall limply on his shoulder. He then held out his free hand palm up, motioning to John Pierre.

The French-Canadian merc, who had worked enough times with Jones to understand the signal, drew his scalpel-sharp tactical knife and placed it in Vigo's outstretched hand.

Vigo turned the blade straight up towards the ceiling and dug the tip of the hollow-ground knife into the soft tissue of Johnston's lower jaw. "Wake up, you pathetic piece of shit," he whispered in the man's ear with an ugly growl as he drew blood with the tip of the titanium blade.

Johnston's eyes fluttered as he moaned. As he instinctively tried to straighten his head, the soft tissue of his lower jaw pressed down on the tip of Vigo's blade. The man's eyes searched the room with panic as he began drawing excited breaths.

"We know your boy, here, assassinated Senator Connie Chavez," Vigo said with a mean, purposeful stare.

"I didn't do it," Johnston whispered aloud.

"The pen with the gold clip was a dead giveaway," Vigo whispered back. Johnston began trembling uncontrollably and his breathing became shallow and frantic as beads of sweat began streaming down the sides of his face.

"This is my last offer, De Bono," Vigo said slowly as Anthony and John Pierre watched with breathless suspense. "It ends here and now and we all walk away. Or, it becomes a blood fight to the finish. What's your answer?"

De Bono's lip quivered as he watched them from the personal safety of his security dome in Geneva. "You are as pathetic as Johnston. I cannot stop you from killing him, and even if you did, he is worthless to me now. Release him and you'll die painlessly. Kill him and you'll spend years begging for death. Either way, you can take your offer to hell for all I'm concerned."

Vigo's eyes glared. "This is for Connie," he said as he thrust the knife up through Johnston's jaw into his head. Johnston's eyes rolled and his body began to spasm as blood began to flow past his lips. Vigo waited a few moments before twisting the blade sharply causing Johnston's body to go limp in death. He then slowly withdrew the knife allowing Johnston's body to sink to the floor at his feet.

Stepping over Johnston's lifeless body, he took hold of the Spitfire cable and, holding up the bloody blade for De Bono to see, said in a blood curdling dark tone, "You'll be looking into my eyes when I gut you like a fat goose. This I promise you." De Bono recoiled with wide, alarmed eyes as Vigo slashed the Spitfire cable in half.

Anthony smiled at Vigo. "Did you really mean that?"

"Ah what the hell," he grumbled. "Let's get the boy and go. We're outta here."

LEBLANC HAD MANAGED to turn all the power systems back on in the silo, including the simple lift elevator that was now rising up to the first level with Ramona kneeling next to Charlie lying unconscious on a stretcher. The elevator came to a jerking halt and she looked up to see a squad of American soldiers surrounding Jeffrey, pointing their rifles at her.

"Put your guns down"; LeBlanc ordered. "These are our people. I told you, the silo is secure." The young squad leader standing next to him ordered his men to put down their weapons and called for his medics.

"Holy hell, Jeffrey," Ramona exclaimed. "What's going on?"

"The cavalry has arrived and the Israelis are on their way to the airport," he beamed. "How is Charlie?"

"It's a nasty wound, and he's lost a lot of blood, but he'll be OK as long as we can get him to a hospital in time."

"You got it," the squad leader replied as two medics arrived. The squad leader had them pick up Charlie's stretcher while Ramona followed alongside, holding a bag of synthetic blood above the wounded orderly's chest. "We've got a chopper on the way," The squad leader said as he pointed towards his Bradley, "I suggest you folks take him inside our M3."

"Thanks sergeant," she said as they trotted towards the gaping, open hatch of the fighting vehicle.

Jeffrey watched them for moment and then turned his attention back upon the squad leader. "The Turks are about twelve minutes out so we need to get rolling. We have a sick boy down there in a biostasis chamber. We'll need your help getting him out of the silo. And be careful not to disturb anything down there. It's a crime scene now."

"You heard the man," the squad leader barked. "Sling arms and follow on me," he ordered as he stepped onto the elevator.

As Jeffrey watched the elevator sink down into the shaft, he heard the familiar sound of a Blackhawk helicopter as it hovered above the main access road beyond the guardhouse. "Ramona," he shouted as they were beginning to load Charlie's stretcher and pointed in the direction of the helicopter. They paused, waiting for the helicopter to land and then started out towards it at a quick pace.

As soon as the Blackhawk's wheels touched down, General George Hennicker leapt out, followed by a young female officer and the Texas Highway Patrol commander. They met Ramona and the medics by the main gate of the guardhouse as the Texas Highway Patrol commander eyed the dead bodies of the Syrian guards.

"This post is too hot to take your wounded," Hennicker shouted over the noise. "Can he make it to Fort Sam in San Antonio?"

"He'll make it," Ramona answered. "I'd like to go with him."

"Of course. You'll fly straight to the hospital, and they've already got a surgical team standing by. I'm also sending Lieutenant Kathy Sullivan, here, along with you. We need to give you new identities, and she'll brief you on the details."

"Thanks, General," she replied as the medics loaded Charlie onto the Blackhawk.

"We take care of our own," he grinned. "Now get your ass out of here." Ramona chuckled and trotted off towards the waiting helicopter.

Hennicker nodded in the direction of the main silo entrance where Jeffrey LeBlanc was waiting beside the elevator shaft. As they walked quickly across the compound, they eyed the bullet holes in the buildings and the stray rounds that had peppered the cockpit of Governor Johnston's Osprey tilt rotor on the landing pad, rendering it useless in the pale predawn light.

Jeffrey watched the Blackhawk lift off from inside the main entrance as Hennicker and his companion entered. "Welcome, General," he said.

"Well, Mr. LeBlanc, it looks like you've had a busy morning. Let me introduce my friend here, Captain Ben Green of the Texas Highway Patrol."

Jeffrey shook hands with the tall, thick-shouldered police officer. "It's a pleasure to meet you."

Not one for banter, Green cut straight to the point. "So what do we have here, Mr. LeBlanc?"

Jeffrey nodded and pointed a finger up. "You'll find two bodies up there."

"I saw them coming in," Green confirmed.

LeBlanc pointed at the large portable building that had once served as the living quarters for the Syrians and Euro mercs. "A whole pack of dead bodies over there and only three bodies down in the silo, including UNE Governor Merl Johnston, his personal secretary, Danielle Peters and a Euro merc. In a few moments, we'll be bringing out a young boy. He was kidnapped by Johnston and Secretary General De Bono."

"No doubt they'll claim the boy was in protective custody," Green replied. "But I've seen enough to declare jurisdiction and to have this place protected as a crime scene." He unclipped the microphone from his shoulder lapel and held it to his mouth. "Put me through to the

Turkish Peacekeepers," he ordered as he switched on the radio's external speaker.

Hennicker and LeBlanc could here Green's communication center routing him through, and after a few minutes, they heard Colonel Bazoglu's voice over the din of his lead Osprey, acknowledging the call.

"Colonel Bazoglu, this is Captain Ben Green of the Texas Highway Patrol. I'm here at silo fourteen, and I'm declaring this a crime scene. The UNE no longer has jurisdiction, and we have matters well in hand, so I suggest you return to your base."

"Captain Green," Bazoglu replied, "Silo fourteen is the sovereign territory of the UNE, and I'm ordering you to withdraw immediately. We will arrive shortly and conduct our own investigation."

"Not so quick, colonel," Green shot back. "We've got clear evidence of a kidnapping and several murders here. I suggest you read the UNE treaty as ratified by the American Congress, because in these cases, local law enforcement authorities take precedence. This is my jurisdiction now, and I'm ordering you to return to your base."

"We have our orders directly from the Secretary General himself and we're coming in. You can take it up with him if you like." General Hennicker winked at Green.

"Standby," Green replied dryly as Hennicker inserted the earpiece of his mobile headset into his ear.

A few moments later, the threat warning lights in Bazoglu's lead Osprey lit up. Sitting in the cockpit just behind his pilots, Bazoglu could see that the radars of three Patriot Missile batteries at Fort Hood had just painted his aircraft and now had a definite lock on them.

"Are you insane?" Bazoglu voice shouted angrily over Green's radio as LeBlanc and Hennicker quietly chuckled.

"No, I'm not," Green replied in a steely voice. "I have jurisdiction in this matter, and it comes straight from the White House. If you try and enter this airspace, I'll order a missile launch, and if you think I can't, you're welcome to try your luck."

"This is an outrage!" Bazoglu barked back. "We know for a fact that Captain Anthony Jarman is there, and I have a warrant issued by an American judge to detain and transport Jarman to a psychiatric facility for the criminally insane. The man is dangerous, and I have direct orders from the Secretary General to get him."

"Not today, Bazoglu. If you don't like it, send me a nasty letter or something," Green replied, "but I will shoot your ass out of the air if you don't turn back right now!"

There was a long static filled pause on the radio as the Turkish colonel chewed on the situation. Finally, they heard a terse reply, "Fine, have it your way. Just remember; it's your funeral. Now stand down your missiles. We're returning to base. Bazoglu out."

Green clipped the microphone back on his shoulder lapel and shook his head. "Man, if this Jarman fellow is really here, my ass will be so far out on a limb right now, I hate to think of it."

Hennicker nodded as he put a finger to his earpiece, "They're turning back," he announced. He elbowed Green in the side. "Don't worry about it, I'm out on the same limb, and if those sons-of-bitches want to mix it up with us, they'll have to come through the President, and he is mighty pissed off about what has been happening here."

TANYA AND ANTHONY knelt beside Russell's biostasis chamber as Boole and Ann-Marie checked and rechecked the restraints, sensor feeds and IV tubes. "What do you think, doc," Anthony asked as he looked upon his son with a deeply pained expression, lovingly caressing his son's face.

"So far, I've only had time for a preliminary look at his records. The chamber data cartridge is pretty complete, and it looks like he's had good medical attention, but from what

I've seen so far, he's suffered a massive head injury. Frankly, I'm surprised that he's still alive."

Anthony sagged, and Tanya wrapped her arms around him, asking, "Is he well enough to be transported?"

"As well as he can be," Boole replied putting a hand on Anthony's forearm. "Anthony, we need to seal the chamber."

Anthony nodded; he and Tanya stood up together, watching silently as Ann-Marie lowered the lid of the chamber. As she snapped the locks into place, Boole tapped the control panel on the lid of the chamber to set the filtered, oxygen rich internal environment to a steady temperature.

"Fortunately," Boole said somberly, "this is one of the best biostasis chambers made, and it can support his body for another seven days without being serviced. Wherever you intend to take him now, you don't have to rush."

VIGO AND JOHN-PIERRE had been standing just outside the room. "Say doc, I have some men out here to help carry the chamber. Should I send them in?"

"We're just about ready to go, here, so bring them in," replied.

As the soldiers filed into the room behind Vigo and John-Pierre, Vigo motioned to Anthony to join him next to the bed. While the soldiers lined up alongside the lightweight titanium chamber, Vigo whispered softly to Anthony. "I just got some news from Jeffrey. He's waiting for you topside with some other folks. Meanwhile, you, John-Pierre and I need to have a private chat here in the control room by ourselves before we go topside. I wouldn't ask if it weren't important."

"OK," Anthony sighed reluctantly. "I'll see him to the elevator and come back."

Following Boole's orders, the soldiers carefully lifted the biostasis chamber and started towards the stairwell at a deliberate pace as Vigo and John-Pierre watched them leave.

Vigo waited until they entered the control room accessway tunnel to the storage room and turned to John-Pierre. "Hey look, you've done a hell of a job here today, and your only thanks is our gratitude and the fact that you're now a marked man. I know you pledged yourself to Jarman and his family, but sometimes we make commitments in the heat of the moment that we later come to regret. If you want to go to ground, I can help you with a new identity or whatever you want."

John-Pierre shook his head. "Major Jones, have you ever known me to back out on anything?"

"No, can't say I have."

"Then I thank you for your offer, old friend, but I meant what I said back there in the control room, and nothing can change that. I know this is hard to explain, but in less than a heartbeat I not only changed; I saw a purpose in life, and I do not need your permission to follow it."

"And what is your purpose now?"

"What else? De Bono."

"As a friend of the family, I have to ask you to set that aside and to follow a different path. You see, I'm about to send Anthony and his family so far away that De Bono could never hope to touch them and I want you to go with him."

"Is it dangerous, this place you intend to send them?"

"No, it is the safest place in the universe if you ask me, but some day he'll have to come back because his destiny is here. The reason why I want you to go is that you need to bond with him so that only a gesture or a nod is all it takes to understand volumes."

"I understand what you're saying. I also had such a relationship with Joe Napolitano, and now he's lying dead out in the tunnel."

Vigo grimaced. "John-Pierre, I'm sorry about Joe, but you know, this is the business we're in. He died like a true warrior. Maybe if circumstances had been different, he'd still be alive, but we can't afford to belabor the point now."

John-Pierre put his hand on Vigo's shoulder. "I know all that. It is just that I will not be here to bury him."

Vigo laid his hand upon John-Pierre's hand. "I will be, and I promise you that he'll be buried with full military honors, and if he has family, I see to it they're taken care of as well."

A proud smile filled John-Pierre's face as he gripped Vigo's shoulder tightly. "Then let me ask you one last favor before I go to this faraway place."

"Sure."

The proud French-Canadian warrior removed his hand from Vigo's shoulder, unclipped his knife sheath from his web belt and handed it handle first to Vigo. "Perhaps this will come in handy when you meet De Bono?"

Vigo smiled and unclipped his own tactical knife end handed it to John-Pierre. "Let's just say you've got more time than I do to put a proper edge on this," he said with a wink.

"It would be my pleasure," John-Pierre replied as he hugged Vigo. "I feel like we've become brothers."

"So do I," Vigo replied warmly as he hugged John-Pierre back, "and it is good to have you in the family."

After a few grunting tugs, they released their grip and Vigo said, "If you don't mind, I need a few moments alone."

"Sure, I'll go to the elevator and escort Anthony back."

VIGO WAITED TILL he heard John-Pierre's footsteps in the accessway tunnel and casually walked down the stairs into the control room. He cleared a spot on the command console table, sat down and pulled his medallion out from under his collar. After taking several deep breaths to calm himself, he held the medallion to his right temple, closed his eyes and directed his thought to JALA.DEE, the mother of JALA.TRAC.

JALA.DEE's weathered and kindly, old face appeared in his mind. "Hello Mother Dee," he greeted her in the familiar manner. "I need to discus a matter of the utmost importance with you."

"I see your thoughts, Vigo," she replied sadly. "So much violence today. This is not the way to those seeking awareness."

"I live to serve those who do, Mother, in the hope that someday I can begin the journey myself. Until then, I must live within my world as it is." He opened his mind fully to her. "I've kept the faith with our agreement. I could have used my medallion today, but I didn't."

"I know," she replied appreciatively. "Still, it pains me to see such violence. Please promise me that you will leave your present path one day, as soon as you can."

"I promise," Vigo replied sincerely. "But today, I seek your help for an extraordinary situation -- one that goes beyond our agreement."

"I've seen this coming for some time," she admitted. "I've watched young Anthony with great interest. He shows much promise."

"As well as a great destiny," Vigo added "So then it comes as no surprise, Mother Dee, that I am asking you for temporary asylum for Jarman and his family on Godschild. I cannot protect him here on Earth until I've dealt with the man who seeks his end and that of his family."

"If you feel it is necessary, it is so granted. How soon must this happen."

"As soon as possible, Mother Dee. Is it possible for your son, JALA.TRAC to retrieve them here, where I am?"

"He is on Godschild now, Vigo. Can this wait for a few days until he arrives?"

"I'm afraid not, Mother Dee."

"Then I will come myself. I am only a few minutes away, but my personal SHEM is small. I only have room enough for five and a small amount of luggage."

"That will be more than enough, Mother Dee; I am very grateful for this, and I know the risk you are taking."

"We do much for love, Vigo, and I sense the deep love you feel for these people. The only real risk is not being able to love and be loved."

"Your words fill my heart with joy, Mother Dee, although it is burdened by the present health of Jarman's son, Russell. He suffers from a terrible head injury. If there is anything you can do to help him..."

"Of course, we'll do what we can." JALA.DEE paused in her thoughts. "What I've been wondering is why the people who kidnapped this boy went to such extreme lengths to do so. Since you know them better than I do, perhaps you can explain this to me?"

"The same question has been crossing my mind for some time," Vigo agreed. "All of this has gone beyond simple political blackmail, although that is how I believe it all began. Perhaps the boy is an Indigo Child like his father, but even that would not justify the blood and treasure they've spilt to keep him. No, there is something extraordinary about this boy. Something they want from him or want to do with him that will advance their plans by long strides. I've pondered this question a great deal and yet, I can never seem to find the answer. Perhaps you will on Godschild if the boy recovers."

"I have an idea in my mind, but it is too early to say. Perhaps once I've had a chance to examine the boy, I may find a clue. If he is as important to these violent people as you say, perhaps the answer may hold the key to his safety and that of his family. We will try."

"You are most kind, Mother Dee."

"You're welcome. Will you be joining us on the trip to Godschild? It has been a long time since you and I have watched a moonrise together."

Vigo could hear the approaching footsteps of Anthony and John Pierre. "Not this time, I'm afraid, but I will do my best to prepare them for the journey in what little time we have."

"Then do so. I shall be there shortly."

ANTHONY PICKED UP one of the padded control room chairs then sat it upright and plopped down in it with a tired grunt. "I feel like a truck just ran over me," he complained as he rubbed his eyes. "So what's on your mind, Vigo?"

"Anthony, I didn't expect to run into De Bono today." He glanced over at John-Pierre. Leaning against a wall cabinet, John-Pierre simply shrugged his shoulders. "I was counting on getting out of here without leaving a trace of ourselves. Now, this whole mess is front page news and De Bono has issued a warrant for your arrest."

"So what; he said he would. Besides, if we go to Russia as planned I'm sure they'll keep him off my back."

"There is only so much they can do, and De Bono has played a trump card. Eventually, they would have to turn you over, as would any UNE member state. Even the non-member states would have to honor the warrant, which by the way, is to have you institutionalized as criminally insane."

"Now that's one right out of the KGB rule book," John-Pierre added. "He can discredit you without the need for a messy trial and keep you pumped full of drugs till you finally die, or till he feels he can have you terminated without risking an incident. This is very dangerous indeed, Anthony. I think you should do exactly what Vigo says now. He understands these things better than either of us."

Vigo picked up another one of the control chairs and used his cap to dust off the broken glass. Rolling it near to Anthony, he sat down and leaned forward. "We don't have much time, so let me explain everything."

"I'm too tired to argue," Anthony replied as John Pierre stepped closely.

Over the next several minutes, Vigo explained his relationship with the Friends and showed them his medallion. Wide-eyed, they listened in stunned silence as he explained his plan with JALA.TRAC to give them temporary asylum on Godschild.

After he finished, John-Pierre was the first to comment. "This is so amazing I can hardly believe my ears."

Anthony looked at him and replied, "This I believe. However, if you were to tell me that one day I'd die in my own bed a happy grandfather and in the arms of my loving wife, I'd call you a raving lunatic."

"All things are possible," Vigo said with a smile.

"Yadda, yadda, so who all is going besides Tanya, Russell, John-Pierre and myself?"

"If asked, I think Dr. Boole will go, but I think you should be the one to ask him, Anthony."

"I can't fault your logic," Anthony said with a groan as he lifted his tired, aching body from the chair. "Let's get going."

AS THE ELEVATOR came to a stop and they found Jeffrey, Dr. Boole and Tanya standing beside General Hennicker.

Anthony leaned his head toward Vigo. "Don't tell me, that's Hennicker?"

"Yup."

They walked up to the small group and Tanya went to Anthony and hugged him. "I think we're in a lot of trouble, Anthony. I'm afraid."

"Don't worry dear," he whispered as he pulled her to his side. "Everything will be OK." He extended his other hand. "It is a pleasure to finally meet you, General Hennicker."

"The pleasure is all mine, Captain Jarman, but I truly wish it were under better circumstances. I hope your boy recovers."

"Thank you general," he replied as they stepped out in the early light of day. "We're all praying he recovers soon. What about the Israelis?"

General Hennicker smiled. "Talk about a sense of timing," he chuckled as he pointed towards the airfield. A moment later, they could hear and see the Flying Circus taking off in a full power climbing turn towards them. Flying over the missile field, Captain Jerome Richard wagged the wingtips of the huge C-130J as everyone on the ground waved goodbye."

"God's speed Shai; we couldn't have done it without you and your men!" Anthony shouted out as the Flying Circus completed its turn taking it on a southerly heading.

"They'll be in Mexico with Darkazani in a few hours," General Hennicker said, "and your wounded man is about to arrive at Fort Sam for emergency surgery. I'm told he'll be OK."

"Ramona is with him," Boole added.

"I'm really glad to hear that," Anthony said as Tanya snuggled close to him. "Say doc, can I have a private word with you?"

"Of course."

Anthony pointed his thumb towards General Hennicker. "Hey Vigo, the general needs to know and so does Jeffrey."

"Know what?" Hennicker and LeBlanc asked with puzzled expressions.

CHAPTER 28

ESCAPE TO GODSCHILD

USING VIGO'S MEDALLION as a homing beacon, JALA.DEE guided her radar-shielded ship, SHEM.GADOK to the silo field. As her ship landed, she saw a small group of people surrounding Russell's oblong biostasis chamber along with several small cases and satchels. A young soldier holding two yellow sticks guided her to a marked spot on the paved road in front of the guardhouse. She slowed her decent to hover just feet above the ground as the landing struts of her circular ship extended and locked into place. As her ship settled down upon the ground, from the side facing the group, a ramp opened from the seamless hull.

Alerted by the hum of her ship, Ben Green left his investigation inside the large portable building that had served as the living quarters for the Peacekeepers and froze at the door. "Holy crap," he muttered to himself.

While the Texas Highway Patrol Captain watched in stunned disbelief, JALA.DEE walked slowly down the ramp and stood next to it on the ground. Slightly shorter than her son, JALA.TRAC, her weathered face showed centuries of keen interests and the building of families. Dressed in a white gossamer robe, her silver-streaked gold hair hung down along her thin shoulders. Her blue-green eyes turned to Vigo as he approached.

"Welcome, Mother Dee; we are grateful for your help."

"And we are most glad to help," she replied. "We haven't much time." She glanced at the group standing next to the biostasis chamber, "I trust the boy is strong enough for the journey to Godschild."

"Yes, Mother Dee. Do you mind if a few soldiers help us carry his chamber into your ship?"

"As long as they are not armed. However, those who will be making the journey are free to bring their own personal weapons if they choose to do so."

"I know your feeling on this, and I've already taken the precaution." JALA.DEE nodded appreciatively and Vigo gave the prearranged signal to Boole who, along with three soldiers, lifted the biostasis chamber and started toward JALA.DEE's ship.

"Just carry it into the center of the ship," she said in a sweet voice as they paused at the lip of the ramp.

"Thank you," Boole answered nervously as he guided the group up the ramp and into the large, saucer-shaped craft.

The interior of the ship was larger than it appeared on the outside; it appeared as an empty shell. The surface of the interior walls was a solid, seamless swirl of pinkish-white material that reminded Boole and the soldiers of the inside of a conch shell.

After placing the biostasis chamber in the center of the ship, the soldiers walked out with amazed looks in their eyes. Boole followed behind and stopped next to JALA.DEE. "Excuse me, but I'll be a member of the group, and I noticed that the ship is empty. Should we bring sleeping bags or something?"

Vigo laughed at the question. "Don't worry, doc. Once you're on your way, she'll make the place nice and comfy, just like home. On my last trip, she turned the inside of the ship into a mountain cabin including a couple of nice, deep chairs in front of a roaring fire. You're in for a real treat, my friend, so just go and get your things."

"Uh-huh," Boole replied numbly.

Vigo then turned toward the small group and said, "Time's a-wastin' folks. Let's get a move on."

Holding Tanya's hand, Anthony walked towards the craft as John-Pierre followed just a few steps behind carrying armfuls of satchels and containers.

They met Vigo and JALA.DEE at the base of the ramp and Vigo introduced the three. JALA.DEE raised a thin eyebrow as he introduced John-Pierre. "This Durand," she said pensively. "I sense there has been much violence with him. Is this wise?"

John-Pierre spoke for himself. "You are right to feel that way. Until this day, I was a man of violence, but through the events of this day, I've gotten a new chance to serve a higher purpose in life."

Her gaze shifted to Anthony and she spoke to him for the first time, "And you want this man to join you on this journey?"

"Yes, JALA.DEE. People can be friends for a lifetime and never know how much one is willing to sacrifice for the other. Today, I shared awareness with John-Pierre, and he saved us all from certain death. I trust him completely."

"Very well," she nodded. "Then you are welcome, Durand. May your path to awareness be fulfilled."

The hum of the ship had troubled Tanya and now she felt a strange magnetic force emanating from it, similar to that of the Mystery Spot. She held Anthony close. "Anthony, I believe I need to stay. I'll have to wait for you here on Earth, my love."

Her sudden announcement caught Anthony completely off guard. "But why?" he stuttered.

"I can't say why," she protested as tears began to form in her eyes. "But I'll wait for you. I love you, Anthony, and I'll wait for you forever."

Torn between being separated from the love of his life and his need to be with his son, Anthony suddenly felt helpless. "Tanya, please don't do this to us," he begged.

JALA.DEE had watched the tender moment between Tanya and Anthony with a sad expression. Normally, she would have remained quiet, but with a love this great, she couldn't resist. She walked up to Tanya and placed her hand on her belly and after a few moments asked, "Have you told him?"

Tanya's eyes opened with surprise. She wanted to pull back, but JALA.DEE's touch was warm and comforting. "I understand your concern. The strange feelings you are feeling here will not trouble you once you are inside my ship, and absolutely no harm will come to your unborn children during the trip to, or on Godschild."

"You're pregnant," Anthony stammered out loud, as JALA.DEE removed her hand from Tanya's belly.

"Next time, try a megaphone!" Tanya shot back, then paused. "Hold on a second," she muttered to herself and turned her attention back to JALA.DEE. "Did you say unborn children as in the plural? As in more than one?"

JALA.DEE smiled warmly, "Twins, a boy and a girl. Both will be Indigo children as you call them and healthy."

Anthony slapped his forehead. "Tanya!" She glanced at him with an annoyed look. "You knew you were pregnant and you came on this mission, and worse yet, you didn't tell me. Excuse me for being the last to know."

Tanya held her head high. "This is not the time to argue, Anthony," she replied hoping to mask her embarrassment.

"You bet your sweet ass we're not going to argue!" With that, Anthony scooped her up in his arms. "You're the one who said that we talk too much, so not another word. Our family is going to Godschild and that is that."

Tanya looked into JALA.DEE's soft blue-green eyes.

"I myself have had eighteen children by three different husbands, and my youngest, JALA.TRAC," she pointed to her ship, "was born in this very ship while I was on an archeological assignment." She wiggled her nose with a loving smile. "You'll be just fine, dear, and we have wonderful medical facilities on Godschild for you and your baby."

Tanya winked at her with a glowing smile, and wrapping her arms around Anthony's neck, kissed him on the cheek. "I know. I know. Shut up and tee off." Anthony chuckled and kissed her as John-Pierre and Dr. Boole finished carrying the last of the baggage into the ship.

Anthony began walking up the ramp with Tanya still in his arms and turned back towards Vigo. "By the way, dear old dad, you're not going to do that crazy slice and dice thing you were talking about with De Bono, are you?"

"Nah, I was just rattling his cage," Vigo replied humorously. "We'll stay in touch, and I'll see you within the year or so. Now get going."

"Vigo, be good to Ann-Marie," Tanya called out as they disappeared into the ship.

Vigo leaned over and kissed JALA.DEE softly on the cheek. "Say hello to JALA.TRAC for me."

JALA.DEE blushed and nodded as she followed Anthony and Tanya up the ramp.

Vigo walked back to the remaining members of the group and stood next to General Hennicker and Ann-Marie.

They watched in silence as the ship began to hum loudly, withdrawing the ramp until it meshed seamlessly back into the hull. A moment later, the ship lifted straight up above their heads, hovered for brief moment, and shot straight up into the early morning light as Ann-Marie drew close to Vigo. "Do you really think he knew you were bullshitting him back there?"

"Who knows, my dear? But I do know this. Three of the people I love the most are on that flying pie tin, and as long as that miserable shit De Bono draws breath they'll never be able to walk the Earth in peace."

"So is Clyde in the market for a Bonnie?" Ann-Marie teased.

"Well, Bonnie my love, somebody's got to drive the getaway car."

THE THREE-DAY TRIP to Godschild on SHEM.GADOK had been comfortable and informative. During the trip, JALA.DEE had given each of them their own medallion and taught them how to use them.

Shortly after leaving the solar system, she fashioned the interior of SHEM.GADOK into a small replica of one of the homes on Godschild, which featured large rooms with tall, domed ceilings, exquisite marble floors and wide, airy arches leading to red-tiled patios. Reminiscent of Mediterranean architecture, the homes were airy and comfortable.

During their meals, she told them stories about the race that had created Godschild. According to the ancient records left behind, they were a small, humanoid race with dimpled, gray skin. She expressed the feeling that they had intentionally built the homes to accommodate taller races and that the material used to construct the homes was stronger than anything she had ever seen during all her adventures -- even stronger than that the Friends used to construct the homes on their own home world.

It amazed everyone how she could change the interior of SHEM.GADOK with a simple touch from a compartmentalized configuration into a single dining room complete with warm meals and delicious wines.

While Tanya and Anthony spent most of the trip sleeping and preoccupied with one another, JALA.DEE chose to spend her time with Dr. Boole. They examined Russell's medical records together, and after learning what she needed to know about human physiology from the doctor, she personally examined Russell at great length. When Dr. Boole chose to rest, she spent the remainder of her time with John-Pierre. Curious about the events that shaped his life and his moment of profound change in the silo she came to feel a new appreciation for Anthony's powers, and in time, she and John-Pierre bonded in a mutually enjoyable relationship.

On the third day, Boole provided JALA.DEE with a small sample of Russell's blood. She placed the tube filled with blood next to the interior wall of SHEM.GADOK and pushed it in. A moment later, the tube appeared from out of the wall, completely empty of its contents.

On the evening of the third day, the group took their meal together, as had become their custom, and it was then that JALA.DEE announced a surprising finding. She had isolated the Mystery Gene and after she explained its significance Anthony immediately realized why De Bono had gone to such great lengths to keep Russell alive and apart from his father.

IT HAD BEEN a week since JALA.DEE and her passengers had arrived, and the whole city was now filled with the hopeful talk of Russell's recovery from his coma.

JALA.TRAC sat alongside Lucinda Chavez and Timmy Watkins on the garden path leading past the home of Anthony and Tanya. Further down the walk, was the main boulevard of Godschild City and its gentle shoreline. Shortly after his arrival, Anthony had found a private moment to explain Connie Chavez's last days and to give her medallion to her only child, Lucinda.

Holding her mother's medallion in her hand, she wept as Timmy held her. JALA.TRAC sat patiently; waiting in silence for the question he knew would come.

Lucinda kissed the medallion, "This is all I have to remember her. I know everyone hopes for Russell's recovery but as I was bringing a basket of fruit to the house I overheard the doctor telling Anthony he'll most likely never recover and that he'll just waste away. JALA.TRAC, we've all suffered so much. Why is it that with all your wonderful technology you cannot save Russell. Why must the innocents die so terribly?"

This was the question he had awaited. "Lucinda, even with all our technology we, too, eventually die. Granted we can live to be many hundreds of your years, but eventually our own bodies cease to accept our own regenerative therapies and we cross over, too, just like you. This is the way of things."

"But you haven't lost your mother," Lucinda said in a low, guilt-tinged voice.

JALA.TRAC shifted himself to face her. "I was hoping you could help me with that, Lucinda, because my mother is dying."

Timmy gasped. "Mother Dee is dying?"

"You will be a young man, Timmy, when that time comes, but yes, she is dying. This is because her body can no longer accept the regenerative therapy, created for us by our ancestors. I'm hoping, Lucinda, that you could help me prepare by sharing your feelings and thoughts with me."

"But you are so much wiser than me," Lucinda said with astonishment.

He took her hand and smiled sadly. "In love, we are all equals."

"Have you talked about this with your mother, JALA.TRAC?" Timmy asked.

"We've talked about it several times," he admitted. "I am not troubled by the fact that she will cross over. We all do eventually, and then we go onto other things. The difference is that I wonder what my life will become without her presence."

"You'll feel an emptiness that nothing can fill," Lucinda replied in a hushed voice. "You'll also feel pride in her and what she has accomplished. Sometimes, I feel my mother standing next to me giving me love and encouragement. Do your people feel the same things?"

"That and more."

Just at the moment, a flash of light caught Timmy's eye and he looked up into the sky. "It's SHEM.GADOK," he exclaimed. JALA.DEE and John-Pierre are back," he exclaimed pointing to the approaching ship.

"She has brought it," JALA.TRAC whispered under his breath.

TANYA SAT DOWN next to Anthony alongside Russell's bed holding a small tray with a variety of hot dishes made of vegetables freshly picked that morning in the city's communal garden. "You've got to eat something, honey. Please, won't you?"

Sitting across the bed, Dr. Boole said, "she's right, Anthony. You haven't eaten since yesterday."

Anthony pushed the tray aside. "I'm sorry, but I just can't."

Boole turned away to look out the large open archway leading out to the patio. Upon their arrival on Godschild, he had tried a new therapy for brain cell regeneration to repair the damage that had been caused by the butt of the Syrian Peacekeeper's rifle. It had not only failed, but now, Russell's EKG was showing a slow, steady decline. Saddened by the fact that he had, with the best of intentions, made things worse, his sense of guilt haunted him.

Tanya slowly put her arm around Anthony and laid her head on his shoulder. "Then perhaps our only hope now is JALA.DEE. When Lucinda brought me your food, she told me that she and John-Pierre returned an hour ago and that she'll be here soon. I know she told us not to put too much hope in her plan, but maybe this is all we have left now."

"I tried and tried, but I can't see him in the garden," he said flatly, as he laid his forehead upon his son's arm. "Oh, Tanya, I'm afraid we're losing him. Maybe it already happened and we're just trying to breathe life back into the empty shell of his body."

"We can't give up hope," Tanya replied kissing him gently on the back of his neck. "Not while there is one last chance."

A HEAVY-HEARTED STREAM of solemn children and adults followed JALA.DEE and JALA.TRAC up the path to the new home of Anthony and Tanya. Leading the procession like a proud flag bearer was John-Pierre, holding an odd-looking plant. Shaped like a large artichoke, its long narrow pedals were white and layered one upon the other like the feathers of a bird. Each petal was delicately crisscrossed with gold colored veins that feathered out to form blue edges.

Lucinda met them at the front door of the house. "Mother Dee, we are happy to see you."

"Thank you, Lucinda; we have come to help Russell."

"Our prayers are with you," she replied as she stood aside.

While JALA.DEE and her son followed John-Pierre into the house, the other Indigo children, along with their parents, streamed around the sides of the home onto the large adjoining patio to begin their prayer vigil.

They entered the large family room adjoining the patio and could see Anthony slumped over Russell's bed in a light fitful sleep as Boole monitored the boy's vital signs on his webpad.

JALA.DEE's first words were to Tanya, who had risen to greet them. "I see you have not rested well and that you need to take nourishment. I understand your grief, but one must always tend to life, and your unborn child depends upon you."

Tanya nodded sadly as JALA.DEE walked to Anthony's side. She placed her hand on his shoulder and waited patiently as he awakened.

"Mother Dee," Anthony said wiping the fitful sleep from his eyes. "I don't think he's with us anymore."

"Until now, I have not said anything, but from your first day aboard SHEM.GADOK, I knew that your son's condition was worsening. That is why I left shortly after bringing you here and why I asked John-Pierre to come with me on a very special mission."

"Before you left on your special mission, you told us not to place great hope in what you could do," Anthony replied. "Is there a reason now to hope?"

"Yes," she replied calmly as she pointed to the strange looking plant that Durand was holding. "John-Pierre is holding what we call a Hadedalo Plant. It comes from our home world and it was genetically engineered millennia ago by our ancients. To this day, we use it to regenerate own bodies until they finally mature to a point where the plant no longer has any effect. For humans, the Hadedalo is very poisonous. However, this particular Hadedalo plant is a rare mutation that lacks the potency we need to regenerate our bodies, but it may help your son, thanks to his special genetic makeup."

"I don't understand," Boole admitted.

"Do you remember during the last day of our trip here to Godschild that I told you about Russell's special gene? The Mystery Gene, as it is known by a few on your planet?"

"Yes, I remember that," Tanya replied.

"I couldn't tell all of you then, but now that we were able to retrieve this extremely rare Hadedalo, I can tell you that there is hope, as well as consequences. But first, I want you to give thanks to John-Pierre for helping us. Normally, I would have harvested this plant myself but I am no longer as agile as I once was. So you must thank John-Pierre, who risked his life with a very dangerous climb."

"It was a walk in the park," John-Pierre said with a blush.

"You're being too modest," JALA.DEE replied. "You gave me a terrible fright when that ledge gave way." John-Pierre shrugged.

Dr. Boole pushed his webpad aside and said. "Mother Dee, you mentioned consequences. What would those be?"

"We have never tried this with a human, but the Mystery Gene which is so uncommon in your race is part of everyone like me, and it is what triggers the regenerative properties of Hadedalo. If his body does succumb to the toxic properties of the plant, Russell's unique genetic makeup should trigger the plant's regenerative properties. If it works, the Hadedalo will completely heal the boy giving him a longer and healthier life expectancy than most humans. But there are other consequences."

Anthony rose up from his chair and stood erect. "Assuming it doesn't kill him, what are they?"

"There are two that concern me very much," JALA.DEE replied with a troubled look. "His powers of precognition will become more advanced and this can be a dangerous thing if one is not spiritually ready for such things. Great care must be taken to mentor him well as he grows, so that his gift does not drive him to insanity. That last consequence and the one that troubles me most is that the Hadedalo Plant will change his genetic makeup forever. While his sexual abilities will be fully developed with strong and fertile sperm, no human ova will accept them. Young Russell will never be able to have children of his own."

Anthony looked at JALA.DEE, then to Tanya. "What do you think?"

Tanya placed a hand on her tummy and said, "It breaks my heart that if he survives, he will never be able to have children of his own. He'll just have to adopt. I say, do it!"

Anthony slowly stood up and walked over to John Pierre, held out his hands and accepted the Hadedalo from him. He studied the plant carefully as he caressed its soft pedals. "Jim, tell me honestly. What are his chances?"

Boole's head dropped as he sighed. "At his present rate of decline, your son will be brain dead within a few days, a week at most. If you're going to do anything, do it now."

Anthony searched Tanya's eyes as a tear began to run down her cheek. "He's my son too Anthony. Just shut up and tee off." He laughed for the first time since their arrival.

He turned to JALA.DEE. "How long will it take before we know?"

"If it works, he'll regain consciousness after moonrise tonight, and after a few days, his recovery will be complete. That is, if it works."

"What do we do next?"

"You must all leave the house. This is a sacred ceremony, and my son and I must be left alone with the boy."

"As you wish, Mother Dee," Anthony replied with hopeful eyes. "We shall leave you now."

FOLLOWING THE HADEDALO ceremony, Boole continued monitored Russell's progress, and by mid-afternoon, the boy's vital signs had improved. Likewise, his brain activity was becoming stronger, and JALA.DEE instructed him to remove the feeding tube she had used to pass a small, continuously trickling flow of Hadedalo juice into the boy's stomach.

The trend was hopeful and continued through the remainder of the afternoon and through to the beginning of the moonrise as the twin moons of Godschild cast their enchanting blue white light on the city.

As long moonbeams began to stretch across the gentle waters of the Godschild sea, everyone in the room held their breath in suspense as Russell's eyes began to flutter.

Anthony pressed his open palms against the sides of Russell's head and began kissing him and repeating the words, "Wake up, son. Come to me, son. I love you so very much."

Russell's eyes opened slowly for the first time. "I can't see," he said weakly.

"It's OK Russell," Anthony said gratefully as Tanya wiped his eyes with a damp cloth. "Give your eyes a moment to adjust. Things will clear up."

"Will I see the moons tonight?" Russell asked.

Anthony looked at Tanya with amazement. The boy had used the plural form, as though he knew, but did he? "Yes, you will," Anthony replied.

"May I," Boole asked, as he stepped in to manage the boy's recovery. Anthony and Tanya stood aside and hugged each other as he tended to the recovering boy.

Standing together off to the side, JALA.TRAC leaned towards his mother, projecting his thoughts to her for a fitting celebration. JALA.DEE smiled, and unnoticed by all, they silently made their way out onto the balcony where they were greeted by a large crowd of well wishers. A cheer began to rise up and JALA.DEE held out her hands to show that everyone still needed to be quiet.

Mindful of the needs of everyone waiting outside, she accepted a tall wax candle in a handmade wicker holder from Jenny Watkins, and then held it out to her mother, Helen. She turned to pass it along to JALA.TRAC and noticed that he was deep in thought, holding his medallion to his temple. She held a finger to her lips, "Shhhh.... Everyone. Quiet, now, until they come out." They all waited in silence, maintaining their prayer vigil for nearly forty minutes till JALA.DEE gestured for them to light their candles.

By the time that the large patio was dotted with dozens of candles, Boole happily announced that most of Russell's sight had returned. "Anthony, I think it's time for you to show him the moons," he said with satisfied smile.

Anthony nodded gratefully and folded back the bed cover. Gently slipping his hands under Russell's body, he cradled the boy in his arms and lifted him up while Tanya simultaneously cradled his head.

Proud and grateful, they both carried him out onto the patio under the magical light of Godschild's twin moons and dozens of flickering candles to face their cheering throng of well wishers. As they stepped out on the patio, JALA.DEE turned to JALA.TRAC with a knowing nod. They held hands and placed their medallions to the temples. Within moments, a dazzling shower of meteorites streaked across the edges of the nigh sky in a festive display of lights that together with the candles and the light of Godchild's twin moons formed a spectacular sight -- a fitting sight for an especially gifted child's first memory on Godschild.

For the first time since that terrible night when he lost his own family, the universe felt right for Anthony Jarman, and never had life been as precious to him as it was in this very moment. He smiled at the Indigo children that now surrounded them then turned Russell to face the twin moons of Godschild. Together, they marveled at the shower of lights Mother Dee and her son now guided.

"It's all so beautiful, papa," Russell exclaimed joyfully.

Tears began welling in Anthony's eyes. "Russell, how do you know I'm your father?" Tanya sighed heavily and began crying as well.

"Momma told me. She's been with me all the time. But why are you crying, Papa? I'm OK, now."

Anthony kissed his son tenderly as tears began to flow freely down his cheeks for the first time in over half a lifetime. "I know you'll be just fine now," he replied as his voice trembled with joy, "and I'm crying because God has given you to me and because I love you so very much, my son.

AUTHOR'S NOTES

The genesis of *Godschild Covenant: Return of Nibiru*, began with my appearance as a government secrecy expert on a PAX Cable Television Network program titled, "Is There a Doomsday Asteroid?" which aired on March 20, 2001. This well-crafted, hour-long program also featured such notable Near Earth Object (NEO) experts as Dr. Brian Marsden, Associate Director of the Smithsonian Astrophysics Observatories; Dr. Duncan Steel, author of *Target Earth*; and Brig. Gen. Simon P. Worden, USAF, Vice Director of Operations, U.S. Space Command. After the program aired, I contacted Dr. Marsden with the help of PAX producer Gail Fallen, and began the first of several intriguing conversations with Dr. Marsden about various NEO issues.

At that time, I was somewhat familiar with the work of Zecharia Sitchin, whose body of research on the planet Nibiru is quite substantial and well-respected. However, in all honesty, I was somewhat dismissive. I simply could not wrap my head around the concept that a planet five times the size of Earth in an elongated, long period orbit around our Sun, traveled through our outer solar system once every 3,600 years. But then, something significant happened.

On July 2, 2001, a group of American astronomers lead by Robert Millis of the Lowell Observatory in Flagstaff, Arizona, announced the discovery of a Kuiper Belt Object (KBO), designated 2001 KX76 (or KX76). The discovery received a broad splash of media attention due to its profound scientific consequence.

While over 400 KBOs have been observed since 1992, KX76 was certainly the Mother of all KBOs due to its sheer size. Reported to be 1,270 kilometers (788 miles) in diameter, it is the size of Earth's moon. No wonder its discovery marveled astronomers and the mainstream media alike.

Why all the hoopla? Prior to the discovery of KX76, the Kuiper Belt was generally regarded as a space junkyard filled with relatively small rocky debris left over from the formation of the planets in our solar system. With the discovery of KX76, it was time to scratch that idea, Hoss, 'cause there's a new sheriff in town!

As my mind raced with KBO possibilities, I phoned Dr. Marsden at the Smithsonian Astrophysics Observatories. At the time, he was busy processing the early data coming in on KX76, but was kind enough to take the time to discuss it with me at length.

It was obvious to him that that KX76 was breaking old theories as fast as it was making new ones, and he mused it would make it even more difficult for astronomers to come to a consensus on how to define the attributes of the planet.

Even more importantly, Marsden expressed the opinion that KX76's discovery also proved that something larger than KX76 could exist in the Kuiper Belt. In other words: this big rock could very well have some planet-sized uncles and aunts floating around the outer reaches of our solar system, in long period orbits around our Sun.

Excited by my conversation with Marsden, I called Steve Russell (co-founder of my web site, YOWUSA.COM) in

Australia. Steve possesses a brilliant, connect-the-dots kind of intellect and has read everything published by Zecharia Sitchin. Of course, he saw this as an excellent opportunity to renew the issue of Nibiru's existence with me.

While I still wasn't ready to jolt on down to the bookstore to swoop up several copies of Sitchin's books, I was finally ready to listen. As Steve began to explain Sitchin's work, the idea of Nibiru began to rattle about in the back of my head, lurking about in search of fertile soil in which to germinate.

I was still struggling with Nibiru when a few days later I received another call from PAX TV producer, Gail Fallen. Gail was working on a new show about the extinction of the dinosaurs 65 million years ago, and she needed to present an alternative theory to that of Nobel laureate physicist, Luis Alvarez.

According to Alvarez's theory, the extinction of the dinosaurs was the result of a massive impact event in an area now known as Chicxulub, Mexico. Alvarez's K-T impact extinction theory has reigned as the golden cow of dinosaur extinction logic for the last twenty years or so.

Gail wanted me to research the K-T Deccan Traps volcanism-induced carbon cycle perturbation extinction theory of Dewey McLean, Professor Emeritus of Geology at the Virginia Polytechnic Institute. McLean's theory would serve as a counter to Alvarez's K-T impact extinction theory. She then wanted me to appear on her upcoming PAX program.

"I'm not a scientist Gail," I protested, "why not interview McLean himself and get it from the horse's mouth?"

"He's too ill to interview and besides," she replied snappily, "you're a former CNN science feature producer and that's good enough for me." Still I protested, but when a successful TV producer like Gail hears a polite "no," it's an open invitation for her to twist your intellectual short hairs with a bugbear of a challenge. Needless to say, I was soon wondering if I had bitten off more than I could chew.

After ringing off with Gail, I poured through McLean's website and other related sites. I immediately noticed that McLean had received a vitriolic level of professional abuse from Luis Alvarez. Now this made me curious! If Alvarez's K-T impact extinction theory was as sound as a sacred cow, why was he hitting McLean below the belt every chance he got? If anything, Alvarez's unprofessional behavior did more to interest me in McLean's theory than anything else.

McLean theorizes that the event that caused the extinction of the dinosaurs was a massive volcanic eruption of the Deccan Traps (in what is now Western India) over 65 million years ago, about the same time as the Chicxulub impact. The eruption was so immense that it defies imagination: it flooded over a million square miles of India and its surrounding areas with layer upon layer of basaltic lava flows. To this very day, evidence of this eruption remains near Bombay, where a 1-1/2 miles-thick lava pile still remains.

At this point, I knew I needed to call in the cavalry and I pulled out Marsden's telephone number. I explained the assignment Gail had given to me and found him to be already well-versed in McLean's theory. Given that we both liked Gail and shared the opinion that Alvarez's ego was roughly the size of his Chicxulub impact event, we set upon the issue with great relish.

After running through a gambit of various scenarios (and a thoroughly enjoyable three-hour dialogue), we managed to build a reasonable scenario for McLean's Deccan Traps eruption theory. We settled on a flyby event of a large object which, while not impacting the Earth, could have triggered a catastrophic event on the scale of the Deccan Traps eruption 65 million years ago. After batting around a few possible object candidates, Marsden settled on Comet Borrelly, the most observed comet in history thanks to the Deep Space One spacecraft.

With a five-mile long nucleus, an object the size of Comet Borrelly could graze the atmosphere of our planet without being captured by Earth's gravity, thereby generating a phenomenal shockwave which could trigger a Deccan Traps-type eruption.

With that all settled, I took great care in preparing a script for PAX and they gladly accepted it without making a single change. In retrospect, that should have tipped me off well in advance of videotaping my interview. It didn't.

After a lengthy pre-production schedule, the show finally aired on January 23, 2001, and I was mortified. Apparently, Gail's executive producer at PAX secretly had a different agenda in mind. He intended to prove that Noah's Flood had caused the extinction of the dinosaurs and used snippets from my interview to do it. In one fell swoop, PAX had cast me down into soundbyte hell. Worse yet, they ignored all the great work I'd done with Marsden. I can remember watching the show and feeling utterly humiliated as I prayed, "please God, don't let Marsden see this insane program." But Marsden did see it, and that basically tore it.

So now, where did that leave me? It left me with a still very credible scenario in which the flyby of a large object past Earth could, in fact, trigger a horrific catastrophic event.

The scenario that I had worked out with Marsden was based on a comet grazing the atmosphere. Yet I continued to wonder about another scenario we had discussed in which a larger, planet-sized object flying through the middle of our solar system causes the same catastrophic results for Earth. I remembered posing that question to Marsden. While he agreed that it was possible, he felt that Comet Borrelly would serve as the basis for a more palatable scenario. The planet-sized object scenario stuck in my mind, however, and that was when the Nibiru seed that Steve Russell had planted in my head finally sprung forth. Curious beyond dismissiveness, I finally took that trip to Barnes and Noble to purchase Zecharia Sitchin's book, *The 12th Planet*. If you have never read this book you should. His work is brilliant!

Five days later after the airing of the PAX program fiasco, I published an article titled, *Did Planet X Kill The Dinosaurs?*, based on the scenarios I'd developed with Marsden and published it on my web site, YOWUSA.COM. This was the first time I'd addressed the issue of Nibiru and from that point there has been no turning back for me, as the existence of Nibiru progressed in my mind from ancient mysticism to scientific possibility. Naturally, the next question to haunt me was, could this possibility become a reality?

With this question in mind, I turned to another YOWUSA.COM co-founder, Dutch Physicist Jacco van der Worp, for fresh ideas. While Jacco was cautious at first, we began discussing how to prove or disprove the existence of Nibiru and he soon warmed to the challenge.

Of course, the first thing that came to mind was that perhaps it had already been observed by the Hubble space telescope. Nope, I knew that was a non-starter. Even if NASA had observed it with the Hubble, news of the discovery could have to filter through an army of intelligence censors with a very clear "need to know" agenda: taxpayers only need to know about things when it becomes patently clear that they're about to fall off the tax roles. So what about amateur astronomers?

Finding an object like Nibiru at the edge of our solar system with a homemade 10" refractor telescope is truly an exercise in blind futility. You really need the big stuff and the federal funding that comes along with it, to take on something of this magnitude.

Then, a thought suddenly popped into Jacco's head that seemed innocuous at first but would later prove to drive us towards more ponderous realties. It was Pluto, the first "Planet X" candidate, and how it was discovered.

Early last century, Percival Lowell founder of the Lowell Observatory in Flagstaff, Arizona, was convinced that he could find the mysterious "Planet X" as he called it, beyond Neptune through mathematics, based on the motions of Uranus and Neptune. Certain of his math, he funded three separate searches for Planet X and on the third attempt, his 26-year-old assistant by the name of Clyde W. Tombaugh discovered Pluto on February 18, 1930 — the first American to discover a new planet! And without using a TV remote, I might add.

Named in honor of Pluto, the Roman god of the underworld (and not Popeye's antagonist), it was later deduced that Lowell's calculations had been in error. After the mass of Pluto had been carefully determined, it became obvious that this newly discovered planet was too puny to cause any changes in the motions of Uranus and Neptune. Consequently, the search for Planet X still continues to this day.

Yet, Lowell's idea of finding an unseen object by the effects it was having on known objects piqued our attention. Could Nibiru (Planet X) — which, according to some, is five times the size of earth — be discovered through its effects upon other planets within our own solar system? If so, then what would be looking for and where, if not Nibiru itself?

To begin with, we know through Sitchin's work that the last flyby of Nibiru occurred during the period known as the Great Deluge in the Babylonian texts or as the Old Testament story of Noah and the Flood. Using that as a base assumption, we set out to find evidence of any unusual atmospheric and seismic patterns in our solar system.

To insure the reliability of our base data, we decided to limit our search to a number of "trustworthy" and mainstream media websites for continual monitoring to include: NASA, JPL, AP, UPI and Space.Com, to name a few. Then, a clear pattern began to emerge. I'll briefly summarize what we found, beginning with Pluto and then work my way inward to Mars.

The following data represents changes from 1995 to 2002, with most of the events centered around 2001-2002. Also keep in mind that in astronomical terms, seven years is a very narrow snapshot in time.

PLUTO: The planet is undergoing global warming in its thin atmosphere even as it moves farther from the Sun and its atmospheric pressure has tripled over the past 14 years, with a dramatic rise in temperature.